Omnibus edition

A RECONSTRUCTED CORPSE

and

SICKEN AND SO DIE

and

DEAD ROOM FARCE

Simon Brett

Back-In-Print Books Ltd

Published by Back-In-Print Books Ltd 2004
ISBN 1 903552 50 8
Previously published in Great Britain by
Victor Gollancz under ISBN 0 575 05641 X and 0 575 05927 3
and 0 575 06488 9

Printed and bound on demand by
Lightning Source.

Back-In-Print Books Ltd
PO Box 47057
London SW18 1 YW
020 8637 0975

www.backinprint.co.uk
info@backinprint.co.uk

When Simon Brett studied at Oxford he became President of the OUDS, appeared in cabarets and directed the Oxford Theatre Group at the Edinburgh Festival Fringe in 1967.

Later he worked as a light entertainment producer for BBC radio and television before taking up writing full time in 1979.

Simon created the Charles Paris and Mrs Pargeter detective series and, to his fans' relief, he is still writing more. He also made a name as the author of the radio and TV series *After Henry*. The radio series *No Commitments*, the best-selling *How to be a Little Sod* and the novel *Shock to the System*, filmed starring Michael Caine, are other fruits of his imaginative mind. He is married, has three children and lives in a village on the South Downs.

This is a Back-In-Print Book.

• This title was out of print for some time but Back-In-Print Books has brought it back in to print because of demand from Simon Brett fans.
• This re-print was produced on demand using digital printing technology.
• Paper and print quality are higher than most conventionally printed paperback novels.
• Digital printing may cost somewhat more but ensures that book titles need not go out of print as long as there are readers who want them.

What other titles are available from BiP ?

Check out our web site at www.backinprint.co.uk for other titles released by Back-In-Print Books Ltd and news about forthcoming titles.

Do you want any other titles?

If you know of a title which is out of print and you think there might be a reasonable demand please contact us.

Back-In-Print Books Ltd
PO Box 47057
London SW18 1YW
020 8637 0975

www.backinprint.co.uk
info@backinprint.co.uk

A RECONSTRUCTED CORPSE

To Ian and Penny,
with thanks for the idea

Chapter One

CHARLES PARIS had never thought that he looked like a murder victim. And for most of his life he didn't. But then someone who looked a little like the actor apparently got himself murdered, and Charles Paris was faced with the unusual prospect of employment.

It was for a programme called *Public Enemies*, one of the rash of 'True Crime' series which had suddenly appeared on British television. Like the others in the genre, the hour-long *Public Enemies* programmes used a worthy, pious, together-we-can-beat-crime approach to pander to its audience's worst instincts of prurience and ghoulishness.

The programme was presented with straight-faced grittiness by self-appointed 'man of the people' Bob Garston who, after lucrative excursions into the lighter areas of television game shows, had returned to what he continuously described as his 'no-nonsense hard-bitten journalistic roots'. (Usually he also managed to get a reference to 'working at the coalface of real life' into the same sentence.)

Public Enemies was produced for ITV by West End Television, in association with 'Bob's Your Uncle Productions'. Bob Garston had, in common with many other successful presenters and writers, formed his own production company to secure a bigger slice of profits and greater control over the shows he worked on. The company's name reflected his game-show identity rather than his serious crime-fighter image, but was retained because its on-screen credit had already appeared on a good few programmes. That put 'Bob's Your Uncle' into an exclusive minority, way ahead of the recent proliferation of other independent production companies which had never made a programme.

Charles Paris had worked for W.E.T. before, but never through an independent producer, and from his first interview for the job, one morning early in November, he was aware of tensions between Roger Parkes, executive producer for the parent company, and Bob's Your Uncle Productions, represented by Bob Garston himself. The presenter had always regarded shows he worked on as private adventure playgrounds for his ego. The involvement of his own production company seemed to him completely to vindicate this attitude, and justify the inexorable imposition of his will on every aspect of the proceedings.

In common with most megalomaniacs, Bob Garston totally lacked the ability to delegate. His management style depended on personally monitoring all details of the production process. The workload this entailed might from time to time threaten to drive him into the ground, but at least doing everything himself allayed Bob Garston's increasingly paranoid fears that somebody might be doing something behind his back.

So he was present even at the interviews to find an actor who resembled the missing Martin Earnshaw, the kind of chore that most producers would have delegated to a casting director. Because Garston was there, so was Roger Parkes. The executive producer had caught on to the presenter's penchant for making decisions behind his back, and now tried to cover every move.

A casting director was present as well, Dana Wilson, fastidiously groomed and languid to the point of torpor. Letting Bob Garston run all the interviews and make all the decisions perfectly suited Dana's inert approach to her job.

Charles Paris had met the casting director before. He'd had a general interview with her some years earlier. Come to that, he'd met Bob Garston too, worked with him on the pilot of *If the Cap Fits!*, the mindless entertainment whose long run had been the foundation of all the presenter's subsequent game show successes. But Charles didn't expect either of them to remember him. The peremptory phone call from the programme's researcher Louise Denning announcing the time of his call had reminded him of the low priority held by good manners in television.

He was proved right. Neither his name nor his face produced the tiniest flicker of recognition from Bob Garston or Dana Wilson.

Charles did sometimes wonder whether he actually looked anonymous. He hoped not. Though actors pride themselves on their versatility, they still like to feel they have a core of individualism, which separates them from the other faces that beam – or more frequently these days scowl – from the pages of *Spotlight*.

But Charles's positive sense of his own identity was frequently undermined. Like most actors, he had the knack of remembering none of the good, but all of his bad notices, and one that rankled particularly had come from the *East Kent Mercury*. 'Charles Paris was apparently in the play too, though he made so little impression that it was easy to overlook the fact.' He would have minded less if he hadn't been playing Hamlet.

Nor was his sense of identity much bolstered by his agent. Maurice Skellern, in a rare moment of analysing his client's strengths and weaknesses, had once said, 'Thing about you, Charles, is you're one of those actors who blends in anywhere. You can play anything.'

'Except major parts, it seems,' the actor had responded bitterly.

'But that's your *strength*, Charles. Stars may do very well when they're on top, but when they run out of star parts they're finished. Whereas actors like you *never* need to be out of work.'

'If that's the case, Maurice, why is it that I'm *always* out of work?'

'Ah, well...' But the agent was never thrown for long. He always had the same excuse at the ready. 'Thing is, Charles, things are very *quiet* at the moment.'

'Been *quiet* for rather a long time, haven't they?'

'Well, yes...that is in the nature of the business, of your chosen profession. And also, Charles...' Maurice had paused, trying to shape his next words in the least harmful way possible. 'The fact is you don't always help yourself...'

'How do you mean?'

'Well, actors do have to *get out there*, you know. See people...hustle a bit...*network*, know what I mean...?'

The only response to this had been a grunt.

'Thing is, with the best will in the world, Charles...' Why is it that people always start like that when they're about to demonstrate lavish amounts of ill will? 'With the best will in the world, I have to say that you do tend to be rather *passive* in your approach to your career.'

'Well, I'm not sure that I'd say –'

'I mean, I do everything I can, *I work my butt off* on your behalf, but you do have to take the occasional initiative yourself, you know.'

The conversation had left Charles, as all conversations with his agent left him, fuming and furious. For Maurice Skellern, an agent who had raised inactivity to the level of an art form, to claim he 'worked his butt off' on behalf of a client was... It made Charles so angry he couldn't finish the thought. And what made him even angrier was the knowledge that there was a lot of truth in what his agent had said.

It actually was through Maurice that he'd been contacted for the *Public Enemies* job. Not that any effort on the agent's part had been required. The programme's researcher Louise Denning had trawled through *Spotlight* looking for faces which resembled the missing – presumed murdered – Martin Earnshaw, had found Charles's in the back section of quarter-page photographs, and simply phoned the agent listed.

No one would have known this, however, from the way Maurice presented the situation to his client. 'You know how I'm always beavering away on your behalf, Charles, never letting any potential opening slip by. Well, some of my groundwork at W.E.T.'s beginning to pay off. After my relentless bombardment of them with reminders about you, they've finally come back to me with something.'

'What is it?' Charles had asked, as ever unable to flatten out the instinctive surge of excitement any chance of work prompted. *This time*, he always thought, this time maybe it'll happen. This time my talent'll be taken seriously, this time I'll be offered something meaty at the National or a major telly series.

But this time was, as ever, another disappointment. To rub salt in the wound, this time the approach had no connection at all with his acting talent. Charles Paris had been short-listed simply because his face fitted. God, it was so humiliating.

Even so, when he went to the interview, he desperately wanted to get the job.

To call the encounter an 'interview' was over-flattering. It was more like a police line-up, which, given the nature of the programme, was perhaps appropriate.

Five potential Martin Earnshaws had been called, and they were told to parade in front of a screen with height-lines marked on it. Charles found the selection process mystifying. Though a couple of the candidates looked vaguely like each other, none of them seemed to bear the slightest resemblance to him. And since he couldn't see the photographs which Bob Garston, Roger Parkes and Dana Wilson so assiduously pored over, he couldn't judge whether any of them looked at all like the missing Martin Earnshaw.

During the selection no attempt was made to treat the aspirants like human beings. Their physical attributes and oddities were anatomised without restraint. They were there simply as set-dressing and the winner would be the one who most closely fitted the preconceived design.

It turned out to be Charles Paris, though Roger Parkes had favoured one of the other candidates. Still, Bob Garston made the decisions and, with that lack of tact only mastered by the totally self-absorbed, bulldozed the executive producer's opinion out of the way. Bob did not even notice the tight-lipped manner in which Roger Parkes walked out of the room, saying he had 'other things to be getting on with'.

Even when informed that he'd got the job, Charles was still treated as if he wasn't there. This didn't surprise him. He'd worked in television long enough to know what to expect. No one even offered to show him a photograph of the man he apparently so resembled.

The casting decision made, Bob Garston bustled off to lean inhibitingly over the shoulder of some other member of the production team, while Dana Wilson suppressed her yawns long enough to take down Charles's details.

'You should actually have them all on file,' he said.

She looked puzzled. 'Why?'

'Well, I have worked for W.E.T. a few times before.'

'Oh really?' This information made not the tiniest dent in the impermeable surface of Dana Wilson's mind. 'Full name...?'

It's strange how some murders are sexy. Not sexy in the sense of being sexually motivated, but sexy in the sense that the media takes them up and keeps on and on about them.

Whether a murder becomes sexy or not depends on the personnel involved. The killing of a pretty woman always attracts the press. Colour photos of her in her prime, snapped laughing in a strapless dress at a disco, can be juxtaposed with bleak shots of the alley or waste ground where she met her end. Newspaper readers enjoy the *frisson* prompted by such contrasts, seeing how quick bright things have come to confusion.

Love triangles also catch the public imagination, regardless of the glamour of the participants. A wife and lover plotting the demise of a husband is a reliable stand-by; while a woman removing her rival for a man's affections is even more popular. When it comes to sexy murders, the public know what they like, and fortunately in this country there are enough people of homicidal tendencies to keep them adequately and entertainingly supplied.

The disappearance of Martin Earnshaw did not fit any of these stereotypes. What made that case sexy was the victim's wife. Chloe Earnshaw was a waif-like blonde of steely determination on whom the media had seized from the moment her husband went missing. Her first press conference, at which, with glistening eyes, she hovered throughout on the edge of breakdown, made the national news on all channels, and from then on she never seemed to be off the screen or out of the papers.

What also made the public interest unusual was that no one knew for a fact Martin Earnshaw was dead. He had certainly disappeared under suspicious circumstances, he had certainly been under threat of death, but as yet no trace of his body had been found. Without the constant appearances of his photogenic wife asserting that he had been murdered, the public would soon have lost interest in the case.

Once Charles Paris had been cast in the role, he tracked down and read everything he could find concerning Martin Earnshaw's disappearance. This was not because he was under any illusions about the part. Dana Wilson had told him firmly that it didn't involve any speaking, so Stanislavskian efforts to get under the character's skin – even if Charles had been the kind of actor to indulge in such excesses – would have been pointless. No, it was just from interest that he delved into the Earnshaws' background.

What he found out was by then well known to any tabloid reader. Charles Paris, always having been more of a *Times* man – and in fact a *Times* crossword rather than a *Times* news man – had been cheated of the more lurid details.

Martin Earnshaw was – or had been – in his fifties, a property developer based in Brighton. Hit hard by the recession, he had endeavoured to refloat his business by borrowing. Because the banks were unwilling to oblige, he had resorted to less respectable sources of funds and got into the clutches of a major-league loan shark.

As his repayments fell further and further behind, Martin Earnshaw had become the object of increasingly violent threats. A few weeks before his disappearance, he was found near his home with facial and abdominal bruising. A strong-willed man, he had apparently not buckled under in the face of these threats, but been determined to expose the extortioners. In fact, he made an appointment to tell a local detective inspector all the details.

That appointment was never kept. The night before it, a Wednesday in early October, Martin Earnshaw told his wife he was going out for a drink, and never returned. It was her assumption and everyone else's – probably even the police's, though they tended to play their cards closer to their chests than the tabloid press – that Martin Earnshaw had been murdered by the men he was about to shop.

All these details were related to the media by the doll-like figure of Chloe Earnshaw. She was his second wife, the first having died some seven years previously. It was a perfect marriage. Chloe was twenty years younger than Martin, they had been together for two years and – at this point during that first press conference the glistening, dark blue eyes began to spill – 'had been intending soon to start a family. Something which now,' she had continued, recovering herself with agonising discipline, 'looks unlikely ever to happen.' She still hadn't lost hope of seeing Martin again, she insisted, but was prepared for the worst.

That worst, everyone knew – and indeed gleefully anticipated – was the discovery of her husband's body.

Official enquiries continued and grew in intensity. But as information dried up and leads proved abortive, the power of television was enlisted to help the investigation. The police, having tried themselves to reconstruct Martin Earnshaw's last evening without much success, had readily accepted *Public Enemies'* offer to reconstruct it for them.

This had necessitated a couple of days filming in Brighton, which was no hardship for Charles Paris. The town had always held a raffish attraction for him, full of memories of the one woman he'd made love to there, along with fantasies of all the other women he'd like to have made love to there. Was it a generational thing, he wondered, a post-war nostalgia, that still made Brighton's air, like that of Paris, heavy with sex? He had only to step out of the train from Victoria to feel the lust invade his mind.

The Black Feathers, in which Martin Earnshaw had last been seen, was in the hinterland of the Lanes between the Royal Pavilion and sea front. It wasn't one of the highly tarted-up pubs of the area, but retained a proletarian – and indeed slightly deterrent – grubbiness.

The landlord and staff, however, had proved infinitely cooperative to the W.E.T. team, led by director Geoffrey Ramage. This was not pure altruism. While a positive disadvantage for someone trying to sell a house, murderous connections in a pub are good news for business. And if those connections are advertised to millions on nation-wide television, the potential boost to trade is enormous. The viewing public is notorious for seeking out any location featured on the small screen, regardless of the context in which it was seen.

In the cause of verisimilitude, Geoffrey Ramage had asked the landlord to get together all the regulars who might have been present on the evening of Martin Earnshaw's disappearance. To Charles's surprise, when he spoke to those who had been assembled, none had any recollection of seeing the missing man.

The actor's instinctive suspicion about this was quickly allayed by further conversation. It turned out that very few of the other drinkers had actually been there on the relevant night, but the lure of television coverage had prompted them to finesse the truth a little.

The sighting of Martin Earnshaw in the Black Feathers had not, as it transpired, come from one of the pub's regulars. An anonymous caller had passed on the information to Chloe Earnshaw, and this had been corroborated by a subsequent telephone call – also unidentified – to the police.

It became increasingly clear to Charles that the Black Feathers was in fact one of those pubs which doesn't have many regulars. In spite of the landlord's attempts to give the impression of a convivial community, the pub was – like Charles's own 'local' in Westbourne Grove – a joyless and anonymous environment.

The landlord himself stoutly maintained that he had seen the missing man sitting with two others on the night in question, though he was vague about further details.

Not for the first time, Charles had brought home to him the fallibility of human witnesses. Recollection is quickly clouded and distorted. From his own experience – and this wasn't just due to the Bell's whisky – Charles Paris knew how difficult he would find it to report accurately what he had been doing even a few days before. So the landlord's vagueness did not surprise him. Cynically, he even wondered whether the man was making up his story. From the point of view of trade, it was certainly in the interests of the Black Feathers that he remembered Martin Earnshaw.

Charles Paris's role in the filming was not onerous, though Geoffrey Ramage, in the self-regarding way of television directors, made as big a deal of it as he could. Dressed in clothes and fake Rolex watch identical to those worn by the missing man, Charles had to sit at a gloomy corner table with two other extras and drink. It could, uncharitably, have been called 'typecasting'.

There was an element of character-acting involved, though, because Charles had to drink draught Guinness rather than the more instinctive Bell's. This was on the advice of Chloe Earnshaw. Her husband, she insisted, had always drunk draught Guinness.

Having Chloe on hand did nothing to drive away the lustful thoughts which Brighton always inspired in Charles. She was there to advise on the filming and they had been introduced by Geoffrey Ramage in the lounge of the hotel that was the *Public Enemies* base.

In the flesh she was even smaller than her photographs and television appearances suggested, but somehow more robust, more curved, more tactile. She was simply dressed in black, as if already anticipating the news she feared to hear, and her blonde hair was scraped back into an artless ponytail.

A tremor ran through her when she was introduced to Charles and an involuntary hand half reached out to touch his arm. She gave a little shake of her head. 'I'm sorry. It's just...They've cast you very well. I mean, you don't really look like Martin, but there's something...Your height, the way you stand, it's...'

Tears once again welled up in the dark blue eyes. 'I'm sorry. I'm not being very brave.'

'Oh, but you are.' The words formed instinctively and were out before Charles was aware of them. 'I mean, you've been very brave from the start – coping with the trauma of your husband's disappearance. And then there's the risk you take by speaking out at all. The same risk that your husband exposed himself to...I mean, that is, assuming what you are afraid has happened to him *has* happened to him.' Her brow wrinkled in pain. 'I'm sorry, I'm saying all the wrong things.'

'No, no. Not at all, Charles,' she reassured him softly.

And Charles Paris was hooked. Just like the rest of the public. There was something mesmerising about the woman's vulnerability. Anyone meeting her in ordinary circumstances would have found Chloe Earnshaw only moderately attractive. It was the knowledge of her jeopardy that gave her such charisma.

The onlooker was drawn to her, but at the same time felt guilty about being drawn to her. She looks fanciable, the thought process ran, but how awful of me to entertain ideas like that about a woman in such distress. It's dreadful to take pleasure from someone else's suffering.

Though of course the pleasure taken from someone else's suffering was the dynamo generating the success of programmes like *Public Enemies*.

Chapter Two

CHARLES PARIS was used to the atmosphere of television hospitality suites, but this one was different. During the transmission of the first of the new series of *Public Enemies*, there was the usual undercurrent of showbiz excitement in the room, the usual panic elaborately disguised as cool, but there was also a more robust coarseness in the general badinage. It was because the police were there.

Public Enemies collaborated closely with the police – Bob Garston kept banging on about *how* closely they collaborated with the police – and the police took this as a licence to bring as many of their number as possible to the W.E.T. studios when the shows were being transmitted. Some of the force justified their presence – the on-screen presenters obviously, the police researchers, those uniformed figures bent over computers and telephones who filled out the background of the set – but others were just along for the ride, attracted by their colleagues' involvement, the glamour of television and the prospect of free drink.

Charles Paris was there just for the free drink. He'd been meant to be there working. Geoffrey Ramage, fresh from the excitements of the Brighton filming, had had Charles called for the live transmission. He was proposing a moody background silhouette of the actor dressed as Martin Earnshaw while Chloe did her latest heart-wrenching appeal.

Geoffrey Ramage was actually always proposing moody background silhouettes. Like all television directors, he really saw himself in the movies and, though his only actual experience in cinema had been doing soft porn, he had been bitten at an early age by the *film noir* bug. The opportunities to indulge this obsession in *Public Enemies* made him feel like a child with limitless credit in a sweet shop.

Charles's only brush with the genre had occurred when a seventies movie he was in had been hailed as 'a British homage to *film noir*' by a critic who didn't realise that the film's budget hadn't stretched to more lights. The actor's own contribution – a mere spit and a cough – had been characterised by the same critic as 'unthreateningly menacing', and Charles had spent a long time puzzling over whether that was a good notice or a bad one.

Geoffrey Ramage's moody background silhouette had been rejected by Bob Garston first thing in the morning, but since Charles Paris had been called, that meant he'd have to be paid another day's fee. The money was nothing to get excited about – Martin Earnshaw was unfortunately not called upon to speak in the reconstruction of his last known movements, so Charles Paris was being paid as a mere extra – but any money was welcome to his morbidly undernourished bank account.

Because he'd written off the day – and because there was the W.E.T. bar at lunch-time and the prospect of free hospitality later – Charles decided he'd stick around and watch the proceedings. Television studios are always full of so many people with unspecified roles that one more or less ligging around wouldn't provoke comment.

So he had a pleasantish day, watching the *Public Enemies* egos battle it out on the studio floor. Roger Parkes was the self-appointed voice of reason, Geoffrey Ramage the self-appointed *enfant terrible*, but Bob Garston rode roughshod over both of them. It was his show, and he wasn't going to let anyone forget it. With no attempt at tact or even awareness that other people might have opinions, the 'man of the people' continued on his workaholic course.

And Charles Paris sat benignly in the bunker of an audience seat, watching the flak fly overhead. He liked the atmosphere of a television studio, and he liked it even better when he had no responsibility for anything that was going on in it.

The free hospitality, when it came, was a bit meagre. Commercial television companies used to lay on wall-to-wall food and drink, so that working on a production would ensure Charles didn't have to go near a supermarket for its duration. The ready availability of spirits even slightly diminished his Bell's whisky bill.

But the new austerity which followed the reallocation of their franchises brought ITV companies' generosity down to BBC standards – or even lower. The only foodstuffs on offer in the *Public Enemies* hospitality suite were crisps and nuts. The booze was limited to wine and beer. And, seeing how vigorously the police hangers-on were getting stuck into that, supplies weren't going to last very long.

Charles wondered whether this parsimony came from W.E.T. or from Bob's Your Uncle Productions. Given the way Bob Garston dominated all other aspects of the production, he probably also controlled the hospitality bill. Its niggardly provisions were certainly in character with his teetotal righteousness.

In the circumstances Charles Paris resorted to an old trick. He took a half-pint beer glass, filled it with wine and sat cradling it unobtrusively in the corner.

He needn't have worried about drawing attention to himself. The police contingent were far too caught up in their own banter and camaraderie to take any notice of anyone else.

There were about a dozen of them. Two were silent, though the remainder made noise enough for many more. Only a few were in uniform, but the others had that distinctive rectangular look which always gives away a policeman.

One of the silent ones was a thickset, mournful-looking man in his forties, who wore plain clothes and was tucking into the booze with a single-mindedness Charles could not but respect.

The other wore uniform, with a few extra flourishes on his jacket which presumably betokened higher rank, and sat apart from the rest, nursing a beer. He was an older man, probably round Charles's age, which in police terms must have put him near retirement. The attitude of his colleagues to him mixed a perfunctory deference with covert insolence. At times they seemed almost to be sending him up. From their banter Charles picked up that the man was called Superintendent Roscoe.

The mob reserved their greatest derision, however, for the colleagues who actually appeared on the screen, and here there was no attempt at concealment. The figure who provoked most raucous response was the one introduced by Bob Garston as 'our resident expert from Scotland Yard – Detective Inspector Sam Noakes'.

'Yeah, and we all know what she's expert in, don't we?' shouted one of the younger policemen.

'Will you let me take everything down for you and use it in evidence, Sam?' asked another fruitily.

'I'm afraid I must ask you to accompany me to the bedroom,' giggled a third, bowled over by his own wit.

The object of their offensive was certainly attractive, but there was about her a toughness which made Charles think they wouldn't have made the sexist remarks to her face. DI Sam Noakes had red hair and those pale blue eyes which the television camera intensifies. Though a detective, she wore uniform, presumably because she looked so good in it. The entertainment element is always paramount in programmes like *Public Enemies*, and there are a good few male viewers out there who are turned on by – and will therefore turn on for – a pretty woman in uniform.

Immediately she started speaking, it was clear that DI Sam Noakes was more than just a pretty face. She had a distinctive voice, deep, with a rasp of efficiency in it, as she enumerated the police successes prompted by the last series, and gave bulletins on the cases that remained unsolved. She was good, and her performance gained an extra glow from the fact that she knew she was good.

Even the sexist banter in the hospitality suite recognised her quality. Through the innuendo ran a thread of respect, at times verging on awe. DI Sam Noakes was already a power to be reckoned with inside the force before television brought her skills to a wider audience.

Public Enemies was scheduled at prime time, ITV Thursday evening, just after the nine o'clock watershed which in theory protected children from sex and violence – and in fact encouraged them to stay up and watch it.

The programme's format was a magazine. Live updates on cases, reports on stolen goods, reconstructions of crimes and appeals for witnesses were intermingled with more general features. These were mostly consumer advice, presented with that distinctive smugness which characterises all television consumer programmes. The subjects covered might be a report on tests for home security devices, tips on how to recognise forged bank notes, lists of the right antique markets to check out for stolen property, and so on.

But for the first programme of the new series, *Public Enemies* did something different. As Bob Garston put it grittily (he put everything grittily – he was constitutionally incapable of speaking without grit): 'We've all watched a lot of television detectives, haven't we, and I'm sure we've all got our favourites. But in fictional crime there are two traditions – that of the professional police detective conducting an investigation and that of the gifted amateur doing the business. On the one hand we've got, if you like...Morse – and on the other, say, – Poirot. Presumably, Sam,' he continued, turning a gritty smile on DI Noakes, 'Morse is a bit closer to the real world than Poirot?'

'Not that much closer, Bob,' she replied with a knowing grin. 'I still want to know how Morse gets hold of that car. Last time I asked down the car pool for a red Jaguar, they laughed in my face.'

Bob Garston let out a gritty chuckle of complicity. 'Yes, but come on, Morse conducts his investigations with all the back-up of computer records and forensic laboratories. Surely that's a bit closer to real police methods than relying on "the little grey cells".'

'We don't actually call it "relying on the little grey cells", but if that expression means respecting intuition and responding to sudden lateral thoughts, then it's certainly a very important part of police investigation.'

'Good, thank you, Sam.' Bob Garston turned smoothly to another camera. 'Well, here on *Public Enemies*, we like to keep you up to date with everything about crime and its investigation, so we thought it'd be interesting to talk to an amateur sleuth, and maybe compare his methods with those of a professional police investigator. So I'm very glad to welcome to the studio – Ted Faraday.'

The shot opened out to include Sam Noakes and a rugged-looking man in his late forties, casually dressed in jeans and baseball jacket. 'Evening, Bob.'

This greeting prompted a roar of obscene responses from the hospitality suite.

'Now, Ted, would you say that your methods as an amateur –?'

'Sorry, I have to interrupt you there, Bob. That's twice you've referred to me as an "amateur". I'm not an amateur. I'm a professional private investigator.'

Bob Garston's face clouded. This was not how the item had been planned in pre-programme discussions, and it rather made nonsense of his neat link about Morse and Poirot. He shoehorned a smile on to his face. 'All right, point taken. Would you say that your methods as a *professional private investigator* differ very much from those used by the real police force?'

Ted Faraday opened his mouth to reply, but before he could say anything, Sam Noakes interposed, 'I think it should be pointed out that Ted is an ex-copper, so his methods are based on the training he had in the Met, anyway.'

Bob Garston seemed glad of this support against Faraday. 'You two know each other?'

'And how!' shouted a raucous voice in the hospitality suite.

'Yes, we do,' Sam admitted.

Bob Garston turned his attention to the private investigator. 'Well, Ted, how do you react to what she says?'

'When I'm allowed to get a word in...' Ted Faraday began with lazy charm, 'I would like to say, yes, I was trained by the Met, and it did teach me some very useful lessons. I would also like to say that, now I'm outside the place, I realise just how rigid it is in its thinking, and how much easier it is to respond rapidly to situations without being strangled by bureaucracy when you're out in the real world.'

The discussion continued. Charles had no means of knowing their past history, but Sam Noakes seemed determined to score points off Ted Faraday. It made for a lively exchange, which climaxed when she coolly announced, 'I think this is all kind of sour grapes, Ted. You'd actually rather be back in the Met than faffing around on your own...assuming you still had the option.'

If ever there was a remark which demanded a follow-up question, that was it, but Bob Garston, concerned about the other items yet to be fitted into the programme, curbed his hard-bitten journalistic instincts and moved on to wrap up the interview.

In the hospitality suite, Charles learned a little more. Faraday was evidently well known to the police contingent and many of his exchanges with Sam Noakes had prompted jokes and barracking. After her last remark one of the policeman shouted, 'Well, you got to be a PI, haven't you, Ted? Should have realised the golden rule – if you want to stay in the Met, keep on the right side of the right people...isn't that right, Superintendent Roscoe...?'

The superintendent looked up from his beer, whose level had gone down very little in the previous half-hour, and smiled. It was a complex smile. Within it were unease and caution, but also undeniably triumph.

'Hey, listen, listen!' shouted one of the policemen and attention returned to what Bob Garston was saying.

'...and we on *Public Enemies* are always trying to find out more about crime on behalf of you, the audience. So we thought we'd hire our own private eye and put him on the Martin Earnshaw case. Are you game to take up the challenge, Ted?'

'If you're prepared to pay my usual rates – plus expenses...you're on, Bob.' Faraday grinned. Clearly this part of the programme had been heavily set up.

Bob Garston turned to the Detective Inspector. 'And, on behalf of Scotland Yard, are you prepared to take up the challenge?'

Sam Noakes also grinned. 'Oh yes.'

'So we'll keep up progress reports here on *Public Enemies* and see whether the real police, with all the resources at their disposal, can be beaten to the solution by the gifted amateur!'

Ted Faraday again winced at the description and would probably have remonstrated, but Bob Garston had already turned to another camera and started reading his next link off the autocue.

The last item on that week's *Public Enemies* was another follow-up on the Martin Earnshaw disappearance. This, needless to say, featured the missing man's wife, currently Britain's favourite sufferer.

Geoffrey Ramage may have been denied the set-dressing of a moody Charles Paris silhouette in the background, but the effect he came up with was still pretty theatrical. Chloe Earnshaw, dressed again in simple black, was shot against a blown-up black-and-white photograph of the Black Feathers. The overhead lighting bleached the colour out of her hair and skin, so that only the deep blueness of her eyes disturbed the monochrome. The light also sparkled off her unshed tears.

What she said was the usual stuff. 'There must be someone out there who knows something about where Martin is. I appeal to them – I beg them – to tell me where he is or what's happened to him. Even if the news is bad, I want to know it. When I know, I can start to rebuild the rest of my life. Please, please, if anyone knows anything – the smallest, smallest thing about Martin...just pick up the phone.'

And all over the country men thought unworthily, 'I wouldn't mind picking up the phone and asking for her number.'

Charles had an unworthy thought too. There was no doubt that Chloe Earnshaw was one of those people whom, as the showbiz cliché has it, 'the camera loves'. Charles Paris couldn't help suspecting that the camera's devotion was reciprocated.

Chapter Three

DI SAM NOAKES had changed into a figure-hugging red dress after the programme. Its colour had been carefully selected to complement rather than scream at her hair. Out of uniform, she still looked good, but softer, less of the disciplinarian.

Her appearance in the hospitality suite was greeted by a tide of catcalls and innuendo which washed off her unnoticed. The silent, heavy-drinking plain-clothes man turned towards her.

'Quite the television star now, aren't you?' he said. 'Police investigation meets game show, eh? What'll it be next, Sam – *Blind Date*?'

She looked at him coolly. 'Well, if it was, I'm afraid I wouldn't pick you, Greg.' It was spoken lightly, but the words stung. Before he could respond, she went on, 'Anyway, I'm a copper. All this television stuff is irrelevant – just means to an end. If it helps solve crime, then I'll do it.'

'Even if it means a "head-to-head play-off" against Ted Faraday?'

'Even if it means that.'

'And so you're doing all this in the line of duty? You don't get any buzz out of just being on the box?'

She shook her head decisively, setting the red hair swaying. 'I just get a kick out of doing my job well, Greg...' The pale blue eyes gave him an even stare...doing it as well as a man would.'

'Better than a lot of them.' The man called Greg looked across the room and murmured intimately, 'Oh-oh, talk of the devil.'

He moved out of the way as Superintendent Roscoe came across to Sam and embraced her with a clumsy, old-fashioned peck on the cheek. 'Another lovely performance, Noakes. Very well done indeed, my dear.' Charles saw her wince at the endearment, but the superintendent didn't notice. 'Whenever I watch this programme, I feel really glad that I backed the suggestion of doing it so strongly in the early days.'

'Yes.' DI Noakes sounded neither interested nor as if she believed him. Her eyes were already over his shoulder, searching out someone else to talk to. Superintendent Roscoe seemed to have the same effect on all his colleagues. Superior in rank he might be, but they all ignored him.

There was a commotion at the door, as more of the production team entered. Sam Noakes, taking advantage of the diversion with a murmured 'Excuse me', moved away from Superintendent Roscoe.

Charles Paris also moved. The booze was getting low and he wanted to ensure a refill before the new influx. He knew it was a bit unfair to take drink from the mouths of people who'd just been busting their guts in the studio, but there are extreme situations in which fairness cannot be the first priority.

He managed to drain what looked like the last bottle of red into his beer glass. That half-filled it, which would have to do.

He was moving away from the bar when he felt a tap on his shoulder. 'Ted.'

Charles turned to find himself facing the plain-clothes officer Sam Noakes had called 'Greg'. The man reacted with some surprise. 'Sorry, I thought you were Ted Faraday.'

'No, I'm Ted Faraday.' The real owner of the identity had just entered the suite.

'Yes, of course you are,' said Greg. 'Just from the back it looked...Ted, this is, um...' He didn't know the name...the guy who played Martin Earnshaw in the reconstruction.'

'Oh, right.'

'Charles Paris,' Charles Paris supplied helpfully.

'Ah. Good to see you.' Charles felt his hand firmly grasped as the private investigator gave him a thorough look. 'Yes, not a bad likeness.'

'Just get you a drink, Ted.' Greg moved to the bar.

'Oh, thanks, I'll have a –'

'Be a matter of what there is, I'm afraid.'

Left alone with Faraday, Charles Paris felt the need to make conversation. 'You know anything special about the Earnshaw case?'

The investigator shrugged. 'No more than anyone else does. Till we find a body...'

'You think that's what will be found?'

'Oh yes, Charles. Somebody knows something. Scotland Yard wouldn't be taking a disappearance this seriously if they weren't pretty damned sure it's a murder.'

'And you think you'll find the body before the police do?'

'I'll give it a bloody good try. Probably easier for me to go underground than someone on the force.'

'But if you're reporting back on the programme every week, isn't it going to be difficult for you to go completely underground?'

'I'll file my reports by phone – or fax more likely. As with all these programmes, the skill is in how much information you give to the public.'

'Bob Garston gave the impression he wanted this story to run through the series. What happens if Martin Earnshaw's body's found straight away?'

A cynical smile tugged at the corners of Ted Faraday's lips. 'Be bloody inconvenient, wouldn't it? Murderers just have no sense of what goes to make a good television programme. Actually, though, there is a contingency plan for that.'

'Oh?'

'If they find the body, then the stakes go higher. It's a race between me and the Met to find the murderer.'

'Do you really approve of methods like this?'

The investigator screwed up his face wryly. 'Well...everything else is showbiz these days. Politics...the Monarchy...why should the police force be any different? And these programmes do sometimes turn up information you wouldn't get from any other source. Anyway, from my point of view, it's bloody marvellous.'

'Hm?'

'For someone who's only recently set up as a PI, this kind of publicity's like gold dust.'

'Yes, but publicity in your line of work could be a two-edged sword, couldn't it? Not much use having a face that's famous from television when you're doing undercover stuff, is it?'

'Don't worry about that. I am *a master of disguise.*' Ted Faraday rolled the cliché ironically round his mouth.

'And when your name's nationally known you'll get a whole lot more enquiries and bookings?'

'Reckon so. And another thing about *Public Enemies* employing me is –' Faraday grinned '– the money's bloody great. That is the big difference from the Met, let me tell you. As a PI, when you get the work, you get properly paid for it.'

'Very nice too.'

'You bet. No, I've really found my feet since I've been out of all that form-filling crap. I wouldn't go back into the real force if they asked me on bended knee.'

'No danger of that happening.' The new voice belonged to Superintendent Roscoe who had sidled into the periphery of their conversation.

Ted Faraday's reaction was interesting. He very positively ignored the superintendent and, talking into the empty air, announced, 'At least in the real world I don't have to deal with superannuated timeservers with no understanding of crime or criminal methods.'

The antagonism hung almost visibly between the two men. Superintendent Roscoe seemed for a moment to contemplate a riposte, but either he changed his mind or couldn't think of anything clever enough to say, because he lumbered off awkwardly to join the fringes of another group.

'Ex-boss?' asked Charles.

Ted Faraday grinned drily. 'You'd make a great detective, picking up subtle nuances like that. Actually, Shitface Roscoe is the reason I left the force.'

'Can I ask why?'

'Too complicated to go into. Let's just say a personality clash. You're never going to find much in common between someone with a bit of imagination and a talentless bureaucrat whose priorities are stifling initiative in others and taking any available credit for himself.'

'Ah,' said Charles Paris. Faraday's answer seemed to have covered the question pretty thoroughly.

The noise in the room abated as Chloe Earnshaw entered. Her television make-up was gone and she looked more vulnerable than ever, as though a layer of protective skin had been removed. There was a momentary hesitation among the policemen who towered around her, before the one Sam Noakes had addressed as 'Greg' moved forward protectively.

'Another very moving appeal, Mrs Earnshaw.'

She turned the blue eyes on him with an air of bewilderment. 'Just so long as it does some good.'

'Yes, of course. I think it's bound to.' He fell back on cliché. 'There must be someone out there who knows something.'

'I hope so.' She look gauchely round the room. 'I shouldn't really have come in here.'

Then why did you? Charles instinctively asked himself, surprised how readily Chloe Earnshaw had prompted another unworthy thought.

'I find crowds difficult at the moment,' she went on.

Then why do you walk into one? Charles's mind unworthily continued.

'Better than being on your own, though,' said Greg. 'At least you can't brood so much when you're with people.'

Chloe Earnshaw gave him a little wry smile, which seemed to announce her infinite capacity to brood in any circumstances.

'Come on,' he said gently, 'let's get you a bevvy.'

As he spoke, he took her arm and led her towards the drinks table. To Charles there seemed something oddly flamboyant about the gesture, as if it were made for the benefit of someone else. And from the glance Greg flashed towards her, that someone else appeared to be Sam Noakes. But either the detective inspector didn't see the move, or deliberately showed no reaction to it.

The noise level in the room rose again as Bob Garston entered, in the middle of an argument with Roger Parkes. Its subject was, needless to say, the programme and, also needless to say, Bob Garston was doing the talking.

'Listen, it's our job to keep *Public Enemies* one step ahead. We're not the only True Crime series on television at the moment, but we're the best and I'm bloody determined we're going to stay the best. We're not going to achieve that, though, if we fill the programmes with half-baked ideas and make-weight features.'

'The public are *interested* in automatic security lights,' Roger Parkes remonstrated wearily. 'It's just the kind of consumer information they want. And it's the kind of feature that's dead easy and cheap to set up and –'

'That's all you bloody think about, Roger – what's easy and cheap. And I'll tell you, items that're easy and cheap *look* easy and cheap. You may have swanned through your career at W.E.T. doing the minimum, taking the line of least resistance, but you're working with *Bob Garston* now. And I care about programmes that have my name on them. I work bloody hard to make myself the best I can be at what I do, and I demand the same kind of commitment from everyone who works for me – *everyone!*'

'But –'

'Even the bloody executive producer! I know that's a title that usually means bugger all – just a way of giving some talentless pen-pusher the illusion of usefulness – but when the production's one *I*'m involved in, then I see to it that everyone pulls their weight!'

'Bob, there's no need to be insulting. I –'

'Listen, television's a competitive business. We've got to do *better* than the opposition – doing *as well* as them is just not good enough. We've got to have new ideas, new approaches, new surprises. We've got to give the audience no alternative but to watch *Public Enemies*. They've got to watch the programme because they know they're missing something if they don't watch it. So we need a dynamic approach, not a line-of-least-bloody-resistance, let's-do-it-because-it's-cheap-and-easy approach!'

'I am giving you all the backing I can,' said Roger Parkes with some dignity, 'but we're only at the start of the series. We have to pace ourselves over the next six weeks. The production team have worked on overdrive for this programme and that's fair enough – it's the first, it needs to make an impact. But they can't maintain that level of energy all the time. We need a few – as you so sneeringly call them – *easy* items to lower the tempo a bit.'

'But we don't want to lower the bloody tempo – that's the way of mediocrity – and only a mediocre mind thinks like that!'

The executive producer was having difficulty curbing his anger, but he managed it. Charles could guess at the motivations which lay behind that restraint. Not least among them, he imagined, was the fact that W.E.T. needed *Public Enemies* for its ratings potential, and if that meant putting up with the manic bad manners of Bob Garston, then so be it. In the changed climate of television, when staff jobs hardly existed, when everyone was only as good as their last short-term contract, the replacement of an executive producer was easily achieved. If he was going to keep his job, Roger Parkes could not risk upsetting the apple-cart.

'Very well,' he said in a conciliatory tone which must have cost him a great deal. 'I'll see to it that everyone gives you all the back-up you require, Bob.'

'Good.' Garston was momentarily appeased, until he saw Geoffrey Ramage entering the hospitality suite and went straight back on to the attack. 'And that everyone includes the bloody director!'

Ramage looked bewildered, still dazed from the exhaustions of the studio day. 'What?'

'*Public Enemies*,' the presenter fulminated on, 'is a piece of serious factual reportage. Its basis is no-nonsense hard-bitten journalism – it's not an excuse for some bloody wanker to audition for the Fritz Lang School of Hard-Boiled Realism!'

Before Geoffrey Ramage had time to respond to this assault, Bob Garston was interrupted by one of the lumbering policemen. 'Hey, the booze has run out. Who's the person who sorts that kind of thing out round here?'

Roger Parkes replied instinctively. He might have a mediocre mind, he might never have made the greatest creative contribution to television, but he was highly skilled in the most important part of a producer's role – getting drinks for people. 'I could organise some more supplies from the bar,' he said.

'No,' said Bob Garston.

'What?'

'Bob's Your Uncle Productions are controlling the budget on this show. We've allocated a certain amount for hospitality. If that's finished, then that's finished.'

'What, you mean you're not authorising any more booze?' asked Roger Parkes in disbelief.

'Exactly,' Bob Garston replied with gritty relish.

It must be wonderful, Charles Paris thought wistfully, genuinely not to care whether people like you or not.

The W.E.T. bar was closed by the time the full impact of the hospitality suite drought had sunk in, so it was a somewhat disconsolate group of policemen and production staff who trickled out of W.E.T. House at the end of the studio day. Some left for public transport, some went to their own cars, others had hire cars organised. There was an official-looking vehicle with uniformed driver for Superintendent Roscoe. And something very close to a limousine waiting for Bob Garston. Whatever budgetary restrictions might apply to other members of the production team, he was a man with star status to maintain.

Charles Paris found himself shuffling through the main door in a group which included Sam Noakes and Ted Faraday. Outside he encountered a phenomenon he hadn't expected for what was basically a documentary series – autograph hunters. The overlap between police work and showbiz was becoming total.

The current focus of their attention was Chloe Earnshaw. She was being fittingly modest, saying 'Oh, you don't want my autograph', but clearly they did. She looked interrogatively at one of her police minders, who shrugged and said, 'Don't want to antagonise them.' So, with a show of reluctance, Chloe Earnshaw signed the few books and bus tickets that were proffered, before being whisked away by her minders to 'a secret location'. (The threats that had been made to her husband and the public way in which she attacked their perpetrators ensured that she was under twenty-four-hour police protection.)

The autograph hunters turned next to the emerging group and there was no doubt who they were after in that lot. However much she dismissed the possibility, in the public imagination DI Sam Noakes had become a star. Hers was the name they wanted in their collections.

One of them asked Ted Faraday for an autograph. He refused, firmly but without rudeness. 'Sorry, in my business you sign as few things as possible.'

'Afraid someone might track you down through your handwriting?' Sam Noakes asked teasingly.

'Maybe.'

'Or – even more worrying – find out your real character through it?'

'Always a risk,' he responded with a lazy grin. There was definitely some undercurrent beneath their banter, though its precise nature Charles could not define.

'Did they organise a car for you, Ted?' Sam asked.

'Offered one. I told them not to bother. Never like being committed to where I'm going to be at the end of an evening.'

Some transient message flashed between their eyes. 'They've done a car for me,' she said casually. 'Fancy a lift?'

Matching her casualness, the private investigator accepted the offer. Charles was aware of a sound behind him and turned to see Superintendent Roscoe and Greg who had just come out of W.E.T. House. They had both heard the last exchange and neither looked particularly pleased about it.

'Good night, Superintendent. Good night, Greg,' Sam called over her shoulder, as she moved elegantly towards the hire car.

Superintendent Roscoe waved an acknowledgement, but the other policeman said nothing. Nor did Ted Faraday, as he nonchalantly followed the female star of *Public Enemies* into her car.

The autograph hunters lingered, hoping to catch Bob Garston when he came out. They'd have a long wait. The presenter had dragged Roger Parkes and Geoffrey Ramage straight down to an editing suite, to watch and make notes on a playback of that evening's *Public Enemies*.

The autograph hunters didn't ask for autographs from Superintendent Roscoe or the man called Greg.

Nor, it goes without saying, from Charles Paris.

Chapter Four

GOT TO BE masochism, hasn't it, thought Charles as he dialled Maurice Skellern's number. I mean, why else would anyone go on ringing someone whose news was always depressing? He tried to think of a single occasion when an unsolicited call to his agent had left him feeling better, but his memory drew a blank. There had been instances – rare instances – when he had rung back after a message from Maurice and received good news, but a call out of the blue had never prompted more than gloomy reflections on the current 'quietness' of the business and on Charles's failure to 'make anything happen for himself' in his chosen career.

He was therefore surprised when he got through to hear his agent in a state of considerable excitement.

'You've no idea, Charles,' Maurice bubbled on, 'how gratifying it is for someone in my profession when all your efforts finally pay off.'

'What?'

'When a talent which you have been nurturing for years – nurturing – finally gets the recognition it so richly deserves. I mean, it makes it all worthwhile – all the anguish, all the hours you spend on the phone trying to make producers aware of your client's skills, all the afternoons when the phone doesn't ring once, all the occasions when you despair that the client's ever going to take any initiative...well, let me tell you – when there's a really big breakthrough, you forget all that.'

'And has there been a really big breakthrough?' asked Charles, trying to sound cool, almost uninterested.

'Oh, I would say so. Yes, I most certainly would say so. No two ways about that.'

'How big?'

'Only *internationally* big. Only *globally* big. Only – and I breathe the word with appropriate respect – only *Hollywood* big.'

'Really?' Charles murmured, hardly daring to believe his ears.

'Columbia Pictures...' Maurice Skellern continued in a deliberately matter-of-fact tone, 'Columbia Pictures, no less, are doing a remake of *The Spy Who Came in from the Cold* – you remember the movie?'

'Of course. Richard Burton.'

'Exactly, Charles. Exactly. Richard Burton as the fiftyish, over-the-hill, crumpled, down-at-heel, unsuccessful spy. Only one small problem – Richard

Burton's dead.'

'Yes. I did hear that.'

'So Columbia wants the new Richard Burton. But not a Richard Burton who's already an established star. They want to *create* the new Richard Burton – find the right person and rocket him to stardom. So their casting people get working and they start looking for someone who can play fiftyish, over-the-hill, crumpled, down-at-heel, unsuccessful. And – inevitably, because of the way he puts himself about in the business – they end up ringing Maurice Skellern. Hello, they say, have you got anyone on your books who can play fiftyish, over-the-hill, crumpled, down-at-heel, unsuccessful? Well, yes, I reply, as it happens I do have on my books the perfect person to play, fiftyish over-the-hill, crumpled, down-at-heel, unsuccessful. And the rest, as they say, will be history.'

Charles could hardly find enough breath in his lungs to murmur, 'So what's the next step?'

'I've shown the Columbia people over here the photograph – they're happy. I've sent them the showreels of work by the actor in question – they're happy. The next step will be to fly him over to Hollywood for final interviews.'

'When?' asked Charles, thinking of the infinite void that was his engagements diary.

'Tomorrow.'

'Oh, my God. It's wonderful news, Maurice, isn't it? I mean, sensational news. Best news I've ever heard in my life.'

'That's very sweet of you to say so, Charles. I'll pass it on to Malcolm. He'll appreciate it.'

'Malcolm?'

'Malcolm Tonbridge. You remember. You met him once at my office.'

'Malcolm Tonbridge? But he's hardly forty, is he?'

'Thirty-eight.'

'And he's not crumpled. I mean, he's quite good-looking.'

'Very good-looking. Positively dishy. That'll stand him in good stead in Hollywood, you know.'

'Yes, but I mean, the part surely demands –'

'Hollywood knows what it wants, Charles. Good heavens, you can't have a character who's meant to be fiftyish, over-the-hill, crumpled, down-at-heel, unsuccessful played by someone who actually *is* fiftyish, over-the-hill, crumpled, down-at-heel, unsuccessful, can you?' Maurice Skellern let out a wheezing laugh. 'Otherwise, well...otherwise even *you'd* be in with a chance, eh, Charles?'

The wheezing laugh continued. Maurice was tickled pink by his little fantasy. It was the best joke he'd thought of for a very long time.

Indulge the masochistic mood while it lasts, thought Charles, as he dialled the number of his wife Frances. 'Ex-wife' would perhaps be more accurate.

Though there was still no official divorce, the 'ex'-ness seemed to be hardening increasingly into permanence.

'Hello?'

'It's me. Charles.'

'Oh yes?' Long experience of such phone calls had brought her response to the point where it had no intonation of any kind. 'What can I do for you?'

'Just rang for a chat.'

'Ah.' There was a silence. 'A chat about anything in particular?'

'No. Just...you know...'

'I don't know unless you tell me, Charles.'

'No. Well, I...Just to see how you are and...'

'Fine. I'm fine.'

'Good.'

'You?'

'Oh, fine, yes. Yes, fine, thank you.'

'Any work?'

'I have actually just done a job.'

'Well, there's a novelty.'

'One of those *Public Enemies* programmes.'

'When's it going to be on?'

'It was on. Last night.'

'Oh. Well, sorry. I missed it.'

'There you go.'

'Charles, if you don't tell me things're coming up, how am I expected to know –?'

'Sure, sure. Sorry, I should have told you, but...the filming kept me very busy,' he lied.

'Hm. What were you doing in the show?'

'I was in one of the reconstructions,' he admitted shamefacedly.

'Charles... After all the things you've said about people who get involved in that kind of stuff... Last time the subject came up, I seem to remember you talking about "actors whose only previous work has been in dandruff commercials".'

'Yes, well, you know...No one'd ever offered me a reconstruction before.'

'Hm. So now I just have to wait and I'll see you in a dandruff commercial, is that it?'

'No one's ever offered me one of those either,' he said, with an attempt at humour.

'But if they did, you would instantly say yes – as you do to everything else.'

'Oh, I don't know. I'd like to think... Yes, I probably would,' he conceded lamely.

'Really, Charles. Why you can't get a hold on your career and...'

She gave up. What was the point of going through all the old arguments again? Raking over old embers. It seemed a long time since those embers had contained even the smallest spark.

Charles could sense her thoughts. Or perhaps he was just transferring his own on to her. Either way, they made him feel achingly empty.

'What were you playing in the reconstruction?' she asked.

'Murder victim. Well, to be accurate, *probable* murder victim. Martin Earnshaw.'

'Oh.' Frances sounded touched. 'Husband of that poor girl who...?'

Charles was surprised that Frances too was under the spell of Chloe Earnshaw. He could understand the male population of the country, but he'd always had great respect for his wife's bullshit-detecting antennae. Probably he was just being over-cynical again. God, why couldn't he take anything at face value? Why couldn't he trust or believe in anything?

'How's work for you?' he asked, trying to shift his developing mood.

'Do you really want to know?'

'Well...'

'It's OK. The school is still standing. I'm still its headmistress. I could provide more detail, but I know you're not really interested.'

'Well, now, I wouldn't say...'

It was another sentence not worth finishing. Frances was right. He wasn't really interested in the minutiae of staff-room politics.

'So...?' She made the word sound like a sigh.

'So,' he echoed. He had had thoughts of fixing a time to meet, asking her out somewhere, but the sterility of the conversation sapped his will. What *was* the point? They really had grown apart now. Separate people. With separate lives. Linked only by a few ambivalent memories. Even those were fading.

And a daughter, of course. Yes, they were linked by a daughter. He was on the verge of asking about her, but again what was the point? He knew Frances would only remind him that he had Juliet's phone number and was quite capable of ringing her himself. The emptiness ballooned inside him.

'Well, anyway, Frances...As I say, I just rang to see that you're OK.'

'And, as I say, I'm fine.'

'Yes. Well...I'll be in touch.'

'Fine.'

'Goodbye then, Frances.'

'Goodbye, Charles.'

Was he being hypersensitive, or had she put the phone down more abruptly than was strictly necessary?

Charles mooched disconsolately along the landing towards the door of his bedsitter. There was the remains of a half-bottle of Bell's in there. At least he thought there was. On those days when he started sipping early, it was always difficult to remember how much there was left.

He was stopped by the sound of the phone ringing. To his amazement, it was Maurice.

The agent's mood had changed totally, its previous euphoria supplanted by a dull gloom.

'What's the matter?' asked Charles.

'Malcolm Tonbridge. Bloody Malcolm Tonbridge.'

'What about him?' A churlishly appealing thought insinuated itself into Charles's mind. 'Columbia haven't gone off the idea, have they?'

'Oh no, Hollywood are as keen as ever. Keener if anything.'

'So?'

'Malcolm just rang me. Said now his career's taking off, he needs to be with a bigger agency.'

'Oh.'

'People who specialise in movies. People who've got "representation on the West Coast". He said he was grateful to me for all I'd done for him, but he's moving into a very specialised area and he needs to be looked after by specialists.'

'I see.'

'God, Charles, I feel a complete failure.'

'Well, I'm sorry, Maurice. But why on earth did you ring to tell *me* about it?'

'Because, of everyone I know, you're the one person who I thought'd really *understand*.'

'Oh,' said Charles Paris, 'thank you *very* much.'

Chapter Five

ONCE, IN A moment of eloquence assisted by Arthur Bell's distillery, Charles Paris had defined the life of an actor as like that of a child's glove puppet, spending most of its life crumpled and forgotten in the corner of a toy cupboard, and only fully alive when a warm hand was inserted into it. At the time the references to inserting warm hands into things had triggered a burst of crude innuendo, but Charles still thought there was something in the image. The hand of course, which animated the actor's personality, was work. Give an actor a job, and suddenly he exists.

Pursuing this image through, it could be said that Charles Paris spent the four days after the first *Public Enemies* programme crumpled up and forgotten in the corner of a toy cupboard. He had made the necessary – or perhaps unnecessary – phone calls, to Maurice and Frances, on the morning after, and didn't feel inclined to ring either of them again. From his agent he would only get more unwittingly dismissive references to his own career and reproachful catalogues of the perfidies of Malcolm Tonbridge.

And from his wife he would get...He didn't quite know what he would get, but he didn't relish it. Something basic seemed to have changed in his relationship with Frances. Ever since he'd walked out – and indeed for much of the twelve years before – the marriage had been an on-off affair, but in the past he had always felt confident that any 'off' would eventually give way to an 'on'. That core of certainty had now gone. The relationship had descended to a new bleakness, and the cold prospect that they might permanently lose contact had become increasingly feasible. Maybe Frances, finally and irrevocably, had had enough of him. Ringing her again would only increase the pain.

He could have telephoned other friends, suppressed his envy to those who had work, indulged in mutual moaning with those who hadn't. He could even have arranged to meet some of the unsuccessful ones, and continued the moaning over too many drinks somewhere. But it all seemed a lot of effort.

So it was the crumpled glove puppet in the corner of the toy cupboard. He was not completely inert. He made it to the overpriced corner shop to buy the basic necessities for his solitary menu, in which toast, baked beans and breakfast slices figured more prominently than most *chefs de cuisine* would recommend. He also stocked up on the necessary bottles of Bell's.

Once or twice, driven by some childhood Calvinist conviction that drinking on one's own was a bad thing, he adjourned to the pub. But the one he always went to, in Westbourne Grove, was, like the Black Feathers, 'local' only in geography. The bar staff, Australians who had always started the job that day, had a religious objection to recognising anyone over thirty.

And the older customers, some of whose faces Charles had seen before, evidently came to the pub for a mystic private communion with their drinks. After twenty minutes sitting shrink-wrapped in his own isolation amidst the music and shouts of the young, drinking alone appeared an infinitely more sociable option.

How long this torpor might have continued was impossible to know, because it was interrupted on the Tuesday morning by a dictatorial phone call from Louise Denning. Charles was commanded to attend a briefing meeting at W.E.T. House that afternoon. As usual in the medium, it was assumed that no one would have any more pressing calls on their time than the demands of a television programme. Charles, who of course had no more pressing calls on his time than the demands of a television programme, would nonetheless have preferred the summons be couched as a question rather than an order.

'Well, I am free as it happens,' he conceded after some invisibly mimed diary-consulting, 'but I thought I'd finished my bit.'

'There has been a new development in the case,' Louise Denning announced mysteriously.

'Am I allowed to know what it is?'

'No. You'll be given all necessary information at the briefing meeting.'

'Oh. Does this mean that I'm going to be involved in more filming? That I'm being booked for this week's show too?'

But Louise Denning was too canny to answer the actor's instinctive question. Though the old-fashioned BBC tenet that an offer of work made over the phone was tantamount to a contract had, in harder-nosed commercial times, gone the way of most 'gentlemen's agreements', incautious words could still pose a risk. 'I'm afraid I'm unable to answer that, Mr Paris,' the researcher replied primly. 'But I'm sure everything will be made clear at the meeting this afternoon.'

They're so bloody arrogant, thought Charles, as he put the phone down. They think everyone'll just drop everything to turn up to their bloody meetings. No contract, no talk of payment, and they expect me just to appear on the off chance. I've half a mind not to go.

But, needless to say, the other half of his mind won. He appeared meekly at W.E.T. House in very good time for the three o'clock meeting.

There's something very pervasive about policemen. They quickly colour the ambience of any situation in which they are involved, and the briefing meeting at W.E.T. House that afternoon was a case in point. The television people – almost all the *Public Enemies* production team – easily outnumbered Superintendent Roscoe, DI Noakes and the man called 'Greg' (who was now identified as Detective Sergeant Marchmont), but the way the three of them sat behind a long table immediately transformed the atmosphere into that of an official police briefing. Even Bob Garston's ego was subservient to the professionals.

Not that the first professional to speak was particularly charismatic. Superintendent Roscoe liked the sound of his own voice, but nobody else appeared that keen on it. The production crew shifted without interest in their seats, and his two colleagues avoided each other's eyes, afraid their superior's long-winded oratory might set them giggling.

'And,' the superintendent announced, homing in on his subject after some five minutes' preamble, 'we – that is I – have taken an unusual decision in these changed circumstances. I have decided that the news should be embargoed until Thursday's transmission of *Public Enemies*. This is not done simply to give the programme an exclusive publicity coup...'

Though, from the gleeful expression on the face of Roger Parkes, it would certainly do that.

'...It is because I have decided that, in my judgement, a shock announcement of that kind will be the most effective way of advancing our enquiries. The relationship between the police and the media has not always been as smooth as one might wish, but here is an occasion where we can mend a few fences by a bit of mutual back-scratching. *Public Enemies* will benefit from the exclusive we are offering, and we in the police can hopefully also benefit from the new information that will come in as a result of these disclosures. I have decided that this is the best way for us to proceed, and I will stand by my decision in the face of any opposition.'

You didn't have to be a very sophisticated psychologist, Charles reckoned, to conclude that someone who asserted so often a decision had been his own was clearly talking about a decision made by someone else.

Bob Garston had been silent too long. *Public Enemies* was his show, after all, and he couldn't allow anyone else more than a brief appearance centre stage. 'Of course, Superintendent, the main opposition we're likely to encounter will be from the boys in News.'

'Of course. This is the kind of information that would normally be broken in a news bulletin, but I have decided it will be more effectively used in your programme. I have no doubt it's the kind of decision that will cause a bit of a furore.'

'That's an understatement,' said Roger Parkes jubilantly. 'ITN will be extremely shirty about this – so will the BBC. It'll get all kinds of flak from the press and could even lead to questions in the House. But don't worry, I'm prepared to defend my decision.'

Oh, I see, so it's *your* decision now, thought Charles. Since the previous Thursday Roger Parkes had changed, seeming to have grown in stature. He even appeared less deferential to Bob Garston, as if he had gained a new ascendancy over the presenter. Charles wondered if it was Parkes who had actually broached the idea of the news embargo and *Public Enemies* exclusive to Superintendent Roscoe. That would explain his new chirpiness – and also create something of a precedent in television – an executive producer coming up with a good idea.

Roger Parkes immediately confirmed Charles's conjecture, as he continued, 'I knew what the stakes were when I first put forward the suggestion, Superintendent.'

Roscoe coloured. He didn't like having the initiative taken away from him in this way. DI Noakes even more studiedly avoided DS Marchmont's eye. The showing-up of their superintendent was clearly regular enough to have become a running joke between them.

'Still, we'd better move on,' said Roscoe brusquely. 'Noakes, over to you.'

She was ready, as ever poised and efficient. Immediately, the audience listened. Superintendent Roscoe didn't carry authority; Sam Noakes did. 'Right, so you've all got the background. What we're dealing with here is extremely secret information. Our approach – embargoing it until it's announced on *Public Enemies* on Thursday – is risky, and it's only going to work if we can guarantee absolute security from everyone involved in the production. You're only here because you're all people who will have to know what's happened in order to do your jobs making the programme.

'But, if that programme's going to happen as we want it to, you're all virtually going to have to sign an Official Secrets Act. If a murmur of this gets to the press before Thursday, a lot of people are going to be left with a lot of egg on their faces. So I want you all to be aware just how high the stakes are. Don't breathe a word of it to anyone – however close they are to you, however much you trust them. If this scheme's going to work, secrecy has to be total – do you all understand that?'

There were murmurs of assent from around the room. Television people love a good internal drama; and the more that drama relies on restricted information, the more they love it. This one promised to be even more exciting than gossip about who'd lose their job next.

'Well, OK,' said Geoffrey Ramage, 'you can rely on all our discretion, no problem about that. We won't tell a soul about the new information, but' – and here he voiced the question of everyone in the room – 'can you please tell us what that new information is?'

'Yes,' said Sam Noakes, professionally slowing the pace of her revelation. 'Of course. We have had a significant breakthrough in our investigations into the disappearance of Martin Earnshaw. Last night in a –'

'Excuse me,' said Sergeant Marchmont. 'Sorry to interrupt, Sam, but we agreed to operate this thing on a "need to know" basis.'

'So?' She was put out at having her narrative interrupted.

'So...there are people in this room who already know all they need to know.'

'What? Who?'

The detective sergeant consulted a list on a clipboard. 'The actor Charles Paris.' Charles looked up in amazement as Marchmont continued, 'He's going to be involved in further filming reconstructing Martin Earnshaw's movements and it's important he understands how secret that is. You do understand that, do you, Mr Paris?'

Greg Marchmont looked round the room to locate the actor.

'Yes, yes, I understand that,' Charles assured him.

'No mention to anyone of where you're doing the filming, no mention even that you're doing it at all – OK?'

'OK. Won't breathe a word to a soul.'

'Someone on the production team'll let you know where you've got to be tomorrow.'

'That's right,' Louise Denning agreed, brusquely efficient. 'You'll get a call at home later on this afternoon.'

'Fine.'

'But that's all you need to know, Mr Paris,' said Sam Noakes, happy to regain the initiative from Sergeant Marchmont.

'You mean I don't get to find out what this new information is?' asked Charles plaintively.

'Sorry. You'll have to wait till nine o'clock on Thursday – along with the rest of the population.'

'Oh. Oh.' Charles rose to his feet. 'So now...I just go, do I?'

Sam Noakes flashed him a professional smile. 'Please.'

Sidling out of the conference room, Charles Paris felt like the boy not picked for either side in playground football. As he opened the door, the unworthy thought of listening at the keyhole crossed his mind, but the presence of a uniformed officer in the corridor put paid to that. The security on this edition of *Public Enemies* was being taken very seriously indeed.

Charles felt extraordinarily frustrated. It was like getting to the end of a thirties detective story and finding the last few pages torn out.

Still, he thought philosophically, there are compensations. First, I will be working again tomorrow. And, second, I have been expressly forbidden to tell anyone I'm working. So maybe I can get away without paying any commission to Maurice Skellern.

The high level of security was maintained during the following day's filming in Brighton. The substantial police presence which kept the general public away from Charles Paris showed just how seriously they were taking it. Nothing would be allowed to leak before the transmission of *Public Enemies* the following evening.

Charles's actual filming was scheduled for after dark, but he was booked for the full day. This he didn't mind at all, as it meant overtime. At ten a car picked him up from Hereford Road to drive down to Brighton. He had assumed that it was one of the hire cars regularly used by W.E.T., and was surprised to discover the driver was a policeman. Presumably this was another reflection of the high security surrounding the operation.

Once in Brighton, Charles was smuggled into the same hotel as before and put up – though he couldn't keep the phrase 'holed up' out of his mind – in a private suite. Here he met Geoffrey Ramage and other members of the *Public Enemies* team, as well as even more policemen. Charles got quite a buzz out of the situation, all the cloak-and-dagger secrecy reminding him of a post-*Ipcress File* espionage movie in which he'd had a small part. It had secured him a memorable notice from the *Observer*: 'Charles Paris's character looked so confused by all the crossing and double-crossing that the bullet which put paid to him on the Berlin Wall must have come as a merciful release.'

A lavish room-service buffet was laid on, but Charles regretfully rationed himself on the free wine. He was, after all, working. The surrounding policemen showed no such inhibitions. It seemed that the line Charles had said in so many stage thrillers, 'No, thank you, sir, not while I'm on duty', was yet another fabrication of crime fiction.

After lunch the reason for his early call became apparent. It was not that his portrayal of Martin Earnshaw required greater psychological depth than it had the previous week, simply that on this occasion the character had to walk. Being filmed sitting in a pub drinking called for limited skills of impersonation, whereas movement needed coaching. To this end, Geoffrey Ramage insisted that Charles watch videos of the missing man.

The only available footage dated from Martin Earnshaw's first marriage, inept wobbly shots of him acting up for the camera on holiday in Majorca. The property developer was then presumably benefiting from the boom of the early eighties. He looked very happy and carefree, anyway, with an almost childlike innocence about his clowning.

Charles wondered idly what had happened to the first marriage. If he had been investigating Martin Earnshaw's disappearance, that was certainly something he would have looked into. But it was a safe assumption that the combined intellects of the entire police force and Ted Faraday had already made that mental leap and acted on it. Charles, who had in his time been involved in investigating a few crimes, was rather enjoying his current position on the periphery of one but without personal involvement.

Martin Earnshaw seemed to walk like most other people of his age and build, but Charles patiently – and literally – went through his paces for Geoffrey Ramage, making minuscule adjustments to stride length and arm swing as required. After an hour or so, the director was satisfied.

To Charles it all seemed a bit pointless. Given Geoffrey's tastes in lighting, he knew that on the final print 'Martin Earnshaw' would appear as little more than a blur.

The evening's task, when it was spelled out to him, did not promise to stretch Charles Paris as an artiste. He had to leave the Black Feathers, and walk – in the approved Martin Earnshaw manner – through a few dark alleys and lanes to the sea front. Once there, he had to walk down on to the beach underneath the Palace Pier.

That was it. Hardly King Lear, but, from an actor's point of view, the part did have a couple of things going for it. First, there were the free meals. And, second, no other actors were involved. It was a one-man show.

Charles was interested to find out the source of the new information about his *doppelganger's* movements. So great had been the appeal to the British public of Chloe Earnshaw's television appearances that her own home telephone had been constantly ringing with offers of new leads. Since many of the potential informants had rung off when answered by a policeman, it had been decided to return Chloe from the 'secret address' to her home. Here she was left on her own, though under heavy surveillance, to answer the telephone. All calls were recorded by the police and checked for authenticity.

The details of Martin Earnshaw's route from the pub to the Palace Pier had come from a woman who refused to give her name. In fact Chloe Earnshaw had been out shopping when the call came through and it was recorded on the answering machine.

The voice quality was muffled, as if the caller had been resorting to the old B-feature cliché of a handkerchief over the receiver. The woman had given no clues to her identity, and police thought it probable that she shouldn't have been in Brighton at the relevant time. Possibly she'd been with a lover. Perhaps she even had some connection with the people responsible for Martin Earnshaw's disappearance. Certainly her muffled message gave the police no means of tracking her down.

Her information, though, they took very seriously, which was why Charles Paris was made to retrace the route she outlined. After the filmed insert had been played in on the following night's *Public Enemies*, Bob Garston would do another of his impassioned, straight-to-camera pleas.

'We do need the woman who gave that information to come forward. We will ensure absolute secrecy for her, but there are a few more follow-up questions we need to ask. Please. We know you're out there somewhere. You've already done the public-spirited thing once by giving that information. Please don't be afraid. Call us again. Who knows, you might be able to tell us that one little, apparently insignificant, detail that enables us to catch these..."*Public Enemies*"!'

For Charles Paris the filming was frustrating. Not because of the actual work – anyone capable of copying Martin Earnshaw's walk could have done that – but because of the knowledge that all the crew around him knew the details of the revelation to be made on the following evening's programme.

He tried, with varying degrees of subtlety, to elicit the odd hint from Geoffrey Ramage, from the cameraman, the Make-Up girl, the police who kept the public away from the location. Not one of them cracked. They'd all taken Sam Noakes's words to heart. The security screen was impenetrable.

Charles Paris, even though he *was* Martin Earnshaw, would, in common with the rest of the British population, have to wait till nine o'clock on Thursday to find out what had happened to the missing man.

Chapter Six

HE WAS NOT called for the following day, so there was no way that Charles could once again see *Public Enemies* in the comfort of a W.E.T. hospitality suite. In common with nine million other members of the British public – or more if Roger Parkes's optimistic prognostication proved correct – he would have to watch in the comfort of his own home.

'Comfort' was not a word readily applied to Charles's Hereford Road bedsitter. He had moved in there when he left Frances, and the room still appeared to be in mourning for their marriage. Maybe Charles had once entertained fantasies of a slick interior-designed bachelor pad to which an endless succession of glamorous women could be lured, but if so, reality had quickly quashed such ideas.

He'd never been good at home-making, drifting before his marriage from one anonymous set of digs to another, rarely bothering even to unpack. Frances it was who had brought into his life the concept of a home as more than somewhere to sleep. She had also introduced him to a love of possessions – not for their monetary value but as a cement of memories, mutual purchases marking off the phases and moods of their marriage.

With the marriage, however, all that had ended. The shared mementoes stayed in their Muswell Hill marital home, an unfinished collection frozen reproachfully in time. And when Frances had finally moved out to her flat in Highgate, many of them just disappeared. Reproducing the same acquisitiveness in his own environment, or even making that environment a little less squalid, would have felt to Charles like a further betrayal of his relationship with Frances. Some perverse, self-punishing instinct dictated that as he had made his bed, so must he lie on it. Except that he very rarely did make his bed when he wasn't changing the sheets. And he didn't do that as often as he should have done.

The room therefore had never fulfilled its promise as a seducer's silken lair. Though Charles had not been without female company since the end of his marriage, not many of the encounters had been conducted on his home ground. Few women had actually been inside the bedsitter. Which was probably just as well.

So it remained very much as it had been when he moved in, all those features about which he'd thought 'that's the first thing I'll change' still unchanged. The grey-painted furniture, the yellow candlewick bedspread bleached now to an unhealthy cream, the sad curtain hiding sink and gas ring, the customary accumulation of glasses and brown-ringed coffee cups – everything gave off a miasma of defeat. It was an appropriate setting for Charles Paris in empty-glove-puppet mode.

That was the state in which he spent the Thursday, trying to pretend he wasn't infected by the same prurient interest as the other nine million who were waiting to watch *Public Enemies*.

His television was of a piece with the rest of the bedsitter – an old portable dating from the days before beige plastic had been appropriated exclusively for computer monitors. To its top was attached a ring aerial, which needed constant realignment to minimise the snowstorms that flurried across the screen.

By the time nine o'clock arrived, Charles found he had got through nearly half a bottle of Bell's, which was bad, even by his standards. Still, it's justified, he thought. I deserve a bit of a celebration. I am, after all, about to watch myself on television. But even he wasn't convinced by such sophistry.

As the applause for the preceding sofa-bound sitcom gave way to a teaser for *Public Enemies* and commercials, Charles realised that once again he'd omitted to tell Frances he was about to be on television. But he didn't feel inclined to do so now. Instead, he poured himself another substantial Bell's.

The credits for *Public Enemies* combined urgency and threat. Crime scenes of mounting violence were superimposed on each other against insistent background music in which jangling guitars mixed with electronic sirens and gunshots. In each of the scenes the criminal appeared as a black void, an evil outline punching, stabbing or slashing at a blurred victim. These outlines froze in place until they all conjoined and blacked out the screen. Over this the blood-red *Public Enemies* logo suddenly appeared.

The blackness melted to blue and fragmented into new outlines, this time of anonymous policemen and women. Out of the middle of this montage a new image took shape and, just as the blood-red words 'with BOB GARSTON' appeared at the bottom of the screen, revealed itself to be a stylised picture of the presenter at his most no-nonsense, hard-bitten and journalistic. It was the gritty face of a man working at the coalface of real life.

The message of the credits was undoubtedly the one that Bob's Your Uncle Productions intended – only one man can find a solution to the rising tide of violent crime in this country, and that man is Bob Garston.

Charles Paris took a long cynical swallow of Bell's, as the image dissolved to zoom in on the real Bob Garston, live in the W.E.T. studio. He sat perched grittily on a high stool, wearing glasses for extra *gravitas*. His light double-breasted suit was beautifully tailored, in a way that eschewed dandyism and maintained the necessary grittiness quotient. It was certainly – and literally – a cut above the square-shouldered suits of the plainclothes men who were part of the presenter's backdrop.

Behind Bob Garston the W.E.T. designer had created a simulacrum of a police incident room, full of telephones, computers, maps and wall charts. Throughout the programme this area was criss-crossed by policemen and women, some in uniform, some not, but all possessed by a desperate urgency to fulfil some unknown mission. The constant, purposeless movement would have been extremely irritating if the viewer saw too much of it, but that was not a problem in a Bob Garston production. Characteristically, the presenter saw to it that he was held in tight close-up for all of his links.

Garston began the programme with even more concerned dramatic urgency than usual. 'Good evening. Tonight on *Public Enemies* we bring you exclusive news on a case that has had the country holding its breath for the past few weeks – the disappearance of Martin Earnshaw. In what is a first for a non-News television programme, *Public Enemies* will bring you information which Scotland Yard have kept secret from all other media until now. We will also get a reaction from Martin Earnshaw's wife to the new breakthrough. That's in a moment, but first a follow-up on last week's report about the security van robbery in Ilford.'

The hook had been baited, the promised revelation cunningly designed to keep millions of hands from straying to their remote controls for the next half-hour. No doubt Roger Parkes hoped that all over the country, extra viewers were being called in from the kitchen. 'Hey, *Public Enemies*'s got something new on the Martin Earnshaw case – and they're going to have that dishy wife of his on again. Bet they've found the body. Come on, love, come and see what's happening.'

The intervening items in the programme seemed particularly dull that week. Bob Garston had even allowed in Roger Parkes's survey of automatic security lights. But the relative tedium was calculated. Between each insert, the presenter wound up the expectation a little more, professionally controlling his revelations with all the skill of a strip-tease artiste.

At last the moment came. Turning with hitherto unplumbed depths of grittiness to another camera, Bob Garston announced, 'And now we come to the latest news on the disappearance of Martin Earnshaw.' But he didn't go straight to the bombshell; still he extended his titillation of the viewing millions. 'We've had a great many very useful calls from members of the public offering new information – and don't forget, our phone lines are open now and continue to be open twenty-four hours a day. The number's on your screen, so if you know anything – anything at all – get in touch. Remember, even what seems to you an insignificant detail could be vitally important to the police investigations – so please pick up your phone.

'We've had one very useful call from a lady who saw Martin Earnshaw leaving the Brighton pub where the previous last sighting of him occurred. She's given us invaluable information for which we're very grateful, but we would urge her to make contact again to...' And he went into his predictable routine before introducing the reconstruction.

Charles Paris watched his own performance dispassionately. The only emotion it aroused in him was mild distaste. Was it really for this that I became an actor? The world is full of wonderful parts in brilliant plays and I end up imitating the walk of a vanished property developer. Have I no pride? Is there no job I wouldn't do for money?

Uncomfortably suspecting that he knew the answers to the last two questions, Charles Paris refilled his whisky glass, which seemed unaccountably to have emptied itself.

At the end of the insert, Bob Garston still prolonged the agony. There were repeated pleas for anyone with information to come forward, further specific pleas to the woman who had seen Martin Earnshaw going to the Palace Pier. Then there was a reminder about the challenge between Ted Faraday and the police from the previous week's programme, and the news that the private investigator had faxed in an update on his progress. 'He's gone undercover, but is very optimistic that he's getting somewhere with his investigations.'

Bob Garston paused and held the silence for a long time. Then, turning to yet another camera, he produced his *coup de théatre*.

'However, Ted Faraday is probably not yet aware of the dramatic new development in the case. I am able to tell you – here, exclusively, live on *Public Enemies* – that a body has been found, which is believed to be that of Martin Earnshaw. Or to be more accurate, *parts* of a body have been found.'

He left another long pause for the gruesome impact of his words to sink in even to the slowest viewing intellect. 'Over to Detective Inspector Sam Noakes for the details.'

The camera found her at the front of the busy incident-room set. She sat, sternly pretty in her uniform, at a functional desk. The camera homed in to exclude the meaningless bustle behind her.

'Acting on an underworld tip-off,' Sam Noakes, with effortless mastery of the autocue, announced, 'police went to a graveyard in the village of Colmer five miles north of Brighton, where there had been apparent desecration of two recent graves. This kind of crime is all too common at the moment, and is frequently thought to be related to black magic practices...'

My God, this story's got everything, thought Charles. All we need now is a coven of naked witches. But his attempt at wry detachment didn't work. He was as surely ensnared by Sam Noakes's narrative as the rest of the silent millions.

'It was found on examination that two recently buried coffins had been tampered with. When opened, police did not discover any harm or desecration to the bodies inside. However...' The detective inspector may have claimed the showbusiness element of her work was merely a means to an end, but she could still hold a pause like a theatrical dame '...they did discover that something else had been placed inside the coffins.' Another silence Edith Evans would have killed for. 'In each coffin they found a human arm.'

Millions of pins, in sitting rooms around the country, could have been heard to drop. Bob Garston gave them time to descend, before he again picked up the narrative.

'Preliminary tests on those severed limbs suggest strongly that they belonged to Martin Earnshaw. His wife has very bravely been to try to identify them and is also of the view that they belonged to her husband. Chloe Earnshaw is obviously deeply traumatised by the experience, but has still agreed to appear – here, live – on tonight's programme. Her reason is a belief in human justice. Her husband has been murdered, and Chloe Earnshaw is determined to help find the *"Public Enemies"* responsible for the crime!'

The grieving wife – now officially the grieving widow – appeared on a separate set, looking frailer than ever between two huge villainous black cut-outs like those in the credits. She was still an elegant figure, in black polo-neck sweater and trousers, the colour now justified by her new status.

Her thin face, again with pale hair scoured back, bore witness to the strain she was under. It seemed even thinner and the highly developed skills of television make-up could not hide – or had perhaps been under instructions from the production team not to hide – the deep circles beneath Chloe's eyes and the redness that surrounded them.

This evidence of her distress made even more unworthy Charles Paris's thought that she still looked fanciable. His guilt was only alleviated by the knowledge that the same unworthy thought had sprung up in a few million other male minds across the country.

'My husband has been murdered,' Chloe Earnshaw began simply. 'That is a terrible truth for any wife to come to terms with, and I don't think it's yet sunk in for me. The reason I feel strong enough to be here tonight talking about Martin is probably that the truth hasn't sunk in yet.

'But the reason that I am here talking to you is that I'm angry. Somebody has taken away the life of the man I love. They've taken him away from me forever. I'll never see Martin again.'

Her voice wavered as the reality of this hit her for the first time. She gulped and recovered herself. 'But I don't believe anyone should be allowed to get away with a crime like that. There still is justice in this country and I want the people who killed my husband to face that justice. They must have friends. They must have wives, girlfriends. There must be someone out there who knows who they are. Please, please, if you know anything...just...get...in...touch...'

The last words struggled out against a mounting tide of tears and, as they finished, Chloe Earnshaw slumped, her head in her hands, weeping bitterly.

The camera, which had closed in on her suffering face, drew back very slowly, till her tiny body dwindled and the two huge cut-outs of *'Public Enemies'* seemed to fill the screen.

Then there was a surprise. Across that stricken image, with no signature tune, the credits started to roll. This was unprecedented. Never before had a production involving Bob Garston ended without a return to the presenter for a closing remark and reminder whose show it was. But in this instance, recognising the strength of the final image, he must have put dramatic television above personal aggrandisement.

It was a surprising decision, given its source, but the right one. As the end credit, 'A W.E.T. PRODUCTION IN ASSOCIATION WITH BOB'S YOUR UNCLE PRODUCTIONS FOR ITV', rolled off the top of the screen and Chloe Earnshaw's tiny white face was lost in black, no one could deny the power of the image.

Nor could anyone deny the power of Chloe Earnshaw's performance. The actor in Charles had to admit, with purely professional admiration, 'She's bloody good.'

Chapter Seven

ROGER PARKES's hopeful prognostications were gratifyingly realised. *Public Enemies*' revelations achieved all the reaction he had hoped for. The Friday's tabloids wallowed in the gruesomeness of the Colmer graveyard find, as ever appealing to that instinct in their readers which forms queues near motorway pile-ups, and as ever dressing up this prurience with 'the-public-must-be-told-the-truth' sanctimoniousness.

There even developed a race between the papers to find a perfect nickname for the crime's perpetrator. The *Mirror* led off with 'The Deadly Dissector'; *Today* offered 'The Sick Surgeon'; while the *Sun* kept things characteristically simple with 'The Bloody Butcher'. Having made their pitches, they sat back and waited to see which name the public would latch on to, each paper hoping that its coining might attain the mythic status of a 'Black Panther', a 'Moors Murderer' or a 'Yorkshire Ripper'.

The sensational Sunday papers, given more time, were able to come up with elaborate features on the story. *The People* brought forward a stomach-turning serialisation of a forensic pathologist's memoirs; while the *News of the World* included a pull-out supplement on other murders involving dismemberment – which no doubt led to many tasteless jokes over Sunday joints.

Far more gratifying, however, to the *Public Enemies* team than this news-inspired coverage was the media reaction to the way the revelation had been made. As Roger Parkes had hoped, there was an explosion of affront from the 'quality' press and television news departments.

ITN attempted through the courts to put an injunction on *Public Enemies*, prohibiting any further 'exclusive revelations'. *The Times*, in a leader headed 'THE TAIL WAGGING THE DOG', waxed lyrical about 'the sanctity of objective factual reporting' which must be protected from 'the iconoclastic vandalism of thrill-seeking entertainment programmes'.

To complete Roger Parkes's happiness, a question was actually asked in the House. A self-important Labour member from South Wales asked whether 'the Government condones the usurpation of journalistic values by televisual sensationalism.' Unfortunately the question received no meaningful answer, since it was asked at one of those moments when the chamber was virtually empty, but nonetheless a point of principle had been established.

Best of all, from the point of view of W.E.T. and Bob's Your Uncle Productions, that Thursday's edition of *Public Enemies* got wonderful 'overnights'. These were the first indications of audience share, ratings which would be confirmed by fuller research a week later, but which indicated that all the elaborately teasing trails running up to the programme had done their stuff. 'The BBC News,' as Bob Garston announced with relish, 'was bloody nowhere – hardly on the map. We bloody stuffed them!'

And, given the amount of publicity that week's programme had generated, the next week's *Public Enemies* looked set fair to stuff the BBC even more comprehensively.

Which was, after all, the whole aim of the exercise.

Charles Paris found it odd being dead. Previously his rendering of Martin Earnshaw had been an impersonation of someone who might or might not have suffered a dreadful fate; now suddenly he was playing a murder VICTIM.

It wasn't of course the first time he'd done that. He'd been killed off early in many creaky stage thrillers, notably one called *The Message is Murder* at the Regent Theatre, Rugland Spa. For another, whose title he had mercifully forgotten, he received a notice which claimed: 'Charles Paris dead was infinitely more convincing than the rest of the cast alive.'

Nor had his defunct performances been confined only to potboilers; he'd also given of himself in the classics. Indeed, his Ghost in a Chichester production of *Hamlet* had been greeted by the *West Sussex Gazette* with the following: 'Charles Paris, as the Prince's father, looked surprisingly corporeal. His too, too solid flesh certainly showed no signs of melting.'

But all these experiences were different from playing the part of a real person who had, until very recently, been breathing, walking and talking. And had now suffered dismemberment. Being Martin Earnshaw did give Charles a bit of a *frisson*.

But it's an ill wind...Martin Earnshaw's murder offered Charles Paris the prospect of continuing employment – at least until the perpetrator of the crime was uncovered. The *Public Enemies* production team had come up with a winning formula, in which the heart-rending Chloe Earnshaw and her late husband were essential ingredients. They weren't about to change that in a hurry. Charles Paris, as the dead man, had become a running character in this soap opera of murder.

Briefly he even contemplated getting on to Maurice Skellern and demanding more money now he was such an integral part of the show, but he decided against it. Instead he – and some bottles of Bell's – passed the weekend around Hereford Road in empty-glove-puppet mode, waiting for the next summons to W.E.T. House.

It came on the Monday morning. Louise Denning, earnestly humourless, announced that he was required for a briefing meeting at eleven the following day. There was no enquiry as to whether he was available. It was again assumed that nothing would impede the ultimate imperative of television.

* * *

W.E.T. Reception was expecting him and Charles Paris was speedily and efficiently escorted upstairs by one of the programme secretaries. Once in the *Public Enemies* outer office, he was asked to wait. He was offered a cup of coffee, though no explanation for the delay. He accepted the coffee, which the secretary quickly brought before disappearing on some unspecified errand to another part of the building.

Charles was left alone, wishing he'd thought to bring his *Times*, so that he could have a crack at the crossword. But he hadn't. He looked around the office for other reading matter. There weren't even any programme files. The conspiratorial secrecy which surrounded *Public Enemies* ensured that all its records were kept under lock and key in an inner office.

Nope, he could see nothing that contained words except for the telephone directories and, compulsive reader though he was, Charles Paris wasn't about to start reading them.

He tried to find something else of interest in the room, but without success. Characterless grey walls and white ceiling; grey desk and typing chair; two low grey armchairs, on one of which he sat; grey telephones, photocopier and fax machine. It was the kind of decor that would have confirmed Kafka's worst fears.

Just as he was thinking that time and life were frozen, that nothing in the world would ever move again, he was surprised by a click. A slight whirring followed, as the fax machine burst into action.

For maybe a minute Charles convinced himself that he would be virtuous and not give in to curiosity. But he was alone in the office, and he was human. He moved casually across to the fax machine and squinted down at the emerging sheet.

The originating fax number began '0273', which Charles had dialled often enough to identify as Brighton, and the ident read 'PRINTSERVE'. Presumably some public fax bureau.

The typed message was short.

GOING UNDERCOVER IN BRIGHTON. FOLLOWING UP VERY PROMISING NEW LEADS. TELL SAM I'M WAY AHEAD OF HER. REPORT AGAIN SOON. T.F.'

Charles didn't think it would be leaping to conclusions to assume that the fax came from Ted Faraday. So, even though the missing persons case had now developed into a murder hunt, the *Public Enemies* contest between the amateur and professional detectives was still on.

A door opened and Charles moved guiltily away from the fax, fascinated suddenly by some detail on the wall calendar. 'Come through,' commanded Louise Denning, never for a second contemplating any apology for keeping him waiting.

The customary level of television manners was maintained inside the room. Bob Garston and Roger Parkes did not even look up when Charles entered, but continued their latest squabble about programme content.

'Well, I still think,' the executive producer was insisting, 'that child abuse is exactly the kind of subject *Public Enemies* should be tackling.'

'Oh yes,' the presenter countered. 'If it's the right sort of child abuse.'

'What do you mean – the right sort? Surely child abuse is child abuse?'

'No, I mean, if we're going to have child abuse on a programme I'm involved in, then it's got to be sexy.'

'But, Bob, for heaven's sake – child abuse is sexy by definition.'

'No, it isn't. It's sex*ual* by definition. I'm talking sexy. *Public Enemies* doesn't want to show yet another kid, shot in silhouette or with the face electronically scrambled, moaning on about how her stepfather touched her up. The public's sick to death of it – they can get all that at home.'

'But child abuse is a criminal offence, and it's a major contemporary social problem.'

'Leave major contemporary social problems to BBC2 and Channel Four – we're talking mainstream television here. Through this Martin Earnshaw thing we've got *Public Enemies* into a ratings position other factual programmes would kill for, and I'm not going to have that threatened by your mimsy-pimsy *Guardian*-reading conscience.'

'It is not just my conscience, Bob, it's –'

'Anyway, there are other programmes that have cornered the market in child abuse. God, I don't want to go into the ring with Esther Rantzen. I do have some standards.'

That final assertion was arguable, Charles Paris reflected, as Roger Parkes picked up the argument again. 'You take my word for it – research shows that child abuse is something the viewers are really concerned about.'

'I don't want them bloody concerned! I want them fascinated, I want them frightened, I want them hooked! While I'm on the screen, I want them to keep watching, I want them to keep their hands off the bloody remote control, for Christ's sake!'

'But –'

'And they're not going to keep watching yet another hushed-voice account of some kid's suffering at the hands of the family pervert. I tell you, nowadays child-abuse victims are as much of a turn-off as...fly-blown babies starving in Africa. Nothing's going to get the viewing public excited about child abuse victims...' Bob Garston paused as a new thought came into his mind '...unless of course we reconstructed some of the actual acts of abuse...'

'But no, we couldn't do that,' he concluded regretfully. 'Might look as if we were being exploitative.'

'But couldn't we –?'

Bob Garston signalled the end of the conversation by looking up at Charles. If he ever had known the actor's name, he'd certainly forgotten it. 'Right, you're going to be needed for more filming this week.'

Charles managed to bite back the instinctive reaction, 'Oh, good.' Instead, he asked, 'Why, have you got new information through from the public?'

Bob Garston wrinkled his nose without enthusiasm. 'Not that much. Plenty of calls, of course, but all pretty bloody vague. No detailed stuff or positive sightings.'

'So there isn't much else you can do with me, is there...?'

'Don't you believe it. We're on to a winner here. We're getting some pretty positive research from your appearances on the show.'

'Oh, thank you,' said Charles, flattered – as any actor would be – by a commendation of his performance.

Bob Garston's next words, however, took some of the shine off the compliment. 'No, apparently the viewers get quite a charge from having a reconstruction of someone who's actually been dismembered.'

'Oh,' said Charles Paris.

A wistful longing came into Bob Garston's eyes. 'Wouldn't it be great if another bit of the body gets discovered in time for this week's programme...'

'Mm,' Charles agreed with a chuckle. 'Maybe the murderer will have the good sense to feed the remaining joints out gradually over the next four weeks – so that you'd have one for each programme...'

'Yes...' The presenter of *Public Enemies* was far too absorbed by this delicious fantasy to realise it had been proposed as a joke. A dreamlike quality came into his voice. 'Yes, wouldn't that be just perfect...'

Roger Parkes decided it was time to assert himself. 'So, about this week's filming, Mr Paris...'

Bob Garston, fearful of any challenge to his command, snapped out of his reverie. 'Yes, about this week's filming. Though we've done Martin Earnshaw in the pub, and we've done him leaving the pub, we still haven't done him leaving home and getting to the pub.'

'Ah. Right. So that's what I'll be doing, is it?'

'Yes. Good thing is we can get Chloe in this one too.'

'Oh?'

'Well, the research on her is still very positive. Getting stronger every week.' Garston looked thoughtful. 'She really has got something, you know...I'd like Bob's Your Uncle to set up another project with her when this lot's finished...'

Charles was incredulous. 'Her own series, you mean?'

'Mm.'

'But wouldn't that require her having a different husband murdered every week?'

Bob Garston looked up sharply, touchy about the possibility of being sent up. 'Look, you just do your work as a bloody extra! Keep your wisecracks to yourself!'

'No, I didn't mean –'

'Another thing...' Roger Parkes chipped in, maintaining the admonitory tone of the conversation. 'The security on this show is getting more and more important. You mustn't breathe a word to a soul about what you're up to.'

'I haven't. I wouldn't.'

'Not even to a wife, girlfriend. No pillow talk – OK?'

'It's all right. I live alone.'

'Oh, that's a blessing.'

Depends on your point of view, thought Charles wistfully. Bob Garston once again hijacked the conversation from his executive producer. 'Right, so we're pretty sure we're going to get very positive viewer reaction from having you in a reconstruction with Chloe.'

'But aren't you in danger of blurring the distinction between fantasy and reality?'

'Exactly.' Garston nodded vigorously. 'That's one of the main aims of programmes like *Public Enemies.*'

Chapter Eight

AN UNMARKED police car arrived at Hereford Road the following morning to take Charles back to Brighton. It was larger than the previous one, almost a limousine. While I was just a missing person, he thought wryly, I didn't qualify for this. Now I'm officially a murder victim, nothing's too good for me.

But he was quickly disillusioned of the idea that the special treatment was just for him. In the back of the car, separated from the driver by a glass panel, sat Superintendent Roscoe and Greg Marchmont. The detective sergeant looked ill at ease, subdued perhaps in the presence of his superior, but Roscoe was almost excessively affable.

He wasn't in uniform, but quickly explained his pale trousers and diamond-patterned pullover. 'Mixing business and pleasure for a couple of days. Keep an eye on the television lot and maybe fit in a bit of golf. Got my clubs in the back, you know. Get ready for retirement, eh? Just think about it, Marchmont, in a few months I'll be able to do this every day...while you lot are still grinding away at the coalface.'

He chuckled. This was a new Superintendent Roscoe, different from the touchy and ignored figure seen before. Charles got the feeling it was Greg Marchmont's presence that had made the change. With Ted Faraday or Sam Noakes and most of the other police, the superintendent had seemed awkward, aware of their contempt. Detective Sergeant Marchmont apparently didn't have that power. In their relationship, Roscoe called the shots.

Certainly the junior officer remained awkwardly silent for most of the journey, only speaking when politeness left him no alternative.

Superintendent Roscoe, on the other hand, was in expansive mood. 'I think this case is going to be my last triumph before I go, you know,' he announced.

Marchmont said nothing, so Charles filled in the silence. 'The Earnshaw case, you mean?'

'Yes. I've a feeling we're very close to the perpetrator.'

'Really? And is that thanks to the television programmes?'

'Well, they don't do any harm, but when this case is finally solved, it'll be down to good old traditional police methods.'

Marchmont stirred a little uneasily at this. Roscoe responded immediately to the unspoken criticism. 'No, I'm fully aware of all the new technology and that – very clever stuff. Genetic fingerprinting, offender profiling, new techniques in forensic pathology, computers, computers and more computers

– all very helpful in their proper place. But they're no substitute for the instincts of an experienced copper.'

From the way he said it, Superintendent Roscoe clearly put himself into this category. 'Young sparks like Noakes and her mates,' he continued, 'are very talented. In a few years they'll be excellent coppers, no question, but right now I'd back someone like me against them every time. They'll start to make real progress when they twig that science can only do so much. There's got to be an intuitive mind working with all that science.'

'But Sam Noakes said as much,' Charles objected. 'On the first programme, when Bob Garston was talking about "the little grey cells", she said the police had to respect intuition.'

'She may have said it, but she doesn't put it into practice. At times when I've passed on my hunches to her, she's been downright rude about them.'

Greg Marchmont again shifted his considerable bulk. Charles surmised that it was the nature of Superintendent Roscoe's 'hunches' rather than the principle of respecting intuition that Sam Noakes didn't like. He also got the feeling that, if she'd been there, Roscoe's defence of his old-fashioned methods wouldn't have got such an easy ride.

'You can have too much science,' the superintendent went on. 'When something's obvious, you don't need to go on wasting valuable resources to produce scientific proof that it's obvious.'

Again Marchmont's body language suggested that, in different circumstances, he would have contested this assertion.

Roscoe continued, relishing the docility of his audience. 'I mean, take the arms that were found at Colmer...OK, you do the basic checks – blood group, that kind of thing – but the most important identification is always going to come from Chloe Earnshaw recognising that they belonged to her husband. Once you've got that, then that's all you need to know.'

Charles thought it was perhaps time to stem the flow of generalisations. 'But surely there's other information that forensic tests can establish? Not just the identity of the victim, but the manner of his death, clues to where it may have taken place, how the body was dismembered, all that kind of stuff...?'

Superintendent Roscoe shrugged. 'Oh yes, fibres from a carpet made in Taiwan and only fitted into a limited edition of thirty-four 1978 Cortinas – that what you mean?'

'Well, there have been famous examples of criminals getting caught on just that sort of evidence.'

'And there have been a darned sight more *less* famous examples of criminals getting caught because an experienced copper has used a bit of gumption.'

'How would you define "gumption"?'

'Common sense. You look at the available information – the broad outlines, not the molecular structure of every speck of dust found on the corpse – and you start to get a feeling of the kind of mind you're up against.'

'The murderer?'

'Right.'

'But surely that's what profiling does. I mean, criminal psychologists work out –'

'You don't need a criminal psychologist to do it. That's the point I'm making, Mr Parrish –'

'Paris, actually.'

'What?'

'My name's "Paris".'

'Oh, right. Well, Mr Paris, I'm saying that anyone of reasonable intelligence who's spent his working life dealing with murderers can produce you a profile at least as well as a bloody criminal psychologist can – except that the copper'll do it a lot cheaper and a darned sight quicker.'

'So have you worked out a profile of Martin Earnshaw's murderer?'

'Course I have.' The superintendent grinned smugly. 'The man who did it –'

'You're sure it's a man?'

'Oh yes. He's very clever – highly intelligent character we're up against here. Also he's a bit of an exhibitionist. He didn't dismember the corpse for the purposes of concealment. Oh no, he did it so that he can control the pace of the investigation. He's going to feed out bits of the body when he feels like it.'

Bob Garston's dream come true, thought Charles, and that prompted him to say, 'So presumably the murderer's delighted by the coverage he's getting on *Public Enemies*?'

'You bet he is, Mr Paris. He's enjoying all that very much indeed. You see, as I say, he's highly intelligent and he likes pitting himself against other intellects. He was always going to be doing that with the police, but now he's also challenging the combined intelligence of the entire television viewing public.'

Charles was tempted to say 'Not much contest', but bit the words back. 'Traditionally, exhibitionists like that tend to get caught because they become over-confident, don't they, Superintendent?'

'Yes, I would agree. Part of the thrill for that kind of murderer is seeing how close to the wind he can sail. He loves almost boasting about his crime, almost actually telling people he's done it and, as you say, it's that temptation that often leads to his downfall.'

'So do you reckon that's what'll happen in this case?'

'Maybe.' The superintendent tapped his teeth reflectively. 'I've just a feeling this murderer may be a bit too canny for that.'

'So do you think you'll get him?'

Superintendent Roscoe beamed a complacent smile on Charles. 'Mr Paris, I told you – this case is going to be the triumph of my career.'

Greg Marchmont again moved uneasily. He wasn't the only member of the force, Charles concluded, who would be relieved when retirement finally came for Superintendent Roscoe and his dated attitudes.

* * *

In Brighton the car drew up outside the same hotel they had used the week before. Probably W.E.T. had some mutually back-scratching discount scheme with the place.

The two policemen and the actor got their luggage out of the boot and carried it inside. Superintendent Roscoe's golf bag was a huge leather job with a zipped hood. It looked brand-new and was evidently its owner's pride and joy. Roscoe refused the hotel porter's offers of assistance, insisting on carrying it himself.

Inside the hotel foyer, Greg Marchmont looked round without enthusiasm. 'Back a-bloody-gain.'

'It's been a week,' said Charles.

'For you it may have been. I was here yesterday. Up to town last night, down here again this morning – like a bloody yo-yo.'

'You were following up on something yesterday, were you?'

The clam-up was instantaneous. 'Sorry, I can't tell you.'

'Sorry, I shouldn't have asked.'

The detective sergeant gave him a bleak smile. Charles noticed how tired and tense Marchmont looked. The case – or perhaps some other pressure – was taking its toll on him.

They went to Reception to check in. Whether being dead had actually enhanced his status or not Charles didn't know, but that week he got a much better room, complete with sea view and minibar.

Geoffrey Ramage and the W.E.T. camera crew were already there. After lunch (in which Charles, relaxing into his role, indulged himself a little more than the previous week) there was some more walking practice to recapture the definitive Martin Earnshaw gait. The director was not easily satisfied and kept making him do it again, but Charles knew this was simply to kill time. Martin Earnshaw had left his home for the last time at seven in the evening, so the W.E.T. crew couldn't start shooting until it got dark. Fortunately, in the intervening four weeks the evenings had drawn in and they left the hotel round four.

The Earnshaws' house was on the borders of Hove, all very middle class and discreet. So middle class and discreet that the setting up of cameras and lights elicited not the slightest reaction from the neighbours. This was in marked contrast to what would have happened in most residential locations. Anything to do with television usually draws an instant crowd.

Still, nobody was complaining. This middle-class restraint of curiosity made Geoffrey Ramage's job a lot easier, and rendered redundant Greg Marchmont and the other policemen delegated to guard the location.

When they arrived at the house, Charles was interested to notice the detective sergeant give a tiny nod of acknowledgement to an apparently empty van opposite. No doubt inside it some of his colleagues were maintaining twenty-four-hour surveillance on Martin Earnshaw's widow.

Chloe, as ever in equal parts fragile and tactile, was expecting them and let them into the house. She neither welcomed the intrusion nor resented it, apparently resigned to the necessity of turning yet another knife in the wound left by the murder. Again she greeted Charles, identically dressed to her husband when last seen, with a piercing, anguished stare. And again his response was unworthy.

Geoffrey Ramage took them quickly through the required actions, with Chloe occasionally interrupting to correct some detail of what was to be reconstructed. Charles found this a new, and rather unnerving, experience. To have Martin Earnshaw's actions described to him by the director was one thing, but to be taken through them by the dead man's wife was something else entirely. Charles was made very sensible of that element in *Public Enemies*, the blurring between fantasy and reality, which Bob Garston so prized.

They were only going to reconstruct what could have been seen from the street. Charles found himself wistfully – and it must be said, again unworthily – dwelling on what Chloe and her husband might have got up to inside the house in the moments before his departure. Why was it this woman always brought his thoughts back to sex? He didn't exactly fancy her, and yet he could not ignore her strong erotic aura.

Still, even the bit seen from outside involved her giving him a goodbye kiss and, as they rehearsed this, Charles realised gleefully that he would be fulfilling a national fantasy. When the reconstruction appeared on Thursday's *Public Enemies*, men all over the country would be envious of Charles Paris.

The kiss, though Chloe insisted on proper lip contact and even a hug and a little pat on the bottom from him, was strangely asexual. It wasn't just because of the circumstances, the lights, the camera crew. Charles had rehearsed enough stage kisses not to be expecting any major excitements. But he was still surprised at how cold and positively antaphrodisiac Chloe Earnshaw's lips proved to be.

Oh dear, he berated himself, another unworthy thought. The woman had just been widowed in appalling circumstances. What was he expecting – that she'd suddenly demonstrate seething passion to a total stranger? He felt guilty and chastened by his reaction.

Charles Paris's latest performance as Martin Earnshaw did not involve much. He had to open the front door, succumb to the kiss from Chloe, and walk off down the road, turning once to wave as she closed the door.

This action, it was hoped, would be the latest prompt to the collective television-viewing memory. Had anyone out there witnessed the scene? Had anyone who had witnessed it seen some other significant detail...like, say, a couple of heavies with butcher's knives lurking in the shadows? Given the apparently total lack of interest in the affairs of others manifested by the Earnshaws' neighbours, it looked unlikely that anyone would come forward.

Still, audience research had shown flashbacks of the living Chloe with her dead husband likely to prove a popular ingredient in *Public Enemies*, so, regardless of their likelihood of advancing the investigation, the scenes would definitely be shown.

A couple of run-throughs and Chloe and Charles were set to go. Then suddenly the heavens opened. Geoffrey Ramage quickly decided they'd delay shooting until the cloudburst had passed. Much as his *film noir* instincts were drawn to dark moody shots through the falling rain, he knew that it hadn't been raining on the evening Martin Earnshaw really left, and it was his brief to reconstruct those events as closely as possible. The director comforted himself with the thought that, after the rain had stopped, he'd still be able to get some pretty damned dramatic effects with light reflecting off the wet pavement.

As the W.E.T. crew busied themselves covering their equipment against the downpour, Charles found himself invited into the house by Chloe Earnshaw. She led him through to a spotless kitchen and offered tea. Just as she was filling the kettle, the telephone rang. Chloe did nothing and after a moment the ringing stopped.

'Ansafone,' she replied to Charles's quizzical look. 'Get lots of calls – most of them from cranks.'

'Couldn't you change the number?'

She looked at him, appalled. 'No! All right, most of them are nonsense, but one of them might be important. One of them might be able to give me some information about Martin.'

'Yes, I'm sorry. Wasn't thinking.'

'It's all right.' She stared searchingly into his face and Charles felt himself transfixed by the intense beam of her dark blue eyes. 'You do look like him,' Chloe Earnshaw murmured. 'Not really like him, but there's something...'

'Ah. Well, sorry...' said Charles lamely.

'Not your fault. And indeed, if your likeness to Martin leads to us getting more information about the murder, then it will have been a very good thing – certainly nothing to apologise for.'

'No.' Still her eyes bored into him, making Charles uneasy. 'It must be awful for you,' he stumbled on, 'just sitting waiting for something to happen, having nothing to do.'

'Nothing to do?' she echoed incredulously. 'But I'm unbelievably busy.'

'Yes, of course you've got the house to look after and –'

'No, not that. I'm busy setting up this support group.'

'Support group – what for?'

'I'm setting up a national support group for the spouses and partners of murder victims,' Chloe Earnshaw replied sedately.

Well, yes, you *would* be, wouldn't you? Even as he had the thought, Charles knew it was yet another unworthy one.

After the filming, Charles changed out of his Martin Earnshaw kit and handed it over to the pretty Wardrobe girl. 'Anyone going out for a meal this evening?' he asked hopefully. 'Well, um...' The girl blushed. 'I'm not sure. I mean, I'm kind of committed.'

Geoffrey Ramage appeared in the doorway behind her and Charles instantly understood the nature of her commitment. The director, given overnight freedom from wife and small family, was going to make the most of it. Judging from the eye contact between him and the Wardrobe girl, it was a set-up job. He'd probably fixed for her to be allocated this particular duty. Some television traditions, like extramarital screwing on location, die hard.

'Oh, fine. Well, probably see you back at the hotel.'

'In the morning, Charles,' said Geoffrey Ramage firmly, emphasising the exclusivity of his and the girl's plans for the evening.

Charles felt a momentary pang of wistfulness – even jealousy – in the car back to the hotel. He thought back to previous location filmings, when he'd set up similar arrangements for himself. In retrospect, none of them had been particularly successful. Indeed, given how rare it was for one to be successful, he wondered why the image of a one-night stand still retained any magic at all.

Charles Paris looked back gloomily on his sex life. There had been some wonderful moments, delirious, peaceful moments of pure pleasure, but their memory was hard to recapture. Something so perfect at the time does not make for good recollection, particularly when recollected in less cheerful mood. Thinking about such moments in the past only prompts mourning for their current absence.

Anyway, sexual highs never last. It's only the continuing relationships that count, he thought morbidly, picking at the scab of his self-pity. Awareness of his cooling relationship with Frances ached like a bruised bone.

There was a message for him back at the hotel. From Louise Denning. 'POSSIBILITY OF FURTHER FILMING TOMORROW (WEDNESDAY). STAY AT HOTEL UNTIL CONTACTED.' She managed to get the same peremptory tone into all her communications.

Oh well, might mean another fee, thought Charles Paris morosely, as he ambled through into the bar.

A small Brighton hotel in late November is not likely to be doing much business, and there was only one other person drinking. A substantial figure sat hunched over the counter with his back to the door. Geoffrey Ramage was off with his quarry for some restaurant foreplay – or maybe they had gone straight up to the bedroom. And the rest of the W.E.T. crew were probably off bitching at everyone else in the business and milking their expenses over a rowdy Italian meal. I suppose I should eat something at some point, Charles reminded himself. Still, couple of large Bell's first.

As he approached the counter, he recognised the other drinker. It was Greg Marchmont, who gave him a deterrent sideways look and returned studiously to his whisky. The bleared look in his eye suggested it wasn't the first of the evening.

The bar was unmanned. Charles's repeated banging at the bell on the counter eventually produced a spotty waiter in a red jacket.

'Large Bell's, please.' And, in spite of the resolutely turned back, he added, 'Get you something, Sergeant?'

Marchmont turned to look at him and, after a moment's hesitation, said, 'I'll have the same, please.'

He took his drink with a murmured 'Thank you', and the spotty waiter left them to it. Doesn't look like being the most convivial evening since records began, thought Charles.

Still, better make some conversational effort. 'Your boss not around then, Sergeant?'

Greg Marchmont looked at him appraisingly, as if undecided whether or not to respond. Charles Paris had seen that look many times before, and always from people who knew nothing about the theatre. It was what he thought of as the 'all actors are poofs' reaction.

But basic good manners just about triumphed. 'No, God knows where he is. Maybe he's found some Masonic function to go to down here.'

The detective sergeant remained surly and didn't volunteer anything else. If the conversation was to be maintained, Charles would have to be the one to keep it going.

'He seemed pretty sure of finding the murderer, didn't he? You know, when he was talking in the car...Sounded very confident.'

'Wankers always sound confident,' Marchmont growled. 'Goes with the territory.'

So his apparent deference to Roscoe only lasted while his superior was actually there. With the superintendent off the scene, Greg Marchmont showed as little respect as the rest of his colleagues.

'And is Roscoe a complete wanker?' asked Charles. Marchmont gave a bitter laugh. 'You better believe it. One of those people who gets promoted for all the wrong reasons. Never done a single thing on his own, but always happy to take the credit for what his staff have done. He's a bloody joke throughout the force.'

'That's virtually what Ted Faraday said, wasn't it?'

'It's what anyone'd say.'

Since the subject had been raised, Charles couldn't resist a supplementary question. 'Why did Faraday actually leave the police? He implied it was because of some run-in with Roscoe...?'

Greg Marchmont gave him another appraising look, and Charles knew that this was a significant one. The detective sergeant was deciding whether to pull out now or to settle in for an evening's drinking with an actor.

At the end of a long silence, Marchmont's gaze shifted to their glasses, which were both empty. 'Same again?'

Charles nodded. Greg Marchmont banged down on the bell. When they were resupplied with Bell's, Charles got his question answered. 'Ted Faraday was always an unconventional operator – tended to have a lot of criminal contacts and sailed pretty close to the wind a lot of the time. Coppers who work that way do sometimes set themselves up.'

'You mean, by getting too close to the criminals they're investigating?'

Marchmont nodded. 'Right. You want something from them, they usually want something from you. So often there's a trade-off for information.'

'What kind of trade-off? Money?'

'Not usually. No, a villain'll tell you what you want to know in return for...well, it can be a straight exchange of information. He tells us about some job one of his mates is planning, we tell him how much we know about what he's up to. Or maybe we agree to turn a blind eye to his next little effort... All kinds of different deals get done.'

'You need them as much as they need you.'

'Oh yes. But sometimes it goes a bit too far...'

'In what way?'

'Well, starts with a trade-off for information. I tell you this, says the villain – in return you don't shop me for that. Only a small step then for the villain to say – you don't shop me for that...in return for *this*...and he bungs the copper a few hundred.'

'Is that what happened with Faraday?'

The detective shrugged again. 'Don't know for sure. But he was well on the way to it. He was investigating a loan-sharking operation, and getting bloody close to the villains who were running it. OK, in order to get that close, he had to pretend he was on their side, he had to look like he was bent...Maybe that's all he was doing. Certainly that's all he *said* he was doing.'

'But he might actually have been bent?'

'There was evidence which could have suggested that. Certainly enough evidence for Roscoe to get him out of the force so quickly his feet didn't touch the ground.'

'But there were no actual charges against him?'

'No. Not enough evidence for that. I mean, opinion's divided. *I* reckon Faraday was straight and still is, but Roscoe'd wanted him out for years and saw his chance. Ted never made any secret of his opinion of our beloved superintendent.'

'Whereas you do...'

'What do you mean?' Marchmont demanded aggressively.

'Well, I've noticed you show a lot of respect to Roscoe when you're with him.'

The detective sergeant looked sullen. 'Yes, well, I can't afford to lose my job. Can't see me setting up as a PI somehow.'

They drank on. The idea of getting something to eat faded from Charles's mind. At midnight the spotty waiter said he was going to have to close the bar. They went up to Charles's room, where, inevitably, he had a half-full bottle of Bell's.

The room was bleak and impersonal. Charles tried to put from his mind all the other anonymous hotel rooms where he'd sat up too late drinking too much with people he hardly knew.

The remains of the bottle didn't last long. 'I'll order another from room service,' Charles announced when it was finished.

'All right,' said Marchmont, 'but I'm afraid it'll have to be on you. I'm bloody strapped for cash at the moment – shouldn't really have spent all that in the bar – so, sorry, if you get a bottle, I won't be able to return the favour – particularly knowing how much over the odds you usually pay for room service.'

'Don't worry,' said Charles with the magnanimity of the very drunk, 'I'm actually in work at the moment. I'll be happy to pay.'

'You get a good screw then, being an actor, do you?'

'Oh yes,' Charles lied.

The room-service bottle arrived – fortunately without notification of how much it was costing. That little surprise would be kept until Charles settled his bill.

The two men recharged their glasses and Greg Marchmont expanded on his financial problems. 'It's the bloody maintenance that kills. God, I should never have got into that divorce.'

'Any kids?' asked Charles.

'Three of the little buggers. God, with what I have to pay for them and for her, I've hardly got a bloody penny to call my own. You divorced?'

'No,' Charles replied, wondering lugubriously how long he would be able to give that answer.

'Keep it that way if you don't want to be ruined for life.'

'Have you remarried?'

Marchmont shook his head. 'No, I've managed to end up with the worst of all worlds. Broke up my marriage to go off with someone else, then as soon as the divorce is all sorted out and definite, she pisses off and leaves me.'

'Ah. It is supposed to put a lot of strain on marriages, isn't it? Police work, I mean. Like the theatre, actually.'

'Hm. Well, I don't know if you can blame the police. I just met someone else and fell for her hook, line and bloody sinker.'

'Someone else in the force?'

'Oh yes.' Marchmont's glazed eyes focused on Charles for a moment. 'You've met her actually.'

He knew immediately who it was. 'Sam? Sam Noakes?' A mournful nod confirmed it. 'Uh-huh. And now she's every telly viewer's favourite bloody wank.'

'Her and Chloe Earnshaw.'

'Hm. Yes, I wouldn't mind giving her one either.' The detective looked dejectedly down into his dwindling drink. 'Sodding women – why do we bother with them? Only leads to bloody heartbreak.'

'Why did Sam leave you?' asked Charles gently.

'Why? Because I wasn't good enough for her, I guess. I was just a DS and didn't show much sign of ever getting above that.'

'So you weren't rich enough?'

'It's not money with her, no. Sam's a control freak. She likes to feel she's in charge. Sex for her is just another way of demonstrating her power. She wanted to prove she was powerful enough to break up my marriage and I guess when she'd done that, I ceased to be a challenge for her, so she moved on. It's the same with her career – she's very single-minded.'

'And good, isn't she?'

'Oh yes, bloody good. Way out of my league. She was same intake as me, actually – came first in the class at everything. No, she can go right to the top.'

'And wants to?'

'You bet. You wouldn't begin to believe that woman's ambition. I used to think she was joking, some of the things she said she wanted to achieve, but now I know it's all for real. It'd give her a bloody orgasm to be first woman Commissioner of Scotland Yard.'

'Regardless of who gets trampled on the way...?'

'Yup.' Tears welled up in the detective's eyes. 'Wish I'd never met the cow. Should've stayed with Maureen and the kids. Now I've lost them, I'm permanently bloody broke, I'm put under intolerable pressure to do a whole load of stuff I don't want to do, I'm –'

'What kind of stuff?'

'Oh, nothing. Doesn't matter.'

'And what do you feel for Sam now?' There was a silence. 'I mean, if she'd have you back, what would you –?'

'Oh, I'd jump. Like a bloody rabbit. Straight back for more humiliation. When you've had a woman like that...you're ruined. I'm still totally obsessed with her. Do anything she asks me, even if...' Marchmont sighed. 'I'm just totally fucked up.' He brushed the back of his hand savagely against his face. 'Come on, pour us another one.'

Charles half filled the glass and the detective downed its contents in one angry swallow.

'When Sam walked out on you...' Charles began tentatively, 'did she walk straight in with someone else?'

'Oh yes,' Marchmont replied bitterly. 'As if I needed it bloody rubbed in.'

'Who did she move in with?' asked Charles, feeling pretty certain he knew the answer.

He was right. 'Ted bloody Faraday,' said Greg Marchmont.

Chapter Nine

CHARLES's hangover the next morning felt like he'd had a face-lift without benefit of anaesthetic. It was as if all the skin had been scoured back and twisted into a little knot of pain at the point where his spine met his skull. So tight had it been pulled that it compressed the brain agonisingly inside his cranium. His head had to be kept at a constant level and moved infinitely gently, like a conjuror's magic ball supported on the edge of a scarf.

The knowledge that DS Greg Marchmont ought to be feeling at least as bad was small comfort. Probably he wasn't, anyway. No doubt a whisky session like that was routine for a hard-bitten copper.

There were certain kill-or-cure options available to Charles, one of which – readily available in a hotel – was a Full English Breakfast. If he could actually get that down him, he knew it would ultimately help. But the dry nausea in his throat cast doubt on whether he could manage that pivotal first mouthful without throwing up.

So he just lay prone, sticky under the sheets, hoping for a blessed return to sleep. He'd woken at five, and deep down he knew that was it for the night. Maybe get a zizz in the afternoon if he had a few drinks at lunch-time.

That was of course another kill-or-cure option – the old 'hair of the dog'. And it was an option that he had been resorting to too often recently. Charles felt grimly virtuous that he and Marchmont had drained the previous night's bottle to its last bead of condensation. Otherwise he knew he'd have been straight at it again.

Anyway, he needed to sober up, not extend the binge. He was, after all, potentially working that day. Although impersonating Martin Earnshaw was not the most complex role he'd ever attempted, playing the dead man drunk might have led to serious misidentifications from the viewing public. And one of Charles Paris's residual professional rules was not to get pissed when he was working. Well, try not to.

The thought of work prompted him to attempt getting up. Further instructions about the day's filming, Charles told himself, might be waiting at Reception. Of course he knew that if W.E.T. really needed him they would have rung through to his room, but he did need some motivation for the potentially hazardous transition from horizontal to vertical.

It took him about an hour and it wasn't easy. Shaving was the real killer. He finished with half a dozen cuts, his head looking, he reflected ghoulishly, rather too much like Martin Earnshaw's might when it was finally discovered. Still, if he was required for filming that day, Make-Up could no doubt patch him up.

It was after half past ten when he got downstairs and they'd stopped serving breakfast; at least he was spared the decision about that option. There was no message for him at Reception, so presumably he'd just have to wait around the hotel until he heard something.

Charles moved through to the lounge and ordered a pot of coffee. He'd try to be strong and put off the first drink of the day as long as possible. The coffee scalded his tongue and he sat there in miserable isolation with the mortifying knowledge that he could blame no one but himself for his condition.

There was no sign of his drinking partner. Greg Marchmont had probably been on duty first thing in the morning, shaking off the night's alcohol like the hard man he was. Oh God, thought Charles, nourishing his self-pity, I can't even hold my liquor like other men.

The couple who came and joined him did little to lift his mood. Geoffrey Ramage and his Wardrobe girl were glowing from the effects of a major sexual work-out. The director exuded the satisfaction of proved masculinity. This was all Charles needed.

He did, however, have a small moment of revenge. Geoffrey and the girl were going through a rather coy farewell routine, about how she was going back to London on the train and how he was driving, and how wonderful it had been and how they'd hope to meet up again soon, when Charles said, 'Oh, hadn't you heard – we might be wanted for more filming today?'

'What?' Geoffrey Ramage looked shocked.

'Had a message last night. More information from the public, I imagine. They may want us to do another reconstruction.'

'Oh,' said the director.

The Wardrobe girl insinuated her hand into his. 'Might mean we have to do another overnight,' she purred.

'Yes,' said Geoffrey; and then, justifiably afraid that the word hadn't sounded very enthusiastic, repeated assertively, 'Yes.'

But his face was a picture, and Charles Paris couldn't help being amused by it. The director was in his late forties. He'd just given his all in a night of sexual passion, secure in the knowledge that, after fond farewells to his bit on the side, he could go home and sleep it off. Now suddenly the spectre had arisen of having to do a repeat performance.

Lunch-time arrived, and there was still no word from W.E.T.. Geoffrey Ramage went to phone Roger Parkes and came back with the news that no decision had yet been made. They were to wait in the hotel for further instructions. But if there was more filming to be done, it would definitely be after dark again.

'Ooh,' the Wardrobe girl giggled. 'Sounds promising.'

Geoffrey Ramage curbed his evident irritation and smiled feebly at her. They all went through to the bar.

The eternal but regrettable fact of life was once again proved true – another drink did make Charles feel unbelievably better. Large Bell's to jump-start the system, followed by a pint of beer to irrigate it. The idea of living another day no longer seemed inconceivable.

After a couple, they were joined in the bar by Roscoe and Marchmont. The superintendent's ghastly leisurewear and bonhomous mood were once again in evidence, but the sergeant still seemed edgy in his superior's presence. Marchmont looked rather the worse for wear, but made no reference to the previous evening, perhaps ashamed of having given so much of himself away to a comparative stranger.

Roscoe decided they'd go through to the dining room to eat. Geoffrey Ramage moved to join them.

'But, Geoff,' whispered the Wardrobe girl, 'weren't we going to eat on our own?'

'No, no. No need to be antisocial,' the director replied breezily.

The Wardrobe girl gave him a sour look as they moved through. Greg Marchmont lingered at the bar.

'Aren't you joining us?' asked Roscoe.

'No. Don't need a full meal, just a snack. Not a big eater at lunch-time.'

'Come on, come on, don't worry about the old exes. This one's on me, Greg.'

Reluctantly, but unable to refuse, the sergeant followed his superior through into the dining room.

It wasn't the most convivial meal of all time. As Geoffrey Ramage responded less and less to her innuendoes, the atmosphere between him and the Wardrobe girl became distinctly frosty. Marchmont, cowed by Roscoe's presence or perhaps embarrassed by Charles's, was monosyllabic. Only the superintendent and the actor showed signs of animation. In Charles this was prompted by the simple blessed fact of feeling human again; what lay behind Roscoe's good humour he had no way of knowing; but the two of them certainly did most of the talking. In their conversation Charles was quite content to take the role of feed. Roscoe liked nothing better than expatiating on his work and how skilful he was at it, so Charles obligingly prompted pontification and reminiscence.

'What always matters...in police work...anywhere,' the superintendent announced at one point, 'is having the right person in charge. Leadership is what counts. If you've got the right person directing the skills of others, co-ordinating their talents, then you're going to end up with an efficient operation.'

There was no doubt, from the way he spoke, that Roscoe regarded himself as 'the right person'.

'Are you actually in charge of the Earnshaw case?' Charles asked obediently.

'Well, of course, there's a chain of command, and mine is really no more than a watching brief, but –' The Superintendent winked knowingly '– let's say not a lot happens on the case that I don't know about...'

Once again, as it had in the car, this boastfulness seemed to make Marchmont uncomfortable. And once again Charles reflected how much less easy a ride Roscoe would be having were any of his other subordinates present. What was the hold the superintendent had over the detective sergeant?

'And I think you said the whole television involvement in the case was your idea?' Charles prompted.

'Oh yes. You see, I recognised from the start that in this case we were up against a criminal of exceptional cunning and intelligence...'

This was patent nonsense. When the case first arose and *Public Enemies* first became involved, there was not even a definite crime to solve. To speak of profiling the criminal at that point was ridiculous. Still, Charles, blissfully marinating in more restorative beer, was content to let the self-congratulation ramble on.

'...so I thought the more resources there were pitched against him, the better. Television, the best brains at Scotland Yard, everything...any criminal who could remain undetected by all that lot was clearly going to be something rather special.'

'But he *has* actually remained undetected by all that lot, hasn't he?' said Charles, introducing the first contentious note into the conversation.

Superintendent Roscoe was unruffled. He smiled benificiently. 'So it might appear, but don't worry, everything's in hand.'

'And you think it'll be the police who get him?'

'As opposed to who?'

'As opposed to Ted Faraday.' A shadow passed over Roscoe 's face at the name. 'I mean, that challenge was put out on *Public Enemies* by Bob Garston, wasn't it? Did you approve of that happening?'

'Well, I wasn't sure that...' The superintendent recovered himself. 'Yes, of course I approved of it. Nothing goes on that programme without my say-so.'

'So do you think Faraday's in with a chance of finding out anything useful?'

'Not a snowball's chance in hell,' Roscoe replied complacently.

Charles remembered the fax he'd seen in the *Public Enemies* outer office. 'But he's still reporting in to W.E.T.. He says he's gone underground here in Brighton and –'

The superintendent's voice was heavy with contempt. 'Ted Faraday's idea of going underground is about as subtle as that of an ostrich. We know exactly where he's hidden himself, don't we, Greg?' Marchmont looked more uncomfortable than ever at this appeal for corroboration. 'If hiding yourself in a rented flat in Trafalgar Lane is going underground –' The irony grew ever weightier '– then he's certainly managed to vanish off the face of the earth. And what a master of disguise he is! No one in the entire country has recognised him, *I'm sure.*'

'So I gather you don't think he's likely to solve the case?'

Superintendent Roscoe laughed heartily. 'I don't know if you're a betting man, Mr Paris...'

'Very occasionally.'

'Well, I will bet you any money you care to mention that Ted Faraday will not contribute in any way to the solving of this case.'

They'd reached the end of the meal. Charles Paris felt welcome waves of drowsiness wash over him. He yawned. 'I'm totally wasted. Let me know if there's any summons from W.E.T.. I'm going up to my bed for an hour.'

'Ooh, there's a thought,' said the Wardrobe girl winsomely. Geoffrey Ramage's face was a study.

It was dark when Charles woke. His head still throbbed and he felt pretty grisly, but he knew it was a grisliness which would evaporate in half an hour, leaving him restored. Must watch the booze tonight, though, he thought. Don't want to start the whole cycle up again. In fact, really, I shouldn't have another drink today. No, I won't. Well, I'll try not to.

He looked at his watch. After five. Surely there wouldn't be anything from W.E.T. so late. And somebody would have rung through to him if he had been needed.

He looked down at the telephone and, on an impulse, rang Frances's number.

'Hello?' Her voice sounded furry, as thought he had woken her.

'Hi. It's me. Charles.'

'Oh.' A silence. 'Any particular reason?'

'No, I just, er...I was in Brighton and I was, er, at a loose end...'

'Oh, *thanks*.'

'Sorry, I didn't mean...'

'It's all right. So what are you doing in Brighton – a dandruff commercial?'

'No, no. Well, you're close. Another of these reconstruction things.'

'Ah.'

'You know he's definitely dead, don't you? And I'm now playing the part of a murder victim.'

'I do read the papers, Charles.'

'Yes. Yes, of course. You getting any reflected glory? People at school saying, "Ooh, I saw your husband on telly last night, doing his well-known impression of a dismembered corpse"?'

'I don't think anyone at school knows you're my husband. Half of them don't even know I've *got* a husband. Anyway, I haven't been in school for the last few days.'

A sudden icicle stabbed at Charles's heart. 'You are all right, are you, Frances?'

'Yes, yes. I've just been getting overtired recently. Touch of flu. Lot of it about this time of year.'

'Mm.' A little silence. 'You're sure that there's nothing –?'

'Charles, Charles, I've got a *touch of flu*.'

'Yes, OK.'

'You're keeping well, are you?'

'Well...Rather hungover this morning, I'm afraid.'

'So what else is new?'

Their conversation dwindled into platitudes and soon ended. Charles felt shaken as he put the phone down. Yes, of course she'd just got flu. This time. But one time it wouldn't just be flu and...They were neither of them getting any younger. He was shocked by how much the thought upset him.

He needed fresh air. On his way out he asked at Reception whether there had been any message for him.

'What name was it?' the adenoidal girl asked.

'Paris. Charles Paris.' She shook her head. 'I'm with the W.E.T. lot.'

'What, for the filming?'

'Yes.'

'Ooh, there was a message about that.'

'What? Was it on? Have they gone off to the location?'

'Erm...' With infuriating slowness the girl shuffled through a pile of message slips. 'Here we are. Message from W.E.T....'

'Yes?'

'From the *Public Enemies* office.'

'Yes...'

'That's that one with Bob Garston, isn't it? I like that. It's the one where –'

'Yes, what was the message?'

''Ere, you've been on that, haven't you? You're the bloke what got killed down here.'

'Well, I play the part of that man in the reconstructions, but I'm not –'

'Fancy that. How spooky.'

'What was the bloody message!'

'All right, all right, keep your hair on.' She consulted the slip. '"NO MORE FILMING. RETURN TO LONDON."'

'And the rest of the crew have all gone?'

'Checked out over two hours ago.'

'And no one thought to pass the news on to me?'

'No.'

The girl had clearly taken a Louise Denning Correspondence Course in Tact and Diplomacy.

'What about the police – Roscoe and Marchmont – have they gone too?'

'Those gentlemen are still booked in.'

Charles asked whether his room was booked for another night and heard with no surprise that it wasn't. 'So I just have to pack my bags and go, is that it?'

'That's it...' the girl assured him cheerfully, as she produced a printed bill, '...just as soon as you've settled *this*.'

And Charles Paris discovered how much a room-service bottle of whisky really cost. It was not a happy discovery.

He was walking disconsolately up towards the station when the headlights of a passing car illuminated a familiar figure some fifty yards away. It was Greg Marchmont, shoulders hunched, looking neither to left nor right and moving purposefully ahead. Charles could easily have caught up, but instead some instinct made him moderate his pace and trail the detective.

It seemed for a while that their destination was the same, as Marchmont strode along Queen's Road. But when he got close to Brighton Station he veered off down the steep tunnel towards the car park entrance. Charles followed, noting with interest that they were in Trafalgar Road.

Greg Marchmont suddenly turned right and, as Charles did the same, he looked up at the street name. Without surprise he registered that it was Trafalgar Lane.

The detective moved steadily forward through the dim lighting, apparently unsuspicious that he might be being followed. He stopped outside a second-hand clothes shop, whose dusty window suggested that it had long since ceased trading. Charles, who had kept a constant fifty yards between them since first spotting his quarry, slid into a doorway and watched.

Marchmont looked up at the shop's first-floor window, from which a little light spilled through a crack in the curtains. He checked his watch and stood for a moment undecided. Then, seeing the lights of a pub a little way down the road, he set off towards it.

When Marchmont entered the pub, Charles was about level with the second-hand clothes shop. The actor took in the broken bell-push beside a side door, which presumably led to the flat over the shop. Light still showed from the window above.

He hesitated for a moment, before following his quarry into the pub. He wasn't quite sure what he was doing, or why he was doing it, but felt he was getting close to something significant. The coincidence of Greg Marchmont going to Trafalgar Lane had to have some connection with Ted Faraday.

The pub was scruffy, with fruit machines and Country music blaring from the jukebox. As he entered Charles saw the back view of Greg Marchmont at the bar ordering a drink. That should keep you in here for a little while, he thought, and give me time to investigate the flat up the road.

There was another reason for getting out. As soon as he'd entered the pub, Charles had found himself facing a short, bespectacled grey-haired man, wearing a neat raincoat and nursing a half-pint of lager. The expression of affront and positive hostility which his arrival brought to the man's face decided Charles to leave the pub as soon as possible.

Outside again, he wasn't certain what to do next. So, maybe he had discovered where Ted Faraday had gone undercover in Brighton...so what? The private investigator wasn't breaking any laws. What he was doing was not Charles Paris's business. In fact, the best thing Charles could do would be to walk back to the station and catch the next train to London.

But, even as he reached this decision, the light above the second-hand clothes shop went out. Charles pressed back into the shadows and watched.

Sure enough, after a few seconds, the door beside the shop-front opened, and a tramp-like figure emerged, swaddled in layers of grubby overcoat, with a large woolly hat pulled down over straggly hair. The face was hidden by a ragged scarf.

The tramp was carrying a large package about three feet long, wrapped in dirty opaque polythene and tied with string.

He locked the door, glanced both ways up the street, and set off in the direction of the station. Charles followed.

There was something strange about the way the man moved. A slight limp, but not a regular limp. The sort of limp in fact that would be used by someone unused to limping.

With a little leap of excitement, the actor in Charles Paris recognised what it was. The walk of someone putting on a limp. The man ahead of him was in disguise.

Ted Faraday's ironic words from the W.E.T. hospitality suite came back to him. 'I am a master of disguise.'

The tramp seemed deliberately to be taking an erratic course. At the end of Trafalgar Lane, he turned left and left again to walk along the parallel Kemp Street. When this met Gloucester Road, he maintained the zigzag, doubling back down Over Road. It was as if he was trying to confuse any potential pursuer, and yet nothing in his behaviour had indicated he knew that he really was being followed.

Charles's mind seethed with possibilities – particularly about the contents of the package. It was clearly heavy, because the tramp kept shifting its weight from shoulder to shoulder.

Charles Paris was concentrating so much on what lay ahead of him that he did not think to look behind. He was only aware of his assailant when his arms were suddenly pinioned.

'You are under arrest,' announced a voice, very close in his ear. 'What!' Charles twisted round in the iron grip sufficiently to see the face of the bespectacled man from the pub. 'What did you say?'

'This is a citizen's arrest,' said the man in his weedy, jobs-worth's voice.

'Do me a favour!' Charles turned back to see the tramp disappearing out of sight at the end of the road. 'What on earth do you think you're arresting me for?'

'Because I recognised you,' said the little man self-righteously. 'I've seen you on the telly. You are Martin Earnshaw and I'm arresting you on a charge of wasting police time by pretending you've been murdered.'

'Oh, for God's sake!' said Charles Paris.

Chapter Ten

THE LITTLE man had got a firm lock on Charles and proved to be surprisingly strong. 'I used to be in the Commandos,' his voice hissed. 'I know about immobilising an enemy. So don't try anything. You won't get away from me.'

'Oh, for heaven's sake!' said Charles. 'This is ridiculous. I don't want to get into a fight. I am *not* Martin Earnshaw.'

'Well, you look like him.'

'Yes, I do look like him. That is the whole point. I am an actor and I got the job of playing Martin Earnshaw in the *Public Enemies* reconstruction for the very simple reason that I *do* look like him.'

'A likely story,' the little man sneered.

'Oh, just let me go!'

Charles tried a sudden movement to jerk himself free, but the hold remained firm. Whether he'd learnt it in the Commandos or not, the little man certainly knew how to restrain a captive. Charles gave up struggling. 'So what are you proposing to do with me then?'

'I'm going to take you to the police station and turn you over to the proper authorities. I know my duty as a citizen,' the little man concluded piously.

'But look, I can *prove* I'm not Martin Earnshaw. My name is Charles Paris. I'm an actor. I have credit cards in my wallet to prove it.'

'You could have stolen those.'

'Why should I?'

'You might have wanted to disguise your identity, so that the police wouldn't get on to you.'

'Look, if I was Martin Earnshaw and was going to disguise my identity, I'd make a darned sight better job of it than this.'

'Ah, so you admit you *are* Martin Earnshaw.'

'No, I don't!' God, this was like arguing with a three-year-old. 'All I'm saying is, if I *was* Martin Earnshaw, I'd have disguised myself by making my face look different, wouldn't I, not just by stealing someone's bloody credit cards!'

'All criminals make that one little mistake,' the little man countered with infuriating complacency. 'And you might have got away with it...if you hadn't had the bad luck to come up against me.'

Who did he think he was, for God's sake – Superman?

'Look, could you just for one moment be sensible? Let go of me and I will *prove* to you that I'm not Martin Earnshaw. I mean, of course I'm not Martin Earnshaw! The man's dead, apart from anything else!'

'*Apparently* dead,' the little man riposted slyly.

'Oh...!' Charles made another attempt to break free. This time a sudden lurch sideways caught his captor off balance, and the two of them fell to the pavement. But the wiry arms kept their grip, still immobilising Charles's own. He tried to roll them both over and use his weight to get the little man – literally – off his back.

It was in the course of this undignified scrabbling that he became aware of a tall figure leaning over them and a ponderous voice asking, 'What's going on here then?'

Charles Paris squinted up to see the outline of a uniformed constable. Never had the sight been more welcome. It carried all the nostalgic *Dixon of Dock Green* reassurance of the good old English bobby on the beat.

'Thank goodness you're here, officer. Would you please ask this gentleman to let me go?'

'Depends rather on the reasons why he grabbed hold of you in the first place, I'd have thought.'

'He got hold of me for all the wrong reasons. It's a case of mistaken identity.'

'Ah, so you admit it!' the little man's voice crowed gleefully from somewhere beneath Charles.

'What is going on here?' the constable asked wearily.

'I've just made a citizen's arrest.'

'Why? What for?'

'Wasting police time. This man is pretending he's someone else – and also pretending he's been murdered.'

'What? Come on, you'd better get up, both of you.'

They shambled to their feet. It wasn't easy, as the little man did not for a moment relax his hold. When they were upright, Charles asked politely, 'Could you ask him to let me go, please?'

'In a minute,' the policeman replied slowly. 'When we know what's what. Very good hold he's got on you there, actually.'

Charles could almost feel the little man glow with pride behind him. 'Yes, well, I was in the Commandos, you know.'

'Really? My dad was in the Royal Signals – Desert War – flushing out Rommel and his –'

Charles was exasperated. 'Look, could we please defer the military reminiscences until I've been released.'

He knew as he spoke that his tone of voice was wrong, and the beady look the constable cast on him confirmed this. 'All right, all right. In my experience, people who make citizen's arrests usually do so for a very good reason. So let's get a few facts first, shall we?' In time-honoured fashion, the policeman drew out a notebook. 'Start with names, eh?'

'My name's Kevin Littlejohn,' said the ex-Commando. Yes, it bloody would be, thought Charles.

'And yours?'

'My name is Charles Paris.'

'No, it isn't,' said Kevin Littlejohn. 'It's Martin Earnshaw.'

The constable reacted to the name and looked closely into Charles's face. 'Yes, you certainly look like him.'

'I *know* I look like him. That is the whole reason why –'

Apparently unaware that he was speaking exclusively in clichés, the policeman announced heavily, 'I think you'd better come along to the station with me, sir.'

'Look, this is *ridiculous!*' Charles repeated yet again to the desk sergeant. 'My name is Charles Paris, not Martin Earnshaw!'

'You look very like Martin Earnshaw,' said the sergeant suspiciously.

'Yes, of course I look like him. How many more times do I have to say this? I am being employed to look like him. The sole reason I was given the job was *because* I look like him!'

'I don't think this bolshie attitude is helping your cause very much, Mr Earnshaw.'

'I am *not* Mr Earnshaw! I am an actor called Charles Paris!'

'Really?' The desk sergeant looked sceptical. 'I've never heard of you.'

'No, all right. Well, maybe I'm that sort of actor. The profession is crowded with actors you've probably never heard of. I mean, I dare say you watch a bit of television, but do you ever go to the theatre?'

'Your tone is getting somewhat offensive, Mr Earnshaw.'

'For the last time, I am *not* Mr Earnshaw!'

The desk sergeant tutted. 'When I think of that poor wife of yours...What you've put her through...it's...well, it's just unbelievable.'

'You know nothing about my wife.'

'Yes, I do. I've seen her on the telly. And you've allowed that poor young woman to believe that you've been murdered and all the time you've been hiding away –'

'I have not. Chloe Earnshaw has nothing to do with me.'

'I don't blame her,' Kevin Littlejohn opined righteously. 'After the way you've treated her.'

God, it was exasperating. The constable who'd brought him into the station had gone back on the beat, but the desk sergeant demonstrated exactly the same bovine incomprehension. And the presence of Kevin Littlejohn didn't help. The little ex-Commando sat, blinking excitedly behind his spectacles, watching every detail of the interview. This was the most exciting thing that had happened to him since the disappointment of the Second World War ending.

The desk sergeant tried a more conciliatory approach. 'Do you have any proof that you are who you claim to be, Mr Earnshaw?'

Charles managed to restrain himself from reacting to the name this time, and said, through clenched teeth, 'I have shown you my wallet. You have seen the credit cards in the name of "Charles Paris". What other proof do you need?'

'You could have stolen those,' Kevin Littlejohn repeated.

'Yes, you could have stolen those,' the desk sergeant agreed.

'Well, what *do* you want then?'

'We just want someone who can vouch for you, who can prove you're who you say you are.'

'There are thousands of people who can do that!'

'Like who?'

As ever in such circumstances, Charles's mind went a complete blank. 'Well...well...Chloe Earnshaw!' he announced dramatically.

'Chloe Earnshaw? Your wife?'

'No. *Not* my wife – that is the whole point! Chloe Earnshaw could take one look at me and tell you categorically that I am not her husband.'

The desk sergeant looked dubious. 'I don't know... I think you've caused her enough suffering already. It'd have to be broken to her very gently that you were actually alive after all this time.'

Charles groaned in frustration. 'Look, can't you get it into your thick skull that –?'

'That is no way to speak to a police officer,' said the desk sergeant, affronted.

'No, it's no way to speak to a police officer,' Kevin Littlejohn echoed. 'In my young day people had respect for authority. That sort of talk wouldn't have been tolerated in the Commandos. We wouldn't have won the war if people had been allowed to talk like that, would we?'

'No,' the desk sergeant agreed.

Suddenly Charles saw a route through this thicket of misunderstanding. Very calmly, he said, 'I'm sorry. I didn't mean to be offensive. But I've just thought of someone who can vouch for who I am. He is someone who is actually here in Brighton at the moment, and he's a senior police officer.'

'Oh yes?' The desk sergeant sounded sceptical. 'Who is he?'

'His name is Superintendent Roscoe. He is in charge of – or at least connected with – the Martin Earnshaw murder case.'

'If it *is* a murder case,' Kevin Littlejohn interposed doubtfully.

Charles managed to curb his reaction to this, and continued evenly, 'Superintendent Roscoe is staying at the hotel I've been staying at for the last couple of days. If you ring him there, I'm sure he will be able to tell you who I am.'

The desk sergeant still wasn't totally convinced, but Roscoe's name had struck some chord and he was prepared at least to call Charles's bluff. 'What's the name of the hotel?' he asked.

He rang through and it was confirmed that Superintendent Roscoe was staying there.

'See,' said Charles, 'see! How would I have known that if I wasn't down here for the filming as I said I was?'

While the hotel receptionist tried to make contact with Superintendent Roscoe's room, the desk sergeant gave Charles a narrow look over the receiver. 'It is not unknown for criminals of a certain exhibitionist type to follow closely the police investigations into the crimes in which they are implicated.'

Charles threw his eyes to heaven. The desk sergeant reacted to something said at the other end and put the phone down. 'He's not there.'

'Well, ring them back and give them a message for him to ring here as soon as he gets in!'

'Don't you order me around, Mr Earnshaw.'

'For the last bloody time, I am *not* Mr Earnshaw!' Charles's anger was by now almost uncontrollable. 'Listen, is it impossible for your single brain cell to cope with the idea that you might be wrong?'

'Don't you be offensive, Mr Earnshaw!'

'No, don't you be offensive!' Kevin Littlejohn parroted.

'Don't you start! I don't care whether you used to be in the Commandos or not, you're now nothing but an officious little nit-picker!'

The desk sergeant came immediately to Littlejohn's defence. 'There's no need to insult someone just because he has a sense of civic duty. Let me tell you, if more people shared Mr Littlejohn's attitude to responsibility, our job would be a lot easier. It's malicious time-wasters like you, Mr Earnshaw, who cause the trouble!'

It was a long time since Charles Paris had been so angry. Maybe the sour, aching residue of his hangover shortened his temper, or maybe it was just the mindless self-righteousness of the two men he was up against that got him going. Whatever the cause, Charles, normally a man to avoid confrontation, found himself shouting back, almost totally out of control. 'I have never encountered such incredible stupidity! All right, anyone can make a mistake, but now you should recognise it's a mistake and bloody let me go! Or can't your Neanderthal mind stretch to take that idea on board!!!'

There was a silence before the desk sergeant said, 'Neanderthal, eh?' Another silence. 'What's that mean then?'

The storm in Charles had blown itself out. 'Oh, never mind,' he sighed wearily.

'Neanderthal,' said Kevin Littlejohn smugly, 'means prehistoric or underdeveloped.'

'Oh, *does* it?' said the desk sergeant, his voice heavy with menace.

Charles Paris wasn't really surprised to be confined to a cell for the night. He submitted passively to the indignities of having his bag and pocket contents inventoried and his belt and shoelaces removed. The desk sergeant assured him grimly that a message would be left at the hotel for Superintendent Roscoe, but Charles wasn't convinced.

Oh well, he thought, as he lay down on the thin mattress under the unforgiving nightlight, serves me bloody well right, doesn't it? Be a long time before I lose my temper again.

The only possible advantage of his situation was that he did – albeit inadvertently – achieve his wish of not having another drink that day.

Charles Paris didn't sleep much during his incarceration, and was quite encouraged to discover that what he missed most through the long watches of the night was not a bottle but a book. He really felt bereft without anything to read; that would be the abiding memory for him of the deprivations of prison life.

Breakfast in the morning was pretty dire and, in spite of Charles's questions, the policeman who brought it volunteered no information about what was going to happen to him. Surely they can't keep me long without charging me, thought Charles, trying desperately to remember what little he knew of the law. Wasn't there something called *habeas corpus* which guaranteed prisoners certain rights in these circumstances?

Yes, surely he'd been in a late episode of *Z Cars* where that had been a significant plot point. He scoured his memory for more detail, but the only thing that had stayed with him was the notice *Stage* had given of his performance. 'If real-life offenders were as ineffectual as Charles Paris's villain, then the battle against crime would be as good as won.'

That recollection didn't help much. Half formed beneath the surface of his mind lurked the anxiety that, however long they decided to keep him in the cell, there wasn't a lot he could do about it.

Relief came late morning when his door was opened by a taciturn constable who led him through into an office. There, to his surprise, Charles found Superintendent Roscoe, dressed in full uniform, sitting on his own behind a desk. The officer looked half amused and distinctly smug.

'Well then...what have you been getting up to, Mr Paris?'

'A misunderstanding. Some old idiot got convinced that I actually was Martin Earnshaw.'

'So I gather. Don't worry, that's been sorted out. They now know who you really are.'

'Oh. Thank you. And indeed thank you for coming here this morning. I'm sorry, I just couldn't think of anyone else whose name would have had the same effect.'

Roscoe inclined his head, accepting the implied compliment. 'But I understand it wasn't just a case of mistaken identity...?'

'What do you mean?'

The superintendent looked down at some notes in front of him. 'Coppers don't like being insulted any more than the rest of the population. What did you reckon – that the desk sergeant wouldn't understand the word "Neanderthal"?'

'He didn't,' Charles couldn't help saying.

'No.' Roscoe examined the notes. 'Had a bit of a problem spelling it too.'

Charles chuckled, but the cold eyes that peered up at him told him the superintendent was not in joking mood. 'Insulting a police officer could be quite a serious charge, Mr Paris.'

'I was just frustrated by his stupidity. Surely it's not very serious?'

'We can, generally speaking, make a charge as serious or unserious as we choose to. Just as we can generally speaking make an investigation as detailed or perfunctory as we choose to. And on the whole you'll find the police tend to look after their own.'

Charles nodded, chastened.

'What I want to know, Mr Paris, is what you were doing round that part of Brighton last night anyway...?'

'Well, I...'

'The message from W.E.T. that you weren't required for further filming got to the hotel early afternoon. I wonder why you didn't just take a train straight back to London then.'

'I was asleep.'

'Oh yes?'

'Nobody gave me the message.'

'Still doesn't explain what you were doing where you were found last night.' Charles was silent, undecided how much he should reveal. 'Mr Paris,' the superintendent went on, 'it's come to my notice, from sources which I have no intention of revealing, that you have occasionally in the past dabbled in a bit of crime investigation yourself...'

'Well...'

'If there's one thing a real policeman hates, Mr Paris, it's the idea of some bloody amateur muscling in on the act.'

'Yes. Right.'

'So please don't tell me your activities last night had anything to do with you trying to do a bit of investigation into the Martin Earnshaw case off your own bat.'

'No. No, that wasn't what I was doing. I'll tell you exactly what happened.'

And he did. He described how he'd caught sight of DS Marchmont and started following him 'just out of curiosity'; and he went right through to the moment when his trailing of the 'tramp' had been interrupted by Kevin Littlejohn's 'citizen's arrest'.

At the end of his narrative there was a silence before Superintendent Roscoe said, 'I see. And no doubt you have a theory about who the "tramp" was...'

'I think it was Ted Faraday in disguise.'

'Do you? And may I have the benefit of your theory about what he might have been carrying?'

'I hadn't really thought about that.'

'It seems to me there's quite a lot you "hadn't really thought about", Mr Paris.' Roscoe was angry now. 'Not least the potential chaos that could be caused by some unqualified amateur getting involved in a professional police investigation!'

'I'm sorry. I didn't mean –'

'I can see to it you're not charged for this lot, Mr Paris –' The Superintendent gestured to the desk '– but if I ever hear that you've been doing anything in this case other than the acting job for which W.E.T. are employing you –' A blunt finger was held in front of Charles's face '– I will see to it that you get put away for an uncomfortably long time. Got that?'

Charles Paris assured the superintendent that he had got that. How much longer the dressing-down might have gone on was hard to know, because he was let off the hook by the appearance of a uniformed constable at the office door. 'Urgent call for you, Superintendent. It's being switched through here.'

'Thanks.' The phone on the desk pinged and Roscoe picked it up. 'What? Where? Has it been cordoned off? Are the public being kept away? OK, I'll be right there.' He put the phone down and picked up his peaked cap. 'I must go.'

'Development on the Earnshaw case?' Charles couldn't help asking.

A stubby finger was again thrust very close to his nose. 'Have you not got the message yet, Mr Paris? Mind your own fucking business!'

Chapter Eleven

IT WAS AFTER one by the time Charles Paris was released from the police station. The desk sergeant, though different from the one who had been on duty the night before, was apparently under instructions to make the prisoner aware of the enormity of his crime. He made a big production of returning Charles's bag, his pocket contents, shoelaces and belt. All of the sergeant's slow actions were accompanied by a litany of reproof and when finally allowed to depart, Charles slunk out of the police station like a beaten schoolboy leaving the headmaster's study.

The first thing he did was find a pub and down a couple of large Bell's. To his annoyance, he found some lines of verse repeating in his head.

I know not whether Laws be right,
Or whether Laws be wrong;
All that we know who lie in gaol
Is that the wall is strong;
And that each day is like a year,
A year whose days are long.

Really, after sixteen hours in a police cell, it was a bit much to be quoting *The Ballad of Reading Gaol*!

He stared out of the pub window at the grey November clouds, trying not do it with 'a wistful eye', nor to think of what he was looking at, *'that little tent of blue / Which prisoners call the sky'*.

And he thought about the case. Up until then any thinking he'd done about Martin Earnshaw's disappearance had been detached, a prurient general interest shared with the millions who watched *Public Enemies*. Nothing about it touched Charles Paris personally; there had been nothing to awake his own dormant investigative instinct.

Now somehow his attitude had changed. It wasn't the activities of Greg Marchmont the night before; it was the sight of the 'tramp' that had done it. Charles felt certain he had been following Ted Faraday in disguise; and that idea fired his curiosity.

The other stimulus to Charles's interest was Roscoe's overreaction to the idea of his involvement. Surely the superintendent wouldn't have made such a fuss unless he thought there was something about the case Charles Paris was likely to find out.

He moved from the Bell's to a pint of bitter and ordered a steak-and-kidney pudding to erase the memory of his police-station breakfast. Then he rang W.E.T. from the pub's payphone.

'Louise Denning, please.'

He was put through to the gallery of the *Public Enemies* studio and the researcher herself answered. 'Yes?'

'Hello. It's Charles Paris.'

'Oh,' she said in a tone of voice that meant 'Why?'

'I thought you might have been trying to contact me.'

'No.'

'It's just that I've been...well, a bit tied up, and, er...'

'I told you – I haven't been trying to contact you,' she repeated in a tone of voice that meant 'Why should I want to?'

'I just thought I should check in...'

'Oh.'

'...you know, to see if I might be needed today for the studio or anything.'

'No, you're not.' And with her habitual charm, Louise Denning put the phone down.

Charles Paris went back to his drink and found his steak-and-kidney pie had just been delivered. As he sat down to eat it, he decided he'd stay another night in Brighton.

Charles had no difficulty booking into a cheap hotel, and amused himself until dark with a bottle of Bell's and indistinct children's programmes on the crackling television. Then he walked back through the dark streets of Brighton to Trafalgar Lane.

It was about six when he got there. Once again the light was on in the flat above the second-hand clothes shop. First checking that there wasn't another Kevin Littlejohn lurking in the shadows, Charles moved into the doorway of a boarded-up shop opposite and watched. He thought he discerned occasional flickers of shadowy movement in the flat, but he couldn't be sure.

After about an hour he got bored. Well, that is not strictly true. He got bored after five minutes, but it was only after an hour that he felt so bored he had to do something about the situation or go mad.

He decided to try an old schoolboy trick – ringing the doorbell and running away. The doorway in which he was hiding was too exposed, so he checked out another further along the road before putting his plan into action. He wouldn't be seen there, but should get a good view of anyone who came to the door.

He pressed the broken bell-push, uncertain whether or not it would be working, then scurried off to his hideaway. There he waited.

Just when he had given up hope, decided that either the bell wasn't working or there was no one in the flat, the door was cautiously opened. The hand that opened it appeared to be wearing a rubber glove.

For a moment Charles feared that, seeing no one there, whoever it was would go straight back inside. But no, a figure in shirt-sleeves stepped out on the pavement and looked in each direction before stepping back inside and closing the door behind him.

The man was out there long enough and there was sufficient light for Charles to recognise Greg Marchmont.

An hour and a half later Charles Paris still maintained his vigil, but with diminished conviction. It was bloody cold, apart from anything else. And what was he hoping to see, for God's sake?

He looked at his watch, registered it was twenty to nine, and suddenly remembered *Public Enemies*.

It was the let-off he'd been waiting for. Convincing himself that he couldn't hope to find out anything about the case without the very latest information, Charles Paris rushed back to his hotel and was snugly settled into his armchair with a large Bell's by the time the opening credits started.

Because of the hotel set's poor reception, Bob Garston looked grittier than ever as he promised 'yet another startling revelation later in the programme – a gruesome new twist in the investigation into the murder of Martin Earnshaw'.

Once again, the audience was teased by trailers through a sequence of more or less irrelevant criminal features until the moment of maximum impact arrived.

Bob Garston back-announced an item about self-switching security sensors and turned gravely to another camera.

'Now the murder of Martin Earnshaw...Police investigations into the crime are of course continuing and we've had another faxed report from our very own private eye Ted Faraday assuring us he's still on the case. But we also have a startling new development.

'On last week's programme *Public Enemies* brought you exclusive coverage of the ghastly discovery of the dead man's arms...' He let the pause linger, relishing it. 'This week another, equally gruesome and appalling find has been made. I regret to have to tell you this...' Oh no you don't, oh no you don't, thought Charles. You're over the moon about it. '...but only today a pair of dismembered legs have been discovered.'

Bob Garston left space for the nation's collective gasp before continuing. 'Early tests suggest that these match the arms found last week. Needless to say, today's discovery is yet another indication of the kind of sick mind behind this appalling crime. This particular "Public Enemy" is without scruples or compassion, a cold-blooded monster...'

And a brilliant television scheduler, thought Charles.

'And I can assure all of you,' Bob Garston went on, 'that I, and all of the other members of the *Public Enemies* team, will not rest until we have tracked down this merciless killer. Don't worry – with the help of you, the public, we can do it!'

After this crusading climax, he passed over to 'DI Sam Noakes for the details of today's macabre discovery'.

She looked as good as ever, though, after what he'd heard from Greg Marchmont, Charles was even more aware of the hardness in her face.

'At just before eleven o'clock this morning,' the detective inspector announced, 'a passenger from a London train arrived at Brighton station. He went to the car park to retrieve his car, but as he was driving away, noticed a polythene-wrapped package which must have been pushed under the vehicle while it was parked. He looked at the package and, becoming alarmed about its contents, summoned the police. The polythene was opened and inside were discovered the severed legs of a man probably in his fifties.'

Sam Noakes left it there. The dramatic impact, all the *Public Enemies* professionals knew, would be greatest without any comment.

The camera cut back to Bob Garston, now so gritty that he could have got a job as a pit-head.

'Needless to say, Martin Earnshaw's wife Chloe is devastated by this latest development. We know, from the letters and phone calls the programme has received for her, how much all of you out there sympathise with her sufferings, and I can assure you that she is very aware of and grateful for... your support.'

The presenter had by now turned up his Sincerity Control almost to danger point. 'And I'm sure you know that the best thing you – and we on *Public Enemies* – can do for Chloe Earnshaw...is to come up with that vital piece of information that will lead us to her husband's killer.

'So...just to see if this jogs anyone's memory – and if it does, remember our phone lines are open twenty-four hours a day – here is a reconstruction – with Chloe Earnshaw pluckily playing herself – of the last time she saw her husband, as he went out..."just to have a drink"...only a few short weeks ago.'

As the reconstruction began, Charles couldn't help reflecting that his double act with Chloe Earnshaw really had now got top billing.

But that thought was swamped by another shocking realisation.

Now he felt certain he knew what had been in the package the 'tramp' had been carrying the night before.

No light showed from the flat when Charles got back to Trafalgar Lane. He pressed long and hard on the bell-push, this time with no thoughts of concealment.

But there was no response. No one came.

He tried the handle. The door was locked, but felt loose and feeble in its crumbling frame. Too excited for caution, Charles Paris threw himself shoulder first at the door. Just like they do in the movies.

There were two shocks. First, how much it hurt his shoulder. And, second, that, in a splintering of rotten wood, the door gave inwards.

He rushed up the dark stairs, certain that the flat was empty. He should have brought a torch, but was reckless now and, when he opened the door to the front room, switched on the light.

The space was completely empty and smelt of detergent. Every surface gleamed. Some of the paintwork was still sticky and the floorboards damp. The cleaning-up job had been extremely thorough.

He searched through the sitting room, tiny kitchen, lavatory and bathroom, but there was nothing. Every trace of recent occupancy had been erased.

Only on the floorboards of the bathroom was there anything that might constitute a clue. The area was damper than its surrounds, and had clearly been subject to even more vigorous scrubbing.

But two stubborn marks had resisted all the cleaner's efforts. Two spots, each about the size of a new penny piece.

They were rusty, the colour of dried blood.

Chapter Twelve

IT WAS A DILEMMA. Charles Paris felt certain he had found out something of real significance in the Martin Earnshaw case, but he didn't know what to do about it. His natural instinct would have been to take his findings to the police, but what police? Of those he knew connected with *Public Enemies*, Greg Marchmont quite possibly had some part in the actual crime, and the terms in which Superintendent Roscoe had warned Charles off further investigation ruled him out as a sympathetic ear.

The only officer he felt inclined to inform was Sam Noakes. From what he now knew of the detective inspector's ambition, Charles reckoned she'd welcome new leads to follow up. To have cracked the case apparently single-handed was just the kind of entry she'd like to see on her CV.

But Charles didn't know where to contact her, and anyway wasn't quite ready to do so yet. He needed to get his own ideas on the case clear first.

These thoughts went through his head as he sat over his hotel breakfast. It was a step up from the police station, but only just. Bacon, egg, shrivelled tomato and soggy fried bread slithered about his plate on a little slick of grease. Nor did the fact that all the other deterrently silent denizens of the tiny dining room were smoking add to Charles's enjoyment.

Also he felt the dull thud of another hangover. He'd needed a few slurps of Bell's to calm him down when he got back the previous night, and they had had a disproportionate effect on his head. It all comes of not drinking the night before, he thought wryly. When you start again, the stuff really does feel powerful. Oh dear, getting back into the old cycle again. Must cut down. Wouldn't be that hard to have a few days completely off the booze, would it, he tried to convince himself.

With an effort he brought his tired mind to bear on the murder of Martin Earnshaw – in which he felt increasingly certain both Ted Faraday and Greg Marchmont were involved, though at what level he did not know. Marchmont, he was sure, had done the clean-up of the Trafalgar Lane flat. The timing and the fact that the detective sergeant had been in shirt-sleeves and rubber gloves made that certain.

But had he been cleaning up after his own crimes or after those of Ted Faraday? The 'tramp' Charles had seen could not have been Marchmont, who was safely ensconced at the time in the pub where Kevin Littlejohn drank, so it seemed a safe bet that it was Faraday in disguise. Roscoe had certainly pointed up the connection between the private investigator and a flat in Trafalgar Lane.

If the contents of the 'tramp's' package were what Charles strongly suspected, Faraday's involvement became even more chilling. Why would he be carrying the dead man's legs, presumably to their hiding place in the car park, if he had not had a hand in Martin Earnshaw's murder?

If he had, didn't the meticulous cleaning-up operation and the stubborn bloodstains that had survived it suggest that, if not the actual killing, then at least the dismemberment had taken place in the flat?

What the private investigator's motive for murder might have been Charles had no idea. But he remembered Greg Marchmont speaking of Faraday's investigation into a loan-sharking operation and his possibly too close involvement with the criminals concerned. It was Martin Earnshaw's escalating debts to loan sharks that were believed to have led to his murder.

Difficult to get much further without talking to someone. Maybe it would have to be Roscoe or Marchmont after all. Charles decided he would check whether the two policemen were still in Brighton, and rang through to the hotel where they had all stayed.

No, the two gentlemen had checked out the previous day.

Fortunately Charles then asked if any other members of the police were currently staying at the hotel or expected in the near future.

'One of them's booked in for tonight,' the girl replied, with a lack of discretion that suggested she was new to the hotel business. 'That lady policeman...you know, the pretty one from the telly.'

'DI Noakes?' said Charles, wondering how Sam would have reacted to her description.

'That's the one. She's arriving after lunch.' A note of doubt came into the girl's voice. 'Ooh, perhaps I shouldn't have told you that.'

'Don't worry about it,' said Charles Paris, as he put the phone down.

There was one small detail of investigation he could undertake on his own before trying to contact Sam Noakes. He consulted the local Yellow Pages. To his surprise, he found no entry under 'Fax', but then he knew that reading Yellow Pages often involved lateral thinking and cross-reference. Indeed, one of his favourite jokes was an entry he'd found in the Yellow Pages: 'Boring: SEE CIVIL ENGINEERS.'

He found what he wanted under 'Facsimile Bureaux'. 'PRINTSERVE' was there, with an address in Churchill Square. He thought of ringing them, but decided an in-person approach might be more fruitful. So he paid his bill and left the hotel without regret. His lips were still slicked with the taste of that breakfast.

As he walked through Brighton, with the sexy whiff of the sea in his nostrils, Charles Paris tried to decide how to conduct his enquiry at the fax bureau. The direct approach might yield results, but he felt an urge to take on a character for the task. Partly he thought it might get a better response, and partly he was just an old ham.

He went into a tatty junk shop and bought a pair of thick wire-framed glasses. As he put them on, he felt the little lift of excitement taking on a new identity always prompted.

Now who...? Perhaps he should present himself as something to do with the police...? That would at least give a reason for his making the enquiry. It would also give him the guilty *frisson* of breaking the law. Impersonating a policeman he knew to be an offence, but Charles Paris relished some kind of quiet revenge for the dressing-down he'd received from Superintendent Roscoe.

But who exactly should it be? Mentally he reviewed his gallery of policeman performances. They divided naturally into three: those who'd had speeches beginning, 'We have reason to believe...'; those who'd said, 'I'm afraid I have some bad news for you, Mrs Blank...'; and those who'd shouted, 'Not so fast!'

His favourites perhaps had been seen at a Soho fringe theatre in the early seventies ('Charles Paris's policeman was clearly intended by the author to provide comic relief in this depressing farrago. His was the only performance that didn't make me laugh.' – *Time Out*), and on an extended tour of a sub-Agatha Christie epic called *Murder at the Bishop's Palace*, in which he'd appeared in Act Three to arrest the murderer all the way from Winchester to Wilmslow and attracted from the *Nottingham Evening Post* the ambivalent notice: 'The cast was completed by Charles Paris.'

For the first he had used a vague burr slightly West of Mummerset, and for the second he thought he'd been using Glaswegian until someone he met backstage congratulated him because 'it's so rare to hear a Belfast accent actually done right'.

As he entered PRINTSERVE he still hadn't decided which of these to plump for and in fact, when he came to speak, found himself falling back on a slightly roughened version of his own accent.

'Erm, excuse me,' he said to the pert-looking girl busy at the photocopier.

She replied with a preoccupied 'Mm?'

Charles went straight into law-breaking mode. 'I'm a police officer.'

'Oh yes?' She turned to face him. 'Have you got any identification?'

Damn. This girl had watched too much television. He reached into his jacket for his wallet, trying desperately to remember what he'd got in it that might vaguely look like an identity card. She wasn't going to be fooled by Visa or Access, was she? Or by the video membership he'd once taken out and then never got round to buying a VCR?

But just as he was contemplating an ignominious retreat from the shop, his hand closed round a piece of paper, which he remembered was a letter confirming his filming schedule from the *Public Enemies* office at W.E.T.. That would have to do.

'As you'll see from this...' He flashed the letterhead at the girl '...I am currently seconded to the *Public Enemies* programme...'

'Ooh yes!' Television worked its customary magic on yet another member of the British public. 'I watched that last night. It's horrible, isn't it? I mean particularly with the Martin Earnshaw murder having taken place right here in Brighton. That poor wife of his...And what kind of sick mind would cut a body up like that? It's almost as if he's actually staging the discovery of the bits in time for the programmes, isn't it?'

This echoed a suspicion which had formed more than once in Charles's mind, but he made no comment, simply pressed on with his enquiry. 'It's about the *Public Enemies* programme that I'm calling, in fact. As you know, we've been asking members of the public to send in information and –'

''Ere,' said the girl. 'You look a bit like him.'

'A bit like who?'

'Martin Earnshaw. The bloke who was murdered.'

'Do I? Really?' Charles Paris screwed up his eyes behind the glasses to look as unmartinearnshawlike as possible. 'Well, nobody's ever said that to me before. Perhaps it's just because the case is on your mind that you're seeing likenesses that aren't there.'

'Perhaps...' the girl reluctantly agreed.

'Now as I say, in the *Public Enemies* office we get information from all over the country and a lot of it comes by fax. Some of these faxes we like to check up on, just to see whether they're authentic or not, and there was one sent from this office earlier in the week...'

'Sent to *Public Enemies*?'

'Yes.'

'Ooh. Which day was it?'

Charles did a quick calculation of when he'd been in the *Public Enemies* office. 'Tuesday. About quarter past eleven.'

'I'll look at the journal,' said the girl.

She quickly found the details on the print-out. 'This is a London number. That the right one?'

Charles checked it against the letterhead. 'Yes.'

'All right then. I can confirm that it was sent from here. Is that all you wanted to know?'

'I wonder if by any chance you can remember who it was who sent it...'

The girl racked her brains and, with a bit of prompting, managed to come up with a rough description.

Though the fax purportedly came from him, her description certainly didn't fit Ted Faraday.

Indeed, the only person involved in the case it could have fitted was Greg Marchmont.

'I know you, don't I?' said Sam Noakes, as she opened the door of her hotel room.

'Well, I'm Martin Earnshaw.' Her eyes narrowed, suspicious for a moment that she was up against a crank. 'That is to say, my name is Charles Paris. I'm the actor who's playing Martin Earnshaw in the reconstructions.'

'Oh, right, of course. Sorry, should have recognised you straight away. Won't you sit down?'

She gestured to the chair in front of the dressing table, and sat herself on the side of the double bed. It was just an ordinary room, more or less identical to the one Charles had had in the same hotel. Sam Noakes had suggested he should join her there to avoid the security risks of the public rooms, and he was sure that was part of her reason. But he also detected in it a kind of feminist bravado, inviting a strange man up to her room to show how unaffected she was by the cautions other women might have felt. There was even perhaps an element of challenge, to test out the reception he'd get if he did try anything on.

Trying anything on, however, was the last thought on Charles Paris's mind. Though Sam Noakes carried a permanent aura of sexuality and looked good in jeans and loose-fitting jumper, he would have sooner tangled with a boa constrictor. Even before Greg Marchmont had told him about her character, Charles had identified Sam Noakes as dangerous territory. Anyway, he wasn't in the habit of making advances in hotel rooms to women he didn't know. Well, certainly not when he was sober.

'So...what is it, Mr Paris? You said when you phoned it was something to do with the Earnshaw case.'

'Yes. It is.'

'Have you been making your own enquiries into it? We've already got one private investigator on the strength. Does every aspiring gumshoe in the country now feel entitled to have a go?'

'If they do, then programmes like *Public Enemies* are as much to blame as anything else.'

She nodded, conceding the truth of this. 'Yes, well, I guess we are encouraging people to be observant, take note of any information that might be useful. What have you got for us, Mr Paris – a clue?'

'Maybe. A lead, anyway. Certainly something that might be worthy of further investigation.'

'Tell me about it.'

And he told her. Sam Noakes listened impassively, her pale blue eyes steady, reacting neither to his mentions of Greg Marchmont nor Ted Faraday. At the end she shook her red hair and asked, 'Why do you think there's any connection between the flat and Faraday?'

'Superintendent Roscoe mentioned Trafalgar Lane when we were talking about Faraday going undercover in Brighton. What he said to Sergeant Marchmont certainly implied that it was from there that Faraday was conducting his investigations.'

'Except what you said implied that his involvement with Martin Earnshaw was rather more sinister than just investigation.'

'Well...'

'Accusing someone of murder is a pretty serious allegation, Mr Paris.'

'I know.'

'...and not one that should be bandied about lightly.'

'No.'

'And I'm not quite sure what it is you're accusing Greg of, but I'd be pretty careful about that too, if I were you.'

'Yes,' Charles agreed humbly.

'It is possible, you see, that you have by chance stumbled on part of the police investigation and completely misconstrued what's been going on.'

'I suppose that is possible, yes.'

'You bet your life it is. Mr Paris, I'm very grateful to you for sharing your opinions with me, and I will be even more grateful if you give me your solemn word you will keep quiet about them to anyone else. This investigation is reaching a very critical stage, and the last thing we need at this point is to have the whole thing screwed up by an amateur.'

She didn't raise her voice or put particular emphasis on the final word, but it still stung. It stung all the more because of its aptness. Charles felt totally excluded. The police investigation was proceeding and he was on the outside, without access to any of their skills or information.

But he felt he had to say something in his own defence. 'Look, I know it was Greg Marchmont who cleaned the flat up; and I'm pretty convinced it was Ted Faraday dressed up as the tramp; so the Trafalgar Lane flat has got to have some connection with the case.'

'I'm not denying it has, but isn't it likely that Greg was cleaning the place up because he had been given orders to do so by his superiors? As to the idea that Ted would use as crass a disguise as the one you describe, that alone – apart from all the other wild allegations you've made about him – means that you're certainly one hundred per cent wrong there. You have absolutely no basis for saying that the man you followed *was* Faraday, do you, Mr Paris?'

Charles was forced to admit that he hadn't.

Sam Noakes smiled, evidently taking pity on him. 'Look,' she said, as if soothing a fractious child, '*Public Enemies* is an exciting programme. It's meant to be an exciting programme, and inevitably members of the public get caught up in that excitement. For someone like you, actually involved in the making of the programme, the temptation to get carried away by the whole thing is all the stronger. But just remember – that doesn't justify making allegations against a hard-working member of the police force, based on nothing more than unsubstantiated guesswork. OK? Television is a glamorous medium, Mr Paris, and some people just can't resist the pull of that glamour.'

Speak for yourself, thought Charles Paris savagely.

If there was one thing he couldn't stand, it was being patronised.

Chapter Thirteen

'I HOPE THE murderer realises just how much hangs on what he's doing,' said Bob Garston grimly. 'We held steady on last week's overnights, but we didn't get the kind of build in the figures I'd been hoping for.'

'Well, there was the first showing of yet another new Michael Caine movie on Sky,' Roger Parkes offered by way of explanation.

'Come on, bloody satellite shouldn't dent our figures.'

'Beginning to. More serious, though, the BBC had started their umpteenth rerun of *Dad's Army* right opposite us after the News. A lot of people probably switched over for that.'

'Why? There can't be a single person in the country who hasn't seen those seventeen times already. *Public Enemies* is giving them something unprecedented in British television, something of today, reflecting all the violence and ghastliness of modern society. I really can't believe that anyone would prefer the anodyne nostalgic claptrap of *Dad's Army* to what we're offering.'

Roger Parkes shrugged. 'The figures speak for themselves. There are a good few millions out there for whom the reason they have a telly is to watch anodyne nostalgic claptrap.'

'But *Public Enemies* is holding up a mirror to the real world!'

'Plenty of people would do anything to avoid the real world. You know there's always got to be tacky entertainment fluff as well as serious journalism on the box. It's not as if you didn't spend all those years doing *If the Cap Fits!*'

Bob Garston seethed visibly. '*If the Cap Fits!* was not "tacky entertainment fluff". It was the best game show of its kind. I make sure that every show I do is the best of its kind.' His expression found new extremes of grittiness. 'But *Public Enemies* is something even more special. In this show I'm going back to my no-nonsense hard-bitten journalistic roots, bloody well working at the coalface of real life.'

'Yes,' Roger Parkes agreed automatically. He'd heard all this a good few times before.

So had Charles Paris. It was absolutely typical of television people, he thought, that the presenter and producer should continue their conversation as if there was no one else in the room. He'd been summoned to a briefing meeting on the Monday morning and already spent an hour sitting in the *Public Enemies* office without anyone taking any notice of him. There seemed no prospect of his being briefed about anything.

Louise Denning swanned imperiously into the room, brandishing some stapled sheets of paper. 'Got the first audience breakdown on last week's show.'

Bob Garston seized the report eagerly and pored over it.

'What's the general message?' asked Roger Parkes.

Louise Denning screwed up her face. 'A lot of people switched over in the middle of the programme. Round twelve and a half minutes in.'

Bob Garston, despite his furious concentration on the report, had heard this. 'See, Roger. I told you that item on how to make an insurance claim after a burglary was a boring load of shit.'

'It's something we get a lot of enquiries about,' the executive producer replied patiently. It was not the first time they had had this argument.

'Yes, well, we should write back to them with the information, not put it on the bloody screen! "Insurance" is one of those instant switch-off words on television. Like "Northern Ireland" or "European Community" or "Bosnia". I'm going to put a total ban on it. No more mentions of bloody "insurance" on *Public Enemies* – ever!' Bob Garston buried himself back in the research.

Roger Parkes raised a wearily interrogative eyebrow to Louise Denning. 'And overall impressions...'

'General view was the punters enjoyed it, but found it a bit the same as last week's programme. You know, discovery of the arms at the end of one, discovery of the legs at the end of the other. General feeling they'd like the contents varied a bit.'

Roger Parkes grimaced ruefully. 'Well, we're really in the hands of the murderer there, aren't we? I mean, there's no question about the fact that he's aware of the programme. He's an exhibitionist and he gets a charge from the publicity, showing how clever he is and all that. So maybe he's also aware of the need to keep building the excitement – and the figures.'

Bob Garston pushed the research report aside with a disgruntled gesture. 'Yes. If only we could contact him and tell him the kind of thing we need...'

'What do you reckon we do need then?' asked the executive producer.

'Some kind of twist on the case, something new...' The presenter tapped his teeth impatiently.

'Well, what're we hoping for this week? Presumably the discovery of the torso...? He's never going to go straight to the head, is he?'

'No, no, that'd be like naming an awards winner before you name the nominees – our murderer's got more sense of theatre than that.'

'You don't think,' Roger Parkes suggested ominously, 'he'll have kept the torso and the head together, do you?'

'No, no, of course he won't. He's not a bloody amateur. Anyone who knows the first thing about dismembering is going to take the head off, aren't they? No, we definitely need the torso this week, but we need a bit of an angle on it.'

'Like...' 'Well, like the torso being found in an unusual place...Or being found mutilated in some horrible way...that'd do. Needs something *sexy* about it...'

'Hm...' Roger Parkes shook his head thoughtfully. 'Of course we do have a potential problem, the way he's feeding us the bits, don't we?'

'What do you mean?'

'Well, if, as we're assuming, we've only got the torso and the head to go...and we get those over the next two weeks, it leaves us with a big hole for Programme Six, doesn't it?'

'I'd thought of that, yes. About the only thing that's really going to pay the series off is if we can actually announce the identity of the murderer in the last programme.'

'Yes, that'd be good,' Roger Parkes agreed. 'Real Hercules Poirot stuff. Invite all of the viewers into the library...A twirl of the moustaches and..."You may wonder why I've asked you all here..."'

Bob Garston was caught up by the idea. 'Like it. The budget'd run to a library set, wouldn't it...'

'If we don't get carried away over the next couple of weeks, yes.'

'Hm...' A new thought struck Garston. 'You don't think that'd look like trivialising the subject, do you?'

'Oh, *no*.'

'Damn, it's frustrating, isn't it? If only we could contact the murderer and tell him what the programme needs...that'd make things so much simpler, wouldn't it?'

Am I really hearing this, Charles Paris asked himself.

He sat ignored in the *Public Enemies* office until a quarter to one, when he thought sod this, I'm going to get some lunch. He announced his intention to anyone who might be interested, but nobody appeared to be.

Lunch was of course preceded by a visit to the W.E.T. bar. Charles wasn't particularly hungover that day, so he went straight on to the beer. He sat down with the welcome pint at a table commanding a view over rooftops towards Regent's Park, and thought about the conversation he had just heard.

What it did bring home to him once again was how high the stakes were in television. For Bob Garston and Roger Parkes *Public Enemies*' audience share was the greatest priority – indeed their only priority. So far as they were concerned, Martin Earnshaw's murder – and his murderer – existed solely to serve that priority. The fact that a human life had been lost was an irrelevant detail.

Charles wondered how far Garston and Parkes would actually go to make their programme successful. The idea that one or both of them was orchestrating the gradual piecing together of the corpse was incongruous, but not totally incongruous.

There remained no doubt that the murderer was aware of his contribution to *Public Enemies*, and indeed was playing up to the demands of the programme. It would be too much of a coincidence for the timing to be accidental. The murderer was someone who understood television, and knew the impact the reports of his actions had.

So Garston and Parkes could not be ruled out. What would a mere murder signify in their cold-blooded pursuit of ratings? Possibly even Sam Noakes came into the frame too. The unravelling of the murder investigation was certainly doing no harm to her public profile. And if she was as ruthlessly ambitious as Greg Marchmont had maintained, was it ridiculous to think of her controlling events, or of having killed Martin Earnshaw herself?

Charles's instinctive answer to this question was no, but, moving on from that thought, he wondered whether Greg Marchmont might have committed the crime on her behalf. The sergeant was clearly still besotted. He'd said he'd do anything for her. Could that anything go as far as committing a murder, either at her instigation, or with a view to regaining her favour? Again it seemed incongruous, but Greg Marchmont's actions did seem suspicious. He had definitely done the cleaning-up job on the Trafalgar Lane flat, and had also sent the fax purporting to have come from Ted Faraday.

The private investigator was someone else whose actions required further investigation. If Faraday had been the 'tramp' Charles followed, then they required very close investigation. But Ted Faraday remained a shadowy figure, only encountered that once in the hospitality suite and since then vanished undercover.

Charles Paris felt confused and out of touch. It wasn't even his investigation, the police presumably had everything in hand, but he was frustrated by the tantalising anomalies and pointers that he had accumulated.

He looked down at his empty glass. Another pint might help. Wouldn't do any harm, anyway.

While he was waiting at the counter behind a drama producer who'd just finished a play and had a shipping order of drinks for his cast and crew, Charles saw a familiar figure come into the bar and look round for someone. It was Sam Noakes, smartly dressed in beige jacket and trousers.

He caught her eye. She recognised him immediately this time. 'Can I get you a drink?' he offered.

'I'm meeting someone, actually.'

'Quick one while you're waiting?'

The barman had just become free. 'OK,' said Sam. 'Dry white wine, please.'

Charles got the drinks and led her across to his table.

'I'll have to leave you when he arrives, Mr Paris.'

'Sure, sure. No problem. Cheers.' They raised their glasses and looked out towards the treetops of Regent's Park. 'So, any dramatic breakthroughs on the case, DI?' he asked in his best American police series voice.

She smiled. He noticed that she had made herself up with some care that morning. 'You know, even if there were, I wouldn't be able to tell you, Mr Paris.'

'Oh, come on,' he wheedled, keeping the tone light. 'I was the one who put you on to the flat in Brighton – don't I at least get told where that fits into the case?'

Her face darkened. 'Very well. You get told that it has nothing at all to do with the case.'

'But –'

'Mr Paris, the flat has been examined and ruled out as having no relevance to our enquiries.'

'When you say "examined", do you mean "forensically examined"? I'm sure those were bloodstains on the –'

'The flat was given all necessary examination. Forensic resources are expensive and only deployed when there is good reason for them to be deployed.' A bitterness came into her tone. 'I would have liked more forensic investigation used in this case – though not into that flat, as it happens...'

'Into the body parts that have been found?'

She nodded. 'Oh, all the basic stuff's been done – confirming the arms and legs belonged to the same person, that kind of thing, but I think more detailed examination could be conducted at this stage.' She shrugged. 'Others don't share my opinion, however. There is a view that more useful conclusions can be drawn when all of the body parts have been recovered. I don't happen to share that view, but –' She shrugged again '– I'm not in charge of the case.'

'And Superintendent Roscoe is?'

'He's in charge of certain aspects of the case.' She couldn't keep the contempt out of her voice. 'At least in name.'

'And he's seeing that it's being conducted in a good, old-fashioned, traditional way?'

Sam Noakes smiled at Charles, and once again he could feel her sexual magnetism. 'You're not going to draw me into criticism of a fellow officer, Mr Paris.'

'Oh...spoilsport.' This prompted a girlish grin, thawing the atmosphere sufficiently for him to probe a little further. 'So did you actually find out what Greg Marchmont was doing in that flat?'

The temperature immediately dropped again. 'Sergeant Marchmont has been taken off the case. He's on sick leave at the moment.'

'Oh. But what do you think he was doing at –?'

'Mr Paris, I thought I'd made clear in Brighton what my views are about amateurs getting involved in police investigations.'

'Yes, but –'

She looked across the bar and rose to her feet. 'You must excuse me. Thank you for the drink.'

His eyes followed her across the room. To his surprise the person she greeted with a little peck on the cheek was Bob Garston. Together they walked through to the executive dining room.

Of course there were a hundred and one programme-related reasons for the two of them to be having lunch together, but something about their body language suggested a more personal motivation.

And why not? Bob Garston was always so preoccupied with work that Charles had never speculated about his sex life. Presumably he had one, though, and no doubt he brought to it the same kind of single-mindedness he did to everything else.

And for Sam Noakes he probably represented a valuable prize. In spite of her apparent poise, she shared the fascination of her colleagues with show business. To be seen around with Bob Garston wouldn't do her image in the force any harm at all.

Also, someone controlling the power of Bob's Your Uncle Productions might be very useful to the burgeoning media career of Detective Inspector Sam Noakes.

Charles took advantage of the W.E.T. subsidised canteen to have roast pork and two veg, followed by treacle roll and custard. With a couple of glasses of red wine. Very civilised.

Then he went back to the *Public Enemies* suite, wondering without much optimism whether his briefing meeting would ever happen.

The office was unlocked and empty, a most unusual state of affairs. The *Public Enemies* team made an enormous production out of their security procedures, constantly punching codes into locks and sliding cards with magnetic strips into slots. Possibly now, midway into the series, everyone was getting lax in their vigilance. Or maybe Bob Garston, distracted by the thought of his lunch date, had forgotten to give his customary exhortations about the importance of security.

Still, it was not an opportunity Charles Paris was going to pass up. He moved quickly across to Louise Denning's desk and started flicking through the card index she kept there. He went straight to 'Marchmont', against whose name the words 'Roscoe's Gofer' had been written, and made a note of the address and phone number.

He flicked on to 'Noakes', and took down her home and office numbers. Against her name had been written the single word 'Star'.

Since he was so close alphabetically, he turned up his own card. Beside his name were scrawled the words 'Corpse Look-alike'. Hm, thought Charles Paris, always nice for an actor to have his artistry appreciated.

He heard a movement in the outside office, closed the index box and sat down. One of the secretaries entered, looking rather guilty, aware that she shouldn't have left the office unattended.

The rest of the production team came back from lunch over the next half-hour, and all studiously ignored Charles Paris. Eventually, round four, Louise Denning announced to the room at large that they'd decided they weren't going to do any more reconstruction on the Martin Earnshaw case that week.

'Does that mean I won't be needed?' asked Charles. The researcher looked at him as if he'd just crawled out from underneath something. 'Well, of course it does.'

'I was told to come here for a briefing meeting, you see.'

'Well, if there isn't going to be any reconstruction, I'd hardly have thought there was going to be any briefing for it, would you?' she asked, heavily sarcastic.

'No. It's just that I've been sitting here for the last two hours, you haven't taken any calls about the reconstruction during that time, so presumably you've known for at least two hours that I wouldn't be needed?'

Louise Denning acknowledged with a shrug that this was indeed the case.

Charles was about to launch into a tirade about common courtesy, but then thought, why bother? She's probably never heard of the word.

The researcher ungraciously gave him permission to leave. 'But don't go away or anything. The situation could change. We might need to contact you.'

As he went out of the *Public Enemies* office, it occurred to him that Bob Garston hadn't come back from lunch yet.

There was no reply from Greg Marchmont's number when Charles tried it from the Hereford Road payphone. He looked at the address he'd scribbled down. Only Ladbroke Groveish...

Why not? Not as if he had a lot else to do.

Greg Marchmont had a basement flat in a rather dingy building. Presumably when married with children he'd owned a house somewhere. This was what he had been reduced to by his infatuation with Sam Noakes.

An arrow painted on the wall identified '57B' and pointed down crumbling concrete steps. Charles went down and pressed the discoloured plastic bell-push. It elicited no response. But then he couldn't hear any ringing, so maybe it wasn't working.

He banged on the door. Nothing. And again. Still nothing.

He moved from the door to the grubby, barred window. Sun-bleached curtains had been drawn across, but did not quite meet. Charles peered through the uneven slit, trying to make out the room's murky interior.

It doubled as bedroom and sitting room. A tangle of sheets and tartan blanket lay on the open sofabed. Clothes, newspapers, glasses and coffee cups littered most surfaces. An old record player perched on a brassbound pine chest. A battered kettle and stained pressure cooker sat on gas rings.

Charles had to admit, with some shame, that it did all look horribly like home.

But there was no sign of anyone in there. He tapped on the window.

Nothing stirred.

DS Greg Marchmont might be on sick leave, but he certainly wasn't at home in bed.

Chapter Fourteen

THAT THURSDAY's *Public Enemies* began differently from the previous ones. Bob Garston and Roger Parkes had taken to heart the public's message about predictability, and completely changed the format of the programme.

Throughout the day trailers had done their teasing work, suggesting the imminence of another sensational first for television. But the viewing audience is canny. In a world where every programme is hyped way beyond its possible value, they have learned to take the claims of trailers with a healthy pinch of scepticism.

When that week's *Public Enemies* started, though, they were left in no doubt they were in for something different. The continuity announcer gave the kind of lead-in that all such programmes covet. 'And now it's time for this week's *Public Enemies* which, because of the nature of the subject matter, contains some sequences which certain viewers may find disturbing.'

Faint hearts immediately switched over to the BBC News and *Dad's Army*. The majority who remained tuned to ITV, pleasantly titillated by the introductory announcement, were then shocked by the absence of the familiar *Public Enemies* signature tune and credits. Instead, they saw a close-up of a knotted string against brown paper.

The image shifted slightly as if in motion and, as the camera drew back, the detail was revealed to be part of a paper-wrapped rectangular parcel about four foot high. It was being pushed on a trolley by a uniformed security guard into what Charles Paris – watching through the customary blizzard at Hereford Road – recognised as the *Public Enemies* office.

During the camera's pull-back, a sonorous voice-over from Bob Garston began. 'On tonight's *Public Enemies* you can witness live a bizarre and horrible manifestation of the criminal mind in action. Yesterday afternoon, *this* package was delivered by a commercial courier company to W.E.T. House. Its label [THE CAMERA LINGERED ON THE LABEL] was addressed to this programme, so it was brought up to our office.

[GARSTON CAME INTO SHOT, AS THE SECURITY MAN STOPPED HIS TROLLEY AND MOVED THE PACKAGE TO THE HORIZONTAL.]

'I myself removed the outer packing from the parcel. [BOB GARSTON WAS SEEN TO CUT THE STRING AND REMOVE SOME OF THE BROWN PAPER]. And I immediately saw this notice stuck on the next layer of wrapping.

[THE CAMERA HOMED IN ON A PRINTED NOTICE ON RED
PAPER, STUCK ON TO THE NEXT LAYER OF WHITE PAPER
WRAPPING THE RECTANGLE. THE NOTICE READ:

*WHY NOT HAVE THE CAMERA RUNNING WHEN YOU OPEN THIS
LITTLE BOX OF GOODIES? YOU MIGHT FIND IT INTERESTING.*
PUBLIC ENEMY NO. 1]

'Because I thought it might serve the public interest by helping to solve a
crime, I decided we would follow the suggestion of whoever it was who had
dubbed himself "Public Enemy No. 1", and we filmed the opening of the
parcel – with sensational results which you will see throughout the rest of the
programme. I should warn viewers of a nervous disposition that they may
find some of what follows...upsetting.

'This sequence you are now watching is a reconstruction. Until we saw the
message we obviously had not thought of having our cameras ready. But
everything else you will see throughout the programme was filmed live –
exactly as it happened.'

The ponderous voice-over stopped, the camera homed in on the printed
notice, and that image mixed to the usual *Public Enemies* opening credits.
Throughout the country millions of viewers thought, if they didn't actually say
out loud, 'That package looks just about the right size to hold a human torso.'

After the credits, Bob Garston gave another little teaser about the opening
of the package, before introducing an innocuous fill-in item on the methods
used by counterfeiters and ways of spotting counterfeit banknotes. It was
pretty dull, but at least it didn't mention the word 'insurance'.

Then, momentously, the presenter announced that they would show the
next stage in the opening of the mystery package.

It had been moved from the office and the trolley was no longer in
evidence. The white-wrapped oblong stood like a gravestone in a studio set of
white tiles and chromium tubes, which suggested the image of a forensic
pathology lab. Uniformed police, including Sam Noakes, stood by, as well as
medical-looking white-coated figures. Everyone had rubber gloves on.

Bob Garston, dressed in white coat and rubber gloves, stepped forward and
talked himself through his actions in the way beloved of regional news
reporters.

'Well, I'll just tear off this sellotape here and pull off this corner of the
paper. I'm afraid I'm going to have to tear it a bit. Ah, it looks like there's
something wooden underneath. Yes, I'll just move a bit more of the paper
and... ah, here we go. Strip the rest off and...There it is.'

With the remains of the paper jumbled on the floor like clothes someone
had just stepped out of, what stood revealed was a wooden chest about four
feet by two feet by two feet.

In silence the camera homed in on this. Then the filmed insert ended and they cut back to Bob Garston live on the regular *Public Enemies* set.

'In a few minutes you'll see the next stage of our opening that package, but first an update on some of the art works that have been recovered following the raid on Birmingham's Merton Frinsley Gallery in July.'

The great British public sat through another more or less tedious item. Only a few hands strayed to remote controls, opting for the familiar warm bath of *Dad's Army*.

Then, after the agony had been extended by a further link from Bob Garston, the programme cut back to the wooden chest in the forensic pathology lab. Garston, in his white coat, watched silently as two uniformed police officers (wearing rubber gloves of course) ceremoniously moved the chest over to the horizontal. The camera moved in on the brass latch that held it closed.

Bob Garston's voice was heard again. 'Don't know whether this is going to be locked or not. We do have a police expert with a picklock on hand if that should prove necessary, but let's see...'

His rubber-gloved hands came into shot. 'It may just be on the latch, so I'll try that first.' The hands fumbled with the latch, pressing in a button and trying to raise the chest's lid. These actions took longer than was strictly necessary, as Bob Garston milked the drama of the situation.

'No, I don't think it's...Oh, just a minute, maybe it's...No. One more try and...yes, I think it is going to open.'

Very slowly he lifted the lid. The camera veered away a little and moved round to peer over his shoulder, almost exactly reproducing the presenter's point of view as he looked downwards.

Inside the chest was revealed a bulky object, wrapped in a tartan rug.

The viewers only had a moment's sight of this, an almost subliminal flash, before they were whisked back to live action in the studio.

Bob Garston, promising 'more of that footage later in the programme', then introduced an achingly boring feature about new anti-theft devices for cars. But *Dad's Army* didn't gain any more viewers. The audience for *Public Enemies* was far too caught up in the ghoulish scenario that was unfolding before them.

The next insert of film was very short. Bob Garston's rubber-gloved hands were seen beginning to unwrap the tartan blanket in the chest, then the camera cut sharply to his face. Sudden shock registered there, as he gasped, 'Quick, police surgeon!'

The programme's final pre-recorded feature – about a group of pensioner vigilantes who had banded together to fight crime on a Newcastle housing estate – seemed to last for ever. But finally Bob Garston cued back to the set with the chest.

It was totally transformed now. Policemen bustled in every direction. There were photographers and men picking at things with tweezers. There was lots of plastic sheeting all over the place. It looked like a classic scene of the crime.

The edges of the tartan blanket spilled out of the chest, so that its contents must have been exposed.

But the camera did not show what was inside. Not quite. It showed everything else, darting around, catching odd angles of the chest, approaching as if to reveal more, then sliding off when it drew close. It was the camerawork of the strip-tease, the technique that was used in all those nude movies of the early sixties which kept avoiding the hairy bits.

And in the middle of all this chaos stood Bob Garston. He was very pale (whether naturally or through the ministrations of the make-up department was hard to know) and he had on the grittiest expression even he had ever attained.

'Ladies and gentlemen,' he announced grimly, 'I can now inform you that the contents of that chest are...' He held the pause with the skill of a professional torturer '...a human torso.' And the programme ended.

Half the country shuddered gleefully in communal shock. But no one was more shocked than Charles Paris. He recognised the tartan blanket and the brassbound chest. He had last seen them in Greg Marchmont's flat.

Chapter Fifteen

IT WAS ONLY a twenty-minute walk, but Charles picked up a cab in Westbourne Grove and gave the driver Greg Marchmont's address. He hadn't worked out what he was going to do when he arrived, just knew he had to get there as quickly as possible.

As he hurried down the stairs he could see a light on through the basement curtains. His excitement took him beyond fear. Some kind of confrontation was now inevitable. He raised his hand to bang on the door.

But then he noticed it was slightly ajar. Charles pushed and the door gave silently inwards.

He stepped into the tiny hall, off which two doors gave, one on to the bedsitting room, the other presumably to a bathroom. The sitting-room door was also ajar.

'Hello?' said Charles softly. 'Is there anyone there? Greg?'

No voice answered him; nor was there any sound of movement. He pushed the door open and sidled into the sitting room.

The first thing he noticed was that the brassbound pine chest was missing. Nor was there any sign of the tartan rug in the disarray of sheets on the sofabed.

Otherwise the room looked even more of a mess than it had the previous day. Drawers of a desk hung open and papers were scattered all over the floor.

Charles bent down to look at these and found all the symptoms of a life fallen apart. There were stern letters from bank managers, statements showing overdrafts galloping out of control, final demands for telephone and gas bills. On Metropolitan Police headed notepaper was a vigorous denunciation from a chief superintendent, assuring Detective Sergeant Marchmont that if there was any repetition of the incident when he was drunk on duty, his career in the force would be at an end.

There was a cold note about late maintenance payments, signed 'Yours, Maureen.'

And a memento of the cause of the trouble. A faded card with a picture of a satisfied ginger cat on the front. Inside were the words: 'Thanks for last night. It was wonderful. Love, Sam.'

Charles moved across to the desk and looked through its remaining contents. There were more, similar letters, more bank statements, a stiff communication from the building society about mortgage arrears.

And down at the bottom, as if they had been hidden away, two documents which brought a dry nausea to the back of Charles's throat.

On one were typed the following words:

'IF YOU'RE LOOKING FOR MARTIN EARNSHAW, YOU COULD DO WORSE THAN OPEN A COUPLE OF COFFINS IN COLMER.'

On the other the message read:

'IF YOU WANT A BIT MORE OF ME, YOU MIGHT FIND SOMETHING PARKED AT BRIGHTON STATION.'

Charles inspected the sheets closely. Plain white photocopying paper. And on the back of each a little circular red stamp, indicating that the sheets had been faxed.

It looked as if Charles Paris had found Martin Earnshaw's murderer.

He scanned the sad, anonymous room – its open wardrobe with jumbled clothes spilling out, its gas rings with kettle and pressure cooker, its silent telephone, its air of seedy despair. And once again he felt how close he himself had come to this.

He moved dejectedly back to the hall, uncertain what to do next. Obviously the police must be contacted. But Charles Paris was disinclined to involve himself in the inevitable fuss which would follow. He was suddenly terribly tired, unable to face a long night of explanations and statements. No, an anonymous 999 call was the answer. Put on a voice, mention the Martin Earnshaw case, give Greg Marchmont's address and let the police procedures take their course.

He decided he might as well take a look in the bathroom. Not that he expected to find out anything else. There wasn't really anything else *to* find out.

He turned the handle, opened the door, and looked inside. Greg Marchmont was slumped on the closed lavatory seat in a parody of drunken collapse. Charles couldn't see the wound, which must have been on the far side of the policeman's head, but blood was spattered over the tiles and cistern and had drenched the right shoulder of his grey pullover.

His right hand dangled, almost ape-like, a few inches above the cracked lino. On the floor beneath it lay a black automatic pistol.

Detective Sergeant Greg Marchmont was undoubtedly dead.

Chapter Sixteen

CHARLES PARIS felt numb, almost detached. His mind wasn't working properly. Ideas floated there loosely, unable or perhaps unwilling to make connections.

He forced himself to go closer to the body. He registered that the spattered blood was still bright red and shiny. It had only just stopped flowing, and had not yet begun to dry and turn brown.

With an even greater effort he leant forward to touch the flesh of Greg Marchmont's hand. It was warm. The sergeant had not been long dead.

Then he noticed on the floor a sheet torn from a notebook. On it were scrawled the words:

'I'M SORRY. I THOUGHT I COULD COPE WITH EVERYTHING, BUT WHEN IT CAME DOWN TO IT, I JUST COULDN'T STAND THE PRESSURE'

There was no means of knowing whether the lack of full stop after the last word was just carelessness or whether the message was incomplete. The dutiful use of punctuation in the rest of the message might point to the second conclusion.

Charles Paris backed away. Ring the police. Dial 999 and get the message across. That was the only coherent thought crystallising in his mind.

He could make the call from where he was. Use Marchmont's phone and then get the hell out of the place. He tried to remember how much Bell's he'd got back at Hereford Road. He was going to need a lot to anaesthetise him that night.

Charles Paris looked at his watch, wondering if he might still find an off-licence open. Twenty-seven minutes past ten. The transmission of *Public Enemies* had finished less than half an hour before. It felt so long ago it could have happened in a previous incarnation.

He moved automatically out of the bathroom, averting his eyes from the corpse, through the hall and back into the sitting room.

He approached the telephone, then hesitated. Was it sensible to make the call from there or might that link him to the place?

Fingerprints. God, his fingerprints were already on the door handles, possibly on the drawers and the papers he had picked up.

A dull panic made its slow progress through him. He was still too traumatised to feel anything stronger.

And with the panic came a new thought, a thought that started as a tiny inkling but quickly grew to a hideous certainty. Maybe Marchmont's message had been unfinished. Maybe it was missing the word 'COOKER'.

Zombie-like, almost in slow motion, as in one of those dreams where you run hopelessly through sand, Charles Paris moved towards the gas rings. He took a handkerchief out of his pocket and wrapped it loosely round the handles of the pressure cooker. Feeling their outlines through the cloth, he eased them apart. He closed his hand round the lid handle and lifted it up.

His intuition was confirmed. In the dry interior of the pressure cooker was a human head.

Mercifully, the eyes were closed, but the shock that ripped through Charles was still intense.

It wasn't the shock, though, of seeing the face of the man he was employed to resemble.

Though discoloured and a little battered, the features were easily recognisable. The head belonged to Ted Faraday.

Chapter Seventeen

CHARLES PARIS tried to piece it together the following morning on the train down to Brighton. His head felt as if it had been scrubbed by an over-diligent housewife with a pot-scourer. There hadn't been a great deal of Bell's back at Hereford Road, but enough. To his shame he'd bought another half at the Victoria Station off-licence that morning and already made inroads into it. The remaining contents sloshed around noisily in the bottle in his sports jacket pocket.

But, Charles told himself, it wasn't the booze that had made him feel so shitty; it was the fact that he'd hardly slept. Every time he closed his eyes, the screen of his mind had filled with that head in the pressure cooker. On the few occasions when he did doze off, he was quickly woken by a dream of the head in even less wholesome circumstances, steaming away with a selection of vegetables. Through the night he had felt – and still felt – as tight as a coiled spring.

After consideration, he hadn't rung the police. He reckoned they would make the discovery for themselves soon enough. Instead, he'd attempted a few futile gestures with a handkerchief to wipe the surfaces where fingerprints might incriminate him, and left Greg Marchmont's flat, slipping the latch and closing the front door behind him.

Through the traumas of the night he hadn't done much coherent thinking, but in the privacy of his empty early-morning railway compartment, he tried to bring an aching brain to bear on the subject.

The night before, his first thought was that Greg Marchmont must have been murdered. The sergeant knew too much and needed silencing. But morning reflection made him question this conclusion.

In some ways, for Marchmont to have been murdered didn't match the rest of the crime. Though he didn't hold much brief for most of what Roscoe had said, Charles agreed with the superintendent that the murderer was an exhibitionist, who got a charge from the way he was manipulating the police, the *Public Enemies* team, and indeed the entire British public.

Everything about the case so far showed meticulous planning skills. Though the crime was grotesque, its perpetrator had brilliantly controlled the flow of information about it, keeping always one step ahead of the official investigations, and providing dramatic climaxes for the weekly *Public Enemies* programmes with all the artistry of an award-winning screenwriter. His technique suggested someone familiar with the workings of police work or television – or, more likely, both.

Greg Marchmont fitted some elements of this profile, but there were others he didn't. For a start, he didn't appear to have enough intelligence or imagination to devise the killer's macabre scenario. Then again, his emotional tension and short temper seemed at odds with the cold-blooded detachment with which the crime must have been organised.

And, even though the faxes in his flat suggested the sergeant had been responsible for passing on information about the body parts to the police, Charles found it easier to cast him in a supporting role than as the initiator of the whole concept.

It seemed more credible that Greg Marchmont had sent the faxes on behalf of someone who had a hold over him.

That might explain his behaviour in Brighton too – clearing up the Trafalgar Lane flat on someone else's orders.

And it could also support the theory that his death was suicide. If Greg Marchmont had not only been responsible for sending the faxes, but also for arranging delivery of the gruesome package to the *Public Enemies* office – and the use of his chest and blanket suggested he was at least involved – then the pressure on him must have been intensifying beyond endurance.

The presence of the severed head in his flat – or maybe the instructions for what he had to do with it – might have proved too much. Stress on that scale could easily have pushed a man in his emotional state over into suicide – and the note he left could be interpreted to confirm such a supposition.

More important than all these arguments was the fact that Marchmont's suicide ruined the dramatic structure of the crime. The murderer's slight lapse, in making his first two discoveries of body parts too similar, had been more than retrieved by his stunning inspiration of the torso in the chest.

Surely the mastermind behind that must have planned some even more sensational *coup de théâtre* for the discovery of the head – particularly given the fact that it wasn't the head everyone was expecting.

But now that dramatic sequence had been broken. Presumably in the next few days Greg Marchmont's flat would be entered and the head in the pressure cooker found. And that discovery would be fed to the media in the usual journalistic way. Given the build-up, it would make a distinctly bathetic last act to the murderer's play.

For a moment, Charles toyed with the idea of the *Public Enemies* office receiving the suggestion that they take their cameras when the door to the flat was broken down. Bob Garston and Roger Parkes would have leapt at the idea, he was sure, and for Geoffrey Ramage, to direct the shot of the camera homing into the interior of the pressure cooker would have been the consummation of all his ambitions. To make the event even more exciting, they could do it as a live Outside Broadcast.

But, appealing though the idea might be to the programme-makers, Charles knew that even in television there are limits, and he couldn't see such a sequence being allowed by the IBA.

It would be another sensational first, though, for *Public Enemies* – the entire ITV audience watching as the camera revealed that the severed head belonged not to Martin Earnshaw, but to Ted Faraday.

That change was the real shock, and Charles's battered mind had not yet worked out all the effects it had on his previous thinking about the case.

One immediate question arose – was there one murder victim or were there two? Did all the scattered body parts belong to Ted Faraday, or was it a kind of 'Mix'n'Match' situation between the dead private investigator and the dead property developer?

The arms had certainly been identified as belonging to Martin Earnshaw. Which was why Charles Paris was once again travelling down to Brighton.

His first thought had been just to ring her up, but then he'd remembered that the police were recording all her calls, so decided on a face-to-face confrontation. The surveillance team might be recording everything that was said in the house as well, but that was a risk he'd have to take.

Even though it was daytime, there was still no one about in the road where Chloe Earnshaw lived. Before he rang the bell, Charles looked across, but no unmarked van was parked opposite. If the police protection was continuing, it now had a more discreet profile.

Chloe Earnshaw did not appear surprised by his arrival on her doorstep. Nor was she hostile. Indeed, she seemed pleased to see someone who had even the most tenuous connection with the world of television.

'I haven't had a single call from that *Public Enemies* lot for nearly a week,' she complained as she led Charles through into the kitchen. 'Tea? Coffee?'

'Coffee, please.' It might help his head a bit. 'You saw last night's programme, did you?'

'Yes.' She busied herself with the kettle.

'Must have been quite a shock for you.'

Chloe Earnshaw shrugged and turned to face him. She was swamped in a big black jumper that came down almost as far as her short black skirt. Tights and shoes were also black. 'Quite honestly, I've had so many shocks since this thing started, I hardly feel them any more.'

If she'd been saying that on camera, Charles reckoned, all over the country people would have been murmuring, 'Plucky little thing.' As before in Chloe's presence, he could feel the sexuality coming off her like a strong perfume. He had to remind himself how very unerotic actual physical contact in the form of their kiss had been.

'Still, if you did see the programme, you can understand why they didn't need you for any more reconstruction or appeals. A rather more dramatic development in the story had broken, hadn't it?'

'Yes, but they could have *told* me they weren't going to need me. I spent most of the week by the phone, waiting for them to call.'

Charles had heard those lines more times than he could recall, though usually from actresses who'd gone up to an interview for a television part and then not heard another word. He was struck by how very like a disgruntled actress Chloe Earnshaw behaved. Her husband's fate had become secondary to her own affront at being ignored by *Public Enemies.*

'They've obviously been very busy,' Charles conciliated, then couldn't help adding, 'and good manners are not something for which television as an industry is particularly well known.'

'Huh.' The kettle had boiled. Chloe Earnshaw turned back to make the coffee, continuing bitterly, 'I don't know – they pick you up, get you all excited, and then drop you – just like that.'

'Yes...When you say "get you all excited", you mean excited about the prospect of solving your husband's murder?'

Charles felt the reproachful beam of those dark blue eyes. 'Yes, of course I mean that.'

'Hmm...And have all the other telephone calls stopped too?'

'Which other telephone calls?'

'The ones from the members of the public.'

'Oh. Oh, those. There never were that many of those. I mean, the programme's phone lines got plenty, but hardly any came through here.'

'Except the one from the woman who'd seen Martin leaving the pub and going to the pier...'

'Oh, yes. Yes, of course, there was that one, but that's about it...'

'I thought you were moved back in here so that you could answer the phone if anyone rang...?'

'That may have been one of the reasons. Sugar in your coffee?'

'No, just black. Thank you. Are the police still recording all your telephone calls?'

Another petulant shrug. 'I don't know. They're supposed to be. Mind you, they're *supposed* to be keeping me under twenty-four-hour surveillance and I haven't seen much sign of that recently either.'

'Well, they wouldn't want to make it obvious, would they?'

'If you're under surveillance by the British police, you *know* you're under surveillance by them. Look, they let you walk in here this morning without any questions, didn't they? You could have been a thug out to murder me for all anyone cares.'

'Mm. But have you actually been told by the police that they're stopping the surveillance?'

'I've been told they're "cutting it down". Some stuff about resources being stretched and personnel being needed for other duties. It seems I've ceased to be a priority with the police as well as with *Public Enemies.*' The disgruntled actress tone in her voice was stronger than ever.

Charles thought about what she'd said. It could just be that the protection of Chloe Earnshaw had moved down the priorities, but, so long as the threat to her safety remained, that was unlikely. She had become such a nationally known figure, that if she came to any harm the police'd never live it down.

A more attractive thesis was that Chloe Earnshaw's protection had been scaled down because the risk to her was perceived to have diminished. Which could possibly suggest that the police knew that it wasn't her husband who had been murdered.

Time for Charles to move on to the reason for his visit. 'Chloe, do you ever consider the possibility that Martin might still be alive?'

It was a cue and Chloe Earnshaw took it like the professional she was. She went straight into television mode. The dark blue eyes misted over as the textbook answer came out. 'Well, of course I sometimes wake up in the morning thinking for a split second that it's all been a ghastly dream, but then reality comes thundering in. I kept thinking Martin was still alive for as long as I possibly could – even when every kind of logic told me how futile such hopes were. But once his arms were found, well...I couldn't pretend any more.'

There were plenty of Equity actresses Charles knew who couldn't have managed that little half-sob in the last few words.

'You identified the arms, didn't you?'

Chloe Earnshaw gave a brave little nod.

'Must've been ghastly for you.'

'Not the greatest moment of my life, no.'

'And...I hope you don't mind my asking this, but what about the other body parts?'

'*What* about them?'

'Did you have to go through the process of identifying them too?'

Chloe Earnshaw shook her head. 'I offered to, but it wasn't thought necessary. Once they'd checked that the various bits matched, that they came from the same body...' Her speech trickled away into quite convincing sobs. 'I think, if the head ever gets found, I'll have to.'

The picture she was building up seemed increasingly odd to Charles, though it did tie in with Sam Noakes's complaints about incomplete forensic examination. He wondered whether the scope of the police investigations into the case had been deliberately restricted.

'Could you...I'm sorry, Chloe, I know it must be painful for you to go back over all this, but I do have a reason for asking...could you tell me a bit more about when you identified the arms...'

She gulped, but gave a resolute little toss of her head. Charles may not have been a television audience of millions, but at least he was an audience. 'Yes, all right. What do you want to know?'

'I want to know how you actually did identify the arms as belonging to your husband.'

'Well, obviously they were his.'

'But how did you know? Was there any distinguishing mark you recognised? A mole? A scar?'

'No, nothing like that. I just *knew*.'

'So there was nothing that made you absolutely certain beyond any possible doubt that they belonged to him?'

'Well...There was his watch.'

'Ah.'

'It's a Rolex – well, it's not, it's a fake Rolex. One of Martin's clients brought it back from Hong Kong for him.'

'And that was still on the arm?'

'Yes.'

'Did you actually spend long looking at the arms?'

'No!' She grimaced. 'It's not something you want to spend long doing.'

'Of course not. So what exactly happened? Were the arms in a mortuary?'

'No, it was kind of a – I don't know, a forensic laboratory sort of place...'

'Here in Brighton?'

She nodded.

'And what...You went into the room and they were lying there on a table?'

'No, they were in a kind of drawer thing, and a woman police officer took me through to look at them.'

'What did she say to you?'

'She said, "There's something we'd like you to look at, Chloe, and I'm afraid it may be bad news." And I said, "What, you mean Martin?" and she said, "Yes, and I think I'd better tell you now – what you're going to see is two severed arms."'

'What did you say to that?'

'I said I felt sick. I *did*.'

'I'm not surprised.'

'And she said, "Don't worry, you won't have to look for long." And then I said I was OK, and she took me through and opened the drawer...and I could see the Rolex through the polythene and –'

'The arms were wrapped in polythene?'

'Yes. And I said, "That's him" and then I rushed out. I thought I was going to be sick.'

'Were you?'

'No, not as it happened, but she took me to the ladies' and I was crying and she...'

Chloe rambled on, but Charles was too preoccupied with his thoughts to listen much. It certainly didn't sound as if the identification of Martin Earnshaw's arms had been the most scientifically elaborate since forensic pathology began. The policewoman had put the thought into Chloe Earnshaw's mind of what she was about to see, and the confirmation of identity had been based on a momentary glimpse through polythene. It was only the fake Rolex that connected the limbs to Martin Earnshaw. And you can buy fake Rolexes all over the world.

If the arms has actually belonged to Ted Faraday, then it was likely that the rest of the body, as well as the head in the pressure cooker, was also Ted Faraday's.

Charles once more became aware of what Chloe was saying. '...but I'm going to see that whoever's done this awful crime is brought to justice. I don't care about my own safety, Sam," I said, "I just want –"'

'Sam? Did you say "Sam"?'

She nodded.

'You mean Sam Noakes? Sam Noakes was the woman police officer who accompanied you when you identified the arms?'

'Yes,' replied Chloe, puzzled by the urgency of his enquiry.

'But –'

He stopped. They looked at each other. Anxiety glinted in Chloe Earnshaw's eyes. They had both just heard the front door opened with a key.

Charles gave Chloe an interrogative look, and she nodded him permission – or something in fact more like an order – to go through into the hall.

Charles Paris pushed the kitchen door gently open.

A man with his anorak hood up stood in the hall. His back was to Charles as he closed the front door.

The man shook the hood off as he turned round.

It is hard to say which of them was the more surprised.

Charles Paris found himself looking at Martin Earnshaw.

Chapter Eighteen

CHARLES HAD been in this situation before, but only in Shakespeare plays.

He'd given his Sebastian in *Twelfth Night* at Norwich ('Sebastian is admittedly a boring part, but he doesn't need to be quite as boring as Charles Paris made him.' – *Eastern Evening News*), and when confronted by his cross-dressing twin Viola (played by a right little raver, as his memory served) had heard the Duke say:

One face, one voice, one habit, and two persons;
A natural perspective, that is, and is not.

Then again, in *A Comedy of Errors* at Exeter, he'd given his Antipholus of Syracuse ('Charles Paris twitched through the play, as if worried he might have left the gas on at home.' – *Western Morning News*) and, appearing on-stage for the first time with his unknown twin brother, Antipholus of Ephesus, had heard the duke (it's a rule in Shakespeare that only dukes get speeches like this) say:

One of these men is Genius to the other;
And so of these: which is the natural man,
And which the spirit? Who deciphers them?

Facing Martin Earnshaw was different. For a start, Charles Paris didn't reckon they looked anything like each other. Mind you, he hadn't thought he looked much like the little raver playing Viola or the old queen playing Antipholus of Ephesus. And in the Earnshaws' hall there was no handy duke ready with a little speech to convince everyone they looked alike – really.

Charles was aware of Chloe moving to his shoulder.

Martin Earnshaw caught sight of his wife and a spasm, almost like fear, ran through him. 'Chloe,' he announced nervously, 'I had to come back and talk to you face to face.'

There was a hissing sound from behind Charles, as Chloe Earnshaw, the nation's favourite tragic widow, spat out the words, 'You bastard! I told you never to dare come back here!'

Suddenly she was past Charles and into the hall, hurling herself at her husband. Martin Earnshaw raised arms to shield his face as her nails ripped towards it. He backed away from her flying feet as they hacked into his shins.

Charles was so surprised that it took a moment before he moved in to get Chloe off her husband. By then she had pulled a horn-handled walking-stick out of the hall-stand and was about to bring it down on Martin Earnshaw's head.

She was amazingly strong and, as Charles pinioned her arms, turned all her aggression on him. He felt the nails gouge into the flesh beneath his eye and the teeth meet through his sports jacket and forearm. It took a full five minutes before he could subdue her.

'It's not something any man's proud to admit,' said Martin Earnshaw, 'that his wife beats up on him.'

'No,' Charles Paris agreed, feeling the bruises on his face swelling.

'A battered husband – I mean, it just sounds so pathetic.'

Each had a pint of beer. They were sitting in the pub in Trafalgar Lane into which Charles had followed Greg Marchmont only a few weeks before. They were there because it was near the station and Martin had arranged to meet someone who was arriving on a train from London.

'Has she been like that ever since you've known her?'

'No, obviously not right at the start. I'd never have married her if I'd seen her in one of those moods. But really, from the moment we were married – even on the honeymoon – she started hitting me.'

'And you never hit her back?'

'No, I'm...I've never really been that kind of person. I was a bit naive, I suppose. My first marriage worked fine, but unfortunately my wife died. I met Chloe and, well...I was very flattered that someone as young and dishy as her was interested in me. She was the one who suggested getting married, actually. I'd never have dared ask her, but...well, I couldn't believe my luck, and I just assumed that everything would be like it was with my first wife. I certainly wasn't left with that illusion for long.' He took a rueful sip of beer.

'Didn't you think about just leaving her, walking out?'

'Oh, of course I did, but it wasn't easy. It takes a long time to believe something like that's actually happening to you. You think things'll change, get better.'

'But they didn't?'

A gloomy shake of the head. 'No. I did make elaborate plans for escape when I first realised what the situation was. I thought of going abroad. I even took to carrying my passport around with me all the time. But somehow...being with Chloe sort of sapped my will. I couldn't...I don't know...'

He shuddered. 'Then there were financial reasons why I had to stay. I'd got a lot of money tied up in the house. I worked from there, apart from anything else. If things'd been better, I could have afforded to get out, but...well, you probably know the property market hasn't been at its brilliant best the last few years.'

'I did just hear about that, yes.'

'And...well...' Martin Earnshaw looked embarrassed. 'The fact is, I'm not the most dynamic person that was ever created. I admit that. With my first wife it didn't matter – she loved me, she gave me confidence, and we had lots of friends, we were fine. I just didn't know how to cope with someone like Chloe. She isolated us as a couple...one by one, stopped me seeing all my friends, everyone I'd known before I met her. It got horribly claustrophobic.

Also I can't pretend – I was absolutely terrified of her. And even though she spent all her time criticising and getting at me, I don't think she wanted me to leave her. I think she wanted me to stay around...'

'As a punch-bag, you mean?'

He grinned ruefully. Charles noticed a matching bruise to his own was swelling beneath Martin Earnshaw's eye. 'Pretty much, yes. And of course working at home made it all worse. I was around all the time, and the work was going badly, and the money was running out.'

'Did you borrow to cover your debts?'

'As much as I could, yes. But that wasn't much. Not a bank's favourite kind of customer – an unsuccessful property developer paying out huge mortgages on properties nobody wants to buy.'

'So did you try anywhere else?'

'What do you mean?'

'Anywhere other than the bank?'

Martin Earnshaw looked genuinely puzzled. 'Is there anywhere other than the bank?'

'Have you heard of loan sharks?'

'Well, I've heard of them, from the press, television documentaries and so on, but I've never met one.'

Charles began to realise the scale on which Chloe Earnshaw had built up her huge edifice of lies. And he also realised how almost every detail of the case had come from her testimony.

It was Chloe Earnshaw who had reported her husband missing. It was Chloe Earnshaw who had said he'd got involved with loan sharks. She had also provided background by telling how he'd arrived home beaten up a few weeks before his disappearance – though, given her propensity for violence, he might well have been seen around with a few bruises.

Charles had a sudden thought. 'Did you have any life insurance?'

'Yes, I did, actually, a couple of quite decent policies. When things got bad, I suggested we should cash them in, but Chloe said no. She said, as my wife, she ought to get some money if anything happened to me.'

Or if the entire country could be convinced that something had happened to you, thought Charles. He could see another reason why Chloe Earnshaw might have been so ready to identify the severed arms as those of her husband.

'How was it that you finally did come to leave her?'

'I don't know. I just snapped. She'd beaten up on me really bad one Sunday evening. I think she'd broken a couple of ribs – hurt like hell.' He rubbed a hand gingerly across his front. 'Still does. And, anyway, I thought, if I let this go on, one day she's going to kill me. So I just said I was going.'

'And what effect did that have?'

'She got hold of a broom handle and went for me even harder. And she was shouting all this stuff – that if I went, I'd never be able to come back – she'd kill me if she ever saw me again. It was terrifying. I thought she'd kill me if I stayed, and all, so I just left – out the front door, gone.'

'And then you went to the pub?'

Martin Earnshaw looked bewildered. 'Went to the pub? What do you mean?'

'The Black Feathers. The pub down in the Lanes.'

'I've never been to a pub in the Lanes in my life.'

'Oh.'

So all the painstaking filming for *Public Enemies* had been reconstructing something that never happened. The sighting of Martin Earnshaw in the pub had just been another of Chloe Earnshaw's fabrications. Charles remembered vaguely that the details were supposed to have been telephoned to her anonymously. Easy enough to make that up.

The subsequent call – from the woman who claimed to have seen Martin Earnshaw walking from the pub to the pier – must have been more difficult to engineer, because by then the police had a bug on the Earnshaw's telephone. Still, not impossible. It had been recorded on the answering machine while Chloe was out shopping, and the voice had sounded as if it was disguised.

The police, who seemed as caught up in the glamour of television as anyone, might not have investigated such a call too closely. So long as it provided some more action for *Public Enemies* to reconstruct, everyone was happy.

'So, Martin, where did you go when you left the house?'

'I just walked. I didn't know where I was going. I was so relieved to be out of there. I just walked. And then, when I kind of came to, I realised I was walking east, out of Brighton, and I thought, that's the way to Newhaven. So I walked on and I'd got a bit of cash on me – still carrying my passport too – so I caught the late-night ferry to Dieppe. And I've been in France ever since.'

'So you don't know what's been going on here?'

'What do you mean?'

'About your disappearance.'

He chuckled. 'Nobody's interested in whether I've disappeared or not.'

Don't you believe it, thought Charles. One day you really must see the audience figures for *Public Enemies* over the last few weeks. But he let it pass, for the time being.

'The obvious question, though, Martin, is – why have you come back now?'

'Ah. Well, you see...' A rather charming coyness came over him. 'In France I met this girl...woman, really. In Dieppe. First day – it must have been meant. I was having a coffee with, like, virtually the last money I had, and she was the waitress, and we got talking and...well, the upshot was...her father'd just died and her mother was having difficulty coping with the farm they'd got...and so, last few weeks, I've just been helping out...'

'Ah.' If Martin Earnshaw'd been hidden away on a French farm, it would explain why no television-watching English tourists had spotted him.

He gave another coy smile. 'And the fact is...Veronique, that's this girl – well, woman...she and I...well, we've become very close. We're going to live together.'

'Oh?'

'She's lovely, she really is. But I thought, I can't just set up with someone else, I've got to tell Chloe...you know, to her face, actually have a confrontation, tell her what's what.'

'Brave thing to do, in the circumstances.'

'Yes. I wouldn't have dared if I hadn't met Veronique. She's given me confidence. Otherwise I'd never have gone near Chloe again – under any circumstances.'

Charles began to realise how safe Chloe Earnshaw had been in her fabrications about her husband's death. She'd got Martin so terrified, he'd have done anything rather than have to face her again. It was only his meeting Veronique that had thrown Chloe's plans. Without a new woman in his life, he'd never have posed any threat to his wife's machinery of self-publicity.

'So you came to Brighton this morning to have the confrontation?'

Martin Earnshaw nodded. 'Yes, Veronique's gone up to London to do some shopping. She thought I was daft, but I said seeing Chloe was something that had to be done.'

'A man's gotta do what a man's gotta do,' Charles rumbled in suitable American.

'Yes.'

'And do you still feel that?'

A quick shake of the head. 'No. Don't know why I ever did. And the great thing is, Veronique won't mind whether I have done or whether I haven't.' He was almost crowing with happiness. 'She is great, you know. Seeing Chloe again made me realise just how great. And how awful things were. When I was in the same room with Chloe this morning, I just felt all my will drain out of me. I couldn't do anything. If you hadn't been there, I'd never have got away from her again.'

Charles Paris grinned. 'Glad to have been of service. Another pint?'

At that moment two people entered the pub. As Charles moved to the bar, he saw a solidly attractive dark-haired woman come in, not together with, but at the same time as, an elderly man.

The woman, from the way Martin Earnshaw hurried to greet her, had to be Veronique. And she looked as nice and warm as he said she was.

The elderly man was Kevin Littlejohn.

He looked at Charles Paris and froze. Then he turned towards the bar and saw Martin Earnshaw.

Kevin Littlejohn did a classic double-take, and fainted.

The two men hurried forward to help.

'What on earth's the matter with him?' asked Martin Earnshaw.

'He just thinks we look alike.'

'You and me?' Martin looked sceptically into Charles's face. 'But we don't look anything like each other, do we?'

'No,' said Charles Paris on a bit of a giggle. 'No, we don't.'

Chapter Nineteen

IT WAS DAFT, he knew, given the fact that there was only a pay-phone there, but he preferred to make his calls from Hereford Road. Or maybe homing back in on where he lived – however unwelcoming it might be – gave him a feeling of continuity, or even of security.

He was back home by four o'clock. Having stiffened the odd sinew with a slurp of Bell's, he got out the paper on which he'd scribbled the numbers from Louise Denning's index, and went to the payphone on the landing.

Stuck to the wall was a message on a yellow sticker. Must have been written by one of the Junoesque – or perhaps Frank Brunoesque – Swedish girls who inhabited the other bedsitters.

'CHARLES PARRISH – JULIET RINGED.'

His first thought was 'Who on earth do I know called Juliet?', before, with shame, he realised it was his daughter. They hadn't spoken for months. Get the difficult call out of the way first, thought Charles, then I'll phone Juliet. Though he had a guilty feeling that the second might not be a particularly easy call either.

He rang Sam Noakes's office number and got through straight away. Her voice was deterrently professional. 'Yes, who is it?'

'Charles Paris.'

'Who? Oh, you're the actor in the reconstructions.' Her voice took on a more forbidding you're-not-going-to-waste-my-time-again-are-you tone. 'What do you want?'

'I've got some more information. On the Martin Earnshaw case.'

'All right. Tell me about it.'

'I think it'd be better if we met.'

She didn't think that was at all a good idea.

'It concerns Ted Faraday. And Greg Marchmont. It's quite sensational stuff.'

She was clearly tempted, but asked, 'What makes you think it's information we haven't already got?'

'I haven't seen anything in the media about it. And once this breaks, even you are going to have difficulty keeping it quiet.'

She decided quickly. 'All right. Come and see me at my office.

Sam Noakes wasn't actually based in Scotland Yard, but in a nearby Victorian building, which showed signs of recent and incomplete conversion into offices.

'Only just moved in here,' she explained when she met him from the lift. 'We were spilling out of the main building. Ours is one of the fastest growing departments.'

'What department is that?'

'It's officially called "Television and Media Liaison". But we're known throughout the force as the "Video Nasties".'

'Oh.'

In the corridor they passed uniformed men and women, who all acknowledged the inspector with the same respect Charles had noticed from her colleagues in the W.E.T. hospitality suite.

'Is Superintendent Roscoe based here too?' he asked.

Sam Noakes grimaced. 'Yes, for about another week. He's extended his retirement till after the end of the *Public Enemies* series. *Then* maybe we'll be able to get some proper work done round here. Come through.'

The inspector led him into a small office sliced off by unpainted chipboard partitions and gestured to a minimally upholstered chair. She sat with her back to the window behind a commendably tidy desk. Her striped shirt and jeans expressed that casualness which takes great care and money.

'And who takes over from Roscoe when he goes?'

'There another old fart sitting in for a few months – but at least he's one who won't interfere so much. Then they'll promote someone permanent. The role of the department's changing so quickly at the moment that they don't want to rush into an appointment.'

'Is it likely to go to someone already working here?'

Sam Noakes gave an enigmatic shrug that didn't rule out the possibility of her being in the running for the job.

Then she straightened up and became businesslike. 'Right, tell me what you've got. It'd better be good.'

'It is,' said Charles Paris. 'Have you heard anything from Sergeant Marchmont in the last few days?'

She shook her head dismissively. 'He's on sick leave. He's got nothing to do with the case now.'

Her unconcern sounded genuine. It was hard to believe that she did know anything about the contents of Marchmont's flat. But then, if some of Charles's suspicions of her were correct, Sam Noakes was highly skilled in deceit.

'What about Ted Faraday? Have you heard anything from him?'

'There've been a few faxes from Brighton – apparently he's still working undercover. *Claims* to be making progress with the investigation, but I've seen no evidence of it so far.'

Again her ignorance of the private investigator's true fate sounded sincere. Again Charles had to remind himself of the deviousness of the criminal he was up against. Somebody had killed Faraday and maintained the myth of his continued existence by faxing reports from him. Or rather by making Greg Marchmont fax reports from him. So the criminal was someone with a hold over the sergeant. By that criterion, Sam Noakes definitely qualified as a suspect.

'Inspector, when Chloe Earnshaw identified the arms as her husband's, I believe you were with her...?'

'Yes, I was.' Noakes seemed suddenly to realise that she was losing control of the conversation. 'Mr Paris, I invited you here because you said you had some information on the case, not so that you could start interrogating me.'

'It's relevant.'

'Bloody well better be.' She sank back into her chair and sulkily allowed him to continue.

'From what Chloe Earnshaw's told me, it seems that her inspection of the severed arms was extremely perfunctory.'

'It's not something you want to bloody linger over. The poor girl had been through hell since her husband disappeared, fearing the worst. Now suddenly the worst had happened. I wasn't about to put her through another major ordeal. The identification was only a formality.'

'Why? Didn't the possibility ever occur to you that the arms might have belonged to someone else?'

'Oh, come *on*. They were found near Brighton. Their owner seemed to have been killed round the time Martin Earnshaw disappeared. The arms belonged to someone the right size, the right age.'

Yes, thought Charles. My size, my age. He remembered how in the hospitality suite Greg Marchmont had mistaken him for Ted Faraday. Faraday, Martin Earnshaw and Charles Paris were all about the same size and the same age.

'And presumably more would be found out about the arms by more detailed forensic examination?'

'Presumably.'

'But you implied when we spoke before, that more detailed forensic examination never took place.'

Sam Noakes looked truculent. 'It was deferred. Until the whole body had been found.'

'The police have great advantages, don't they, in organising how a case is pursued?'

'Of course we do. That's our job.'

'But, if a policeman – or woman, with privileged information, wanted to control the direction of enquiries...by, say, ensuring that the forensic investigation was inadequate, it wouldn't be difficult to do, would it?'

'Perhaps not. But why would they *want* to do it?'

Charles shrugged. 'Any number of reasons... To make their own role in the proceedings look more important than it actually was...? To impress a television audience...'

'What are you actually saying, Mr Paris?'

'I'm just thinking round the case. Asking, really, whether, when you were with Chloe Earnshaw looking at the severed arms, it ever occurred to you for a moment that they might belong to someone other than her husband?'

'Of course not. Look, the investigation was under way. We'd got the public's interest through *Public Enemies* – finding those arms was just the breakthrough we needed.' The pale blue eyes sparkled as she became caught up in the excitement of recollection. 'And the way we broke the story on that week's programme...now that was really something.'

It could have been Bob Garston or Roger Parkes speaking. Charles realised just how much her instincts as a member of the police force had been swamped by the values of television.

'So...' he hazarded gently, 'if Chloe Earnshaw hadn't identified the arms as belonging to her husband...?'

'Well, it would have screwed up bloody everything, wouldn't it!' Sam Noakes realised this was a bit indiscreet and hastened to cover up. 'Anyway, she identified him from his watch.'

'A fake Rolex? Plenty of those about. And presumably you had descriptions of all the stuff he was wearing when he disappeared?'

'Of course we did.' A hard, resentful light came into the pale blue eyes. 'Mr Paris, what are you suggesting?'

'Just that if someone in the police force wanted Chloe Earnshaw to identify those limbs as her husband's, it wouldn't have been very difficult to fix it so that she did.'

'But they *were* her husband's! Nobody needed to fix anything. And I may tell you, Mr Paris, that the kind of allegations you seem to be making against the police are not –'

'The arms don't belong to Martin Earnshaw,' said Charles Paris calmly.

'*What!*'

'I spent lunch-time today in a Brighton pub, drinking beer with Martin Earnshaw.'

This revelation completely winded her. The inspector gaped at Charles, incapable of speech. He took advantage of the silence to press on. 'I also know what's happened to Greg Marchmont and Ted Faraday. I'm afraid it's not good news in either case.'

'What do you mean – what's happened to them?'

'I know they were both your lovers.'

'So bloody what!' Her eyes blazed. 'I'd like to know what my private life has to do with you.'

'Greg would have done anything for you, anything you asked...'

'So...'

'Did you ever ask him to do anything...?'

'Like what?'

'Anything illegal?'

'No! Listen, Greg and I lived together for a while, but it didn't work out – end of story.'

'Then you joined up with Ted Faraday.'

'So? What business is that of yours?'

'And is that relationship still going on?'

She smiled now, a superior smile of sexual confidence. 'We still see each other from time to time. We're both grown-ups, you know. We see other people and when work and what-have-you permits, maybe we'll spend the odd night together. There are other friends with whom I have similar relationships.'

'Is Bob Garston one of them?'

She gave him a feline smile. The attraction of boasting about her sexual power overcame her instinct for discretion. 'You don't have to be a man to have control over your own sex life, you know.'

Her mood changed. She realised how much she was allowing herself to be side-tracked by vanity. 'Come on, you said you had some information. If you have, tell it to me. Otherwise, get the hell out of here!'

'One more piece of information I want you to tell me, then I'll tell you mine.'

'What?' she asked sullenly.

'Greg Marchmont nearly got kicked out of the force a little while back, didn't he?'

'Yes.'

'For being drunk on duty?'

'That's right. He'd really gone to pieces over the last year.' She gave Charles a stubborn look, daring him to make any accusations. 'And it wasn't my bloody fault. If he couldn't cope with us splitting up, then that was his problem, not mine. I needed to move on.'

Story of your life, thought Charles. You'll always need to move on. And up. And if a few Greg Marchmonts get washed up in your wake...well, that's just their bad luck.

But all he said was, 'So why wasn't Greg Marchmont kicked out?'

She shrugged. 'I don't know. It was odd. He seemed all set to get the boot, then suddenly he was staying on. Guess someone interceded for him. Must have a friend in high places.'

Yes, thought Charles Paris, he must.

He looked across at Sam Noakes and thought again how beautiful she was. How beautiful and how completely heartless. And he replied to the insistent enquiry in her pale blue eyes.

'The solution to this case – or at least part of the solution to this case – is in Greg Marchmont's flat. You'd better send someone over there right away.'

'But is Greg all right?' she asked, suddenly anxious.

'No,' said Charles Paris. 'He's dead. And so, I'm afraid, is Ted Faraday.'

The news caught her like a slap in the face. Moisture gathered in her eyes.

In the brief instant before she regained control, Detective Inspector Sam Noakes looked human.

Chapter Twenty

CHARLES TOLD her more about what to expect in the flat, but Sam Noakes's brief moment of vulnerability was past. The fact that both dead men had been her lovers had become irrelevant. She appeared to have no problem stomaching the most gruesome details.

'You should have reported this immediately you found it,' she reproved him. 'You have a duty to –'

'I think there have been duties inadequately fulfilled on both sides,' said Charles evenly.

She held his gaze with defiance, but after a moment looked away and let it pass. 'You say you think Sergeant Marchmont's death was suicide?'

'Looks that way to me. It also makes more sense in the logic of the whole case that he did it himself.'

'Would you care to expand on that?'

Charles Paris shook his head. 'I'm sure the last thing you want at this point in your investigation is to hear the theories of an amateur.'

With a little nod of her head, she acknowledged the point scored. 'So you have no idea who committed the original murder, Mr Paris?'

He shrugged deferentially. 'I always leave that stuff to the police, Inspector.'

She picked up a phone on her desk. 'I'm sure you can find your way back to the lift.' Charles rose and she ignored him as he walked to the door of her office. 'Hello, Noakes here,' she barked into the telephone. 'I need a car – like fast!'

Charles made his way slowly to the lift, knowing he had no intention of leaving the building yet. He asked a uniformed policewoman for directions.

There was no one in the outer office. A typewriter shrouded by a dusty cover suggested there hadn't been a secretary there for some time. Compared to the bustle of the rest of the building, the area was very still. It wasn't where the department's action happened.

Charles Paris knocked on the inner door, and a startled voice told him to come in.

Superintendent Roscoe was sitting by the window, and the movement of his swivel-chair suggested he'd been looking out of it before Charles's arrival. The office he occupied was large and might in time be luxurious, but the decorations were half done. There seemed to be no air of urgency about finishing them. The superintendent would be gone in a couple of weeks, after all. No point in making an effort for someone just working out his time.

Roscoe recognised Charles immediately, and seemed pleased to see him. The intrusion of anyone into his solitude was welcome.

He gestured to a seat. 'So to what do I owe this pleasure, Mr Paris? You haven't been doing your own amateur investigations again, have you?'

'I have found out a few odd things, yes. Been talking to Greg Marchmont.'

'Ah, poor Marchmont. He's been off sick for the last few days. Pressure was getting to him a bit.'

'I'm not surprised.'

'What do you mean by that?' Roscoe asked sharply.

But Charles Paris wasn't quite ready to go into the attack. 'I just meant that it's a stressful job, being a policeman, isn't it?'

'Yes. You have to be pretty tough to get through.'

'But you have, Superintendent – got through – all the way through to retirement.'

'Nearly.'

'Which is something Greg Marchmont won't do.'

'I don't see why not.'

The reaction was so instinctive that Charles now knew Marchmont's death had been suicide. The Sergeant couldn't cope any more with the pressure that had been put on him. But, even as he shot himself, he must have known that his death would also destroy the person who had imposed that pressure.

'Greg Marchmont won't make retirement, Superintendent,' said Charles in a level voice, 'because he's dead.'

'What?'

'He didn't mind sending anonymous faxes about the whereabouts of the body parts. He even coped with cleaning up the flat in Trafalgar Lane...where you had butchered Ted Faraday. He wasn't keen on arranging the packaging and delivery of the torso, but he did it. The head, though...the head was too much.'

Superintendent Roscoe was staring at him with horrified fascination. 'Marchmont isn't really dead,' he murmured. 'He can't be. It'd ruin everything.'

'I'm afraid everything is ruined already. So, unless you tell someone, we'll never know how you were intending to spring the revelation of the head on to the great British public.'

There was a sudden movement as Roscoe reached to one of his desk drawers. Charles found himself looking down the barrel of an automatic pistol, very like the one that had killed Marchmont.

'I could still make the arrangements myself. I can get rid of you, Mr Paris, with no problem, and if you're the only person who knows about Marchmont's death, then –'

'Ah, but I'm not.' Charles sounded considerably more laid back than he felt. 'No, I'm afraid Sam Noakes is on her way to Marchmont's flat – even as we speak.'

A spasm of anger crossed the superintendent's face and the gun wavered dangerously in his hand. Then, listlessly, he dropped it on to the desk. 'If I don't get to the payoff, to the final act of the drama, then the whole thing's been a waste of time.'

'Why did you do it, though, Superintendent?'

'To prove that I could.' A spark of energy glinted in his eye. 'To show all those smug young bastards that I could run circles round them. You may imagine I don't know how they think of me, but I do. Boring, incompetent old Roscoe. He can do bugger all as a policeman and won't it be a bloody relief for everyone when he finally retires. But I showed them. By God, I showed them! They all agreed that they were up against a criminal with a brilliant mind, but they didn't know just how brilliant.'

As he spoke, the glee of his self-regard mingled with the bitterness of an entire career spent without respect or affection from any of his colleagues.

'And, of course, it enabled you to get rid of Ted Faraday.'

'Yes.' Roscoe nodded with relish. 'The smuggest of all the young bastards. Thought he knew it all, thought he could do it all, thought he could mix with crooks and get away with it...kept saying he "understood the criminal mind". Well, he didn't understand my criminal mind. You should have seen the expression in his eyes when he realised I'd got him, when he realised I was going to kill him. That made the whole bloody thing worthwhile.'

'You killed him in Brighton?'

'In the flat, yes. Made him suffer for an hour or two, after I'd told him I was going to do it. Then I strangled him.' The superintendent let out a little giggle at the recollection. 'Beautiful job, sweet as a nut.'

'And you planned the whole *Public Enemies* thing, feeding the bits of the body to them.'

'Yes...' Roscoe nodded proudly. 'It's my job, after all. "Television and Media Liaison". The job they all said I couldn't do. But I bloody showed them. Produced the best set of "Video Nasties" ever.'

'And you *intended* that everyone should think the body was Martin Earnshaw?'

'Oh yes, you bet. And it was wonderful how willing everyone was to believe it. Those two tarts – Chloe Earnshaw and our brilliant little sexpot Sam Noakes – oh, they lapped it up. I only had to plant the idea in their heads and they were away, like a pair of bitches on heat. Anything to ensure they got another appearance on precious bloody television. Bob Garston and the *Public Enemies* lot were just as easy to convince. They didn't give a shit about the truth, so long as they got something to make the public switch on. It's amazing how easy it is to make people believe what they want to believe.'

'And meanwhile you controlled the investigation – stopped it going into too much depth when you didn't want it to, limited the amount of forensic examination, all that?'

'Yes, I'd do that and they'd all say, "Bloody Roscoe – always putting the dampers on everything – boring old fart – God, he's so thick." And all the time I was making them dance to my tune like a bunch of bloody puppets.'

He chuckled again at his own remembered cleverness. 'And I kept saying things to them, like "I've a feeling you're very close to this murderer", stuff like that...and they never bloody knew how right I was!'

'When we were going down to Brighton, you told me the criminal was an exhibitionist.'

'Exactly! I remember. And I told you that the case was going to be the triumph of my career. And...' He giggled on the edge of hysteria '...oh, I was sailing close to the wind then. Do you remember what I had in the boot of the car that day?'

'Well, I...Your golf clubs.'

'I've never played golf in my life.'

'But...So what was in...? Oh my God,' said Charles, as he realised the implication. 'The legs?'

Superintendent Roscoe grinned complacently. 'Yes, I bought the golf bag in Brighton. I put the legs in and took them up to London and back again – in a bloody police car, for God's sake – just for the fun of doing it!'

'And it was you in disguise who I followed when you were going to plant the legs in the station car park?'

Roscoe looked at him in surprise. 'Yes, that was me. I was really sailing close to the wind then – I enjoyed that. And then when you were banged up down in Brighton, you told me all about it...and I could hardly stop myself from telling you it was me you'd been following.'

'But most of the dirty work you got Marchmont to do for you?'

'Mm. He was only still in the force on my say-so, and his life was so fucked up the job was about the only thing he had left. I knew he'd do anything I told him, anything. And once he'd started, he was implicated. An accessory to murder – no way he was going to blab about it then.'

'Except he couldn't stand the pressure.'

'No. The stupid bugger!' Roscoe slammed his fist on the desk in frustration. 'He's screwed up the whole bloody thing!'

'But if he hadn't...? If you'd managed your final coup – and got the discovery of the head announced on *Public Enemies* – what then?'

The superintendent sighed. 'I hadn't really thought that far. Just do it, round off the whole perfect sequence – that was all I'd thought about. Oh, I don't know, I might have staged a neat little suicide for Marchmont *after* the end of the series. There was enough evidence pointing in his direction for everyone to think he'd done the lot. I could have fixed that, but...' His eyes grew distant and unfocused. 'I hadn't really thought beyond finishing it...my final triumph. Retirement?' He screwed up his face. 'I don't think I'd be much good at retirement. Being in the police's been my life. Maybe I never was much good at it, but it was my life...'

Charles brought the superintendent out of his reverie by asking, 'And what had you got in mind for the final *Public Enemies*? How were you going to stage the revelation of the head?'

'Well, I was...' Roscoe stopped, and a sly smile came to his lips. 'I'm not going to tell you. We all have our professional secrets, after all.'

'Ah. Right. And now...?'

'Now?' The superintendent spoke as if he didn't understand the word.

'Yes, what are you going to do now?'

'Oh.' He looked bleakly out of the window. 'I hadn't really thought.'

'I mean, there's no way your involvement can be kept quiet now. I don't mean that I'm going to say anything, but I'm pretty sure Noakes and her lot will start to put two and two together. Once it's known that the murder victim's Ted Faraday and not Martin Earnshaw...'

'Yes, yes...Oh, I'm sure they'll work it out. They may not be quite in my class, but they're not stupid.' Superintendent Roscoe sounded bored now, as if he were speaking of something which didn't involve him at any level.

'Well...' Charles shrugged. 'I guess how you play that is up to you.'

'Hm.' Roscoe nodded abstractedly. 'Yes, I guess it is.'

He was silent, locked away in his own thoughts.

Charles Paris rose from his chair. Just before he got to the door, he looked back, but the murderer was miles away, in a world of his own.

It was while he was waiting for the lift that Charles Paris heard the muffled crack of a gunshot.

Chapter Twenty-One

HE TOOK IN a few pubs and an Italian restaurant on the way back, so it was nearly midnight when he finally reached Hereford Road. As he walked past the payphone, he remembered that he'd never rung Juliet, and his shame was increased by the sight of another sticker, bearing the message: 'CARL PARRIS – PLEESE RING JULIETTE.'

It'd have to wait till the morning. Juliet might not have minded a call at that hour, but her husband Miles, insurance maestro and heavily backed favourite in the Most Boring Man In Britain Stakes, certainly would.

It wasn't a good night. Charles's thoughts churned blackly and his brief moments of sleep were crowded with images of dismembered daughters. Drinking more Bell's to try and shift the mood probably didn't help either.

He waited till half past eight to ring Juliet. 'It's me, Charles.'

'Oh, Daddy, I've been trying to contact you for days.'

'Yes, well, I've, er, sort of been...you know.'

'I just didn't know if you knew about Mummy...'

'Knew what about Mummy?'

'She's in hospital.'

'Hospital? Why?'

'Oh, just for some tests.'

Frances looked very pale and thin with her dark – now dyed dark – hair spread out over the pillow. But she managed a grin when she saw who had come to visit.

'Charles, you shouldn't have bothered. I'm not going to be in here long.'

'But I...I couldn't not have come to see you.'

She didn't look totally convinced by this.

He sat down at the bedside. 'I haven't brought you anything, I'm afraid. You know, grapes or...'

'I'll survive.'

He desperately wanted to ask her why she was there, what was wrong, but somehow the words wouldn't form themselves into the right order.

He took her hand. She didn't resist. He fondled it in his, feeling the reassuring ridge of the kitchen knife scar on her thumb, and was swamped by the knowledge of how much she meant to him.

Frances's hand returned the pressure. He kissed her thin lips.

* * *

The last episode of *Public Enemies* was, inevitably, an anticlimax. The news media were not going to let themselves be upstaged again and were hungry for revenge.

The story broke on the Saturday, so the weekend papers and television news bulletins took great pleasure in producing ever new revelations about the death and dismemberment of Ted Faraday. All their reports made references to *Public Enemies*, the television programme which had devoted nearly a whole series to investigating the wrong murder.

By the following Thursday the public was sick to death of the story and of the very mention of *Public Enemies*. They voted with their feet – or rather with their remote controls – and the ITV ratings plummeted. *Dad's Army* had never been so popular.

Bob Garston and Bob's Your Uncle Productions, realising that the prospects for another series of *Public Enemies* had been seriously jeopardised, started developing a new True Crime format called *The Sex Offenders*. This would reconstruct historic and current sex crimes with the same public-spirited grittiness which had characterised *Public Enemies*. The thinking was that an appeal to the public's prurient fascination with sex, as well as to their prurient fascination with violence, could not fail.

Bob's Your Uncle Productions did not mention the new idea to Roger Parkes, whose contract at W.E.T. had not been renewed. Geoffrey Ramage, however, thought he was in with a chance of being employed because in his time he'd directed quite a few blue movies.

The Sex Offenders, however, fell foul of an increasingly puritanical IBA, and was abandoned at an advanced stage of preparation, after Bob's Your Uncle Productions had spent a considerable amount of development money.

Bob Garston, so recently flavour of the month, suddenly couldn't be given away with soap. His girlfriend, Detective Inspector Sam Noakes, very quickly left the sinking ship and started an affair with a junior cabinet minister who was very strong on law and order issues.

Her police career continued to advance, but not as quickly as had once been prophesied. When the new head of the 'Video Nasties' department was announced, it wasn't Sam Noakes. Her involvement in the *Public Enemies* debacle had left a permanent black mark against her.

The true story of Ted Faraday's death never emerged. The police closed ranks and, though the suicides of Greg Marchmont and Superintendent Roscoe were reported, no connection was ever made between them and the private investigator's murder.

So far as the public knew – and it was a thought which gave them a deliciously unpleasant *frisson* – the man who had killed and dismembered Ted Faraday was 'still at large'.

Chloe Earnshaw was not prosecuted for wasting police time. Though her fabrications had cost them hundreds of thousands, it was reckoned impossible to proceed against her without raising embarrassing questions about the force's own shortcomings during the investigation.

Martin Earnshaw became a kind of folk hero. His simple manner and the tag of 'The Man Who Came Back From The Dead' made him ideal tabloid fodder. And when he married his beloved Veronique, the paparazzi gave the occasion almost as much coverage as a royal divorce. The couple retired happily to her family farm, where they bred Limousin cattle and children.

Chloe Earnshaw, almost as discredited as Bob Garston but still drawn to publicity like a moth to flame, tried to set up a charitable trust to help victims of tabloid character assassination. She arranged a major launch, featuring a couple of minor film actors, three rock musicians, a television weather girl and innumerable soap stars.

Unfortunately, though the event was well organised and publicised, no press arrived to cover it. Chloe Earnshaw should have realised that she would never get away with biting the hand that had so lavishly fed her.

Within a year, the public had completely forgotten the name of Chloe Earnshaw. And that hurt more than any of the supposed sufferings during her brief camera-flash of fame.

The tests on Frances were inconclusive. 'There's nothing to worry about,' said the consultant jovially, 'or if there is we haven't found it!'

She said she felt fine, but still tired easily. Her husband made all kinds of extravagant promises that he'd keep more closely in touch with her, that he'd really try to rebuild their relationship.

But Charles Paris remained Charles Paris, and the road to hell is paved with empty bottles of Bell's.

He went back into empty-glove-puppet mode, and his so-called 'career' returned to its customary stasis. The theatre was, as Maurice Skellern put it, 'very quiet', and nobody seemed to be making television drama any more. Or those who did seemed determined not to employ Charles Paris in their productions.

Sometimes, when things were really bad, Charles would walk through the streets of London and, if he saw someone of approximately his build and age, would think idly to himself, 'If I killed that man, I might be employed to play him in a television reconstruction of the murder. But is it really worth the hassle?'

Generally speaking, the answer he came up with was no.

SICKEN AND SO DIE

To Michael

SIMON BRETT

Chapter One

THINGS WERE actually going rather well for Charles Paris. Basically, it was a matter of work. He had work, he was in work, he was working. For an actor, a job is the switch that turns the personality on to full power. Without it Charles Paris existed. He had all the components of himself: his cynicism, his gloom, his apologetic lusts, his drinking, his deflated air of defeat. But with a job all those elements fused and he was energised, sustained by a galvanic charge that even incorporated optimism.

What was more, he was doing good work. He was playing a good part in what promised to be a good production of a good play. *Twelfth Night* by William Shakespeare; plays don't come a lot better than that. Nor, for a slightly frayed, unravelling actor in his late fifties, do parts come a lot better than Sir Toby Belch.

Playing a major Shakespearean role made Charles feel that perhaps his career had come back on course – or perhaps finally come on course. The theatre offers no obvious career structure – indeed its ups and downs make investing in the National Lottery look a secure bet – but there are certain milestones to which all actors aspire. To play Sir Toby Belch in one's late fifties is a necessary notch carved on the bedpost of a career, a qualification which opens up the possibility of a Henry IV, a Prospero, or even the ultimate prize of a Lear, in one's sixties.

Charles had played big parts in Shakespeare before, but the time or the production had never been right. He had been too young when cast as *Macbeth*, badly directed as Henry V and, as for his leading role in *Julius Caesar*, well, even Charles himself agreed with the estimation of the *Lancashire Evening Post* that 'here was a Mark Antony to whom even Vincent Van Gogh wouldn't have lent an ear.'

But this *Twelfth Night* felt right. Only a week into a five-week rehearsal period, but the whole production had a glow of confidence about it, a growing conviction among the company that they were involved in a show that was going to be successful.

This was something of a surprise because the director was not the most dynamic in the history of the theatre. In fact, Charles Paris had always considered Gavin Scholes rather ineffectual. They'd worked together a good few times, most recently on *Macbeth* at the Pinero Theatre, Warminster, where Gavin had been Artistic Director.

Charles had assumed that at the end of his contract there Gavin would have retired to nurse his hypochondria and irritable bowel syndrome; but the *Director* had confounded expectations by developing a very successful subsequent career as a freelance. This was proof once again that charisma and innovation in the world of theatre count for less than good old-fashioned competence. Gavin Scholes' productions might not set the world on fire, but they told their stories clearly, they came in on time and stayed within their budgets. These were virtues that appealed to production companies.

The current *Twelfth Night* was being mounted by Asphodel Productions, a touring management who had risen to prominence during the previous five years. Their recipe of simply narrated classics – frequently Shakespeare and almost always A-level set texts – had proved extremely successful. Clever, uncluttered set design had made their productions mobile and suitable for all kinds of different performance spaces. One week they'd appear in a conventional theatre, the next a school gymnasium, then a library, a leisure centre, a church hall or a warehouse. As the company's fame spread, so did the range of their touring venues, which now included foreign destinations.

They were poised for greater recognition. They needed one breakthrough production to capture the attention of the national press, and Asphodel's name would be firmly fixed on the British cultural map.

The designated tour for *Twelfth Night* was characteristic of the company's current outreach. It began in early August. The first six performances would be open air, in the gardens of Chailey Ferrars, an Elizabethan mansion in Hertfordshire; they would be presented as part of the nine-day Great Wensham Festival.

Thereafter the show would move on to a studio theatre in Norwich for two weeks. Seven performances in a Billericay leisure centre would be followed by three in a public school's own theatre near Crawley and three on the boarded-over swimming pool of a Reading comprehensive. After a week in a converted Methodist chapel near Cheltenham, the company had a few days' break before the high-spot of the tour – three performances at the University of Olomouc in the Czech Republic. Back in England, two weeks in a former corn exchange in Warwick, a temperance hall in Swindon and a prefabricated sports dome in Aldershot would then climax in the relatively sedate booking of three weeks back at Gavin Scholes' former base, the Pinero Theatre in Warminster.

For Charles Paris all of this represented, with rehearsals, the rare phenomenon of nearly five months' guaranteed work. It also offered the prospect of recapturing the excitement of constant change which had largely vanished from the theatre since the demise of weekly rep.

As well as being cautious in his interpretation of plays, Gavin Scholes was also conservative in his casting. He liked working with people he knew, their familiarity cushioning him against the potential 'difficulty' of actors he didn't know. When he had to introduce new members into this charmed circle, he favoured performers suggested by actors he did know. He particularly liked to use recommended young actors at the beginning of their careers; they were eager and biddable, and unlikely to question the authority of their director.

Charles Paris recognised that this approach was uninventive and prevented Gavin's productions from reaching the creative heights, but the system was not one he was going to complain about, since he was one of its beneficiaries. However suitable Charles Paris might be for Sir Toby Belch, he couldn't see the National or the RSC suddenly going out on a limb and casting him in the role. They'd go for someone much more starry and voguish. Come to that, Charles couldn't see himself getting the part in any lesser company where an old pal's act was not in operation.

So he was all in favour of Gavin Scholes' 'safety-first' casting policy. It brought another benefit too; there were other members of the *Twelfth Night* company with whom Charles had worked before, which is always – or, depending on the individuals involved, perhaps 'usually' would be a better adverb – a comfort to any actor. Two of the cast of Gavin's *Macbeth* were also in the new production.

Russ Lavery had come a long way since playing Fleance and Young Siward in Warminster. That had been his first job in the theatre, and then his undoubted talent had been obscured by a callow, puppyish approach to the business. But four or five years of solid stage work and small television parts had preceded the breakthrough when he'd been cast as Dr Mick Hobson in ITV's *Air-Sea Rescue*.

The show, now into its third series and showing no sign of flagging in the ratings, had turned a young actor of identical talent to at least a hundred of his contemporaries into a household name and a household face. *Air-Sea Rescue* had brought Russ Lavery all of the bonuses of money from escalating fees and foreign repeats, fan mail from half the nation's teenage girls, lucrative offers for personal appearances and voice-overs, and the possibility of saying in interviews that 'I get sent lots of scripts, but I don't like to commit myself to a project unless I feel it is a really exceptional piece of work.'

It also enabled him to say in interviews that 'I really feel the need to get back to my theatrical roots', which explained his appearance in Gavin Scholes' *Twelfth Night*. The fact that he was playing the relatively small and ungrateful part of Sebastian did his image no harm at all. Rather, it demonstrated what an unstarry star Russ Lavery was, and how serious was his dedication to his art. The presence of a well-known television name in the cast of *Twelfth Night* wouldn't do any harm at the box office, either.

The other familiar face in the company provided Charles Paris with even greater cause for celebration. John B. Murgatroyd was an actor against whom Charles had frequently bumped in his theatrical career, and the experience had always been a delightful one. John B. was a clown, a great giggler, in whose company Charles had often been reduced to incapable hysterics and behaviour which would have been judged immature in a primary school. John B. was a terrific person to have around any production.

In the Warminster *Macbeth* he had given his distinctive and stunningly versatile interpretations of both Lennox and the First Murderer. In *Twelfth Night* he was playing Sir Andrew Aguecheek. Since most of Sir Toby Belch's scenes included the wan and winsome knight, Charles was relishing the prospect of building up his double act with John B. on-stage as well as off.

And it wasn't just the work that was going well. For once, Charles Paris's emotional life was also looking promising. He wasn't experiencing the tense, manic uncertainty of a new love affair, but the solid comfort of an old one.

Charles had been married to Frances for twelve years before he finally walked out. He had used all kinds of justifications, about the incompatibility of an actor's lifestyle with the institution of marriage, about the need for them both to develop outside the claustrophobia of cohabitation, but the real motive for his departure had been self-punishment. He'd been having affairs away from home, and he felt guilty about them. Walking out on Frances – and their daughter Juliet – had been a kind of public penance for his misdemeanours.

It had also, he'd hoped at the time, been a bid for freedom. On his own, he would be able to follow up on the emotional hints and half-chances that other women offered. What he'd done was hurtful, but necessary to his fulfilling the imperatives of his own personality. Marriage had been part of his growth, but a part that he had outgrown.

Of course, it hadn't worked out like that. The freedom for which he had given up Frances proved illusory. Yes, he followed up on the other women. He had some good sex and some bad sex, he made some good friends, he even at times imagined himself in love, but all the relationships left him ultimately empty. There was still a void in his life that only Frances could fill.

He'd worried the situation through in his head more times than he cared to count, and almost always came back to the same basic problem. He liked Frances.

That was aside from loving her, which he sometimes did, or from time to time feeling towards her an infuriation which qualified as hatred. But the liking remained constant; that was the invisible chain that held him to her.

For a total split from a lover, there needs to be a two-way pressure. Not just the overwhelming attraction for the new love-object, but also a distaste for the old. Constant comparisons then become inevitable. The new love is not only wonderful, she is also so much more wonderful than the one you are leaving. In fact, when you catalogue the faults, deficiencies and inadequacies of the old love, the only remarkable point is that you stayed with her so long. Why did you put up with someone so unsuitable for all that time?

But such a natural process of fission is rendered inoperable when you still *like* the old love, when you worry about her, think about her, want to discuss things with her. The loving and the hating are relatively easy to cope with; it's the *liking* that makes the whole thing impossible.

And that, Charles had come to realise ruefully, was the state of play in his relationship with his wife. Whatever else there might be happening in his sex-life – and at times there had been quite a bit – he still felt linked to Frances.

Whether she felt the same obligation, he was never quite sure. And even in those moments when he did feel quite sure, he was also aware of how much she resented the encumbrance. At times she seemed very distant from him. At times he knew for certain that she had had other men. But did the fact that none of them had gone the distance mean that Frances's relationships were hobbled by the same restrictions that cramped his own?

Charles Paris knew that he wanted a closer intimacy with his wife, but he could never be certain how much she shared that ambition.

The circumspection of her attitude was not without justification. Charles could not claim to be the most assiduous of men in the protocol of marriage. Even ignoring the fact of his having walked out on his wife – and he could recognise that that was a significant blot on the marital copybook – his behaviour since then would not always have inspired confidence in a potential partner.

He did have a tendency to get distracted. The intention to ring Frances, make contact, fix to meet up, was always there, but when he got involved in a production, when he was away for a while, it was remarkable how the weeks, and even the months, could slip past without his acting on that intention.

There had also been one or two regrettable incidents when he had fixed a rendezvous and been prevented by circumstance – or occasionally drink – from fulfilling his part of the arrangement: the small matter of turning up at the agreed place at the agreed time.

Charles could fully sympathise with Frances's scepticism when he spoke of a closer future between them.

And it wasn't as if she didn't have a full life. Now independent, with her own flat in Highgate, she had risen through the hierarchy of education to become headmistress of a girls' school. She was a caring mother and a solicitous grandmother. What possible incentive could she have to make room in her well-ordered life for a man whose moody personality took over any environment like a wet Labrador?

And yet at the moment she *was* making room in her life for Charles and, at the moment, the experiment seemed to be working.

It was all down to the builders, really. When he left Frances, Charles had moved into a dingy and soulless bedsitter in Hereford Road, 'Just in the short term, you know, till I find somewhere more suitable', and he was still there. Or at least he would still have been there had not the new landlord of the house embarked on the long-overdue transformation of the bedsitters into 'studio flats'.

Once the work was completed, the existing tenants would be given first refusal to continue residency at increased rents, but obviously they all had to move out while the builders gutted the property. Charles, remarkably, had moved in with Frances.

It was convenient – particularly since the *Twelfth Night* rehearsals were taking place in a church hall in Willesden. It was also logical – or it would have been for a couple whose marital history was less chequered.

But the most astonishing thing about the arrangement was that it seemed to be working. They were actually getting on rather well.

Maybe it was age. Maybe they had both matured, and could be more tolerant of each other. Maybe both had learned and been enriched by the traumas of their long separation.

The best part for Charles was that Frances had let him back into her bed. The ease and familiarity of their lovemaking glowed in him through the days like a personal heart-warmer. He didn't feel lonely. It was a long time since he hadn't felt lonely. A long time since he had had someone to go home to at the end of the day.

One unexpected side-effect of this domesticity was that Charles was drinking less. The automatic loose-end recourse to the pub at the end of rehearsals seemed less imperative, and the too-many nightcaps of Bell's to deaden the end of the day were no longer necessary. He and Frances would share a bottle of wine over dinner, but often that was the sum total of his day's intake. For Charles Paris, that made quite a change.

His new circumstances generally made quite a change.

It was early days, mind. Less than two weeks they'd been cohabiting, and neither of them wanted to threaten the fragility of what was happening by talking about it.

Promising, though. Somehow, Charles felt confident that the thoughts going through Frances's mind matched his own. It still wasn't too late for them to make something of their lives together.

Yes, Charles Paris reflected, as the train sped towards Great Wensham and the *Twelfth Night* photocall, things are actually going rather well.

Chapter Two

THE FORMAL Elizabethan gardens of Chailey Ferrars could have been designed as a setting for *Twelfth Night*. Their geometric patterns offered a choice of avenues down which Malvolio could walk. Their statuary, low walls and neatly clipped box trees offered manifold hiding places from which Sir Toby Belch, Sir Andrew Aguecheek and Fabian could observe the steward picking up the letter from 'The Fortunate Unhappy' and falling for Maria's trick to make him believe his mistress Olivia loved him.

The Asphodel production of the play was not to be performed in the formal gardens, however. They were far too precious, far too carefully maintained, to be overrun by actors and picnic-toting members of the public. The acting area for *Twelfth Night* was further away from the house, in a walled field at one end of which a natural amphitheatrical shape had been enhanced by the construction of a grass-covered mound and the planting of a semicircle of trees around it. For performances a wooden stage was erected on the mound and the backstage area cordoned off with hessian screens.

It was the Chailey Ferrars Trustees who imposed conditions on which parts of the estate could be used. They were a body of men and women of prelapsarian conservatism, who saw it as their God-given mission to resist every proposed change to the house or gardens. They would really have liked the public excluded totally from the premises, but had been grudgingly forced to accept the financial necessity of paying visitors.

At first the Trustees had resisted the overtures of the Great Wensham Festival Society to stage plays at Chailey Ferrars. But by the third year, having seen how much other businesses had benefited from the new custom attracted by the festival, they had agreed to very limited access to the grounds for two public performances of *Much Ado About Nothing*. Again, grudgingly, they had had to concede that the experiment had not led to wholesale vandalism of their precious property, and that, as well as being an artistic success, it had indeed proved rather profitable to the Trust.

From then on the Chailey Ferrars Shakespeare had become a regular feature – in fact, the main focus – of the Great Wensham Festival, though the Trustees never allowed its continuance to be taken for granted. Each year the Festival Director, Julian Roxborough-Smith – or, in the event, his administrator, Moira Handley – had to go through an elaborate square dance of application and supplication until the Trustees – with an ever-increasing number of cautions and provisos – agreed to let the Chailey Ferrars grounds be used for yet another Shakespearean production.

It was a measure of Moira Handley's skilful management of the Trustees that, though there would never be any possibility of the play being staged in the formal gardens, she had elicited permission for the *Twelfth Night* photocall to be held there.

As an even greater concession, the Trustees had allowed the accompanying press conference to be conducted in the Chailey Ferrars dining hall. The magnitude of this honour was continuously emphasised, though, since Asphodel were being forced to pay well over the odds for the Chailey Ferrars in-house catering services, the Trustees' attitude did seem a little hypocritical.

Still, Charles Paris wasn't that worried. A photocall and a press conference had to mean a few free drinks.

He had been unperturbed by the prospect of a visit to Great Wensham, though many of the other company members had made a big fuss about it. Gavin Scholes objected to losing a day's rehearsal, even though his presence at the press conference was written into the contract between Asphodel and the Great Wensham Festival. His wardrobe mistress resented the demand for costumes to be worn at the photocall; she grumbled that it was only local press, anyway, surely they could be fobbed off with rehearsal stills. But again a fully dressed on-site photocall was written into the contract.

These complaints, however, were as nothing to those raised by the cast. Few of the principals wanted to drag out to Great Wensham for some bloody photocall; they regarded a day without rehearsals as a day off, and at the beginning of several months' intensive work they weren't going to miss out on that.

Russ Lavery was particularly vehement in his refusal when Gavin Scholes tried to cajole him into being part of the outing. Up until that point he had been very meek and unstarry at rehearsal – except for one violent blow-up with the wardrobe mistress who'd wanted to give Viola's and Sebastian's costumes shorter sleeves than Russ Lavery thought appropriate. Needless to say, the star had won; the sleeves were lengthened.

But the press conference prompted another tantrum. Russ's agent had set up a meeting for that day with a Hollywood director who'd got a project he might be interested in. When Gavin rather tentatively pointed out that 'availability for promotion of the production' was written into Russ's contract, he was nearly blown out of the water.

'I don't have to make myself available for bloody local hacks!' the star of *Air-Sea Rescue* stormed. 'My publicist and I spend most of our time *avoiding* publicity, not courting it.'

'It's not going to be just local coverage,' Gavin asserted. 'The festival press officer I spoke to said they've invited all the nationals as well.'

'I don't care if they've invited the Pope, Barbra Streisand and Nelson Mandela,' said Russ Lavery. '*I* won't be there.'

So the party who actually did attend the photocall and press conference were the amenable ones who tended not to make a fuss, like Charles Paris and Tottie Roundwood, the actress who was playing Maria; and those who were desperate for publicity in whatever form it came – Vasile Bogdan, who played Fabian, Sally Luther, the production's Viola, and Talya Northcott, whose first professional job this was.

Talya had been cast in the non-speaking role of Olivia's Handmaiden, with the additional responsibility of understudying all three female parts. For someone so new to the profession, just working in the theatre was profoundly exciting. And any newspaper picture of her in costume would be religiously snipped out and scrapbooked by the worshipping 'Mummy' to whom her conversation frequently reverted.

Vasile Bogdan, a gloweringly handsome dark-haired actor in his twenties, may have had an obscure European name, but spoke without any trace of an accent. He was fiercely ambitious, and his own opinion of his talents manifested itself in a slight contempt for the rest of the company. His *Twelfth Night* casting in the ungrateful role of Fabian was a stage which he considered himself to be passing through only briefly on his way to greater things. An opportunity to get his photograph in a newspaper – any newspaper – was not one that at this phase of his career he would ever pass up.

Sally Luther's relationship with the publicity machine was more complex. In her early twenties she had been the tabloids' darling. A pretty blonde ingenue, she had been cast effortlessly, straight out of drama school, as one of the leads in the ITV sitcom *Up To No Good*. In that show she had charmed the nation through four series, and become a familiar presence failing to answer the questions on showbiz quizzes, guesting daffily on game shows and manning phone-lines on charity telethons. She described the interior of her flat to colour supplements, her kind of day to the *Radio Times*, and her first kiss to teenage magazines. She had all the trappings of stardom: a fan club, a rose named after her, and even the unwanted attentions of obsessive fan letters and a mysterious stalker. The public loved her, she could do no wrong, and she made a very good living.

Sally Luther's fall from this state of grace was not dramatic. No messy break-ups from famous boyfriends, no arrests for drunken driving, no allegations of drug abuse. She just slowly dropped out of the public consciousness. *Up To No Good* was not recommissioned for a fifth series. The pilot for a new Sally Luther sitcom was rejected. Guest appearances in other sitcoms became more spaced out and finally dried up.

The public did not fall out of love with Sally Luther; they simply forgot about her. Without a weekly reminder of her face on their television screens, she slipped imperceptibly out of the collective memory.

She wasn't out of work. She wasn't broke. She didn't crack up. She was just brought up hard against the fact that she'd had a lucky start, and if she was going to continue in the business, then she'd have to rebuild her career from scratch.

And she'd have to rebuild it from different elements. The baby face that had floated her through her early twenties had grown harder and more lined. The natural blonde of her hair had darkened to a light brown. She could of course have kept the colour artificially, but decided not to. The new Sally Luther was not going to be a clone of the old.

She had never been as stupid as she appeared on the screen. She applied her considerable intelligence and pragmatism to starting again.

Charles Paris admired the determination with which Sally Luther had hit the comeback trail. She had immersed herself in stage work, learning the basics of a trade which her television success had bypassed. She had taken small parts in out-of-the-way theatres, slowly building competence and experience. She had worked her way up from being a pretty face to a respectable actress, and the Asphodel Productions' Viola was the highest point yet of her reconstituted career.

It was Charles's secret opinion that Sally Luther, even with all her grafting away, was not really a good enough actress to play Viola. But he respected her professionalism and enjoyed working with her.

The Trustees of Chailey Ferrars grudgingly – it was the adverb with which they performed their every action – allowed the *Twelfth Night* cast a small room off the ground floor administrative office in which to change. So, amidst coffee machines and photocopiers, and in cramped proximity to Vasile Bogdan and the three – mercifully small – actresses, Charles Paris donned his Sir Toby Belch costume.

He was pleased that Gavin Scholes was doing the play in what he, Charles, thought of as the 'right' period – in other words, contemporary with when it had been written. Charles Paris had had enough of gimmicky productions of Shakespeare. He'd been in a nineteen-twenties flapper-style *Love's Labour's Lost*; he'd worn cut-off jeans as Bardolph in *Henry V*, a pin-striped suit as one of the tribunes in *Coriolanus,* a hippie kaftan as Lancelot Gobbo, and even a tutu in a hopelessly misconceived cross-dressing *All's Well...* ('*All's Well That Ends Well*, but here was a production which neither started nor ended well. In fact, so far as this critic's concerned, it would have ended much better three hours before it actually did' – *Financial Times*).

What a relief, after all that, to be playing Shakespeare in appropriate dress. Gavin Scholes' lack of imagination did have its advantages.

Also, for once, Charles actually had a new costume. For most period productions of his career he'd been dressed in something hired from a theatrical costumier or tatted together from whatever could be found in Wardrobe. He'd become accustomed to other men's clothes, to walking around in the aura – or, in certain regrettable instances, the smell – of another actor.

But Asphodel employed a pukka costume designer for all their shows. This was partly so that the costumes could reflect a production design concept; but there were practical reasons too. A four-month engagement justified the expense of specially made costumes, and the company was also shrewdly building up its own wardrobe stock which was increasingly hired out to other managements. There were astute business brains behind Asphodel Productions.

Charles Paris liked his Sir Toby Belch costume. The designer's overall theme was muted greys and silver, which reflected *Twelfth Night*'s underlying melancholy – and also pointed up even more the virulent shock of Malvolio's yellow cross-gartering.

And the designer had not succumbed to the common error of making Sir Toby scruffy. The man was a gentleman of the court, after all, so Charles Paris was dressed in charcoal velvet doublet and hose, piped with silver and slashed with oyster-coloured silk. He had a silver-frosted ruff and a small charcoal hat with a fluffy pale-grey feather. As Charles donned the costume in the Chailey Ferrars office, he did feel rather pleased with himself.

He felt particularly pleased that the costume's generous cut rendered his own paunch inadequate and forced him actually to pad for the role. This gave Charles a spurious sense of righteousness, as did the fact that he also had to redden his face with make-up. The Bell's whisky may have taken its toll, but it had not yet sufficiently ravaged his complexion for him to play Sir Toby without cosmetic help. All encouraging stuff.

As well as a specially made costume, Charles had had a customised beard constructed by Wig Creations, and this too gave him a sense of being pampered. As he peered into the tiny mirror, the familiar alcohol smell of spirit gum in his nostrils, and pressed Sir Toby's luxuriant moustache on to his upper lip, Charles Paris felt good.

His self-satisfaction must have expressed itself in his body language, because Tottie Roundwood, reaching round to pull up the zip of her jet-black Maria costume, grinned and said, 'Yes, very handsome indeed.'

Charles grinned back. 'Let me.' He reached across to help her with the zip.

Tottie Roundwood was probably around the fifty mark, short, plumpish, dark hair beginning to be streaked with grey. She was one of those actresses capable of enormous fireworks on stage, but quiet and reserved the rest of the time. Charles liked her, though he knew little about her, except that she was interested in some system of alternative medicine. Reflexology? Healing? Homeopathy? One of those, anyway, he couldn't remember.

He patted her shoulder to indicate that the dress was secure, and reflected on the total lack of sexual charge the contact gave him. Actors and actresses are so used to sharing dressing rooms that gender becomes irrelevant. Charles couldn't help noticing out of the corner of his eye that Sally Luther still had a pretty good body, though.

To his surprise, this little glancing thought made him feel guilty. There was a tiny pang of disloyalty to Frances, with whom he'd made tender and extended love the night before. Obviously his wife's body had to give Sally Luther's twenty years, but it was still looking pretty terrific. And, he concluded virtuously after a covert look at Talya Northcott slipping into her costume, I don't fancy that really young one at all. Neat little figure, nice blonde hair maybe, but it doesn't do a thing for me.

Goodness, thought Charles Paris, I am changing. If this goes on, I'll soon be positively uxorious.

Gavin Scholes came bustling into the office. 'OK, are you set? The press – such as they are – are all here, and we're ready to go.'

Chapter Three

'...BUT PERHAPS the Shakespeare is the jewel in our crown – though of course the Great Wensham Festival is a crown of many jewels – as you will be able to see from the press releases that are on the table over there. Anyway, we of the Festival Society are absolutely delighted to welcome, for the third year running, Asphodel Productions. I'm sure you all enjoyed their *Midsummer Night's Dream* and *As You Like It* and I am confident that we can look forward to the same qualities of robust storytelling in this year's *Twelfth Night* – whose performance, incidentally, is made possible by the generous sponsorship of Mutual Rel –'

At a warning cough from a dark-haired woman beside him, the Festival Director, Julian Roxborough-Smith, hastily corrected himself. '– of a variety of national and local businesses which you will find listed in the press release. I would also like to acknowledge at this point the invaluable contribution made by Hertfordshire Arts Network, without which the scope of the Great Wensham Festival would be considerably less broad.

'As you see, some members of the *Twelfth Night* cast have been good enough to join us today. Yes, they are in costume – those aren't their normal street clothes.' A little pause for the even littler joke. No reaction. 'But before we become more informal and you get a chance to chat to them, I'm going to call on *Twelfth Night*'s director to say a few words about the production. Ladies and gentlemen of the press, will you please welcome Mr Gavin Scholes.'

'Lady and gentleman of the press' might have been more accurate, Charles reflected. Though there were lavish amounts of sandwiches and other snacks – and a gratifying number of wine bottles – laid out in the dining hall of Chailey Ferrars for the press' conference, there did seem to be a marked lack of press.

A bored-looking man in his fifties held a notebook and pencil, but had not yet heard anything he deemed worthy of recording; and an earnest-looking girl, barely out of her teens, pointed a cassette player with great concentration at whoever happened to be speaking. Otherwise, a single photographer, burdened down by a shoulder bag of camera impedimenta, shifted from one foot to the other at the back of the hall, with the expression of someone who should already have moved on to cover the local primary school's Wildfowl Week.

Julian Roxborough-Smith's address was unlikely to have stirred much excitement among the press, even if more of them had been present. It was not what he said that was uncharismatic; it was the manner of his saying it.

The Festival Director had one of those languid, slightly theatrical voices which suggests he is doing everyone a favour by speaking at all, and imparts an unintentional tinge of contempt to everything. He was a tall man pushing sixty and turning to fat. His sandy hair was thinning. He wore a suit in broad pin-stripe. The thick-framed glasses and spotted bow-tie seemed to accentuate rather than obscure the nondescript nature of his face.

'*Twelfth Night*,' Gavin Scholes began, 'is one of the most charming of Shakespeare's comedies, and yet at the same time it is one of the darkest. The treatment meted out to Malvolio alone prevents the play from being the jolly romp which it is sometimes portrayed...as,' he added uneasily, having got a little lost in his syntax. 'And in my production I have deliberately emphasised the –'

'Look, if you want to have any photographs, we're going to have to do them now,' a harsh voice interrupted from the back of the dining hall. 'I'm already running late.'

Since with no visual record the press conference would be even more of a non-event than it was already, the photographer's bad manners won the day, and the five costumed cast members were trooped out to the formal gardens to strike Elizabethan poses against the statuary.

They were shepherded by a small, anxious woman who had identified herself earlier as Pauline Monkton, press officer for the Great Wensham Festival. She kept apologising for the lack of press at the conference and, while apologies were certainly in order, the way she went on about it quickly became wearing.

'I mean, I don't know what you can do,' she said plaintively. 'They all got invited – the nationals and everything. They had their invitations *weeks* ago. And they did say RSVP, but, do you know, hardly any of them have even *bothered* to reply. I mean, once you've invited them and given them all the information, well, what else can you *do*?'

Hire a professional publicist or public relations company, would have been Charles's answer. He had encountered the fatal touch of the amateur at other arts festivals, and he knew it almost never worked. Publicity is a hard-nosed cut-throat business, there are any number of highly sophisticated organisations out there lobbying for media coverage, and one earnest middle-aged woman sending out invitations – even with RSVP on them – doesn't stand a chance. Goodwill can only go so far. If you want a job professionally done, you have to pay a professional to do it.

Local newspaper photographers, as a breed, are not the subtlest of people, and what the one from the *Great Wensham Observer* was really after was a bit of cleavage. He managed to get a meagre ration from Tottie Roundwood, lolling lasciviously on Sir Toby Belch's lap. He tried to persuade Talya Northcott to take up a provocative pose, but was quickly deterred by a righteous blast of political correctness. And he was disappointed to find Sally Luther (whose tits had once been quite famous) doubled up to the neck in her male Cesario rather than her female Viola costume. Her face was framed by a pageboy-cut blond wig, identical to the one Russ Lavery would wear as her twin Sebastian.

Gavin Scholes fussed around, objecting to details like the fact that in the play Fabian would never put his arms round Viola – least of all when she was dressed as a man – but he was ignored. The photographer just pressed on, taking his clichéd shots against the garden features, and constantly looking at his watch. He wasn't an exemplar of the Cecil Beaton school of photography – his was more the railway station booth approach. After about five minutes he shoved his camera back in its bag, pulled out an old envelope on which he scribbled down the cast's names – in a way that didn't inspire confidence he'd got them right – and hurried off to do the Wildfowl Week.

Sally Luther. had been a bit tight-lipped about the perfunctory nature of the photocall, but then she had plenty of better-orchestrated ones to compare it with. Charles Paris was unworried. In his new, benign mood, little worried him, and he quite enjoyed being photographed – even for the *Great Wensham Observer*. He felt secure in his costume, secure in his role, secure in his life.

And after the photographs would come the interviews. Yes, he quite relished the idea of expatiating on his past career and his current interpretation of Sir Toby Belch. Local newspapers, he knew, were always desperate to fill space, so he'd be allowed to spread himself. It was about time Charles Paris gave an in-depth interview.

When they went back into the dining hall, he was waylaid by the earnest young girl with the cassette recorder even before he had time to get a drink. 'Tell me, Mr Parrish,' she asked, 'what's it like working with Russ Lavery?'

The press didn't stay long. They did routine interviews with Sally Luther and left, saying they'd got all the biographical information they needed on file or they'd get it from the press release.

Vasile Bogdan glowered even more darkly at their ignoring him, and Talya Northcott looked pretty miffed. She had quite fancied the idea of a nice personality interview with her for Mummy's scrapbook.

Tottie Roundwood, of a naturally equable disposition and someone who'd been around the business a long time, was unflustered by the disregard. And Charles Paris couldn't complain about lack of attention – even if his whole interview had been about working with Dr Mick Hobson of *Air-Sea Rescue*.

The two reporters departed having drunk only one glass of mineral water. The girl had that. The man had nothing. The accountable nineties were really wreaking havoc with journalistic stereotypes. Still, that does leave an awful lot of wine to be consumed by those who've remained, thought Charles comfortably.

Not many did remain, apart from the *Twelfth Night* representatives. For form's sake, Gavin had staged a weary little tantrum to Julian Roxborough-Smith about the lack of press presence and the waste of a day's rehearsal; and then the festival's Artistic Director had gone off, scolding a still-apologetic Pauline Monkton for the lack of response to her invitations. 'But they did all have RSVP on them,' she wailed as they left the dining hall.

The locals who stayed to drink with the *Twelfth Night* company were all involved in the festival, and the majority of them were volunteers. Apart from Julian Roxborough-Smith, the society only had one paid employee who, in common with most people working in 'the Arts', was paid a pittance for her services. She was the administrator, Moira Handley, the one whose cough had saved her boss from a gaffe over the festival's sponsorship.

Moira was fortyish, thin, with short dark hair. She wore black jeans, a sloppy red jumper, and that expression of sardonic long-suffering which Charles had seen on the faces of so many stage managers over the years. It said, 'What you're asking for is totally impossible, but don't worry, I'll do it somehow.' It was a coping expression.

Charles had always found that look very reassuring, because of the rock-solid competence it implied. Not only that, he'd also always found it rather sexy. His career had encompassed some very pleasant interludes with stage managers. Their attitude to sex he'd found equally practical; and they didn't cling.

As he talked to her, Charles realised he could quite fancy Moira Handley. Or, that is to say, were he not now totally fulfilled in his relationship with Frances, he could have quite fancied Moira Handley. She wasn't wearing a wedding ring, he noticed.

Moira was talking about her boss. 'You won't see much of Julian once the festival's up and running. I mean, he's put in an appearance today, he'll be there at your first night, I'm sure, pressing the flesh of the sponsors, but that's about it.'

'So he won't interfere artistically with the production?'

'Good heavens, no. He reckons the Shakespeare runs itself. His background's music, anyway.'

'Oh?'

'Used to be a mildly successful baritone. Was shrewd enough to move towards management before the voice went.'

'And what does he do when he's not directing festivals?'

'Not a lot. Pretty full-time job he's got doing the two of them, anyway.' Charles looked at her quizzically. 'Julian also runs the Barmington Festival – or should I say has another bunch of volunteers in Barmington who run the Barmington Festival for him.'

'I don't detect a note of criticism in your voice, do I?' he asked archly.

'By no means. Julian Roxborough-Smith's very highly thought of in the Arts world. On lots of advisory panels, you know, that sort of thing. No, he is reckoned to be wonderful – a perfect, cultured human being – by everyone…who hasn't worked with him.'

Charles wondered if it was the drink that was making the administrator indiscreet, but decided not. Moira Handley, he felt instinctively, was one of those people who were totally honest. She wouldn't edit her views on Julian Roxborough-Smith according to the company she was in; she'd say them to his face if he was incautious enough to ask for them.

'What makes him so difficult to work for?'

Moira puffed out her cheeks in a kind of 'take your pick' expression. 'Well, in common with a lot of people who run arts festivals, he has a total inability to delegate. Julian will apportion work to others to make more time for himself, and then waste the time he's gained by looming over the shoulder of the person he's appointed to do the job. He will agree to binding decisions made in committee one day, and take the exact opposite course the next. He will independently commit the festival to undertakings for which he has neither the mandate nor the budget. He's an autocrat who's big on the notion – though not the practice – of consultation.'

Charles shrugged. 'There are a lot of people in the theatre who're totally impossible to work with. Doesn't stop them being very successful.'

'I know.'

'Something about channelling all that energy.'

Moira shook her head ruefully. 'Doesn't hold up with Julian. He is the possessor of a very small amount of energy, which he husbands very carefully. In fact, Julian is basically extremely lazy. Divides his time between booking artistes who've appeared at the Great Wensham Festival for the Barmington Festival and artistes who've appeared at the Barmington Festival for the Great Wensham Festival.'

'But *somebody* must get the festivals happening.'

'Oh yes, somebody does.' She gave Charles a cool, appraising grin. 'But that somebody isn't Julian Roxborough-Smith.'

Charles chuckled. 'Well, from the tone of what you've said, I wouldn't imagine you'll be working for him a lot longer. Is this the first time you've done the Great Wensham Festival?'

Moira looked shocked. 'Good heavens, no. I've been working with Julian for the past sixteen years.'

'Hello. I'm Carole Whittaker from HAN.'

'Ah,' said Charles, taking the thin hand the girl thrust towards him. She had, he noticed, an unnervingly offset hennaed hair style – clearly expensively sculpted – and small black-rimmed granny glasses. 'I'm sorry – what's HAN?'

'Hertfordshire Arts Network.'

'Oh yes, Julian said you're one of the sponsors – right?'

'Not exactly. HAN's a body whose remit is to provide seed-corn funding which can enable and empower companies to input adequate community outreach and attain quality feedback in an arts context.'

'Ah. Right.'

It was Charles Paris's first encounter with Artspeak.

Because the trains from Great Wensham back into London were frequent, and because the day's rehearsal schedule was shot to pieces anyway, there didn't seem much point in the members of the *Twelfth Night* company stopping drinking. They deserved it. They'd been dragged all the way out to Hertfordshire for nothing; they might as well get some benefit from the day. And, after all, the booze was free.

Only Sally Luther, rigidly disciplining her career back on course, stayed with the mineral water.

The others – even Vasile's glowering could evidently be converted into smiles by sufficient alcohol – just got gigglier and gigglier. Charles was quite relieved John B. Murgatroyd wasn't there. The level of giggliness might then have become unacceptable.

Not that there was anyone left except the catering staff to find anything unacceptable. Moira and the other Great Wensham Festival Society representatives had long gone back to their offices, leaving the theatricals to get more and more boisterous.

Even Tottie Roundwood came out of her shell for once, the wine making her as raucous offstage as her Maria was on. In the illogic of alcohol, it suddenly seemed essential for her to convert everyone present to vegetarianism. Immediate support arrived from Talya Northcott who said she'd been vegetarian since she'd started drama school, '– and I've persuaded Mummy to give up meat too.'

'Charles,' Tottie demanded, 'do you eat meat?'

'Guilty as charged,' he replied. 'But I do eat vegetables too.'

'Do you? Good.' She spread her hands broadly over the Chailey Ferrars catering. 'You'd eat the vegetable stuff in that lot?'

'If it was something I liked, yes.'

Talya Northcott snatched up a plate of mushroom tartlets. 'Would you eat one of these?'

'I would if I was hungry. I'm not hungry at the moment.'

'Go on!' She thrust the plate up under his nose.

'What's going on over here?' Gavin Scholes, also in bonhomous mood, ambled towards them.

'Go on, eat it, Charles!'

He grinned, shaking his head away from the proffered delicacy. 'Tottie and Talya are on a crusade, trying to persuade me to take up vegetarianism.'

'Oh God, why?'

'The more relevant question is: why not?' Tottie Roundwood countered. 'Why aren't you a vegetarian, Gavin?'

'Because I like meat! I actually like the taste of bloody meat!'

'What about cooked meat?' asked Charles facetiously.

'Any meat. I'm a meat-eater. I'm a carnivore.' His voice wobbled over the word. He was actually quite pissed. Maybe relief from the tensions of rehearsal made him more susceptible.

'But you like vegetables too,' Tottie persisted.

'Yes, I like vegetables,' Gavin agreed, *'in their place.'* He paused, then giggled. 'And their *place* is beside a dirty great big slab of meat!'

'No, come on, you taste this.' Tottie Roundwood picked up one of the mushroom tartlets.

'Yes,' Talya urged. 'Go on.'

'This is purely vegetable and yet the taste is a hundred per cent more subtle than any meat you're ever going to find.' Tottie Roundwood pressed the tartlet towards the director's mouth. 'Go on, eat it.'

'I'm too full,' said Gavin. 'Too full. There's so much meat in my stomach that there's not *mush room* for anything else.'

This ancient pun made him laugh even more loudly – yes, he really was pissed – and Tottie took the invitation of his open mouth to cram in the mushroom tartlet. Talya Northcott giggled; she was quite pissed too. Gavin spluttered for a moment, but swallowed the delicacy down.

'Well, what do you think?' demanded Tottie. 'What do you think of the taste?'

'I think it...' There was a silence before Gavin Scholes bawled out, '...needs a bit more meat with it!'

The alcohol endowed this sally too with infinite wit, and they all giggled even louder. It was then that the Chailey Ferrars catering staff decided they had had enough. Discreetly, they started tidying up and edging their guests towards the door.

Charles dozed on the train back to London. At St Pancras, since he seemed to have revived a taste for the stuff, he downed a couple of large Bell's. That evening he fell asleep halfway through the meal that Frances served him in front of the television.

So he didn't see the pursed expression on his wife's face as she closed the sitting room door and went alone to her bed.

Charles Paris had a wretched headache the next morning when he arrived at the rehearsal room to the news that Gavin Scholes had been taken ill with severe abdominal pains.

Chapter Four

'HE'S ALWAYS had problems with his digestion,' said Charles. 'One of those nervy types for whom everything goes to the stomach. Some people react to stress by getting depressed, some by getting migraines –'

'And some by getting drunk,' John B. Murgatroyd interrupted. 'Same again?'

'Well, shouldn't really.'

Charles glanced at his watch, but John B. had already whipped up the two pint glasses and was on his way to the bar, throwing one of Sir Toby Belch's lines over his shoulder as he went. '"O knight! thou lackest a cup of canary: when did I see thee so put down?"'

What the hell, thought Charles. Couple of lunch-time drinks aren't going to hurt. We're not doing any proper rehearsal today, anyway. The assistant director, who had taken over in Gavin Scholes' absence, was an uncharismatic youth whose approach to the cast was too tentative to command respect. Asphodel Productions hadn't yet told him whether he'd be taking over permanently as director of *Twelfth Night*, but his unassertive manner suggested he thought this was unlikely. And the more he thought it was unlikely, the more unlikely it became.

Anyway, Charles reassured himself, he and John B. weren't the only ones who'd defected to the pub. Across the bar sat Sally Luther with Chad Pearson, the chubby West Indian who was playing Feste (which was about as controversial as Gavin Scholes' casting was ever likely to get). Also present were Sally's in-house fan club. These were the two youngest members of the company, who were both fresh out of the same drama school (another testament to Gavin's lack of adventure). One was Talya Northcott and the other an assistant stage manager/walk-on, who was called, unbelievably, Benzo Ritter.

It certainly wasn't the name he was born with – in fact, Talya thought he'd said it was a nickname from school. He must've chosen to use it, either because there already was an Equity member with his given name, or – more likely – because he thought it would look better on a theatre programme.

If that was the reason, Charles didn't share the opinion; but he knew young actors have always been prone to exotic excess, building fantasies of their stage names glowing above the titles of plays and television series. It was a harmless exercise of the imagination, and one with which even a cynical old ham like Charles Paris could still empathise.

For a young actor, the possibilities of a showbiz career appear infinite. Each job, however minor, is the next rung on the inevitable climb to becoming the new Olivier. They all know they're going to get to the top; it's simply a question of how long the process is going to take.

Charles, in whose battered heart such fatuous ambitions could still be ignited by a sudden phone call or a good rehearsal, couldn't yet judge whether Benzo Ritter had the talent to realise his dreams. As well as being an ASM, the young actor had been cast as one of the officers who arrest Antonio in Act Three, Scene Four. He was the Second Officer, which was unfortunate for him, because the First Officer has the lion's share of the lines.

All Benzo had to say was:

"'Antonio, I arrest thee at the suit
Of Count Orsino,"'
"'Come, sir, away!"'

and

"'Come, sir, I pray you go."'

On their second appearance in Act Five, Scene One, the First Officer is the only one who speaks. So the only opinion Charles had formed was that Benzo Ritter, in common with most young actors in their first parts, had a tendency to make too much of his minimal contribution to the play.

There was no immediate glow of talent, such as Russ Lavery had shown in his first job, Gavin Scholes' *Macbeth* at Warminster. Still, learning to act is a long process, there's a lot of luck involved, and Benzo Ritter might yet make it to the top of the profession.

Certainly he and Talya Northcott seemed willing to learn. They watched rehearsals avidly, particularly when their idol, Sally Luther, was involved. Sally took their devotion in good part; it seemed to amuse her rather than anything else.

The conversation at the other table appeared animated, though, Charles noticed with a small twinge of guilt, they were all on the mineral water. The twinge lasted a microsecond until John B. Murgatroyd returned from the bar.

'Sorry, they were fresh out of canary,' he announced, putting the two full pint glasses down on the table. 'Had to make do with bitter.'

'Oh well. "Needs must when the devil drives."' Charles Paris took a long swallow. Nice stuff, beer. Three pints'd have him peeing all afternoon, but it was nice stuff.

'Irritable bowel syndrome,' he announced.

John B. Murgatroyd cocked a quizzical eyebrow. 'You too, mate?' he said.

'No, irritable bowel syndrome is what Gavin was told he'd got last time he went to the doctor about it. He's always been – a bit of a hypochondriac, and he seemed quite relieved to actually have a name given to his condition.'

'So he's got an irritable bowel, has he?'

'I guess so.'

'I must introduce it to my grumbling appendix,' said John B. 'I'm sure they could have a wonderful time moaning away at each other.'

Charles gave the joke a token chuckle, then looked pensive.

'Mind you, what Gavin's got now sounds a bit more serious than just irritable bowel. I mean, that wouldn't put him right out of the production, would it?'

'I suppose it depends how irritable it is. If his bowel's absolutely bloody furious, then I'd imagine –'

Charles shook his head. 'Wouldn't be hospitalised with just that. Wouldn't be all this talk of "tests". No, I reckon it sounds a bit nasty.' He took another substantial swig of beer. 'Oh well, no doubt we'll get more details in time.'

His tone was rueful. The news of Gavin's illness had cast a shadow, threatening his uncharacteristically upbeat mood of recent weeks. Maybe things have been going too well, he thought gloomily; it can't last.

'Come on, Charles, perk up.' John B. quoted Sir Toby again. '"I'm sure care's an enemy to life."'

'Yes, I'm sure it is too.'

The other *Twelfth Night* party were moving across to the door. Benzo Ritter, Charles noticed, glowed with excitement. Was it just the thrill of being in a professional production, or had it something to do with being with the undoubtedly dishy Sally Luther?

'You two coming?' asked Chad Pearson in his lilting, Caribbean tones.

'In a minute.' Charles raised his glass. 'Just finishing this.'

'See you then.' Charles watched Chad and the others out of the pub, then turned back to confront an exaggerated expression of reproach on John B. Murgatroyd's face. 'What's up?'

'You just don't care, do you?' said John B. in a voice of camp petulance. 'I just give, give, give, all the time, and you just take, take, take.'

Charles grinned, wondering what this latest performance was in aid of.

'I mean, I don't ask a lot, Charles, but I would have thought there are certain basic reciprocal rules of friendship that just *ought* to be observed.' John B. Murgatroyd flicked back a piqued eyebrow and gave a little snort of martyrdom.

'What are you on about, you idiot?'

'Well, I'd have thought it was obvious. We came into this bar – what, an hour ago? – and I bought us two drinks. When we'd drunk those, *you* went and bought us two more. When we'd drunk those, I went and bought two more. And now...' John B. drained his beer glass and turned to his friend with a smug grin. 'Your round, I think, Charles?'

'But we shouldn't...' All too easily, Charles Paris caved in. 'Same again?'

'You bet.'

The following morning Charles had another headache. The trouble was, once he started drinking, he did have a tendency to continue. Stupid habit, he could recognise that. And it was already proving destructive. Frances had been a little less than forthcoming at breakfast. Mustn't slip back into the old ways, he told himself. What he'd got going with his wife was far too important to be jeopardised by a little carelessness on his part. Pull yourself together, Charles.

The assistant director was even less assertive that morning. Something in the doomy way he put the cast through their paces suggested he now definitely knew he wasn't going to take over the production on a permanent basis.

They were doing Act Five, the final scene, for which Gavin Scholes had done a rough blocking the previous week. The action was complicated, with all the principal characters – except Maria – coming on, in turn, to tie up the various threads of plot. As a result here was a lot of hanging around for everyone.

Charles himself didn't have much to do. Sir Toby Belch's only contribution to Act Five is to be led in, drunk and bruised, by Feste, to say a few bad-tempered, truculent lines, and be led off again. In Charles's current state, little acting was required.

While the rest of the cast were reminded of their moves, he sat slumped on a chair, head aching too much even to contemplate *The Times* crossword. Tottie Roundwood sat beside him, but mercifully did not seem in a mood to chat. Charles's mind alternated wearily between two familiar poles – swearing he'd never touch another drop of alcohol, and looking forward to the first life-restoring drink at lunch-time.

John B. Murgatroyd seemed unaffected by the excesses of the day before. Indeed, he was infuriatingly bouncy and on top. He'd probably been sensible and not continued drinking into the evening. If only Charles could learn to do that...

The atmosphere in the rehearsal room was bad, even for those who weren't hungover. Though the *Twelfth Night* company had all bitched behind his back about Gavin Scholes' lack of imagination, they had found him an unchallenging, reassuring presence. They liked the way he only gave them minimal notes on interpretation; few actors object to being allowed to play parts as they want to play them. And, while he was around, they'd all shared in the communal warmth of a show that felt good, a production that was going to work.

Without him they were bereft, and their mood was further weakened by the faltering suggestions of the assistant director. Tensions came to the surface.

The one in whom they were most evident was Russ Lavery. Having taken the decision to 'get back to his theatrical roots' in the surprisingly minor role of Sebastian, he had been extremely obedient and self-effacing under Gavin's direction. Except for the blow-up over attendance at the press conference, he had demonstrated none of the starry behaviour that might be expected from someone so used to being the centre of attention.

With Gavin removed, however, Russ Lavery became a very different creature. He seemed wound-up, impatient when the assistant director spent time with other actors. Suddenly he seemed to think that Sebastian was the only person in the play who mattered. He injected into the rehearsal room that unease that only a discontented star can bring. Even when he was sitting silently away from the action, no one could be unaware of his seething resentment.

The awareness was greatest in the assistant director, who looked frankly terrified, and winced visibly, anticipating an outburst, every time Russ Lavery shifted in his chair.

Charles Paris was reminded of a story – maybe apocryphal, maybe not – about the great Edith Evans. One day at rehearsal she decided that the director had been taking too much interest in a speech delivered by one of her supporting actors, so she swanned up to him and demanded, 'And what am I meant to do in this long pause while he's talking?'

The cast member of whom Russ Lavery seemed most jealous was Sally Luther. Every time the assistant director gave a note for Viola, the star of *Air-Sea Rescue* sighed with exasperation, as if commenting on the incompetence of someone who needed so much guidance. This was completely unfair. It was early days of rehearsal, and the notes Sally was given were largely technical ones relating to movement or position, but Russ still implied that she was at fault.

Charles suspected a hidden agenda in all this. Maybe Russ Lavery and Sally Luther had known each other before. Maybe it was some resentment born of television, the rising star not liking to be yoked with the forgotten one. Perhaps Sally Luther's presence in the company was too vivid a reminder of the fickle nature of the medium that had puffed Russ Lavery up so high.

Whatever the cause of the friction, it was strange that it had never manifested itself before.

The climax of bad feeling came at the moment when Viola – dressed in male clothes as 'Cesario' – and Sebastian come face to face and catalogue the coincidences of their lives.

"'My father had a mole upon his brow,'" said Sally Luther.

"'And so had mine,'" Russ Lavery agreed.

"'And died that day when Viola from her birth
Had numbered thirteen years.'"

Sally stopped. 'Do you think she should be sad here?'

'Sad?' echoed the assistant director uneasily.

'Yes, I mean sad because she's remembering her father who she loved and –'

'Oh, for Christ's sake!' Russ Lavery erupted. 'She's not bothered about her father now! She's over the moon because she thought Sebastian was dead and she's found him alive!'

'But has she actually realised Sebastian's alive yet? Is she actually sure that –?'

'Sally, of course she's bloody sure! You have to remember – Viola's not as stupid as you are. You've got to play her intelligent, for God's sake. Tricky for you perhaps, but maybe it'll help if you think of it as a character part!'

The whole rehearsal room reeled at the sheer rudeness of Russ's attack. The assistant director, the one who should have defused the atmosphere, stood fidgeting awkwardly. But one voice did leap to Sally Luther's defence. Surprisingly, it came from the Second Officer.

'Russ, that was an unforgivable thing to say. Apologise at once.'

'What!' The television star rounded on Benzo Ritter. 'And just who the hell do you think you are, to speak to me like that?'

The boy stood his ground 'And just who the hell do you think you are, to speak to Sally like that?'

'I am an experienced actor with a lot of good work under his belt – not some incompetent teenager with no talent and a silly name!'

'Now, listen, Russ, don't you dare –'

'Stop it! Stop it!' came another voice, as the two squared up to each other. 'Let's just get on with the rehearsal, shall we?'

It was Sally herself. She was a pragmatist. Russ Lavery had been extremely offensive to her, but Sally saw that as his problem rather than hers. Certainly nothing to stop the rehearsal for.

Benzo Ritter and his opponent edged away from each other. With bad grace, Russ Lavery resumed his rehearsal position. The younger actor gazed hopefully at Sally Luther, perhaps seeking some accolade for his intervention, but she didn't look at him, just took her place facing Sebastian. She was not going to let temperament and bad manners from other members of the company get in the way of her performance.

'Hmm,' murmured Tottie Roundwood to Charles Paris. 'That young man may not be going the best way to further his theatrical career.'

'How do you mean?'

'Russ Lavery thinks of himself as very important, because of the television and everything. Trouble is, he probably is quite important – now Gavin's not there to rein him in a bit.' She shook her head. 'No, I would say this show is in serious need of a Director.'

Charles nodded. 'Wonder who it'll be? Not him, will it?' He nodded towards the assistant director, who stood awkwardly chewing his fingers and looking down at his copy of *Twelfth Night*.

'No way.' Tottie Roundwood grinned confidently. 'Don't worry. I'm sure Asphodel will get someone *good*.'

The rehearsal dragged on through its uninspiring course. There were no more open confrontations, though an undercurrent of resentment remained. Gavin-Scholes' patterns of movement and tableaux were more or less accurately recreated, and at last the stage area was emptied of all characters except for Feste, the Clown.

Chad Pearson moved forward to centre stage, sat down cross-legged, and began to sing.

"'When that I was and a little tiny boy,
With hey-ho, the wind and the rain;
A foolish thing was but a toy,
For the rain it raineth every day...'"

As he sang through to the end of the song, the room stilled. He had a beautiful light voice, and the tune either was, or sounded like, a traditional English one. Singing, Chad Pearson ceased to be a short, tubby West Indian and became a natural part of Shakespeare's world; there seemed no incongruity at that moment about the presence of a black Feste at the Illyrian court. It was not just voguish casting against ethnic stereotype. He felt right in the part, and the song was the day's only moment of genuine theatre.

The cast left for lunch in slightly improved spirits.

The 'go on, you'll feel better if you have a drink' voice in Charles's head beat the 'I'm never going to touch another drop of alcohol' one. Again. But he and John B. Murgatroyd did only have a couple of pints each, so they felt relatively virtuous.

In fact their sense of virtue was a little specious. They had been contemplating a third pint, but just at that moment Benzo Ritter, in his assistant stage manager role, appeared in the pub, ordering everyone back to the rehearsal room. A representative of Asphodel Productions had just arrived. With an announcement to make.

'...and I'm afraid the hospital can't see any prospect of Gavin returning to work in the short term. I'm sure he will make a complete recovery, but it's going to take time.

'And time, with just three weeks till this production starts a four-month touring programme, is something we don't have a lot of.'

The man from Asphodel Productions, whose name Charles hadn't caught, wore a dark suit and looked more like an accountant than an impresario. Probably he was an accountant. They seemed to be running most areas of show business nowadays.

Charles felt a twinge of regret for the more colourful characters he had worked for in the past. His memory instantly summoned up a gallery of producers, agents, managers and fixers. A rogue's gallery, it had to be said. Many of them had fabricated completely indefensible contracts. Many had inexplicably disappeared just when the company was due to be paid. Many had screwed everyone they worked with – particularly the leading ladies. But Charles Paris couldn't help feeling nostalgic for the dead, gone days.

Probably, his cynicism told him, nothing had changed that much, anyway. Nowadays the producers wore suits and had their deals checked and authenticated by lawyers, but they were still out for as much as they could get. Show business management, like horse racing and boxing, has always attracted its share of shady characters – not to say crooks.

'So,' the Asphodel Productions man went on, 'we need to appoint a director as soon as possible.' He looked across at the assistant director, who hung his head in a rather shamefaced way. 'And while we very much appreciate the way you've held the fort, Nick, for the last couple of days, as you know, we need to look for someone with a bit more experience for a production of this scale. Don't worry, what you've done for us has not gone unnoticed and your day will definitely come.'

I doubt it, thought Charles, realising that it was the first time he'd been aware that the assistant director's name was Nick. The boy had so little charisma that even his name didn't register. But the quiet way in which he took the news of his demotion showed he had been told of it beforehand.

'We have been very fortunate, however...' the Asphodel executive continued,'...very, very fortunate...to secure the services of someone we've been keen to work with for a long time...One of the most dynamic and exciting new directors currently working in the British theatre.'

Oh dear, thought Charles Paris, I don't like the sound of this.

'I say working in the British theatre, but in fact a lot of his work has been abroad and he's only recently come to this country. But I'm sure all of you who know how much of a stir his vivid and radical reinterpretation at the Old Vic of *She Stoops To Conquer* caused will not need me to tell you his name.'

There was a murmur of stunned appreciation from the cast, though Charles wanted to say, 'I need you to. Please, please. I don't know who you're talking about.'

The information came, anyway. 'I'm referring of course to Alexandru Radulescu. He had been due to return to Romania shortly, but when he heard of our problems, he very graciously deferred his plans. Alexandru will be starting work with you tomorrow morning, and I think it's extremely exciting news.'

From the expressions around the room, a lot of the cast shared this opinion. In particular, Russ Lavery, Vasile Bogdan and Tottie Roundwood were positively ecstatic at the news. The name had impressed Talya Northcott and Benzo Ritter too. Sally Luther, Charles noticed, looked considerably less keen.

'So, though of course we at Asphodel are very sorry about Gavin Scholes' illness, I feel that this particular ill wind is going to blow us all a great deal of good. Alexandru Radulescu is the sort of director whose productions really put a company on the map. And, when I talked to him about the project this morning, he was already full of ideas. He's as excited about the whole thing as all of us at Asphodel are. He says he's been dying to get his hands on Shakespeare for years.'

Oh no, Charles Paris inwardly groaned. Anything but that.

Chapter Five

'THAT'S NOT the point, Charles.'

'But I'd have thought –'

'No,' Frances steamrollered on. 'I am not criticising you for coming back late. You're a grown man, for God's sake. It's up to you how you spend your time, who you drink with – that's your business. What I am objecting to is you coming back late to my flat.'

'If you're trying to get rid of me...'

'I am not trying to get rid of you. All I'm saying is that if you're going to be staying here with me...' Charles noticed that she hadn't said 'living here with me,' '...then we have to have certain ground rules. It's just a matter of information. All I'm asking is that you let me know when you're likely to be in, if you're likely to be in. All you have to do is pick up a phone.'

Frances caught the expression in Charles's eye and pursed her lips ruefully. 'Yes, yes, yes. I know I'm sounding just like a nagging wife, but I'm afraid once we put ourselves into a cohabiting situation I'm going to come back with all the things wives usually nag about. It's not what I want, Charles. I don't want to be forced into a stereotype.'

'No, no, I can see that.'

'Look, my life is actually very well sorted at the moment. I've got used to living on my own. I've actually got quite efficient at it. And I don't want to be taken back to square one.'

'I don't want to take you back to square one. Honestly, Frances.' He took her hand, comforted by the familiar ridge of the old kitchen-knife scar. 'I'm thinking in terms of square five at least. Maybe even square six.'

She shook her head wryly.

'And then, who knows, we might find that there's a ladder on square six leading straight up to square seventy-four.'

'More likely a snake to send us thumping down to square one again.' But at least she smiled as she said it.

Charles tightened the pressure on her hand. 'Look, Frances, I really mean what I'm saying now. This last couple of weeks has been the best thing that's happened for years. For me, nothing has ever replaced what there is between us.'

'Though you've tested out a good few options on the way to that conclusion, haven't you, Charles?' said Frances with a beady look.

He shook his head in exasperation. 'Yes, all right. But that's over now. That part of my life's behind me.'

'Oh yes?'

'Yes. Other women…All that other women have ever shown me is that you're the only woman who's right for me. You're what I want, Frances.'

'Are you talking permanence here, Charles?'

'Yes. Well, possibly…Maybe…I mean, obviously not in the short term.'

'Oh, no. Obviously not.'

'Nothing's going to happen quickly. I just feel that there's such a bond between us we should test it out, see how strong it really is. Try and get back together.'

Frances was silent, but her expression didn't show wholehearted conviction about what he was saying.

'Look, I know there've been times in the past when I've been inconsiderate, when I've hurt you…'

He let the pause lengthen. Then Frances said suddenly, 'I'm sorry. You're not expecting me to disagree, are you?'

'No, of course I'm not.' Mind you, some token contradiction wouldn't have hurt. 'But this time I am really determined to make it work. We've got so much to give each other, and I think we should try to make the best of the time we have left, and make the best of that time…together.'

'The trouble with actors,' said Frances, removing her hand, 'is that they're all full of shit, and full of half-remembered lines from shows they've been in. Go on, tell me, where did that last line you said come from?'

Charles looked shamefaced. 'Comedy called *The Twang of a Heartstring*. Hornchurch in the early seventies. Can still remember quite a lot of the lines from it, actually.'

He could also still remember the review that the *Hornchurch Herald* had given his performance. 'If Charles Paris was meant to be Love's Young Dream, it suggested Love had been eating rather too much toasted cheese before going to bed.'

He took her hand again. 'All right, what I said was garbage, but the intention wasn't garbage. I'm really determined to make this work, Frances.'

Her face was still a conviction-free zone. 'Even if it means making concessions?'

'Of course.'

'Living by the rules I dictate?'

'Sure.'

'Allowing me to continue having a life of my own? To have parts of my life that are not your business?'

'Yes, all that.'

'Mm.' Frances was pensive for a moment, then came to a decision. 'OK, let's give it a whirl.'

'Great.' Charles squeezed her hand.

'Right,' she went on briskly. 'Tonight I don't want you here.'

'Oh?'

'Till after midnight. You can come back then.'

'Thank you.' A silence. 'May I ask...?'

'I thought you'd just agreed to allow me to have parts of my life that're not your business.'

'Well, yes, but –'

'All right then. I've got a friend coming round.'

'Oh. Anyone I know?'

'No, Charles. Nobody you know.'

After Frances had gone to school, Charles was left with a little niggle of disquiet. Not jealousy, surely? No, she'd just been playing a game with him. It was a small revenge for her. You come back late and pissed, I'll be mysterious about some unnamed friend I've got. Tit for tat.

What worried him more was that the niggle might presage a shift in his mood. He'd been so positive the last few weeks. Everything had been going so well. Now, suddenly, there was the professional threat of the unknown in the form of Alexandru Radulescu, and, privately, a new edginess in his relationship with Frances.

Oh well, if I'm going to go down, I may as well go down properly. To compound his mood, he rang his agent, Maurice Skellern.

'Yes, I had heard. I do keep my ear to the ground on my clients' behalf, you know, Charles.' Maurice's voice was full of reproach at the idea that he wasn't aware of *Twelfth Night*'s change of Director.

'And do you know anything about him?'

'Not a lot. Hasn't been in this country long. Comes from Bulgaria, doesn't he?'

'Romania.'

'Same difference. And he's done a couple of productions over here that've got the chattering classes very excited. Gets all those reviews which use words like "radical" and "mould-breaking".'

'Yes,' said Charles gloomily. 'And "Radulescu's production made one feel one was seeing an entirely different play."'

'That's right. Now what paper was that in?'

'I just made it up.'

'Really? I could have sworn I've read it somewhere quite recently.'

'You probably have.' Charles groaned. Might as well lower his mood even further. 'Anything on the horizon...you know, workwise...?'

The reproach in Maurice Skellern's voice was now ladled on with a towel. 'Greedy, Charles, greedy. Let me get my breath back. After all, I've got you a five-month contract with Asphodel.'

'Gavin Scholes rang me direct and offered me that, Maurice. I told you about it.'

'Ah, maybe, but I was the one who sorted out the deal.'

'You accepted the first offer they made.'

'Charles, Charles, when will you realise? What I do is a very finely tuned business. Involves a lot of very delicate decisions. Sometimes you have to push like mad, scrabble for more and more money from them. Other times you have to be subtle – sit back, hold your fire, live to fight another day.'

'Funny it's always other clients you do the scrabbling for. When it comes to me, on the other hand, you always seem to be holding your fire.'

'Charles, that's very cruel. If I didn't know you so well, I'd find that extremely hurtful. You've no idea how much I do behind the scenes on your behalf.'

'I've a nasty feeling I have, Maurice.'

'Charles, trust me...' How many times must Maurice have said that over the years. And every time Charles'd heard the words, they had prompted the identical reaction. 'I assume you're joking.' And yet, in all their long associations, he'd never once vocalised the thought.

'If I didn't know what I was doing,' Maurice went on, 'ask yourself – would you still be one of my clients after all these years?'

Yes, thought Charles Paris, savage with self-contempt, I would.

'"Approach, Sir Andrew. Not to be abed after midnight, is to be up betimes, and diluculo surgere, thou knowest –"'

'"Nay, by my troth, I know not; but I know that to be up late is to be up late."'

'"A false conclusion!"' Charles bellowed, wishing he hadn't been up quite so late the night before. It had been stupid to engage Frances in conversation about how she'd spent her evening. The sensible course would have been to take the hint of her closed bedroom door and go off to sleep in the spare room. And that's what he would have done if he hadn't drunk so much. Still, he told himself with the wounded logic of someone who knows he's in the wrong, it was her fault. If she turfs me out and I'm not allowed back in till after midnight, how does she imagine I'm going to spend the evening?

'"I hate it as an unfilled can,"' Charles continued, thinking how much he'd welcome a filled can to irrigate his desiccated brain. He felt a bit gutty too; that really meant he'd had too much the night before. '"To be up after midnight and to go to bed then is early; so that to go to bed after midnight is to go to bed betimes. Does not our life consist of the four elements?"'

'"Faith, so they say,"' John B. Murgatroyd's Sir Andrew Aguecheek weedily agreed, '"but, I think, it rather consists of eating and drinking."'

And sex, thought Charles wistfully. He shouldn't have put his hand on Frances's shoulder the night before. He should have respected her privacy rather than trying it on. His behaviour had been juvenile and crass and she'd been absolutely right to tell him to leave her alone. Oh God. He hoped he hadn't cast a permanent blight over his prospects of making love to Frances again. Why was he capable of such total idiocy?

'"Thou art a scholar,"' Sir Toby Belch went on. '"Let us therefore eat and drink. Marian, I say! A stoup of wine!"'

The assistant director stopped them there. He was still in charge of the first part of the morning's rehearsal. Alexandru Radulescu had a meeting at the National Theatre and wouldn't be with them till about twelve.

'Just like to take it from the top again...' the assistant director suggested nervously.

'Anything specific wrong?' asked Charles, hoping that the hangover wasn't spoiling his performance.

'No, not really. Just need a bit more contrast between you, I think. Sir Andrew really is knackered. All he wants to do is go to bed. So we need more of Sir Toby jollying him along. Be more of a party animal, Charles.'

'Right, OK.' It was a good point. In fact, the assistant director's ideas were all good; he just didn't have the personality to put them across with sufficient definition.

Even through his hangover, Charles knew that the double act with John B. was going well. They looked good together. A long willowy Sir Andrew Aguecheek and a more substantial – thanks to the padding, Charles kept reassuring himself – Sir Toby Belch. A kind of Don Quixote and Sancho Panza in reverse. Then of course Charles would have his ruddied face, and John B. would make his as pale as milk. Yes, they'd look great.

It was so good to be working on a classic. The relationship between Sir Toby and Sir Andrew had a kind of mythic quality. The crafty drunkard and the ineffectual dupe. The parts Shakespeare wrote were so solid, almost tactile, and yet with infinite nuances to be explored. Even the lines were easy to learn because they felt so right. Charles was really going to enjoy Sir Toby Belch – or at least he was as soon as he'd got rid of his hangover. His guts felt distinctly squittery. He had a nasty feeling he was going to have to rush to the Gents before too long.

They pressed on through Act Two, Scene Three. Chad Pearson joined them and his rendering of another of Feste's songs again reduced the rehearsal room to silence.

"*'O mistress mine! Where are you roaming?*
O! stay and hear: your true love's coming,
That can sing both high and low.
Trip no further, pretty sweeting;
Journeys end in lovers meeting,
Every wise man's son doth know.'"

They worked through to the end of the scene, though the cement-mixer rumbling of Charles's stomach was getting louder and louder. He felt sure everyone could hear it. Thank God I'm not doing a radio, he thought.

He just made it to the end. "'Come, come, I'll go burn some sack; 'tis too late to go to bed now. Come, knight; come, knight.'"

'Very nice,' said the assistant director. 'Very nice indeed. Erm, I'd just like to –'

'Sorry, must dash,' panted Charles Paris.

It was a close call getting to the Gents in time and, as he squatted back exhausted on the lavatory, he swore he'd never touch another drop of alcohol. It was insane, putting his body through this kind of punishment.

Charles was pulling up his trousers when he heard the sound of two men coming in to use the urinals. Instinctively, as everyone does in that situation, he froze, embarrassed to give away his presence in the cubicle.

The men were talking, but in a language Charles had never heard before. One of the voices was familiar, though. Yes, in spite of the words, the deep tones were recognizable as those of Vasile Bogdan.

It seemed reasonable to assume that he was talking Romanian; and that the man he was talking to was Alexandru Radulescu.

Charles couldn't be sure, but in amongst the strange words, he thought he heard the director mention Gavin Scholes. There was a sound of zipping-up, then the footsteps and voices moved away.

Vasile Bogdan let out a harsh laugh as the door was opened. Then, in English, he said, 'I told you it would be all right, Alex. Gavin's out of the way, and you've got the job.'

Chapter Six

'OK.' ALEXANDRU Radulescu moved his spread hands outwards in a that's-enough-of-that gesture. '*Twelfth Night* is a play about sex.'

Well, only partly, thought Charles. It's more a play about romance, romantic ideals and how they frequently mismatch with reality.

'*All* plays are about sex,' the director continued in his heavily accented voice. 'All life is about sex, if you like, and so of course Shakespeare, who reflected life, writes only about sex...'

Now just a minute, hang on there. In Charles's view, Shakespeare wrote about everything. That included sex, sure, but to call sex his overriding obsession seemed an unnecessarily simplistic and Freudian interpretation.

'...and nowhere is that more true than in *Twelfth Night*. When I first read the play...'

Which was probably last night, was Charles's instant reaction. He was having no difficulty being uncharitable to this small, wiry, dark-eyed Romanian. It wasn't just from suspicion raised by what he'd overheard in the Gents. Alexandru Radulescu had a deliberately provocative manner. He seemed to enjoy putting people's backs up. As yet none of the company had raised any objections to what he was saying, but when that did happen, Charles felt the director would enjoy slapping them down.

'When I first read the play, I thought, sex, sex, sex – that's what's happening here. Exciting young sex with Sebastian.' He flashed a smile at Russ Lavery, who grinned back knowingly. 'Sebastian and Olivia, yes, but also Sebastian and Antonio.'

Charles groaned inwardly. He hated productions that imposed twentieth-century values on the society of Shakespeare's time. In the sixteenth century there had been a strong tradition of masculine friendship and loyalty. A line like Antonio's to Sebastian, 'If you will not murder me for my love, let me be your servant', did not imply a full-blown homosexual affair, though Charles had a nasty feeling that's how a director like Alexandru Radulescu would interpret it – no doubt with lots of gratuitous male kissing and mime of sexual congress. The good burghers of Great Wensham weren't going to like that.

'There is also old sex: disgusting geriatric groping between Sir Toby Belch and Maria.'

Now just a minute...Charles had always thought there was something rather heartwarming in the relationship between Sir Toby and Maria. He tried to assess how old Alexandru Radulescu was. Early thirties, perhaps. Certainly of the age that reckoned sex was turned off like a bathtap at the age of fifty. Huh, he's got a thing or two to learn. But that thought brought a pang of unease, reminding Charles of the previous evening's scene with Frances.

'But there is also – and most important of all – an uncertainty about sexual identity. This is at the centre of the play: Viola searching for her own sexuality by the experiment of cross-dressing...'

No, no, no, that isn't at the centre of the play.

'...Orsino being brought face to face with his homosexuality through his infatuation with Cesario...'

No.

'...Malvolio's obsession with Olivia, which is fetishistic and can only find expression through bondage in the form of yellow cross-garters. This is what Shakespeare meant us to take from *Twelfth Night*.'

No, it isn't. That's just what you want to impose on *Twelfth Night*.

'Right, so bear all this in mind as we work on the play. Sex, sex, sex.' Alexandru Radulescu looked across to the assistant director. 'OK, maybe we should start.'

'Yes, well, we've just rehearsed Act Two, Scene Three. Would you like us to run through that, and maybe we can see places where, you know...the sexual element can be emphasized a bit...?'

'What!' Alexandru Radulescu stared at the young man, appalled. 'You think I am just going to pick up the left-overs of someone else's production?'

'Well, it's all been blocked. The cast know their moves and lines. I mean, we do only have three weeks before we open and –'

The director drew himself up to his full – not very great – height. 'Alexandru Radulescu does not collaborate! When Alexandru Radulescu directs a production, he does it his way. And, anyway, Alexandru Radulescu does not just direct, he *reinterprets* a play.'

It'll end in tears, thought Charles Paris. It'll end in tears.

'It could have meant anything,' said John B. Murgatroyd. They were sitting over drinks at the end of that day's rehearsal. John B. had a pint of bitter; Charles was on the large Bell's. For him beer spelt relaxation, and an afternoon in the company of Alexandru Radulescu had rendered him desperate for whisky.

'"I told you it would be all right,"' John B. quoted again. 'Vasile probably just meant that Alexandru had cracked the British system – made himself the natural candidate to take over when Gavin got ill.'

'Equally it could have meant that their plan to *make* Gavin ill had worked.'

'Oh, for heaven's sake, Charles. You're the last person I'd have expected to be a conspiracy theorist. What, so you've also got proof that Kennedy was assassinated by Elvis Presley and Marilyn Monroe because he threatened to tell Martin Luther King about their love-child – is that right? You're being paranoid.'

'Don't you think this afternoon's events justify a little paranoia?'

'Hmm...' John B. Murgatroyd took a thoughtful swallow of his beer. 'It'll probably be all right. Look, he hasn't got time to make too many changes. I'm sure he's mostly talk – that sort always are. What we'll end up with is a straight telling of *Twelfth Night* with a couple of trendy flourishes.'

'You have the sound of someone trying very hard to convince himself – and failing. I've worked with Directors like this before,' said Charles darkly.

Various unpleasant memories bubbled to the surface of his mind. Charles Paris liked the words a playwright wrote to be the mainspring of a production; he couldn't stand Directors who regarded the text as an obstacle that had to be negotiated on the way to their personal glorification.

Wincing, he remembered a production of *Richard III*, in which Richard alone remained handsome and upright, while all the other characters had been played with various disabilities. The Director's point, that deformity is in the eye of the beholder, might have had some validity in another context, but it sure as hell made nonsense of Shakespeare's play. Charles rather treasured the notice the *Wigan Gazette* had given of his one-legged Duke of Clarence (Jesus, he'd been grateful to be killed off so early – the strapping was agony): 'Charles Paris's resolute swimming in the malmsey-butt suggests a promising nautical future for him as Long John Silver.'

'Oh God,' Charles groaned, dragging himself out of this unwelcome recollection, 'just wait till Alexandru Radulescu starts exploring the homosexual subtext of Sir Toby Belch's relationship with Sir Andrew Aguecheek.'

'Now, the opening dumb-show...' were the first words with which the new director began the next day's rehearsal.

'But there isn't an opening dumb-show,' Sally Luther objected. Charles had been about to make the same point, but the coward in him was relieved she'd got the words in first. No point in antagonising Alexandru unnecessarily. Charles had a gut feeling there would be plenty of other issues over which he'd really *need* to take issue with the Director.

'The dumb-show,' said Alexandru patiently, 'is a very common feature of Elizabethan theatre. Many plays were started with a dumb-show, prefiguring the action to follow. Indeed, the play that Hamlet organises to be performed before King Claudius begins with a dumb-show,' he concluded as if closing the argument.

Charles couldn't let that go by. 'Yes, but the whole point there was that Shakespeare was deliberately presenting an archaic convention. In the same way that the First Player's language is dated and overblown, the dumb-show is put there to show how unfashionable this particular troupe of travelling players are. Shakespeare always knew what he was doing. If he'd intended *Twelfth Night* to begin with a dumb-show, he'd have specified a dumb-show.'

He didn't look directly at Alexandru Radulescu until the end of this speech. What he then saw was chilling. The Director's black eyes were two focused pinpoints of hatred. Up until that moment their relationship had been wary but polite; now Charles felt he had made an enemy for life.

'God, that's all I need,' Alexandru spat out the words. 'Actors who think they're experts on Shakespeare. Listen, *I* do the thinking round this production. All that's required of you is to say the words the way I tell you to.'

Charles felt as if his face had been slapped. He wanted to come back, fierce and hard, with the fact that he *did* actually know quite a lot about Shakespeare, that he'd got an Oxford degree in English to prove it, that... But he restrained himself. Time enough. No need to go out on a private offensive. Soon the rest of the company were bound to join forces in resistance to Alexandru Radulescu's fatuous innovations.

But no other members of the cast made any complaint about the idea of the dumb-show. It was understandable that the youngsters like Benzo Ritter and Talya Northcott might eagerly lap up Alexandru's suggestions, but the more mature cast members also seemed placidly content to do as they were told.

Charles often marvelled at the ridiculous hoops actors will go through at the bidding of a forceful personality. *Twelfth Night*'s assistant director, whose ideas were actually rather good, could not command obedience; while Alexandru Radulescu, whose ideas were clearly crap, could lead the entire company by the nose. Sometimes Charles could empathise with Alfred Hitchcock's well-known view that 'actors are cattle'.

The only objection that did arise was when Alexandru Radulescu announced that for the opening of the play the stage area would be converted into a huge double bed. And the objection came, not from a cast member, but from the Asphodel representative, who had appeared to see how rehearsals were going.

'No,' he said, quietly but firmly.

The Romanian whirled furiously round at him. 'What!'

'No room in the budget for more scenery. You've got to work with the sets as built, and with the costumes as already made.'

'But how am I expected to express my vision of the play if I am saddled with unimaginative sets and traditional costumes?'

The Asphodel accountant shrugged his shoulders. 'That's your problem. It was made perfectly clear in our agreement that you had to work with the existing sets and costumes. There isn't the time, apart from there not being the money, for any changes to be made.'

'But this means I will have to compromise my entire artistic perception of the play!'

The accountant shrugged again. 'Well, there you go,' he said coolly.

Charles Paris wished some of the cast had the nerve to take that approach to Alexandru. Because it clearly worked. Faced with a will as strong as his own, the director could only huff and puff petulantly.

'I thought you employed me because I would bring something fresh, something radical to this production. People who employ me do so because they know they will get a play that has the Alexandru Radulescu stamp all over it!'

'I'm not interfering with your stamp,' the Asphodel man replied without changing his lazy intonation. 'I'm just saying that that stamp will have to appear with the existing set and costumes. That's all. I'm not going to interfere with what you do artistically.'

'But for a director like me, the art comes in the *total* look of a production. It is not just the acting – it is the movement, the music, the setting, the clothes the actors wear!'

This bluster produced no more than another shrug. 'You knew the deal when you started, Alex. I'm here to control the budget, and I say you can't change the sets or the costumes.'

Though the director huffed and puffed a little more, it was only token resistance. He knew he couldn't beat the money men. But his defeat seemed to make him determined to put his cast through more irrelevant hoops of artifice.

'Right, the dumb-show,' he announced again, once he'd given up grumbling as a bad job. 'As I said yesterday, *Twelfth Night* is a play about sex, and I want the opening mime to reinforce this message. So it will take the form of a ritualised orgy.'

Charles Paris shook his head in disbelief.

'In this way we will show the different cross-currents of love and lust between the characters, as they come together in different combinations.'

'How do you mean "come together"?' He hadn't wanted to ask the question, but couldn't help himself.

'I mean, obviously, Charles, come together as in acts of sexual congress.'

'Simulated sex?'

'Exactly.' With the word, Alexandru Radulescu turned a withering look on Charles. What was more worrying was that most of the cast also directed withering looks at him. Good God, they actually seemed prepared to go along with this madman's ideas.

'And,' the director continued, intrigued by a new thought, 'if we can't afford new costumes, then maybe we do without costumes...Yes!'

Charles's mouth dropped. 'Are you suggesting we do all this simulated sex without any clothes on?'

'Of course.'

'But –'

'No.' Once again the authoritative monosyllable came from the Asphodel representative.

'You said you would not interfere with the *artistic* content of my production!'

'This is not artistic, this is financial. A *Twelfth Night* that opens with a naked orgy will be death at the box office – particularly at Great Wensham. Sorry, you can't do it.'

This second rejection produced only minimal remonstrance from Alexandru. He knew when he was beaten. If things started to get really out of hand, Charles comforted himself, the Asphodel man would be the person to talk to.

The Director, accepting his defeat, moved on. 'So, we will think which characters have lusts towards which others, yes?' He looked ingenuously at his cast. 'Please, you tell me. I don't want to impose my ideas on you. I want you all to contribute to this production. I am a director who believes very much in ensemble thinking.'

That was patent nonsense; the man was clearly an unhinged autocrat. But once again none of the cast drew attention to his hypocrisy. They seemed happy, even flattered, to be part of this illusory consultation process. A lot of them sat forward eagerly as they tried to think of potential sexual connections within *Twelfth Night*. Benzo Bitter and Talya Northcott were particularly enthused. This was what they had gone into the theatre for – the creative white heat of workshopping in the rehearsal room.

'Well, there are the obvious sexual attractions you've already mentioned, Alex,' said Vasile Bogdan. His readiness to come forward suggested it was not the first time he had played this game. Vasile seemed very familiar with Alexandru's methods. Charles would have to check out whether the two Romanians had worked together before. There was something going on between them.

And he couldn't forget the words that he had overheard. In spite of John B. Murgatroyd's scorn for the idea, Charles still wondered whether Gavin Scholes' accident had been engineered. He'd have to investigate further.

'Sebastian and Olivia,' Vasile went on. 'Viola's lust for Orsino. Orsino's lust for Cesario. Toby's for Maria. Malvolio's kinky obsession with Olivia.'

'And of course Orsino's obsession for Olivia at the beginning of the play,' Benzo Ritter contributed. 'I mean, he's totally gone on her, can't think about anything else. Waking, sleeping, his thoughts, his dreams are full of nothing else – just Olivia.'

'This is good.' Alexandru Radulescu nodded enthusiastically. 'And then, when he sees Viola/Cesario, it all vanishes. One obsession is instantly replaced by another. This is showing us, I think, the fickleness of obsessive love, infatuation, whatever you want to call it.'

'I don't think it's saying *all* obsessive love is fickle. I mean, there are passions which endure and are rather magnificent in their –'

But Alexandru seemed unwilling to listen to more of Benzo's theories – presumably because they didn't coincide exactly with his own. 'Yes, yes, yes.' His eyes darted round the company. 'What else have we got in the play? What other couples, what other sexual cross-currents, eh?'

Vasile Bogdan picked up the cue again. 'Well, we have Antonio's gay thing for Sebastian.'

Alexandru nodded enthusiastically. 'Yes, let's keep going on this gay thing. There are other characters in the play, I am certain, who are attracted to their own sex. Who do you think? Come on, it is obvious – no?' Alexandru

Radulescu looked round the faces, exasperated by their slowness in reaching the obvious.

'Well,' said Sally Luther. 'I hope you're not suggesting that Olivia's attraction to Cesario means that deep down she's a lesbian?'

'Why do you hope I am not suggesting this?'

'Because it's a ridiculous idea. It makes nonsense of the play's resolution when Olivia marries Sebastian.'

Good for you, Sally, thought Charles. Thank God somebody's not going along with all this garbage.

The director looked piqued. 'No, it does not, Sally. It makes *sense* of this. Both Olivia and Sebastian are bisexual, you understand. The two heterosexual halves of them match together and make the play's resolution, but the other halves of them are still ambiguous, unresolved. It is those sexual ambiguities which Shakespeare would have explored had he written a sequel to this play.'

'What – a sort of *Thirteenth Night*?' John B. Murgatroyd suggested.

A couple of the cast snorted at this, but the expression on Alexandru Radulescu's face showed that there weren't going to be many giggles round the production now he was in charge. Benzo Ritter and Talya Northcott also turned reproving stares on John B. Murgatroyd; so far as they were concerned, he was being inappropriately trivial in the presence of genius.

'Please, don't let's waste our time in silliness,' the director said primly.

You're a fine one to talk, thought Charles.

'So that is one gay element we have isolated, right. But there is another, very obvious one we haven't mentioned yet.' Again Alexandru looked round the semicircle of faces. 'Come on, very obvious indeed.'

It was Tottie Roundwood who spoke finally. As she did so, she looked at the director with a respect that verged on devotion. 'Could you possibly mean...Sir Toby Belch and Sir Andrew Aguecheek...?'

'Yes,' said Alexandru Radulescu. 'Exactly.'

I don't believe this is happening, thought Charles Paris.

Chapter Seven

ALEXANDRU Radulescu's mind made a butterfly's look like a model of consistency. He behaved like a child playing in a toyshop of ideas; and perhaps, after the artistic restrictions he'd experienced in his native Romania, that was how he felt. He came into rehearsal every morning brimful of new thoughts, derived from anything he'd happened to have observed, or heard, or seen. He was into everything just deep enough to get the soles of his shoes wet.

For instance, he saw a mime artist busking in Covent Garden and was so impressed that he brought the guy in to advise the cast on movement. Then in an Indian restaurant, by chance, he heard some Eastern muzak which he decided had an authentic 'dying fall'. He immediately engaged a sitar player to do the *Twelfth Night* music. Worse than that, he got the musician to reset Feste's songs in some approximation to raga style. Chad Pearson gamely tried to ride the unfamiliar rhythms. He succeeded pretty well, but at the expense of audibility. The atmospheric, melancholy words of the songs were lost.

In a way it was all very exciting – so long as you didn't care about Shakespeare's *Twelfth Night*. Charles Paris did, and he found the rehearsal process agonising. Every few minutes, it seemed, some other felicity of the play was sacrificed or obscured for a theatrical effect.

Even Charles had to admit, though, that most of the effects were very striking. Alexandru Radulescu had an inspired visual sense. He created patterns of movement which were mesmerising and dramatic.

But it was all independent of the text. He would have made as interesting a spectacle of the *Yellow Pages* as he was making of *Twelfth Night*. And Charles Paris would have much preferred them to be doing the *Yellow Pages* than a text he had cherished since his schooldays.

The production's opening moments were typical of the Radulescu approach. The dumb-show had survived and refined into something far less crude than first envisaged. All of the play's characters took up positions in the blackout; then, to intricate Indian rhythms, moved like blank-faced automata into a variety of physical combinations. Their bodies had become inhuman, like components of some intricate metal puzzle. The mime, though it still had copulatory overtones, had taken on a universal and emblematic quality. But the precision of their ensemble movement could not fail to arrest an audience's attention.

The sitar music continued as the cast froze into a tableau, facing out front, chilling the audience with the blankness of their stares. Alexandru Radulescu had wanted this moment to echo his sketchy understanding of Noh Theatre, and only the vigilance of the Asphodel accountant had stopped him from commissioning traditional Japanese wooden masks for the entire cast.

While his fellow-actors stayed immobile, Orsino then stepped forward and, with his staff, struck the stage three times (a convention borrowed from classical French theatre). He then intoned:

'If music be the food of love, play on;'
'On, on, on, on...'
the rest of the rigid cast echoed in unison, their words tapering off to silence.

'Give me excess of it, that, surfeiting,
The appetite may sicken, and so die.'

'Die, die, die, die...' came the dwindling echo.

'That strain again!'
'Again, again, again, again...'
'It had a dying fall.'
'Fall, fall, fall, fall.'
'O!'
'It came o'er my ear like the sweet sound
That breathes upon a bank of violets,
Stealing and giving odour.'

'Odour, odour, odour, odour...' This time the echo was as soft as breath.
'Enough! no more.'

Suddenly Orsino slammed his staff down on to the ground. All of the cast, except for the Duke and Curio, scattered off to the sides of the stage with the exaggerated, flickering movements of silent film.

The Indian musician let out a long lamenting twang from his sitar, and Orsino was left to continue his speech in relatively traditional manner until Alexandru Radulescu's next theatrical sensation.

The effect was undeniably dramatic, but it had nothing to do with *Twelfth Night*.

Charles's position within the production was tense and difficult. Sir Toby Belch was a part he'd longed to play all his life, and he was now at the ideal...erm, maturity...to do it justice. He wouldn't get another crack at it. And he didn't want this chance buggered up by a director with no sensitivity to Shakespeare.

John B. Murgatroyd and he had prepared tactics over various long sessions in the pub. Basically, they both intended to play their parts as they had been playing them under Gavin Scholes' direction – and, in their view, as Shakespeare intended them to be played.

So, though they listened politely to Alexandru's suggestions, and even went through the motions of trying out his new ideas, after a couple of runs at a scene they would revert to doing it exactly the way they had before. This did not make for a good atmosphere between the two actors and their Director.

A typical moment of conflict occurred when they were rehearsing Act Two, Scene Three. Maria, having described her plans to dupe Malvolio, has just exited, leaving Sir Toby Belch and Sir Andrew Aguecheek united in admiration for her ingenuity. The following lines then ensue:

SIR TOBY: Good night, Penthesilea.

SIR ANDREW: Before me, she's a good wench.

SIR TOBY: She's a beagle, true bred, and one that adores me...what o' that? [HE SIGHS.]

SIR ANDREW: I was adored once, too. [HE SIGHS ALSO.]

SIR TOBY: Let's to bed, knight.

Charles and John B. ran through the lines as they had rehearsed them under Gavin. Alexandru Radulescu, his little body contorted into a knot of concentration, watched intently. As soon as Charles had said his "'Let's to bed, knight,'" the director waved his hands in the air.

'OK, OK, we stop. There is a lot here. It is a very good moment this, I think.'

'Certainly is,' Charles agreed. For him it was the most poignant moment in the play, one of the many in *Twelfth Night* where farce is suddenly shaded with melancholy. He loved the wistfulness with which John B. Murgatroyd played his "'I was adored once too,'" and was pleased with the way he, as Sir Toby, put his arm around the ineffectual knight's shoulder and led him off. It was a brief instance of closeness between the two characters; for a second Sir Toby suspended his cynical campaign of exploitation and showed Sir Andrew a flash of human sympathy.

That was not, however, how Alexandru Radulescu saw the exchange. 'Yes, very good,' he repeated, looking down at his script. 'As ever, Shakespeare tells us everything. It is all in the text, if only you look hard enough.'

Actually, you don't have to look that hard, thought Charles. Usually the meaning in Shakespeare's lines is limpidly self-evident. Still, he was relieved that the director was finally recognising the pre-eminence of the actual words.

'Now, obviously,' Alexandru went on, 'there are references here to the past, things that have happened before the play starts.'

'Yes,' Charles agreed.

'Sir Andrew talking about having been "adored once too" John B. contributed.

'...and,' the director concluded triumphantly, 'an unequivocal confirmation of the homosexual relationship between the two knights.'

'What!'

'What!'

Alexandru became excited as he expounded his textual analysis. 'You see, they talk about Maria. Sir Toby says she's "one that adores me – what of that?" In other words, he is saying, "She fancies me, but what of that? Since I'm gay, she's wasting her time."'

'No, he is not saying that. He's praising her.'

'Praising her? How do you get that? What does he describe Maria as? A "beagle". This is not very flattering, I think. He is saying she is very ugly. He is saying she is a *dog*.'

'"Dog" didn't have that meaning at the time Shakespeare was –' But the director was too preoccupied even to hear counter-argument. Then Sir Andrew, all pathetic-like, reminds Sir Toby that they used to have a thing going. '"I was adored once too," he says – doesn't he?'

'Yes, he does, but he's not referring to Sir Toby.'

'Oh no? Then why is it that Toby's next line having been reminded that he's been neglecting Sir Andrew emotionally is: "Let's to bed, knight." I mean, how overt do you want this to be? "Let's to bed, knight" – you can't have a less ambiguous sexual proposition than that, can you?'

'Yes, of course you –'

'No, come on. What did you used to say, back in the days when you were seducing women, eh?' Charles rather resented that implication. 'If you said "let's to bed", or "let's go to bed", it meant "I want to screw you" – yes?'

'Look –'

'Yes or no? Did it mean "I want to screw you" or not?'

'Well, yes, in that context it probably did, but –'

'See!' The director spoke with the satisfaction of an ontologist into whose sitting room God has just walked.

'But, Alexandru, that is not what it means in this context. Such an idea makes nonsense of the relationship between Sir Toby and Sir Andrew. They're talking about Maria and what a great woman she is. What they're saying is in total admiration of her.'

'I think not. Look at the text, Charles. That is what you must always do when you are dealing with the work of a great genius like Shakespeare – look at the text.'

That's rich, coming from you.

'And when we look at the text, what do we see? "Good night, Penthesilea." Who is this "Penthesilea", by the way?'

'Penthesilea,' said Charles patiently, 'was the Queen of the Amazons. Hence, any forceful or effective woman. Sir Toby describes Maria by that name as a tribute to the skill with which she has set up the plan to fool Malvolio.'

He looked up, anticipating apology in the Director's face, but instead saw glee. Wagging a triumphant finger, Alexandru shouted, 'You see, you see, that proves it! You've said it out of your own mouth! "Amazon" means "any forceful or effective woman". In other words, a dominant woman. In other words, the dominant mother whose sexuality so frightened the son that, in self-protection, he became homosexual.'

'That is psychological claptrap. Apart from anything else, it's been proved that there's no connection between –'

'What is more,' Alexandru rolled on with satisfaction, 'Amazon often means lesbian. Hmm, I think maybe we are also getting the key to Maria's character here...'

He looked thoughtfully across to Tottie Roundwood. To Charles's annoyance, she didn't immediately point out what balls this all was. She looked pleased, even honoured, to be sharing the wisdom of the guru.

'OK.' Alexandru clapped his hands. 'Let's run through the lines again, bearing in mind what we now know.'

'We don't know anything we didn't know before,' Charles protested.

'No? So what are you saying? Are you saying that there is no attraction between Sir Toby Belch and Sir Andrew Aguecheek? Are you flying in the face of William Shakespeare's text?'

'No, I am not. I am saying there is affection between them, and this is the moment in the play where that affection is most overtly expressed – but *that is all!*'

Alexandru Radulescu's mouth pursed in annoyance. 'It is very difficult, you know, for a director to direct when his actors will not take direction.'

'I'll take direction as well as the next actor,' said Charles with dignity. 'But not when I think what's suggested is destroying the sense of the whole play.'

The black eyes sizzled up at him. 'It is not impossible for this production to be recast,' the director hissed.

'Oh yes, it is,' said a cool unemotional voice. Thank God, thought Charles, that the Asphodel accountant was once again monitoring rehearsals. 'Budget doesn't allow it. Sorry, Alex, you work with the cast you've been given. They're all contracted, so, except in case of illness or accident, they all do the full four months – OK?'

Charles Paris met the stare of Alexandru's ferocious black eyes and could see the rich variety of illnesses and accidents they were wishing on him.

Chapter Eight

CHARLES was annoyed. For many reasons. Not least among them was that Alexandru Radulescu was efficient. All the arguments Charles wanted to bring forward – that this endless mastication of the text and addition of gratuitous business slowed down the whole production process – were defused by the fact that the schedule was well up to time. Considering his late start on the production – and the amount of new stuff he was bringing into it – Alexandru Radulescu was showing himself to be a very well-organised Director.

Even, Charles Paris was forced grudgingly to admit, a rather good Director. Not for this show, of course, not for *Twelfth Night*. Nor in fact for any show where the text was important. But for the presentation of spectacle, of individual theatrical moments independent of a play's overall structure or the internal logic of characters, Radulescu came up with the goods. This guy should be directing musicals, thought Charles sourly. It wouldn't matter there.

But still his major source of annoyance was the way the director imposed interpretation on the text. In the second week of rehearsal, Alexandru became obsessed with the sexual ambiguity of Viola and Sebastian.

'They express, you see, the male/female duality that is inherent in all of us. They look identical, and yet one is male and the other female. Yet, at the same time, both are attracted to their own sex. And both can inspire attraction in their own sex. I feel this is something we need to explore.'

Charles had become very wary of the Director's use of the word 'explore'. It invariably led to the discovery of something that had never been there in the first place. But there was no dissent from either the two characters who were being discussed, or from anyone watching the rehearsal. The three who seemed always to be on hand, Tottie Roundwood, Benzo Ritter and Talya Northcott, nodded enthusiastically at Alexandru's latest suggestion. Presumably they all paid such rapt attention because they hoped to pick up from the Romanian's table crumbs of genius that might help their theatrical development. Such an idea seemed to Charles excusable in the naive youngsters; Tottie, he would have thought, was old enough to know better.

'Now,' the director announced. 'I think it will help enormously if Viola and Sebastian play some of each other's scenes –'

'What!' Sally Luther was very quick to pounce on this idea. Was Alexandru suggesting that they share out the scenes between them? She had come a long way on the path-of her rebuilt career to get the part of Viola. A leading part.

She wasn't about to sacrifice any of the character's preciously won lines. Sebastian was an important, but minor, character in the play – even when he was being played by the star of ITV's *Air-Sea Rescue*.

The star in question, Russ Lavery, was, unsurprisingly, much more intrigued by the suggestion. 'I think it could be good, Alex. Exploring the duality of the other character could give us a new dimension on how we play our own parts.'

'Yes, that is my idea.'

'I can't see why you're not keen, Sally,' said Russ ingenuously.

She ignored him, but demanded suspiciously, 'Alex, what are we talking about here – testing this out as a kind of rehearsal method or actually playing some of each other's scenes in performance?'

'Oh, only as a rehearsal method,' the director reassured her. But the pensive expression on his face added an unspoken gloss: 'For the time being...'

And, to Charles's annoyance, the idea did work rather well. Russ Lavery sat in on rehearsals for Viola's scenes and every now and then took over for a run. Sally Luther did the same on Sebastian's scenes. It was a gimmick, but it enriched both performances. Their speech patterns and body language grew more alike. The concept that in Illyria the twins could be mistaken for each other became less fanciful.

And, again to Charles's annoyance, the experiment was somehow fitted in without putting the rest of the production behind schedule. Much as he would have liked to dismiss Alexandru Radulescu as a time-wasting poseur, he couldn't.

It was an afternoon rehearsal in the third week. Outside the rain fell, matching Charles's mood. The first week's atmosphere of excitement had dissipated. Perhaps it would have gone anyway by this stage of the production, but Charles couldn't help feeling wistful for the days when Gavin Scholes had been in charge.

What upset him was being out on a limb. While he had never been one of those actors who can see nothing outside the show he's currently working on, Charles Paris had always been a popular member of the companies he was in. Not one of the most boisterous ones, a bit quiet sometimes, possibly even a loner, but one of the team. What Alexandru Radulescu had achieved was to make him unpopular.

The trouble was that the rest of the cast had been charmed by the Director, colonised, subsumed. They had begun to share Alexandru Radulescu's self-belief. They thought his ideas were good. They thought *Twelfth Night* would be a better production for its Director-transplant.

Even Sally Luther, once she had been assured none of her lines were at risk, had started to get excited about the changes.

Only Charles Paris and John B. Murgatroyd held out for the old ways, and John B.'s allegiance was definitely wavering. Charles knew the attitude he'd taken wasn't doing his image in the company any good. It showed his age, his inflexibility. He would overhear cast members talking about how exciting it was to 'get a different perspective on a classic, rather than just relying on old-fashioned storytelling.' Then he would look away to avoid their gaze of mild contempt at someone who still valued 'old-fashioned storytelling'.

He also knew that ultimately his intransigence wasn't helping his cause. Although Alexandru Radulescu's directorial method relied on a cataclysmic clash of styles, the one style that would stick out like a sore thumb amidst all the innovation would be the traditional. And Charles was giving a very deliberately traditional performance.

He couldn't see quite how the problem would resolve itself. Come the performance, Charles Paris would look as if he were in an entirely different play from the rest of the cast. The fact that he still felt confident he'd be in *Twelfth Night*, while the rest were in something else entirely, would not lessen the incongruity.

For many of the younger members of the cast, this was their first Shakespeare, anyway. Actors like Benzo Ritter and Talya Northcott felt no obligation to preserve anything, because they weren't aware that anything needed preserving. So long as Alexandru Radulescu gave each a few individual moments of flashy theatricality, then everything was fine by them.

So what should Charles do – knuckle under, sacrifice his pride, give a performance as Sir Toby Belch that he knew to be totally wrong, and support Alexandru Radulescu's conspiracy to upstage Shakespeare?

Something of that order might have to happen eventually, but Charles Paris was determined to resist the moment as long as possible.

He was also feeling low about Frances. There had been no more direct confrontations, she had been polite – even pleasant – to him, but he got the feeling she was counting the days till he'd be off to Great Wensham and out of her hair.

Perhaps he was being paranoid about that. What was undeniably true was that she hadn't yet readmitted him to her bed.

Off the main hall where they rehearsed there was a little scullery which the company called the 'Green Room'. The name was appropriate. It had the same atmosphere as backstage, the same coffee jars and cups and spoons, the same sugar spills and biscuit tins.

Usually there was also the same assemblage of actors and actresses, sprawled over chairs sipping coffee, perched against tables bitching about their agents, hunched over crosswords, books or knitting. But the room was unoccupied when Charles Paris went in there that afternoon.

Everyone else was watching the rehearsal. They wanted to see Alexandru Radulescu's latest experiment. It was Act Three, Scene Three, the first entrance of Sebastian and Antonio, and Alex (as they all now sycophantically called him) had decided he wanted Sally Luther to play Sebastian, 'Just for this run, you understand, love, just for this run.'

Sally, since the exercise involved her having more lines rather than fewer, readily agreed. And Russ Lavery, after looking momentarily miffed, also fell in with the suggestion. He was, after all, a serious actor 'getting back to his roots in the theatre.' Directorial experiment excited him; when next interviewed for *TV Times*, he'd tell them how much he enjoyed 'playing with ideas in the rehearsal room, just picking something up and seeing how far you can run with it.'

The cast, fascinated to see how Alex's latest invention would work, clustered around to watch the two-handed scene. Even John B. Murgatroyd stayed, wistfully – now almost desperately – wanting to hunt with the pack. Only Charles Paris emphasised his isolation by making for the Green Room. He'd hoped to slip out unnoticed, but everyone saw him go.

The kettle was empty. He filled it and switched it on. Waiting for it to boil, he flicked moodily through the pile of books that someone, trying to tidy the place up, had piled on a central table.

Most of it was predictable rehearsal reading. A Dick Francis. A Joanna Trollope. A compendium of crosswords. A dog-eared analysis of Nostradamus's predictions. Some swot had even brought in *Shakespeare's Festive Comedy* to do some background reading on *Twelfth Night*.

But the book that didn't fit – and the one that interested Charles – was old and green-covered, probably a late nineteenth-century publication.

It was *An Elementary Handbook of British Fungi* by William Delisle Hay, FRGS.

And there was a torn-paper marker in the chapter entitled 'On the Chemistry and Toxicology of Fungi.'

Chapter Nine

THERE WAS a break in rehearsal and all the company came milling in. They made coffee and formed little knots of chatter round the Green Room. Vasile Bogdan and Tottie Roundwood expatiated enthusiastically on Alexandru Radulescu's latest ideas. Sally Luther and Benzo Bitter were huddled in deep but inaudible conversation on a sofa in the far corner. Other actors loudly acted and emoted. Charles watched closely over the rim of his coffee cup, but nobody claimed the book on British fungi.

The rehearsal recommenced, but he stayed behind to maintain his vigil, until summoned by a rather testy assistant stage manager. Sir Toby Belch was late for his entrance with Maria and Fabian in Act Three, Scene Four. Malvolio had been left suspended at the end of his monologue and the momentum of the action had been lost. Everyone was waiting for him.

As Charles scurried shamefacedly into position, he could feel the general disapproval. And it may have been paranoia, but he could have sworn he heard someone muttering 'not so good after lunch these days.' Which was annoying, because he actually hadn't had a drink that lunch-time.

As a result he was flustered and cocked up his opening line. Instead of '"Which way is he, in the name of sanctity?"', his mouth said, '"Which name is he, in the way of sanctity?"'

'God, that doesn't even make sense,' Alexandru Radulescu said contemptuously. 'What can a director do when he's saddled with actors who don't understand the text?'

This was an infuriating criticism for Charles, given his love of Shakespeare. But it was also, in the current circumstances, unanswerable. Alexandru had scored a point, and enlisted yet more company support against Charles Paris.

They played the scene, and Charles knew he wasn't doing it very well. Not nearly as well as he'd played it in previous rehearsals. The trouble was that the general resistance to his performance was getting to him. Charles shared the undermining weakness of far too many people – he liked to be liked. An atmosphere of disapprobation wormed away at his confidence. He started to wonder whether perhaps he should be playing Sir Toby as Alexandru demanded. He even started to wonder whether he actually had any talent at all as an actor.

Act Three, Scene Four is a long one, and one of Sir Toby Belch's biggest, as he hurries on and offstage setting up the elaborate mechanics of the duel between Sir Andrew Aguecheek and 'Cesario'. It was a scene Charles usually enjoyed playing, but not that afternoon. His mind was in the Green Room, wondering who – if anyone – had picked up the book on British fungi.

When, at last, he could leave the stage, his exit line proved prophetic. "'I dare lay any money, 'twill be nothing yet.'"

For nothing was what he found. The book of British fungi was no longer in the Green Room. And there was no way of knowing who had reclaimed it.

Charles Paris could not remove from his mind the image of the dining hall at Chailey Ferrars, of Gavin Scholes swallowing down a mushroom tartlet.

Doing the full run of the play meant inevitably that they overran their designated rehearsal time, but this gave rise to no objections. Alexandru Radulescu, showing surprising awareness of British union rules, kept checking with the company's Equity representative that he had permission to continue. The Romanian showed an annoying degree of tact for someone Charles would like to have dismissed as an insensitive megalomaniac.

The run wound through to its end, gathering momentum. Sir Toby Belch did the little he had to do in Act Five. He approached, 'Bleeding, led by the Clown', and let out his few petulantly drunken lines before being taken off to have his wound dressed. Again, Charles felt unhappy about what he was doing. And again he was getting paranoid. He felt sure, after Sir Toby had said, 'I hate a drunken rogue', he heard a voice murmur, 'Takes one to know one.'

The play's final loose ends were tied up in neat matrimonial bows; though, of course, this being an Alexandru Radulescu production, the bows were not tied very tight. The impression left after the play's end was that the characters faced lives of serial infidelity – with partners of both sexes.

Then Chad Pearson, alone on stage, came forward to sing "'When that I was and a little tiny boy...'" The words, to Charles's continuing annoyance, remained indistinct, but the moment was still theatrical, the wailing Indian music compounding the melancholy that lies at the heart of *Twelfth Night*.

The general view at the end of the run was that it had gone very well for this stage of the production. There was even the beginning of communal excitement, restoring the feeling of the first week under Gavin Scholes. Since it was late, a popular suggestion spread of everyone going off to 'an Indian for a bite to eat.'

There was much discussion as to how many were going. A hard core committed themselves immediately, while some thought they ought to get back home, but lingered and were persuaded. Sally Luther was among these.

'I really shouldn't,' she said. 'My flat's in a hell of a mess and we're going to be away for months...'

'Oh, go on, do come,' urged Benzo Ritter. He sounded truculent, his tone implying that she'd be letting him down if she refused.

Sally looked across at the boy and grimaced. 'Oh, all right, I'll come.'

Benzo looked marginally more cheerful.

Charles was torn. He didn't really want to go. He'd enjoyed many riotous post-performance dinners over the years, but he wasn't in the mood that evening. Also, he had a vague recollection of having hinted to Frances that he might take her out for a meal. He was always better on a one-to-one basis, and a little fence-mending with his wife was certainly overdue.

Also, he wasn't that keen on Indian food. That is to say, he liked it while he was eating it, but he didn't like the aftertaste that seemed to stay in his mouth for the ensuing twenty-four hours. And, pathetically, his stomach was very old-fashioned about spicy food. As a result, he would never go to an Indian restaurant by choice and, on the rare occasions when he did, always had to be guided through the unfamiliar menu.

So there were a lot of arguments for just slipping away at the end of rehearsals with a casual, 'Got to meet someone for dinner. See you in the morning.'

Against that was, once more, the dreadful pressure of wanting to be liked. Fences certainly needed to be mended with Frances, but he didn't want to break any more with the *Twelfth Night* company. These were the people he was going to be spending the next four months with. Some kind of working relationship with them had to be recaptured. Charles Paris didn't relish being ostracised; it wasn't his style.

A measure of how far his isolation had already gone was that, as all the cast shuffled off chattering and pulling on their coats, it was only John B. Murgatroyd who asked, 'You're not going to come, are you, Charles?'

If ever there was a question expecting the answer no, that was it.

'Yes,' Charles Paris replied. 'I'll come.'

'So let me get this right – is it the Khurma that's mild and the Vindaloo hot?'

'Yes, yes, yes,' said John B. Murgatroyd dismissively and turned to his right to talk to Talya Northcott.

'And the Madras is somewhere in the middle?' asked Charles. He felt rather pathetic for not knowing. And he also worried that John B. Murgatroyd was only sitting next to him out of pity. His friend'd much rather be the other side of the table, in the raucous sycophantic crowd that surrounded Alexandru Radulescu. The director was flanked by Russ Lavery and Vasile Bogdan. Sally Luther and Tottie Roundwood spread out from them. Benzo Ritter was beside Tottie; he looked a little marginalised – rather the way Charles felt.

Chad Pearson, seated beside Sally, was in the middle of some scatalogical anecdote about a slow-witted Jamaican immigrant. It was all right for him. He was black. Anything he said against black people was politically acceptable.

Chad reached his punch-line with immaculate timing, and the area around him erupted with laughter. When it subsided, Alexandru Radulescu was full of congratulations. 'Excellent, Chad, excellent. You are very good comedy actor. It is a pity that Feste doesn't have more comedy in the play. Maybe we work out some extra business to use your talents properly – eh?'

Chad Pearson responded to this with some line in his dumb Jamaican patois, which again set the table on a roar. Charles wasn't near enough to hear what was said. He hadn't been near enough to hear more than the odd word of the original story. His spirits sank lower. Pity Osbert Sitwell had used the title *Laughter in the Next Room* for a volume of autobiography. It would have suited Charles Paris's memoirs. Not of course that there was anything worth remembering in his life. A long timetable of missed buses and wrong roads followed.

Oh God, he must get out of this cycle of self-recrimination. There was an unhealthy indulgence in it, a picking away at the scabs of his discontent, willing them to reinfect themselves.

A waiter was slowly working his way round the table, taking orders. There was so much hilarity, so much backchat, so much flamboyance, so many changes of mind, that it was hard for him to pin the diners down to final decisions, particularly on the minutiae of bhajees, naans, chapatis and pappadums.

'I must just nip off to the Gents,' John B. Murgatroyd announced. 'Order me a Chicken Vindaloo, Charles. With a tarka dal. And pilau rice. And, as for you, my dear...' He turned a sexy beam on Talya Northcott, '...I'm sure Charles will keep you conversationally on the boil till my return.'

The pretty little actress gave Charles a token grin and then turned determinedly to talk to the person on her right.

I'm too old, he thought. Why should I imagine a young woman would be interested in me? Why should I imagine any woman would be interested in me?

Even Frances. He'd really screwed up with Frances. The one lifeline that was offered for his declining years and he had deliberately swum away from it. He should be with her at that moment, making it up with her, telling her how much she meant to him, telling her that she was the only woman he'd ever really loved and that he'd definitely try in future to – 'Yes, please, sir?' The waiter's voice broke into this self-indulgent spiral of misery. 'Have you decided?'

'Oh yes.' John B.'s instructions had completely vanished from Charles's head. He grasped at the menu, hoping it would remind him. 'Now my friend wants a tarka something. Not *Tarka the Otter*, I know, but –'

'Tarka dal,' supplied the waiter, and wrote it down.

'And he wanted a...Vindaloo, I think...'

'Prawn Vindaloo is very good, sir.'

'Yes, fine. And I'll have the...which is the mild one?'

'Khurma is mild. Or...' A note of contempt came into the waiter's voice '...Dupiaza is so mild it hardly deserves the name of a curry.'

'Chicken Dupiaza for me, please,' said Charles wimpishly. He also wanted to order some of those nice crispy round things, but he couldn't remember whether they were chapatis or pappadums. Unwilling to show himself up further, he didn't ask for either.

'And boiled rice for both of you, yes?'

'Er, yes, fine,' said Charles, and took another long swallow of wine.

He knew there was little chance of shifting his mood, but at least he could numb it with alcohol. Pity he hadn't had the chance to put down a few large Bell's before they got to the restaurant. Wine worked, but it took so much longer. And you needed a lot more of it. Charles Paris refilled his glass.

The large order from the *Twelfth Night* company seemed to have thrown the restaurant into confusion. Maybe they were short-staffed, maybe there was some crisis in the kitchen... For whatever reason, the food took a long time to arrive. The actors drank more, ordered extra bottles, and grew ever rowdier.

As a result, there was a lot more confusion – genuine and engineered – when the food finally came. People couldn't remember what they'd ordered. Some mischievously claimed things they hadn't ordered, while others rejected dishes that they had ordered. It was the kind of mayhem that Indian restaurateurs are presumably used to when they have in a large party of over-excited thespians.

'Who's the Chicken Madras?' 'King Prawn Biryani, anyone... ?' 'Whose are the Dupiazas?' 'Someone's stolen my naan.' 'Oy, get the chutney down here.' 'I'm missing a chapati.' 'I definitely did order a Sag Aloo.' The sound level rose higher and higher.

But slowly order was imposed on the orders. The joke of pretending to have got the wrong food wore thin, metal dishes were reallocated around the table, wine glasses recharged, and the serious business of eating began.

'What the hell's this?' John B. Murgatroyd demanded when the only meal left that could possibly be his appeared in front of him. 'Charles, what did you order me?'

'Vindaloo – that's what you wanted, isn't it?'

'Yes, Chicken Vindaloo, not prawn. For God's sake, I'm allergic to shellfish. If I eat these now, I'll be throwing up all over the place in three hours' time.'

'Oh, I am sorry. I wasn't concentrating. Look, you have mine. Mine's chicken.'

John B. Murgatroyd scrutinised the proffered dish dubiously. 'What is that?'

'Chicken Dupi...duppy – doopy – something...'

'Dupiaza?' John B. had caught the waiter's note of contempt.

'Yes.'

'Oh God.' Charles's order was picked up and waved over the table as John B. Murgatroyd shouted out, 'Anybody fancy swapping a Chicken Dupiaza for something stronger?'

Howls of derision, 'I've already got one', 'No Way' and, 'Forget it' greeted this suggestion.

'Order something else,' said Charles. 'I'll pay. Look, I'm sorry if –'

'God, no. If it takes them this long to get things cooked, I'll be waiting all night. I'll eat this.'

John B. Murgatroyd dumped a portion of Chicken Dupiaza on to his plate, then saw the rice. 'Oh, shit. I did say order pilau.'

'I'm sorry. I –'

But John B. Murgatroyd turned his back on his friend, and spent the rest of the meal strenuously and unambiguously chatting up Talya Northcott.

Leaving Charles feeling even more wretched. Particularly as he found the Prawn Vindaloo inedibly hot.

John B. Murgatroyd clearly thought he was on to a winner. The intentions of his chatting up became more overt as the evening progressed. He only spoke to Charles once, when Talya had slipped away to make a phone call.

'I think the old John B. magic's working again,' he leered. 'I think a serious, steamy bonking session is going to prove unavoidable. God, it's hell, you know, being fatally attractive to women.' He grinned smugly. 'But I've learned to live with it. Ah, my dear,' he greeted the returning Handmaiden, 'you just put your beautiful little bottom back down there.'

Why is it, Charles asked himself bitterly, that one always feels jealous of someone who's clearly about to score? It doesn't make any difference if you find the object of their attentions utterly repulsive. It doesn't even matter how well your own sex-life's going at that precise moment... Not of course that mine's going at all right now... His mind readily – even eagerly – supplied the gloomy thoughts, and the cycle of self-hatred started up again.

They'd got to the stage of bill-paying. Everyone was keen to leave. Those who didn't reckon they were on a promise, like John B. Murgatroyd, were simply tired. It'd been a long day's rehearsal, and they had to start again at ten in the morning. Another ten days and *Twelfth Night* would be opening at Chailey Ferrars. They all needed to conserve their energy.

Dividing up the bill was, as ever, complicated, and the communal mood was by now scratchier. The company's two teetotallers objected to contributing to the wine; the vegetarians, Tottie Roundwood and Talya Northcott, insisted they'd only ordered small vegetable curries; all the usual wrangles developed. And, as always, somebody – in this case the company manager – produced a calculator and started working it all out.

Sally Luther, exasperated, slammed a twenty-pound note down on the table and left. Benzo Ritter's eyes followed her like a rejected spaniel's. She hadn't even said goodbye to him. Charles felt a moment of sympathy for the young actor. Infatuation's tough when you're that age, he recollected.

'I'll pay for yours,' said John B. Murgatroyd, flamboyantly placing a twenty and a ten-pound note on Talya's side plate.

'Oh, thank you very much,' she giggled.

John B.'s proprietorial hand was on her shoulder. 'Come on, let's move. See you, Charles,' he threw back as they strolled to the door.

Wistfully, Charles watched them across the room. Then Olivia's Handmaiden walked up to an elegantly dressed woman in her sixties, who was standing by the coat-rack. Introductions were made and the new arrival graciously shook John B. Murgatroyd by the hand. Talya Northcott also shook her host politely by the hand; then she and the woman who was undoubtedly 'Mummy' left.

Charles Paris did not need the explanation John B. gave as he came stomping back to the table; he had read it all in the little pantomime by the door. 'Only rung up her bloody, sodding mother, hadn't she? Oh, shit! Fucking, pissing shit!'

'All-round entertainer,' said Charles.

'What?'

'Well, shit that can fuck and piss could surely get bookings at any venue in the...' But John B.'s face suggested he was in no mood to pursue verbal fantasies. Charles looked at his watch. 'Pubs're still open. Fancy a quick one?'

'That's what I thought Talya bloody Northcott was going to say,' John B. Murgatroyd muttered. 'Oh yes, what the hell? Let's see how many quick ones we can fit in before they close.'

Chapter Ten

'WHAT WE'RE doing isn't working, you know,' said John B. Murgatroyd, as he sat down with their second round of drinks. The pub had been recently refurbished, decked out with all those brass rails, coloured glass lamps and sporting prints which are meant to give character, but are now so familiar they drain it all away.

'It is,' Charles protested. He took a substantial swallow from his large Bell's. 'We are doing the play as Shakespeare intended it to be done. We are making sense of our scenes.'

'We're still sticking out like sore thumbs in this production.'

'That's the production's fault, not ours. Everything else is just flashy theatrical tricks; *we* are actually telling the story.'

'Still sticking out like sore thumbs.' John B. Murgatroyd took a reflective swig from his second pint.

'So what are you suggesting – that we cave in, do as Alexandru tells us, make nonsense of the play?'

'Well –'

'Listen, I'm not denying he's talented. He is. He has some very good ideas. *Some* very good ideas. But not all his ideas are good. And it needs someone to stand up to him and tell him that. He'll listen.'

'I doubt it.'

'He listens to that guy from Asphodel. When he was told he couldn't change the sets and costumes, OK, Alexandru stamped his little foot, but he accepted it. Thank God he did. Otherwise, no doubt, we'd be doing *Twelfth Night* in cycling shorts and kimonos. But you see, a firm hand works. We've got to stand up to him about the way we play our characters.'

'We just look wrong. I was noticing during the run this afternoon. The two of us looked totally out of place.'

'That's because the place is wrong, not our performances.'

'Maybe. It doesn't matter which, anyway. It's still going to give the audience a strange feeling, as if they're watching something unfinished.'

'Listen, John B.,' said Charles. The alcohol had made him more forceful and confessional than he might have been under other circumstances. 'My career as an actor hasn't been great. I've had my chances, OK. Most of them I've screwed up. I've never made it to the top rank. At my age it's very unlikely now that I ever will. I can accept that. I have accepted that.

'But it doesn't mean I've run out of ambition. There are still things I want to do professionally, still things I believe I *can* do professionally. And playing Sir Toby Belch is one of them. It's a part I've always wanted, and one I know I can play well. Under Gavin I was getting the chance to play it well. Now that's being threatened. It's impossible for me to give a good performance with Alexandru directing.'

John B. Murgatroyd shook his head ruefully. 'The production was looking pretty good this afternoon. Even you must admit that.'

'Yes, moments looked OK, I agree. Some of the effects are stunning, but it's all at the expense of the play – and at the expense of the actors. You know, no one in the cast is going to get any decent notices out of this.'

'Well, I don't know. I'd have thought –'

'All the notices will be about the production. They'll talk about "Alexandru Radulescu's radical new interpretation", "Radulescu's brave vision". Directing for him's nothing more or less than an ego-trip.'

John B. Murgatroyd squirmed uncomfortably. 'But if it *works*?'

'Do I gather from this, John B., that you're about to start playing Sir Andrew Aguecheek differently?'

'Well...maybe.'

So Charles Paris had lost his one supporter in the *Twelfth Night* company. From now on it was just him against the massed forces of Alexandru Radulescu's creatures.

There was a morose silence while they sipped their drinks. Charles finally reopened the conversation. 'Going back to what I was saying about Gavin's illness...'

His friend groaned. 'Oh no, Charles! All I want to do for the rest of this evening is to get smashed out of my skull. I don't think I've got the energy for any more conspiracy theorising.'

'No, listen.' And Charles told John B. Murgatroyd about the book he'd found in the Green Room.

'Well, so what? So, somebody in the company's interested in British fungi, or possibly in old books; who can say? I don't think we should drag in the CID quite yet, Charles.'

'But, taken in conjunction with what I heard Vasile say to Alexandru, and the fact that I saw Gavin eating a mushroom tartlet the day before he was taken ill –'

'Pure coincidence.'

'I'm not so sure. I think I'm going to go and have a word with Gavin.'

'Fine. Good. You do that. Give him my love.' Across the room the landlord, with a lack of charisma that matched his pub's door, rang a bell and dolefully called 'Time'. John B. watched him with disappointment. 'Why do they always do that just when you're getting a taste for the stuff?'

'Mm, rotten,' Charles agreed. Then an idea came to him. 'Tell you what...You could come back to my place for a nightcap.'

'Your place? But you're miles down Westbourne Grove way, aren't you?'

'Not at the moment. I'm staying in my wife's flat.'

'Ah.' John B. Murgatroyd was attracted by the idea. 'Are you sure she won't mind?'

'Oh no,' said Charles. 'She won't mind.'

Frances was far too well brought-up to let John B. Murgatroyd see if she did mind, but Charles knew her well enough to detect a slight resentment on their arrival. It wasn't so much the fact of his appearing on her doorstep at eleven, clearly drunk, in the company of someone she'd never met before, also clearly drunk; Charles got the feeling it might have more to do with his not having been there earlier to take her out for dinner. Maybe what he'd thought of as a to-be-confirmed possibility had been a definite arrangement. That would certainly justify Frances's frostiness.

But he admired the way she didn't let on to John B. His friend was made to feel extremely welcome, and not allowed to sense any edge in her refusal to join them for another drink on the grounds that she had to be up early in the morning.

Charles watched her go somewhat mournfully. He had a feeling that when he did finally make it to bed he'd find her bedroom door once again closed. All in all, he had made rather a cock-up of the evening.

'Lovely woman,' John B. Murgatroyd commented as he slumped on to her sofa. 'You never told me you were married. Recent thing, is it?'

'No, we've been married quite a time,' replied Charles, unsnapping the top of a new bottle of Bell's. 'You all right on the Scotch?'

'You bet. Seal in the beer. So, how long?'

'How long?'

'How long've you been married?'

'Oh God.' Charles totted it up in his head. Surely it couldn't be that long. He rechecked the figures. No, it was. He told John B.

'Jesuuuus! Lots of people don't *live* that long.'

'No. Well...'

'And you've actually been together all that time?'

'Mm. Pretty much.' Charles handed across a large Scotch. 'I mean, inevitably there have been gaps...with me working in the theatre and...you know...'

'Well, good on you, mate. And good on her too, eh?' John B. Murgatroyd raised his glass in salutation. He was already too fuddled to ask why, if Charles was locked into an ongoing marriage to Frances, he actually lived on his own in a bedsitter in Hereford Road.

They drank on steadily, their conversation, in the way of such conversations, circling round the same points and recycling them. They both agreed – many times – that *Twelfth Night* was a 'bloody good play.' They both bemoaned – many times – the fact that they hadn't been allowed to act their parts as they ought to be acted. John B., who had by now given up all pretence that he was going to continue his resistance to Alexandru Radulescu's ideas, said dolefully – many times – how little he was going to enjoy the rest of the rehearsal period. While Charles Paris asserted vehemently – and many times – that he was going to continue playing Sir Toby Belch the way Shakespeare had written the character.

It was about half-past one. They were at that stage when the conversation filled with lacunae as one or the other dozed off. Getting a taxi for John B. had been mentioned at least four times, but the effort of moving to the phone seemed insuperable to both of them.

Then, suddenly, John B. Murgatroyd sat bolt upright on the sofa. His hand shot up to cover his mouth. 'My God, I think I'm going to be sick!'

Charles stumbled to his feet. 'I'll show you where the bathroom is.'

But John B. didn't make it that far. In the middle of Frances's neat hall, all over her new oatmeal carpet, he began to spew his guts out. He clutched at his stomach and sank down against the wall, but still the flow spurted from his mouth.

Charles heard the door of Frances's bedroom open behind him and turned apologetically. She was standing, belting up her dressing gown, with a hard look in her eyes.

'I'm sorry. Just a little bit too much to drink. He's not usually...' Charles babbled.

Frances moved across to assess the damage to her carpet. Charles followed uselessly behind her.

'Good God!'

The shock in Frances's voice made him look down. Amidst the mess that still pumped relentlessly out of John B. Murgatroyd's mouth he could see bright flecks of blood.

'I'm going to call an ambulance,' Frances announced.

Chapter Eleven

'THEY WANT to keep me in for tests,' said John B. Murgatroyd sullenly.

He looked drained, wrung out like an old floorcloth. Presumably the drip that fed into his arm was part of the hospital rehydration process.

It was the evening of the following day, the first time the patient had been deemed well enough to have visitors. Anyway, Charles couldn't have got to the hospital earlier. He'd been locked into a heavy day of hungover rehearsal. Without John B. there for support his own performance had seemed even more at odds with what was going on around him.

For that day an assistant stage manager had read in Sir Andrew Aguecheek's lines, but with just over a week till the show opened, a decision about the future had to be made quickly. Alexandru Radulescu had agreed to hold fire on this until the following morning. John B. Murgatroyd's consultant was going to see him then and would pronounce on the actor's chances of getting back into the show. Looking at the shrivelled figure sunk into the pillows, Charles Paris didn't put those chances very high.

'Have they given any suggestion of what they think it might be?'

John B. Murgatroyd shrugged feebly. 'Food poisoning's as far as they'll go at the moment. They've sent off some of my stomach contents to the labs for a biopsy; is that the word?'

'I'm surprised they could find any contents left in there.'

John B. didn't even smile. He was very low.

'Still, if it was food poisoning, probably as well you chucked it all out.' There was a silence. 'And you've no idea what it might have been?'

'You were there, Charles. Your guess is as good as mine. Something in the curry, I suppose. If I'd had the prawns, I wouldn't have been surprised – I've always been allergic to them. Still, chicken can be dodgy if it's been reheated, can't it? Or maybe I've developed an exciting new allergy to something I've never been allergic to before. I don't know.' He spoke without interest.

'And the thought hasn't occurred to you that it might be something else?' Charles prompted.

'Well, the ward sister puts it down purely and simply to alcohol. I thought I'd flushed most of that out of my system, but apparently I was still reeking of the stuff when I was brought in here. A somewhat puritanical lady, the ward sister – as I'm discovering.'

'We had a lot last night, but not more than we've had on plenty of other occasions without worse effects than a sore head.'

'Exactly.' John B. Murgatroyd nuzzled sideways into his pillow and yawned weakly. It was a fairly unambiguous hint that Charles should leave.

'But you don't think there's anything suspicious about it?'

'What, Charles?' A light of understanding came into the sick man's eye. 'Oh, for God's sake,' he said wearily. 'You're not still on about that. Leave it alone.'

'But it's getting more than a coincidence. Gavin Scholes, whose departure opens up the possibility of Alexandru Radulescu taking over, suddenly gets ill with abdominal pains. You, who're one of the two actors who's opposing the way Alexandru's directing the show, suddenly get ill with abdominal pains. Call me a conspiracy theorist if you like, but at least there seem to be grounds for my having a conspiracy theory.'

'Charles, as I said, leave it alone. It's happened. I'm ill. Whatever the reason, it looks like I'm out of the show.'

Charles began a token remonstrance, assuring his friend that he'd soon be fine and – 'Don't bother. Look at me. There's no way I'm going to open in *Twelfth Night* next week, is there?'

'Well –'

'So I've got to come to terms with that. It's a real bugger – I was looking forward to doing the show – but there it is.'

'Oh, come on. Surely you want to get even with whoever did this to you.'

'I don't think anyone did anything to me. It was just bad luck.'

'At the very least, you could sue the restaurant, or get the health inspectors out to them or –'

'Charles, I don't want to do anything. I want to forget about it, and just get better. OK?'

Charles Paris looked at his friend's exhausted face. The freckles stood out unnaturally against the surrounding pallor. It was no longer a sparkling, comical face. John B. Murgatroyd looked crumpled and defeated. And, Charles suddenly realised, there was another emotion also on display.

'You're frightened, John B., aren't you?'

The anaemic attempt to shrug off his suggestion was more telling than an admission.

'But if you're frightened, that must mean you believe there's some truth in what I've been saying. You wouldn't be frightened unless –'

'Charles, I'm frightened because I'm forty-four years old, and for the first time in my life I've come up against the possibility of real illness. Suddenly losing control of your body like that is a real shock. Abdominal bleeding could be a symptom of any number of extremely nasty conditions, one at least of which begins with the letter "C". If I look frightened, I'd say I have every justification for looking frightened.'

It was a good speech, but it didn't fool Charles. 'No, you're frightened because you think someone in the company poisoned you. That's why you want to lie low, why you don't want to argue. You're afraid if you make a fuss, they'll try again.'

'Crap, Charles. And please stop going on about it. I'm feeling really shitty. All I want to do is close my eyes and shut out the world.'

'Yes, yes, OK,' Charles began to feel guilty for hounding a man in such reduced health. 'I'm sorry. I'll be off. See if I can make my peace with Frances.'

'Oh. Look, I'm sorry about her carpet. It came on so suddenly, I just didn't have time to –'

'It's not her carpet I need to make peace with Frances about.'

'Ah. OK. Right. Well, good luck.'

'Thanks.' Charles stood up. 'Hope you sleep well and...you know, wake feeling better.'

'Yes. Sure I will,' said John B. Murgatroyd without conviction. 'And thanks for coming, mate.'

'No problem.' Charles moved awkwardly towards the door.

'Of course, there is one thing...' John B. Murgatroyd's weak voice stopped him.

'Hmm?'

'If one did go along with your crap conspiracy theory...'

'Yes?'

'...and really believed that someone in the *Twelfth Night* company put poison on some of the food last night...'

Charles was silent, alert.

'...and deliberately targeted the Chicken Dupiaza...Well, I didn't order that. So it wasn't me they were out to get, was it? They were out to get you.'

He was determined not to have a drink until Frances came back. She was late. It was agony.

But he needed to talk to her. And he needed to be sober when he talked to her. In less than a week he'd be off to Great Wensham; then all over the place for more than three months. Things had to be sorted out before then.

He was sitting in the middle of the sofa, feeling very conspicuous and only partially dressed without a drink in his hand, when he heard the front door. It was half-past twelve. Frances came into the sitting room, as if to turn off the lights. He noticed she was smartly dressed, in softer and more feminine style than her headmistress mode. She reacted with surprise to his presence, and asked tartly, 'Couldn't sleep?'

'No, I just...I wanted to talk.'

'Oh. Really?' Her eyes immediately moved to her watch. 'Can't be long. I'm exhausted and school will open the same time in the morning, regardless.'

'Yes.' He had to get the important fact in quickly. 'I haven't had a drink all day.'

'Well, there's a novelty,' said Frances. 'Let's hope Arthur Bell and Sons can survive this temporary blip in their profits.'

She still didn't sit down, but lingered by the door as if keen to be away.

'I've been to see John B.'

'How is he?'

'Pretty washed-out.'

'But conscious?'

'Oh, yes. On a drip. The consultant's going to see him in the morning. Know his immediate prospects then.'

She nodded. 'They got any idea what it was?'

'Talk of food poisoning.' In the past Charles had sometimes shared with Frances his suspicions about criminal activities; now there were more important subjects to discuss. 'I don't think he's going to make it for the show.'

'Ah. Bad luck for him.'

'Mm. You have a good evening?'

'Yes, thank you.'

She deliberately hadn't volunteered any more information, which should have been a signal to him, but Charles couldn't stop himself from asking, 'What did you do?'

'Had dinner with an American friend.'

An interrogative 'Ah?'

'Someone I met at an international teachers' conference.'

'I didn't know teachers had international conferences.'

'Well, you learn a little something every day, don't you, Charles? If you ever showed any interest in my work, I might have told you that, as a headmistress, I get invited to an increasing number of conferences of one kind and another.'

The rebuke was justified. 'And do you go to many of them?'

'If the subject's interesting and I can fit it into my schedule, yes.'

'And this American you met tonight...does she teach in the States?'

'He. Yes.'

'Ah.' A silence loomed between them. 'Frances, about what happened last night...'

'I thought we'd just been talking about what happened last night. John B. Murgatroyd's conscious and on a drip.'

'I meant before he got ill. The fact that I brought him back here for a drinking session. The fact that I forgot you and I were meant to be going out together, or that it was as definite an arrangement as...It was insensitive.'

'Yes,' Frances agreed.

'And I wanted to say I'm sorry. And it won't happen again.'

'No, I shouldn't think it would.'

Charles looked up, blinking with hope. Did she actually believe him? Had she accepted that he really, genuinely intended to turn over a new leaf?

'I shouldn't think it would,' Frances went on, 'because by this time next week you'll be away doing *Twelfth Night* at wherever it is, and I wouldn't imagine even you would have the gall to do a repeat performance here in one of the intervening evenings.'

'Frances –'

'And, after that, who you bring back to drink at wherever you may happen to be staying...won't be my problem.'

'Oh, Frances.' He took in the familiar outline of her face, and realised how much he loved her. Had always loved her. Would always love her. Tears prickled at his eyes, and he wasn't even drunk. 'I really thought we could get back together this time – you know, make it work.'

'So did I, Charles,' said Frances softly. Then, with a sharp 'pity we were both wrong', she turned on her heel and left the room.

Charles did have a drink then. Quite a few, actually.

There was no surprise in the rehearsal room when the message from the hospital came. John B. Murgatroyd was going to be out of action for at least a week, and probably a lot longer. He would be unable to play Sir Andrew Aguecheek for the Great Wensham Festival.

'I have of course been prepared for this eventuality,' Alexandru Radulescu announced to the hushed company.

Oh yes? For how long, Charles wondered.

'And I do not at this stage wish to introduce new members into our cast. We have a good ensemble feeling here. Almost all of us...' Charles looked down to avoid the inevitable glances cast in his direction '...are working together well to make a production that is really going to register with its audience.'

If not with lovers of *Twelfth Night*, Charles thought for the thousandth time.

'So I am not going to regard John B.'s accident as a problem. I am going to look on it instead as a positive creative opportunity. It can spur us on to a new pitch of excitement in the show, if we accept the challenge we are offered. So, we will have someone new to play Sir Andrew Aguecheek...'

During the pause which Alexandru Radulescu left for dramatic effect, Charles tried to predict who would get promoted. Since he had so many scenes with Sir Andrew, the outcome was of considerable importance for him. Mind you, he didn't think there was much chance of getting anyone who'd play the part right. Even John B. Murgatroyd had been on the verge of defecting to Alexandru Radulescu's camp, and the rest of the company were already firmly installed there.

He looked round the room. Everyone was expectant, but the most feverish glow showed on the faces of the youngest male cast members. Benzo Ritter, in particular, sparkled with anticipation. Charles felt sorry for the boy. He knew how potent the mythology of the theatre is. One day you're a walk-on... One of the leads is taken ill...The director points at you...You rise magnificently to the challenge... And a star is born.

If that was what was going through Benzo Ritter's mind – and it almost certainly was – then he was due for a disappointment. None of the male attendants or officers had shown sufficient talent to justify their promotion to a part as important as Sir Andrew Aguecheek. No, the logical thing, Charles reckoned, would be to move Vasile Bogdan up into the role and give Fabian to the best of the walk-ons.

In spite of his arrogance and self-regard, Vasile was a good actor. As Fabian he was in a lot of the Sir Toby/Sir Andrew scenes, so would be familiar with the lines and moves. He was tall too, which was right for the part. His complexion was a bit dark, but that could be paled down with make-up. And presumably he'd be given John B. Murgatroyd's floppy blond wig, so that his hair could, as the text demands, hang 'like flax from a distaff.'

Charles didn't relish acting so closely with Vasile. The young man was totally under Alexandru Radulescu's spell; he'd play everything exactly as the director told him. Charles knew he was probably being old-fashioned about it, but he didn't relish the homosexual kiss which would inevitably get grafted on at some point. Also, though he hadn't yet cleared his mind on the subject of poisonings within the company – if there had been any, then Vasile Bogdan was way up any possible list of suspects.

Charles was so carried away in his thoughts that it was a moment before he took in Alexandru Radulescu's next words. 'I'd like you to play the part, Chad.'

'What!' The word was out of Charles Paris's mouth before he had time to think.

'What's wrong? You have some objection, Charles?' The Director's black eyes turned on him, teasing, challenging him to make a fool of himself.

'Well, it's just...'

'I hope you're not suggesting Chad is not good enough to play the part.'

'No, not at all. I have a great respect for Chad. He's a very fine actor.'

'Thanks, mate.' The West Indian beamed a cheery grin at him.

'It's just...'

'What?' asked Alexandru Radulescu, feeding out more line to his victim.

'It's just that Chad's wrong physically.'

'Physically?'

'All the references to Sir Andrew in the play are about him being long and thin. Even the name "Aguecheek" suggests he's thin. The first line Sir Toby says about him is: "He's as tall a man as any's in Illyria." At the end he's described as "a thin-faced knave". I mean, Chad, as I say, is a terrific actor, but there's no way you're long and thin, is there?'

He turned his appeal to the subject of the conversation, who grinned again and said, 'No way.'

'Don't you think you're being a bit literal, Charles?' suggested Alexandru Radulescu gleefully. 'Surely what one's trying to do in the theatre is to excite, to surprise the audience by doing something different? They come to the theatre with certain expectations.'

'In this case the expectation that they're going to see *Twelfth Night* by William Shakespeare.'

'OK. And it's up to us to surprise them. They expect Sir Andrew Aguecheek to be tall and thin – then he isn't. They are surprised, yes?'

'Yes, but it's wrong. And it's not just that,' Charles plunged on. He knew he was getting into deeper and deeper water, but he couldn't stop himself. His resentment had been building from the moment that Alexandru Radulescu took over the production. 'Sir Andrew's meant to be *pale*. That's what "Aguecheek" means. Just before his first entrance Sir Toby even calls him "Sir Andrew Agueface", which is a comment on his washed-out complexion. Then his hair's described as hanging like flax, there's the line about him not having "so much blood in his liver as will clog the foot of a flea." It's obvious that the Sir Andrew Aguecheek Shakespeare intended was tall, thin and anaemically pale.'

'*Pale*?' echoed Alexandru Radulescu quietly. 'Charles, you're not saying Chad's the wrong colour, are you?'

Which of course *was* what Charles was saying; but was also, in the theatre's current climate of political correctness, totally unsayable.

Chapter Twelve

NOW THAT HE was identified not only as an actor unreceptive to the Romanian boy-wonder's ideas but also as a racist, Charles Paris's position within the *Twelfth Night* company became even more uncomfortable. Normally, in the week before a show's opening, he would share in the communal mood, the giddy excitements when everything seemed to be coming together, the swooping despairs when it all fell apart. Now, though he was aware of all that going on around him, Charles felt painfully isolated from the process.

But he still thought he was right. He was still of the opinion that Alexandru Radulescu was systematically destroying the finely tuned comic machinery of *Twelfth Night*. And no amount of pressure towards political correctness would ever convince him that Sir Andrew Aguecheek should be played by a short, tubby West Indian. He had seen some very successful mixed-race casting in Shakespeare productions, but only where the individual actor was right for the individual part. Alexandru Radulescu's choice of Chad Pearson had been simply perverse.

So had his elevation of the Indian sitar player to Chad's part (another disappointment to the dreams of Benzo Ritter). Alexandru's arguments that the most important function of Feste the Clown was to provide music were let down, in Charles's view, by the fact that the Indian could not act for toffee. His accent was so strong that few of his words were comprehensible, particularly in the songs, which were his supposed *raison d'être*. And his singing style demonstrated none of Chad Pearson's magical charisma.

But Charles was too canny to point any of this out. He'd already offended the Afro-Caribbean contingent; he wasn't about to take on the Asian lobby too.

Even under pressure of the last week of rehearsal, the director still managed to find time to experiment, and Charles was once again grudgingly forced to admire Radulescu's efficiency. Alexandru continued to explore the Viola/Sebastian duality, constantly recasting their scenes in rehearsal so that Sally Luther and Russ Lavery became as familiar with each other's roles as they were with their own.

And the benefit of the exercise was evident in both performances. Greater depth and texture came into their interpretations, and the possibility of the one being mistaken for the other became infinitely more plausible.

Yes, even Charles admitted, some of Alexandru Radulescu's ideas were very good indeed. It was the rest of them that drove him mad.

The latest example of the Director's sheer gratuitous gimmickry affected the production's wardrobe. Charles had assumed, after the intervention of the Asphodel representative, that at least the sets and costumes were sacrosanct. But he had reckoned without Alexandru Radulescu.

The first hint of trouble came when they were rehearsing Act Two, Scene Three, in which the late-night carousing of Sir Toby Belch, Sir Andrew Aguecheek and the Clown is interrupted by a furious Malvolio entering with the line, 'My masters, are you mad?'

'This is not working,' Alexandru Radulescu interrupted, waving his arms discontentedly. 'We are not getting enough offence. Why is Malvolio so angry?'

'Because we are making a drunken row late at night in a court that he runs on rigidly puritanical lines,' Charles answered, reasonably enough.

'Yes, but we need more than this. When he comes in, Malvolio's eyes should be offended by what he sees.'

'Surely three drunken men singing bawdy songs is offensive enough?'

'No, no. We need something visual. The three should look in a way that somehow outrages his sensibilities. It is something they are wearing, or how they are wearing it...'

'Well, they could have their doublets undone and drink spilled all over them.'

'Yes, this is good, Charles, good.'

'Oh.' He was taken aback. It was the first time since they'd met that Alexandru Radulescu had described any of his ideas as 'good'.

'Doublets undone – yes, good, I like it. And with their doublets undone, what is it that Malvolio sees?'

'Well, their shirts, grubby linen, I suppose...though I'm not actually sure that it would be grubby. I mean, Sir Toby may be an old rake but –'

'No.' The lines around the black eyes tightened, as they always did when the director produced another of the 'radical ideas' for which he was so famed. 'What Malvolio sees under their doublets,' he pronounced triumphantly, 'are T-shirts.'

'T-shirts?' came the feeble echo from Charles Paris.

'Yes, T-shirts. They would offend his puritan sensibilities I think, no?'

'Yes, they probably would. They'd also confuse him totally, I would imagine, since they weren't due to be invented for another three hundred years.'

But, as ever when Alexandru Radulescu was following the thread of a new idea, he did not even hear counter-arguments. 'Excellent, good, yes. They are wearing T-shirts that would offend his puritanism. "Legalise cannabis", this would be a good one, I think.'

'What?'

'Or "Fuck the Pope". You can, I think, get T-shirts that say "Fuck the Pope".'

'Except it's a sentiment that Malvolio, as a puritan, would probably agree with, anyway,' Charles couldn't help objecting.

'Good point, good point. So we won't have that one. "Guns 'n' Roses"!'

'What?'

'You will have a "Guns 'n' Roses" T-shirt under your doublet. That would certainly offend Malvolio.'

'But, Alexandru...'

It was hopeless. Once the director had got the bit between his teeth, nothing could stop him galloping over the horizon with his latest brainwave. Anachronisms began to erupt all over the play.

Viola, as Cesario, was taken out of doublet and hose and put into doublet and Levi's, 'To stress the refreshing informality of her approach to Olivia.' Antonio was to wear a leather peaked cap and biker's jacket over his puff-sleeved shirt and slashed hose, 'To emphasise the gay thing.' Benzo Ritter and the First Officer were armed with pistols in holsters, 'So that the audience realise the real threat to Antonio.' Feste, in his disguise as the parson Sir Topas, was given a clerical dog-collar and, of all things, a laptop computer on which to note down Malvolio's answers to his questions. Maria, when flashing a leg, would reveal sexy stockings and a suspender belt.

It was only with reluctance that Alexandru Radulescu was dissuaded from having Orsino deliver his opening 'If music be the food of love...' while listening to a Walkman.

It was the end of their last day's rehearsal in London, the Saturday. Sunday off, then all reassembling at Chailey Ferrars on the Monday morning for a no doubt agonising sequence of technicals and dress rehearsals before the Tuesday night opening. They'd done a full dress run in the rehearsal room that day and the general view was that it had gone very well.

Charles Paris did not share that general view. Chad Pearson had been encouraged to put all kinds of new business into his performance as Sir Andrew Aguecheek, and the whole balance between the dominant, manipulative Sir Toby and his petulant dupe had been lost. Alexandru Radulescu's policy of 'challenging accepted stereotypes' had resulted in something merely eccentric.

The homosexual kiss had not yet been written in, but it had already been discussed. Charles had the ominous feeling that its inclusion was only a matter of time. And no doubt if, when the moment arose, he objected, he would be once again branded as racist. And homophobic. People of Charles's age found mere survival tricky, bulls in the china shop of modern political correctness.

The cast dispersed quickly at the end of the run. Benzo Ritter was once again left droopy, like a rejected spaniel, as Sally Luther shot off with only the most perfunctory of goodbyes. But everyone was in a hurry. Once they moved to Great Wensham, the tour had effectively started. Most of them had sex-lives to put on hold or partners to placate.

Charles Paris, wondering whether his partner could ever be placated again – and indeed even whether the word 'partner' was still appropriate – lingered. He'd persuaded Frances to let him take her out for dinner that evening, but he didn't approach the encounter with enthusiasm.

Then on the Sunday she was going to visit their daughter Juliet, husband Miles and three grandchildren. Charles had been assured that he'd be welcome too, but somehow didn't see himself going. So he recognised he was close to some sort of goodbye to Frances.

How permanent a goodbye he couldn't be sure, but he didn't feel optimistic. He tried to pinpoint the moment during the last few weeks when things had started to go wrong. It really all dated from Gavin Scholes' illness. Uncertainty over the change of director had got Charles drinking again, and the drinking had once again been a contributory factor to his soured relations with Frances.

As he moved morosely towards the Green Room to pick up his bag, the decision formed in Charles's mind to stop for a couple of large Bell's on the way back to the flat. He'd a feeling he might need bracing for the evening ahead.

He was about to enter when he heard the sound of voices from inside. He wouldn't have stopped if he hadn't heard a mention of his own name. In the event, he loitered out of sight and listened.

There was no problem identifying the speakers. Charles immediately recognised the dark, guttural sounds of Vasile Bogdan and the lighter, lilting tones of Chad Pearson.

'No, Charles Paris is in a different play from the rest of us,' said Vasile.

'Well, he's a traditional kind of actor,' Chad Pearson offered in mitigation. He had an exceptionally amiable disposition; it really hurt him to think ill of anyone.

'Yes, but he's getting in the way of what Alex is trying to do. His scenes just aren't working.'

'He'll be fine. Everything'll shake down when we get into the run.' Chad Pearson still didn't want the boat rocked. 'It's too late for anything to be done about it, anyway.'

'Is it?'

'What do you mean?'

'Well, you're playing Sir Andrew Aguecheek, aren't you?'

'Sorry, Vasile? I'm not with you...'

'Until last week Sir Andrew Aguecheek was being played by another actor who didn't fit into Alex's scheme of things. Then fortunately he got ill, and now you're playing the part.'

'Yeah, well, I feel rotten about poor old John B., but it's an ill wind.'

'Yes. Wouldn't it be great if another ill wind could just...blow away Charles Paris?'

'But if that happened, who'd play Sir Toby Belch?'

'I could do it,' Vasile Bogdan replied. 'I'd do it bloody well, actually...if only Charles Paris wasn't around.' There was a silence. 'Still, better be moving.'

Charles backed away from the Green Room door and tried to look as if he was fascinated by a copy of the *Daily Mail* somebody had left lying on a chair. But he knew it was a bad performance, and the look Vasile Bogdan gave him in passing only confirmed it.

He knew his words had been overheard. In fact, Charles got the distinct impression Vasile had only spoken as he had because he *knew* Charles was listening.

His words had been a deliberate threat.

'It's just the predictability, Charles.'

They were in a Hampstead bistro they'd often been to before. Soon Charles would feel the need to order a second bottle of wine. On previous occasions they'd happily knocked back two and then moved on to the Armagnac. But this evening Frances was only sipping at her glass. The order for a second bottle was likely to prompt a sigh and a raised eyebrow.

'How can you call me predictable? You can accuse me of a lot of things, Frances, but not that. We make an arrangement – I may turn up, I may not turn up. I say I'll call you tomorrow, and you may not hear from me for three months. That's the secret of my great appeal – you never know where you are with me.'

Had he looked into her face earlier, Charles might not have completed the full speech. He'd clearly chosen the wrong tack. Light-hearted irony was not what the occasion demanded. Frances shook her head wearily and pushed the hair back out of her eyes.

'It's the predictability of your unpredictability I'm talking about, Charles. That's what gets me down. I mean, how many new dawns am I expected to greet? How many times am I supposed to believe in you as a born-again dutiful husband? How many good intentions am I meant to listen to, while all the time I hear the Hell Paving Company truck revving away in the background?'

Charles grinned at the conceit, then looked serious. 'Look, I do mean everything I say at the moment I say it.'

'Well, thanks. That's a lot of help, isn't it? I'm sure a goldfish is surprised every time it does a circuit of its bowl and sees the same bunch of weed.'

'What's that supposed to mean?'

'That, OK, maybe you do mean everything you say at the moment you say it, but that doesn't mean you're always saying it to the same person.'

He looked puzzled, so she spelt it out for him. 'Charles, it's very difficult for me to believe anything you say to me – anything caring, anything about loving me, for instance – when I know the next day – or the day before – you'll either say or have said exactly the same words to someone else.'

'Oh, Frances, that was ages ago. I've grown out of all that. I now know what I want in life, and it's you.'

'So all those other women...?'

'There never were that many, and none who really meant anything to me.'

'Must've been nice for them to know that, mustn't it?'

'Frances. You should never worry about me and other women.'

'I agree. And, generally speaking, I've found the best way of not worrying about them is to close my mind to the fact of their existence. Which is a lot easier to do when I'm not being constantly reminded of the fact of your existence.'

'You mean when I'm not around?'

'In a word, yes,' she replied brutally.

'But, Frances...' He knew he was sounding pathetic. He didn't want to sound pathetic, but that was how the words came out. 'There's still so much between us.'

'Is there? Listen, Charles, what you don't realise is that things change. I change. You think I'm just the same person. You go away, have an affair, and when you get bored with it or she gets bored with it, you think you can come bouncing back and I will still be exactly where you left me. Life doesn't work like that. Every pain takes its toll. Each time you've hurt me it's left a mark – and strengthened my defences against you, against the same things happening again. I'm a lot stronger than I was when you first walked out, Charles.'

'I know. That's part of your appeal for me.'

'I haven't built up that strength for *your* benefit. Rather the reverse, actually. I've built it up for me, so that I've got the strength to lead my own life – on my own – which is what I was doing, quite cheerfully, until, a few weeks ago, you shambled back into it.'

'You were pleased to see me. You welcomed me.'

'Yes, you're right. I did manage to forget about the past. I managed to forget the predictability. Once again I deluded myself that – this time – it'd all be different.'

'And it has been.'

'Has it, Charles? Oh, the first two or three weeks were fine, yes, I agree. But would you say the last two have been very different from the way it always was?'

'Well.' Charles looked away from her and, as he did so, caught the eye of a passing waiter. He lifted up the empty wine bottle. 'Could we have another one of these, please?'

On the landing back at the flat, he put his arms round her. 'Good night,' Frances said. 'As you know, I'm going to Juliet's tomorrow. I don't suppose you...?'

He shook his head.

'No, no, I thought not. Well, Charles, I hope everything goes well at Great Wensham.'

'Mm. Thanks.' He'd had plans for organising first night tickets for her and...But it all seemed a bit pointless now.

'...and keep in touch, eh, Charles?'

'But not too much in touch?'

She looked up and the pain in her eyes burnt into him.

He still had his arms around her. He really wanted her. Maybe if they made love it'd sort everything out.

He squeezed her tighter. 'Frances...'

'What?'

What indeed? There was no point in trying to make love to her if she didn't want to. It wasn't just an act of sex he wanted; it was the coincidence of two people who really wanted to have sex with each other.

Slowly he released his hold. 'I'll ring, you know, keep you up to date with how things're going.'

'Mm.' The disbelief in her monosyllable was not quite overt. 'Take care, Charles.'

She leant forward and gave him a soft peck on the cheek. Then her bedroom door opened and closed, and she was gone.

Charles Paris went through into the sitting room and poured himself a large Bell's.

Chapter Thirteen

HE WOKE IN the spare bed, tired and headachy. The stableyard taste in his mouth suggested he'd passed out before cleaning his teeth the night before. Nausea lurked in the cobwebs at the bottom of his throat. Why did he do it? Convivial drinking with other people was at least fun while it was happening; drinking alone was nothing more nor less than self-punishment.

There was an empty stillness in the flat. He glanced at his watch. After ten. God knows what time he'd fallen into bed. He didn't want to move, but his straining bladder insisted.

Being upright didn't help the headache. In the bathroom he peed copiously, sluiced his face in water and cleaned his teeth. The mint wasn't strong enough to swamp the other taste in his mouth.

The door to Frances's bedroom was closed. He knew she wasn't there, but still tapped on it before entering. The room seemed almost clinically neat, the edges of the bedspread regulated into neat parallels.

The whole place smelt of Frances. A strong whiff of her favourite perfume in the air suggested she might only just have left. Maybe the closing of the flat's front door was what had woken Charles.

He sat on the bed, hunched in misery. This time he really had screwed up. Frances had given him a chance, and he'd blown it. What was more, it felt ominously like a last chance. They'd made no plans to meet again.

He could have stayed there, marooned in self-pity, all day, but he forced himself to stand up. His weight had left a semicircular indentation on the bedspread. He smoothed it out. The bed was once again a rigid rectangle, as if Charles Paris had never been there at all.

He got dressed and tried to drink some coffee, but gagged on it. Savagely, he took a long swig straight from the Bell's bottle, recognising as he did it – and almost revelling in – his self-destructive stupidity.

Then he went to the phone and rang Gavin Scholes.

When he reached the neat terraced house in Dulwich, Charles was surprised to discover that Gavin had developed a new wife. The former one had walked out after many years in Warminster because, although he only lived a mile from his work, her husband was never home. Gavin was so obsessed with the Pinero Theatre that he gave little sign of having noticed his first wife's departure.

The new one was on the verge of walking out too when Charles arrived. Only temporarily, though her tone of voice implied a more permanent separation was not out of the question.

'Sorry to appear inhospitable,' she said, 'but I have so few opportunities to get out at the moment that I have to snatch every one that comes along.'

'You mean Gavin's too ill to be left on his own?'

'No. I mean that Gavin *thinks* he's too ill to be left on his own – which, in terms of how much freedom it gives me, comes to the same thing.'

'Ah.'

'He's in the sitting room – through there. I'm going for a walk in the park. Can you stay for an hour? I won't be longer than that, I promise. But please don't leave him till I come back.'

Through her brusqueness, a genuine anxiety showed. However much she tried to dismiss Gavin's illness as hypochondria, deep down she was worried about him.

The director was certainly doing the full invalid performance. Dressed in pyjamas and dressing gown, he sat in an armchair facing french windows which opened on to a punctiliously regimented garden. (That must be the new wife's doing; Charles couldn't imagine Gavin Scholes showing an interest in any activity outside the theatre.)

Beside the patient, Sunday papers lay unopened on a table, which also bore a bottle of Lucozade and a basket of grapes. The attention to detail was maintained, in spite of the summer weather, by a rug over Gavin's knees. The room even contrived to carry a hint of hospital disinfectant.

'How're you doing?' asked Charles.

It was an incautious – though probably unavoidable – question. Whatever the reality of Gavin Scholes' illness, he was certainly obsessed by it, and Charles did not escape the blow-by-blow – or perhaps twinge-by-twinge – account of every last bowel movement.

Gavin finally drew breath long enough for Charles to ask, 'And what does your doctor reckon it is?'

The director shrugged. 'Bloody hopeless, doctors these days. You never catch one committing himself to an actual opinion. It could be this, it could be that, better have some more tests...Never get a straight answer out of them.'

'So you've had tests, have you?'

'Oh yes.' Gavin spoke as a connoisseur of tests. Clearly his health was the one subject which could threaten the exclusivity of his obsession with theatre.

'And have they found anything?'

He shook his head. 'Nothing definite as yet. They can see I'm ill, but none of them has a clue what it is. My GP even had the nerve to suggest the whole thing was psychosomatic.'

'Well, you have always been a bit prone to that sort of thing, haven't you?'

'What do you mean?' Gavin was incensed by Charles casting doubt on the authenticity of his precious symptoms.

'I mean you have suffered from irritable bowel syndrome in the past, you know, when you've been stressed or –'

'Irritable bowel syndrome is not a psychosomatic disorder,' said Gavin, still offended by the suggestion. 'It's a genuine illness – and absolutely crippling for those who have it. I've been a sufferer for years.' Then, to compound his martyrdom, he added, 'Mind you, what I've got now is considerably more serious than that.'

'Hmm.' Time to move the conversation away from Gavin's cherished symptoms and get on with a bit of investigation.

'There hasn't at any point been a suggestion that it might have been something you ate?'

'Something I ate?'

'Yes. That caused you to be ill?'

'What, just food poisoning?' Gavin's tone dismissed the unworthy idea. 'No, what I've got is much more serious than that. Anyway, if it was food poisoning, I'd have recovered by now.'

'It depends what you'd been poisoned with.'

'And I'm sure some of the tests would have picked it up if that's all it was.'

'That may not have been what the tests were looking for.'

'I don't know why you're harping on about this, Charles.'

'I was just thinking...The day before you were taken ill, we'd done the photocall and press conference at Chailey Ferrars.'

'Yes. So?'

'Well, I was just wondering whether you might have been poisoned by something you ate from the buffet.'

'Why? Did other people who were there get ill?'

'No.'

'Then why should I have done? What am I supposed to have eaten that caused this, anyway?'

'I did notice you have a mushroom tartlet.' As he said them, Charles realised how stupid his words sounded.

'Yes, I remember it. Why should that have made me ill?'

'Well, suppose the tart had not been made with mushrooms, but with some form of poisonous fungi...'

Gavin Scholes looked at Charles in blank amazement. 'Why? Why on earth should it have been?'

'I've just been thinking...The timing was odd. You get ill, you can't continue directing *Twelfth Night*...'

'Yes.' Suddenly Gavin understood what Charles was hinting at. 'Are you suggesting that I was deliberately poisoned to get me out of the way?'

'That's exactly what I'm suggesting.'

'Well, it's absolute, total rubbish.' The invalid was very offended now. An insinuation of foul play was the ultimate insult to his precious symptoms. 'I am genuinely ill, Charles, not the victim of some crazed poisoner. Honestly, you really mustn't let your imagination run away with you like this.'

'No. No. Sorry,' said Charles.

Asking Gavin Scholes the questions he had come to Dulwich to ask did not prove easy. The director had become highly skilled at finding in any unrelated sentence a cue for further medical reminiscence. If Charles mentioned Sir Toby Belch, Gavin was prompted to details of his wind problem. Talk of the rehearsal room unearthed the coincidence that the laboratory to which his stool sample had been sent was also in Willesden. And even the word 'production' was picked up when Gavin said, 'Goodness, you've no idea the production they made of giving me my barium enema.'

Charles noted that Gavin had developed the true hypochondriac's possessiveness. Everything was '*my*'. Not just '*my* barium enema', but also '*my* consultant', '*my* enterologist', *my* proctologist', and so on. Charles got the feeling Gavin would only be truly happy when he was qualified to talk about '*my* operation'. He began to see why the new wife seized every opportunity to get out of the house and away from the unending litany of medical minutiae.

What was striking, though, was that Gavin Scholes showed absolutely no interest in how *Twelfth Night* was going. While he had been in charge, the play had consumed his every waking thought; now it was out of his hands, he might never have had anything to do with the show. He did not even express regret at the illness which had taken him away from the production. Why should he? That illness had provided him with a subject of much more consuming interest than anything the theatre could offer.

Gavin's medical monologue ensured that Charles had no problem staying an hour; indeed the promised time was almost up before he managed to shoehorn in the other questions he'd taken the trip to ask. And the only way he finally succeeded was by interrupting an account of catheterisation with the words: 'Vasile Bogdan!'

The surprise was sufficient for Gavin Scholes to stop in his tracks and say, 'What?'

'I wanted to ask you something about Vasile Bogdan.'

'Oh. Why?'

'I just wondered how he came to be in the company.'

'Well, he's a good actor, isn't he?'

'Yes, but you hadn't worked with him before, had you?'

'No. I don't only work with people I've worked with before, you know, Charles.' Gavin sounded aggrieved, though the implied criticism had been justified. He only employed actors he had worked with before or actors recommended by actors he had worked with before.

Which was why Charles next asked, 'So who recommended Vasile to you?'

'He auditioned for me,' Gavin replied, still a bit huffy at having his casting methods questioned.

'But someone must've suggested his name for you to audition him.'

'I'd heard good reports of him. I looked him up in *Spotlight*, thought he had an interesting face, so I asked him to come along for an interview.'

'But who –?'

'It's not as if he was completely unknown, Charles. He'd got quite a track record for good work. Even West End...Well, that is to say, the Old Vic.'

'What'd he done at the Old Vic?'

'Oh, nothing very big, but apparently he was good.'

'You didn't see him?'

'No.' A defensive look came into Gavin's eyes. 'When you're busy directing, it's difficult to get to see every show that opens, you know.'

'Sure.' The director was notorious for never going to see any productions other than his own. 'So what was the play Vasile was in?'

'*She Stoops to Conquer*. Just played one of Tony Lumpkin's drinking cronies, I think, but, as I said, supposed to be very good.'

'That was the production Alexandru Radulescu did, wasn't it? Another of his "revisualisation" jobs.'

Gavin shrugged. 'Don't know. As I said, I didn't see it.'

'So who was it who recommended you should audition Vasile? Was it someone who you'd already cast in *Twelfth Night*?'

'Yes. And I thought he sounded an interesting actor, so I saw him. I'm always on the lookout for new talent,' Gavin lied.

Charles patiently repeated his question yet again. 'So who was it who first mentioned Vasile's name to you?'

'Russ Lavery,' the director replied. 'You know, Russ told me he'd once been taken ill with abdominal pains. Only an appendix in his case, obviously not as serious as what I've got. In fact, my consultant was just saying to me a couple of days ago, "If only we were dealing with something as straightforward as an appendix, we'd know where we stood. As it is, Mr Scholes, your case has got me completely baffled. I wouldn't be surprised if you get written up in *The Lancet*, you know. You have an extraordinarily interesting...'

And Gavin Scholes was back on track. Charles extricated himself with difficulty once the new wife had returned. And as he left, he felt more than a little sympathy for the look of resigned panic he saw in her eyes

Chapter Fourteen

THE GREAT WENSHAM Festival had been started ten years previously, on a great wave of local enthusiasm. Like many such enterprises, it had been the brainchild of one determined and charismatic individual, a local woman, who, having brought up a family, was looking for something different to consume her inexhaustible energy. The complexity of setting up an arts festival was exactly the sort of challenge she relished. By a mixture of charm, bullying, cajolery and sheer bloody-mindedness, she set up the whole thing from a standing start within a year.

And local people still talked back to the first Great Wensham Festival. There had been a raw excitement about it, the novelty of multifarious plays, concerts and exhibitions all being crammed into one week, a sense of danger. For seven days Great Wensham had ceased to be another boring little Hertfordshire town and had come to life. Local people were caught up in the communal fervour. Many volunteered to help make the festival happen; many more flocked to the scattered venues, and almost all of the artistic events were sold out.

Buoyed up by that success, the second year's festival was even more exciting. The one week was extended to two. The programme was larger and more varied; more local buildings were commandeered as venues; the recruitment of volunteers grew ever wider. Famous names were engaged to appear; national reviewers came to write about the shows. The town filled with cultural tourists; business boomed. The summer festival became established as a high spot in the Great Wensham social calendar.

That was in the early eighties, when the idea of a local arts festival was original. But over the years every tinpot town in the country started to develop its own comparable event. Artistes and agents grew cannier; the network of festivals became just another booking circuit. As it had been in the days of music hall, the same performers took the same performances round the country, often unaware that their appearance was as part of a 'festival'. It all became predictable and not a little dull.

For Great Wensham, the rot set in when the prime mover behind the early successes left the area. Her marriage broke up – due in no small measure to the pressures of running the festival – and she moved away. Recognising that the initial thrill of that kind of festival had gone forever, she developed a new and successful career as a concert agent.

Without her dynamism, the Great Wensham Festival might have been expected to shrivel away to nothing. But by then the committees had taken over. The Great Wensham Festival Society had been born, representing the great and the good of the area. They rather liked the idea of their town continuing to host a nice, safe, contained, one-week festival. The shopkeepers were particularly keen.

By this time a new breed had appeared in the Arts world – the professional festival administrator – and it was to one of these that the Great Wensham Festival Society turned in their hour of need. Julian Roxborough-Smith was already running the Barmington Festival with apparent success; inviting him to take over Great Wensham was a logical step.

And so, with Moira Handley at his side to do all the actual work, Julian Roxborough-Smith started his familiar routine of juggling artistes between the two events. Since he also acted as agent for quite a few of the performers involved, he did rather well out of the arrangement.

The Great Wensham Festival continued to happen every summer. But the excitement, the energy, the danger had gone.

The *Twelfth Night* tech run at Chailey Ferrars had been scheduled to start at eleven on the Monday morning. The obvious objection that the effects of the lights could not be judged in daylight was supposed to have been countered by a light-plotting session – without the cast – on the Sunday evening.

Gradations of lighting for an open-air production are always pivotal. During the first half of *Twelfth Night*, scheduled to start in daylight, the levels would be slowly built up, so that when the interval came almost all the illumination was artificial. And by the start of the second half, night would have fallen. All these subtleties of shading were due to be plotted in the Sunday evening session.

The theory was that during the dress rehearsal, scheduled as per performance for seven-fifteen on the Monday, levels could be tweaked, spots repositioned and the lighting plot generally adjusted. Recognising that this might be inadequate provision, the cast, after consultation with their Equity representative, had been asked to hold themselves in readiness for a couple of hours of fine-tuning on the lights after the dress rehearsal ended, which should be around ten-thirty.

The Asphodel production of *Twelfth Night* did not actually run three and a quartet hours. The playing time was just over two and a half, but a forty-five minute interval was mandatory at Great Wensham, so that the locals could enjoy what they all referred to as 'a Glyndbourne-style picnic'.

Alexandru Radulescu had stamped his little foot a lot when he heard this demand, insisting that 'my productions are about ensemble work and my cast cannot be expected to keep their concentration with a three-quarters of an hour gap in the middle of the play.'

But to no avail. Going to see the Great Wensham Festival Shakespeare was a social rather than an artistic event for the local audience. In fact, most of them would have preferred to watch a brass band and fireworks, but if they couldn't have that, Shakespeare'd have to do. Whatever the entertainment offered, the demands of their picnics took unquestioned priority.

They made a big deal of the occasion. Some parties would arrive hours before the performance started, weighed down with folding tables, chairs, hampers, linen, cut glass and even, in a few cases, candelabras.

The timing of their actual eating varied from group to group. Some tucked into a three-course dinner immediately on arrival. Others took pre-prandial drinks and maybe their starters before the play began, then ate the bulk of their meal during the interval. Yet others munched and swilled throughout the entire performance.

The three-quarters of an hour interval was incorporated into the proposed schedule of technical and dress rehearsals for *Twelfth Night* 'to give us a bit of a time buffer.' However – and it seems there's always a 'however' in the theatre where tech runs are concerned – everything got hopelessly behind.

The fault lay not with Asphodel. Their backstage team was compact and highly efficient. The production company knew the pressures of touring and accordingly hired the best staff available. They all arrived at the agreed time on the Sunday afternoon, ready to erect *Twelfth Night*'s cunningly minimalist set on to the stage, and to adjust the lights in the towers and gantries which surrounded it.

But when they got to Chailey Ferrars, there was no stage on which to erect the set. The scaffolding towers and gantries were in place. So was the metal load-bearing shell which covered the natural grassy mound; but the acting area, the boarding which should have been fixed on to this structure, was absent.

The problem was one of demarcation. Though the scaffolding was supplied and erected by outside contractors, construction of the staging was the responsibility of the festival volunteers. In previous years this group had been organised and co-ordinated by Moira Handley, whose judicious mix of bullying and flattery had built up a dedicated band of recidivists. Every year when re-approached about helping with the festival, they all began by saying, 'No way, never again.' Every year they relented, and by the final event had built up a tightly knit community with its own jargon and camaraderie. Many of them, in spite of the mandatory grumbles, took their annual holiday over the festival period and regarded its two weeks as the high-spot of their year.

However – another 'however' – during the run-up to the current festival, Julian Roxborough-Smith had piled yet another duty he should have undertaken himself on to the long-suffering shoulders of Moira Handley. He asked her to organise the guest list for one of the final festival events, the all-important Sponsors Dinner and Chamber Concert, and Moira, in a rare moment of complaint, had objected that she really had far too much on her plate to take on anything else.

In a fit of pique at this unexpected resistance, Julian Roxborough-Smith had responded, 'What've you got on your plate then?'

'Organising the festival volunteers, for a start.'

'Oh, for heaven's sake, Moira. You do make heavy weather of everything.' Which was possibly the most unjust criticism ever levelled.

'Julian, you've no idea how much time it takes – how many phone calls, chatting them all up, keeping them sweet, working out their rotas. You should try it some time.'

Stung by her tone, the festival director had responded, 'All right, I will. I will organise the volunteers this year. Then we'll see what you're making so much fuss about.'

And indeed they did see what she was making so much fuss about. Within a week Julian Roxborough-Smith had alienated the local roofing contractor who co-ordinated all the heavy-work volunteers. Then, by an injudicious display of temper, he'd reduced to tears the little old lady from the tobacconist who masterminded the box office. Incapable of admitting he was in the wrong, he reported to Moira that both of these essential supports to the festival had resigned in fits of temperament.

He'd then issued invitations to virtually everyone he met to take over various festival functions which already had incumbents jealous of their precious little areas of responsibility. So more noses were put out of joint.

Finally, as the festival approached, he produced a volunteers' rota so inflexible that it made Masonic ritual look impromptu. And, all the time, whenever Moira enquired about how the volunteer organisation was going, Julian Roxborough-Smith brushed her off with a dismissive, 'Oh, for heaven's sake, woman, it's all in hand.'

As a result, it was only the weekend before the festival opened that Moira realised exactly how out of hand the whole organisation was. The lack of staging at Chailey Ferrars was symptomatic of total chaos at all the festival venues.

With superhuman energy – and at a time when all the other bubbling crises of the festival were reaching boiling point – Moira threw herself into rebuilding the volunteer network. Some would never be reclaimed. The roofing contractor and the little old lady from the tobacconist had been alienated for good. Other reliable standbys, when not asked to participate, had either used up all their outstanding leave entitlement or had actually gone away on holiday over the festival period.

But Moira's skills of persuasion were exceptional and by the Monday morning, the day before the opening of the whole event, she had in place a workable infrastructure of volunteers.

Typically, Julian Roxborough-Smith did not thank her. In fact, if the subject of the chaos came up, he implied that it had been an error in Moira's organisation rather than his own.

The result of all this for the Asphodel *Twelfth Night* was that by the time the stage was in place, it was late Monday afternoon. With no time available for preparatory work on the lighting plot, the tech run began at six forty-five.

And it had been raining in Great Wensham since the Saturday morning.

'What's a drunken man like, fool?' Olivia demanded.

'Like a drowned man, a fool, and a madman,' the Clown replied. 'One draught above heat makes him a fool, the second mads him, and a third drowns him.'

'Go thou and seek the crowner, and let him sit o' my coz, for he's in the third degree of drink – he's drowned.'

Olivia's words could not have been more apt. The 'coz' in question, Sir Toby Belch, was drowned indeed. He would have given anything to be 'in the third degree of drink' too, but Charles Paris hadn't touched a drop all day.

The rain had by now soaked through the thick charcoal velvet on his shoulders and was trickling down his back, between his stomach and its padding, everywhere. His tights felt as though they had been recently painted on to his legs. Water still dripped incessantly off the brim of Sir Toby Belch's hat, from which the light-grey feather dangled like a dead fledgling.

The canvas awning under which he stood offered no protection; it was as porous as a sieve. The allocated wing space was very cramped and suddenly pitch-black after the brightness of the lights on-stage. The trees surrounding the stage area were thought more important by the Chailey Ferrars Trustees than the comfort of mere actors, whose entrances and exits had to be fitted around them. A kind of hessian tunnel led off from the stage towards the caravans which served as dressing rooms. Because of the trees and limited sight-lines, the tunnel was very narrow and actors had to press themselves against the walls to get off stage. Needless to say, the hessian was also wet.

On-stage it was even wetter. Olivia blinked to keep the water out of her eyes. It dribbled off the ends of her straggled hair, sending little rivulets into her ample *décolletage*. The bell-tipped horns of the sitar-playing Feste's head-dress drooped limply down around his ears.

Still, Charles had actually exited. Unless there was a sudden summons back, he would be free to go off and find some shelter. And a drink. He'd been very good all day, but now, hell, he needed one for medicinal purposes if nothing else.

'Hold it there for a moment, can we?' Alexandru Radulescu immediately dashed his hopes. The Director's voice came out of the darkness, beyond the lights which illuminated the crosshatching of rain as it fell relentlessly on to the stage.

Charles peered out into the auditorium – though 'field' might have been a better word to describe what he was looking at. Julian Roxborough-Smith's cock-up over the volunteers meant that the raked audience seating had not yet been delivered. The Director, assistant director and lighting designer huddled round a camping table in the middle of a space which would have served well as a location for a movie set in World War One trenches. A single sheet of polythene covered the three of them.

'Can we just go back to before Toby's exit...'

Shit.

'Positions for "Lechery! I defy lechery..."' Charles shambled soggily back on-stage. 'And can you just hold that tableau while we adjust a couple of the parcans...?' Alexandru's voice continued.

Oh God. Moving the lights took forever. Someone would have to climb up one of the scaffolding towers and fiddle about with the angle of the beam until the lighting designer was satisfied. And unfortunately Asphodel's lighting designer was a perfectionist.

Charles, desperately willing the guy would settle for second – or even third – best, held his position. Damp was now creeping down his tights into his boots.

He sneaked a look at the watch he should by rights have taken off – and must remember to take off the following night. Alexandru Radulescu would probably applaud the anachronism, but Charles was determined not to give him the opportunity. He'd already secretly decided to ditch the Guns 'n' Roses T-shirt for the first night. He knew he'd get stick from the director afterwards, but had promised himself he'd give at least one performance of Sir Toby Belch as Shakespeare had intended the part to be played.

The watch revealed it was nearly quarter past nine. God, and they'd only reached Act One, Scene Five. Charles wished he'd gone straight off and got lost after his exit. By now he could be sitting somewhere dry with a large Bell's in his hand. But he knew his professionalism wouldn't let him do that; he'd be letting down the rest of the company. He only had to wait a few minutes and then Sir Toby was off till Act Two, Scene Three.

The few minutes while the parcan was adjusted seemed more like hours, but eventually even the lighting designer was happy with the new setting. 'OK.' Alexandru Radulescu's voice came through the rain. 'Take it from after Sir Toby's exit.'

'That mean I can go to the dressing room?' asked Charles.

'Yeah, yeah, sure. We're moving on.'

The alacrity with which Sir Toby Belch moved to get offstage was ill-judged. Losing his footing on the wet boards, he skidded and fell hard on his bottom, prompting a trickle of uncharitable and disembodied laughter.

It was as he hurried off, pressed against the clammy walls of the hessian tunnel, that Charles remembered he hadn't got anything to drink in his dressing room. Oh shit, shit and again shit.

He had had one of his misplaced attacks of righteousness that morning. Deciding that the booze had been at least a contributory cause of his cool parting from Frances, he had made yet another vow to cut down. He shouldn't be drinking on a rehearsal day, anyway.

So there was no comforting half-bottle of Bell's tucked away in his jacket pocket in the caravan. (The word 'caravan should perhaps be explained at this point. In a theatrical context it might be expected to describe a lavish trailer of the kind used by Hollywood stars on location. But no. The caravans parked at the back of the stage at Chailey Ferrars were old, green-stained, noisesome and damp. They were also horrendously overcrowded. Three served the entire *Twelfth Night* company. There was really only room inside for the costumes, not the actors who were going to put them on.)

Charles got the feeling that actors weren't very high on the priority list for the organisers of the Great Wensham Festival. No one had greeted or welcomed the *Twelfth Night* company when they arrived, and they had been left to find their own way around the facilities. It made them feel like strolling players, newly come to the next barn they were due to storm.

He emerged from the end of the hessian tunnel slithering in the mud. A solitary working light hung in a tree spread a meagre glimmer over the scene. As he squelched off in the direction of the caravans, Charles met someone coming towards him. She was recognisably a woman, dressed in a navy plastic anorak, which was sleek with rain. On the front of the anorak was the white logo of the Great Wensham Festival. This was a fanciful combination of the letters 'G', 'W' and 'F' together with a shape that might have been a waterfall, or a scallop shell…or possibly a unicorn. It was a piece of amateur artwork which explained instantly why major corporations will spend millions to get a good logo.

She looked up into his face, and Charles recognised Moira Handley, the festival administrator.

'Oh hi,' he said.

'Charles Paris, isn't it?'

'You have a very good memory. We only met the once at the press conference.'

'Ah, maybe, but I've lived with you for nearly six months.' Seeing the puzzlement in his face, she laughed. 'Well, lived with your photograph.'

'Oh.' That was flattering. Charles Paris didn't have that many fans, but all comers were welcome – particularly when as attractive as Moira Handley.

Her next words quickly disillusioned him. 'It's one of my jobs to get all the programme copy together, so my office is spilling over with photos and biogs.'

'Ah. Right.'

'God, you look drowned.' She giggled. 'How's it going out there – the underwater *Twelfth Night*, starring Esther Williams as Viola?'

'It is absolutely disgusting,' Charles replied, 'but I don't see anyone stopping it. If the show's to open tomorrow, we've somehow got to get through this tech.'

Moira nodded. She understood the imperatives of the theatre. 'Yes, if it's still like this tomorrow evening, we'll have to cancel, but the show has to be ready to go up.'

'Which means you can cancel a performance, but not the tech.'

'Exactly. I'm surprised you're doing it in costume, though.'

'Alexandru insisted. So did the lighting designer. Said you can't judge the overall effect unless everyone's dressed as they will be for the show.'

'Which is true, of course. What was the wardrobe mistress's reaction?'

'"Resigned", I think would be the word. I mean, the costumes have in theory been designed to cope with anything the elements can throw at them…I just don't envy her trying to get everything dry for tomorrow night.'

'No.' Moira lingered for a moment, as if about to move off. Then she said suddenly, 'Don't suppose you fancy a drink?'

'Those,' Charles replied, 'are the most wonderful words I've heard all year.'

Chapter Fifteen

CHARLES followed her. On the back of her navy anorak was printed in white: 'MUTUAL RELIABLE – FOR ALL YOUR FINANCIAL NEEDS – AND FOR THE GREAT WENSHAM FESTIVAL.' Above the words was the professionally designed MUTUAL RELIABLE logo on which a large corporation had spent millions.

The Portakabin into which Moira led him was a few steps up in comfort from the dressing room caravans. One side was filled with desks on which piles of posters, handouts and programmes threatened to overwhelm the computers and telephones; on the walls planning charts outlined elaborate schedules and rotas with coloured strips and stickers; everywhere, papers bulged from the open drawers of battered metal filing cabinets.

On the other side of the room a dead sofa and a couple of terminally ill armchairs huddled round a table scattered with coffee jars, coffee cups and coffee stains. The impression was one of controlled chaos.

'Is this the main administration office?' asked Charles.

'No, it's the Chailey Ferrars outpost. The main office is in the town, but so much needs doing out here, we have to have somewhere.'

As she moved towards one of the filing cabinets, she noticed a figure hunched in a chair, almost totally obscured by the mountain of paper on her desk.

'Oh, hi, Pauline.' A small, harassed face peered out over the debris. 'Charles, did you meet our press officer?' asked Moira, as she produced a bottle of red wine from a drawer.

'Yes. At the photocall. Hello...er...?' The name had gone completely.

'Pauline,' she supplied. 'Pauline Monkton. I recognised your costume from last time, anyway.'

'Except it wasn't soaked through then.'

'No.'

Moira was now over at the grubby little sink, swilling out two glasses. Only two, Charles noticed. Pauline wasn't going to be invited to join them. Good.

'Surprised you're still here,' the administrator observed. Was Charles being hypersensitive to detect a hint in the voice that perhaps the press officer should be on her way? Moira had stripped off her MUTUAL RELIABLE anorak, and he was aware of the firm outline of her body in its jeans and Guernsey sweater. Oh dear. The old stage manager syndrome was getting to him once again.

'Just came in to check the answerphone, Moira, see if any more of the press have said whether they're coming or not tomorrow. I mean, I've sent them all invitations with RSVP on, and none of them has even had the courtesy to ring back.' Clearly Pauline Monkton's approach to publicity hadn't changed a lot in the last couple of weeks.

'We must know how many so we've got the right number of seats reserved for them, Pauline. You'll have to do a ring-round in the morning and check who is actually coming.'

'Oh, will I?' asked Pauline pathetically.

Moira was implacable. 'Yes.' She sat down on the dead sofa and gestured Charles to join her. She slopped wine into the two glasses on the coffee table 'Was there anything on the answerphone?'

'Something from…Saniserve, I think it was…'

'What?' The administrator was instantly alert.

'They said they'd tried to deliver at four this afternoon, but there was nobody around to let them in.'

'Oh, shit!' Moira was furious. 'Shit, shit, shit!'

'Is it important?' asked Pauline mildly.

'Yes, it is bloody important! Julian assured me he'd got someone lined up to wait for them. Oh, bugger, and there won't be anyone in their office now till the morning.'

'What were Saniserve trying to deliver?' asked Charles cautiously.

'Only the most important thing in the entire operation. That without which the show cannot go ahead.' He looked at her quizzically, as he sifted through the possibilities. Extra lights? Back-up generator? Fire extinguishers?

'Portaloos,' Moira announced. 'We've got nine hundred people booked in tomorrow. At the moment there are no seats for them to sit on to watch *Twelfth Night*, but that's OK – we could still go ahead with the performance. But if we've got no toilets for them to sit on, then we might as well forget the whole thing!'

'Oh.'

'Charles, you may think a festival like this is about the plays and the concerts and the performers who come together down here. It isn't. All it comes down to basically is seats and lavatories – that's the bottom line.'

He grinned at her inadvertent pun, and was pleased that, through her annoyance, she could see the funny side too.

'But, if worst comes to worst, can't the audience use the loos inside the house?'

Moira's hands shot up to her face in mock-horror at the suggestion. 'Inside *Chailey Ferrars*?'

'Uhuh.'

'Charles, you could have the entire audience in the terminal stages of dysentery and the Trustees would still not let them inside Chailey Ferrars out of opening hours – and unless they'd bought entry tickets.'

'Ah, dealing with dinosaurs here, are you?'

'Good heavens, no,' said Moira. 'They're not nearly as far advanced along the evolutionary track as dinosaurs.'

Charles chuckled. He liked her cynical turn of phrase. And she was very tactile.

'Better be on your way, Pauline,' Moira called across the room. 'Big day tomorrow. You'll need your sleep.'

'Oh, I don't think I'll sleep a wink tonight,' said the press officer, gathering a sheaf of papers on her desk. 'The thought of all those press people coming.'

'Or not coming,' Moira suggested.

'Mm. I think I'd prefer that. If I actually knew that none of them was coming, then I could relax.'

Once again Charles was forced to question whether Pauline Monkton had the right priorities for someone in the job she had been given.

'Still raining out there, is it, Moira?'

'Pissing down.'

'I'd better take another of these.' Pauline Monkton reached to a pile of polythene-bagged plastic anoraks. She split one out of its package and slipped it on, revealing the MUTUAL RELIABLE logo on the back.

'You seem to have plenty of those,' Charles observed.

'Yes,' Moira agreed. 'Bye,' she said in response to Pauline Monkton's muttered 'See you in the morning.' The press officer scuttled out into the dark, holding her hood up against the continuing downpour.

Moira Handley looked at Charles Paris and grinned. He grinned back, as she picked up the conversation. 'Bit ironic having all those anoraks, actually, since we've now lost Mutual Reliable as a sponsor.'

'Really?'

'They supported the festival last year – seemed all set to do it again – then suddenly backed out three months ago. Needless to say, just after we'd had the preliminary programme printed – with their name all over everything.'

'Why'd they back out?'

Moira Handley spread out her hands and made a little plosive, 'Pff. Didn't reckon they were getting enough out of it. Sponsorship's not undiluted, altruistic charity, you know. All sponsors want a *quid pro quo*. It was decided at Mutual Reliable that they weren't getting their *quid* – or is it their *quo*? – out of the Great Wensham Festival, so...' She shrugged. 'Now they're sponsoring a golf tournament instead.'

'Oh?'

'The majority of the corporate clients would much rather get hopelessly pissed in a marquee at a golf club than have to sit through three hours of Shakespeare.'

'So who's sponsoring the festival now?'

Moira shrugged again. 'A hotch-potch of local firms and, let's say, anyone we can get our hands on. Anyone who'll stump up a few bob. And in the mean time we have to go round scratching Mutual Reliable logos off everything in sight – and trying to offload the plastic anorak mountain.' She gestured to the pile. 'We're handing them out all over. You fancy one?'

'For the rest of the rehearsal, you bet. And Alexandru'd probably think it was great. He seems determined to get as many anachronisms into this production as possible.'

'I don't detect a little hint of criticism there, do I, Charles Paris...'

'What? Heaven forbid.' But he could tell she saw through his denial. 'Anyway, even if the director sanctioned an entire production of *Twelfth Night* in Mutual Reliable anoraks, I somehow don't think the lighting designer would allow it.'

'No.'

Charles still felt soggy, but better in the warmth of the Portakabin. The wine was slipping down a treat too. And he didn't think he was completely misreading the signals in Moira Handley's shrewd brown eyes.

He looked round the room. 'So this is your domain, eh?'

'Part of it. Won't be able to shift from here much till your show's opened tomorrow night.'

Charles listened to the rain drumming on the flat roof. 'If it *does* open tomorrow night. Don't suppose you've got nine hundred of those anoraks, have you – one for each member of the audience?'

''Fraid not.' She picked up from what she'd been saying before. 'So I'll be staying here tonight...'

'Will you?' asked Charles foolishly.

'Mm.' She offered him an enigmatic grin. 'More wine?'

'Please.'

After she'd filled the glasses, there was no doubt that she ended up closer to him on the dead sofa.

'You married, are you, Charles?'

The direct question gave him a straight choice. If he really meant what he kept telling himself about his need to get back with Frances, then he should say 'Yes'. To say 'No' would show up the hollowness of all his fine protestations.

In the event, he replied, 'Well, still technically, but...How about you?'

A firm shake of the head. 'Never appealed. The thought of committing myself to one man...The thought of only ever making love to one man for the rest of my life...Well, not for me, I'm afraid.' Slowly but definitely, she put her hand on Charles's knee. 'The thought of making love to lots of different men, though... The thought of making love to any man I fancy...That I find more attractive.'

'Mm...Yes, it's a good philosophy, that. Good approach to life, really,' he agreed fatuously.

Moira gave another of her little shrugs. 'Workable, anyway.'

'Right.' There could be no doubt about her signals now. Charles, rendered doubly cautious by the existing climate of political correctness surrounding all interpersonal relationships, still couldn't find any ambiguity in what she said.

He looked into her eyes. They were sharp and teasing, daring him to take action. His face moved towards hers.

Their lips were almost touching when they were stopped by an electronic crackling. It came from a field telephone on a desk.

A voice emerged through the bacon-sizzling sound. 'Does anyone know where the hell Charles Paris is? He's needed on stage *immediately*.'

Chapter Sixteen

HIS BOOT-SOLES skidding in the mud, Charles Paris hurried back through the trees towards the stage. Rain still dripped obstinately from the branches and sheeted across the open spaces below. He wished he had taken one of the Mutual Reliable anoraks, after all.

As he had the thought, someone dressed in one came hurrying towards him. It was a woman; the thin working light caught on the water-shiny plastic outline of her breasts. Though the head was averted against the weather – or perhaps against him – Charles could see straggling blond hair flicker out from under the anorak's hood.

The woman said nothing to him, possibly hadn't even seen him, but turned abruptly away between the trees in the direction of the cast caravans.

Charles pressed forward, feeling an idiot. For him to have missed his cue was a serious black mark. A tech is hell for everyone, a major test of company patience, but it is the duty of all cast members to be on hand – or at least somewhere whence they can be quickly summoned – at all times. There are enough technical problems to slow the process down without lost actors screwing things up. Charles didn't anticipate a warm welcome when he made his belated entrance.

On top of that, he was feeling stupid about what had happened with Moira. He berated himself for the weakness of his will. She was attractive, she appeared to be amenable – even enthusiastic – but he still shouldn't have responded so easily. His sole aim in life should be to make it up with Frances, for God's sake.

Charles dived into the hessian tunnel which led to the stage. It seemed even narrower and clammier than it had before.

He skidded to the wing area and almost cannoned into Sally Luther, dressed in her soggy Cesario costume. Her blond wig dangled in tendrils like overcooked pasta.

'Oh, I'm so sorry, Sally.'

'Where the hell have you been?'

'Got delayed.' He popped his head out on to the stage and shouted, 'Sorry, Alex! I'm here now!' then smartly popped back in before the director could start bawling him out.

Sally Luther moved on to the stage and shouted, 'Can I get back to my dressing room now he's here, Alex?'

'No.'

'Oh, for God's sake! We've already been doing this scene for half an hour.'

'Sally, I'm sorry, but we need the bridge between the scenes, because we've got to do the lighting change and move the chairs. We'll have to go back on the end of your scene. Take it from "O time, thou must untangle this…" Oh, just a minute –' He had been interrupted by the lighting designer. 'No, we've just got to reset a couple of lanterns. Could be five minutes. Nobody leave the stage…And that includes you, Charles Paris, you unprofessional bastard!'

Charles was stung by the words. To be called unprofessional is the worst insult any actor can receive – particularly when he knows the aspersion is justified. He shrunk into the wings against the damp hessian, as Sally Luther and Chad Pearson came off stage to join him.

'I wouldn't get too close to that if I was you,' the actress advised.

'Mm?'

'There's a holly bush or something behind it. I was standing there a minute ago and I got quite a nasty prick through the hessian. Just in the fleshy bit of my thigh – really stung.'

'Oh. Right. Thanks.' Charles moved further away from the screening, and saw that he was now directly in view of half the audience (assuming that the Chailey Ferrars *Twelfth Night* ever did have an audience, an idea which at that moment seemed a laughable fantasy). 'Tight on sight-lines, isn't it?' Charles observed as he shrank back into the wings.

'OK, we're set!' Alexandru Radulescu's voice bawled out from the darkness. 'Back to "O time, thou must untangle…", Sally. And make sure you're ready for your cue, Charles bloody Paris!'

Sally Luther ventured back into the downpour to complete her soliloquy at the end of Act Two, Scene Two.

"O, time, thou must untangle this, not I!

It is too hard a knot for me t'untie."'

Shaking her head wearily – and to the sound of doleful sitar music – she moved off into the wings where Sir Toby Belch and Sir Andrew Aguecheek waited. Charles had always thought it a clumsy bit of blocking from Alexandru Radulescu to have her exit the same way they were about to come on, but he didn't think this was the moment to raise the point.

'Thank God for that,' Sally Luther muttered as she passed. 'I'm not in the next scene.' And she hurried off towards the 'dressing rooms'.

Charles Paris and Chad Pearson made their entrance and then had to wait in the rain for further adjustment of the lights. The *Twelfth Night* tech wound on its weary course. At the current rate of progress, Charles reckoned they'd be lucky to finish before four in the morning.

And a wicked, but unsuppressible thought inside him conjectured what kind of response a knock on the Portakabin door at four in the morning might get.

* * *

In the event, he never found out. The tech was not allowed to run its full course.

In the middle of Act Two, Scene Four, Orsino had just asked 'Cesario', 'And what's her history?'

Sally Luther replied,

'"A blank, my lord. She never told her love,
But let concealment like a worm i'the bud
Feed on her –"'

Suddenly she clutched at her throat and started gagging. She fell down on to the wet stage.

After what seemed an age, an ambulance made it across the muddy grounds of Chailey Ferrars to pick up the invalid and take her to the local hospital.

And on the next morning's radio and television news bulletins it was announced that Sally Luther was dead.

Chapter Seventeen

THE TECH HAD ended in chaos with less than a third of the play rehearsed, so it was no surprise to have a company call for ten o'clock the following morning, the Tuesday, the day *Twelfth Night* was due to open. Very few in the cast expected that opening to happen as scheduled.

Charles Paris had gone back to his digs and slept little. (Somehow, in the circumstances, knocking on the door of Moira's Portakabin had seemed inappropriate.) He made a point of getting back to Chailey Ferrars early in the morning.

The weather had miraculously changed. As if Sally Luther's death had been some ritual sacrifice to propitiate the rain gods, the Tuesday dawned bright and clear. Underfoot remained muddy, but the growing warmth of the sun promised to dry out the sodden field.

Moira's prodigious organisational skills were paying off. As Charles arrived at nine-thirty, groups of men were bolting together the metal structure of a raked auditorium. Women and boys were unloading stacks of chairs from a drop-side truck. Already the front few rows were fixed in position. So the audience would have seats to sit on that evening – though whether there would be a show for them to watch was more doubtful.

At the back of the auditorium stood two Land Rovers towing large caravans with the name 'Saniserve' printed on their sides. Moira had sorted that out too. Not only would the audience have seats to sit on, they would also be able to relieve themselves. There was nothing to stop the first night performance from going ahead – except its lack of a central character.

Charles Paris knew exactly what he needed to do. He went straight up on to the stage to the wings through which he had exited and entered the night before. In the daylight the tented area looked untidy and amateur. The hessian drapes hung damply down, but already, where the beams of the sun caught them, a thin steam was beginning to rise.

Charles tried to remember Sally's exact words. Something about being careful, not standing too close to the drapes... About a holly bush... About feeling something prick through... Something stinging her upper thigh...

He probed gingerly along the soggy fabric hanging, but could feel nothing pressing through from behind. He went backstage to check. The hessian screen, shabbier from this side and supported on irregularly angled tent-poles, stood proud from the surrounding trees and shrubs. There was no holly bush for Sally Luther to have leant against.

Which meant that if something had punctured her skin, it must have been pushed through the drape from the other side. And Charles Paris didn't find it fanciful to think that something might have been a syringe.

This was serious now. Gavin Scholes could possibly have been struck down by a genuine illness. John B. Murgatroyd's attack might just conceivably have been accidental food poisoning. But Sally Luther was dead, and it seemed very likely that she had been murdered.

Charles kicked himself for not taking action earlier. If he'd voiced his suspicions, the poor girl's death might have been averted.

On the other hand, the familiar question arose of who he should have voiced his suspicions *to*. Previous experience had taught Charles that the police have a distinctly sceptical attitude to intimations of murder – particularly when they come from members of the theatrical profession. That all actors are self-dramatising and effete – and probably gay – seemed to be an enduring conviction amongst the British constabulary.

He would need unanswerably solid proof of wrongdoing before he could take his accusations to the proper authorities. And at the moment he had no proof at all, only vague suspicions and a few, inadequately connected, links of logic.

There was also his position in the company to consider. Charles Paris was already unpopular enough, without starting to spray around accusations of murder. He needed to be extraordinarily certain of his facts before he challenged anyone. A misplaced allegation of serious criminality from one cast member to another could prove to be a very inauspicious opening to a three-month tour.

There was of course a strong chance that if Sally Luther had been murdered the police would soon be on to the case. A death as sudden as hers must inevitably demand a post-mortem, and if its finding showed she had been injected with poison, then the *Twelfth Night* company would quickly be swamped by inquisitive police officers.

But if, for some reason, that didn't happen... Charles had to find out more.

The Great Wensham Festival officials had turned out in force for the ten o'clock call on stage at Chailey Ferrars. The Festival Director was there, along with Moira Handley and Pauline Monkton. Asphodel's accountant was also present, flanked by Alexandru Radulescu, the lighting designer and the assistant director.

Alexandru was the most overtly irritated by Julian Roxborough-Smith's long-winded oration, tapping his hand crossly against his knee, anxious to be active.

'...a terrible tragedy of the kind which I am glad to say is unprecedented in the history of the Great Wensham Festival. On behalf of the Festival Society – and of course of our sponsors – I will be sending appropriate condolences to Miss Luther's family.'

The company, in the front rows of audience seating, were as impatient as their Director. They wanted to know what decisions had been made, and they wanted to know as soon as possible. All were twitchy. Only Talya Northcott looked serene, as her mind formulated the dream that was about to come true. 'UNDERSTUDY RISES TO TRAGIC CHALLENGE – A STAR IS BORN!' Mummy would really enjoy telling her friends about that. The scrapbook would fill up very quickly.

'One point I should mention,' Julian Roxborough-Smith ground on, 'is that there are always people who feed on and try to benefit from disaster – I refer of course to the press – and it's not impossible that, after what's happened, Great Wensham will become the target of the tabloid hacks. The Chailey Ferrars staff will be doing their best to keep these scavengers out, but in the event that any of you are approached by journalists, I would ask you to say nothing, just address all enquiries through the festival's press officer...'

Pauline Monkton squirmed at the thought of more limelight and responsibility.

'...who I am sure is better qualified to handle such enquiries than you are.'

The panic in the press officer's eyes cast doubt on the truth of this assertion. 'We've had lots of calls already, Julian,' she whispered breathlessly, 'and I really don't know what to say to them. I think, if I just leave the answerphone on then they'll probably stop ringing after a time.'

Annoyance tugged at the corner of the Festival Director's mouth, but he was too professional to give his press officer a public dressing-down for wimpishness and general incompetence, so moved smoothly on.

'If, on the other hand, you are approached by the police – and I don't at this stage know whether there is likely to be any form of police investigation – I would obviously rely on you all to co-operate fully.'

'However...' He sighed and adjusted his floppy bow-tie '...with every setback – even one so terrible and shocking as this – the question that must follow on from any tragedy is: "Where do we go from here?" I've just come from a meeting with your director and...' He clearly didn't know the name of the person to whom he gestured...this gentleman from Asphodel Productions, at which meeting we discussed the various options that are open to us.

'While I support in principle the old adage that "the show must go on," I am sure that you will all agree the show should only go on if the performance is of a standard that will not do discredit to your own high professional standards. Now in this instance a variety of potential scenarios offer themselves to us if we –'

'Oh, for Christ's sake, get on with it!' Alexandru Radulescu's patience was exhausted. 'We're incredibly pushed for time, and you're just wasting more of it with all this long-winded crap!'

Julian Roxborough-Smith was so unused to anyone speaking to him like this that he could only gape and straighten his bow-tie. Charles noticed that her boss's discomfiture brought an irrepressible grin to Moira's lips. She'd enjoy seeing that kind of thing happen more often.

The Asphodel representative suavely interceded to cover up Alexandru's rudeness. 'I'm sorry, Mr Roxborough-Smith, we're all obviously under a lot of stress.'

The Festival Director was still too shocked to do more than mouth back, so the accountant slid quickly on, 'And Alex does of course have a point. Time is of the essence, so I think, if it's all right with you...' He didn't give Julian Roxborough-Smith time to say whether it was or it wasn't '...I should hand straight over to our Director, so that he can put forward to the cast his proposed solution to the current crisis: a solution which – in keeping with most things Alex does – is extremely *radical*.'

Charles groaned inwardly, as the small figure of the director stepped forward. The black eyes gleamed with fanatical zeal.

'Friends, fellow-workers, fellow-artistes,' Alexandru Radulescu began. 'In no way do I wish to diminish what has happened. It is a terrible thing. Sally was one of us – we have lost her. At the proper time we will mourn her properly. But for now my priority must be *Twelfth Night*.'

Why suddenly? Charles's cynical mind couldn't help supplying the question. It never has been before.

'This is not just my priority – it is *our* priority. And it is a priority which Sally – of all people – would have respected. The show, as Julian has said, must go on. The question is how soon it goes on. My proposal is that we open tonight as scheduled.'

A collective gasp of astonishment rose from the company. They were all troupers, but surely what their director was suggesting was impossible.

Talya Northcott voiced the communal objection. As understudy to Viola, she had more reason than most to be anxious. 'But, Alex, we just haven't got time. I mean, I know the lines all right, but I'd have to go through all the blocking and –'

'Besides,' the lighting designer chipped in, 'we haven't done the tech on the second two-thirds of the show. We've only got the roughest kind of plotting done for that.'

'You can continue plotting as we rehearse,' Alexandru announced magisterially.

'But look, that'll be daylight. We won't be able to judge how the –'

'That is what we will do.'

He did not raise his voice, but the words were a testament to the strength of the little man's personality. The lighting designer was silent as his director repeated, 'We will open tonight, as scheduled.'

'But don't you think that shows a lack of respect for Sally's memory – as if we don't think her death's important?'

This latest objection, from Benzo Ritter, was slapped down as firmly as the others. 'I do not think so. She was an actress. She would understand.

229

Tonight's performance will not be a disrespect to Sally Luther – it will be a tribute to Sally Luther.'

Alexandru Radulescu knew he had everyone's attention and he played his scene to the full. 'As I say, we will open tonight, as scheduled...' He turned to Talya Northcott '...But I am sorry, my dear, you will not be playing Viola.'

Like Julian Roxborough-Smith before her, the girl was stunned into silence. She too mouthed hopelessly. Charles felt sure she had already been on the phone to Mummy about her big break, and Mummy had already rung round all her family and friends. Some embarrassing calling back was going to be necessary.

'I have said before,' Alexandru continued, 'that what some people regard as problems, I see as positive creative opportunities. All through rehearsal we have been saying that *Twelfth Night* is Shakespeare's exploration of the potentialities of human sexuality...'

Charles's knee-jerk reaction – 'No, it isn't!' – once again remained unspoken.

'....and a solution to our current problem which extends the range of this exploration occurred to me very early this morning. It will need some revised blocking towards the end of the play, but this is not insuperable. You see...' He turned again to the stricken Talya. '...we already have someone in the company who is fully rehearsed in the part of Viola. Yes, my friends, we will open *Twelfth Night* tonight with the parts of Sebastian *and* Viola both being played by Russ Lavery!'

There was another gasp from the company, which quickly gave way to delighted applause. Charles Paris looked round the semicircle of faces to gauge reactions. Apart from Talya Northcott, who could not suppress her tears, Benzo Ritter seemed to be the only one downcast by the news, presumably because he still thought it betokened disrespect to his lost idol.

Vasile Bogdan and Tottie Roundwood were ecstatic in their appreciation for another stroke of Radulescu genius. Chad Pearson shook his head, chuckling at the audacity of the solution.

And on the face of Russ Lavery was an expression of unambiguous triumph.

Chapter Eighteen

THE REST OF the day was a tribute to the organisational skills of Alexandru Radulescu. He started by rehearsing Act Five, the only moment in the play where Viola and Sebastian, brother and sister, are both on stage at the same time.

He must have been up all night devising the blocking for this confrontation. Inevitably it involved the use of a double. Talya Northcott, who had been cast for her physical likeness to the compact Sally Luther, was awarded this role (the nearest she was ever going to get to playing Viola), but all the lines were to be spoken by Russ Lavery. Mummy and the large party of family and friends she had conscripted for the first night, were due for a disappointment.

In Alexandru's revised blocking, by ingenious use of the entrances and exits, by a lot of crossing behind the emblematic trees of the simple set, Viola and Sebastian appeared, reappeared and changed roles as in some elaborate conjuring trick.

When the Duke, upstage of the identical pair who faced him, said in wonderment:

'One face, one voice, one habit, and two persons!

A natural perspective, that is and is not',

few of the company would have disagreed with him. The director had created another moment of theatrical magic.

Even Charles Paris, who thought this new twist only served to push Shakespeare's play further out of true, could not help but be impressed.

Given the opportunity, Russ Lavery demonstrated what an exceptional actor he was. After the popular success of *Air-Sea Rescue*, in which he played an amiable but two-dimensional character, there had been a tendency in the profession to dismiss him as 'very limited – plays the one part fine, but that's it.' Russ Lavery's work on *Twelfth Night* that day refuted any such criticism.

As he had begun to in the experiments during rehearsal, he created two totally different characters for Sebastian and Viola. The physical likeness was obviously there; there were vocal similarities – though Viola's voice was lighter and more feminine; but he differentiated the two so subtly that throughout the play there was never any question which of the twins had just come on stage.

In most productions of *Twelfth Night*, much effort is expended to make two people of different sex – frequently also of different height, bulk and colouring – look alike. In Russ Lavery's performance – or performances – the likeness could be taken for granted, and so he was able to emphasise the differences between the two characters.

For anyone who knew anything about the theatre, the development was fascinating to watch. Russ Lavery's performance as Viola had come on so much from the sketchy outline he had revealed in previous rehearsal exercises.

It was almost as if he had prepared for this moment, as if he had known he would be playing the part.

The inhospitable nature of the Chailey Ferrars Trustees for once proved a benefit. During the day of rehearsal they kept the estate firmly shut, so that the horde of tabloid journalists, drawn to Great Wensham by Sally Luther's name and the whiff of potential scandal, was unable to get near the *Twelfth Night* company.

In fact, the only way they could get into Chailey Ferrars was by buying tickets for the evening's performance. This was good news for the box office, and also had the beneficial side-effect of introducing to Shakespeare people whose only previous contact with English literature had been 'GOTCHA!', 'PULPIT POOFTAHS!' and 'QUEEN: IT'S BEEN A BUM YEAR!'

Because of the intense rehearsal pressure, the grounds were not to be opened to the public until six-thirty, three-quarters of an hour before the performance. This caused a great deal of disgruntled harrumphing from hamper-laden regulars, who could not understand why something as minor as getting the performance right should be allowed to abbreviate the time they spent setting up their picnic tables.

The change in the weather had been maintained. The weekend's downpours had left the Chailey Ferrars lawns glowing with health; the surface moisture had dried off and the worst of the mud crusted hard. The audience seating was in place, chairs joined together in the requisite manner and passed as safe by the fire officer. The Saniserve lavatories were fixed and plumbed, ready for the worst the bladders and bowels of Great Wensham could throw at them. Volunteers were in position behind the bars of the refreshment tent, from which the spicy aroma of mulled wine fought for dominance with onion soup. Outside, under an awning, charcoal glowed beneath the grills which would soon be busy cooking hamburgers.

In the Patrons' and Sponsors' marquees (behind which were special Patrons' and Sponsors' superloos that played music and sprayed perfume), uniformed waitresses waited to dispense food and alcohol – the Sponsors' only tangible reward for putting money into the Arts. By the entrance gates, programme-sellers and usherettes, wearing sashes with the appalling 'GWF' logo on them, massed in readiness. Men in Mutual Reliable anoraks criss-crossed the auditorium, talking importantly into two-way radios.

Six-thirty arrived. Incredibly, the Asphodel company had just completed a full run of *Twelfth Night*. The new moves and business in Act Five had worked without a hitch. Alexandru Radulescu gave very few notes, thanked the cast for all their hard work and instructed them to 'fuck the bastards rigid!'

The great and the good of Great Wensham, at that moment admitted through the gates of the car-park into the Chailey Ferrars grounds, were unaware of this exhortation – which was probably just as well, because they were a very strait-laced bunch.

They hurried in, outpacing each other with their tables and hampers, desperate to secure the best pitches on the grassy slopes behind the seating. And they settled down to enjoy their picnics and... 'Which one is it this year...? Oh yes, *Twelfth Night.*'

The British notoriously love underdogs, they love stories of plucky little Britishers triumphing against overwhelming odds, so the first performance of the Asphodel *Twelfth Night* started on a wave of goodwill. The Great Wensham audience might not know a great deal about Shakespeare, but they were good on television drama and sitcoms, so the news of Sally Luther's death had shocked them all. The fact that the person stepping into the breach – as they were informed by a printed slip handed out with their programmes – was none other than Russ Lavery, who played Dr Mick Hobson in *Air-Sea Rescue*, ensured the production a sympathetically partisan reception.

But it wasn't just a softened-up audience that made the show go so well that night. And it wasn't just the communal spirit-of-the-blitz, let's-do-a-good-one-for-poor-old-Sally spirit that lifted the company to new heights. Alexandru Radulescu's production actually worked.

All the apparent perversities of his interpretation were ironed out in actual performance. The seemingly unconnected sequence of theatrical moments developed their own rhythm and momentum, as if they were part of some meticulously prepared master-plan. It still wasn't Shakespeare's *Twelfth Night*, but it was a fascinating theatrical experience.

What made it perfect for Great Wensham was that the production was experimental without being impenetrable. Somehow the outline of the story remained intact, so the audience's attention was held throughout. The show manifested a kind of licensed *enfant terriblisme*, which would enable the great and good of Great Wensham to say at drinks parties, 'Oh, I'm not against experimental theatre, you know. I mean, we saw that very radical reinterpretation of *Twelfth Night* at the festival, and we enjoyed that a lot, didn't we, darling?'

Even the company member most opposed to Alexandru Radulescu's innovations, Charles Paris, was forced to concede that the evening worked as a piece of theatre. To his annoyance, he even found himself caught up in the impetus of the production. His performance as Sir Toby Belch shifted away from the traditional – in his view, 'right' – way of playing the part towards the style Alexandru Radulescu had been trying to impose on him. A more than friendly relationship with Sir Andrew Aguecheek emerged – though it stopped short of the mooted homosexual kiss. And under his doublet Charles Paris did wear his Guns 'n' Roses T-shirt.

But the show's real triumph belonged undoubtedly to Russ Lavery. The improvement shown in the day's rehearsals was maintained through the evening. He must have been utterly exhausted, but an adrenaline high spurred him to ever greater achievement. The rest of the company were infinitely supportive to him and when, at the end of the performance, he came forward to take his solo bow, they joined in the audience's ecstatic ovation.

Russ Lavery, glowing with realised ambition, bowed and bowed again. He'd 'gone back to his theatrical roots' and grown from the experience. After his fourth solo bow, since the applause showed no signs of abating, he stretched out a hand into the wings and gestured the director to join him.

The tiny figure of Alexandru Radulescu bounced on-stage and took Russ Lavery's hand. They bowed together, incandescent in their mutual triumph.

Then the actor stepped forward and, managing eventually to still the audience, announced, 'Thank you very much, ladies and gentlemen. I'd just like to say, on behalf of the entire company and crew, that we dedicate tonight's performance to the memory of a great actress and a very dear friend – Sally Luther. We love you, Sally – and we did it for you!' As Russ stepped modestly back, the audience erupted into an even more vigorous ovation. For them the evening had had everything: a sensational news story, a star familiar from television, an 'understudy triumphs' backstage drama – all overlaid with the righteous, self-justifying glow of having 'seen some Shakespeare.'

All of the company were invited by Julian Roxborough-Smith to have a post-performance drink in the Patrons' marquee. After the traumas and hard work of the previous thirty-six hours, they had earned it.

Charles Paris, who hadn't touched a drop since the wine he'd shared with Moira Handley in her Portakabin, eagerly seized a glass of red from the tray of a passing waitress.

'It's refreshing to see a production which conceptualises from an alternative learning base and challenges the diktats of traditional authoritors, isn't it?'

If he hadn't recognised her face, Charles would have known instantly that the granny-spectacled woman speaking to him was Carole Whittaker of HAN.

'Erm...well...yes,' he hazarded.

'Radulescu has an almost post-modernist attitude to the text *qua* text, synergising a kind of input to Shakespeare whose outreach goes beyond the microcosm of received and conformable educational data – don't you agree?'

'You're not wrong.'

'So his extrapolations from the atavistically protected corpus of words known conveniently as *Twelfth Night* come to represent a parallel but diverse textual statement.'

Charles Paris thought he almost understood that bit. 'You mean he's created a *Twelfth Night* that is different from Shakespeare's *Twelfth Night*?'

'At the most primitive level, yes. But at the same time a process of inter-textualising is at work, so that not only the verbalisation is transformed, but the received definition of the media-related categorisation in which the opus partakes is also challenged.'

'Hm. Too right.' Charles nodded. 'Erm...Will you excuse me...?'

Carole Whittaker seemed unworried by his abrupt departure and moved to share her thoughts with Sir Andrew Aguecheek. Charles would always treasure the image of growing puzzlement that spread across Chad Pearson's genial features.

Alexandru Radulescu was moving round the room, gathering plaudits and spreading congratulations. He came face to face with Charles, and grinned. 'Coming better, yes...? I was right about how Sir Toby should be played – no?'

'Well...' To have agreed would have been total hypocrisy. In performance Charles might have come closer to Alexandru's views, but he still didn't believe the director was 'right'. He salved his conscience by avoiding the direct question and making a general comment. 'Thought the whole thing went wonderfully well – congratulations.'

The conversation might have continued, had Alexandru Radulescu not been swept away by Julian Roxborough-Smith to meet Great Wensham's mayor, 'who is also a past president of the Great Wensham Rotary Club.'

Charles found himself face to face with Moira Handley. She grinned, but he noticed the tight lines of tiredness around her eyes. 'Very good,' she said. 'I gather it went very well.'

He experienced the little pang all actors feel at such moments. 'You mean you didn't see it?'

'Saw the first ten minutes and most of the last act. We have got other performances on, you know. I had to put in an appearance at a Bach piano recital and a one-man show about W. B. Yeats.'

'Ah.'

'Then tomorrow it's Palestrina in St Michael's Church, a lecture on stained glass at the community centre, literary lunch at the Marlborough Hotel, bagpipes in the town square, Mozart in the Corn Exchange, the Amateur Operatics' *Brigadoon*... A few other events I've forgotten, finishing with alternative stand-up in the big top.'

'Busy schedule.'

'You could say that.'

'Well, if you have time in that busy schedule for a quick drink at some point?'

Moira Handley shook her head ruefully. 'Don't see it, Charles.'

'Oh.'

'I think we had a moment, you know, but I think it's probably passed.'

'Mm. Probably.'

He might have been left standing there pathetic and awkward if Pauline Monkton hadn't bustled up. She was bubbling with enthusiasm and self-confidence.

'Well, talk about press coverage, eh?'

Moira turned her quizzical gaze on the press officer, but said nothing.

'Couldn't have been better. All the nationals here. I think the secret with publicity...' Pauline Monkton confided knowingly, '...is not to bother about the RSVPs. Oh yes, put them on the invitations, by all means, but if nobody replies, don't worry about it. Doesn't mean they're not coming. Oh no, publicity is about targeting the right individuals. Get the right press list, distribute invitations to the right people, and they'll come, no problem. Even spread it among their fellow journalists. Do you know,' her voice dropped to an awed tone, 'there are press here tonight who I *didn't even invite*.' She nodded complacently. 'Shows they got the message this was a first night that just shouldn't be missed.'

Charles and Moira exchanged looks, and he could tell they shared the same thought. The press presence at Great Wensham that evening had nothing to do with Pauline Monkton's strategy – with or without RSVPs. It was prompted entirely by the news of Sally Luther's death. But neither of them would be so cruel as to tell the press officer that.

Moira was summoned away to sort out some other cock-up over the volunteers, another task which Julian Roxborough-Smith had assured her he had 'completely in hand'. Charles, left on his own, scooped up a second glass of wine from a waitress's tray, and looked around the scene.

It was really remarkable how little Sally Luther's death had impacted on the *Twelfth Night* company. Sure, at that moment they were all caught up in the communal euphoria of having got the show on against the odds, but he'd have expected a little more introspection. Instead, it seemed as though Russ Lavery's formal acknowledgement of the death had closed the subject. Sally Luther need never be thought about again.

The only person who still seemed affected by her absence was Benzo Ritter. The boy's face looked stressed, but even he was perking up. A few more drinks and he too would be able to forget his infatuation – at least for a little while.

Charles Paris wondered whether Sally Luther's murderer was in the marquee at that moment. If his theory was right, if her death had been one in a sequence of poisonings, then that was likely.

The perpetrator must have been present at the Chailey Ferrars press conference after which Gavin Scholes had become ill, in the Indian restaurant which did for John B. Murgatroyd, and around the stage during the *Twelfth Night* tech the previous evening.

The only people who qualified were Talya Northcott, Tottie Roundwood and Vasile Bogdan. Talya had not come to the Sponsors' marquee for a drink; she had been taken away by Mummy to have her wounded pride soothed with assurances that she would have made a much better Viola than Russ Lavery.

But Charles noticed his other two suspects were in the marquee talking together, and he edged through the crowd in their direction. Standing with his back to them, pretending interest in a poster-size festival programme, he listened to what they were saying.

'A triumph,' Tottie Roundwood enthused. 'He's got exactly what he wanted.'

'Oh yes,' Vasile Bogdan agreed. 'And I think we can confidently state that he wouldn't have got it without our help, don't you?'

Chapter Nineteen

ONE NAME dominated the news pages of the next day's tabloids: Sally Luther. The death of a pretty actress – prettier in the archive photographs they reprinted from her sitcom heyday – was a good popular story.

Her career was recapitulated and analysed. The days when her face was a fixture on the nation's television screens were recalled, together with tales of the fervour she inspired in her fans. At her peak she was the recipient of a massive postbag, including the usual creepy, obsessive letters that beautiful public faces inspire.

She'd even had the ultimate showbiz accolade of a stalker, who followed her around for some months. Unusually, she had been pursued and spied on by a woman rather than a man. Though this made her feel less threatened, it was still unnerving. Eventually she had called in the police, and her action had the right effect; the pestering instantly ceased.

As well as recalling her career, the papers were lavish with tributes to Sally Luther from other showbiz names. The television executives who'd turned their backs during the eclipse of her popularity all came forward to say what a fine actress and delightful person she had been, how much they'd loved working with her, and how disappointed they'd be not to work with her again.

The circumstances of her death were described, but few details were known beyond the facts that she'd been taken ill on stage during rehearsal and had died in hospital. One of the papers tried kite-flying the expression 'mystery illness', but if they hoped that would give rise to speculation about AIDS, they had reckoned without the affection in which Sally Luther had been held. For the great British public – particularly after her death – she represented the squeaky-clean girl next door; they would never dream of associating her with something as squalid as AIDS.

But if Sally Luther had colonised the front of the papers, the Arts pages were dominated by two names – Alexandru Radulescu and Russ Lavery.

The Asphodel production of *Twelfth Night* got an astonishing amount of coverage. Neither Pauline Monkton's cunning 'targeting of the right individuals', nor the additional interest given by Sally Luther's death was sufficient to explain the number of national critics who had been at the first night.

The reason was Alexandru Radulescu. He was – at least for a few months – the current vogue name, and no one who mattered in British theatre wanted to risk missing his latest production. Even if it meant forsaking the West End for the comparative wilds of Great Wensham, they had to be there. No doubt Radulescu and the Radulescu style would soon be condemned as 'dated' and 'meretricious', but during his brief moment in the sun he was the director who could do no wrong.

His revisualisation of *Twelfth Night* was hailed as 'mould-breaking', 'daringly different', 'a radical reinterpretation of what had always been thought of as a safe old play' and 'an evening of pure theatre that challenges the spectator's every preconception.'

Charles Paris could have spit.

He wasn't surprised that an untutored audience would go for Alexandru's flashy tricks, but he was amazed that professional critics could be seduced by such modish claptrap. Surely they should respect Shakespeare's text, and recognise when it was being traduced – that was their job, for God's sake! Critics should uphold the enduring values of the great British literary tradition, not be a prey to every new fad that comes along.

Even as he had the thought, Charles Paris realised how impossibly reactionary it sounded. Maybe he really was past his sell-by date. Maybe the values he represented were going the way of the dinosaurs. For a moment he was undermined by the appalling possibility that Alexandru Radulescu might be right.

But if the director was one of the golden boys of British theatre, there was another coming up fast to share the limelight. Russ Lavery had the kind of reviews even he – and his ego was of no mean proportions – would have been too bashful to write for himself.

The words 'star' and 'genius' were bandied about like small change. 'A truly great Shakespearean performance,' one critic enthused. 'To be at Chailey Ferrars last night was to know what it must have been like to witness the debut of Garrick or Kean.'

Oh, for heaven's sake, thought Charles. What is going on here? He would never be able to understand the random cycle of critical opinion. He had rehearsed many shows he thought excellent, and then seen them suffer savage dismemberment by the critics. He had been in productions he regarded as total shit, which had received rose-scented notices. It made no sense at all.

All he knew about criticism was that the only reviews he remembered were the bad ones. Over the years he must have had a good few laudatory notices – come on, he *must* have done – but all that stayed with him were of a type with the one he'd once received from *Plays & Players*: 'Charles Paris was also in the cast, though why is a question which neither the director nor the playwright seemed prepared to address.'

The cast were given the chance of a lie-in on the Wednesday morning, but there was a rehearsal call for two o'clock in the afternoon. The triumph of the first night had been the product of luck, adrenaline and a sense of occasion. There were still details in the production that needed to be gone over and fixed.

Needless to say, most of these moments involved Russ Lavery. He was the one who, in his role as Viola, had suddenly taken on a lot of new scenes and, though his first night performance had been stunning, at times he had been flying on a wing and a prayer.

Most of Viola's important scenes were with Orsino or Olivia, so Sir Toby Belch and his cronies were not called for rehearsal till five o'clock. Charles Paris, who had risen after his landlady had stopped serving breakfast, reckoned that the late call justified a pub lunch.

He wandered out looking for the centre of Great Wensham, but found that, in common with many other English country towns, its centre had been removed. Where one might have expected a characterful town square was a brick-paved pedestrian shopping precinct, featuring Marks & Spencers, Currys, Next, the Body Shop and all the chain-store names that appear in every other English town and city.

Still, he found a pub, Ye Olde King's Head, which looked as if its construction had been completed the day before. He bought a pint of beer, ordered a lasagne, and sat down with his drink. A compilation of *Hits of the Sixties* was playing just too loud in the background.

Damn, he'd meant to buy a *Times*. Then he could have had a go at the crossword until his food came. Without a paper, though, he couldn't avoid thinking about Sally Luther's death.

He was convinced she had been murdered, poisoned by a fatal injection pushed through the hessian screen in the wings at Chailey Ferrars.

He was also convinced that her death was the culmination of a sequence of poisonings. Gavin Scholes, John B. Murgatroyd, Sally Luther.

The question was: who had gained from that sequence of events? The obvious beneficiary of Gavin's removal had been Alexandru Radulescu, who took over the production of *Twelfth Night*. But the director could not have been directly responsible for the first poisoning because he had been nowhere near Chailey Ferrars when it happened.

The idea of Radulescu having someone doing his dirty work for him, though, was quite appealing. And if he'd had an accomplice, then the obvious candidate for the role was Vasile Bogdan. That would certainly explain the conversation Charles had overheard in the Gents at the Willesden rehearsal room.

But when Gavin's poisoning was considered in conjunction with Sally Luther's death, the main beneficiary was undoubtedly Russ Lavery. Because of those two events, he had achieved the Sebastian/Viola double role which had restored his credibility as a stage actor. Was it possible that such an outcome had been planned from the start?

But Russ hadn't been at Chailey Ferrars either. Indeed, he had made a great public scene about not wanting to go to Chailey Ferrars. Could all that fuss have been deliberately set up to distance the actor from anything that might happen there?

If Russ was involved in Gavin's poisoning, then he too would have needed an accomplice. Maybe Vasile Bogdan also fitted that role...? It was Russ Lavery, Gavin had told Charles, who recommended Vasile as a suitable member of the company. Had there been a mutual exchange of favours between the two actors?

Or were they both involved in a conspiracy with Alexandru Radulescu?

The element that didn't fit into any of these possible scenarios was the poisoning of John B. Murgatroyd. In rehearsal he'd been proving unreceptive to the Director's ideas, but surely that wasn't sufficient reason to have him removed? The only person who had benefited directly from John B.'s illness was Chad Pearson who inherited the role of Sir Andrew Aguecheek, but Charles had great difficulty including Chad in any list of suspects.

On the other hand, suppose John B. had been right when he suggested that his poisoning had been a mistake? And that the intended victim had been Charles Paris...

That was a chilling thought, which prompted another, even more frightening.

Suppose Sally Luther's death had also been a mistake...

At the time she was stabbed with the syringe, she shouldn't have been in the wings anyway. She was only there, sheltering from the rain, while they waited for Charles Paris, who had missed his cue.

The person who should have been there in that cramped space, pressed against the damp hessian, was Charles Paris himself.

Now the sequence of crimes had a logic. Gavin Scholes had been poisoned so that Vasile Bogdan would have the director he wanted. To get the part he wanted, Vasile'd have to remove Charles Paris. He'd made one attempt at the Indian restaurant, and another during the tech run. On each occasion he had caught the wrong victim.

But he was unlikely to let that stop him trying again.

Charles Paris's lasagne was delivered to his table. He looked down at the greasy, yellow, microwaved slabs, and he didn't feel hungry.

Chapter Twenty

THE RAIN did not return and the Wednesday evening was idyllically warm.

It was positively hot in the caravan dressing room as they waited for the 'beginners' call. Charles felt uncomfortable in his thick Sir Toby Belch costume. He also felt uncomfortable because Vasile Bogdan was there too. Still, no immediate danger – they weren't alone together. Russ Lavery, Benzo Ritter and Tottie Roundwood were also present, lounging around, pretending they weren't nervous and glancing idly through the newspaper reports of Sally Luther's death.

'Dreadful business, isn't it?' said Charles, for want of something else to say.

The others agreed it was.

'She was so young.'

Russ Lavery, wearing a dress for Viola's first appearance in Illyria and sitting in a neat feminine pose, nodded uneasily. 'Kind of thing happens too often for my liking. Chum of mine, only my age, just got married, suddenly keeled over a couple of months back. Heart attack. Dreadful.'

From the nodding reactions of the others, it seemed no one thought there was anything suspicious about Sally's death. But, since he'd raised the subject, Charles dared to probe a little further. 'I wonder what she died of?'

'Heart? Brain tumour?' Tottie Roundwood suggested. 'Usually one of those when it's as unexpected as that.'

'What do you think, Vasile?'

The only reaction he got was a shrug of the shoulders.

Charles decided to be even braver. 'Funny nobody's suggested the possibility of foul play...'

'Foul play?' Benzo Ritter echoed.

'Yes, foul play. Murder.'

'Don't be morbid, Charles,' said Tottie mildly.

Vasile Bogdan's reaction was anything but mild. 'That's a filthy suggestion!' he stormed. 'The poor girl's not been dead twenty-four hours. What on earth made you say that, you bloody fool?'

He'd gone too far. Charles tried to ease the situation with a *Twelfth Night* quote. '"Now Mercury endue thee with leasing, for thou speakest well of fools."'

Vasile, about to come back with a fierce rejoinder, was stopped by a tap on the caravan door. 'Act one beginners, please.' And they all trooped out for the opening dumb-show.

* * *

Thanks to the day's newspaper coverage – both sensational and artistic – all of the fixed seats for *Twelfth Night* were taken and spectators on folding chairs and rugs were densely spread over the surrounding slopes. Some of the audience that evening found the production a bit bizarre – it wasn't Shakespeare's play as they knew it – but the newspaper critics had told them it was good, so it must be. Anyway, they all enjoyed their picnics.

Charles Paris was very wary throughout the performance, watchful whenever Vasile Bogdan was in sight, and watching out for him when he wasn't. He knew he had to find some proof to back up his suspicions, and a plan was forming in his head as to how he might achieve that.

The show was a bit second-nightish. The audience wouldn't have noticed anything amiss, but the cast knew they hadn't quite scaled the peaks of the previous performance. There had been an inevitable sense of anti-climax, which many of the company proposed to counteract by a meal at the Great Wensham Tandoori.

Charles Paris, mindful of what had happened after the last communal Indian meal – and with his own plans for the rest of the evening – said he wouldn't join them. Nobody made any attempt to dissuade him from his decision.

In the cramped caravan, he removed the Sir Toby Belch costume and put on his street clothes. He felt the reassuring weight of a half-bottle of Bell's in his jacket pocket. What he was planning to do could well require some Dutch courage. In his other pocket were a pencil torch and a screwdriver.

Charles got a lift with the rest of the company in the festival minibus, which stopped outside the Great Wensham Tandoori. Studiedly dilatory in getting out of the bus, he was able to check who went into the restaurant.

He ticked off Alexandru Radulescu, Vasile Bogdan and Tottie Roundwood in the crowd that passed through the door. Good, that gave him at least an hour while they had their meal.

An hour, Charles reckoned, would be long enough. He reached into his pocket for the Bell's and prepared to snap the seal, but found the metal cap already loose. Dear oh dear, he must have had a swig earlier. Never mind. He braced himself with another long swallow.

The house that Tottie, Vasile and Alexandru were renting was on the outskirts of the town, conveniently without near neighbours. Charles had been prepared to use his screwdriver to force a lock or break a pane, but fortunately he found a downstairs window insecurely latched. Carelessness seemed to accompany hot weather.

After another emboldening swallow of Bell's, Charles Paris was quickly inside. His pencil torch showed he was in the sitting room. He moved through to the hall and up the stairs. Though not certain what he was looking for, he felt sure he was most likely to find it upstairs.

There were four doors – presumably three bedrooms and a bathroom –

leading off the small landing. Charles opened one, and flashed his pencil light across the room.

His eyes were immediately caught by a pile of books on the bedside table. Drawn by the line of his torch beam, he approached them.

One looked ominously familiar. Light reflected from the dull gold lettering on the green spine: Hay – *British Fungi*.

The other books were more authorities on the same subject. Charles took a triumphant swig from his Bell's bottle. He felt vindicated. There had to be something in this room that would positively incriminate Vasile Bogdan.

He swung his beam across the room to a rack of small opaque glass jars. Each seemed to contain a dry powder and was neatly labelled in a calligraphic hand. He moved forward to read the contents.

'Aconite', 'Arsenic', 'Belladonna'...Good God! He just had time to register that he'd found an entire poisoner's armoury before his attention was snatched away by something behind the rack.

A dress drooping from a coat-hanger.

He moved the torch beam round, revealing more dresses, skirts and blouses, some of which he recognised. The dressing table was littered with pots of face cream and make-up.

He was in Tottie Roundwood's room.

Just as he formulated this thought, Charles Paris heard the sound from downstairs of the front door opening.

Chapter Twenty-One

HE CAUGHT THE strong whiff of Indian food before he heard the voices. Damn, he should have considered the possibility of their having a takeaway. Still, presumably they'd eat in the dining room or kitchen. That should give him a chance to make a run for it out of the front door.

'Shall we eat this upstairs?' said a voice, dashing his hopes. It was Tottie Roundwood who had spoken, but a new Tottie Roundwood. The voice was sultry, even sexy.

'Have we got a corkscrew?' asked a male voice Charles also instantly recognised.

'No need,' she replied. 'This Italian plonk has a screw-top.'

'Good. Upstairs we go then.'

The landing light was switched on, sending a blade of brightness across the room in which Charles was cowering. The smell of the takeaway came ahead of the footsteps mounting the stairs. He looked desperately round. There was a window, but he didn't fancy launching himself into the dark from the first floor.

Hide under the bed, that was the only answer. Just as he'd done in that terrible adaptation of a French farce, *Follow Me, Fifi!* ('About as funny as an attack of shingles' – *Western Evening Press*).

Charles was under the bed with a faceful of dust before he remembered what had happened next in *Follow Me, Fifi!* A couple had come in, lain down on the bed and started making love.

The footsteps paused on the landing. There was the sound of a long, succulent kiss.

'Your place or mine?' Tottie Roundwood's voice asked throatily.

Oh God, thought Charles, please. This isn't a French farce I'm involved in; it's a case of murder.

After a pause which seemed endless, the man replied, 'Mine. We can enjoy my music, yes?'

'Yes.' Tottie chuckled. 'Amongst other things.'

The footsteps moved across the landing, away from Charles. A door opened and closed.

He gave it five minutes, then eased himself out from under the bed. There was dust all over him, he knew, but that was the least of his worries. He ran his torch beam once again over the books about fungi and the set of small jars. Making a quick decision, he pocketed the one labelled Aconite. Then he edged his way towards the door.

It creaked at the first gentle pull, and Charles froze. But there was no reaction from across the landing. He drew the door to him and stood exposed by the light.

He took a step towards the stairs. Still nothing. From the closed door opposite came the sound of Gregorian chant.

That was not the only sound, though. In profane counterpoint to the music, Charles could hear the mutual gasps of a couple making love.

He paused for a moment close to the door. A moan from Tottie changed into a little shriek. 'Oh, you are a wonderful lover,' she murmured. 'These last six months have been the best time of my life, Alex.'

With great care, Charles moved down the stairs and across the hall. He turned the latch on the front door and closed it gingerly behind him, then padded softly off down the garden path.

His caution was probably unnecessary. Tottie Roundwood and Alexandru Radulescu sounded far too involved in each other to be aware of anyone else.

At the end of the street, Charles Paris slipped the half-bottle out of his pocket and rewarded himself with a substantial swig of Bell's.

He deserved it. Now at last he had some solid proof of wrongdoing. He didn't know much about the subject, but felt pretty sure that aconite derived from some form of poisonous fungus.

He also had a new suspect. If Tottie Roundwood had been having an affair with Alexandru Radulescu for the past six months, a great many previously inconsistent details fell into place. There is little a besotted woman nearing her fifties won't do to keep the affections of a younger lover.

Charles wondered how much Alexandru had been involved in the planning. Or had it been a Thomas à Becket scenario? Did Alexandru just intimate the outcome he desired, and leave Tottie to make it happen?

The director must have been in contact with Asphodel, so that he knew they wanted to work with him. Then he just tipped the wink to Tottie, and she got Gavin Scholes out of the way. Vividly the picture came back to Charles of the dining hall at Chailey Ferrars, and the actress forcing a mushroom tartlet into Gavin's mouth.

Then perhaps Alexandru had intimated that he was getting tired of Charles Paris's intransigence about how Sir Toby Belch should be played...? Which had led to the poisoning in the Indian restaurant...

Unless...A new thought came to Charles. The scene at the restaurant was suddenly very clear to him. When John B. Murgatroyd had received his wrong order, he had called out down the table, 'Anybody fancy swapping a Chicken Dupiaza for something stronger?'

And amongst the raucous responses, someone had shouted back, 'I've already got one.' Now, suddenly, Charles knew that that voice had been Sally Luther's.

In other words, the poisoning of John B. Murgatroyd had not been aimed at Charles Paris. It had been the first attempt on the life of Sally Luther.

It had failed; but the second, the injection of poison at Chailey Ferrars, had succeeded. Probably all Alexandru had said was, 'Wouldn't it be great if I could actually have Russ Lavery playing both parts?' And Tottie Roundwood, unhinged by her infatuation, had taken the hint.

Another detail fell into place. Amidst all the upheaval that followed Sally Luther's death, Charles had forgotten the woman he had seen hurrying through the rain when he was on his way from Moira Handley's Portakabin to the stage. But now that image too was crystal clear to him.

It must have been the murderer he had seen. Vasile Bogdan immediately left the reckoning. Even if he had been disguised in women's clothes, he was far too tall.

But the height and the gender were absolutely right for Tottie. True, Charles'd caught a glimpse of blond hair spilling from the anorak hood, but what actress doesn't have access to a range of wigs? She must have committed the crime only moments before, stabbed Sally through the hessian, and be running away from the scene.

And if that was the case, then – But his thought processes were suddenly halted. With no warning at all, he was seized by violent nausea.

And as the entire contents of his stomach – and what felt like most of the stomach itself as well – spurted out of his mouth on to the pavement, one of Olivia's lines from *Twelfth Night* resonated in his head.

> 'How now!
> *Even so quickly may one catch the plague?'*

But quotation immediately gave place to one appalling, heretical thought in Charles Paris's mind.

Somebody's poisoned my Bell's!

Chapter Twenty-Two

HE WAS LUCKY. The violence of his vomiting saved him from worse harm, flushing his body out as effectively as a stomach pump.

But it left him drained and feeble, slumped on the pavement. He was glad the good burghers of Great Wensham kept sober hours. They would not welcome dust- and puke-covered strangers littering their tidy streets.

The desk sergeant at the police station to which he staggered wasn't very welcoming either. The sight of a dust- and puke-covered stranger presenting him with a half-bottle of Bell's, a jar of powder and some garbled story about a serial poisoner brought out his highest level of scepticism.

And DI Dewar, the bored-looking detective to whom Charles was passed over, looked equally disbelieving.

'So let me get this right, Mr...Parrish was it?'

'Paris.'

'Paris, then. You are saying that the contents of this bottle have been adulterated with some fungoid poison?'

'So I believe.'

'And that it was done deliberately by someone trying to kill you?'

'Yes.'

'When would they have had the opportunity to put the poison in the bottle?'

'It was in my jacket pocket hanging in the dressing room right through the performance.'

'And you weren't there all the time?'

'No, I was acting, for heaven's sake.' Surely that'd be obvious even to someone who didn't know anything about the theatre.

The detective gave him a look that suggested raising his voice hadn't been a good idea. Charles didn't care that much what the detective thought. He felt ill and weak; all he wanted to do was crawl into a warm bed.

The detective tapped his pencil on the desk tetchily. 'You implied you had an idea who this person who's trying to kill you might be...?'

Charles gave an ambivalent shrug.

'But you're not going to share your suspicions with me?'

'No.'

'Why not?'

A good question, and yet Charles didn't yet feel certain enough to point a finger at Tottie Roundwood. In spite of the chain of logic he had worked out, she might still somehow prove to be innocent, and it can prove tricky to mend fences with someone you've accused of murder.

No, it would be better to go one step at a time – first get the whisky tested for the poison, then look for the culprit.

'I'm not absolutely sure who it is,' Charles replied evasively.

'You mean there are a lot of people it could be?'

'Well...'

The detective had his little joke. 'Have a habit of making yourself unpopular with your workmates, do you, Mr Parrish?'

'Look, I'm sure there is something criminal going on. And I think it's related to Sally Luther's death.'

'Really?' Now he had got the detective's attention. 'That case is currently under investigation, Mr Parrish.'

'You mean you've got proof that she was poisoned too?'

But Charles's eagerness was quickly slapped down. 'Listen, if you think I'm about to give you information on the state of an investigation, then you have a very false idea of how we in the police force go about our business. Miss Luther's death was unexpected, so a post-mortem was required. We will be kept informed of any developments that may concern us.'

And that was all the detective would give. His attitude remained wary. There was a strong chance he was dealing with a crank. He had an instinctive distrust of theatre people, which Charles's appearance and unlikely story had done little to dispel.

DI Dewar did grudgingly say, however, that he'd arrange for the contents of the bottle and jar to be analysed. He took the address of Charles's digs, confirmed how long the company was going to be in Great Wensham, and said he'd be in touch.

Charles felt so weak he called a cab to take him back to his digs. When he got there, he lay on the bed in his clothes and instantly passed out.

He stayed in the following morning. For one thing, he was still feeling very battered after the poisoning. His throat burned and his stomach muscles felt as though they had been pulled inside out.

He was also not keen to get back among the *Twelfth Night* company until he had to. Whoever had poisoned the whisky – and he was assuming it had been Tottie Roundwood – was going to realise that he had escaped, and might well be moved to make another attempt on his life.

And he was hoping to hear something from the police before he had to go out to Chailey Ferrars for the evening's performance. Once the poison in the whisky had been identified, then the whole machinery of official criminal investigation could be set in motion, and Charles Paris would cease to be under threat.

He tried to read a book, and toyed with the crossword, but his thoughts kept slipping past the words. He wanted to talk to someone. Frances. But he didn't feel up to the inevitable recriminations such a call would involve.

He couldn't concentrate; he kept coming back to Tottie Roundwood. How much of what had happened had she planned? Had she known from the start that Alexandru wanted to direct *Twelfth Night* with Russ Lavery playing the double role, or had the elements of her plan come together piecemeal? How had she got into the company in the first place?

Well, that at least was a question he could get answered. And it would give him something to do. He went to the phone and dialled Gavin Scholes' number.

The new wife answered. In an appropriately hushed voice, she said, 'Yes, I'm sure he'd like to talk to you. But not for too long. Be careful you don't tire him. Phone for you, Gavin,' she called out.

Another extension was picked up. 'Hallo?'

'Morning, Gavin, it's Charles Paris.' Then, unthinking, he asked, 'How are you?'

'Not so bad, all things considered,' the director replied nobly. 'It's quite a relief, actually, to have had it confirmed.'

'Had what confirmed?'

'Oh, didn't you know?' Then, with considerable pride, he announced, 'I've got cancer.'

'Oh. Gavin. I'm so sorry.' The condolence came out automatically, but Charles's mind was already racing with the implications of the news.

'That's very kind of you, Charles.' A great complacency came into Gavin's voice. 'I was pretty certain that's what it was from the start, but my consultant just wasn't convinced. Goodness, the barrage of tests I've been through – you just wouldn't believe it. I mean, first I had to –'

'Gavin, are you saying that it was cancer you were taken ill with after that day at Chailey Ferrars?'

'Yes, of course I am. Stomach cancer. That's what I told my consultant straight away. But would he listen? Now of course he's very apologetic and says he should have paid more attention to me from the start, and he's moving heaven and earth to get the radiotherapy under way but...'

Charles did not manage to get off the phone for half an hour. For a hypochondriac like Gavin Scholes the diagnosis of a life-threatening disease was a vindication of his entire life. No one could doubt him any more. He really was ill.

In the event, Charles didn't ask about how Tottie Roundwood had come into the *Twelfth Night* company. It didn't seem relevant.

Because if Gavin Scholes had been ill with cancer from the start, then he hadn't been poisoned at Chailey Ferrars. His inability to continue as director had been purely accidental.

And the logic of the case Charles Paris had been building against Tottie Roundwood totally fell apart.

Chapter Twenty-Three

'MR PARRISH?'

'Paris.'

'Yes. This is Detective Inspector Dewar from Great Wensham. We met last night.'

'Right.'

'I'm calling because we've had the lab results on the items you brought in.'

'Yes?' Charles was very tense. After the collapse of all his previous thinking about Tottie Roundwood's involvement in the case, he was fully prepared to be dismissed as a self-dramatising crank. The sceptical tone from the other end of the phone was not encouraging:

'Well, let's start with the powder in the jar. That was indeed a preparation made from a vegetable substance...'

'Yes?'

'...though not in fact from a fungus...'

'Oh. But aconite *is* a poison, isn't it?'

'Can be. What was found in that jar, however, would have purely medicinal applications.'

'Oh.'

'Something to do with homeopathic medicine. Not a subject on which I'm an expert, Mr Parrish.'

'Nor me.' Though he knew that Tottie Roundwood was. He shivered at the thought of how close he'd come to making public accusations against her.

'No. However, Mr Parrish, it appears that while the plant from which this powder originated is potentially poisonous, at the concentration in which it appears here, it is completely harmless. Or even, I suppose, beneficial, if you happen to be one of those weirdos who believes in homeopathic medicine.'

The scepticism had given way to downright contempt. 'Now we come on to the contents of the whisky bottle...'

Charles prepared himself for a serious dressing-down about wasting police time and being a hysterical theatrical crackpot. But, to his surprise, DI Dewar continued, 'Traces of poison were found there, Mr Parrish.'

'A vegetable-based poison?'

'No, no. A chemical poison. Mercuric chloride.' There was a silence. 'It seems you had a very lucky escape, Mr Parrish.'

'Yes. And it also seems pretty definite that we have a poisoner in the

Twelfth Night company, doesn't it?'

The detective was too canny to commit himself to an opinion on the subject. 'What makes you say that?'

'Well, when you put what's happened to me – or nearly happened to me – together with Sally Luther's death...' DI Dewar did not react. 'Come on, the two must be connected, mustn't they?'

'Must they?' He was not giving anything away. 'Clearly, Mr Parrish, we need to talk to you further.'

'Yes. When?'

'Right away.'

'The problem with that is...' Charles Paris looked at his watch '...it's now five forty-five. I have to be at Chailey Ferrars in three-quarters of an hour to get ready for tonight's performance of *Twelfth Night*.'

'Mr Parrish, if you're suggesting that a play,' the word was larded over with distaste, 'should take precedence over a police investigation...'

'I'm not. I'm fully aware of how serious this is. All I'm saying is that if I'm not there for the performance because I'm being interviewed by the police, it will cause very considerable disruption – and will also provide a warning to any guilty person in the company that your investigation is drawing close.'

There was a silence before DI Dewar conceded, 'You may have a point, Mr Parrish.'

'So that means you do think someone in the company is guilty?'

But again the detective wouldn't be drawn. 'What time does your play finish?'

'It comes down at ten-thirty.'

'And at that time all of the company members will be around Chailey Ferrars?'

'Yes. Why, are you thinking of questioning everyone then?'

'Mr Parrish.' The detective's stock of patience was quickly becoming depleted. 'We are in the habit of conducting investigations in our own way. And we are not in the habit of providing information to irrelevant members of the public on how our investigations are going. We will speak again soon, Mr Parrish.'

And the phone was put down with some force.

Charles hadn't eaten anything since his poisoning of the night before. To his surprise, when his landlady suggested some scrambled eggs before he went out to the show, the idea appealed.

She was a good landlady, with that quality that more landladies should manifest – unobtrusiveness. She brought his scrambled eggs into the dining room and left him on his own to eat them. From a rack by the fire he picked up a copy of one of the previous day's broadsheet newspapers.

It was, inevitably, full of Sally Luther, but provided a less hysterical assessment of her importance than the tabloids had. Her death prompted a feature on the nature of media celebrity, in which one paragraph in particular caught Charles's attention.

Sally Luther also suffered from the disadvantages of being public property. She received a disturbing sequence of letters from an obsessed male fan, whose infatuation for her soured into violent fantasies. She also inspired the attentions of a young woman, who took to following her around at a distance for some months. Though Sally frequently tried to engage her in conversation, the girl always ran off when approached.

This was a nuisance, but little more. However, the harassment became more worrying when Sally's pet cat was found poisoned. And then the mysterious girl began to stake out Sally's block of flats. The actress was justifiably unnerved by the sight every night of 'a young blonde woman, her face hidden by the hood of her anorak, standing immobile under the street lamp opposite.' Sally had been unwilling to call in the police before, but the new development changed her mind. Though the police never managed to catch the stalker, their presence ensured that the nuisance quickly ceased.

I wonder, thought Charles Paris. I wonder...

The image was vivid in his mind of a young woman hurrying through the rain, and a straggling wisp of blond hair escaping from a Mutual Reliable anorak.

Chapter Twenty-Four

TALYA Northcott was sitting with a cup of coffee at a table in the shade of one of the fine old oak trees at Chailey Ferrars. Now the weather had improved, the Green Room – literally green amidst the trees – had moved into the open air. Evening sunlight dappled through the oak leaves, sparkling on Talya's fine blond hair and the silver brocade of her Olivia's Handmaiden costume.

Charles Paris, in his Toby Belch gear, took a seat beside her. 'Lovely evening, isn't it?'

'Oh yes.'

'Twenty minutes till beginners...'

'Mm...'

'You enjoying doing the show?'

Her mouth twisted into annoyance. 'Not as much as I should be.'

'Ah. Yes, of course.' He had momentarily forgotten about her being the passed-over understudy for Sally Luther. 'No, that was rotten luck. Don't worry, everyone in the theatre's had bad breaks from time to time.' He grinned. 'Me more than most maybe.'

She gave him a look which suggested bad breaks for someone like him might be justified, but not for her. Mummy's solicitude had certainly produced one very spoilt and self-obsessed young lady.

'Also, Talya, I mean, you must recognise that Russ Lavery is a *name*, and I'm afraid *names* count for a lot in this business.'

'That's not the point. I was contracted to play Handmaiden to Olivia and to understudy all the female parts.' She sniffed irritably. 'I'm going to get on to my agent. I reckon Asphodel's in breach of contract.'

'I don't know that making a fuss will do much good.'

'Perhaps not, but *it'll make me feel better*,' she said with considerable venom. 'And what's so great about Russ Lavery, anyway? All right, he's in the telly series, and he plays that one part OK – not that it's very hard. But it's daft having him playing Viola. It goes absolutely against the text of Shakespeare's play.'

In different circumstances Charles would have agreed with her and joined in a mutual moan about Alexandru Radulescu's massacre of *Twelfth Night*. But this wasn't the moment.

'You admired Sally very much, didn't you...?' he probed gently.

'Yes. She was a role model for me. She was the kind of actress I want to be

– and will be,' she added, then went on resentfully, 'She would have been much better as Viola than Russ will ever be. I would have been much better as Viola than Russ will ever be.'

Charles was about to ask when she'd first met Sally, but Talya continued on another burst of anger. 'It's not fair. I should be playing that part. After everything I've done, I should be playing that part!'

'When you say "everything you've done" –?'

But Talya Northcott was too infuriated to listen. 'It's ridiculous that Viola should be played by some pathetic male television star with a drug problem!'

'With a drug problem?' Charles echoed.

Talya Northcott looked sheepish. She'd said more than she intended. But a what-the-hell defiance came into her face. 'Yes. Russ Lavery's into hard drugs. I know.' A thought came to her. 'And I've half a mind to tell the press about his little habit...That'd sort him out, wouldn't it? Really do something to his "Mr Clean" image.'

'What do you base your knowledge on?' asked Charles.

'I've *seen* him doing hard drugs.'

'When?'

'The night of the tech. The night Sally died. After his first Sebastian/ Antonio scene – Act Two, Scene One – Russ came back into the caravan where I was and he was in a filthy mood – very tense and twitchy.'

'Was it just you in the caravan?'

'No, I was there with Vasile and Chad.'

'And how long did they stay there?'

'What?' She didn't like having her narrative interrupted. 'What does that matter?'

'Please, just tell me.'

An exasperated sigh. 'All right, let me think...Well, Chad went to do his clown bit in Act Two, Scene Three, and then Vasile was there till Fabian's first proper entrance – Act Two, Scene Five. You know that – you're in the scene, for God's sake!'

'Yes,' Charles agreed meekly. 'You were telling me about Russ...?'

'Right. Well, as I say, he came in after his scene in an absolutely vile mood, and he twitched around for a little while, and then he stormed out again. And the reason he did that was because he needed a fix.'

'What makes you so sure?'

'Because I saw him. Out of the caravan window. He'd stopped under a tree out of the rain and I saw him pull something out of that pouch he has on his costume.'

'What did he pull out?'

'It was a syringe.'

'Ah,' said Charles Paris. 'Was it?'

Chapter Twenty-Five

THAT NIGHT Sir Toby Belch went through the comic machinations of the first half of *Twelfth Night*, but the actor playing him was on automatic pilot. Charles Paris remained detached, his mind forging links in a new chain of logic.

With Gavin's illness explained, the two remaining crimes had clearly both been aimed at Sally Luther, and Russ Lavery was the one who had benefited most from her death. Alexandru Radulescu, as the current licensed iconoclast of the theatrical establishment, would have got the same reviews if Sally had remained alive. The doubling of Sebastian and Viola was just one more *coup* in a production full of innovation (or perversity, if you shared the Charles Paris view).

But for Russ it was a career-making change. Now, to add to the fame and money brought by television, he had the artistic respectability that only a high-profile theatrical performance can give. The value of that is incalculable, and might well make an ambitious actor contemplate all kinds of criminality.

The more Charles thought about Russ, the more details fitted. He cast his mind back to Gavin Scholes' production of *Macbeth* at Warminster. Fresh out of the Webber-Douglas acting school, Russ Lavery had been callow and naive. He had also attached himself with doglike devotion to an older actress, the somewhat precious Felicia Chatterton.

Was it fanciful to imagine that that was not his first comparable infatuation? At a younger age might not the hypersensitive Russ Lavery have become similarly fixated on Sally Luther?

Because, as Charles watched Russ on-stage as Viola, he was struck again by how superbly the actor played a woman. It wasn't just his mannerisms; he seemed to take on the complete female identity. The ease with which he'd done that, from the first experimental moment of role-swapping in rehearsal, suggested that he had practice in cross-dressing.

And that would explain the incongruity of Sally Luther having been followed by a woman all those months. Surely with stalkers it was a sex thing. In the famous examples of such incidents, the actresses had always been pestered by men.

Mentally Charles kicked himself. He should have thought of this earlier. After nearly a month of Alexandru Radulescu's harping on sexual ambivalence, his mind should have made the jump more readily. It was all there in *Twelfth Night*; the whole plot hinged on the ambiguity of gender.

Charles had planned to confront Russ Lavery at the end of the show, but two factors made him move his plans forward.

The first was his own danger. The confirmation that Charles's half-bottle of Bell's had been poisoned also confirmed that the murderer saw him as a threat. After one failure, another attempt on his life seemed a certainty. And Sir Toby Belch had an uncomfortable amount of booze-swigging to do throughout the play. To poison the contents of his tankard in the wings would not be difficult. Charles gave himself a mental note under no circumstances to let any of the fluid he was meant to quaff touch his lips.

The other pressure on his plans was the appearance of Detective Inspector Dewar backstage during the first half of *Twelfth Night*. Since he was in plain clothes, there was little chance of anyone but Charles knowing his mission. When, however, a message went out during the interval requesting all the company and crew to assemble briefly at the end of the show, Charles reckoned the murderer might become suspicious that someone was on to him.

There was also pride at stake. Charles Paris had got so far down the road of investigation that, for his own satisfaction, he wanted to have his theory proved correct. The police could then move in and arrest the culprit, but Charles didn't want them to upstage him by having their denouement first.

No, he would have his confrontation during the interval.

That August, the evenings remained warm even after the sun had gone down, and few of the cast chose to spend their interval in the stuffy caravans. They sat outside under the working lights in the *al fresco* Green Room or lolled on the grass. The long interval was still a bone of contention. It was hard to keep up concentration, and they looked forward to moving on to the studio theatre in Norwich, where the running of *Twelfth Night* would not be dictated by the demands of picnickers.

Russ Lavery, who, because of his onerous double role, was more concerned about threats to his concentration than most, had formed the habit of sitting quietly in one of the caravans for the full duration of the interval; and it was there that Charles Paris found him.

Russ looked up without enthusiasm. He had a glass of mineral water and an open copy of the play in front of him. 'I'm concentrating. What do you want, Charles?'

'I want to talk about Sally Luther's death.'

A sigh. 'I'd have thought everything to be said on that subject had already been said.'

'The police are investigating it, you know.'

'So? They'd be likely to investigate any unexplained death, wouldn't they?'

Russ Lavery sounded very calm, as if he had deliberately damped down his pulse and heart rate to improve his concentration.

'They think it was murder.' Charles hadn't actually had that in as many words from DI Dewar, but he thought the implication was clear.

'Huh. Someone always thinks every unexplained death is murder. But why would anyone want to murder Sally? Was she screwing some other woman's husband, or what?'

If this was a pretence of innocence, it was a very convincing one. But then, Charles reminded himself, he was dealing with a consummately good actor.

'There are motives other than sexual jealousy,' he said.

'I'm sure there are.' Russ now sounded simply bored.

'Professional jealousy, for example. Or professional advantage.'

'I don't know what you're talking about.'

'Russ, when did you first meet Alexandru Radulescu?'

'Hmm? I don't know. Six months ago...'

'And did you talk together about *Twelfth Night* then?'

'We talked about a lot of plays. Alex has got a lot of exciting ideas.'

'But did the idea of doing *Twelfth Night* with Sebastian and Viola doubling come up then?'

'I can't remember. It may have done.'

'Did it?'

'Yes, I think it did. Just as a speculative idea. I certainly never thought it'd happen.'

'But now it has happened...'

'Yes.'

'...thanks to Sally Luther's death.'

'Yes.' Russ Lavery was silent for a moment as the idea took root. 'Good God. You're not suggesting Alex killed her, are you?'

'No, I'm not.'

'Then I don't see what you're talking about, Charles.' He looked genuinely puzzled.

'Russ, on the evening of Sally's death, you were seen holding a syringe...'

Up till this point Russ Lavery's cool had been unchallenged, but Charles's words really shook him.

'Oh, God,' he murmured. 'How did you find out? You didn't see me.'

'No, somebody else did.'

'Look, Charles, you mustn't shop me about this.' Now there was a naked plea in Russ's voice.

'Why shouldn't I?'

'Because it'd ruin my career.'

'Yes, I think it probably would,' Charles agreed evenly.

'But you don't know the pressures that drive someone to that kind of thing. Oh yes, I've been doing well the last few years, and everyone's jealous and thinks what a lucky fellow Russ Lavery is. But in this business doing well is not good enough. You have to do *better* all the time, have something new on the horizon, always be moving on.

'So, yes, at the moment they're still talking of further series for *Air-Sea*

Rescue, but the ratings only have to fall half a million and they'll pull the plug on it as quick as breathing. Look what happened to Sally's series – just suddenly, thank you very much, goodbye. And actors who haven't got something else lined up when that happens can have a very sticky few years.'

'So is that why you did it?'

'Yes. It made me feel better.'

'Really?'

'And it still does make me feel better. Look!'

Suddenly Russ Lavery pulled up the sleeve of his doublet. The reason for his tantrum with the wardrobe mistress was now clear. He didn't dare to show a forearm that was a wasteland of scars and punctures. 'I'm ruining my body. I'm putting my life at risk. But it helps – it really helps me! Without this my whole life's a mess. With it I can just about cope.'

'Ah,' said Charles Paris. 'Right. That's what you used the syringe for?'

'Yes. What else?'

'And Sally Luther?'

'Sally Luther wasn't into drugs.' Russ's bewilderment was so genuine that Charles's suspicions crumbled away. 'No, she somehow managed to cope with all the pressure, when it was all happening for her, and during the even more difficult time, when it all started to fall apart. I admired her for that, because I'm afraid...when it all goes wrong for me – and it will, it will, it does for everyone – well, I'm worried that I'll just do more of this.' He gestured feebly at his ravaged arm.

Charles Paris looked at the handsome wreck in front of him. Russ Lavery wasn't a murderer, just an actor paying the price of his celebrity. That was what Sally Luther had done too, though in a different way. She had died because she had inspired too much public affection. Russ Lavery was killing himself because of his fear that the public affection he inspired would one day trickle away.

There are times, Charles Paris thought, when there's a lot to be said for being an unsuccessful actor.

Chapter Twenty-Six

SIR TOBY BELCH had to do his first scene of the second half, Act Three, Scene Two, before Charles Paris could go into action. He found DI Dewar waiting in the administrative office Portakabin. Moira Handley was not there, though another detective was.

'You're not watching the show?'

The curt headshake showed exactly what the inspector thought of the theatre.

'Listen,' said Charles. 'I've got an idea...'

Both detectives looked sceptical, but did at least hear him out.

'I'm very doubtful it'll work,' said DI Dewar finally.

'But isn't it worth trying? It can't do any harm, can it?'

The inspector was silent for a moment, then conceded, 'Well, I suppose not. All right, you can have a go.'

'I mean, who have you talked to so far? Who does actually know why you're here?'

'Just the company manager.'

'Oh,' said Charles. 'If you told him, then probably everyone *does* know already.'

But they didn't seem to. There was genuine surprise from the actors to whom he murmured the reason for their call after the show. Mind you, he only had to mention it to a couple and he knew it'd be round the whole company within minutes.

"'A great while ago the world began,
With hey-ho, the wind and the rain;
But that's all one, our play is done,
And we'll strive to please you every day.'"

The sitar-player's enunciation had improved over the run, and the final moment of *Twelfth Night* still retained its magic. The Great Wensham audience, having greatly enjoyed their picnics, erupted into applause.

As the cast came forward to do their curtain calls, Charles counted them. All present and correct. If the murderer was going to make a move, it hadn't happened yet.

The cast had been told to get out of their costumes and reassemble on stage as quickly as possible. Charles, as he had arranged with DI Dewar, stayed in his Sir Toby Belch gear and hurried down the side of the auditorium to the box office, a rectangular shed which stood by the gates into the theatre field.

The inspector was in there, looking out over the mass of Great Wensham folk trooping towards the car-park laden with rugs and garden furniture. Overhead working lights beamed down on the faces as they passed. One or two were talking about *Twelfth Night*; the majority were discussing their picnics.

'If this doesn't work, it's a bloody waste of time,' he grumbled to Charles. 'Or if the person we're looking for has already left.'

'Everyone was at the curtain call.'

'Hmm. Well, we'll see...'

It was hard to concentrate on the individual faces that streamed past. Charles was tempted by a couple of blond heads, but neither looked quite right. DI Dewar's grumbling about time-wasting grew more vociferous.

Charles had almost given up when he saw what he had been hoping to see. The audience flow had dwindled to just a few stragglers. Be-sashed usherettes and festival volunteers in Mutual Reliable anoraks milled around the seating, picking up rubbish, chatting and giggling.

And someone with their anorak hood up was walking briskly towards the exit. The face was hidden, but a wisp of blond hair escaped the hood.

'There,' Charles murmured.

He slipped out of the box office and waited in the shadows beside it. Then, just when the hooded figure was about to pass, he stepped out into its path.

'Good evening,' said Charles Paris.

The speed with which his throat was grabbed stunned him. He felt himself pushed back against the counter of the box office, and could feel his assailant fumbling for something in his pocket.

In the glare of the working light he saw a syringe raised to stab at him.

'You bastard! This time you won't get away!' the murderer screamed.

Charles Paris closed his eyes.

'I'll have that, thank you very much.'

It was DI Dewar's voice. Charles opened his eyes and saw his assailant's wrist caught in the inspector's vice-like grip. The two arms swayed in conflict for a moment, as if wrestling.

Then the inspector's started to win. It forced the other down towards the box office counter. As it drew close it slammed the loser's hand against the wood.

There was a little cry as the syringe dropped, and Charles felt the pressure on his throat slacken.

He reached across and grabbed the free arm. The murderer was now held by DI Dewar across the box office counter and by Charles from outside. In the struggle, the anorak hood slipped back, pulling the blond wig with it.

Charles found himself looking into the furious face of Benzo Ritter.

Chapter Twenty-Seven

HIS ATTACK on Charles, witnessed by DI Dewar, was sufficient cause for the police to arrest the boy, and while he was in custody his other crimes were investigated.

His handwriting was matched to the threatening letters Sally Luther had received at the height of her television fame. Faced with that fact, he confessed to everything.

Yes, he had been the 'woman' who trailed the star. He loved her, he needed to be near her. But, he explained, he'd been very immature at the time. Later he realised that the only way to be with his idol was to earn her respect as an equal.

That was why he had gone into show business. When she met him as one of her profession rather than an anonymous admirer, he knew she was bound to succumb, to feel as much for him as he did for her.

But that was not what had happened. In the event, when he declared his passion, she had laughed at him. He couldn't tolerate that. Other people might find out, they might laugh at him too.

So it was only logical that Sally Luther would have to die.

He'd always been fascinated by poisons. Indeed, his school nickname 'Benzo' had been based on an illicit experiment he'd done in the chemistry lab with nitro-benzene. Mind you, he told his interrogators proudly, he'd used atropine from belladonna when he'd poisoned Sally's cat.

He'd used the mercuric chloride in powder form in the Indian restaurant, surreptitiously shaking some over one of the Chicken Dupiazas in the confusion of the food's arrival. The fact that he had poisoned the wrong person he regarded as an inconvenience rather than a tragedy.

Then he had employed the same poison in solution to inject Sally Luther and adulterate the Bell's whisky. The reason for his turning his murderous attentions to Charles Paris, it emerged, was due to another misunderstanding. It happened when, a few days previously, Charles had raised the subject of Sally Luther's death in the dressing room caravan. To defuse a potential confrontation with Vasile Bogdan, he had quoted from *Twelfth Night*: "'Now Mercury endue thee with leasing, for thou speakest well of fools!'"

Benzo Ritter had taken this reference to 'Mercury' as evidence that Charles knew the poison he was using, and that had led him to doctor the half-bottle of Bell's. The boy had been extremely irritated that Charles Paris survived that attempt.

At no stage during his questioning and subsequent trial did Benzo Ritter demonstrate any feelings of guilt or remorse.

At the trial, psychological reports ruled him to be insane, and he was committed to a secure institution.

Benzo Ritter's absence made little difference to the Asphodel production of *Twelfth Night*. A new Second Officer was found and the play set off from Great Wensham on its triumphant tour.

Charles Paris did not enjoy the experience. His performance moved a little closer to what Alexandru Radulescu wanted, but Charles felt uncomfortable eternally marooned between two stools. He still longed to play Sir Toby Belch as Shakespeare had intended the part to be played, but didn't think he was likely ever to get another chance. As Moira Handley had said in a different context, the moment had passed.

Charles didn't really feel part of the tour. His resistance to the communal hero worship of Alexandru Radulescu isolated him. John B. Murgatroyd had been his closest ally in the company, and though the invalid made a full recovery from his poisoning, he did not rejoin the show. As *Twelfth Night* criss-crossed the United Kingdom – with a diversion to the Czech Republic – Charles Paris felt marginalised and lonely.

Alexandru Radulescu did not return to Romania, but stayed on to impose his personality and perversity on more classic English texts. He continued to be hailed as a genius, until one day a new *enfant terrible* took the British theatre by the scruff of its neck, and the Radulescu style seemed suddenly meretricious and old hat.

Russ Lavery's career went from strength to strength. He managed to combine television popularity with serious critical respect for his theatre work. And the British public adored him even more after his much-publicised battle with heroin addiction.

Julian Roxborough-Smith added another artistic directorship to his portfolio. He was appointed to run the West Bartleigh Festival and thereafter, in his usual dilettante fashion, spent his time rebooking the same artistes for all three festivals. Since he still acted as agent for many of these artistes, he made rather a good living.

And Moira Handley, needless to say, continued to do all the work.

Gavin Scholes' cancer required surgery, granting him his lifelong wish of being able to talk about '*my* operation'. It was followed by a course of radiotherapy, which seemed to work. He apparently made a complete recovery, though, as he kept telling his new wife – and anyone else incautious enough to listen – 'it might just be a temporary remission.'

* * *

Charles Paris had intended to ring Frances during the tour, but somehow didn't get round to it.

Back in London it was nearly December and cold. Unequal to the upheaval of finding somewhere new, Charles had agreed with his landlord to continue at Hereford Road, paying the exorbitantly increased rent. The conversion from bedsitter to studio flat had managed to keep the essential features of the original space – in other words, its total lack of charm.

There wasn't any work around either. He'd spoken to Maurice Skellern, who'd once again said that things were 'very quiet'. Charles watched what was left of the money he'd made from *Twelfth Night* slowly dwindle. He signed on again at the Lisson Grove DSS.

After a week of mooching round his bedsitter – no, studio flat – he finally rang Frances. And he found she had exciting news.

'I'm doing an exchange programme with a school in the States.'

'What does that mean?'

'My deputy stands in as headmistress, an American teacher comes over to my school and I go and teach in California for a year.'

'Oh. When does this happen?' Charles asked bleakly.

'Starts in January.'

'How was it arranged?'

'Through an American friend.'

'The one you met at the international teachers' conference?'

'That's right.'

'What, so he'll be over here while you're there, will he?'

'No, it's another member of staff I'm swapping with. My friend will be in California,' Frances replied crushingly.

And once again it seemed inconceivable that things had ever gone well for Charles Paris.

DEAD ROOM FARCE

To David and Jacqui

Chapter One

THAT September morning Charles Paris had his trousers round his ankles, but it was for entirely professional reasons. He was taking part in the final London rehearsal for the forthcoming three-month tour of *Not On Your Wife!*, a new farce by the prolific British farceur, Bill Blunden. Charles was playing Aubrey, the older lover of Gilly, wife of Bob, the advertising executive who was pretending that his young mistress Nicky was in fact the property of his hapless neighbour, Ted, played in this Parrott Fashion production by the well-loved comedy actor, Bernard Walton. In the scene they were rehearsing, Charles Paris, as Aubrey, had just arrived for a bit of illicit afternoon pleasure with Gilly...

The set is the sitting rooms of the two flats, divided by a common central wall, The flats are identical in dimensions, and both have French windows opening on to a balcony running along the back of the stage. Gilly and Bob's flat (Stage Left) is smart and fashionable; Louise and Ted's (Stage Right) scruffier and more lived-in. Louise sits in her flat in an armchair, reading a magazine. (The lights on this area are dim; the lights are up on Gilly and Bob's flat.) Gilly, an attractive redhead in her thirties, has just let in Aubrey, her wealthy lover, in his fifties. As soon as they enter the room, they go into a clinch.
AUBREY: I'm sorry I couldn't come any quicker.
GILLY: I never want you to come any quicker.
AUBREY *(after a tiny pause to give the audience time to pick up on the innuendo)*: I got tied up.
GILLY: You naughty boy! And I thought I was the only woman in your life.
AUBREY *(tiny pause)*: No, no, one of the secretaries at the office had made a cock-up and I had to have her on the carpet.
GILLY *(tiny pause)*: I don't think you're making things sound any better, Aubrey. *(starting to undo the buckle of his trouser belt and pulling him by the belt towards the bedroom door)* You're going to have to make it up to me. In bed. *With her spare hand, she opens the bedroom door.*
AUBREY: Oh dear. I'm not sure that I'm up for this.
GILLY *(as she pulls him through into the bedroom)*: You'd better be!
They disappear into the bedroom. The door slams shut behind them. There is a moment's silence, then the doorbell is heard. It rings a second time. Gilly comes bustling out of the bedroom, followed by Aubrey. He has his trousers round his ankles, to reveal boxer shorts that are a bit too young for him.

AUBREY: Oh Lord, who could it be?

GILLY: I don't know, do I? But, whoever it is, they can't see you here. I'm a respectable married woman.

The doorbell rings again.

AUBREY *(trying to run in three directions at once and finding it difficult with his trousers round his ankles)*: Oh, goodness! Where can I go?

GILLY *(pointing to the French windows)*: Over there.

AUBREY: Over there? But we're on the fifth floor. *(letting out a wail)* I'm too young to die!

GILLY: No, I didn't mean over the rail. *(hustling him towards the French windows)* I just meant on to the balcony. You can come back in when whoever it is has gone.

AUBREY: But suppose they don't go? Suppose it's your husband. He might never go. He lives here.

GILLY *(opening the French windows)*: He also has a front door key, so he wouldn't use the bell, would he?

AUBREY: He might have lost it.

GILLY *(pushing Aubrey out on to the balcony)*: Not as much as you seem to have done, Aubrey.

AUBREY *(as she closes the French windows on him)*: Ooh, my good Gawd! It's cold enough out here to freeze the ba...

The closing of the French windows cuts off the end of his line. Running her hands through her hair to tidy it, Gilly hurries towards the door to the hall. On the balcony, Aubrey, shivering and still with his trousers round his ankles, scurries off towards Stage Left. Unable to proceed further in that direction, he scurries back the other way. He has just gone out of sight behind the central division between the two flats, when Gilly returns from the hall, ushering in Willie, a flamboyant interior designer, who wears a brightly coloured silk suit with a diaphanous scarf floating around his neck.

WILLIE: Ooh, I'd nearly given up on you. I thought you must've been having a bit of an afternoon snooze. Go on, were you having a bit?

GILLY: Very nearly.

WILLIE *(tiny pause)*: I'm your interior designer. *(reaching out to take her hand and give it a flamboyant kiss)* I'm called Willie. *(coyly)* Not without reason.

GILLY *(tiny pause, gesturing to the flat)*: Well, here's the flat. This is about the size of it.

WILLIE: As the bishop said to the actress. *(looking round the flat with disapproval)* Oh dear. Who on earth did this for you? These designs have got all the razzmatazz of a civil servant's Y-fronts.

GILLY: That's why they need changing.

WILLIE: That's what the civil servant's wife said.

Gilly watches anxiously, as Willie continues to look disparagingly round the flat. On the balcony, Aubrey's head has appeared behind the French windows, peering nervously round from the central division.

WILLIE *(still facing out front, taking out a notebook)*: Maybe we should start with those dreadful 1950s French windows. Hm, is the balcony only as wide as the windows themselves? *(He turns to face Gilly.)* Or do you have a bit on the side?

GILLY *(guiltily)*: No, I certainly don't! What on earth gave you that idea?

WILLIE: Well, let's see just how bad these windows really are. *(He swings round in a flamboyant gesture. Just in time, Aubrey's head disappears behind the central division.)* What do you keep on the balcony?

GILLY *(very quickly)*: Nothing.

WILLIE *(moving towards the balcony)*: I bet you do. Everyone does. I bet you've got some revolting old crock out there...

GILLY: No, I haven't!

WILLIE: Some mouldy old creeper that took your fancy...

GILLY: No.

WILLIE: Well, let's have a look!

He throws the French windows open. Gilly covers her face with her hands in horror. As Willie opens the windows, Aubrey appears suddenly on the balcony outside the French windows of Louise and Ted's flat. (The lights now go up to half-full on Louise and Ted's flat.)

WILLIE *(picking up a flowerpot with a shrivelled plant in it)*: See, I knew I'd find some wizened old weed out here.

GILLY *(her hands still covering her eyes)*: It's all right, I can explain everything. He's the window cleaner!

WILLIE: What?

GILLY: Yes, and his ladder fell down!

WILLIE: His ladder?

GILLY: Yes. *(taking her hands away from her eyes and seeing what Willie is holding)* Oh, that kind of weed. Yes, yes, of course.

Willie gives her a strange look. (The lights go down on Gilly and Bob's flat and up to full on Louise and Ted's.) Aubrey, afraid of being seen by Willie, opens the French windows, and steps into the other flat. He still has his trousers round his ankles. Louise looks up from her magazine in horror.

LOUISE: Oh, my goodness! *(thinking he's the escaped prisoner, 'Ginger' Little)* Are you Little?

AUBREY *(looking down at his boxer shorts)*: Quite possibly. But it is very cold out there.

LOUISE: No, I mean – are you 'Ginger'?

AUBREY: Certainly not! *(He pulls his trousers up.)* Nothing funny about me. I'm as straight as the day is long.

LOUISE: But today's the shortest day.

AUBREY: You don't need to tell me. *(He turns away from her modestly to try to zip himself up. As soon as his back is turned, Louise reaches in panic to a drawer in a desk beside her chair.)* Ooh, it was so cold out there. Goodness, I thought I'd –

LOUISE *(producing a pistol from the drawer and pointing it at Aubrey's back):* Freeze!
AUBREY: Exactly. *(He turns back to face Louise. Seeing that he's looking down the barrel of a gun, he throws his hands up in the air.)* Aagh!
His trousers once again fall down.

The general feeling about the run-through had been pretty good. At the end, Rob Parrott, of Parrott Fashion Productions, who had watched it, was cautiously complimentary. True, there was a lot still to do; and true, everything would be different when they actually got the show on to the proper set in Bath; but at least for the time being *Not On Your Wife!* seemed to be in pretty good shape.

The director certainly thought so. But then David J. Girton was not the most demanding of taskmasters. His background was in BBC Television Light Entertainment. Until recently he had been a staff producer/ director with an extensive portfolio of inoffensive sofa-bound situation comedies behind him. But the changing world of the BBC in the 1990s had seen him edged out, still brought back on contract to produce the occasional series – in particular, the relentlessly long-running *Neighbourhood Watch* – but now with freedom to 'do other things'.

Not On Your Wife! was one of those 'other things'. David J. Girton had worked a lot in television with the show's star, Bernard Walton, and that was the reason for his appointment. Bernard Walton's contract stipulated that he had director approval and, rather than going for a dynamically creative figure, the star had opted for someone who wouldn't interfere too much with the way he intended to play his part.

Because there was no question who was in charge of the production, Bernard Walton dictated the pace and emphasis of rehearsals. He selected which bits should be worked on in depth (the scenes he was in) and which should be hurried through on the nod (the scenes he wasn't in). And the whole schedule was fitted around his commitments. The reason their last London rehearsal was on a Thursday was simply that Bernard Walton had a long-standing commitment to play in a charity Pro-Am golf tournament on the Friday.

As well as having the star's approval, David J. Girton was treated with easy tolerance by the rest of the company. Many of them were comedy actors he already knew from television, though he hadn't worked before with Charles Paris, who Bernard had suggested as a possible Aubrey. Charles had appeared at the end of the first afternoon of auditions, and been extremely flattered when the director had cancelled the second day's calls and offered him the part on the spot, expressing his opinion that the actor demonstrated the requisite quality of 'seedy gentility'. At the time Charles had seen this as a reflection of his own brilliance, but closer acquaintance with David J. Girton suggested it might have more to do with the director's constitutional indolence.

Because, the longer rehearsals went on, the clearer it became that this production of *Not On Your Wife!* had been entrusted to a seriously lazy man. The business of television sitcom, in which David J. Girton had learnt his comedy skills, was, for an experienced hand, not a particularly onerous one. True, the studio days could be stressful, and there was always the risk of flouncing and door-slamming from the various service departments involved. But, for someone who'd been around such a long time and who always worked with the same tolerant studio team, a long-running sitcom did not present an over-taxing work schedule. Daily rehearsals from ten to two, and a camera script in which only the lines changed from week to week, had left David J. Girton with plenty of time to enjoy the good food and wine which had contributed to his substantial girth.

So, doing theatre rehearsal hours – usually from ten to six with the statutory Equity coffee and lunch breaks – gave him the impression he was working hard. To have actually worked hard during those hours would, to David J. Girton, have seemed like gilding the lily. He was content to block out the play's basic moves, take long lunch hours, lop a bit off the end of the working day, and basically let Bernard Walton get on with it.

This suited most of the actors very well. It certainly suited the star. Bernard Walton reckoned he 'knew about comedy', and worked tirelessly on his own part, incorporating his familiar repertoire of elaborate takes and reactions, without any reference to the other actors around him.

This behaviour, which in more serious areas of the theatre would have been regarded as appallingly unprofessional and selfish, was accepted amiably by the rest of the cast. They were all old comedy hands, who knew better than to get into competition for laughs with their star. Many of them had been in plays by Bill Blunden before, and were aware that his dramatic structures offered each cast member an unchanging ration of funny moments. So long as those moments were played right, the laughs would come. Only the star was allowed to embroider his part. And any attempts to upstage him would simply throw out the predictable but durable mechanism of Bill Blunden's plotting.

So David J. Girton, as director, was content to be a chubby, bonhomous presence around the rehearsal room, and to punctuate the days with his two catch-phrases, 'Anyone fancy a little drink?' and 'Anyone going out for a meal?'

The take-up he got on the second question was smaller than that he got on the first. David J. Girton's eating habits were expensive. Long training with a flexible BBC expense account had provided him with a compendious list of smart restaurants, which were beyond the means of most of his cast. Bernard Walton, and the others who could have afforded it, tended to duck the eating invitation. They were professionals, concentrating on the show. They'd be happy to go out for lavish meals between projects, or to celebrate high points of the current production – first night and so on – but they didn't aspire to them, as their director did, on a daily basis.

A good few of the cast, however, were happy to take up David J. Girton's invitation to 'a little drink' – particularly because he hadn't yet broken his old BBC habit of hurrying to the bar and buying the first round. So that was what happened on the day of the last London rehearsal for *Not On Your Wife!* The director, keen to top up his own alcohol level, issued the customary 'Anyone fancy a little drink?', and most of the company were happy to take up his offer.

Bernard Walton was one of the exceptions. 'S-sorry,' he said, with the familiar and studied stutter which had been the dynamo of his comedy career. 'Got to get into the dickie bow for this AIDS charity do at the Shaftesbury.'

'I can't make it either, I'm afraid, David,' apologised the youngest member of the cast, Pippa Trewin, who played Louise. She was a pretty enough and perfectly competent young actress, though Charles had been surprised that she'd got a substantial part in such a major tour straight out of drama school.

He was even more surprised at that moment to see Bernard Walton give Pippa a discreet little wave and mouth, 'See you later, love.'

Maybe her casting wasn't such a surprise then, after all. Charles had known Bernard Walton for a very long time – he'd directed the young actor in his first major role, as Young Marlowe in *She Stoops to Conquer* – and in all that time Charles'd never heard the faintest whiff of sexual gossip about him. In the relationship maelstrom that is the theatre, Bernard was one of the minority who had stayed locked into his original marriage. Indeed, it was a subject on which he frequently waxed boring in television chat-shows and magazine interviews.

Charles's view had always been that Bernard was not that interested in sex. The all-consuming passions of the star's life were his career and, more recently, his desire to get a knighthood for 'charitable work and services to the theatre'. Any woman who could put up with his whingeing and worrying on all the time about those two subjects would have no difficulty in staying married to him.

But, thought Charles wryly, Bernard Walton wouldn't be the first star to have maintained a front of devoted domesticity and had a vibrantly active alternative sex-life going on. Nonetheless, the whispered words to Pippa Trewin did still seem out of character. Apart from anything else, dalliances with young actresses weren't recommended for an actor with his sights set on a knighthood.

Still, the conjectural infidelity of Bernard Walton wasn't Charles Paris's problem, and, besides, he was in no position to contemplate first-stone-casting. Charles's own sex-life was currently moribund, and he was at that worrying stage of a man's life, his late fifties, when 'moribund' could easily become 'over'. Maybe he never would make love to a woman again. The current frostiness of his relationship with Frances, the woman to whom he was still technically married, offered little hope of a rapprochement, and there weren't currently any other contenders for the role of Charles Paris's bed-mate.

The only detail about the whole sad subject that gave him the occasional flicker of optimism was that, although nothing was actually happening, he hadn't lost the desire for something to happen. He still woke up randy in the mornings, and the flash of a leg, an image on the television, the glimpse of a woman on a poster, could still work their old, predictable, frustrating magic.

These were his thoughts as Charles Paris made his way through to the cloakroom at the end of rehearsal. The coat that he lifted off its hook felt lopsidedly heavy, and Charles remembered with relief that he'd got a half-bottle of Bell's whisky in the pocket. Not a full half-bottle, probably a half-full half-bottle, but it was still a reassuring presence. He had a sudden urge to feel the slight resistance of the metal cap turning in his hand, the touch of upturned glass against his lips, the burn of the liquor in his throat.

He looked around. He was alone in the cloakroom. Just a quick sip...? But no. Someone might walk in, and there are certain reputations no actor wants to get in a company – particularly at the beginning of a three-month tour.

It wasn't as if he didn't need a pee, anyway. Charles slipped on his coat and went through into the Gents'. Once there, although the pressure was only on his bladder, he ignored the urinals in favour of a cubicle. He went in and locked the door.

Just one quick swig. To make him more relaxed when he joined the rest of the company.

Mm, God, it was good. He felt the whisky trickle down, performing its Midas touch, sending a golden glow right through his body. Mm, just one more. Lovely.

And a third. But that was it. Charles Paris knew when to stop. He firmly screwed down the cap on the bottle, thrust it deep into his coat pocket, and went off to join the rest of the company in the pub.

'Sorry, old boy. Didn't have time to get to the cash machine and it's my round. Don't suppose you could sub me a tenner?'

'Of course.' Charles opened his wallet expansively. It was Thursday; he'd just been paid. 'Help yourself.'

'Well, I'll take twenty, just to be sure. But you'll have it back tomorrow, promise. If there's one thing I can't stand, it's being in debt to anyone.'

'No problem.' Charles was feeling in a generous mood. His Bell's level had been topped up by a double from David J. Girton's first round, and then a couple more. Now, ever the one to know how to moderate his drinking, Charles Paris was on the red wine. And that seemed to be slipping down a treat too. He was feeling really bloody good.

The beneficiary of his bountiful mood had taken the two ten-pound notes, folded them and stuck them firmly in his inside pocket, before handing the wallet back.

'You're a saint, Charles,' said Ransome George. He was one of those actors, of indeterminate age, who was never out of work. Though he was not the most intelligent or subtlest interpreter of a part, Ransome George's face was, quite literally, his fortune. It was a funny face, in repose a melancholy boxer dog, in animation an affronted bullfrog. He had only to appear on stage, or on a television screen, for the audience to start feeling indulgent, for them to experience the little tug of a smile at the corner of their lips.

He was also blessed with intuitive comic timing. Whatever the situation, some internal clock told him exactly how long to hold a pause, when to slam in quickly with his next line, when to extend the silence almost unbearably. And he never failed to catch the reward of a laugh.

That was all Ransome George could do. Whatever the part, whatever the play, the performance was identical. Whether the lines were spoken in Yorkshire, Cornish, Welsh, Scottish, Transylvanian – or an approximation to these, because he wasn't very good at accents – they would be delivered in exactly the same way. And they'd always get the laughs. That guarantee he carried with him made Ransome George – or 'Ran', as he was known to everyone in the business – an invaluable character to have in comedy sketches.

In a full-length play his value was less certain. Though a good comedy performer, Ran was not in truth much of an actor. He was good at individual moments, but couldn't lose his own personality in a character throughout the length of a play. This deficiency perhaps mattered less in farce than it would have done in more serious areas of the theatre, but Charles Paris was still quite surprised at Ransome George's casting in *Not On Your Wife!* Still, Ran seemed to have worked a lot with Bernard Walton over the years. Maybe the old pals' act, a phenomenon all too common in the theatre, had been once again in operation.

In *Not On Your Wife!* Ransome George was playing the part of Willie, the flamboyant (for 'flamboyant' in British farce scripts, always read 'gay stereotype') interior designer. He wasn't playing the part particularly gay – indeed he was delivering the Standard Mark One Ransome George performance – but the laughs were inevitably going to be there.

Whether Ran was in reality gay or not, Charles Paris did not know. But from the way the actor, boosted by the loan of twenty pounds, homed back in on the dishy young assistant stage manager, it seemed unlikely. Charles did notice, though, that the girl had just placed two full glasses on their table. It wasn't Ran's round yet.

Somewhere in the back of his mind came a recollection: he'd heard somewhere that Ransome George was surprisingly successful with women. In spite of his cartoon face and shapeless body, he could always make them laugh. And rumour had it he'd laughed his way into a good few beds over the years.

The thought threw a pale cast of melancholy over Charles, as he compared his own current sexless state. His eyes glazed over, looking out at, but not taking in, the bustle of the busy pub.

'Come on, it's not that bad,' a husky voice murmured in his ear.

'Sorry?' He turned to face Cookie Stone, the actress playing Gilly, who'd just moved across to sit beside him. Though not as cartoon-like as Ran's, Cookie's face too was perfect for comedy. A pert snub nose had difficulty separating two mischievous dark brown eyes, and her broad mouth seemed to contain more than the standard ration of teeth. But her body, Charles couldn't help noticing as she leant her pointed breasts towards him, was firm and trim.

He reckoned Cookie must be late thirties now, maybe a bit more, and, like Ran, she was never out of work. She'd started in her teens as the female stooge for television comedians, playing all those roles – secretaries, nurses, receptionists, shop assistants – that the sketches of the time demanded. And she'd always got the laughs by her mixture of sex and mischief. The body was undeniably sexy, but the jokey face – by no means traditionally beautiful – suggested another dimension to her character, an ironic awareness of the roles in which she found herself.

This quality had stood Cookie Stone in good stead when the priorities of comedy changed, when political correctness emerged as an issue, and women comedians started to take a more central role. That revolution had put out of business many of the pretty little things who'd formerly adorned television comedy. It was now unacceptable for a woman to be on screen simply because she was sexy, and for that to be the basis of an item's humour. But an actress who could look sexy while at the same time, by her expression, giving a post-modernist gloss to her sexiness, was worth her weight in gold. So there had been no blip in the career of Cookie Stone.

But her ranking in the comedy business hadn't changed. After a decade of playing stooge to a series of male comedians who commanded the lion's share of the show's funny lines (not to mention its budget), she now played stooge to a series of female comedians who commanded the lion's share of the show's funny lines (not to mention its budget). Cookie still had no power; she had simply changed bosses.

And, in a way, that was fair. Cookie Stone had no originating talent, but she was a very good mimic and a quick learner. She absorbed the comedy technique of everyone she worked with and, as a result, had become a consummately skilful comedy actress. Her every take, her every pause, her every intonation, had been copied from another performer, but her armoury of them was now so large, and her skill in selecting them so great, that she was almost indistinguishable from an actress of intuitive comedy skills.

'I was saying, Charles...' she continued, in a favourite voice, the humorous right-on feminist learnt from one of the first female stand-ups to do menstruation jokes on television, 'I was saying that, like, you really look as though you've just had a fax saying the world's about to end.'

'No. Rubbish. Someone just walked over my grave, that's all. You OK for a drink?'

Cookie raised a half-full glass of red. 'Cheers, I'm entirely OK, thank you,' she slurred, in the remembered voice of a comedian who'd killed himself with exhaust fumes after rather nasty tabloid allegations about rent boys.

They talked and had a couple more glasses of red wine, and then looked round and realised there was nobody they recognised left in the pub. The rest of the *Not On Your Wife!* company had all gone home, or on to eat. Maybe some of them, flushed with the success of the day's rehearsal and the fact that it was pay-day, had even gone to join David J. Girton at some smart restaurant.

Charles and Cookie could have had another drink, but it seemed the moment for him to say, 'You fancy eating something?' He wasn't sure whether he was hungry or not, but he knew some kind of blotting paper was a good idea.

Outside the pub, they swayed on the kerb. 'Where we going then, Daddy?' asked Cookie, in the voice of an American comedian who'd been given her own short-lived series at the moment when television had first fallen in love with female stand-ups.

'Erm...' A taxi drew up in obedience to Charles's wavering hand. 'I know.' He couldn't think of anywhere else. There was an Italian on Westbourne Grove, just round the corner from his tiny studio flat.

Inside the restaurant, he ordered a bottle of Chianti Classico. They also ordered some pasta – at least he was fairly sure it was pasta, though he had no recollection of eating it. Maybe it was one of those evenings when at the end of the meal impassive waiters had gathered up virtually untouched plates.

Charles did remember them ordering a few sambucas, though, and joking as they blew out the blue flames that rose from the top of their glasses. He remembered Cookie's head leant close to his across the table, her tongue constantly licking over her prominent teeth as she talked. And he remembered, in a fit of righteousness, ordering each of them a large espresso 'to sober up a bit'.

He also remembered listening with great concentration to Cookie Stone, though he was a little vague about what she actually said. He knew, however, that it was said in many different voices, that there was a lot about the actor's identity, and how every actor hid his or her true, snivelling, abject self under the comforting carapace of fictional characters, and how few men bothered to probe into what the real Cookie Stone was like, and, generally speaking, what bastards men were, and how all most of them wanted was just to get her back to their place for a quick shag.

And Charles remembered being very understanding and very sympathetic to Cookie, and saying she was right, yes, she was right, she'd really put her finger on it, and how if only men and women talked more, communicated more, then maybe there'd be a bit more understanding between them and they'd be able to break away from these old-fashioned stereotypes. Men and women were both people, after all, that was the important thing about what they were, people. Men and women were people.

He must also have paid the bill at some point, presumably with a credit card. He couldn't actually remember doing it, but the fact that he and Cookie were allowed to leave the restaurant suggested that the relevant transaction had somehow taken place.

For the life of him, he couldn't remember the conversation that must have ensued on the pavement outside the restaurant, the precise form of words – and who they were spoken by – which led to Cookie Stone going back to his place.

He must have been drunk, though, for that to have happened. To let someone else see the shambles of old newspapers and grubby clothes in which he lived, he must've had a few.

Charles had recollections of finding an unopened bottle of Bell's at Hereford Road, and of opening it. He had recollections of charging a couple of glasses, then of moving a pile of newspapers and books off the bed, and of lying down on it with Cookie.

But of what happened next, he couldn't be exactly sure. Certainly, when he woke at three-fifteen, she was entirely naked. She lay on her back, breasts pointing firmly upwards, and snored nasally. Charles was wearing his socks and, somewhere round his shins, telescoped trousers and briefs.

But he didn't have time to explore further. His head was drumming, his throat was as dry as a desert of sandpaper, and he felt violently and urgently sick. He just managed to make it to the bathroom, where he threw up loudly and copiously into the toilet bowl.

Charles Paris finished the day, as he had begun it, with his trousers round his ankles, though this time it was not for professional reasons.

Chapter Two

IT WAS'NT GOOD. It really wasn't good. The words swam in front of his eyes, and if there's one thing you don't want when you're being paid to read a book for audio cassette, it's the words swimming in front of your eyes.

In the not-inconsiderable annals of Charles Paris's hangovers, this one stood out. He'd never felt as bad as he did at that moment. He knew whenever he had a hangover he thought he'd never felt as bad as he did at that moment, but this was on a different scale. It really was.

Everything felt dreadful. His whole body ached. The joints, particularly knees and elbows, ached even more than the rest of his components. There was a pain and stiffness at the back of his neck that rendered him incapable of moving his head without moving the rest of his body too, like some awkward cardboard cut-out. The dryness in his mouth had moved on from sandpaper quality to the feeling of having been sand-blasted. His eyes stung as if he'd spent a couple of hours underwater in an over-chlorinated pool. And his digestion felt seriously at risk. The jacuzzi of his stomach threatened to overflow at any moment, and without warning of which direction that overflow might take. His guts complained at their treatment with rumbles that wouldn't have sounded out of place in the third rinse of a dishwasher cycle. And a rumbling stomach doesn't help an audio book recording either.

He could have tolerated the sickness of his body, if his mind had not also been infected. While his mouth continued to pronounce the swimming words on the page, his mind seethed with self-hatred and recrimination. Why on earth had he let himself get so drunk? He must've been aware of the way he was going, why hadn't he put a brake on it?

He was such a fool. A man in his late fifties behaving like a teenager at his first grown-up party. And it was hideously unprofessional – the worst insult that can be levelled at an actor – for him to get so wasted the night before he was to start on a whole new area of work. Getting the contract to record an audio book could be a breakthrough into a different, and possibly lucrative, market; he mustn't screw it up.

At the bottom of all these anxieties, lurking like some evil predator in the depths of a murky pool, lay the question of what he'd said the night before. Worse than that, what he had *done* the night before.

Cookie Stone. What had happened between him and Cookie Stone? He knew the position in which they'd found themselves at three-fifteen, but what had been the precise sequence of events that had led up to that?

Various possibilities presented themselves. One – the most unlikely – was that they'd just gone to bed together for a cuddle, mutual support for two lonely people, and by agreement nothing else had happened. A second scenario – also, he feared, unlikely – was that they had enjoyed a long session of abandoned, passionate and satisfying love-making. The third – and the one towards which he was unwillingly inclining – was that they had prepared to make love, gone through all the soft-talking and the anticipatory blandishments, that they had started to make love, and then that he had proved incapable of completing the process, and fallen into a drunken stupor halfway through.

Charles had a horrible feeling that that was what had happened, but his memory could offer him no help on the subject. His recollection of the previous night's events, after their departure from the Italian restaurant, was, to use the most generous adjective possible in the circumstances, hazy.

And there hadn't been much chance in the morning for Charles and Cookie to compare notes. He had woken in a sweat of panic at 6.33, suddenly aware that he was supposed to be catching the 7.15 train from Paddington to Bath for the day's recording. In the rush of his own dressing and incomplete ablutions, and of hurrying Cookie through her reduced morning ritual, there hadn't been any opportunity for an assessment – or more likely a post mortem – of the previous night's encounter. They had parted with their stale mouths joining in a dry kiss and a cheery 'See you Monday', but no mention had been made of any relationship in which they might be considered to be involved.

And, as so often after an unsatisfactory skirmish with a member of the opposite sex, all Charles could think about was his wife Frances. Though there seemed almost nothing now left between them, he still felt as if he had betrayed her. There was even, at the back of his mind, the appalling thought that at some point during the events of the previous evening, he'd found a message from Frances on his answering machine. Surely that couldn't be true, surely that was just the guilt getting at him?

Even worse, though, was the fear that he'd actually phoned his wife back, just a quick call to establish contact, and that she'd said she wouldn't talk to him until he was sober.

No, that bit couldn't be true, he felt sure. It was just his mind providing another prompt of guilt to add to the muddy swirl of self-recrimination. But, hallucination or not, it wasn't a thought that improved his mood.

As it had transpired, in spite of his heroic rush to the station, Charles had just missed his train at Paddington and had to wait nearly a full hour for the 8.15. He'd hung mournfully about the concourse, clutching a copy of *The Times* he didn't feel up to reading, and wishing the owners of the privatised station had made more seats available. At one point he contemplated the rough remedy of a Full English Breakfast, but the smell of food as he entered the cafeteria brought nausea back to his throat and he had had to hurry out again.

The train had arrived in Bath on time, at 9.38, but there had been a queue for taxis and, as luck would have it, the driver Charles finally got seemed to be spending his first day in the city. The address of the studio was not familiar to him and, when they at last reached the relevant road, they had difficulty finding the right building. The studio was a recent conversion, and its name had not yet been put up outside.

As a result, instead of arriving in good time for a relaxed chat before the contractual ten o'clock start of recording, Charles had bumbled in at ten-twenty, panicked and deeply hungover. His producer said it really didn't matter, missing the train could have happened to anyone, but the girl who seemed to be looking after the technical side looked less than amused.

But then, if anyone was going to sympathise with Charles Paris's condition, his producer was that person. Mark Lear himself was certainly not unacquainted with the bottle. Charles had known him for years, and they had worked together when Mark was a BBC Radio producer of Further Education, a department which had later become known as 'Continuing Education' and no doubt gone through a whole raft of other name-changes in the years since.

Mark Lear had always been a licensed BBC malcontent, continually moaning about the Corporation and asserting that he wasn't going to stay, that soon he would be 'out in the real world, doing my own thing'. Well, in the late 1980s, along with a great many other members of the BBC staff, he got his wish, though not perhaps in the way he would have wanted. Mark Lear had been offered an early retirement package that didn't carry the option of refusal, and at the age of fifty found himself being taken at his word and having the opportunity to 'do his own thing'.

The 'thing' he chose to do – or perhaps 'chose' is too positive a word to describe the way he drifted into it – was to set up an audio production company with its own tiny recording studios in Bath. It was an initiative Mark Lear could never have managed on his own. However much he banged on about BBC bureaucracy stifling his creativity, about his longing to shake the dust of the place off his heels and be his own boss, in reality he revelled in the cosiness of a big institution. Whether he'd had much initiative when he started his career was questionable, but twenty years in the Corporation had drained any he did have out of him. Mark Lear would never have started his own company without someone else to push him.

The person who had done the pushing was the girl behind the control panel in the studio that morning. Her name was Lisa Wilson, and two things about her relationship with Mark quickly became apparent. First, it was not exclusively professional. And, second, in their business venture she was at least an equal partner.

Charles reckoned he could piece together how Mark and Lisa had met. As a producer in the BBC, Mark Lear had always taken full advantage of the regular supply of attractive single girls who worked there, and his wife

Vinnie had either remained in ignorance or, more likely, turned a blind eye to his serial infidelities. For many years, Mark had enjoyed a very convenient life-style, using the excuse of 'late bookings in the studio' to cover his philanderings, and always returning to the safety of the elegant Hampstead house which Vinnie's private income had bought them. The set-up was not one that Mark had ever had any need – or indeed desire – to alter.

The impetus for change, when it did come, came from Vinnie. She fell in love. She felt she'd done her duty by their three daughters, who were by then off at university, and for the first time in her life, Vinnie Lear behaved with total selfishness. She had no choice. The love she felt for her new man was unanswerably powerful. Within three months – in spite of Mark's self-justifying whingeing, in spite of their children's reactions, including the development of an eating disorder in the youngest, Claudia – the divorce had been finalised, the Hampstead house sold, and Vinnie had moved in with her new lover. Within another three months, Vinnie Lear, now insisting on being called 'Lavinia', had had her face and body expensively remodelled by plastic surgery, and remarried.

Mark Lear, for whom these events coincided with early retirement, spun reeling into a small flat in Pimlico. Once again, he'd achieved what had been long wished for. He'd said frequently to anyone who'd listen – and particularly to his sequence of young paramours – that what a free spirit like him really needed was 'my own pad, a bachelor place where I can just, you know, like, be myself'. And, in case this might raise in his listeners any inconvenient ideas of potential cohabitation, he would swiftly add, 'but of course, I couldn't do that, you know, because of the children'.

The reality of freedom, the realisation that there were now no restrictions on his free spirit, did not prove to be quite the nirvana Mark Lear had hoped for. No longer being in the BBC had reduced his supply of nubile young women. And those he did manage to lure out to Pimlico, though quite happy to have a bit of quick sex, proved less willing to listen to the witterings of a worried fifty-year-old – and deeply unwilling to provide any domestic back-up for him. Mark had been spoilt by living with Vinnie, and assumed that anyone vouchsafed the rich gift of his body would feel automatically obliged to reciprocate by doing his washing and cooking. But the single younger women he encountered in 1990s London were unaware of any such obligation.

It didn't take Mark Lear long to realise that, if he was going to find someone else to look after him, it would have to be in the context of another ongoing relationship. And it was around the time this message sank in that he met Lisa Wilson.

She was some twelve years younger, and had also worked in BBC Radio. She had never been on the staff – in the organisation's changed climate almost everyone worked on short contracts – but Lisa had shown sufficient flair and energy to be in demand and be offered many such contracts. Her departure from the BBC had been voluntary. She genuinely wanted to set up her own business.

Since this decision coincided with the establishment of her relationship with Mark Lear, since he was an experienced producer, and since he had come out of his divorce with a lump sum from the sale of the house, it seemed logical for the two of them to set up in partnership.

Lisa had organised everything. She it was who had done the research and costings for the project, and who had made the economic decision that they'd do better out of London. She had found the premises in Bath, she had designed and overseen their conversion into studios. She had dealt with planning problems and building regulations. She had sorted out the insurance, checking quote against quote. She had arranged for the fixing of the security systems the insurance companies demanded – window-locks, dead-bolts on the outer doors – and on the studio and cubicle doors too, because valuable equipment might be stored in there.

It was Lisa Wilson too who had touted for work to keep the studios filled. She had selected where to place advertisements. She had had business cards and flyers printed. She had relentlessly followed up any contacts which might result in bookings.

And Mark, apart from the occasional whinge about moving out of London, had been content to be swept along in Lisa's wake. His skills, after all, were on the creative side of things; his sensitive mind couldn't be cluttered with managerial details.

But even in the studio, the environment in which Mark's skills were supposed to blossom, Lisa was taking the dominant role. When Charles arrived, Mark, who seemed to be nursing a hangover of his own, had been quite content to natter away for a while over a cup of coffee. It was Lisa who had pressed for them to start recording, pointing out that they only had two days to complete a full-length book.

The work in question was not one that Charles Paris would have read for anything other than money. It was entitled *Dark Promises*, and written by someone called Madeleine Eglantine, with the rest of whose oeuvre he was unfamiliar. The book was one of those standard-issue romances, in which the right man and woman meet in Chapter One, and are then kept apart for two hundred pages by misunderstandings and external circumstances, until being joyfully reunited, and presumably married, in the last chapter. Charles, who was of the view that everything necessary in the romantic genre had been achieved by *Jane Eyre* and *Wuthering Heights*, found it difficult to summon up much interest in the characters. The heroine, despite Madeleine Eglantine's constant assertions of how strong-willed and feisty she was, came across as totally insipid. And the hero, although there were frequent references to his 'struggles with his own demons', seemed plain dull. Nor could Charles find much good to say about the author's prose style.

Still, it was work, and work that could lead to other work. Lisa Wilson had organised a deal with a publisher to record a whole series of such romances.

The audio book market was a growing one, and it would be handy for Charles to join that select list of not-very-famous but reliable actors who spend much of their time in the intimacy of small recording studios reading books out loud.

It was an opportunity, and Charles wished he was feeling less shitty as he faced that opportunity. He thanked God that he had actually done his homework on the book a few days before. If he'd left it till the train that morning, the text would have seemed more alien than it already did.

Even without the hangover, he wouldn't have found it easy. As a bit of a writer himself, Charles found the book's style awkward, and kept wanting to change sentences to give them greater fluency. But he wasn't allowed to do that. Every time he deviated by a word from Madeleine Eglantine's text, Lisa Wilson would put down the talkback key from the control cubicle and say patiently, 'Sorry, can we go back on that?'

'But what I said was much better,' Charles had complained the first few times. 'I mean, it's not as if we're dealing with Shakespeare here, is it?'

'Sorry,' Lisa had responded firmly. 'We have to do the book as printed.'

'Oh, OK.' And Charles reread the unamended text.

What with these interruptions, and the fluffs caused by a tongue that seemed to be the wrong size for his mouth, and the retakes necessitated by intrusive stomach rumbles, the morning's reading made slow progress.

Charles hadn't realised how difficult it would be. He was an experienced actor, after all. But most of his work had involved other actors, whose performances his own could bounce off. Acting with others shared the burden; the maximum pressure was sometimes on one, sometimes on another. But in that tiny, airless studio, he was on his own. It was just Charles Paris and Madeleine Eglantine. His concentration had to be total all the time.

In fact, the part of the proceedings Charles had found most difficult had arisen before they even started on Madeleine Eglantine's text. Once Lisa Wilson had checked Charles's voice level and made a few adjustments to the settings in the control cubicle, she had said, 'Can we start by doing the cassette numbering?'

'Sorry?'

'We have to get you to do the announcements that come at the beginning and end of each side. "Side One" – "End of Side One" – "Side Two" and so on.'

'Just that?'

'Mm. With this book you'll have to go up to "Side Twelve". Six cassettes, you see. If you could just do them all on the trot, leaving, like, a couple of seconds' pause between each announcement...?'

Charles Paris chuckled, which was an unwise thing to do with a hangover like his. The chuckle seemed to shake together all the bits of him that hurt. Nevertheless, he managed to say, 'Well, that doesn't sound too difficult.'

'OK. Tape's rolling. In your own time.'

Charles left a silence and then intoned, 'Side One...'

His pause was interrupted by Lisa's voice on the talkback. 'No, sorry, can you do it again?'

'What was wrong with it?'

'Too much intonation.'

'Oh dear.'

'They should have no intonation at all. Just completely flat. No rhythm. Like the football results.'

Charles Paris tried again. 'Side One...'

'No, sorry. You're still making it sound like it means something.'

'Well, it does. It means "Side One".'

'Yes, but you're making it sound like "Side One" has some hidden significance.'

'OK. I will try to bleach the words of all significance. Is the tape still rolling?' Through the glass, Lisa Wilson's blonde head nodded. Pretty girl, thought Charles, I could envy Mark a bit of that. Even as he had the thought, came the recrimination. How on earth, after what had happened the night before, could he ever again find the nerve to have a sexual thought about any woman? 'Side One...'

'Sorry,' Lisa's voice broke in. 'Still sounds a bit actorish.'

Charles Paris found it very hard. He sounded 'actorish' because he was an actor. And an actor is trained to give significance to words. To be asked to bleach them of all intonation and rhythm was to be asked to unlearn decades of technique.

He made another attempt. 'Side One...'

'Nearly,' said Lisa. 'Getting close. Just one more try and I think we'll be there.'

As Charles Paris struggled to get his tongue round Madeleine Eglantine's prose, he realised he was feeling worse. The hangover showed no signs of shifting. The pain across his eyebrows was intensifying.

Partly, it was the claustrophobia of his setting. The premises that Lisa Wilson had had converted into studios had been the ground floor of a corner shop. There were now, crammed into the space, a tiny reception, small sitting area, kitchenette, toilets and two recording studios. The larger could just about accommodate a small drama production or a musical group. It was walled with movable acoustic screens, which could be set up to muffle the recorded sound, or reversed to show a shiny surface which produced a more echoey or 'live' sound quality.

The other studio, in which Charles Paris was working, was little more than a cupboard, separated from its tiny control cubicle by thick double doors. There was just room inside for one chair, and a cloth-covered table with a cloth-covered book-rest on it. Beside this stood an Anglepoise lamp, a jug of water and a glass. The studio's walls were heavily upholstered with dark sound-proofing material, which seemed to press down and take away more of the available space.

'It's very dead in here,' Lisa had said, when she first showed Charles inside. 'This is our dead room. That's what you want for an audio book. No ambient atmosphere. It makes the sound more intimate.'

As he read on, Charles was increasingly aware of how quickly intimacy could become claustrophobia. The narrow focus of light on the book intensified the feeling of encroaching darkness around him. The air he breathed felt stale and recycled.

'I'm sorry,' he said, about three-quarters of an hour into the session, after a particularly messy sequence of fluffs. 'Do you mind if I just come out and get a breath of air?'

'No, of course not,' said Lisa. 'Apologies, I should have thought. We try to open up the studio doors every half hour or so, but because we started so late, I forgot.' She pulled the two heavy doors open. Their draught-excluding strips hissed against the carpet. 'Come on, Charles, stretch your legs.' She shook her head in apology. 'Sorry. The air conditioning in there isn't working. Well, it is working, but we can't use it.'

'Oh?'

'Boring and technical, but they swore blind they'd installed a system that was completely silent. Sadly, as soon as we switched it on, it started to hum. Not very loud, but enough to come across on the tape. They should be here to sort it out tomorrow.' Lisa looked with sudden sharpness across to Mark. 'You did ring the engineers, didn't you?'

'What?'

'The engineers. To come and sort out this air conditioning.'

'Oh...' Mark said vaguely.

'*Did* you call them? Go on, Mark, *did* you?'

'Yes, of course I bloody called them! For Christ's sake, Lisa, stop treating me like a child.'

'So when are they coming?'

'Tomorrow. They're coming to-bloody-morrow!'

Charles Paris cleared his throat uneasily, and Lisa realised this wasn't the moment for a domestic row. 'Sorry, Charles. Would you like a coffee or something?'

'Please.'

While Lisa went off to make the coffee, Mark Lear, who had hardly stirred from his chair all morning, grinned knowingly at his friend. 'Could do with something stronger than coffee, I dare say, couldn't you?'

'Well...I have got a little bit of a hangover this morning,' said Charles, with breathtaking understatement.

'Me too. Incidentally, sorry about the stuffiness. I'll put the air conditioning on now, to cool the studio down.' Mark Lear threw a switch. 'You see, it's all right so long as we're not actually trying to record. And, so long as we remember to open the studio doors every half hour or so, you'll be fine.' He chuckled. 'Basic rule of production – don't suffocate your artistes.'

Lisa returned with the coffee, and also a printed list on a laminated plastic sheet. 'Sandwiches,' she announced. 'If you say what you want, Charles, I'll ring through and then they'll deliver round lunch-time.'

'Oh, I think we'll go to the pub,' said Mark. 'It's so much easier.'

Lisa looked peeved, and spoke as if this was not a new argument. 'It may be easier, but it always takes longer, and we're already behind...'

'See how far we've got by one o'clock,' said Mark. 'If we've picked up a bit of time, we'll go to the pub.'

Maybe that wasn't the reason why the morning's second session of reading was more fluent than the first. Maybe Charles Paris was just getting into his stride. But the prospect of a drink was a real incentive.

Throughout the morning Lisa had given the orders, but as the hands of the studio clock approached one, it was Mark who said, 'OK, let's break it there. Well, we've done pretty well. Think we've earned lunch at the pub.' He turned defiantly to Lisa as he said the words, daring her to challenge him.

She didn't. She held back, and replied lightly, 'As you wish.'

'You coming?'

The blonde head shook. 'Got a few phone calls to do. And a bit of editing.' As Mark and Charles gathered up their coats, she couldn't help saying, 'Be sure you're back by two.'

'Of course,' said Mark. And then, with the slightest edge of irony, 'Of course, my dear.'

As a general rule, Charles Paris tried to avoid having a lunch-time drink when he was working, particularly working on something that required as much concentration as *Dark Promises*. But this time he wouldn't be having a drink for purely recreational reasons; it was a medical necessity. His system cried out for irrigation, and that had to be a pint of bitter.

As he felt the first mouthful go down, he knew his decision had been the right one. God, it made him feel better.

Chapter Three

HE WAS QUITE good. Really. At least he reckoned he was. Just a couple of pints, and two sandwiches to do the blotting-paper job. And it was only a few minutes after two – well, two-fifteen – when they got back to the studio.

But Lisa Wilson's face was unamused. It wore the kind of unamused look that, from primeval times, wives have perfected to greet husbands coming home later than they promised. Charles reflected that Mark Lear had maybe not landed so perfectly on his feet, after all. The attractions of a younger woman were presumably avid sex and blind adoration, not the cross-armed resentment of an aggrieved spouse.

'OK, straight through to studio,' Lisa said brusquely. 'We're behind schedule.'

'Yes, just nip for a pee,' said Charles. He wasn't sure this was a good idea. A pee so soon after two pints of bitter could frequently be the precursor to a busy sequence of pees. Still, he did feel the need.

When he came back, Lisa was bringing Mark up to date on the phone calls she had made during the lunch break. 'I think you should follow up on it.'

'Yes, yes,' said Mark breezily.

'No, soon. I've found out that the market's there. I thought we'd agreed that you would do the follow-up on those kind of openings.'

'Yes, sure, sure.'

She lifted the cordless phone off its base and held it out to him, along with a business card. 'There's the number.'

'Yeah, I'm not going to do it right now.'

'Why not?'

'Because it's only half-past two. Everyone knows publishers don't get back from lunch till three.'

'You could leave a message.'

'Not on a Friday afternoon. They all go home early on a Friday. POETS. Piss Off Early – Tomorrow's Saturday.' He sniggered at the recollected BBC joke.

Lisa didn't share his amusement. 'I think you've got an outdated concept of how publishers work these days, Mark. It's a hard-nosed, accountable business, like everything else.' She waved the cordless phone in front of him. 'Come on, are you going to do it?'

'No,' he snapped. 'Will you kindly allow me to be the judge of how I conduct my own business!'

'Our business,' said Lisa. But she didn't press further. She put the phone back on its base, and they both seemed aware of Charles for the first time. Lisa answered the unintended interrogation in his expression. 'Possibility of more work,' she explained. 'A lot of publishers going multimedia. CD-ROMs.'

'Ah,' said Charles, to whom these expressions were vaguely familiar, but not subjects of which he had a full understanding.

'A lot of CD-ROM reference packages need an audio component,' she elaborated. 'Pronunciation dictionaries, that kind of thing.'

'Uh-uh,' said Charles, sounding as if he knew what she was talking about.

Lisa Wilson looked at her watch with a degree of exasperation. 'OK, we'd better get on.'

Charles was incarcerated back in the studio, which was quite pleasant at first because the air-conditioning had been on throughout the lunch break. He set off again up the North Face of Madeleine Eglantine's prose. It was currently the Second World War that was keeping *Dark Promises'* perfectly matched lovers apart. Not only that, but the hero was also now at risk from the blandishments of a tempestuous Italian partisan beauty. Since the tempestuous Italian partisan beauty and the heroine seemed interchangeably wet, and the hero's dullness was unalleviated, Charles Paris still found it difficult to summon up much interest in the proceedings.

But the drink had helped. His body's individual components felt more as if they were part of some functioning whole, and the pain behind his eyes had lifted. There were a few fluffs arising from his reduced sense of inhibition, but not as many as there had been before lunch.

At least that was how the afternoon's recording started. After three-quarters of an hour, however, the alcohol was beginning to wear off, the air had grown stale, and Charles felt his energy flagging. The dull headache had returned, his tongue seemed again swollen and ungainly, Madeleine Eglantine's writing increasingly indigestible. As he stumbled to the end of a page on which there had been some dozen stops and starts, Lisa Wilson threw in the towel. 'I've got to change the reel. Take a coffee break there.'

'OK,' said Charles gratefully. 'And let me have some air, eh?'

'Sure. Let him out, Mark.' Lisa, preoccupied with the large reel-to-reel tape recorder, turned her back to the studio.

There was no response and Charles noticed, through the refraction of the double glass, that his friend had gone to sleep. Lisa spotted this at the same moment and, though Charles couldn't hear the words she actually used to wake Mark up, by a combination of lip-reading and simple deduction he managed to piece them together.

Mark Lear rose to his feet, stretching, and pulled open the double doors. 'Want to come out?' He twiddled the key of the door's dead-bolt, and asked inanely, 'Or would you rather I incarcerated you in there for good?'

'No, thanks,' said Charles, rising from his seat and going through into the relatively fresh air of the cubicle. He too stretched out his arms. 'Always worst bit of the day, early afternoon. That's when most of us are at our biorhythmically lowest.'

Lisa flashed a sharp look at Mark. 'With some people, it's hard to tell.'

Her partner ignored the gibe. 'Do you want a coffee, love?'

'Please.'

'Did you get a sandwich at lunch?'

'Wasn't time,' Lisa answered shortly, as she reached for the telephone.

'You've got a good business partner there,' said Charles, when they were through in the sitting area and the kettle had been switched on.

'Oh, yes,' Mark agreed casually. 'I've always been lucky with my back-up.'

It was a splendidly dismissive remark, the kind that a BBC producer might often have made about his secretary. Charles wondered whether Mark was genuinely unaware that Lisa was doing all the work within their partnership. But maybe that was just a reflection of another old BBC tradition. There had always been plenty of producers whose offices had been run entirely by their secretaries, and it had been a point of honour that that fact was never acknowledged. Charles wondered idly how the balance of power operated in Mark and Lisa's personal relationship.

His head was now aching horribly again. His mouth was dry and the dryness permeated his body; parts of his anatomy seemed to grind unlubricated against other parts. Mark saw the hand Charles passed painfully across his brow and said, 'You need a top-up.'

'Hm.'

'Alcohol level. Dropping below critical. Serious malfunction could result.'

The conspiratorial tone and the pseudo-scientific jargon made Mark Lear sound like a naughty schoolboy, and this image was reinforced when he showed Charles the half-bottle of Teacher's he had hidden in the cistern of the Gents' lavatory.

Mark took a long swig. 'Wonderful. Ideal storage place.' He winked. 'No ladies come in here, by definition, and the water keeps the whisky perfectly chilled.' He proffered the bottle to Charles. 'Go on, this'll pick you up.'

'I'm not sure that I should...' Apart from anything else, he was a Bell's man. He'd never really been that fond of Teacher's.

'Go on.'

Charles's hesitation went the way of most good intentions. And the injection of alcohol did give him a predictable lift. But something about the whole episode felt shabby. Two middle-aged men in the Gents', hiding from a woman to take illicit sips of booze...there wasn't much dignity in the scenario.

Of course, it put Mark in a worse light than it did him. Mark had actually set up this private cache of whisky to hide his drinking from his partner. Charles would never have done that. He didn't hide his drinking from anyone. But then, even as he had the thought, he realised that was probably only because he lived on his own. It's easy enough to be overt when you know there's no one watching. If he had been cohabiting with someone who monitored his every sip, he wondered how long it would be before he resorted to subterfuge. He had an uneasy recollection of a bit of covert swigging towards the end of the time when he and Frances had lived together.

Mark Lear led the way back to their coffees with a smug, got-away-with-it smile. He produced a packet of Extra-Strong Mints from a pocket, and popped one into his mouth. 'Hide the evidence, eh?' He grinned as he offered the packet across.

Charles felt uncomfortable. There was something too calculating in all this, too cunning. He knew he drank too much, but he felt there was a degree of spontaneity about his drinking. Surely his own approach had never been this cold-blooded...? He did, nonetheless, take one of the Extra-Strong Mints.

Mark Lear grinned. 'Should keep us going till the end of the day's recording. The old "maintenance dose", eh?'

Charles resented the implication. He didn't like the way Mark spoke of their two problems as if they were the same. Mark was clearly an alcoholic, who was in chemical need of a 'maintenance dose'. Whereas Charles, on the other hand...But he knew the exaggerated pique at his friend's words rose from a suspicion that they might be all too applicable to himself.

On his way back to the cubicle, Charles thought he caught a flash of suspicion in Lisa's face as she looked at her partner and Mark averted his eye. But the moment didn't last. Lisa had clearly been busy on the phone during their absence.

'I've talked to the publishers.'

'Oh yes?' Mark sounded Olympian, detached. He was glad to have staff to sort out the minutiae for him, and glad they kept him up to date with their progress.

'They're doing a version of a Thesaurus on CD-ROM and, yes, they are accepting tenders for the audio content.'

'That's good,' said Mark smugly, as if all his careful planning was about to come to fruition.

'I've fixed a meeting for Thursday afternoon. You'll be free, won't you?'

'Not sure,' Mark replied, with the air of a man in whose diary an empty space was an endangered rarity.

Lisa's lips pursed. 'Well, we'd better get on. Find out what new excitements *Dark Promises* has in store. Through you go, Charles. Afraid I'll have to switch off the air conditioning again.'

The last session of the recording was the most constructive of the day. Charles Paris was more fluent, he found the rhythms of Madeleine Eglantine's prose less alien, and a good few pages got safely recorded. Only in the last half-hour, after five-thirty, did his concentration go. Sheer tiredness took over. His voice became croaky, and the fluffs proliferated.

At ten to six, Lisa Wilson gave up the unequal struggle. 'OK, let's call that a wrap. Well done, Charles. Last bit was very good.'

'Thanks.' He acknowledged the compliment with a tired grin. But inside him was the lurking fear that the recording wouldn't have been so good without that mid-afternoon injection of alcohol. Had he really reached the stage when he needed a 'maintenance dose'?

As he went through into the cubicle, he ached all over, but it was a better ache than that brought on by the hangover. This was the tiredness of having achieved something.

'Only about twenty pages behind where we should be,' said Lisa, with a hint of approbation in her voice. 'You picked up the pace quite a bit.'

'Well done,' Mark agreed. 'I'd say that deserves a drink.'

Charles saw the tiny spasm go through Lisa's face, as she bit back her instinctive response. She had been living with Mark long enough to know that direct confrontation wasn't the best way of dealing with him.

'You coming, love?' her partner asked, a slight tease in his voice, once again daring her to express disapproval.

'No,' she replied lightly. 'Got to do a Sainsbury's run when I finish in here.'

'OK. Well, if I'm not home when you get back, we'll be in the Queen's Head.'

'Fine,' said Lisa Wilson, and only someone who, like Charles Paris, had witnessed her relationship with Mark throughout the day, would have known that what she meant was actually far from 'fine'.

'Happy coincidence.' Charles raised his glass, took a long swig and felt the warm glow of a second large Bell's irradiate his parched system. 'I mean, your studio being in Bath and our show opening in Bath.'

'What is the show? I know you told me, but I can't remember.' Mark Lear was also on the whisky, which he was downing as if the world's supplies were on the verge of exhaustion.

'*Not On Your Wife!*'

'Don't know it.'

'Well, you wouldn't. It's a new play. By Bill Blunden.'

'Oh.' The monosyllable contained all that snobbish resistance the playwright's work usually inspired in people with university educations. Bill Blunden may have been an audience-pleaser, but he didn't strike much of a chord among the intelligentsia. When, every now and then, Sunday newspaper reviewers took it into their heads to rehabilitate farce as an acceptable medium of entertainment, they would home in invariably on Feydeau, Pinero or perhaps Ben Travers. Bill Blunden was too ordinary, too mechanical; his plays were mere clockwork toys designed to entrap laughter. He would never attain intellectual respectability; his only comfort would have to remain the huge international royalties which his plays brought in.

'And you're touring it, Charles, is that right?'

'Mm, three months. Fortnight in Bath, then single weeks. Bill Blunden always takes his shows on the road, works on them, does lots of rewrites, sharpens them up.'

'With a view to the West End?'

'Ultimately, yes. But some'll have three or four tours before he's happy.'

'So you haven't got a West End option in your contract?'

'Nothing so grand, no. They did check my availability for three months hence, but that's as far as it went.'

'Oh, right.' Mark Lear chuckled with sudden recollection. 'Checked with your agent, eh? I've just remembered, when we last worked together, you were with this incredibly inefficient agent...what was his name? Maurice Skellern, that's right. He was a kind of a joke throughout the whole business, the worst agent since records began.' Mark shook his head and chuckled again. 'Who represents you now?'

'Maurice Skellern,' Charles Paris replied.

'Oh.'

'I hope today was all right...?' said Charles tentatively. 'I mean, the recording.'

'It was fine.'

'I felt awful, arriving so hungover and –'

'Don't worry, we've had many worse through the studio.'

'I didn't think the studio had been open that long.'

'Well, no, not through that studio, but when I was at the Beeb...' A hazy look came into Mark Lear's eyes. 'I remember once doing a play with Everard Austick, and he was virtually on an intravenous drip of gin.' The retired producer let out a little melancholy laugh. 'Good times we had, back in the old days...'

Charles could see what had happened. In Mark Lear's mind, the BBC, the institution he had spent all the time he worked there berating, had become a golden city in his recollection. Now he wasn't there, it was perfect. For Mark, perfection would always be somewhere he wasn't. Charles suspected that the same pattern obtained in his friend's private life too. While he had been with Vinnie, all his young girls on the side had represented the greener grass of happiness. And now he was with Lisa...Charles wondered where Mark's fantasies hovered now.

'No, but I hope the recording was all right. Lisa didn't seem very happy with what I was doing...' Charles ventured.

'Don't worry about Lisa. She gets very po-faced about the whole business. What she doesn't realise is that the creative process should be *fun*. She's always clock-watching and budget-watching...and number-of-drinks-watching. Do you think, if I'd had that kind of attitude, I'd ever have produced any of the great programmes I did when I was at the Beeb?'

Charles Paris was too polite to ask which 'great programmes', as Mark went on, 'No, creativity is a wild spirit. It's the untutored, the anarchic, the bohemian. That's what creates art – danger, risks being taken in the white heat of rehearsal – not a bunch of accountants poring over spreadsheets in offices.'

Charles searched for a safe, uncontroversial reaction, and came up with 'Hm.'

Mark Lear shook himself out of his 'misunderstood artist' mode. 'Right, same again, is it?'

'Maybe I should move on to the wine...'

'Time enough for wine. A couple more large Scotches first.'

Well, Charles comforted himself, it wasn't as if he hadn't worked hard. He'd earned some kind of reward. No, all things considered, his first day of reading an audio book hadn't been too bad. And *Dark Promises* by Madeleine Eglantine was by no means an easy read.

As for the hangover, well…that'd probably been mostly nerves. There was a definite pattern to these things. Charles's hangovers always seemed to be at their worst on days when he had something important to do. Days when he was relaxed, when he wasn't stressed, he could wake up feeling fine, however much of a skinful he'd had the night before. He never quite knew whether it was the challenge of a difficult day ahead that exacerbated the hangover, or whether his anxiety pushed him to drink more the night before such difficult days. Either way, he knew he was feeling better now.

It wasn't a bad achievement, actually, fitting in a couple of days' reading in the middle of the rehearsal schedule for a play. That was the kind of thing stars did. 'Doing a telly on that free Sunday before we open,' actors like Bernard Walton would say airily, while the rest of the cast would sit, shrouded in misery, thinking, 'There's no justice. The bugger's already being paid twenty times more than me for this show, *and* he's cleaning up with a quick telly as well.'

Charles Paris's current position wasn't quite on that financial scale, but it was still rather heart-warming. Mark Lear had specifically asked for him to do the reading of *Dark Promises*, and had been happy to fit the dates into the brief break in the *Not On Your Wife!* rehearsals when the show transferred from London to Bath. That was quite a novelty in Charles Paris's theatrical career – shoehorning bookings into a busy schedule, rather than planting tiny, distantly spaced oases of work into the arid wastes of his diary.

And he put from his mind the thought – no, the knowledge – that Mark had turned to him only because he was familiar, someone who wouldn't shake the boat, someone who was safe.

The third large Bell's was as welcome as its predecessors. Must watch it tonight, something in the recesses of Charles's mind mumbled, just moderate intake tonight – OK? But who was going to listen to a voice like that, when the alcohol tasted so good?

'Who's directing this tatty show of yours?'

'David J. Girton.'

'David J. Girton? From the Beeb?'

'Right.'

'Good Lord. Presumably he's left the old place?'

'No longer on staff. Gather he still goes back to work on individual projects on contract.'

Mark Lear let out a harsh laugh. '"Individual projects on contract"? Oh, that's what they all say. It's the equivalent of that movie euphemism, "having a script in development", or "consulting" in advertising, or "wanting to spend more time with your family" if you're a politician. Means he's out on his ear.'

'No, David did say he was going back to produce another series of one of his long-running sitcoms next month. I think it's called *Neighbourhood Watch*.'

'Oh?' The news clearly pained Mark. It was all right so long as all his former colleagues were in the same boat, so long as they'd all been unceremoniously dumped, as he had. But he didn't like the idea that one of them was still reckoned to be of value to his former employer. The thought brought a new viciousness into his tone. 'He's a lucky bugger, that David J. Girton.'

'Oh?' Charles prompted innocently.

'Yes, a few years back he was extremely fortunate not to lose his job.'

'What happened?'

'Bit of financial fiddling.'

'But surely that was always common practice in the Beeb? I thought doing your expenses was one of the most purely creative parts of the job.'

'David's fiddling was on a rather bigger scale than that.' In response to Charles's interrogative expression, Mark was about to say more, but changed his mind. 'Let's just say, he was lucky to keep his job.'

'Ooh, you do know how to tease,' said Charles in the voice he'd used as the outrageously camp Gorringe in *Black Comedy* in Ipswich ('One of the best arguments for heterosexuality I've seen in a long time' – *Eastern Daily Press*).

'Who's in the cast then, apart from you?'

Mark Lear raised an eyebrow at the mention of Bernard Walton. 'He's quite a big name. They must have hopes for the West End if he's involved.'

'Oh yes, I should think Bernard's secure, but the rest of the company might change a bit on the way. Bill Blunden's shows have a reputation for touring with a cheapish cast, which gets more upmarket when the show "goes in".'

'So you think you might not stay the course?'

'I'd like to, obviously, but...'

'Hm.' Mark Lear nodded his head thoughtfully. 'Well, of course, Charles, you always have been a cheapish actor...' He seemed unaware that he might have said anything mildly offensive. 'And if Maurice Skellern's still your agent...' His grimace completed the sentence more effectively than any words could have done. 'Bernard Walton, though,' he went on. 'Well, you should be all right. He's definitely bums on seats, isn't he?'

'That's the idea. Though apparently the box office advance isn't as good as they were hoping for.'

'Probably pick up by word of mouth.'

'Maybe. You ever work with Bernard, Mark? I'm sure he did radio back in the early days.'

Mark Lear shook his head. 'No. I was first aware of him on the telly. That ITV sitcom...forget the name...

'What'll the Neighbours Say?'

'That's the one. So who else have you got in the cast?'

Charles continued his run through the dramatis personae of *Not On Your Wife!* His friend reacted to the mention of Pippa Trewin.

'Do you know her, Mark? Have you worked with her?'

Mark shook his head in puzzlement.

'It's pretty unlikely you would have done, actually. She only finished drama school last year.'

'Hmm...No, I know the name in some connection, can't remember where.'
Charles pointed to Mark's whisky glass. 'That rotting the old brain, is it?'
But his friend didn't respond to the jocularity in the question. 'Perhaps it
is,' he replied slowly. 'Certainly there's a lot of stuff I don't remember these
days. Not that it matters much. I'm not doing much these days that's *worth*
remembering.' With an effort, he shook himself out of this melancholy
downward spiral. 'You have that problem, Charles? The old memory? Can
you still remember your lines?'

'Pretty well.' It was true. Memorising lines was simply a matter of practice,
and Charles hadn't lost the knack. When that facility went, then it really
would be time to cut down on the booze.

Strange, he contemplated, how many of his thoughts these days finished
with the phrase, 'then it really would be time to cut down on the booze'. If he
ever actually screwed up a job because he was too drunk or too hungover to
do it, then it really would be time to cut down on the booze. If he ever woke
up somewhere and genuinely couldn't remember how he'd got there, then it
really would be time to cut down on the booze. If he found he was
consistently impotent, then it really would be time to cut down on the booze.

And yet he'd been close to all of those situations. A harsh critic might say
he'd been *in* all of those situations. The prospect of having to cut down on the
booze was stalking Charles Paris, a looming, distant shadow on the horizon,
but a shadow that was drawing closer all the time.

This sequence of reasoning always prompted the same two thoughts in
Charles. First – but if I gave up the booze, it'd ruin my social life; everything
I do in my leisure time involves drinking.

Second – *could* I actually give up the booze if I wanted to?

And, that particular evening, the two recurrent thoughts were joined by a
third. What *did* happen between me and Cookie Stone on Thursday night?

Mark Lear continued asking Charles about the cast of *Not On Your Wife!*
The other name that prompted a reaction from him was Ransome George.

'Old Ran. He still up to his old tricks?'

'Which tricks are those?'

'Borrowing money. Sponging. He always used to be entirely blatant about it.'

'Oh,' said Charles.

'Had a terrible reputation. You'd think everyone in the business must've
heard about it, but he'd still always manage to find some innocent sucker to
bum a fiver off.' Mark chuckled, shaking his head at the follies of
humankind. 'There's one born every minute, isn't there?'

'Ah,' said Charles.

Mark Lear was caught by something in his tone and looked up sharply. 'He
hasn't tried to touch you, has he? You haven't fallen for the old "left my
wallet at home" guff, have you?'

'Good heavens, no,' said Charles.

Mark looked thoughtful, then chuckled again. 'Well, your company seems to have more than its fair share of skeletons in its cupboards.'

'What do you mean?'

'David J. Girton...' Mark mused, 'and Ransome George...'

'What? Do you know something bad about Ran? I mean, apart from the fact that he bums money off people and doesn't pay it back?'

'Oh, yes,' replied Mark, enjoying the power of telling his story at his own pace. 'Yes, I know something very considerably worse about Ransome George than that. Goes back to the early 1970s, I suppose...'

But suddenly the producer's manner changed. The slyly conspiratorial was replaced by the irresponsibly drunk. Charles followed Mark's eyeline to see that Lisa Wilson had just entered the bar. She looked stern, a mother come out on to the recreation ground to tell her son it was bedtime – and no arguments.

As if it was some ritual the two of them had been through many times before, Mark played up to the image. He whinged to Lisa like an eight-year-old about what a spoilsport she was, and how she wouldn't let him have a life of his own, and how he was a grown man, for God's sake, and at least Vinnie never treated him like – 'Well, I've got to be off, anyway,' said Charles. He didn't want to get caught in crossfire of a domestic argument. 'Haven't checked in at my digs yet.'

'OK,' said Lisa. 'Ten sharp in the morning, for more *Dark Promises*.'

'Sure,' said Charles. 'I'll be there. Can't wait. You never know – tomorrow may be the day that either the heroine or the hero shows a spark of character...'

And he left Lisa Wilson to gather up her recalcitrant charge. Somehow, Charles reckoned that the minute he'd left, Mark Lear would turn all docile and follow her obediently home. But he also reckoned, once Mark had got home, that he would continue drinking.

Charles Paris's accommodation had been sorted out from London. The stage door of the Vanbrugh Theatre, Bath, kept a digs list, and he'd easily found a suitable landlady who had a vacancy for a couple of extra nights before most of the *Not On Your Wife!* company arrived.

She was a pale, anonymous woman – Charles Paris never seemed to end up with the larger-than-life, characterful landladies who people theatrical legend. The one in Bath was possessed of either a permanent sniff of disapproval, a bloodhound's nose for alcohol, or a bad cold. She showed him the room, which was fine, offered him an evening meal, which he declined, and directed him towards a late-opening supermarket, where he bought a chicken pie and, it has to be admitted, another half-bottle of Bell's.

By his standards, he didn't reckon he'd had that much, but the effects of alcohol are cumulative and, as he slipped, later than intended, into a drunken sleep, Charles Paris knew he'd have another hangover with which to face his second day of reading *Dark Promises* by Madeleine Eglantine.

His last thought, before he surrendered consciousness, was once again – What *did* happen between me and Cookie Stone?

Chapter Four

COOKIE Stone sidled up to him at the Vanbrugh Theatre in Bath on the Monday afternoon, and winked. 'I remember what you said on Thursday night.'

Charles Paris smiled weakly. He wished to God he did.

Fortunately, there wasn't much time for embarrassment. The rest of the day ahead promised to be too busy for reminiscence or recrimination. The cast of *Not On Your Wife!* was about to rehearse the play for the first time on set, and they all knew that, whatever standard the show had reached in the rehearsal room, on stage everything would be different.

The schedule for the next two days was tight. The get-in to build the set had happened on the Monday morning. (In the old days, Charles Paris reflected nostalgically, that would have taken place on the Sunday, but now prohibitive overtime rates made any theatre work on Sundays a rarity.) On the Monday afternoon the lighting director would work out a basic lighting plot, to be tweaked and refined during the tech. run, which was scheduled to start at five, and to take as long as it took. Fortunately, *Not On Your Wife!* was not a complicated show from the technical point of view. The basic set of the two adjacent flats, once built, did not change throughout the play, and the lighting plot was a simple matter of switching between the two acting areas.

The Tuesday morning was to be reserved for final adjustments to the set and lights. The company would then be called at twelve o'clock for notes arising from the tech. run. At two-thirty they would start a full dress rehearsal, which everyone in the company knew would not be enough to drag the show back to the standard it had reached on the previous Thursday in London.

Then, on the Tuesday evening at seven-thirty, *Not On Your Wife!* would face its first-ever paying audience, amongst whom would be critics from the local press. This last detail, when announced, had distressed many of the cast – particularly Bernard Walton. The show, he argued, would be terribly rough on the Tuesday night. Give it a chance to run itself in for a couple of performances before admitting the press. But for once the star didn't get his own way. The view of Parrott Fashion Productions, relayed through the company manager, was that, yes, the show might have rough edges, but, more important, they needed to get newspaper reviews as soon as possible. *The Western Daily Press*, as its title implied, came out every day, but Bath's other local newspapers had midweek deadlines. If their critics came any later than the Tuesday, the notices wouldn't make it into print until the Thursday week, by which time *Not On Your Wife!* would have only four more performances to do in Bath, before the whole caravan moved on to Norwich. The company manager apologised to Bernard Walton for this fact of life, but stood firm. The star might have total artistic control, but when it came to purely commercial considerations, he had to give way. Advance booking for the show wasn't as good as they'd hoped, and Parrott Fashion Productions insisted on a Tuesday press night.

It was clear on the Monday that the show's director was more than a little out of his depth. Though he'd got by all right in the rehearsal room, actually getting a play into a theatre presented different challenges to someone whose main experience had been in television. Up until that point in the production, David J. Girton had abnegated his directorial responsibilities to Bernard Walton and the rest of his cast. But the decisions he faced now were technical rather than artistic, and he needed someone else to whom he could abnegate these new burdens.

Luckily for David J. Girton, the perfect person on whom to offload all such matters was conveniently to hand. He was the company manager, the one who had explained to Bernard Walton the necessity of a Tuesday press night. His name was Tony Delaunay, and he had worked for Parrott Fashion Productions for years. He was small, with short blonded hair, and always dressed in a black suit which somehow gave the impression of being more casual than a suit.

Tony Delaunay had run more touring productions than most people – though obviously not David J. Girton – had had hot dinners. He was a creature of the theatre, who'd worked as a scene shifter while still at school. In his late teens, he'd tried to make it as an actor in a variety of low-budget London productions, before recognising that his skills lay on the technical side. He had graduated through the ranks of assistant stage manager, deputy stage manager and stage manager to take on ever more responsibility. He could do lighting plots, he could build sets, he could pacify local stage crews, he could mollify furious designers and wardrobe mistresses, he could mediate between stingy managements and poverty-stricken actors. He had saved the bacon of Parrott Fashion Productions on more occasions than he cared to remember. He was the all-purpose theatrical Mr Fixit, and nothing surprised him.

So, effectively taking over the technical direction of a new Bill Blunden farce from a Director whose main expertise was in television presented no problems to Tony Delaunay.

But he didn't crow. He didn't rub in the fact that the show's designated director was incompetent. Tony Delaunay had no ego; he was the ultimate pragmatist. *Not On Your Wife!* was due to open to a paying audience on the Tuesday night. Parrott Fashion Productions paid him to ensure that that happened, and Tony Delaunay would see that it did.

David J. Girton quickly recognised his good fortune in having the company manager there to do all his work for him, and arranged his own movements on the Monday accordingly. Deciding, with some justification, that a director couldn't be of much use during the get-in, he had appeared in the Vanbrugh Theatre at noon to see how things were proceeding. Comforted by the fact that Tony Delaunay had everything in hand, David J. Girton decided to slip away for 'a little drink and a bite to eat'. And, since he was in Bath, after a couple of 'little drinks', he decided his lunch had better take place at the Hole in the Wall restaurant.

After lunch, he felt so exhausted, he slipped back to his hotel to put his feet up for a few minutes. He didn't know much about lighting, anyway. He'd only get under the lighting director's and Tony Delaunay's feet if he was in the theatre. The art of directing, after all, was the art of delegation. Respect the individual skills of all the members of your team, and you become a well-respected director. That had been David J. Girton's approach in television, and it had worked well enough for him there. It had also perfectly suited his natural indolence.

When he returned to the Vanbrugh Theatre, around four-thirty, he found that Tony Delaunay and the lighting director had finished their plotting, and that the entire company was ready for the tech. run to begin. David J. Girton gave them a few rousing words of the 'Have a good show' variety, and allowed Tony Delaunay to start the run. Then, rather than slowing the process down by interfering – he had always prided himself on being a minimalist director – David J. Girton sat quietly at the back of the auditorium and watched the show unfold.

The run – in comparison to the majority of tech runs – went very smoothly. That was of course down to Tony Delaunay. He managed the cast efficiently, speeding through easy sections of the text and bringing his meticulous concentration to bear on the play's more difficult moments. Observing all the required Equity breaks, he reached the final curtain just before nine o clock in the evening. The cast members, who'd been fully prepared to work through into the small hours if necessary, were massively relieved.

As the final curtain fell, David J. Girton was seized by a late burst of energy. He strode down the auditorium from his perch at the back with an authoritative cry of, 'Could we have the house lights, please? And tabs up? All company remain on stage, please.'

The cast stayed obediently on stage. They'd all – with the possible exception of Pippa Trewin – been through the process many times before. Tech. runs were a stage of a production which required infinite patience. There was no room for temperament or thespian ego. However many times you were asked to repeat something, however many notes you were given, you just put your head down and got on with it. So the *Not On Your Wife!* company remained on stage, ready for a long screed of directorial notes.

'Well...' said David J. Girton, with a bonhomous, avuncular smile, 'pats on the back all round, I'd say. Bloody well done, the lot of you. I've kept a pretty low profile today...' (that was something of an understatement) 'because I don't believe in interfering on the technical side. There are plenty of people around the studio – erm, around the theatre – who have their own very considerable skills, and I'm not the person to put my oar in and tell them what they should be doing. Pats on the back to all you technical chaps too, by the way.

'So all I want to say, really, is: Keep up the good work. Tough day tomorrow. We've got a dress rehearsal in the afternoon, and the call for that is...?' 'He turned round helplessly to the company manager.

Tony Delaunay was, as ever, ready with the relevant information. 'There's a company call scheduled for twelve for notes, and the dress rehearsal's two-thirty, so the "half" for that'll be one fifty-five.'

'Oh, well, I don't think we need the twelve o'clock call, do we? Seems a bit much to break into everyone's lunch hour.' There were a good few restaurants in Bath that David J. Girton hadn't tried yet.

But actors' stomachs are not their main priority when a show's about to open. 'I think we should stick with the twelve o'clock call,' said Bernard Walton. 'There are a couple of bits we need to run. That tablecloth biz in Act Two for a start...'

David J. Girton saw a potential lunch disappearing over the horizon. There was a serious risk he might have to make do with a sandwich. 'Do you really think we need to...?'

'Yes,' said Tony Delaunay with unshakeable authority. 'Twelve o'clock call, as per schedule, for notes and the bits that need running.' He turned deferentially to the director. 'Anything else you want to say, David?'

'No, thanks. Just...all have a good night's sleep and see you at twelve tomorrow...that is, of course, unless anyone fancies going out now for a bite to eat?'

None of the cast did. They were tired, for one thing. Also, most of them were husbanding their touring allowance and didn't want to blue any of it so early into the schedule. Maybe after the first night, a company meal might be in order.

Before they all dispersed, Tony Delaunay, unthanked by the director for his superhuman efforts during the day, but apparently unworried by the omission, shouted for attention. 'Sorry, just one more thing. Another call to add to your schedule. I've just been talking to Rob Parrott at Parrott Fashion, and he's not happy about the advance. Show like this ought to be getting more bums on seats in a town like Bath. So we'll be recording a commercial for local radio.'

He nipped an incipient murmur of grumbling in the bud. 'Of course, anyone who's involved will get paid. I'll talk to your agents.'

'When are we going to have to do this?' asked Bernard Walton truculently.

'Well, since we've got the matinée Wednesday, it'll have to be on Thursday some time. Won't involve all of you...obviously you, Bernard, and one other, I would imagine.'

'Oh, we do want a lot of voices involved.' It was typical of David J. Girton that he should suddenly become assertive over a detail that didn't matter.

'Well, I don't think Parrott Fashion –'

But the director had got the bit between his teeth. 'Yes, Tony,' he went on self-importantly. 'We need a lot of voices for this commercial. I'll let people know who's going to be involved.'

Tony Delaunay betrayed only the slightest reaction of annoyance, clearly deciding that this was not something to take issue about in front of the entire company. 'OK. Anyway, just wanted to warn you about the commercial. I'll let you know more details as soon as we've sorted out a recording studio and that kind of stuff. Thanks. And I think we can break everyone there...' Tony Delaunay turned, with proper deference, to the director. 'If that's all right with you, David?'

David J. Girton, his brief moment of assertiveness past, looked up from his study of *The Good Food Guide*. 'What's that?'

'OK if we break them?'

'Sure, sure.'

'Right, that's it for today!' said Tony Delaunay. 'See you all at twelve tomorrow.'

The *Not On Your Wife!* company started to drift off into the wings. Charles Paris heard Bernard Walton saying to Pippa Trewin, 'So are they coming?'

'Hope to. I talked on the phone today.'

'Oh well, we must go out for a really good dinner, just the four of us.'

'That'd be lovely, Bernard.'

Once again, Charles was puzzled. Though there was certainly some relationship between the star and the ingenue, he still couldn't quite define it. But he had more pressing concerns on his mind; Ransome George was beside him as they crossed into the wings. 'Er, Ran, about that twenty quid...'

'Haven't forgotten about it, dear boy. Go to the cash point first thing in the morning.'

'Well, I'd be grateful if you could, because the thing is –'

'Don't you worry. First thing in the morning,' said Ransome George grandly and speeded up on the way to his dressing room.

Charles was about to follow, but suddenly found himself face to face with Cookie Stone. She grinned at him, and gave another wink. 'Wondered if you fancied going out for a "little drink" and "a bite to eat"...' 'She was a good mimic; she had caught David J. Girton's tone exactly. '...and whatever else is on offer?'

There was no ambiguity in the final phrase. Charles Paris felt himself colouring, as he desperately tried to muster some excuse. 'Erm, maybe...' he said feebly. Then, with a brainwave, 'Just got to check something with Tony first.'

He found the company manager in the auditorium, talking on a mobile phone. Tony Delaunay raised a hand to acknowledge that he'd seen Charles, and continued his conversation. Its subject was guarantees and percentages; no doubt he was again talking to his boss at Parrott Fashion Productions.

'Yes?' he said, as he switched off his phone at the end of the call.

'Just a thought, Tony...Don't know whether you've got a studio sorted out for recording the radio commercial?'

'No, I was going to ask around. Why, have you got any ideas?'

'It's just I've been recording an audio book in a studio down here. It's run by some people I know. They've got the full set-up, state-of-the-art technical stuff. I thought, if you hadn't got anywhere sorted...'

'Have you got their number? I'll call them. If they offer me a reasonable rate, then that'll be one less thing I have to sort out.' Charles handed across one of the newly printed cards that Lisa Wilson had given him at the end of the *Dark Promises* recording on the Saturday. 'Thanks.'

Charles reached the dressing room he shared with a couple of the other minor actors. There was no one else there, but his haven didn't remain secure for long. He heard a discreet tap on the door, and a 'Come in' admitted Cookie Stone.

'Ah,' said Charles. 'Hi.'

She leant her face forward, lips puckered over her prominent teeth, waiting to be kissed. He chickened out and planted a gentle peck on each cheek. If she felt any disappointment, she didn't show it. 'So, how about this evening then, Charles?'

'Love to,' he said, 'love to. Thing is...you know I was doing that audio book over the weekend?'

'You mentioned it, yes.'

'Well, there were a couple of retakes we didn't get round to – only tiny bits – but since we've finished earlier than expected this evening...well, I just rang through to the studio, and they're still there...so I'm going straight over now to get it sorted.'

'This time of night?'

He coloured. It did seem pretty unlikely. 'As I say, it's only a couple of tiny bits,' he floundered. 'And they're up against a tight deadline.'

He didn't sound very convincing, but Cookie Stone took his words at face value. 'OK. Very starry, though,' she observed with mock-deference. 'You fitting in bits of other work round the play schedule. Be off playing in charity Pro-Am golf tournaments next.'

'I don't see it. Even this audio book's not my usual style, I can assure you.' It was against Charles's nature to claim charisma he didn't possess, so he confided, 'I only got involved in this because Mark Lear –'

'Who?'

'Mark Lear. He's the producer. Why, do you know him?'

'No,' Cookie replied firmly. 'I've never heard of him.'

'Oh. Well, I've known him from way back. Old friends and confidants, know what I mean?'

'I suddenly understand why you're recording for him then. Jobs for the boys, as ever in the theatre?'

'That's it, I'm afraid.'

'Or jobs for the relatives,' said Cookie Stone, with sudden venom. 'That's the way to get on in this bloody business, get born into one of the great theatrical dynasties.'

Charles chuckled. 'Trouble is, that's one of those things we don't have a lot of control over, do we? Rest of us must just scratch a living the best we can, eh?' Cookie's expression was beginning to take on an amorous cast, so he cleared his throat and said quickly, 'Anyway, I thought it'd be easier to get these retakes done now, because we don't know how the schedule for the rest of the week's going to pan out, do we?'

'No, no, we don't,' Cookie agreed. She nodded, accepting the situation. 'Oh, well, make it another night, eh?'

'Sure,' said Charles, once again weak. Then, falling back on the traditional actor's defence of a funny voice, he assumed the one he'd used for *Every Man in His Humour* in Belfast ('Charles Paris seemed to have drifted in from another play' – *Plays and Players*). 'Make it another night,' he echoed.

Cookie Stone proffered her face to him again. This time he planted a kiss on the tip of her upturned nose. It was a kiss without attitude; it could have been an expression of deep affection, it could have been merely avuncular. 'See you in the morning,' said Cookie, and left the dressing room.

He didn't feel good about the glibness with which the lies had slipped out. It reminded him of times he'd lied to Frances. Lying never felt good, but the more readily the lie is accepted, the more of a heel its perpetrator feels. Cookie didn't matter to him – or at least he didn't think she mattered to him – so lying to her shouldn't cause him too much anguish, but he still didn't feel good about it.

The thought of Frances hurt like a jaw-deep toothache. In his brain remained a residue of the recollection that he'd rung her the night he'd got drunk with Cookie. Surely it couldn't be true. Cookie had been in the flat with him; he wouldn't have rung Frances with Cookie there, for God's sake, would he? But the thought remained, and it deterred him from ringing his wife again.

As if to give some kind of substance to the lies he'd palmed off on Cookie, Charles stopped at the stage door and dialled the number of Lisa and Mark's studio. Probably be no one there at that time of night, but if there was, better warn them that he'd given their names to Tony Delaunay.

Also, there was something in him that wanted to talk to Lisa Wilson. He couldn't have got off to a worse start, but he liked to think that, by the end of the *Dark Promises* recording, he had to some extent rescued himself in her estimation. In spite of the Friday night's drinking, his Saturday hangover had not been so bad (maybe supporting his theory that anxiety aggravated the condition), and on the second day he'd felt more at home in the world of audio book recording. He liked to think he'd completed his reading of Madeleine Eglantine's deathless work in a style that had been, at the very least, professional.

Certainly, at the end of the recording, Lisa Wilson had said, 'Well done. We must get you in to do another of these.' It could merely have been routine courtesy, but Charles liked to think there had been a bit more to the compliment.

There was another thing, too. He couldn't deny that, over the two days of close proximity, he had come to find Lisa Wilson increasingly attractive. He knew he shouldn't be thinking about women. The chaos of his relationship with Frances, the ill-defined nature of the one he had with Cookie Stone, the fact that Lisa was Mark's girl anyway, and the disaster-littered history of Charles Paris's emotional life should have stopped him from ever feeling another stirring of lust in any direction. But it hadn't.

'Hello?' Lisa answered. Given her character, it was no surprise that she should be working late.

'It's Charles Paris. I rang because I was talking to the company manager of our show and –'

'Tony Delaunay.'

'Yes. You mean he's been on to you already?'

'Mm.' Tony certainly didn't hang about; no doubt that was one of the reasons for his success as a company manager. 'Yes, we've fixed it.'

'To do the *Not On Your Wife!* radio commercial? Great.'

'He beat me down a bit on price...'

'No surprises there. He's a shrewd operator. Parrott Fashion Productions run a tight ship...which is the polite way of saying they're so mean that when they open their wallets moths fly out.'

'Still, it's new work,' said Lisa. 'Might lead to something else, you never know. Getting the studio used, anyway. So, many thanks for the introduction.'

'No problem. The cue came up and it seemed daft not to act on it.'

'Much appreciated.'

'Is Mark there?' asked Charles. He didn't particularly want to speak to Mark, but etiquette dictated that it was really Mark who was his friend, not Lisa.

'No, I'm just finishing up here. He's in the pub.'

'Ah.'

Charles thought he'd bleached the monosyllable of all intonation, but Lisa still picked up on it. 'Yes, I must go and drag him out soon. Otherwise he won't be fit for anything tomorrow.'

'Mark always enjoyed a drink,' Charles observed uncontentiously.

'It's got beyond "enjoying".' There was bitter experience in Lisa Wilson's voice. 'I'm not sure that he does enjoy it now. He just goes on drinking, in a kind of blur of self-hatred. It seems to be part of some death-wish.'

'You're exaggerating,' said Charles lightly.

'I wish I was. My father was an alcoholic,' Lisa confided. 'I've seen it all happen before. And I'm not enjoying going through it again.'

'Ah,' said Charles. There didn't seem a lot else to say. Lisa Wilson sighed. 'Anyway, I'd better go and do my nagging-little-woman routine and extract Mark from the pub. Hm, I just hope he manages to keep off the stuff on Thursday.'

'Thursday?'

'That's when you're doing your radio commercial. I'm going to be in London, at this publishing meeting...'

'Oh yes, you mentioned it.'

'...so Mark will be in charge.'

'Come on, Lisa. He'll be fine. You're talking about a man who spent over twenty years producing radio programmes for the BBC.'

'I know,' she said gloomily, 'but I don't think you've any idea how much he's degenerated since they kicked him out.'

'I thought it was "voluntary redundancy" –'

'Kicked him out,' Lisa repeated. 'Mark's never really recovered from that. Totally knocked the stuffing out of him.'

Charles could only manage another 'Ah.'

'Anyway, I must get on. Thanks again for mentioning us to Tony Delaunay.'

'No problem. See you, Lisa.'

''Bye.'

He put the phone down, feeling disproportionately sensitive. He'd said 'See you', and she'd only said "Bye'. Did that mean she didn't want to see him? Did that mean her talk of further audio books had just been professional flannel?

Charles knew his reaction was ridiculous. He just felt exposed, nerve endings too near the surface of his skin. It was a combination of factors, the tensions of a play about to open...the ugliness of his relationship with Frances...the stupid situation he'd got himself into with Cookie...And Lisa Wilson's talk about Mark had raised the old worry about his own drinking.

His behaviour the previous week had been appalling, and the blame for it could be fairly and squarely attributed to alcohol. If he hadn't drunk so much, none of it would have happened. He must cut down.

But not quite yet. There was bound to be a pub on the way back to his digs.

Charles Paris was about to go out through the stage door, when he was surprised to hear voices coming from the Green Room. He thought all the company would have hurried off as soon as they could. He moved closer to the Green Room door.

He was even more surprised to hear that one of the voices belonged to Bernard Walton. 'Listen,' the star was saying, 'it's even more important at the moment that you keep quiet about the whole thing.'

'Don't worry,' Ransome George's voice cajoled lazily. 'No problem. I'll keep stumm.'

'The thing is, there's this guy who's going to be around for the next couple of days, name of Curt Greenfield. He's writing a biography of me, and it would be very awkward if he found out anything that –'

'You have my word, Bernard. There's no danger I'll say a dickie bird.'

'Good.'

The star didn't sound totally reassured, so Ransome George went on, 'Listen, it's not in my interests, is it, Bernard? I don't want to spoil the arrangement we have at the moment. It's suiting us both fine, isn't it?'

'Well...' Bernard Walton wasn't convinced about that.

Ran chuckled. 'Well, it's suiting me fine. No, your secret is absolutely safe with me, Bernard. There's no way I want anyone sharing it. I'd be extremely miffed if I thought anyone was sharing it.' He dropped into a punch-drunk boxer's voice. 'In fact, I'd do a mischief to anyone I thought was trying to share it.'

'OK. Fine.' Bernard Walton sounded partially reassured. 'Well, look, I'd better be on my way...'

At the sound of movement, Charles Paris glided silently away from the Green-Room door. He didn't want to be caught eavesdropping.

Bizarre, though, what he had heard. There was now something else in his mind of which he couldn't make sense.

As he'd intended, Charles Paris found an anonymous pub on the way back to his digs. He started with a couple of large Bell's. After a busy day's technical rehearsal, he felt he'd earned those. Then he moved on to the wine, at some point interrupting the flow with an unmemorable portion of shepherd's pie. When 'last orders' were called, he had another large Bell's as a nightcap. And the half-bottle back at his digs still contained enough to drown him into sleep.

Chapter Five

ON THE Tuesday, there was a lot of tension in the *Not On Your Wife!* company, and it rose to a crescendo in the break between the afternoon's dress rehearsal and the show's first performance at seven-thirty. It wasn't that the dress rehearsal had gone particularly badly; it was something else that was bugging people.

Every cast of every play that's ever been put on has been nervous of facing an audience for the first time, but the *Not On Your Wife!* company were suffering from an anxiety unique to the world of comedy. In the rehearsal period for most plays there are predictable fluctuations in company confidence. The day of the read-through is always tense and tentative, with cast members insecure, sniffing round the unfamiliar, each masking his or her individual paranoia in standoffishness or forced joviality. In the next few days confidence usually builds. The company begins to bond, they get excited about the work they're doing, they start believing that they could be involved in a really major success.

The next downturn regularly occurs when they 'come off the book', because actors don't all learn their lines at the same rate. But once the text is firmly assimilated, there is another upswing. Yes, they are involved in something good; the show's really going to work. That mood is unfailingly dashed as soon as the company gets into the theatre and starts working on the actual set. That is why technical rehearsals are always so ghastly. But, as the best productions run up to the first night, there develops a nervous bubble of thrilled anticipation. The show's not ready, they need more rehearsal, but if everything comes together, if they have a following wind and a sympathetic audience, then it could be wonderful.

In comedy, while all of this regular pattern is followed through, the stakes are much, much higher. The play that seemed so hilarious at the read-through, the play whose stage business frequently made the entire company collapse in hysterics during the early stages of rehearsal, becomes dull by familiarity. In the week before it opens, when all concentration is on the technical aspects of the production, the play seems about as funny as a bowl of cold sick. And, as the moment of first exposure to a paying audience approaches, the awful fear creeps into the mind of every company member: 'Suppose they don't find it funny at all? Suppose nobody laughs?'

There is no escape. The average 'straight' play with a couple of mildly humorous lines in it will be hailed by the critics as 'witty'; but when a show's billed as a 'comedy' or a 'farce', nothing less will suffice than continuous laughter. A farce company is so horribly exposed. Everyone has experienced the personal humiliation of telling a joke which gets no reaction.

Charles Paris had also had the personal experience of being in a farce whose audience would have got more laughs at a funeral. The show had been loosely adapted from some French original, under the title of *Look Out Behind You, Louise!* It had completed its three-week run in Newcastle to tiny and stony-faced audiences, before being finally put out of its misery. And it had elicited from the *Gateshead Gazette* the following notice: 'But for the word "farce" on the poster, I would have assumed the play to be a serious documentary about the casualties of "care in the community".'

It was *Look Out Behind You, Louise!* whose dark shadow lurked in the back of Charles Paris's mind, as the first performance of Bill Blunden's new farce drew ever nearer. But each member of the company had his or her own comparable nightmare of failure. Privately, they all twitched with terror.

Generally speaking, the first night of *Not On Your Wife!* didn't go too badly. The play didn't get all the laughs it should have done, but it did get some laughs. There was something to build on.

And at least, for the company, that dreadful moment of presenting a comedy for the first time was past. They breathed a communal sigh of relief.

On the Thursday lunch-time, when Charles arrived at the studio, it looked as though Lisa Wilson's vigilance had been insufficient. Mark Lear was extremely drunk. He must have spent the morning taking continuous top-ups from the bottle in the Gents'. Charles hated to think how high Mark's 'maintenance dose' might be.

They had arranged on the phone that Charles should arrive before the other members of the *Not On Your Wife!* company involved in the commercial. It had been Mark's suggestion. 'Come round twelvish. We'll have a couple of pints before we do the recording.' The rest of the actors were called for two o'clock.

He had agreed to the earlier meeting because there had been a quality almost of desperation in Mark Lear's voice. Charles was determined, though, that, whatever Mark might do, he himself wouldn't drink. He had woken up in his digs that morning with yet another hangover, and there was a show to be done in the evening. He needed all his wits about him. Under the circumstances, it would have been deeply unprofessional for any actor to drink at lunch-time.

But somehow, once they were actually inside the Queen's Head, it all seemed less important. The very smell of the beer was heady and seductive. And Charles knew how much better a pint would make him feel. Just the one pint, mind, just to counter the morning's dehydration. Charles Paris knew when to stop.

Besides, Mark Lear needed him. The desperation Charles had heard on the phone was intensified in the flesh. Mark looked haggard and dispirited. To let a man in that condition drink alone would have been inhuman.

Charles got the first two pints and ordered sandwiches. After they had both taken greedy gulps from their glasses, he said, 'You don't look too good, Mark. Anything the matter?'

'You name it. Where shall I start?'

'Well, let's start with the most important. Will you be in a state to produce this commercial this afternoon?'

His question prompted anger. 'Of course I bloody will! What do you take me for, Charles? When I was at the Beeb, I'd do huge, elaborate, three-day productions and not draw a sober breath the whole time. And they were bloody good, bloody good programmes!'

'That's all right then,' said Charles soothingly. 'So that's not what's upsetting you?'

'No.'

'Which means it must be something else?' Mark Lear was silent. 'If talking about it's going to help...I'm happy to listen. If, on the other hand, you don't want to talk about it, that's entirely up to you.'

Of course Mark wanted to talk about it He had never been much of a one for the stiff upper lip, for buttoning in his emotions. That wasn't his way. If he had a problem, then other people were bloody well going to hear about it. Mark Lear had always craved sympathy, ideally from a wide-eyed young girl, but when one of those wasn't available, anyone with open ears would do. At that moment Charles Paris fitted the specification.

'Oh, I don't know, Charles, it's all such a bloody mess.'

'What is?'

'Everything. I mean, the way everything's gone wrong in the last couple of years. I'm out of the BBC...'

'Just as you always said you wanted to be.'

'I know, I know. But somehow it's different on the outside. And now I've lost Vinnie and the kids.'

'Again you always said you wanted freedom.'

'Yes, but I don't know...I just feel...I mean, I was never that great a father, but at least I had contact with them.'

'And now you don't see them at all?' suggested Charles, feeling an unexpectedly strong and sudden pang of guilt about his own daughter. When had he last seen Juliet? Or his grandchildren, come to that?

'No,' Mark replied. 'I suppose I should make the effort, but...well, the kids don't seem that interested in seeing me. They only hear Vinnie's side of things, obviously, but...anyway, two of them are off at university.'

'I thought all three of them were.'

'No, Claudia, the youngest...she's having some time out. She had this eating disorder...which I think was kind of started by us splitting up...so at the moment she's living with Vinnie and the new husband...though I can't imagine that makes her situation any less stressful. Oh, it's all such a bloody mess,' Mark repeated abjectly. 'I feel so guilty. Perhaps I should have stayed with Vinnie.'

'I gathered that wasn't an option.'

'Well...Maybe if I'd tried harder at the relationship?'

'It wouldn't have worked,' said Charles firmly. 'Vinnie is out of your life for good. And come on, cheer up. It's not as if you haven't got a rather good replacement. I wouldn't mind having...' He nearly said 'Lisa', but changed it to 'a girl like Lisa around. You're a lucky man.'

'I know, but...'

'But what?'

Mark Lear shook his head self-pityingly. 'It's just not working. I mean, it's not the same. I think she's had enough of me.'

'Anything particular make you say that?'

Mark grimaced. 'A girl like her...well, she's going to have had other boyfriends, isn't she...'

'I would assume so. She's very attractive.'

'...in the past.' Mark seemed not to be listening to what Charles said. 'Boyfriends in the past. She's talked about them, told me everything. There was this married man she had a long affair with...and quite a few others...in the past.' His eyes misted over as he picked away at the scab of his unhappiness. 'But how can I be sure they are all still in the past? How can I be sure she isn't still seeing them?'

'Mark, Lisa is living with you and has gone into partnership with you on the studios. Short of having your babies, I don't know what more she can do to express commitment.'

'No, but...I don't know. With her, sometimes I just feel so old. I mean, what woman's really going to want someone of my age?'

Mark had chosen the wrong person to put this question to. Perhaps it might have gone down well with one of his nubile totties; for Charles Paris it was too uncomfortably pertinent to his own situation.

'You've got Lisa,' he said brusquely. 'You're being given a second chance. If I were you, I'd be down on my knees thanking the Lord for His generosity.'

'Hmm.' Mark Lear's mood was too entrenched to be shifted so easily. 'I don't know, Charles...I just don't seem to have anything to look forward to...I can't really see the point of going on.'

'Oh, Mark, for God's sake...You're only fifty. You could have half your life still ahead of you.'

His friend shuddered. 'What a repellent thought.'

Charles continued trying to jolly Mark out of his gloom, but he recognised it was a hopeless task. Having been in that trough so frequently himself, Charles knew one could only wait for the mood to shift. And, though at the time he could never believe it would, ultimately it always did. Or, the depressive in him qualified pessimistically, it always had so far.

Mark Lear clearly didn't want to be shaken out of his gloom that day. He was in a bleak, self-destructive mood. Charles had only one more pint, but Mark kept ordering double Scotch chasers to go with his beer, and left the sandwiches untouched. As the hands of the clock approached two, he didn't have the air of a man capable of producing his hand from his pocket, let alone a radio commercial.

And one thing he said in the course of his maudlin ramblings stayed with Charles for the rest of the day. 'I feel afraid, actually afraid. I don't know what it is, Charles, but I feel as though something awful's going to happen. I feel as if someone's out to get me.'

They got back from the Queen's Head a little after two, to find the other *Not On Your Wife!* actors waiting outside the studio. The atmosphere was scratchy. Since the beginning of the week their schedule had been punishing, and the previous day they'd done a matinée as well as an evening performance. The fact that they were being paid to do the radio commercial was not enough to raise their spirits, and the general mood was not improved when they realised that the man who let them into the studios was extremely drunk.

David J. Girton had won his point about having a lot of voices for the commercial. Though the expense involved went against all the penny-pinching instincts of Parrott Fashion Productions, it was an issue on which the director had proved surprisingly intransigent. Perhaps, finally recognising that he wasn't having much influence on the actual production of *Not On Your Wife!*, he was determined to have his one moment of assertiveness over a detail.

As a result of his insistence, therefore, the actors who had been called were Bernard Walton, Ransome George, Cookie Stone and Pippa Trewin. David J. Girton was also present, of course, though in a bad mood. He'd won his point about the number of actors, but had failed in his attempt to make the call later than two o'clock. As a result, he'd had to rush his lunch at Popjoy's to be there in time.

The mood of the assembled company went down another notch when they realised that Tony Delaunay was not present. The company manager it was who would be bringing the text of the commercial they were to record. That was being organised by the Parrott Fashion Productions office, and was to be faxed through to the Vanbrugh Theatre. But there had been some hitch at the London end, with the result that Tony Delaunay, who was never late for anything, was late.

The company members drooped around the studio, whose sitting area did not boast enough chairs to accommodate all of them, while Mark Lear stumbled about, trying to locate microphones and reels of tape. His antics and slurred speech did not inspire confidence. Charles wished to God Lisa Wilson was there; she'd have got everything sorted out within seconds.

There was a communal sigh of relief when Tony Delaunay came hurrying in, but it turned to a communal groan of exasperation when he announced that there were a couple of points in the script which still needed checking with Parrott Fashion Productions. He immediately dialled through to London. The actors looked even more bad-tempered, as Mark Lear continued to fumble around the studio.

'Hope we're not all going to be crammed into that little dead room of yours,' Charles said to Mark jovially, trying to lighten the atmosphere. He turned to the rest of the actors. 'Last time I was in there, there was no air at all; after half an hour I just couldn't breathe. It was some problem with the air conditioning.'

No one seemed particularly interested in what he was saying, but Mark responded, 'We're going to be in the big studio. Just as soon as I've got it all rigged up properly.'

'But the air conditioning in the little one has been fixed, hasn't it?'

'Not yet,' Mark responded tetchily. 'That's another bloody thing I've got to sort out.' And he blundered through the open door of the larger cubicle to stare hopelessly at the rows of switches, faders and jack plugs. For the first time, the anxiety struck Charles that Mark might not actually know how to work the equipment. As a producer at the BBC, he would always have had a team of studio managers to sort out the technical minutiae for him; and from what Charles had seen, in their new studio Lisa Wilson dealt with that side of things. He began to regret his recommendation to Tony Delaunay.

And he felt very glad that the company manager was still on the phone to London. So far as the cast was concerned, the lack of a final script was what was preventing the recording from getting under way. They seemed not to have noticed that the studio wasn't yet properly rigged for them to start work.

Continuing his attempt to ease the atmosphere and doing his bit to help, Charles took orders for coffee and went off to fill the kettle.

Mark Lear tried to go through into the larger studio, but found it was still locked. He had some problem finding the key to the dead-bolts, but eventually managed to open the heavy double doors and go inside.

From over by the kettle Charles heard Bernard Walton's petulant drawl. 'Isn't it bloody typical? You work your guts out for weeks on a play, the whole complicated machinery runs like bloody clockwork, and then when you get to a minor detail – like this wretched radio commercial – it all screws up. I mean, why on earth did we have to come out to the bloody suburbs of Bath to record this thing, anyway? You'd have thought they could have found a studio nearer the centre. I wonder who was responsible for choosing this godforsaken hole?'

Charles kept quiet. In the corner of the room, Tony Delaunay continued to wrangle with the Parrott Fashion Productions office.

David J. Girton, still sour with lunch-withdrawal symptoms, looked across towards the studio, from which Mark was just emerging, and seemed to see him for the first time. 'Hey, you're Mark Lear, aren't you?'

'That's right.'

'David J. Girton.' He stretched out a hand. 'We met way back at the Beeb. I started in radio, before I went across to telly. Used to see you hanging round the Ariel Bar, didn't I?'

Mark Lear took the proffered hand and grinned slyly. 'I used to see *you* hanging round the Ariel Bar.'

'Gone, you know, that bar. Gone with all its memories of post-production celebrations, failed seductions and drowned sorrows. That whole Langham block's back to being a hotel now.'

'I know,' said Mark. 'I've only been out of the Beeb eighteen months or so.'

'Oh, right. You couldn't stand the atmosphere under Chairman Birt either?'

'You could say that.'

'No, it's all changed.' David J. Girton shook his head mournfully. 'Old days, they used to say BBC top management was like a game of musical chairs, except when the music stopped, they added a chair rather than taking one away. Now, when the music stops, they take away two chairs, or three. Haven't seen blood-lettings on that scale since Stalin's purges.'

'You're still involved, though, I hear?' Mark Lear swayed slightly as he spoke, picking out his words with great concentration.

'Yes, I go back on contract from time to time. When they want a new series of *Neighbourhood Watch*. I know all the cast and the writer so well.'

'All right for some.'

'You haven't been asked back then?' asked David J. Girton smugly.

'Oh no. No, they're well and truly finished with me. Definite one-way ticket to the scrap-heap in my case.'

'Ah,' said the director. There didn't seem a lot else to say.

'Mind you...' A nostalgic glaze stole over Mark Lear's bloodshot eyes. 'I remember those times back at the BBC. Particularly the early days...You were left to your own devices then, just allowed to get on with things in your own way. Now there's a whole raft of middle management and accountants standing between the producer and any kind of real creativity.'

'Couldn't agree more.' David J. Girton grinned. 'Sounds like you're well out of it, Mark, old man.'

'Maybe.' For a moment Mark Lear was immobile, eyes still filmed with recollection. Then he lurched forward suddenly, as he continued, 'Sometimes think I should write a book about the Beeb as it was in those days. Yes, I think I should do it, tell a few home truths. Show the BBC...not like everyone presents it on all those bloody nostalgia programmes...like it really was...all the scams, all the fiddles, all the under-the-counter deals that went on. Shee, I remember some of the things I used to get involved in, moonlighting on other jobs...Of course, it all had to be terribly secret then, the BBC owned one's soul, it wasn't *nice* to work for commercial companies outside. Whereas now...your bonus is probably calculated according to how many other organisations you work for. Yes, I think I've got some interesting stories in me...You'd be surprised the unlikely things unlikely people got involved in. Some they certainly wouldn't want to be reminded of, I'm sure. Actually, the whole thing'd make a bloody good book...I can see the cover now..."Mark Lear takes the lid off the BBC in a way that –"'

He may have had further literary ambitions but he didn't get the chance to expatiate on them because at that moment, finally, Tony Delaunay put the phone down, and waved the precious Parrott Fashion-approved text for the radio commercial.

It was a simple enough forty-second spot, in which Bernard Walton expressed his view that *Not On Your Wife!* was the funniest play he'd ever been in, and the other cast members asked him questions about who else was in it, where it was on, and what the Vanbrugh Theatre's box office phone number was. Even though they were being paid, everyone except Bernard was rather miffed that they'd been dragged out for the recording. They'd each got such a tiny 'cough and a spit' in the commercial that they'd never be identified personally. One voice, any voice – even an anonymous voice like Charles Paris's – could have been used to read all Bernard Walton's feed-lines.

'Let's get this knocked on the head as quickly as possible,' said Tony Delaunay. 'I've got a lot to do, and I'm sure you all want a break before "the half".' The assembled company mumbled agreement. The company manager turned to David J. Girton. 'Will you be producing the recording, David?'

But the director's moment of assertiveness had passed, and given way once again to his customary languor. 'No, no,' he said rather grandly. 'I have complete faith in you, Tony.'

The company manager nodded, without comment, and turned to Mark. 'OK, through into the studio with them?'

'Sure.' Mark Lear moved clumsily across to hold back the double doors. His disoriented sullenness had suddenly given way to a kind of giggly euphoria. 'Through you come, my luvvies!' A few of the cast bridled – they didn't like being called 'luvvies' – but nobody said anything. 'Come on, into the studio! Let's commit this deathless piece of drama to tape!'

He looked piercingly at Cookie Stone as she passed through. 'I know you, don't I? We've met before, haven't we?'

'I don't think so,' she replied.

'At the Beeb? Didn't you ever work for Continuing Education?'

'No.' Cookie dropped into a Brooklyn 'Broadway Babe' voice. 'I never got the breaks. From birth I was just a no-hoper. I never made it into Continuing Education.'

But by then Mark Lear had lost interest in Cookie, in favour of Pippa Trewin. Something of the old charm he'd focused on so many young women came back into his manner, as he murmured, 'And who are you?'

'Pippa Trewin.'

'Oh, *you're* Pippa Trewin,' he said. 'Well, well, well. I know all about you.' And he fixed her with a beady, challenging eye. The girl looked away, annoyance twitching at the corner of her mouth.

'Can we get on, please?' demanded Tony Delaunay from the control cubicle.

'Yes, of course.' Mark Lear stumbled through to join him. Tony put the talkback key down, and spoke through into the studio. 'All gather round the one mike, I imagine. OK, one run and we should be able to take it.'

They were cramped around the microphone. A green light flicked on and Bernard Walton started speaking. Through the double glass, Charles could see Tony Delaunay and David J. Girton in the control cubicle, both looking confused. Tony turned to Mark Lear beside him. Their dumb show made it clear that no sound was coming through from the studio. Charles saw Mark turn helplessly to a bank of sockets and reach, without conviction, towards a jack plug.

In one seamlessly efficient movement, Tony Delaunay's hand swept up to a row of switches and adjusted them. 'OK, just give me a couple of words for level, Bernard,' his voice crackled through the talkback.

'From the minute the script of *Not On Your Wife!* arrived, I knew I was reading the funniest play that –'

'OK, fine.' Tony Delaunay's fingers flickered across the control desk, doing a little more fine tuning. Beside him, Mark Lear had sunk back into his chair, eyes almost closed, happy to surrender responsibility to the company manager. 'Give us a read and then we'll go for a take,' said Tony.

'Just a moment,' Bernard Walton objected.

'What is it?'

'This line: "the sauciest, sexiest, smuttiest show in town"...'

'What about it?' the talkback demanded.

'Can we lose "smuttiest"?'

'The text of the ad has been cleared with Rob Parrott. Not sure that we ought to make any changes.'

Bernard Walton was adamant. 'Look, I don't want my name associated with anything "smutty".'

'It's only a word, Bernard. It goes with "saucy" and "sexy".'

'No. "Saucy" and "sexy" are all right. "Smutty" is something else again. "Smutty" is unwholesome.'

'I don't think it's going to worry anyone.'

'Listen, Tony, I've lent my name to this new campaign for standards in television. To the Great British Public, Bernard Walton represents Family Values, the kind of entertainment you wouldn't be ashamed for your kids to see. Bernard Walton is not associated with anything "smutty".'

At this point Tony Delaunay's unfailing pragmatism once again took over. Rob Parrott might want the word "smuttiest" in the commercial, but Bernard Walton saw it as a potential threat to his knighthood. Persuading the recalcitrant star to include the word could take up valuable time. 'OK, lose "smuttiest",' said the talkback. 'Do we need another word in there?'

'No, it'll flow all right with just "sauciest, sexiest show in town".'

'Right you are. OK, let's go for a read.'

Mark Lear lay slumped in the chair beside Tony Delaunay. He appeared to be asleep. Certainly he took no interest in what was being recorded in his studio.

The commercial was done in two takes. Tony Delaunay had got the small reel off the tape machine and left the building almost before the cast streamed back into the sitting area. 'Where's a phone?' demanded Bernard Walton. 'I need a cab.' He turned to Mark. 'Have you got a number for a taxi firm?'

Mark looked up blearily, and Charles was glad he'd noticed a printed card stuck on one of the notice boards. 'Here's one,' he said, handing it and the cordless phone across to Bernard.

'Hm...' David J. Girton stroked his hands down over his ample belly. 'Don't suppose anyone fancies a little drink? I noticed there was a pub that's open all day by the –'

'No,' Cookie replied shortly. 'We've got a show to do tonight. I'm off to my digs for half an hour's kip.' And, without a look or word to anyone, she left the building.

'Oh, for God's sake!' Bernard Walton slammed the aerial back into the phone with annoyance. 'Half a bloody hour for a cab! "In the middle of the school run rush,"' he mimicked. 'What do I care about bloody school runs? I'll see if I can find a cab on the street.'

And the star stumped out.

'Er, Ran,' Charles murmured. 'About that twenty quid...'

'Just off to the cash point now, dear boy.' And Ransome George too was suddenly gone.

'I should be off,' said Pippa Trewin. 'Meeting my agent for tea.'

David J. Girton chuckled. 'Oh, right. Mustn't keep the agent waiting, must we? Particularly when that agent's...' And he mentioned the name of one of the biggest in the business.

What is it with this girl Pippa Trewin, wondered Charles, as he watched her neatly and demurely leave the studio. She's had the best start in the business of any young actress I've ever heard of.

Now there were only the three of them left – Charles Paris, Mark Lear and David J. Girton. 'Well,' said the director diffidently, 'what *about* a little drink...?'

He was preaching to the converted. Charles made a token remonstrance about having to do a show that night.

'Nonsense. Some of the best performances I've seen have come from people with a couple of drinks inside them. Freddie in *Neighbourhood Watch* gets through a whole bottle of white wine during every recording of the show.'

Oh well, thought Charles Paris, if the *Director* says it's all right...

They had only a couple. Scotch this time for Charles, he didn't want to keep peeing during the performance. David J. Girton drank wine, forcing the Queen's Head to open a rather better bottle than their house red. Mark drank whisky, and drank it with a dull, silent determination.

Suddenly, after two drinks, he rose to his feet in a panic. 'Only left the bloody studio unlocked, haven't I? God, after all those provisos the insurance company made about security. See you,' he called back at them as he hurried out of the pub.

'It seems to me your friend has a bit of a drinking problem,' said David J. Girton sleekly, as he downed the remains of his second glass of Australian Shiraz. 'Another one?'

Charles looked up at the clock. It was twenty-five to four. Plenty of time to sober up before the show. 'Why not?' he said with a grin.

It was after four-thirty when they left the Queen's Head. Charles didn't reckon it was worth going back to his digs, so he shared a cab with David J. Girton into the Georgian splendours of the centre of Bath.

That night's performance was better. There were more laughs, and the whole show was more relaxed. Charles certainly felt his Aubrey had improved. Oh dear, was he reaching the point where he could only give of his best when he'd got a few drinks inside him?

One thing about the performance was interesting, though. In the Vanbrugh Theatre's audience that night was one of British theatre's most distinguished couples. The famous actress Patti Urquhart and her equally famous husband Julian Strange had come all the way from London to see *Not On Your Wife!* And what's more, afterwards they went out to dinner with Bernard Walton and Pippa Trewin.

Chapter Six

'IT'S FOR YOU, Mr Paris.'

His landlady hadn't become any less anonymous as the week went by. Nor had she quite eradicated the sniff of disapproval with which she always approached him. There had been a slight thawing in her manner when he'd organised her two seats for the Thursday night (without mentioning that the advance at the box office had been disappointing and the performance was being heavily 'papered'); but any brownie points he might have gained there had been cancelled out by the hour at which he'd arrived back after the show.

Still, the call to the phone was a welcome distraction. Charles had decided that morning to go for the kill-or-cure option on his hangover and have the Full Breakfast his landlady offered. But, though Charles had started on the fry-up with commendable vigour, the further he got into it, the more his enthusiasm waned. There is something baleful in the expression of a congealing fried egg, and he didn't think he could face its reproaches much longer. He was glad to leave the egg's recriminations for the phone in the hall.

'Hello?'

'Charles, it's Lisa Wilson.'

'Oh, hi.' On the spur of the moment, he couldn't think of any reason for her call, but he was nonetheless pleased to hear from her. Could it be that his success with *Dark Promises* was to lead so soon to another booking? It didn't sound that way, though. There was something odd in her voice, a tension he had not heard before. Up till then in their dealings, Lisa Wilson had always been in complete control; now she sounded as if she was on the verge of some kind of emotional outburst.

She still hadn't responded to his 'Oh, hi.' 'What's the matter, Lisa?' he asked.

'It's Mark...' She gulped, and the sound could have been a sob.

'What about him?'

'He's dead.'

'What?'

'I got back from London this morning. I stayed over, you see.' She gulped again. 'He was in the studio.'

'Which one?'

'The one you used. The little dead room.'

'What'd happened to him?'

Now her sobbing was unrestrained. 'He'd...suffocated. I...I don't know exactly what happened...There was an empty whisky bottle in there with him. The doctor thinks he must've passed out from the booze. That's really why I was ringing, Charles...You were there to record the radio commercial, weren't you?'

'Yes.'

'Had Mark been drinking? He swore to me that he'd lay off the stuff, at least till the commercial was recorded, but...Had he been drinking when you saw him, Charles?'

It was impossible to deny that Mark Lear had been drinking, and drinking heavily.

'Oh, God.' Lisa's voice cracked in anguish. 'He must've passed out while he was in there, and been too insensible to wake up when there wasn't enough air. It's my fault. Just like it was with my father...' Another huge sob welled up.

'What?'

'I let my father go out and drive when he'd had far too much to drink. He had a crash, hit a tree...He died three days later in hospital. God, I feel this is my fault too. If I hadn't stayed over in London, I'd have found Mark in time. I could have prevented it.'

'You mustn't think like that, Lisa. You mustn't blame yourself. It just happened, that's all.'

There was unrestrained sobbing from the end of the phone. Then, with a great effort of will, Lisa Wilson regained control of herself. 'Charles, I want to see you, talk to you about it.'

'Sure. Where are you?'

'I'm at the studio now. There are police here, and ambulances, and all kinds of...I'll ring you, OK?'

'Yes.'

'I mean, it's quite possible the police will want to speak to you, anyway – you and the other people from the *Not On Your Wife!* company who were here yesterday afternoon.'

'Why? Is there any suspicion of foul play?'

There was an infinitesimal pause before she replied, 'No, I don't think so. But I guess they always check everything out. Have to, don't they? See if it's just an accident...or I suppose...' she gulped again '...it could be suicide...or...'

She didn't complete the thought, but left it dangling, tantalisingly, in the air.

'I'm frightfully sorry,' said Charles. 'It's an awful thing to have happened. You must be in shock.'

'Yes, I think I probably am a bit. Shock and guilt.'

'You have no reason to feel guilty.'

'Don't I? You don't know the half of it, Charles.' She let out a harsh laugh, which broke down into a sob.

'Just hang on in there, Lisa. Don't blame yourself. There was nothing you could have done. And, when things're a bit more sorted out, call me to fix a time to meet. Obviously we've got a show tonight...there'll be a matinée too on Saturday, but just leave a message with my landlady – OK?'

'OK. Thanks, Charles.'

He cleared his throat and then said, 'It may seem indelicate to ask, under the circumstances, but was your day in London good?'

'What?' she asked sharply.

'Your meeting with the publishers. Did you get the job?'

'Oh yes. Yes, we got the job.' Sobs once again threatened. 'Not that it actually seems very important now...'

'No, of course it doesn't. Look, I'm awfully sorry...You take care of yourself.'

'Sure.'

Back in the dining room, Charles's fried egg looked even colder and more accusatory. He pushed the plate back. His landlady didn't say anything, but her look demanded an explanation.

'I'm sorry,' said Charles Paris. 'I've just had some bad news. A friend of mine's died.'

Chapter Seven

AS IT TURNED out, Lisa and Charles didn't meet till the Sunday. By then, *Not On Your Wife!* had done another three performances, and the show was definitely getting better. The cast were more prepared for where the laughs were going to come, and their timing had improved considerably. The overall pace of the production had picked up, the audiences seemed to be enjoying themselves, and David J. Girton was very pleased with the way everything was going.

Bill Blunden, the playwright, was not so positive in his approval, but then it was not in his nature to be positive. He worked on his play scripts like a mechanic tuning a Formula One car engine. He tweaked here, he tightened there, he constantly dismantled, adjusted and rebuilt his creation. He'd watched every performance so far, making extensive notes about the audience's reaction to each line and each moment of comic business. And he'd been sitting up late in his hotel room, rewriting and reshaping the script. As yet, the cast had not been given any of the changes he was proposing to make, but there was a full company call scheduled for the Monday morning at eleven, and everyone had to be on standby for possible extra rehearsals during the second week of the Bath run.

Charles Paris's performances as Aubrey on the Friday and Saturday were workmanlike, but not inspired. He garnered the ration of laughs his part was allocated, but did not grow in comic stature as some of the other actors were beginning to. Charles was on automatic pilot for *Not On Your Wife!*; his mind was preoccupied with Mark Lear's death. The news of the tragedy had filtered through to the Vanbrugh Theatre, but prompted little reaction in the company.

For Charles Paris, though, the death had been a body-blow. Mark had never been a particularly close friend, but he was someone Charles had known for many years, and his sudden absence prompted gloomy reflections on human mortality. There was also a sense of shock. It was so recent. On the Thursday, Charles had been drinking with Mark at lunch-time; less than twenty-four hours later, the man was dead.

There were also uncomfortable parallels to be drawn. Charles Paris didn't yet know the detailed circumstances of Mark's death, but there seemed little doubt that excessive drinking had played its part. There had been too many occasions in Charles's life, particularly recently, when, for the same reason, he hadn't been entirely in control of his actions. Mark Lear's death gave him a there-but-for-the-grace-of-God *frisson*. Charles Paris knew his own drinking was getting out of hand. He could all too easily have been the victim of a comparable accident.

His reaction to this realisation, however, was not admirable. Instead of immediately cutting down on – or, ideally, completely cutting out – the booze, on the Friday and Saturday Charles actually drank more. It seemed that whisky was the only resource he had, the only palliative that could, however briefly, deaden the pain of the thoughts whirling around his head.

Also, he was into one of those cycles of cumulative drinking when the only way he could achieve all he had to was by continuous topping-up. The sequence of half-bottles of Bell's at his digs became a sequence of full bottles. On the Friday and Saturday nights – when he'd woken up at three, his thoughts too troubled for further sleep – he'd had recourse to the whisky. And he'd even taken a couple of solid slugs in the mornings before going down to face his landlady's breakfast.

Charles Paris knew he must stop, but he wasn't quite ready yet to do that. His current dosage was necessary, medicinal even. Wait till he was feeling a bit stronger, then he'd really take the drinking in hand.

The result of his mounting intake was that when, according to pre-arrangement with Lisa Wilson, he arrived at the studio at eleven o'clock on the Sunday morning, he was in the grips of another stinking hangover.

She too looked in a dreadful state, but presumably for different reasons. There were dark circles under her eyes, and her mouth was a thin line of tension.

Though he had never touched her before, it was instinctive for Charles to wrap an avuncular arm around her shoulders and put his lips to her cheek. She gave no sign of objecting.

'I'm sorry,' he said. 'You must have had a terrible couple of days.'

She grinned wryly. 'Known better. Would you like some coffee?'

'Please.' While she crossed to switch on the kettle, Charles looked around the studio space. 'No police tape or seals or anything like that. Does that mean they've finished their investigations?'

'I guess so,' she replied from the other side of the room. 'We'll find out for sure at the inquest, but they seemed fairly confident it was an accident...though one of them was asking about the possibilities of suicide.'

'Would you say Mark had a death-wish?'

She crossed to the table with two mugs of coffee. 'At times.'

'Yes.'

Something in Charles's intonation made her look up sharply. 'What do you mean? What did he say on Thursday?'

'Well...we had lunch in the Queen's Head.'

'He told me he wasn't going to drink.'

Charles shrugged. 'You said so on the phone. I'm sorry. At the time I didn't know he'd promised you to lay off.'

'No reason why you should have done. So what did he say?'

'He was just in a maudlin mood. Self-pitying. I'm sure you know what he could be like...' Lisa Wilson nodded with feeling. 'Well, Mark was saying that life was a mess and that kind of stuff. But I don't know that that would qualify as having a death-wish. I mean, he didn't talk about suicide or...He was just gloomy, depressed if you like.'

'Hm...' Lisa fiddled with the handle of her coffee mug. Charles hadn't seen her in a state like this before. He suddenly realised it wasn't simply shock she was suffering from; she was actually nervous of something. Not of him, surely?

'Did Mark say anything about me?' Lisa asked diffidently.

'He did mention you, yes.'

'What did he say?'

'He implied that...that things weren't...Look, I'm sorry, the state of your relationship is none of my business. I –'

'What did he say?' she insisted.

'He, sort of, said that he was too old for you and that things weren't going too well.'

Lisa nodded her head slowly. 'Did he say anything about other men?'

'Other men?'

'Other boyfriends of mine.'

'Yes, he did, um...he said that you must have had other boyfriends in the past.'

'*And?*'

'And perhaps you still kept in touch with some of them.'

'Oh. Oh God.' Her blonde head sank down on to the table, and her shoulders shook with sobs. 'I should have come back. I could have saved him. I shouldn't have stayed in London overnight.'

'Come on, Lisa, you had things to do. You were having that meeting with the publishers, trying to get work.'

She looked up at him, her eyes smudged with tears. 'My meeting with the publishers finished at five o'clock. I spent the rest of the evening – and the night – with an ex-boyfriend.'

'Ah. Did Mark know that was what you were doing?'

'Yes, otherwise he wouldn't have...' She recovered herself, and shook her head. 'I think he may have suspected.'

Charles nodded. That would certainly make sense of some of the things that had been said in the pub. 'But you can't blame yourself for that,' he urged. 'It was just bad luck that you were away when he passed out in the studio, just incredibly bad luck.'

She shook her blonde head decisively. 'No, it was more than bad luck.'

There was a silence. Charles's head was still drumming with a dull, low pain. He took a long swallow from his coffee. It had gone cold. Oh, he needed a drink.

Lisa Wilson sat up straight and flicked her head briskly from side to side, as if to flush out morbid thoughts. 'Incidentally, do you want some work, Charles?'

Her question got every actor's knee-jerk response. 'Yes.' Then, 'What? Not another finely chiselled literary gem from the deathless Madeleine Eglantine canon?'

'No. It's what I went to London about. This CD-ROM thing. The Thesaurus.'

'I remember you mentioning it. I didn't quite understand what it was about.' The advances of computers and the information revolution they had brought about had rather passed Charles by.

'A lot of CD-ROM reference works these days are multimedia,' Lisa explained patiently. 'So when you look up a word or phrase, you hear it as well as seeing it.'

'I think I'm with you so far.'

'Well, to get all those words and phrases so that they can be heard, someone has to record them.'

'And that's the contract you've got?'

'Exactly. Does recording that kind of thing appeal to you?'

'I am gobsmacked,' said Charles, 'chuffed, over the moon, delighted, ecstatic, jumping for joy, happy as Larry, glad all over, jumping for –'

'Yes, all right. You've got the idea. Well, the publishers need a whole Thesaurus recorded – and pretty damned quickly. I was thinking...now your show's up and running, you'll be free during the days, won't you?'

'Most of the time, yes. May have the odd call for rewrites and extra rehearsal of bits and pieces, but basically I should be free.'

'Well, in that case, we should be able to get the whole lot recorded before you move on to...where's your next port of call?'

'Norwich.'

'Be good if we could get it all done, wouldn't it?'

'Yes,' said Charles, thinking of the money. 'How many words and phrases are there in a whole Thesaurus?'

'About a hundred thousand in this one.'

'Jesus,' said Charles Paris. 'And they all have to be spoken absolutely straight? No inflection, no vocal colouring?'

'None at all.' There was a gleam of amusement in her voice as she asked, 'Do you think you could do it, Charles?'

'Well, I could have a go.' He grimaced. 'Remember, though, you're dealing with someone who couldn't say, "Side One – End of Side One" without sounding "actorish".'

'Dead,' said Charles Paris into the microphone. Then he left a two-second pause, and went on, 'Deceased' – two-second pause – 'Defunct' – two-second pause – 'Died out' – two-second pause – 'Dead and gone' – two-second pause – 'Inert' – two-second pause – 'Lost and gone for ever' –

Lisa Wilson's voice came through the talkback before he completed the next two-second pause. 'No, I'm sorry, that had intonation in it.'

'What?'

'"Lost and gone for ever".'

'What kind of intonation?'

'Well, you were almost singing it.'

'*Singing it?*'

'Yes. Like in *Clementine*. "Thou art lost and gone for ever, dreadful sorry, Clementine."'

'Oh, sorry, yes. I wasn't aware I was doing it. It's something so deep and atavistic, it's almost impossible to get it out of my mind.'

'Well, you must *try*,' said Lisa's voice firmly.

'Yes, OK.'

They had started recording more or less straight away. For one thing, the publishers' deadline was tight, but also Lisa Wilson was in need of displacement activity. Work, any kind of work, might stop the repetitive churning of guilt and horror in her mind. She'd quickly agreed an hourly rate with Charles and, as soon as she'd set up the small studio, they had started recording. They reckoned they could get an hour in before they broke for lunch.

It was still stuffy in the little dead room. Lisa had arranged for the air conditioning engineers to come the next day, and the police had offered no objection, which presumably confirmed that their investigations were at an end. But the airlessness in the studio cast a shadow over Charles. It did not allow him to forget that he was sitting in the very seat where Mark Lear had breathed his last.

Trying to blank that memory – and indeed all received memory – out of his mind, he once again pronounced, 'Lost and gone for ever.' He must've got it right, because there was no further interruption. 'Non-existent' – two-second pause – 'Obsolete' – two-second pause – 'Passed away' – two-second pause – 'Released' – two-second pause – 'Six feet under' – two-second pause – 'Dead as a dodo' – two-second pause – 'Dead as a doornail' – two-second pause – 'Dead as mutton' – two-second pause – 'Dead as –'

'No, sorry, Charles,' Lisa's voice broke in again. 'You're getting a rhythm to the words. You're making them sound like a catalogue.'

'Well, it's bloody difficult not to,' Charles Paris complained. 'Bloody hard – bloody tough – bloody arduous – bloody challenging – bloody problematic...'

They broke at one. 'Shall we go to the pub?' Charles suggested.

One look at Lisa's face told him it was a bad idea. 'Not if we're going to do any more recording this afternoon.'

'No, no, OK.' But, God, how his body screamed out for a quick injection of alcohol. 'Don't you drink at all, Lisa?'

She shook her head.

'Health reasons? Or don't you like the taste?'

'No. No, I like the taste all right. I like the taste very much indeed. Too much.'

'Ah.'

'I used to drink a lot, but then... I stopped.'

'Was that after your father was killed?'

She nodded. The recollection was still powerful enough to deprive her of words. 'Yes, I stopped then completely. I could see the way I was going. I didn't want history to repeat itself.'

'No. Was it easy to stop?'

She let out a harsh little laugh. 'Easy? No, it wasn't easy. It still isn't easy. Still, when I see people drinking on television, when I smell a glass of wine, when I…No, it's not easy.'

'Cohabiting with Mark can't have made it any less difficult.'

'True.' She grinned wryly. 'Mind you, compared to the other difficulties of cohabiting with Mark, the booze was kind of a detail.'

'Ah. So how did you give up? Just will-power? Or did you go to Alcoholics Anonymous or something like that?'

'No, I suppose it was just will-power. Well, I say "just willpower". Shock helped too.'

'Shock?'

She nodded. 'My father's death. We were very close. He did mean an enormous amount to me.'

'Presumably part of the appeal of someone like Mark? The older man?'

'I didn't have you down as an amateur psychologist, Charles.'

'No, well, most actors…it's kind of part of the job.'

'I didn't need Alcoholics Anonymous,' Lisa continued. 'When I'd seen how destructive the booze could be, when I'd seen what it'd done to my father…I didn't need any Twelve-Step programme. I was there in one step.'

'So presumably you tried to stop Mark drinking too?'

'Tried. Early on in our relationship, anyway.' She jutted out a rueful lower lip. 'Huh. I think I probably made it worse in his case. He drank more to get back at me.'

'What do you mean – "get back at you"?'

'Well, increasingly he kind of couldn't hold his own with me in the normal ways. I mean, the break-up of his marriage and being kicked out of the BBC…I didn't realise, when we first met, how much those two events had taken out of him. They'd totally destroyed his confidence. So, in our business venture here, I'm afraid Mark was really just a passenger.'

'That was rather the impression I got.'

'And then, in our private life…' She coloured. 'Well, I guess that wasn't very equal either, not after the first flush of meeting each other, anyway. And the booze was the one thing that Mark felt gave him a kind of power over me.'

'Power?'

'Yes. Constantly challenging me. Challenging me to have a go at him about it, to become the stereotype of the nagging little woman. And he knew how strong my taste for the stuff was too, so he was challenging me to keep off it. Yes, it was the only area in which Mark felt he had power over me.'

'Hm. If you don't mind my saying so, you don't paint a very rosy picture of your relationship.'

'No, Charles, I don't. It started, as many of these things do, quite romantically. There were warning signs, but I made that classic woman's mistake of recognising certain qualities I didn't like about a man, and imagining that I could change them. Things didn't get really bad until we moved down here. I suppose I'd changed too. Over buying this place and getting it converted...well, somebody had to be assertive or nothing would have got done.'

'And that person wasn't Mark?'

'No. I made all the important decisions. I had to. So I guess he felt he was being even further marginalised. But I struggled on, trying to make the relationship work. We were in it together, I thought things would improve.' She sighed. 'But they didn't. They were never going to, so long as he went on drinking that much.'

Lisa shook her head in disbelief at what she was about to say. 'The awful thing is, Charles, that when I realised Mark was dead...along with all the shock and guilt and everything else...a little bit of me was actually relieved.'

'Ah.'

'It's a dreadful thing to say.'

'No. No, it's quite understandable.'

'And that bit of me – that disloyal, traitorous bit – was saying, "Now you've got another chance. Now you've got the possibility of something in your life to look forward to." I'm sorry. I know it's an awful thing to feel.'

'We don't have control over what we feel, Lisa. I think it's very honest of you to admit it.'

'Hm.' She sat back in her chair, somehow eased by the confession, and looked piercingly into his eyes. He'd always thought hers were blue, but this intense scrutiny revealed them to be a pale, unusual grey.

'You drink too much, don't you, Charles?' she said evenly. '

Well...Well, I suppose...I mean, I do sometimes have rather heavy sessions when I'm under pressure and go through bouts of –'

'All the time,' said Lisa.

That almost made him angry. 'You've no idea. You've no basis for saying that. We met less than a week ago and –'

'I can tell,' she said.

There was no arguing with the certainty in her voice. 'Well, yes, all right, I probably do, but –'

'Why?'

'Oh, for God's sake, Lisa! You don't have to ask that question. You understand the compulsion. You know why people drink.'

'Maybe I do, in general terms, but why do *you* drink?'

'All right. I drink to...I drink to make life different.'

'Drink doesn't make life different.'

'I know. Nothing makes life different, but drink makes life *seem* different, and that seems to me the best deal that's on offer.'

'Is life so dreadful?'

'Most of the time I'd say, "yes".'

'And it hasn't occurred to you that it might be your attitude to life, the way you see life, that's actually dreadful? That life itself is entirely blameless?'

'That is possible, of course it is. However, the fact remains that I'm me, and I have only one way of seeing life.'

'And it looks better to you through the bottom of a glass of whisky?'

'Undoubtedly.'

Lisa Wilson shook her head in exasperation. 'But, Charles, just think how much of your time you *waste* by drinking.'

'It gets me through it,' he responded doggedly. 'Without the booze, life would just take so long.'

'Hm. And have you ever tried to give up? I mean, seriously tried?'

'I've tried to cut down from time to time. I've gone whole days without a drop,' he added virtuously.

'But never *really* tried?'

'If you mean by that, have I ever joined something like Alcoholics Anonymous, then the answer's no. I couldn't stand all those smug, self-righteous people swamping me with the patronising zeal of the converted. No, thanks. If I decided to give up, I'd do it on my own.'

'But could you –?'

'Actually, I heard this joke,' Charles interrupted, trying to lighten the atmosphere. '"Friend of mine used to have a drinking problem, so he joined Alcoholics Anonymous. He still drinks, but under another name!"'

Lisa Wilson was not to be deflected by humour. 'Could you actually give up, Charles?'

'Give up booze? Of course I could.' His head was aching more than ever now. All he needed was a drink to melt away the pain. 'It's just that I don't want to,' he concluded.

She sat back, with a cynical curl to her lip.

'And what's that expression meant to mean, Lisa?'

'Just that I don't think you could give up.'

'Of course I could.'

'Yes?'

Her patent disbelief was beginning to annoy him. 'Yes, of course I bloody could! Just like that. All right, I won't have another drink till I leave Bath.'

As a smile of satisfaction spread over Lisa Wilson's face, one thought dominated Charles's mind. It was: Oh my God, what have I said?

'Good,' said Lisa quietly. Then she stood up. 'There's a corner shop along the road. They're open every day of the week, and do sandwiches and Cokes and all that stuff. Shall we grab some there to have for lunch?'

'Yes,' said Charles Paris, without enthusiasm. 'All right.'

* * *

They were again seated either side of the table, this time with their packets of sandwiches and their drinks. Lisa's bottle of mineral water was sparkling; Charles's was still – he found when he was recording that the fizzy stuff made his stomach rumble even more.

Lisa again seemed ill-at-ease, as she had done earlier in the day. It was as if there was something she had to say to him, and clearly it wasn't about the booze, because she'd already said that. Finally, after a long silence, the words burst out.

'Charles, when I came into the studio on the Friday morning, when I found Mark...'

'Yes?'

'There were a couple of things I didn't tell the police about...'

'What?'

'I told them I found Mark in the studio dead...which was true. And that I'd found the bottle of whisky in there with him. What I didn't tell them, though...' she was having difficulty in framing the words '...was that the door to the small studio had been locked.'

'Locked?'

She nodded. 'From the outside. The key was still in the bottom dead-bolt. I unlocked them both, then wiped the key with a handkerchief, and hung it up on the hook where it always goes. And I... didn't tell the police.'

'Why not?'

'I wasn't thinking. I was feeling guilty.' She looked into his eyes, wondering whether she dared confide in him. Deciding to take the risk, she went on, 'The man...the man I spent Thursday night with...he's married. I didn't want all that to come out.'

'But why should it have come out?'

'If I'd told the police everything, then, when they'd investigated, they couldn't have helped finding out.'

'Why? Was there something else that –?'

'Also,' she interrupted him, 'other people maybe knew that things weren't too good between Mark and me...I suppose I was afraid that the police might have thought I had something to do with shutting him in, that I wanted to do away with him, that...I'm sorry, I wasn't thinking logically. It was very stupid of me.'

Charles Paris looked thoughtful. 'Don't worry about that,' he said. 'But this does change the situation, doesn't it?' Lisa Wilson nodded miserably. 'Because if you didn't lock him in...'

'Yes.'

'...then somebody else did...'

'I know.'

'...and that means that Mark Lear was murdered.'

Chapter Eight

AFTER LOUISE has gone through into the bedroom, Aubrey triumphantly closes the door, and locks it. He pulls up his trousers and does them up, then crosses to the French windows. As he does so, the lights dim in Louise and Ted's flat, and come up in Gilly and Bob's flat, where Gilly is just seeing Willie out.

GILLY: And when my husband Bob comes back, you can try out your designs on him.

WILLIE (*very camply*): Don't tempt me.

He goes out into the hall. Gilly turns back into the room to see Aubrey appearing on the balcony from behind the central partition. She rushes across to open the French windows.

GILLY: Aubrey! I was worried you might have dropped off!

AUBREY : And I was worried something might have dropped off. I was in serious danger of joining the Brass Monkey Brigade out there.

GILLY (*putting her arms around him*): Don't worry about that, my darling. I'll soon have you up to scratch again.

AUBREY (*lasciviously*): It wasn't actually 'scratch' I was thinking of being up to, Gilly.

GILLY (*leading him towards the bedroom*): Ooh. Shall we get up to something else instead then? Now, where were we? Shall I just pick it up where I left off?

AUBREY (*enthusiastically*): Sounds good to me!

They disappear into bedroom. The door slams shut behind them. A moment's silence, then doorbell is heard. It rings a second time. Gilly comes bustling out of bedroom, followed by Aubrey. Again his trousers are round his ankles.

AUBREY: Oh no! The fates seem to be against us today! What am I getting myself into?

GILLY (*hustling him across to push him into a cupboard which stands against the central partition wall*): You're getting yourself into this cupboard, that's what you're doing!

She closes the cupboard door on him, and hurries across to the door to hall. The cupboard door opens: Aubrey emerges, trying to pull trousers up. As he gets out, he hears banging from behind him. He turns and looks dubiously at cupboard. There is a further banging noise. He realises where it comes from.

AUBREY: Oh, no! It's Louise banging on the bedroom door in the other flat!

GILLY (*heard from the hall*): No, do come in, Ted, by all means.

Hearing the voices, Aubrey, still with his trousers round his ankles, hurries back into the cupboard. The banging sound from the other flat ceases. The cupboard doors close behind Aubrey, just as Gilly ushers Ted into the sitting room.

GILLY: No, Ted, of course it's not inconvenient.

TED: I hope I didn't arrive when you'd got your hands full.

GILLY *(after a momentary take)*: No, no, good Lord, no.

TED: It's a bit embarrassing.

GILLY: Well, yes, it is, I agree, but... *(realising he's not talking about her situation)* Oh, is it, really?

TED: Yes, you see, I was worried you might have heard something.

The sound of Louise knocking on the bedroom door of the adjacent flat is heard again.

GILLY: No, no, I haven't heard anything. *More loud knocking from Louise.*

TED: You're sure you haven't heard anything?

GILLY: Not a thing.

TED *(looking curiously at the cupboard which conceals Aubrey)*: It's peculiar. I'd have sworn there was a banging noise coming from that cupboard.

GILLY: From that cupboard? Nonsense!

More loud knocking is heard from the adjacent flat. Gilly rises to her feet and hustles Ted through towards the bedroom.

GILLY: No, the acoustics in these old flats are most peculiar. The sound seems to come from over there, but in fact it comes from over here. *(She pushes Ted through into the bedroom.)* You have a listen to that wall over there. Then you'll hear where the banging really comes from.

Gilly closes the door behind Ted, and rushes across to let Aubrey out of the cupboard. He still has his trousers round his ankles.

GILLY: You idiot, Aubrey! Why on earth were you making that knocking noise?

AUBREY: I wasn't!

GILLY: Yes, you were.

There is once again a knocking sound from Louise's bedroom door.

AUBREY: See!

GILLY *(looking curiously at the empty cupboard)*: There's something most peculiar going on here.

AUBREY *(reaching down to pull up his trousers)*: At least I'll be glad to get my trousers on.

There is a sound from the hall of the front door being opened with a key.

BOB *(from the hall, angrily)*: Gilly! Gilly! Where the hell are you, Gilly?

GILLY *(panicking)*: Oh, my God, Aubrey! It's Bob! Quick, hide under here!

She lifts up floor-length cloth that covers dining table. Aubrey, still with his trousers round ankles, scuttles underneath table. Gilly drops the cloth to hide him and smoothes it down nonchalantly as Bob comes storming in from hall.

BOB: Gilly! I have reason to believe that you are entertaining a lover here this afternoon!

GILLY: A lover, Bob? Me? Don't talk nonsense!

BOB: I know there's a man in here, and I'm going to find him!
He looks furiously round the room for a hiding place. As he does so, the door from the bedroom opens, and Ted, looking slightly bewildered, comes in.
TED: About this banging, Gilly...I don't seem to be getting any.
BOB *(turning on his heel to face Ted)*: Oh, my goodness, no! You, Ted! My best friend!

'"Well, you know what I think, Willie. When my husband Bob comes back, you can try out your designs on him."' Bill Blunden read the line out at dictation speed, with all the animation of the Directory Enquiries electronic voice. 'Have you got that, Cookie?'

Cookie Stone nodded, her pencil completing the latest amendment to the already-much-amended script. The entire company had had an eleven o'clock call the morning after their first night at the Palace Theatre, Norwich. They all knew they'd been summoned for more rewrites, more tinkering, more fine-tuning from Bill Blunden.

Tony Delaunay sat at the back of the auditorium, silently watching what was going on. Now they were in Norwich, he was in charge of the show, officially as well as de facto. David J. Girton had returned to the BBC to start pre-production planning for the next series of his long-running sitcom, *Neighbourhood Watch*. He would reappear for the odd night on the tour, but his work as nominal director of *Not On Your Wife!* was – unless the show did ever make it into the West End – virtually finished.

'I just think the new line's got more rhythm,' said the playwright.

'OK.' Cookie was a professional; she'd been through this process many times before. She didn't pass judgement on the changes she was given, just learnt them and delivered them.

'Try it tonight. See what reaction you get.'

'Wilco, Bill. Roger and out,' she said in the voice of a Second World War ace.

'So it doesn't change your cue, Ran. Line's a bit longer, that's all.'

'Young Ms. Stone building up her part again,' said Ransome George, getting his laugh from the rest of the company. As usual, the line itself wasn't funny; but there was some alchemy in his timing and intonation.

'Then, Charles...'

Charles Paris looked up and tried to concentrate. He could no longer blame the booze for the fact that his mind kept wandering, but it did. It kept wandering back to Mark Lear and the circumstances of his death. It kept wandering back to the possibility – or even likelihood – that someone in the *Not On Your Wife!* company had caused that death.

'Yes, Bill?'

'"Brass Monkey Brigade" still not getting the laugh, is it?'

'No. I just wonder whether the audience is catching on to the reference. "Cold enough to freeze the balls off a brass monkey"...I mean, do people still use that expression?'

'I think they do,' said the playwright cautiously, 'but I've got another suggestion, anyway.'

'Oh, right. Good.'

'Try…"And I was worried *something* might have dropped off. And let me tell you – it's a long time since *I*'ve sung soprano!" and make sure you hit the "I"… since *I*'ve sung soprano" – OK?'

'Do you really think that'll work any better?' asked Charles.

There was a rustle of reaction around the auditorium. This was bad form. Bill Blunden was the playwright, after all, he was the expert on farce. For a member of the company – except of course for Bernard Walton, who had star's privilege – to offer an opinion on a rewrite was simply not done.

But Bill Blunden didn't seem worried by the lapse of etiquette. 'Try it tonight,' he said evenly.

'OK,' said Charles, and caught a grin from Cookie Stone. That caused him a pang of guilt. She kept catching his eyes these days, as though they shared something other than the coincidence of appearing in the same theatre programme. In Bath she'd kept her distance, respecting his state of shock following Mark Lear's death. But now they were in Norwich, she seemed to be drawing closer to him again, spurred on perhaps by the memory of some intimacy of which he had no recollection.

'Then I think we can sharpen up the exit sequence to the bedroom,' Bill Blunden droned on. 'You and Cookie, Charles…If Aubrey makes his line: "It wasn't actually 'scratch' I was thinking of being up to, Gilly"…and then goes on: "Do you think we can still manage a little something?"…and, Cookie, as you lead him to the bedroom, you make your line simply:

"Don't worry, it'll all soon be in hand!"'

'OK, love,' said Cookie. 'What, and cut the other lines?'

'Mm. And then, Charles, you just come back with: "Sounds good to me!"'

'Right you are,' said Charles. 'Sounds good to me!'

But it didn't really. Charles Paris didn't enjoy this constant juggling with innuendoes; he liked comedy that came out of character, rather than the mechanical deployment of double entendres. Still, Bill Blunden's international royalties showed that he was doing something right. British farce was a distinct subgenre of the theatre; and, whether Charles Paris liked the medium or not, it was one over which Bill Blunden had complete mastery.

'Now, Bernard…' the playwright continued, turning his focus towards the star, 'still not quite getting the boffo on "…got your hands full", are we?'

'No. Got a woofer at the last Saturday matinée in Bath, but then I did the face.'

'Hm, I think we can get it just with the line, actually…' said Bill Blunden.

'Not with the current line, we can't,' was Bernard Walton's tart response.

'No, I agree. So I've got a suggestion which may sort it out. After Gilly's cue: "No, Ted, of course it's not inconvenient…try saying: "You weren't working, were you? I'd hate to have arrived when you were on the job." Try that.'

Bernard Walton grimaced. 'Bit contrived, isn't it? I mean, obviously I can get the laugh with an expression or a take, but I'd like to feel I was getting a bit more help from the line.'

'Try it tonight,' Bill Blunden wheedled. 'See if it gets the boffo tonight, eh?'

'Oh, all right,' said Bernard Walton. 'For want of anything better.'

'Now,' the playwright continued metronomically, 'still not getting as big a laugh on the word "banging" as we should be getting, are we?'

Charles Paris had reviewed the circumstances of Mark Lear's death on the train up to Norwich the Sunday afternoon after the Bath run finished. He'd talked a bit about it with Lisa Wilson during the preceding week, but they hadn't had much opportunity for detailed discussion. At the studio their days had been full; they'd been deeply involved in recording yet more Thesaurus words and phrases; and then he'd had to rush off to do the show in the evenings. The one night he had organised a ticket for Lisa to see *Not On Your Wife!*, though she'd come for a drink afterwards, they'd been joined by Cookie Stone and some other company members, so they couldn't talk about Mark's death, except in general terms.

The after-show drink had, incidentally, been a mineral water for Charles. Though he had deeply regretted the bold pledge he had given to Lisa, he had stuck to it.

His reasons had been mixed. For a start, the abstinence was the result of a long-held conviction that his drinking was getting out of hand; considerations of health alone suggested a cutback was in order.

Then there was the fact of Mark Lear's death. Whether he had died by accident or by murder, in either case alcohol had been a contributory factor. If he hadn't been so drunk, he would have been in a better condition to protect himself. His example loomed like a dark shadow over Charles. Mark Lear's death had been a warning, a final warning. Get your act together, Charles Paris, or you could be next.

Not drinking because of Mark's death also presented a horizon, something to work towards. *When* I've found out the truth of how Mark died, Charles comforted himself, *then* I'll allow myself to drink again. Somehow making the term of trial finite made it seem marginally more tolerable.

There was also Lisa, the fact that it was to Lisa that he had made his promise. The more Charles saw of her, the more he liked her. He didn't exactly have sexual ambitions in her direction – or if he did, he managed to convince himself they were inappropriate. She was his friend's girl, after all, currently traumatised by that friend's death. Charles Paris was far too old for her, anyway. Given the shattered state of his relationship with Frances – not to mention the totally undefined nature of his relationship with Cookie Stone – he was in no position to be entertaining any kind of sexual ambitions.

But it was the little spark of desire that kept him off the booze. If he hadn't fancied Lisa Wilson, he could never have done it. Because it was hard. God, it was hard. That first Sunday had been awful, his hangover had screamed out for the relief of a little top-up. He'd survived the lunch-time – when Lisa was actually there, the danger of backsliding was very much less – but after they'd finished their recording session and he'd gone back alone to his digs, the pain had been almost intolerable. That Sunday evening had been one of the longest he had ever experienced.

The knowledge that there was a third of a bottle of Bell's sitting in the bottom of his wardrobe made the pain all the more excruciating. Just a little sip was all he wanted. Just one little sip, and then he'd screw the cap on again and put the bottle away.

But something in him knew the sipping wouldn't stop there. And something else in him managed to resist the urge. The reward for his abstinence was one of the best nights' sleep Charles Paris had had for years. So, but for the dark shadow cast by Mark Lear's death, Charles had faced the Monday ahead with more optimism than he could usually muster. He actually enjoyed – rather than just managing to get through – his landlady's breakfast.

But the two major alcoholic pressure points of that day had occurred before and after the show. Before was not so difficult. The biorhythmic urge to have a drink between six and seven was diminished by the fact that he had a show to do. Though recently he had been slipping into the habit, the professional in Charles Paris knew that drinking before a performance was a bad thing. So getting through that night's *Not On Your Wife!* without alcohol had not been too arduous.

Not having any alcohol after the show, however, had been agonising. There was no righteous reason not to drink then. He'd just done a performance, for God's sake! He'd given of himself in the role of Aubrey. He deserved a bloody drink! And everyone else in the company was going off to have a drink after the show. It would have been positively antisocial not to join them.

So he did join them and, somehow, with physical pain, he managed not to drink anything other than mineral water. Not wanting to admit the real reason for his abstinence, he invented a stomach upset to explain it away. The session in the pub was purgatory, but he managed to survive.

That wasn't the cure, though. If he'd imagined that, having cracked one night, he'd broken the back of the problem, Charles Paris would have been wrong. It was still agony for him not to have a drink. The urge for a quick restorative injection of alcohol did not leave him. And, after that first blissful night, his old disrupted sleeping pattern reasserted itself. So it wasn't just the booze that kept him awake.

Still, Charles Paris thought to himself on the train to Norwich, I am managing. My health and my wallet must be feeling the benefit of not drinking. Perhaps my mind's clearer...? Possibly I'm even giving a better performance as Aubrey...

But he wasn't entirely convinced. All he really knew about not drinking was the fact that he hated it.

It was to take his mind off the gnawing ache for a drink that Charles Paris had started reviewing the circumstances of Mark Lear's death.

On his mental video he reran the tape of the Thursday in the recording studio. If the death had been murder, then there were two significant moments during that afternoon. The first had been his own doing. It had been he, Charles Paris, who had drawn attention to the stuffiness of the small dead room and perhaps inadvertently suggested part of a murder method to the perpetrator. Mark's unlocking of the dead-bolts on the studio doors had supplied the other necessary element.

The other significant moment had arisen when Mark started on about the book he was going to write that would 'take the lid off the BBC'. At the time Charles had put this down as drunken rambling, but with hindsight he realised that Mark's words could have been seen as a challenge, and a challenge to one individual person in the studio. What was it he'd said exactly? 'You'd be surprised the unlikely things unlikely people got involved in. Some they certainly wouldn't want to be reminded of now, I'm sure.' If someone present that afternoon, someone with a dark secret connected with the BBC, had recognised the challenge that was being thrown out, then it was entirely possible they might have contemplated silencing Mark Lear for good.

Charles again went through the list of people who'd been present when Mark issued his ultimatum (if that was indeed what it had been). The list ran: Bernard Walton, David J. Girton, Tony Delaunay, Ransome George, Cookie Stone and Pippa Trewin. Which one of them had Mark Lear been threatening?

The person with the most obvious BBC connections had been David J. Girton – and Mark had mentioned some financial malpractice that concerned the director. On the other hand, David J. Girton was the one person who couldn't have gone back to the studio to lock Mark Lear in the dead room. Any of the others might have done, but he had the perfect alibi: Charles Paris. He'd spent the afternoon drinking with Charles, and they'd shared a cab back to the Vanbrugh Theatre.

So it had to be one of the others. Once again, Charles concentrated on the list. Ransome George. Yes. As well as fingering David J. Girton, Mark had also implied that there was a skeleton in Ransome George's cupboard.

And then of course there was the strange fragment of conversation Charles had overheard between Ran and Bernard Walton in the Green Room after the Bath technical rehearsal. 'Your secret is absolutely safe with me.' That's what Ran had said. And then he'd gone on to imply that he'd be angry if anyone else knew about the secret.

There was something odd going on between Bernard Walton and Ransome George. And given the dearth of other candidates, perhaps they'd have to be promoted to prime suspect status.

But what was the 'secret' they had mentioned? How was Charles going to find out more about their murky pasts? Gossip was what he needed, good old-fashioned dirty theatrical gossip.

By the time his train had reached Norwich, Charles had made a decision. He needed to ring his agent.

Chapter Nine

'MAURICE SKELLERN Artistes.'

'Maurice, it's Charles.'

'Long time no hear.'

Charles bit back the instinctive response – And whose fault is *that,* Maurice?, as his agent went on, 'So how you doing, Charles? Enjoying that tour I set up for you?'

'You didn't set it up for me. I was interviewed for it by Parrott Fashion Productions because Bernard Walton had mentioned my name. All you had to do was negotiate the contract. And then you accepted the first figures they mentioned without any argument. That is not my idea of "setting things up".'

'Don't be picky, Charles. Anyway, how's it going? It's the *Romeo and Juliet*, isn't it? And don't tell me, don't tell me – you're playing Friar Tuck.'

'I think Friar Lawrence is the character you have in mind, Maurice.'

'Oh well, same difference.'

'However, the show I'm in is not *Romeo and Juliet*. It's the first run of a new farce by Bill Blunden, entitled *Not On Your Wife!*'

'Yes, I knew that, Charles. Of course I knew that. I was only having a little joke with you.'

'Oh yes?' That Charles certainly didn't believe. 'All right then – test question. Where am I calling you from? Where've we got to in the tour?'

'Well, I...Look, honestly, Charles, without the contract in front of me, I'd find it very difficult to say. I mean, I suppose you imagine you're the only client I have to worry about all the time – and in a way I'm flattered that you think that, because it's a tribute to the kind of exclusive, personal service I'm giving you – but the fact remains that you're only one amongst many highly respected, highly valued clients. And if I could give you the chapter and verse of where every one of them is at any given moment...well, I tell you, Maurice Skellern's feats of memory would be in *The Guinness Book of Records*.'

The whole speech was so outrageously at odds with the truth that Charles Paris hadn't got the energy to start arguing. 'I'm in Norwich, Maurice,' he said dully.

'Yes, of course you are. Vanbrugh Theatre.'

'That's in Bath. That was last week. It's the Palace Theatre in Norwich.'

"Course it is. You know, Charles, what a lot of my clients do...'

'Hm.'

'...when they're on tour, they send me kind of itineraries...you know, week-by-week lists of digs where they're staying, contact numbers, that kind of thing.'

'Ah.'

'Or a lot of them have mobile phones. Do you have a mobile phone, Charles?'

'No, I don't.'

'Oh, you should. Wonderful invention, the mobile phone, for people in your profession, Charles. Means you need never be out of contact with your agent, never be out of the swim of the showbiz maelstrom.'

'I see. But since you never ring me, Maurice, I'm not quite sure what would be the point of my sending you itineraries...or of having a mobile phone, come to that.'

'No. No, well, right. For someone like you, Charles, I agree, it's probably not so important.' There was a silence, then the agent continued in an aggrieved voice, 'Incidentally, I hope you're not hassling me about more work, Charles. I've just set up this tour for you, there's no need to be greedy.'

'No, in fact, I wasn't ringing about work, Maurice. I was after some gossip.'

'Ooh.' Maurice Skellern's tone changed instantly. Its grudging note gave way to pure enthusiasm. 'Who d'you want to know about? Young Kenneth and his latest dalliance with –?'

'No, Maurice. It's not current gossip. It's very old gossip. Possibly going back more than twenty years. Don't know if it'd be possible for you to track down something that long ago.'

'Wouldn't rule it out, Charles,' said his agent with quiet pride. 'I do have quite a network, you know.'

Though sadly not one to procure work for this particular client, Charles Paris thought.

'Who is it?' asked Maurice Skellern eagerly. 'Who do you want me to get the dirt on?'

'There are a couple of names – well, no, three, actually – and the connection is through the BBC – probably BBC radio – and, as I said, we could be talking twenty years ago...'

'What makes you think there's some dirt there?'

'A few things a friend of mine said. Mark Lear – sadly dead now. He used to be a producer in Continuing Education at the Beeb.'

'I remember the name.' Maurice's voice grew heavy with reproach. 'I seem to recall you once worked for Mark Lear, and tried to keep the fact from me. Tried, in fact, to cut out my commission...'

The accusation was left hanging in the air and, to his fury, Charles found himself feeling guilty. 'Yes, OK, well, it's the same guy I'm talking about. And the two I want the dirt on are someone who's now a television producer called David J. Girton...'

'Oh, I know him. Does *Neighbourhood Watch*, doesn't he?'

'That's right.'

'Yes, I've put quite a few of my clients up for parts in that.'

But never me, thought Charles resentfully. You never put me up for a part in it, did you? Still, making that kind of point to Maurice had never been worth the effort, so all he said was, 'I think we could be talking about when David was also working in radio. Some financial fiddle, maybe...'

'Leave it with me. If there's anything to find out, I'll find it out. You said there were three names?'

'One of the others is Ransome George.'

'Ah, dear old Ran.' Maurice Skellern let out the same affectionate chuckle that the actor's name prompted throughout the business. 'How is the old reprobate?'

'Much as ever, I gather.'

'Yes...The dirt you want on him isn't just the fact that he borrows money from everyone and never pays it back, is it? Because he's always had a reputation for that.'

'No, no, I'm sure what I'm after is something more serious.'

Maurice Skellern chuckled again. 'Ran's always been incorrigible on the old dosh-borrowing front. You'd think his reputation in the business would have preceded him and everyone would be forewarned, but, oh no, apparently he still manages to find the odd sucker who'll stump up a tenner.'

'Does he?' said Charles Paris shortly.

'OK. Leave it with me, Charles. I'll see what I can root out, and get back to you. Oh, you'd better give me a number where I can contact you in Bath.'

'Norwich.'

'In Norwich, right. You see, Charles, it would have helped if you'd given me a detailed itinerary...or had a mobile phone. Then I'd be able to get back to you whenever I wanted to.'

Yes, be nicer if you needed to do that because of work rather than gossip, thought Charles Paris. Then he remembered, 'Oh, I haven't told you the third name, have I, Maurice?'

'No, that's true.'

'Still talking round the same time. About twenty years ago, and with a radio connection, possibly through Mark Lear. It'd be in the very early days of this guy's career...'

'Who're we talking about?'

'Bernard Walton,' said Charles Paris.

'Why aren't you drinking?' asked Cookie.

They were sitting in an Italian restaurant near the stage door of the Palace Theatre. It was the Wednesday. They were well into the Norwich run of *Not On Your Wife!* They'd done a matinée that day as well as an evening performance. They deserved a treat.

'Oh, you know...' Charles replied casually, 'just seeing if I can do without.'

'And can you?'

'So far.' He grinned. Now he actually was alone again with Cookie Stone, it wasn't nearly as bad as he'd feared. He'd built up all these images of her rounding on him, accusing him of having behaved appallingly to her in London, but there had been none of that. She just seemed pleased to be with him; and he found her company strangely relaxing.

'Well, I hope you don't mind if I do.' She gave him a toothy grin and raised a glass of red. The candlelight from adjacent tables sparkled and refracted seductively through the wine.

'No, no. I'm not a proselytising teetotaller or anything like that. I'm just having a rest from drinking myself.'

'But the attraction of having a drink's still there?'

'Oh yes,' Charles Paris replied, in one of the greatest understatements of his life. 'The attraction's still there.'

'This doesn't seem to be a very heavy-drinking company, does it?'

'No, maybe not. Mind you, old Ran was pretty far gone last night.'

'Really? Didn't know he was into the booze.'

'Well, last night he was. Came back to the cottage, you know, one I'm staying in with a couple of the stage management bods, and Ran was so far gone he had to stay the night.'

'Ah.' Cookie Stone's face took on a cynical twist, as her voice dropped into cartoon canary, 'Doing dat old twick, is he?'

'What old twick?'

She was instantly back into her normal voice. 'It's one he's used a good few times before, I gather. I bet he pulled it at somebody else's place on Monday night.'

'You've lost me.'

'What Ran does, Charles, when he's on tour, is to keep ending up in other people's digs. Sometimes he'll just leave it too late to get a taxi back; sometimes he'll do the too-much booze routine – as he did with you; and on occasions he's been known to joke his way into young actresses beds...all for the same reason.'

'Which is?'

'So that he doesn't have to pay for digs. He's managed to get through whole weeks without touching his touring allowance.'

'Really?'

'Oh yes, Charles. I'm afraid Ransome George is the original sponger. He knows all the wrinkles. And of course you know about the way he keeps borrowing money from people?'

'Heard something about it, yes.'

'Never pays it back, never has done.' Cookie chuckled. 'It's incredible, really, that someone with a reputation like that can still get away with it. You'd have thought there couldn't be a single person left in the business who didn't know about his little habit. And yet every production he's involved in, he still manages to find some dickhead who's stupid enough to lend him a fiver.'

'Really?' Charles was beginning to get sick of that particular litany. 'But,

Cookie, you've never heard of anything really bad about Ran, have you?'

'How do you mean – really bad"? I would imagine the dumbos who haven't got their money back reckon that's bad enough.'

'No, I meant anything...criminal?'

Cookie Stone shook her head. Her red hair brushed gently against her face. In the candlelight, her eyes didn't seem so close together, and her face softened into a kind of beauty.

Charles Paris lightened the tone of the conversation. Though Mark Lear's death remained on his mind, he didn't want to sound too inquisitorial. 'Quite a boring company all round, isn't it, actually? Boring company in a boring place.'

'Norwich?'

'Hm. Doesn't seem the hub of the universe to me. I have this theory that the most boring places in England are places that aren't on the way to anywhere. It's as if it's the pressure of knowing that the only people who go there are people who actually have to go *there,* rather than being on their way to somewhere else, that makes those places so dull. It's the same with bits of eastern Kent...and bits of Cornwall, I suppose...and, of course, all of Wales.'

Cookie grinned a crooked grin, and dropped into a husky Mae West voice. 'So, if you and I are in a boring place, I guess we're reduced to making our own entertainment, eh?'

Charles Paris wasn't quite sure whether or not this was a come-on, but to his surprise her words prompted a trickle of physical interest. He moved hastily on to less dangerous ground. 'No, I suppose what I meant about this company being boring is that none of them seem to have any dark secrets, do they?'

'Well, no dark secrets which aren't extremely badly kept dark secrets,' said Cookie.

He cocked his head interrogatively. 'Who're you talking about?'

'Let's say a young lady called Pippa Trewin...'

'What about her?'

'Oh, come on, Charles, you *know*.'

'I don't think I do.'

'Young actress fresh out of drama school, gets a lead part in the new Bill Blunden farce, gets one of the best agents around, keeps having to rush off to see television casting directors about new series, movie casting directors about new movies...do you think that's just the result of her exceptional talent?'

'No. Well, if it were, it'd be a first in this business.'

'Exactly. All down to having the right contacts, isn't it?'

So his suspicions had been right. There *was* something going on between Bernard Walton and Pippa Trewin. There couldn't be any other reason why she was in the show. Charles would listen with new cynicism to the next interview in which Bernard waxed lyrical about the perfection and sanctity of his long-running marriage.

'Knowing the right people, that's what gets you ahead in this business.' Cookie Stone hadn't finished. A hobby-horse was being mounted. Her mouth contracted into a tight purse of resentment, as she went on, 'God, I've got more talent in my little finger than that kid, but do I get put up for the kind of parts she does? And, if I make it to an interview, am I the one who ends up being cast? Am I hell?'

'Oh, come on, who's ever pretended that this business is fair?' Somehow it seemed only natural for Charles to reach out and stroke Cookie's hand as he gave this reassurance. His reward was a warm sparkle from her eyes. 'The people who make it, Cookie, are the ones who use every contact they've got. Like old Bernard himself. Do you know, I directed him in his first major stage role.'

'Did you?'

Charles nodded. 'Young Marlowe in *She Stoops*...Cardiff, way, way back.'

'Oh?' Cookie looked at him shrewdly. 'So is that why *you're* in the show?'

'What do you mean?'

'We were talking about contacts. Are you in *Not On Your Wife!* because of the old pals' act with Bernard?'

'Oh, I don't think so.' But, even as he denied the allegation, Charles Paris had a recurrence of the nasty feeling that it might be true. It was Bernard Walton who'd suggested that Parrott Fashion Productions should see him for the part of Aubrey, so perhaps it was to Bernard that he owed his casting. Not the first time he'd had cause to be thankful in that direction. Charles wouldn't have minded if he thought Bernard Walton offered such gestures out of pure altruism, but they seemed to be made solely to provide an opportunity for the star to patronise his former mentor. At least, thank God, Charles thought, Bernard's already been done on *This Is Your Life*; there's no longer any danger of me being wheeled out as the unknown actor 'who was awfully influential in the early days of my career'.

'You know someone's writing a biography of Bernard?' said Cookie.

'Yes. I did hear it mentioned. Seems inconceivable, though. I wouldn't have thought Bernard had been around long enough to provide sufficient material.'

'Don't you believe it. Plenty of showbiz names to be dropped, I'm sure. And with the telly and stuff, there are a lot of punters out there who'd want to read that kind of book.'

'Have you heard if it's going to be a warts-and-all job, a proper exposé?'

Cookie Stone laughed away the idea. 'No way. *Authorised* biography, or near as dammit. Another stepping stone towards Bernard's knighthood, all carefully calculated, I bet. There'll be nothing in the book to sully the image of Showbusiness's Mr Squeaky-Clean.'

Mind you, thought Charles, the revelation of an affair with an actress young enough to be his daughter might sully the image of Showbusiness's Mr Squeaky-Clean. Charles wondered if, by any chance, Mark Lear had known about that particular liaison.

Cookie had the wine bottle poised over her glass. 'I feel pretty selfish, sitting here slurping away on my own. Sure I can't tempt you, Charles?'

For a moment his resolve held. Then he pushed his glass forward. 'Oh well, just the one.'

Boring town though Norwich might be, it was a good place for theatrical digs. As well as some excellent inner-city addresses, the stage door list at the Palace Theatre also included a few in the countryside around. Charles Paris and his stage management friends were staying in one such, but it wasn't nearly as pretty as the tiny cottage outside which the taxi deposited him and Cookie Stone soon after midnight that evening. It was a crisp October night, and an early frost sparkled on the thatch.

'One of the nice things about touring,' she said in response to his expressions of admiration, 'is getting to stay in places you could never in a hundred years live in permanently.'

It was clear once they were inside the cottage that Cookie was a home-maker. All actors approach touring in different ways. Some see it as an opportunity to explore the countryside, taking advantage of their National Trust membership to visit sites of interest. Others use it to develop hobbies such as collecting books or antiques. Some fill their free afternoons catching up on films at the local cinemas; others wile them away in betting shops. Bridge-loving actors have been known, if they've found three like-minded people in the company, to spend an entire three months playing cards.

Some notice where they are and get a lot of feedback from the constant change of surroundings. For others, like Charles Paris, one place looks much like another.

And for him, touring always meant living out of a suitcase. Literally living out of a suitcase. Whether in digs or a rented house, away from home he made no pretence at personalising his environment. (Mind you, the few people who'd seen his studio flat in Hereford Road would probably say he'd made no pretence at personalising that environment either.) For Charles, touring meant one big suitcase, containing books, a bottle of Bell's (or at least it always had until his Lisa Wilson-inspired conversion) and three changes of clothes. While he was wearing one set, the other two remained, more or less folded, in the suitcase, except for their occasional – and not quite frequent enough – trips out to the launderette.

Cookie Stone, however, did not belong to that school of touring. The row of old production photographs on the cottage mantelpiece, the cuddly toys on the back of the sofa, the artfully scattered magazines on the coffee table, all showed her to be someone who enjoyed making any space her own. Maybe she was one of those actresses who was away so much, so often on tour or on location, that she had to take her home with her and stake her claim, set up her camp afresh, in each new setting. Or maybe she was just an old-fashioned homebody.

As soon as they were through the sitting-room door, Cookie had crossed to the drinks tray and lifted a bottle. 'It's Bell's, isn't it, Charles?'

'Well, back in the days when I was drinking...yes, it was Bell's.'

She shrugged. 'You've had half a bottle of red wine already tonight.'

'Mm.'

She held the bottle by its neck and let it sway gently from side to side. 'Up to you...'

Again his resolution was short-lived. 'Yes, I can't think of anything I'd like more.'

'Oh, I hope there's *something* you'd like more,' said Cookie, in a Marilyn Monroe little-girl voice, as she poured Scotch into two tumblers. 'How do you like it? With water or...?'

'Ice, if it's convenient. Otherwise, on its own.'

'Ice is perfectly convenient.' Crossing towards the kitchen, Cookie Stone chucked over a box of matches. 'If you could just do the fire...'

The grate had been neatly laid. Shredded newspaper underneath kindling, lumps of coal and a log on top. As he put a match to the paper and watched orange shoots of flame lick upwards, Charles wondered if Cookie had a fire set in the cottage every night. Or was it only when she was expecting company?

She brought in the drinks, and they sat side by side on the sofa. 'Clink, clink,' said Cookie. They clinked their tumblers together.

Then Charles took a long swig of Bell's. God, he had missed it. God, it tasted wonderful.

He wasn't sure quite how they started touching, whether he moved first, whether she moved first. It didn't seem to matter; neither of them thought it was a bad idea.

'We're grown-ups, after all,' said Cookie, as they withdrew from their first long kiss. 'And it's not as if we haven't done this before.'

'No, for two people of our age to have got through life without having kissed anyone before would be pretty bizarre,' Charles agreed fatuously.

'I didn't mean "kiss anyone". I meant it's not as if we haven't done this *together* before.'

'No. Right.' He chuckled knowingly, but really wished he could remember exactly what they'd done before. How much they'd done before.

Still, this was no time for piecing together the past; his body was getting too interested in the present. His hand slid naturally down to the surprising firmness of Cookie's breast. 'You've got the body of a teenager,' he murmured into the soft redness of her hair.

'Oh God!' said Cookie in her best Hammer Horror troubled heroine mode. 'We must find this teenager and give it back to her!'

'No, we mustn't.' Charles's hand was slipping down from the breast. 'First we must check all the bits are where they should be, to make sure we've got the right body.'

The fire's warmth was spreading now, and their clothes seemed to slip away without embarrassment. Cookie let out a little gasp as Charles's hand found the soft centre of her. 'Do we want to go upstairs to the bedroom?' she murmured.

'Don't see the necessity. Very nice down here.'

They both chuckled at the double meaning. Her hands were doing their bit too. She held him just hard enough, stroked him just softly enough. She knew what she was doing.

'Oh, you're beautiful,' Charles mumbled, as the waves of pleasure mounted. 'Beautiful.'

Cookie contradicted him. 'No. I may be sexy, I may be attractive, I may have a good body, my face may "have character", but there's no way I'm beautiful.'

'Oh yes, you are,' said Charles Paris, as the imperatives of their bodies grew unanswerable. 'You're beautiful, Cookie Stone, you're beautiful!'

It was good. As they subsided into the nest of discarded clothing on the hearth-rug and the firelight airbrushed away the blemishes of their bodies, both of them lazily untwitched.

The only tiny nagging question in Charles's mind remained: Was that the first time I've made love to her, or did it happen in London too?

'Well...' Cookie purred on a wave of fulfilment. 'That was better than the last time.'

A remark which, unfortunately, did not help clear up Charles Paris's confusion.

He felt good the next morning when he returned to his digs. The alcohol had left him with no hangover, and it was a long time since he'd had good sex – or any sex, if the truth be told.

Also there was a message at the digs for him to ring Maurice Skellern. Maybe he was getting closer to finding out who had murdered Mark Lear as well.

The only slight cloud on his horizon was the news from one of his fellow lodgers that, taking advantage of Charles Paris's absence, Ransome George had spent the previous night in his bed.

Chapter Ten

'NOTHING ON Bernard Walton or David J. Girton yet...'

'Oh, well, thanks for trying, Maurice.'

'But give me time, give me time. I did get something on old Ran, though.'

'Ah.'

'I mean, his is a complete history of fiddles and not paying back money he's borrowed and all that stuff...'

'I know.'

Maurice chuckled down the phone. 'And I dare say nothing's changed in that department over the years. He's still finding idiots stupid enough to –'

'Yes, yes,' said Charles briskly. 'What've you actually got on him?'

'All right, all right. Let me get there. Notice, incidentally, Charles, that I haven't asked why you want this information. I've been very restrained.'

'Yes, and your restraint is much appreciated, but I'm sorry, I have to get off to the theatre shortly, so if you could just let me know what you've found out...'

'Of course. Now, the Mark Lear you mentioned, he had a lot of money, right?'

'His wife, Vinnie, had a lot of money, yes.'

'Hm...Well, I think some of it could have ended up in Ransome George's pocket.' Maurice Skellern let the information settle, saying nothing more, challenging Charles to prompt him. Charles resisted the temptation and let the silence extend itself until, with a disgruntled edge to his voice, Maurice went on. ''Ran got involved with some people who were making porn tapes...'

'Videos?'

'No, it was just audio tapes in those days. Ran may have started by acting in them, I don't know, but he certainly got involved in the business side too. Now the thing is, I've found out that certain BBC radio personnel were brought in to help produce the things...'

'And was Mark Lear one of them?'

'Can't be sure about that yet, but, if he was, that'd be your connection, wouldn't it?'

'Could be.' Charles was unable to hide the disappointment in his voice. He'd been hoping for more concrete information.

'It's also a fact, Charles, that some of the BBC people were encouraged, by Ransome George I think, to invest in the company that was making and marketing these tapes. And, when the inevitable happened, they lost their stakes.'

'By "the inevitable", you mean when the company went bust?'

'Exactly. As a lot of those seedy little operations did. Mind you, my information suggests that Ransome George himself may not have lost money. In fact, I'm pretty sure he creamed off quite a lot.'

'That would be in character. By the way, Maurice,' Charles asked curiously, 'where do you get your information from?'

'Ah, now I can't tell you that, can I?' The agent's voice was heavy with reproach. 'I just happen to have certain rather useful specific skills.'

Not for the first time, Charles wished Maurice's 'specific skills' included getting work for his clients. But all he actually said was, 'Well, thank you for that. Much appreciated.'

'I'm still working on it,' said Maurice. 'Still talking to people. I think it's quite possible I'll be able to tell you more soon...maybe definitely tie in Mark Lear's name with the porn tape company.'

'Be great if you could.'

'So where do I find you, if I need to get in touch?'

Charles Paris thought it inappropriate at that moment to pass further comment on an agent who didn't know where his clients were working. 'Leeds next week. But I'm going back to Bath on Sunday.'

'Really?' Maurice Skellern's antennae had instantly picked up the possibility of unpaid commission. 'You working and not telling me, Charles?'

'No, no, Maurice, of course not.' He chuckled, then lied, 'No, my visit to Bath is purely social.'

Despite Charles's complaint that Norwich wasn't on the way to anywhere, the city's train service was not bad. The 9.05 on the Sunday morning got into Liverpool Street at 10.58, giving him time to get round the Circle Line to Paddington and catch the 11.30 to Bath, where Lisa Wilson had arranged to meet him with her car at the station.

The early start had not gone down well with Cookie Stone. She had had in mind dinner after the show, bed and then a lazy waking up to Sunday papers and sex, the kind of indulgence that most established couples enjoyed. She was too much of a professional to argue against Charles's apology that he needed an early night on his own because he was working the next day, but she clearly didn't like it.

That reaction, which he couldn't keep out of his mind as he sat in the safety of the train from Norwich to London, was symptomatic of his relationship with Cookie. He had known from the start that he shouldn't have got involved there. Years of experience should have taught him the unwisdom of becoming entangled with anyone on a long tour, and the more time he spent with Cookie Stone, the more he realised how seriously he'd blundered by becoming entangled with her in particular.

It wasn't that he disliked Cookie. He was fond of her. She was enthusiastic and good at sex; she had a remarkably well-preserved body. And, even though her taste for funny voices could become wearying, she was entertaining company.

What was wrong with her, however, was the old performer's problem – insecurity. Charles, of all people, could sympathise with that. He'd been through every kind of angst about his talent as an actor and his adequacy as a human being. But in Cookie's case, the insecurity manifested itself in a particularly difficult way.

He didn't know her full history of previous relationships, but it seemed clear that at some point in her life she had been badly let down by a man – or, perhaps, at several points in her life she had been badly let down by several men.

This, coupled with the insecurity of a woman who'd grown up knowing she'd never be conventionally good-looking and always have to make her mark by personality, charm, vivacity or sex, left her as raw and vulnerable as a peeled shrimp. If only Charles Paris had known the rod he was making for his own back, he would never have called Cookie Stone 'beautiful'.

That was what had done it. A word he'd used in the heat of extreme physical urgency had fulfilled Cookie's lifelong dreams. It was the plot of every Barbra Streisand movie. At last, she thought, she'd met a man who found her beautiful, a man who really cared for her for herself.

In fact, Cookie Stone had fallen in love with Charles Paris.

He'd only realised this over the previous few days, and it had come as rather an unpleasant shock. For Cookie, though, the emotion was of longer standing, as she told him during one of her endless talkative times in bed when he'd rather have gone to sleep.

She'd fancied him from the moment she'd seen him at the *Not On Your Wife!* read-through. 'And then of course,' she'd gone on, I knew things were going to be wonderful between us...after what happened that night in your flat in London.'

For Charles Paris, remarks like that weren't helpful. 'That night in your flat in London' remained a closed book to him, and however much he scoured his memory, it refused to give up its secrets.

He was left in one of those awkward situations, like having forgotten someone's name, not admitting to the fact straight away, and then getting so far into conversation with them that the admission that you didn't know who they were became insulting. Except with Cookie, it was worse than a name. To have forgotten someone's body, to have forgotten making love to someone, not even to be sure whether or not you *had* made love to them, now that was really insulting. And the longer Charles put off owning up to his uncertainty, the more potentially insulting it became.

Unfamiliarity with the circumstances of its commencement was not the only problem he had in his relationship with Cookie Stone. Perhaps it was a hangover from the days when he'd still been cohabiting with Frances, but so far as affairs were concerned, Charles Paris's inclination was always to tick the box for 'No Publicity'. 'Why,' he had been heard to say speciously, 'do we want the whole world to know about something that's only important to us?'

Cookie, on the other hand, did want the whole world to know. Charles couldn't possibly have anticipated the weight of expectation she brought with her. All her previous disappointments had been cancelled, all her aspirations met, the moment he had called her 'beautiful'. Having quickly established that he was no longer in any meaningful sense married to Frances, Cookie could see no reason why they shouldn't shout their love from the rooftops.

At the very least she saw no reason why they shouldn't shout it to the assembled company of *Not On Your Wife!* Charles had managed so far to manufacture reasons why they should be discreet, but his fabrications couldn't last for ever. And the idea that any liaison could remain a secret for long in the gossip-machine of a touring theatre company was laughable. Besides, Cookie deeply wanted to tell everyone.

This threw Charles into an agony of awkwardness. It was not the first time in his life that he'd regretted a penis-driven impulse, but in the current case Cookie's galloping insecurity made the situation worse than ever. Any hint he gave to her that he was less than wholehearted in his commitment would throw her back into an anguish of rejection.

Cookie Stone's life was locked in a cycle of self-fulfilling prophecies. Charles Paris had started feeling he'd like to back out of the affair within forty-eight hours of its starting (and, so far as he was concerned, the starting point had occurred in Norwich), but even a man who had wanted the relationship to go the distance would have had his resolution tested by Cookie's constantly voiced anxieties.

'You don't really care about me,' she'd keep saying. 'You don't really think I'm beautiful. You're really just like all the other men, aren't you, only interested in the physical side, and when you lose interest in that then you'll lose interest in me. You don't really want this relationship to go anywhere.'

She repeated the litany so often that even someone madly in love with her might pretty soon start believing what she was saying.

And to someone like Charles Paris, who was far from madly in love with her, what Cookie said was all too painfully accurate.

Oh, shit! Why on earth did he allow himself to get caught in these situations? And he had another hangover, too.

It frequently happens that men in unsatisfactory physical relationships start to idealise women with whom they have platonic relationships, and that is exactly what Charles Paris ended up doing on the train from Norwich to London. He was really looking forward to seeing Lisa Wilson. It would be comforting to be with a woman he could just chat to naturally, without any of that confusing lust nonsense.

'Unfaithful,' Charles read without intonation, and left the statutory two-second pause. 'Perfidious' – two-second pause – 'faithless' – two-second pause – 'disloyal' – two-second pause – 'inconstant' – two-second pause – 'unprincipled' – two-second pause – 'double-dealing...'

This particular section of the Thesaurus was not doing anything to improve his mood, and he was relieved to hear Lisa Wilson's voice through the talkback saying, 'OK, got to the end of the reel. I should think you're pretty knackered. Shall we call it a day?'

'Please,' he said gratefully. The air conditioning in the studio was working now, but its atmosphere remained claustrophobic.

'Fancy a coffee?'

'And how!'

'Got anywhere?' asked Lisa, as they sat either side of the table over coffee and chocolate digestives.

'Got anywhere?' Charles echoed guiltily.

'I meant about Mark's murder.'

'Ah.'

'Because I kind of got the impression you were thinking about investigating it, Charles.'

He nodded. 'Yes. I've got to find out what really happened. You still haven't said anything to the police?'

She shook her head firmly. The blonde hair flurried and resettled. Natural blonde, Charles couldn't help thinking. Not like Cookie Stone's dyed red. And Lisa's face was innocent of make-up...unlike Cookie's, which never faced the day without a good half-hour of cosmetic concentration. Oh dear, thought Charles guiltily, once you admit the first hint of criticism, how quickly the floodgates open.

He didn't look forward to re-meeting Cookie in Leeds. He'd have to put an end to the affair as soon as possible. He'd have to fulfil all her gloomy prognostications, crush her like a snail without a shell, and show her that he, Charles Paris, was, like all men, just another shit.

And then, worse than that, for another two months he'd have to be with her on stage through all the ribald whackeries of *Not On Your Wife!*

Oh dear. One thing was certain, though. He'd never, ever get into a comparable situation again.

Charles had to drag himself out of his gloom to concentrate on what Lisa was saying. 'No, it's bad. I know I should say something to the police, but... well, I told you where I was the night Mark died.'

'The married man?'

'Yes, and...I don't know whether the marriage would survive if his wife found out.' She sighed. 'There are kids and everything.'

'Say no more.' He took a sip of coffee. 'You're right, though, Lisa, Mark's death has been nagging away at me. Still, I may be getting somewhere on it, I'm not sure. Tell me, did Mark ever talk to you about pornographic cassettes?'

'What, are you suggesting we needed naughty videos to spice up our sex-life?'

'No.'

'Actually, towards the end it could have done with a bit of spicing up,' she mused.

Charles didn't pick up on that, but went on, 'I'm talking about audio cassettes. Long time back, possibly as much as twenty years, Mark may have got himself involved in producing them.'

A spark came into Lisa Wilson's eye. 'Do you know, he did mention something about that. I've just remembered. Apparently, they used to use wet newspaper.'

'Wet newspaper?'

'Yes, for sexy sound effects. All the liquid sloshings about of sexual organs.'

'Good grief.'

She chuckled. 'Wonderful the things you learn how to do in the BBC, isn't it?'

'Remarkable,' Charles agreed. 'But did Mark mention any of the other people he was working with, you know, when he was producing these cassettes?'

'Don't think so. Can't recall any names. No, he just said he was moonlighting from the Beeb when he did it. In those days a BBC contract was totally exclusive. You weren't allowed to work for anyone outside.'

'Least of all if you were making porn cassettes.'

'Right.' Lisa fixed her grey eyes on his. 'Does that lead you somewhere – the fact that Mark was mixed up in the porn business?'

'Could do, yes. Ties in with something he said about moonlighting the afternoon he died. Yes, it could be very important.'

'Good. But you can't give me a name, say in which direction your suspicions are heading?'

Charles shook his head. 'Wouldn't be fair. Not till I've got a bit more information.'

'OK. I will wait on appropriate tenterhooks.' She reached across to the packet. 'Another chocolate digestive?'

'Why not? Who knows when I will eat again?'

'Are you going up to Leeds tonight?'

'No. I'll probably go back to London. The trains are fine in the morning. We've got a four o'clock call tomorrow, just to familiarise ourselves with the stage. No complete run-through.'

'Ah. So you're not pushed for time?'

'No.'

There was a companionable silence, broken only by the munching of chocolate digestives. As Charles had anticipated on the train, it was comforting to be with a woman he could just chat to naturally. And, as for all that confusing lust nonsense...well, he couldn't deny there was a bit there, but thank God at that moment it wasn't relevant.

'So how're you managing without Mark?' he asked solicitously.

Lisa Wilson grimaced. 'Distressingly well. I'm afraid the feeling of relief has continued, and now I'm even ceasing to feel guilty about it.'

'Good.'

'Yes, I suppose so. Certainly a darned sight easier to run this place without Mark drifting aimlessly around all the time.'

'Hm. And...tell me if it's no business of mine...but is the affair with the married man still going on?'

'Good Lord, no.' Her hair spread outwards and reformed again as she dismissed the idea. 'No, that was really over a long time ago. Which was why it would have been so awful if it had come out at this point. I mean, there were times when it was very intense, when his wife would really have had something to worry about. But now...no. The heavy emotional bit had run its course. Our last encounter was just down to sex.'

'Ah. Right.'

'I'm afraid, you see...' she grimaced again as she chose her words '... sex between Mark and me had been more or less non-existent for some time...since we moved down here, I suppose. It was partly his confidence was shot to pieces and...well, the booze. He was drinking so much he just couldn't do it. And I'm afraid that wasn't good enough for me. I needed some physical attention. So I went back to a former lover for...what shall we call it? A quick fix? A quick service? I'm not proud of the fact, but that's what I needed at the time.'

Charles cleared his throat in a way that he hoped didn't sound embarrassed, and once again found himself transfixed by Lisa's grey stare. 'Apropos of nothing...how're you doing on the booze, Charles?'

'Ah...Well...'

'You promised me you'd give it up completely.'

'Yes, I know, I...'

'I see.' She sat back, letting out a long sigh of disappointment.

'Yup. 'Fraid I have backslid.' He fell back again on a funny voice – the one he'd used in an ill-fated play based on the career of John Wayne ('Thank God the Duke is dead and thus spared the knowledge that this sad travesty of his life has been perpetrated' – *South Wales Echo*.)

Lisa just looked at him. Charles found her silent reproach more painful than if she had said something. 'I will try to get off it again, but...well, sometimes it's difficult.'

'Difficult, but worth doing. How long did you stay off?'

'Till last Wednesday.'

'Oh, terrific! Big deal!' Her voice was weighed down with sarcasm.

'It's a kind of occupational hazard in the theatre for –'

'Don't give me that crap! If you really wanted to stop, you could stop.'

'I know. I've proved it.'

'Proved it? Ten days? Come on. You've got to do better than that to convince me.'

'I think I could do better than that. I'm sure I could do better than that. But I don't think I could do it for ever.'

'Why not?'

'I don't know. Just "for ever" sounds so...final.'

'It is final.'

He shook his head ruefully. 'No, never going back on the booze...I'm afraid that's unthinkable.'

'Why?' asked Lisa.

'Well, I mean it's just...there are certain things, there are certain occasions, which one cannot imagine without a bit of alcoholic lubrication.'

'*One* cannot, or *you* cannot?'

'All right, *I* cannot.'

'Like?'

'Well, OK – sex. I mean, I cannot imagine going to bed with a woman without having had a few drinks first.'

'Why, are women that terrible?'

'No, no!' he said hastily, before noticing the twinkle in Lisa Wilson's eye. 'No, I suppose I mean it's just...I don't know, a matter of relaxation. A couple of drinks, a bit of...I guess for me drink has always been a part of foreplay.'

'The trouble is, that kind of foreplay can so easily mean there's no afterplay. As I found with Mark.'

'Yes, OK. I don't mean too much. I just mean a couple of drinks, to calm the atmosphere...'

'There are other forms of foreplay.'

'I know that.'

'And all those sex manuals and how-to-keep-your-man's-interest articles in women's magazines are always recommending that couples should try new forms of foreplay...'

'I know that too. There's a whole sequence in Bill Blunden's *Not On Your Wife!* on that very subject.'

Charles Paris found himself transfixed by the steady gaze of Lisa Wilson's grey eyes, as she asked, 'Are you actually telling me, Charles, that you have never been to bed with a woman when you weren't drunk?'

'No, by no means. What I'm saying is that I can't recall having gone to bed with a woman without having had a couple of drinks beforehand.'

'Well, maybe you should try it one day. It'd be a new experience for you.'

He chuckled, shrugging the idea off. 'Yes, maybe I should.'

'How about today?'

For a moment he thought he'd misheard, but he hadn't. The even beam of her grey eyes was still focused on his face.

'Erm...well...nice idea,' he said lamely.

'Why not, Charles? We fancy each other, don't we?'

'Well, I fancy you, but I wasn't sure that –'

Take it as read.'

'Good. Um... Thank you.'

'My pleasure.' She reached out and took his hand. 'At least I hope it will be.'

'I'll do my best,' said Charles. Then a sudden panic hit him. Suppose his best wasn't good enough? He'd managed all right with Cookie, but then Cookie was in love with him. Lisa Wilson was a younger woman, in her sexual prime, a woman of a different generation too, who probably had strong views on her sexual rights. He kept reading things in newspapers – even in *The Times*, for heaven's sake – about how assertive modern women had become in the bedroom. God, he needed a drink! That was why he needed a few drinks before sex, to take away performance anxieties.

One of Lisa's fingers was stroking the back of his hand. The action itself wasn't erotic, but the potential it implied was. He felt the reassurance of a stirring in his scrotum. Maybe she was right. Maybe it would be rather interesting to experience sex that hadn't been well marinated in alcohol.

'One thing...' said Lisa.

Oh dear, thought Charles. He had grown up in a generation for whom women saying 'One thing...' before sex usually presaged some mini-lecture on men not taking advantage, and women not being cheap, and commitment being terribly important, and other antaphrodisiac caveats.

'Yes?' he responded with foreboding.

'I don't want any commitment involved here. We're talking about physical pleasure, two people who fancy each other giving and receiving pleasure. No emotional entanglement – OK?'

What man had ever heard more heart-warming words? It was the ultimate masculine fantasy come true. 'OK,' Charles Paris agreed enthusiastically.

They went back to her flat. It was wonderful. Perhaps – heretical though the concept might be – it really was better without the booze.

When he left for the station early on the Monday morning, Charles Paris was more than a little in love with Lisa Wilson.

Chapter Eleven

AS LOUISE goes through to the bedroom to change, the lights go down on Louise and Ted's flat, and up on Gilly and Bob's flat. Ted is sitting on the sofa with Nicky. He is embarrassed; she is all over him.

NICKY: And I just think you're such a good man, Ted.

TED: Oh, really, it's nothing.

NICKY: No, but to agree to pretend to your friend's wife that your friend's mistress is your mistress...I don't know what you call a man who does that kind of thing.

TED: An idiot?

NICKY *(vindictively)*: Mind you, it doesn't reflect very well on the friend, does it? So Bob's ashamed of me, is he?

TED: No, no, I think he just doesn't want Gilly to find out about you.

NICKY: But he told me he did want Gilly to find out about me. He said he wanted to have me out in the open...

TED: Really? Be a bit cold this time of the year.

NICKY *(not hearing what Ted said)*:...but instead he actually wants to have me under wraps.

TED: Probably be warmer, wouldn't it?

NICKY *(furious)*: Huh. Bob's a two-faced rotter. Still, two can play at that game. *(reaching for Ted's tie and drawing him towards her)* If he wants to tell people I'm your mistress, then I'd better become your mistress, hadn't I?

TED *(appalled)*: What!

NICKY *(giving him a kiss on the lips and rising from the sofa)*: Yes, you just give me a couple of minutes, Ted, and then come through to the bedroom – and I'll really have my revenge on Bob. *She sets off towards the bedroom.*

TED *(weakly)*: But, Nicky, wouldn't that just be using me as a sex-object?

NICKY *(as she goes through into the bedroom)*: Yes! Any objections?

As she goes off, Ted rises to his feet and stands irresolute.

TED: Ooh-er.

He decides his best defence is going to be escape, and hurries off towards the door to the hall. Just as he gets there, however, Gilly comes in from the hall, furiously angry. Ted backs away as she advances on him.

GILLY: Do you know what I've found out about that slug of a husband of mine?

TED *(falling backwards on to the sofa)*: No, no, I don't.

GILLY: That chit of a girl who he said was your mistress...

TED: Oh, no.

GILLY: ...is actually his mistress.

TED *(weakly)*: Really? Are you sure?

GILLY: What do you mean – am I sure? Surely you'd have noticed whether or not you had a mistress?

TED: Oh, I don't know. It's the kind of thing one could easily forget.

GILLY: If you think that, then you've clearly never had the right sort of mistress.

TED: I've never had any sort of mistress.

GILLY *(intrigued)*: No? Goodness, Ted, your life must've been very dull.

TED *(miserably)*: Yes – and I liked it that way!

GILLY *(furiously)*: Ooh, Bob's made me so furious. *(She sits beside him on the sofa)* Do you know, I've half a mind...

TED: That's about all I seem to have at the moment.

GILLY *(thoughtfully)*: I've half a mind to get my own back on Bob – in the appropriate way.

TED *(with foreboding)*: 'In the appropriate way'?

GILLY: Huh. Bob's a two-faced rotter. Still, two can play at that game. *(reaching for Ted's tie and drawing him towards her)* If he's saying you've got a mistress, then you'd better have a mistress, hadn't you?

TED *(appalled)*: What!

GILLY *(giving him a kiss on the lips and rising from the sofa)*: I'll just get us some champagne, Ted, and then we'll go through to the bedroom – and I'll really have my revenge on Bob.

As she goes off into the kitchen, undoing her blouse, Ted rises to his feet and stands irresolute.

TED: Ooh-er. Back home, I think.

He turns to go out through the French windows. But as he opens them, Louise appears on the balcony in front of him, dressed in a sexy negligée. She comes into the room, closing the doors behind her.

LOUISE: I knew you'd be here, Ted darling.

TED *(backing away and falling back on to the sofa)*: What?

LOUISE: Ted, I've been reading this magazine article about putting the excitement back into your sex-life...

TED: Really? I'm not sure that my sex-life can cope with any more excitement.

LOUISE *(coming to sit lasciviously beside him on the sofa)*: ...and it says that couples who've been together a long time should liven things up by making love at unexpected times in exciting new places...

TED: I'm quite happy with the boring old places, Louise darling.

LOUISE *(taking hold of his tie and pulling him towards her)*: I'd have thought a neighbour's flat was definitely an exciting new place.

She suddenly reaches for the buckle of his belt, and starts to undo it. Ted struggles to get free.

TED: Louise! Darling! I don't want to make a big thing of this.

LOUISE: I do – and, what's more, I seem to be succeeding.

Ted manages to break free from her and stands in the middle of the room, clutching at his trouser-belt. Louise stands up, and throws off her negligée to reveal that she is dressed in sexy bra and pants.

LOUISE: Ted, you don't always have to have a boring sex-life, you know.

TED: Ooh-er.

At that moment Nicky appears from the bedroom door, dressed in sexy bra and pants. At the same time Gilly appears from the kitchen door, holding a bottle of champagne and also dressed in sexy bra and pants.

LOUISE, GILLY AND NICKY *(all at the same time)*: Come on, Ted. I'm ready for you now.

TED: Ooh-er.

He throws up his hands to his face. Unsupported, his trousers fall down around his ankles. The three women watch in amazement as he falls over backwards in a dead faint, as...

THE CURTAIN FALLS FOR THE END OF ACT ONE.

'I'm still not happy about that "big thing" line,' Bernard Walton complained at the 'rewrites call' on the second day of the Leeds run.

'It's getting the laugh,' Bill Blunden countered.

'Well, it isn't, actually. The laugh comes on Louise's line: "I do – and, what's more, I seem to be succeeding."'

'I'm sorry, Bernard. You can't have all the funny lines.' This insinuation really offended the star's professionalism. 'I am not asking to have all the funny lines, Bill! I'm a team player, always have been. Ask anyone in the business, and they'll all tell you Bernard Walton works as part of an ensemble!'

The rest of the *Not On Your Wife!* company, who worked on stage every night getting no eye contact or feedback from Bernard, might have questioned the accuracy of this, but none of them would have dared voice what Bill Blunden said next. 'I haven't seen much evidence of it. Your performance as Ted seems to me entirely self-centred. You're in a hermetically sealed little world of your own.'

'What the hell do you mean? How dare you, a mere writer, have the nerve to tell me –?'

Tony Delaunay moved quickly to stem Bernard Walton's fury. The company manager was ever-present, ever-watchful, always ready to ease over any little difficulties the current Parrott Fashion production might encounter in its circuit of the country. 'Sorry, sorry, can we just cool it, please? Bernard, if you just say what your problem with the line is...'

'My problem with the line,' the star replied in a voice of icy restraint, 'is that it's been shoe-horned into the script with no real logic and motivation, and that all it basically is is just a knob-joke. "I don't want to make a big thing of this." "I do – and, what's more, I seem to be succeeding." What is that about if it's not about an erection?'

'Of course it's about an erection,' said Bill Blunden. 'That's why it's getting the bloody laugh!'

'All right. Well, I suppose I'd rather be in a play that got its laughs from genuine wit and character, rather than from jokes about erections.'

This belittling of his playwriting skills was too much for Bill Blunden. 'Are you trying to tell me I don't know how to write comedy? Shall I tell you how many productions of my plays there were, world-wide, last year? Go on, you guess how many. You just try and have a bloody guess!'

'Look, let's not turn this into a shouting match,' Tony Delaunay eased in again, as ever smoothing the way, mollifying offended egos. 'Is your problem with the line itself, Bernard, or the fact that it's you who says it?'

'Well, all right. I suppose it is the fact that I'm involved in the exchange,' the star conceded. 'My audience doesn't expect to hear Bernard Walton doing primary school smut.'

'Sod *your* audience!' snapped Bill Blunden. 'Let's think about the play's audience, shall we, for a change?'

'No, no,' Tony Delaunay's conciliatory voice once again intervened. 'Bernard has got a point. He's the star of this show, his name's above the title, and people who come to see it have certain expectations because of his name. He shouldn't be having to deliver lines which are at odds with his public image.'

'Thank you, Tony.' Bernard Walton sat back, vindicated, but the playwright still looked unhappy, so the company manager continued his fence-mending.

'Look, Bill, Bernard has to be doing material he's comfortable with. He's a public figure who has been bold enough to take a stand against declining standards of decency in entertainment and –'

'Are you saying that *Not On Your Wife!*'s indecent?'

'No, Bill, no. I am not saying that. I am saying that Bernard's position is particularly sensitive at the moment, given the current national debate about moral responsibility in the arts – not to mention the fact that Bernard is currently having a biography written about him, so we don't want any adverse publicity. You know how the tabloids love the kind of "Anti Porn Campaigner Spotted in Sex Club" type of story, and we –'

'Are you comparing my play to a sex club?'

'No, I'm not.'

'Oh, I see. You're just afraid this could prevent him from becoming *Sir* Bernard Walton, is that it?'

There was total silence in the theatre. Though everyone knew about the star's campaign for a knighthood, it was not a subject to be mentioned out loud. Bernard himself seemed about to make some response, but thought better of it. Needless to say, it was Tony Delaunay who defused the tension. 'All I'm saying, Bill, is that we have to be extra-cautious at the moment. Adverse publicity of any kind could affect our takings at the box office.'

This appeal to his wallet finally silenced the disgruntled playwright. The company manager continued, 'And don't forget, everyone, that our director's coming to see the show again this week. David'll be in Wednesday evening, so make sure that's a good one. Which reminds me...on the subject of Bernard's biography, the guy who's writing it...' He hesitated, trying to remember the name.

'Curt Greenfield,' Bernard Walton replied.

'That's right...Curt Greenfield. Some of you may have met him when he was in Bath. Anyway, he'll be up here in Leeds on Wednesday, tomorrow. He's going to be around the theatre to get some atmosphere stuff, background, you know. So can I remind you all of what I said when we started rehearsing – no unauthorised talking to the press about anything. If someone wants to interview you about the show, check it out with me first – OK? And the same goes for anyone talking to Curt Greenfield about Bernard.'

'Yes, so keep quiet about Bernard's secret past as a belly dancer – and his sex-change!' Ransome George shouted out.

As always, he got his laugh. Not wishing to appear as someone who couldn't take a joke, Bernard Walton allowed the sally a thin smile. But he didn't look very amused by it. Instead, he said in a tired, we-are-here-to-work-after-all type of voice, 'So, Bill, if you could think of a replacement for those couple of lines for Ted and Louise... I'd be most grateful.'

The playwright was struck by instant inspiration. 'How about Ted says: "Louise! Darling! I can't stick it out any longer", and Louise says, "Oh, I'm sure you can, Ted"?'

'It's still a knob-joke,' Bernard Walton objected.

When the meeting ended, the company drifted away. It was only twelve o'clock, and they weren't due back at the theatre till six fifty-five, the 'half' for that evening's performance. As they moved off, Charles heard Bernard Walton saying to Pippa Trewin, 'Fun at the weekend, wasn't it?'

'Yes, really enjoyed it.'

'Heard any more about the film?'

'I've had a recall,' she replied excitedly. 'It's down to three girls now, my agent says. Going to see the producers again Thursday morning.'

'You'll walk it,' said Bernard Walton. 'Oh, and do give Dickie my best when you see him.'

Charles caught Cookie Stone's eye, and realised that she had heard the exchange as well. She grimaced. For her it was just another manifestation of the unfairness of a business in which it wasn't what you could do, it was who you knew.

For Charles, though, it had other potential meanings. Tony Delaunay's words about Bernard's image brought home to him again how damaging news of an affair with a girl barely out of her teens could be. But was the secret sufficiently important for the star to murder someone who threatened to expose it?

Charles noticed that Cookie Stone was still looking at him, and gave her a weak grin. The situation between them was far from resolved. After his magical night with Lisa, Charles Paris had arrived in Leeds full of the determination to make an immediate and final break with Cookie. He'd tell her she was a wonderful person and a great lover, and somewhere out there was the right person for her, and he was only sorry it wasn't him. He'd really enjoyed their time together, but now they'd have to think of it as no more than an enchanting interlude. It was over.

But seeing her in the flesh had made such directness impossible. He'd fudged around, using all the traditional vague masculine excuses for inadequate emotional commitment, phrases like 'taking a bit of time to adjust to things', 'needing a bit of space' and 'not wanting to rush things, letting the relationship find its own pace'.

And each time Cookie had asked him a direct question, like 'Do you mean this is the end for us?', he'd retreated from the hurt in her eyes and come up with some time-buying formula, such as 'No, no, of course not. Let's just see how things pan out.'

But he knew it was only a holding operation. At some point he'd have to grasp the nettle, and confront the inevitable unpleasantness. Still, he had so far managed to defer any actual sexual encounter between them in Leeds. Fortunately, Cookie was staying in a B & B with a rather old-fashioned landlady and Charles, as he confessed wryly, was staying with 'an old friend, someone who knows my wife…so you know, might be a bit awkward'. And then, feeble fool that he was, he'd lost any ground he might have gained there by saying, 'Still, always next week in Birmingham, isn't there?'

In fact, when he said he was staying with an 'old friend', he had been telling only half of the truth. Ruth was an old friend, but she'd never met Frances. And Ruth brought her own problems.

He'd been shocked, when he saw her, by how old she looked. It had been a good few years since they'd met, but surely not enough to justify the lines on her face, the thinness of her grey hair. Ruth's body had always been thin, but now the word was 'gaunt'. Her clothes hung uneasily about the jutting edges of her thighs and knees, shoulders and elbows.

He made no comment on her appearance, but she gave him one of her familiar sharp, cynical looks and said, 'A bit greyer, but I see it's the same old Charles Paris.'

'What does that mean?'

'It means you look the same – just ever so slightly on the turn.'

'Thank you.'

'And it probably means you are the same. Still drinking too much?'

'I have been cutting down on that recently.'

She barked out a short, disbelieving laugh. 'Won't last. And I assume you're not back with the wife?'

'Well…'

'I see. Still juggling with a series of women, are you?'

At most times during recent years he could have denied the allegation hotly. But, given what had been happening the last couple of weeks...silence seemed the best option.

'I see,' she said again, in a tone of despair at the unerring predictability of humankind – or of mankind – or of Charles Paris, anyway. 'You're in this show with Bernard Walton?'

'That's right. *Not On Your Wife!*'

'He's good, Bernard Walton. Makes me laugh on the telly.'

'Mm. Well, of course, I can organise tickets for any night you fancy.'

'Thanks. I'd enjoy that. Free most evenings these days, but I'll let you know.'

'Fine. Are you still working?'

'No, no, I stopped that.'

'Ah. And you aren't in any kind of, er, permanent...?'

'Relationship?' That got the derisory laugh it deserved. Though there had been quite a few men in Ruth's life since her divorce from a central heating systems salesman, none had raised her opinion of the subspecies.

The look she fixed on him was as it had ever been, expecting nothing, because she knew that expectations with someone like Charles Paris could only lead to disappointments.

After the first performance in Leeds, Charles didn't have a drink with the company, and when he got back to Ruth's semi in Headingley, he saw that her bedroom light was on and the door ajar. On previous occasions those signs had been tantamount to an invitation, and he did hover on the landing for a nanosecond of indecision.

But no. God, no. His life was complicated enough at the moment. The last thing Charles needed was to start hurting someone else. He'd spent the previous night with Lisa. Then he'd had a rather sticky confrontation during the day with Cookie. And somewhere, lurking in the mists of guilt that filled his mind, was an indistinct image of Frances. Charles Paris went straight to his own bedroom.

'The Beeb was never very generous,' said David J. Girton. 'Almost mythic reputation for meanness, actually. All the comedians used to come on and say to the audiences, "I'm wearing my BBC suit today – small checks!" Boom-boom!'

He and Charles were in the theatre bar after the Wednesday night's performance. The director had managed to fit in a large dinner at the Queen's Hotel before the show, so all he was now in need of was a few 'little drinks'. He was on the red wine again, a Chilean Cabernet Sauvignon he'd got the barman to open specially. Very acceptable, David J. Girton had opined after the first sip. Charles Paris, who was sharing it with him, did not disagree.

'No,' the director went on, everyone was strapped for cash in those days, so, although it was deeply against BBC rules and potentially a sacking offence, a lot of moonlighting went on. Pop music was really booming, for one thing, and some of the Radio One stage managers made a very healthy living from producing commercial sessions for various bands.'

'And was Mark Lear into that?' Charles prompted.

'No, music was never really Mark's thing. All the stuff he produced was speech-based. Mind you, he got involved in his own unofficial, don't-say-a-word, readies-in-the-back-pocket work as well.'

An interrogative movement of the head was all Charles needed to make David J. Girton continue. 'The porn industry was also expanding exponentially at the time. Mark got involved in producing dirty audio cassettes.'

Good to have it confirmed. Maurice had been getting very close to the truth. Might be bugger-all use as an agent, but the quality of his gossip was impeccable.

'And presumably, for that kind of work, Mark would have been paid a fee per session?'

'I assume so. As I said, readies in the back pocket. Nothing official, nothing that ever appeared on the old taxman's books, that's for sure.'

'No, of course not.' Charles took a long sip of red wine before remembering that he'd told Lisa he'd stay off the stuff. Oh well, too late to make changes that evening. And it was only wine, after all, not spirits. He went on, 'Tell me, David, I heard a rumour that Mark actually got involved in the management side of the porn tape business, put money into the company...Ring any bells?'

David J. Girton shook his head. 'No reason I would have heard if he had done, though.'

'No. You've no idea what other actors and actresses he might have been working with on these tapes, have you?'

'No idea. Anyone who was around at the time, I would imagine. Not many young actors would object to picking up the odd unofficial tenner for a quick session at the microphone, would they? And with that kind of stuff, there wasn't much danger of them ever being identified from their performances.'

'Why not?'

'Not many actual words involved, I would imagine. Lots of panting, groaning, and the odd grunt of "I'm coming!" Hardly Shakespeare.'

'No. Not to mention the wet newspapers.'

'Ah, you heard about that?' The director chuckled. 'Yes, Karen Cohen was telling me about that.'

'Karen Cohen?'

'Actress who's in *Neighbourhood Watch*. Don't you know her?'

'Know the name.'

'Well, she's a...what shall we say? She's a larger-than-life character. Larger than life in every way. Foul-mouthed, utterly disgusting, very funny. She's always telling us at rehearsal about her wicked past. I'm sure she makes half of it up, just to shock people, but it can be very entertaining. Anyway, she mentioned that wet newspaper thing. She says she did a lot of porn tapes back in the early 1970s – and I think she's probably telling the truth about that.'

'Well, could you ask her if she's got any names for other actors who were involved?'

'Sure.' David J. Girton looked at him with curiosity. And with something else as well. A caution, a guardedness, had come into his manner. 'Why do you want to know all this?' he asked. 'Are you writing the definitive history of moonlighting in the BBC?'

'No, no,' Charles came up with a quick lie. It was distressing how glibly he could sometimes lie. 'No, I was just talking to Mark's girlfriend about it. You remember – Lisa Wilson from the studio in Bath?'

'Didn't meet her.'

'No, no, of course you didn't. She wasn't there that Thursday afternoon. Anyway, she just wants to find out all she can about Mark's past. I suppose it's her way of coping with the bereavement.'

He felt marginally guilty about attributing these spurious motives to Lisa. On the other hand, in the cause of finding out how Mark died, she probably wouldn't mind.

David J. Girton's anxiety had passed. He'd decided that his own moonlighting wasn't the subject of Charles Paris's investigations. Relaxed, he chuckled at another recollection. 'Karen's very funny when she gets going on her days as a porn star. Because she did a lot of video work as well as the audio stuff. Featured in lots of little epics catering for those whose tastes run to the "bigger woman".'

'Ah.'

'Well, if you'd ever seen Karen, you'd know it was perfect casting.' He giggled. 'She said some of the "bigger men" she worked with were so fat she had difficulty actually finding their dicks, let alone doing anything with them!'

'And she's not ashamed of talking about that stuff?'

'You try and stop her. No, "shame" and "inhibition" are two words Karen Cohen just does not understand. She takes great delight in talking on chat-shows about the most intimate details of her life.'

'Whereas other actors might try to cast a veil over some of the things they did just for the money?'

'Too true. Come on, Charles, I'm sure there must've been a few jobs in your past you wouldn't exactly boast about...'

'In my case, that's rather an understatement, David.' Charles Paris tried to think which of the many had been absolutely the most embarrassing. Could it have been his performance as a burnt chip in an advertisement for cooking oil? Or his rendering of the role of a turd in an experimental work entitled *Sewer Fantasies* ('An evening of which I would like to flush away all memories' – *Time Out*). Charles wasn't even sure whether he'd boast about recording over a hundred thousand words and phrases for a Thesaurus on CD-ROM.

'And with those tapes that Mark Lear produced,' David J. Girton went on, 'there might be even more reason for the actors involved to keep quiet.'

'Why? Just because they were porn?'

'No, Charles, because they were gay porn.'

Chapter Twelve

'MAURICE, I've now got information that definitely ties Mark Lear in with the audio porn cassettes.'

'Really?' Down the telephone his agent's voice sounded disgruntled. 'I was getting close to a result on that myself.'

'So if I can tie in the Ransome George strand, you know, prove that he got Mark Lear involved on the financial side...'

'Yes, all right, Charles. *If* you can do that, so what? How's that going to help you?'

'I'm not sure...'

He wasn't. All he knew was that Ransome George was now at the top of his list of suspects. Everything seemed to come back to Ransome George. First, there was his character, entirely amoral, out to get any money he could by any means.

Then there was the conversation Charles had overheard him having with Bernard Walton in Bath. Ran knew something that Bernard wanted him to keep quiet, and Ran, presumably because of some financial arrangement with the star, also wanted to keep it quiet. If the challenge Mark Lear had thrown down in the studio threatened that cosy little set-up, then Ran was quite capable of using any means to neutralise that threat.

What the secret was that Ransome George and Bernard Walton shared, Charles didn't know. Bernard certainly couldn't have had anything to do with the porn tapes, because Mark had specifically denied ever working with him. But the tapes were the link between Mark and Ran.

Charles was confident that it would soon all be clear to him. Though he hadn't got the fine detail of motivations worked out yet, he felt certain that Ransome George had murdered Mark Lear.

'Maybe it'd make things easier,' he was aware of Maurice Skellern's voice going on, 'if you told me why you were trying to get this information.'

'Yes, yes, perhaps it...No, I'm sorry, Maurice. Have to keep quiet about it for the moment. I think I'd better talk to Ran.'

'All right, but when you're with him, just make sure you don't open your wallet.' Maurice's laugh wheezed away at the hilarity of the idea.

'Yes, yes, all right, very funny. Anything on the other names I mentioned?'

'Nothing that ties them up with Mark Lear, no. David J. Girton may have been involved in some overnight expenses fiddles, but no worse than most

BBC producers of the time got up to.'

'What about Bernard Walton?'

'Nobody's ever got anything on Bernard Walton – well, except for insincerity, egotism and being a workaholic. Anyway, all those just go with the territory of being a star. Otherwise, dear old Bernard remains Showbusiness's Mr Squeaky-Clean.'

'Never anything dubious on his sex-life?'

'Charles, the general view is that Bernard Walton doesn't have a sex-life, that he's so obsessive about his work Mrs Walton would get more action in a nunnery.'

'But they've got three children, haven't they?'

'Yes, and the consensus is that those three times were the only three times it's ever happened. I mean, I'm not one to spread gossip, but...'

Why is it that people say things like that, Charles wondered. Why do they say exactly the opposite of what they mean? Why do the shiftiest characters in the world always begin sentences with 'Honestly...' and 'Trust me...'?

But, as Maurice Skellern rambled on with more details about the supposed aridity of Bernard Walton's sex-life, Charles Paris was reminded of something else he had to check up on. He must find out precisely what place Pippa Trewin had in the star's life.

He finally located Ransome George in the pub near the stage door before the show that evening. He indicated Ran's gin and tonic glass. 'Another one of those?'

'If you're buying, Charles, I would be honoured.' He did it in his obsequious-funny voice. Had there been other people there to hear it, the line would have got its certain laugh.

They settled with their drinks. Instinctively, Charles had bought himself a large Bell's. It was only as he was carrying the glasses back to their table that he remembered his pledge to Lisa. Oh well, time enough. If he didn't drink on the Friday or Saturday, then when they met on the Sunday, he'd have survived nearly three days without booze.

Anyway, he was conducting an investigation. He had to relax the person he was pumping. If Ran noticed Charles wasn't on the Bell's, that might put him on his guard.

Even as he shaped these justifications, Charles Paris knew they were nothing more than the casuistry of the alcoholic. He raised his glass to Ran. 'Cheers.'

'Down the hatch.' Again, the timing and the voice were funny. It was difficult to consider someone who could be so consistently funny in connection with a murder enquiry. But then so impermeable was Ransome George's humorous defence that it was difficult at times to think of him as a human being, or to get near the real human being who must lurk somewhere in the middle of all the funny faces and funny voices.

'Was talking to my agent about poor old Mark Lear...' Charles began.

'Uh-uh.' Ran's reaction was entirely without attitude. He didn't sound anxious or guilty. He didn't sound anything. 'Who is your agent?'

'Maurice Skellern.'

Ransome George just giggled.

'Maurice used to know Mark way back in the early 1970s,' Charles lied. 'I gather you did some work for him back then...'

Ran didn't deny it. 'Odd little bits here and there, yes.'

'Agent mentioned something about some audio porn tapes...'

'So?'

'Do you remember making those?'

'Vaguely. I've done all kinds of stuff over the years. Never been out of work for more than the odd month.'

'Lucky you.'

'Partly luck. Partly grafting away, following up leads, making the right friends, you know how it is.'

'Oh yes. Were you actually involved in the production company that made the porn tapes?'

For the first time there was a wariness in Ransome George's eye. 'May have been. Why you asking?'

'To be quite honest, I think there was something funny about Mark Lear's death.'

'Funny?'

'Not to put too fine a point on it, I think someone may have helped him on his way.'

Ran nodded slowly, weighing the idea. 'I suppose it's possible. What's this got to do with the porn tapes?'

'Well, that afternoon Mark talked about writing a book, exposing things that went on in the BBC, or amongst people who had BBC connections... Do you remember?'

'Uh-uh.'

'And in retrospect I've come to the conclusion that what he was actually doing was issuing a threat. He was saying he would expose something he knew about someone.'

'Who?'

'That's what I don't know. Obviously someone who was in the studio that afternoon.'

'Mm.' Ransome George caught his eye. 'You're not looking at me, are you? I never worked for the BBC.'

'Not on the staff, I know, but you did the odd radio as an actor.'

'Very few. Pretty quickly realised my face was going to be my fortune and concentrated on the telly.'

Charles took another sip of his whisky. It did taste good. The idea that he could ever give the stuff up permanently seemed more remote than ever. 'I've just a feeling, Ran, that what happened to Mark is somehow tied in with events at the BBC in the early 1970s.'

Ransome George shrugged, without much interest in the subject. 'Maybe.'

'So I want to find out all the detail I can, particularly about the time when Mark was involved in producing those porn cassettes.'

'Well, good luck. I don't see that it has anything to do with me.'

'You were involved in making those cassettes, so you could fill in a bit of the background.'

'Yes, possibly I could. Doesn't mean I will, though, does it?'

'Why not?'

Ran didn't answer that straight away. Instead, he asked, 'What kind of stuff do you want to know?'

'Anything. Everything. Names of the other actors involved, for a start.'

'It'll cost you.'

'What do you mean – it'll cost me?'

'I'd have thought the words were clear. We live in a consumer society. Most things have a price. Information's certainly a marketable commodity. I've got information you want. So, to get it, you're going to have to pay me.'

'How much?'

Ransome George stretched out a ruminative lower lip. 'Say five hundred quid per actor's name.'

'What? But I haven't got that kind of money.'

'Didn't think you had. Means you haven't got that kind of information either, doesn't it?'

Charles was too dumbfounded by this reaction to press his point. Instead, he said, 'Incidentally, Ran, talking of money…there's still the small matter of that twenty you borrowed from me on the last day of rehearsal in London.'

Ransome George looked up, his face full of shock and injured innocence. 'Oh, now come on, Charles…'

'What?'

'I paid you back that money when we were in Bath. Don't you remember, just before the first night? You were hurrying to your dressing room and I thrust a twenty into your hands.'

'I don't remember that.'

Ransome George hit his head with the heel of his palm in annoyance. 'Oh no, you must've left the note in the pocket of your costume. I bet one of those little sluts in Wardrobe nicked it.'

The awful thing was that, for a moment, Charles actually believed it. He'd underestimated Ransome George as an actor.

'So what was it like directing Bernard Walton in his first major role?'

There was something creepy and slightly unwholesome about Curt Greenfield. He was late thirties, a showbiz journalist who'd developed a lucrative second string as a paste-and-scissors 'biographer to the stars'. An uneven beard straggled round his chin. His clothes were sweatshirt, denim jacket, jeans and incongruously new-looking cowboy boots.

Curt Greenfield had no social graces, made no attempt at small talk. He hadn't offered coffee or a drink when Charles appeared in the theatre bar for the interview officially sanctioned and arranged by Tony Delaunay. All Curt Greenfield wanted was quick, quotable answers to his questions. Answers that could be shoved straight into his book with the minimum of editing.

'Well, he was quite inexperienced,' Charles replied, 'but he had got something.'

'Star quality?' asked Curt Greenfield, ever eager for the cliché.

'I wouldn't say that. More a stage presence. Even back then, when he was on stage, the audience found it difficult to concentrate on anyone else.'

Charles saw the biographer write down 'Star quality', then look up and ask, 'Why in particular did you cast him? What was it about Bernard that so impressed you?'

'Well, his stammer was certainly part of it.'

'So you'd say Bernard Walton's speech impediment, something which to many people might appear as an obstacle, in his case proved the springboard to stardom?'

'No, I'm not sure that I would say that,' said Charles, reluctant to have his views reduced to journalese.

Curt Greenfield ignored the objection. 'And was the Cardiff production when you first met him? You didn't know him as a child? You didn't know any of the Miles family or –?'

'I met him first at the London auditions for that production of *She Stoops to Conquer*.'

'By which time he was already "Bernard Walton the actor"?'

'I suppose you could say that. He hadn't got much experience at that stage, but he had been around a bit.'

'Hmm...' Curt Greenfield didn't reckon any of that was worth writing down. His hopes for charming, winsome reminiscences of the star's boyhood were not to be realised. 'Anything else?' he asked restlessly. 'Any little anecdotes? Any stories that show what a popular member of the Cardiff company Bernard Walton was?'

'No, I can't think of any of those.'

The biographer shrugged. 'Oh well, if I put something like..."Bernard Walton's infectious high spirits made for a relaxed and convivial backstage atmosphere", that should cover it.'

'Not really. I think that'd give rather a misleading impression of –'

'And he's been generous to you over the years, I gather?'

'What do you mean?'

'Helping you out. Seeing you got the odd small part in shows he's been involved in. Not forgetting the lesser figures who helped him on the way up.'

'No, I wouldn't put it like that. I'd say –'

But Charles knew his protests were in vain. Curt Greenfield had arrived with his interview virtually written. Nothing that was actually said was going to change it.

The biographer closed his notebook with an air of finality. 'That's it. I'll see any quotes I use are attributed to you by name.'

'But will the words be what I actually said?'

Curt Greenfield looked at Charles in total incomprehension. He didn't understand the question. Then he sat back, with a reptilian expression, and said, 'By the way, you know what I'm writing about Bernard is, like, the official, authorised biography."

'I got that impression. Be closer to a hagiography, I gather.'

'Mm?'

'A "hagiography" is the life of a saint.'

'Ah.'

'A biography devoid of criticism.'

'Oh, right, get your drift. I'm with you. And because it's that kind of book, that's why your nice camp little company manager...Tony...?'

'Tony Delaunay,' Charles supplied.

'That's right. Well, that's why he's been so co-operative to me, setting up all these interviews. Anything that builds up Bernard Walton's image is presumably good for Mr Delaunay's business.'

'I guess so. Good for Parrott Fashion Productions.'

'On the other hand...' Curt Greenfield began slowly, 'if there's any other stuff you've got on Bernard Walton...'

'What kind of stuff?'

'Let's say stuff that's less flattering, less hagi...whatever you said, less "Lives of the Saints" stuff, eh? Well, I'd be interested to hear that too.'

'So you've taken a commission to write a book that's a whitewash, but in fact you're going to make it subversive, is that right?'

'No, no, Mr Paris. The book will be exactly what the publisher wants...and, incidentally, what Bernard Walton's management wants – they've put some money into the project too – but, while I'm doing all this research, while I'm meeting all the relevant people...well, if there's any dirt around on Bernard Walton, I've probably got a market for that too.'

'You'd sell it on anonymously?'

'Oh, you bet. So, if there is anything...?'

Charles shook his head.

'I'd pay, if it's good. Ransome George gave me some good stuff.'

Suddenly Ran's remarks about paying for information began to make sense. 'What? What did he tell you?'

Curt Greenfield smiled an oleaginous smile. 'Now, come on, Mr Paris. I'm the one who paid for the information, not you.'

'Yes. Of course.'

'So if you have got any stories that might show the sainted Bernard Walton in less of a stained-glass window light, I'm very happy to discuss terms.'

'No, no, I don't think I've got anything,' Charles said distractedly. 'When did you talk to Ransome George? Yesterday?'

'No. I caught up with him when your show was in Bath. We had a very productive three hours of chat there one afternoon.'

'Which afternoon?'

'Erm...The Thursday, I think.'

'What time on the Thursday?'

'Three-thirty he came to my hotel.'

'It was just the two of you?'

'Yes. Well, most of the time. Tony Delaunay popped in...I don't know, half-past four, fivish, I suppose...just to see that everything was OK. He'd set up the interview, you see.'

'Hm. Can you be absolutely sure it was the Thursday?' asked Charles.

The biographer wrinkled his forehead. 'Fairly sure.'

'I mean, for instance, did Ransome George say he'd come from recording a radio commercial?'

'That's right. He did.'

Damn, thought Charles Paris. Because if Ransome George was in a hotel with Curt Greenfield telling tales out of school about Bernard Walton, then there was no way he could have been in a studio murdering Mark Lear.

It was something to do with Bernard. Charles kept coming back to that fact. His thoughts distracted him from whatever Cookie Stone was saying over dinner on the Saturday night after the show.

He shouldn't have been there with Cookie, anyway. Delaying the clean break, trying to let her down gently, wasn't going to work. It would only build up troubles for him later, because, from the bits of her monologue he caught, Cookie Stone was still as deeply in love with Charles Paris as ever.

His mind homed back in on Bernard Walton. It must be some secret in the star's private life, something Mark Lear had found out about. But what? Well, he still hadn't fully investigated the Pippa Trewin connection. Maybe there had been company gossip on the subject...? It was quite possible that he'd missed it. Charles Paris had incredibly unresponsive antennae for gossip.

'Cookie,' he said suddenly, 'about Pippa Trewin...?'

Cookie Stone looked surprised. She had been in the middle of saying how wonderful it was to be with someone to whom you didn't have to explain everything, someone with whom you felt companionable enough to share silence, someone whose every thought you could anticipate...But she hadn't anticipated that Charles's thoughts would be currently centred on Pippa Trewin.

'What about her?'

'How long has her affair with Bernard Walton been going on?'

'*What!*' Cookie let out a screech that turned every head in the restaurant. Then, in an elaborate stage whisper, she went on, 'What on earth are you talking about, Charles?'

'Well, they seem to be very pally, they keep talking about mutual arrangements, they seem to see each other over the weekends...Apart from anything else, ask yourself: "Why is Pippa Trewin in the show, anyway?"'

'Pippa Trewin is in the show,' said Cookie Stone icily, 'because she has better contacts than anyone else in the business.'

'Yes, but Bernard must be getting some payback for –'

'Bernard Walton is her godfather.' The frost hadn't left Cookie's voice, as she went on. 'Her parents are Patti Urquhart and Julian Strange. That is why she's with a top agency, that is why she's got a fast track to television casting Directors and movies. That is why her career is set fair, and why for the rest of her professional life she will continue to take parts that should be going to other, more talented, actresses who happen to have been born to different parents.'

'Oh,' said Charles Paris. 'I think I've been a bit stupid not to realise that earlier.'

God, that wasn't the only way he was stupid. As they left the restaurant, Cookie had said, 'I don't care about my bloody po-faced landlady. I'll never have to see the old bag again after tomorrow morning. Come back to my place.'

And like a fool, he had done so. He blamed the hurt in Cookie's eyes, which had been intensified by the furious sense of professional injustice their talk about Pippa Trewin had revived. But the only thing he could really blame was his own spinelessness.

And then, because of his tiredness, because of the prospect of seeing Lisa Wilson the next day, because of his confusion about Mark's death, Charles hadn't been very good in bed. And, although that was completely his fault, Cookie had blamed herself and started asking questions on 'Don't you love me any more? Have you stopped fancying me?' lines.

So, amidst all the recriminations and the angst, very little sleeping had taken place that night.

Charles's return to Ruth's house, early on the Sunday morning, to pick up his things, had exacerbated the feeling of being an emotional disaster area, unable to move in any direction without causing more pain.

Ruth didn't pass any comment on his overnight absence, but her expression didn't need words to back it up. All she said was: 'There was a message for you last night from a Lavinia Bradshaw. Wants you to ring her. Another of your women, I suppose?'

'Lavinia Bradshaw? I don't know anyone called Lavinia Bradshaw.'

'Oh no?' said Ruth, disbelieving.

'No, I don't. I really don't.'

He packed his bits in silence, and they almost parted in silence. But when he got to the door and looked back, Charles was astonished to see that Ruth was crying. Tears poured unchecked down her lined, grey face.

'What's the matter, love? What is it?' He put his arms around her, and felt the unnatural thinness of her body against his. 'What is it?'

'Oh, Charles, I just thought...you...I thought you, the eternally unreliable, eternally selfish, eternally randy...I thought you would...But now I'm too ugly and sick even for you to fancy me...'

She broke into a long wail. 'No, no,' he said, patting the sharp ridge of her shoulder. 'No, of course not. I just didn't think I should take advantage of you...I thought...'

There are some situations in which one can do nothing right. Charles Paris had been in a good few of them during his lifetime. He'd been exercising restraint, trying to do the decent thing, and all the time Ruth had actually been *wanting* him to make love to her.

God, Charles Paris thought savagely on the train down to London, am I capable of doing *anything* that doesn't hurt someone?

Chapter Thirteen

'END,' Charles Paris intoned, then left the required two-second pause, and went on, 'Ending' – two-second pause – 'Conclusion' – two-second pause – 'Finale' – two-second pause – 'Closure' – two-second pause – 'Curtain' – two-second pause – 'Termination' – two-second pause – 'Halt' – two-second pause – 'Payoff' – two-second pause – 'Last words – God, I wish they bloody were!' he concluded in exasperation.

Nothing came from the talkback. He looked up through the glass. Lisa Wilson's head was bowed. She showed no reaction to his lapse. Was she being professional, or was there actually a deterrent factor in her lack of response?

Charles focused his eyes back on the photocopied list of words, which swam before him. Even without his hangover, the task would have been hard. It was incredible how much concentration doing individual words demanded. The text of a play or a book at least had a logical sequence to it, there was a continuity of thought which could be followed through. With the Thesaurus, he had to start from scratch with each new word or phrase.

'Swansong,' he continued. Two-second pause. 'Coda'–two-second pause – 'Boundary'–two-second pause–'Terminus–two-second paus –Where the rainbow'–

He was suddenly and unexpectedly ambushed by giggles. 'I'm sorry, Lisa...It's just..."Where the rainbow ends" sounds so...I don't know, so showbiz!' Another burst of giggles ran through him. 'I mean...all the others are kind of doomy and dreary...and then suddenly you get to...' He dropped into a little Shirley Temple voice: '"Where the rainbow ends"! Yippee! Yippee! "Somewhere, over the rainbow..." I'm sorry...'

He looked, through his uncontrollable tears of laughter, into the cubicle and saw, with relief, that Lisa was also incapacitated. Her eyes were streaming too.

'I'm sorry,' Charles managed to say again. 'It's just hysteria...It's like...like "gate fever"...you know, that thing long-term prisoners get when they're about to be released...A hundred thousand bloody words and phrases we've done...suddenly the end is actually in sight and I just...'

He broke down again. Lisa Wilson's voice came giggling through the speaker into the studio, 'You'll never make it to the end...It's like the horizon...the nearer you get to it, the further away it moves.'

'Or one of those classical myths...Who is it? Tantalus having the bunch of grapes constantly whipped away when his mouth gets near them...'

'Or Sisyphus pushing that bloody stone up the hill...'

'And watching it roll all the bloody way down again? Oh, I'm sorry, Lisa, I'm just completely gone...I can't do the next phrase. I literally cannot say the words, "Last g-g-g-g..."'

He went again. By the time Lisa's voice next came through the speaker, she had regained a degree of self-control. 'OK, Charles. Enough. The phrase is, "Last gasp".'

'Yes,' Charles Paris agreed soberly. 'Last g-g-g-g-g...'

And still he couldn't shape the word.

'Joke over,' Lisa's voice announced sternly. But, through the glass, Charles could see her mouth was still twitching uncontrollably.

'Yes,' he said. With enormous concentration, he emptied his mind of everything, bleached the words he had to say of all meaning or connotation, and managed to pronounce, 'Last gasp' – two-second pause – 'Last lap' – two-second pause – 'Home straight' – two-second pause – 'Last t-t-t-t-' But this time it was the word 'trump' that wouldn't come.

Once again the two of them had dissolved into hopeless giggling.

'I can't believe it's all done,' said Charles Paris, as he finally staggered out of the studio just before seven that evening.

'Well, it is.' Lisa indicated the high pile of marked-up tape boxes. 'I've checked. Every single word and phrase recorded. So, in a few months' time, everyone who consults that particular CD-ROM Thesaurus will hear the dulcet tones of Charles Paris wafting out of their computer's speakers.'

'Yes.' Charles hesitated before his admission. 'It seems somewhat late in the day for me to ask this, Lisa, but what exactly is a CD-ROM?'

'How long have you got?'

'Well...'

'Because I could give you an extended scientific description of the technology and potentialities of CD-ROMs, or I could just say they're a means of storing information which can be presented on a computer screen with illustrations in sound and pictures.'

'That'll do.' Charles reached out his arms behind him, joined his hands, and stretched. 'God, it really gets you in the small of the back, that kind of concentration.'

'Still, you can stop concentrating now. As I say, all done. Congratulations.'

'Thanks. Ooof.' He sank gratefully into a chair. 'Really calls for a drink, doesn't it?'

'I'll make us some coffee,' said Lisa Wilson tartly.

'The police have been round again,' she announced, when they were settled either side of the table, making inroads into another packet of chocolate digestives.

'Really?'

She pursed her lips. 'Still hasn't been an inquest yet. The first one was adjourned for a month, to give the police time to make more enquiries.'

'So we're not the only ones to suspect murder?'

'I'm not sure about that. I think they're concentrating more on suicide.'

'Oh?'

'Well, you see, they don't know the one detail that we know – namely that the studio door was locked...'

'Because you haven't told them.'

'Exactly. But, if you rule that out as a consideration, then, given Mark's depressed mental state...suicide must look like a possibility. You know, he takes a bottle of Scotch, shuts himself into a space which he knows has no air supply...'

'But why's this suddenly come up now? I thought the police were satisfied at the time that it was an accident.'

'I don't think they'd made up their minds, but I reckon they'd have been happy to accept that explanation. No, someone has been stirring things up.'

'Who?'

'Who do you think?'

Charles shrugged. 'Search me.'

'Oh, come on, it's obvious. The widow.'

'Mark's ex? Vinnie?'

'Sure.'

'But I thought she'd given up all interest in him.'

'All interest in him as a human being, yes. But not all financial interest in him.' In response to Charles's puzzled expression, she continued, 'Mark was heavily insured, and the beneficiaries of the insurance are his children. That situation wasn't changed by the divorce. I think his widow's view – not unreasonably – is that, since it was her money that paid all the premiums, she should ensure that her kids get what's due to them.'

'Ah. But if Mark was found to have committed suicide.'

Lisa Wilson nodded. '...then the insurance company wouldn't pay up. I reckon Mark's widow must've started making the claim, and then the insurance company – who, like all insurance companies, would do anything rather than actually shell out any money – became suspicious about the circumstances of his death. And I reckon they're the ones who've got the police taking another look at what happened.'

'That'd make sense. Has Vinnie talked to you about it?'

Lisa gave a firm shake of her blonde head. 'No. She wouldn't talk to me about anything. She may not have wanted Mark any more for herself, but she was damned if anyone else was going to have any rights in him.'

'So you never even met her?'

'No. And, of course, I've only heard Mark's side of the story...but I do get the impression that she is one very strong-willed lady.'

'Yes, I suppose she always was. I didn't meet her that often, but she was strong, you're right. I think a lot of people who're born with money are strong. Of course, when I knew her, she was channelling all that strength into keeping the family together.'

'I gather she still is. Mark's no longer part of the equation – he ceased to be from the moment she walked out on him – but I think she'll still be ferocious in support of her offspring. The old "lioness with cubs" syndrome. Which is why she'll fight any suggestion that Mark committed suicide. She'd regard it as him having the last laugh on her – there's no way she's going to allow that to happen.'

'No.'

'From everything I've heard about her,' said Lisa, 'she's a truly terrifying woman. I don't envy Mr Bradshaw.'

'Mr Bradshaw?'

'That's her new married name.'

'Of course! She's Lavinia Bradshaw.'

Lisa looked at him curiously. 'Yes. So...?'

'It's just that a Lavinia Bradshaw has been trying to make contact with me.'

'Ah. She's probably found out that you were here the afternoon Mark died. She'll want to see if she can get anything from you to scotch the suicide theory.'

'Well, I'll let you know what she says.'

'Thanks.' There was a silence. Lisa's grey eyes locked on to him, as her hand reached across and rested lightly on top of his. 'Talking of Scotch, Charles.'

'Hm...'

'How've you been doing this week?'

'On the booze front?' He grimaced wryly. 'Well, I cannot put my hand on my heart and say it's been a week of total abstinence.'

'Ah. Why not?'

'I'm sorry. I've had pressures and...'

'I see,' she said in a tone that meant: yes, she saw, but no, she didn't *approve*. She withdrew her hand from his.

'The thing is...'

'Don't worry, Charles.' She let out a little sigh of exasperation. 'You don't have to explain. Remember, I've lived with two alcoholics.'

'I'm not an alcoholic!'

Her grey eyes challenged him. 'No?'

'No. I can stop. I just...'

'...don't stop,' she supplied. 'Or at least not for long.'

'No...Well...I...'

Lisa Wilson stood up from the table. 'Which train are you getting back to London, Charles?'

He was dumbfounded, as all the carefully fostered fantasies of the previous week crumbled around him.

'Well, I wasn't sure that I was going back. I thought –'

'Charles,' said Lisa firmly. 'What happened last Sunday night was good. We both enjoyed it. It answered a need in both of us. But it was never intended to be the start of anything long-term.'

'No. I know that,' he said miserably.

'As I recall, I spelt out our "terms of engagement" at the time. No commitment, no emotional entanglement. And I also seem to recall that you were very keen to accept those terms.'

'They're terms men have been trying to get from women since the race began.'

'Exactly. And also, generally speaking, the terms men have tried to impose on women since the race began...'

'All right. Possibly.'

'So you can't really complain when I act according to those terms, can you?'

'Look, are you making a political point here? Is this part of some kind of feminist agenda that you –?'

'No, Charles, it isn't. What I am saying is that what happened last week was very good –'

'But if it was so good –' he protested.

'It was what was needed at the time,' she steamrollered on. 'I enjoyed it, and it's a memory I will always treasure.'

'Me too.'

'Good. But it wasn't the start of anything. We lead different lives, we're very different people. What we're going to do shortly is part – with a big, friendly hug – and we'll certainly see each other again from time to time...but, so far as any physical relationship between us is concerned, that's over. Nice while it lasted, but not to be repeated. OK?'

'OK,' Charles agreed mournfully, and got out the little timetable of trains back to London.

Just before he left, as they had their 'big, friendly hug', he asked, 'Lisa, if I hadn't had any booze during the week...? I mean, is it because of the drinking?'

'No,' Lisa Wilson replied firmly. 'With you, the drinking's just a symptom of everything else.'

'Oh,' said Charles Paris. 'Right. Thank you.'

The digit '2' was glowing on his answering machine when he got back to Hereford Road. He replayed the messages.

The voice on the first was dauntingly upper class and authoritative. 'Charles, this is Lavinia Bradshaw. We met when I was married to Mark Lear. Could you get back to me urgently, please?' She gave a London number. 'I'm calling on Sunday morning, having, I gather, just missed you in Leeds. I'll be up till half-past eleven tonight, so could you get back to me? It's important that we meet before you leave for Birmingham tomorrow. Message ends.'

Yes, as Lisa Wilson had said, she was a very strong-willed woman. And she'd done her research on his movements; maybe she'd got all that detail from Maurice Skellern. When Charles had met Vinnie before, with Mark, it had always been on social occasions and perhaps then her ferocity had been masked. But now there was no gainsaying her. He'd have to call back. Besides, Lavinia Bradshaw might, unknowingly, hold the key to Mark Lear's murder.

Checking on his watch that it was only just after eleven, he let the tape play on for the second message.

It was a full drama queen performance from Cookie Stone. 'Charles darling, I feel so miserable about last night, and about how we parted this morning. I just have to see you. I'm in Crouch End. It doesn't matter what time you get in, what time you receive this message…you just have to call me. You must.'

Oh, shit! thought Charles. Why do I get myself into these situations? And why can't I get myself out of them with any kind of grace? He thought of the relative elegance with which he had just been dumped by Lisa Wilson. The rejection was still hurting, but he couldn't deny the fact that it had had style. Why couldn't he find within himself the skills to let down Cookie Stone in the same way?

He rang Lavinia Bradshaw. While he dithered about what time he would be leaving for Birmingham in the morning, she announced she'd be round at Hereford Road at nine-thirty. As on the recorded message, her tone of voice did not countenance the option of disagreement.

Then, for a full ten minutes Charles held firm. He checked through the flat and found there was a quarter-full half-bottle of Bell's. He hadn't searched it out because he was going to drink it, just to assess the degree of temptation it offered. Because what Lisa had said to him had hurt. Charles Paris *could* stop drinking whenever he felt like it. It was just that he very rarely felt like it.

For a moment, he contemplated pouring the whisky down the sink, but that did seem an excessively melodramatic gesture. Also, that would be making things too easy. He had to prove to himself that he could keep off the booze, whatever temptations there were around him. Then, after…what?…a month…two months…six months…he could go back to Lisa Wilson and...

He knew that scenario would never be completed. The sexual relationship with Lisa was over. But he still wanted to keep off the booze. He'd been really offended by her saying that it was 'just a symptom of everything else'.

At the end of the ten minutes, Charles gave in and rang Cookie Stone. He was determined to be strong and sensible, to be supportive, but to leave her with no illusions about the true state of their relationship.

And he might have done all that, if she hadn't cried. Two minutes later, as he put the phone down, Charles realised he had agreed for Cookie Stone to come round to Hereford Road. God, he was an idiot!

She arrived within the half-hour, clutching a bottle of Glenfiddich. And although he managed to resist the whisky, Charles Paris didn't manage to resist Cookie Stone's body.

It was realising the depth of her pain and her need that did for him, though he wasn't helped by her assertion, 'After all, this is where it all started.' For Charles Paris the obscurity which surrounded their first encounter had not lifted at all.

But he succumbed to Cookie's need for reassurance. 'You do really care for me, don't you? You understand the real me, don't you – not the flamboyant jokey front I present all the time? You really do find my body beautiful, don't you?'

And Charles – weak Charles – supplied all the reassurances that his words and his body could provide. And, with its own infuriating irony, his perfidious body conspired to dig the hole he was in even deeper, performing exceptionally well.

Chapter Fourteen

CHARLES WOKE up at quarter to seven in the morning, which meant that some sleeping must have taken place in the course of the night, but it didn't feel that way. He ached as though his body had been through the full cycle of an industrial carpet-cleaning machine, and the minute he showed signs of life, Cookie made him go through another spin.

Again, he was surprisingly effective, but his performance didn't give him the warm glow it might sometimes have done. Sex without love is never good, but sex without love with someone who's in love with you is worse, intensifying the accompanying guilt and self-hatred. Why is it, Charles pondered – not for the first time – that women so often identify sexual attention with love? In his experience, intense and continuous sexual activity was usually a sign of one partner trying to prove or justify something to the other. His most satisfactory physical relationships – like the one he and Frances had once shared – had involved a lot more stillness and stroking and cuddling than manic screwing.

The thought of his wife brought the inevitable pang of guilt, this time stronger than ever. He hadn't been strictly faithful to Frances since early on in their marriage, but he had rarely got himself into the kind of bedroom farce tangle he was in now. Cookie...Lisa...Ruth...What was he playing at? Was he going through some Final Benefit Night before the Eternal Safety Curtain crashed down and locked itself permanently in place?

One reason, Charles knew, why he made love with such avidity to Cookie Stone was that, for a while at least, it stopped her talking. But not for long. The most recent orgasm had hardly shuddered itself away, before she started up again. 'It worries me, Charles, that you sometimes seem so distracted when you're with me.'

'You shouldn't bother about that. It's what I'm like. I drift off. I lead a very full fantasy life, you know.'

If that had been intended as a joke, it was the wrong joke for the moment. Cookie's prominent teeth jutted forward ruefully, as she said, 'Full of other women, I bet.'

'No, no, of course not.'

'I bet it is. I do worry about you and other women...'

'You have no cause to. I mean, I still have a very strong bond with my wife, but...' Good idea to slip that in. Frances might prove a useful argument when the final breaking-off with Cookie eventually happened. 'I'm afraid the feeling I still have for my wife prevents me from committing myself fully to another woman...' he could say at the appropriate moment, then adding, '... even one as wonderful as you, Cookie.'

But, the minute he had the idea, he felt shabby. He did still care for Frances, but to use her as some kind of bargaining counter to get out of his other messy entanglements was disgusting.

Cookie's jealousy, however, had not been defused. 'I was worried about you and that woman in Bath.'

'Woman in Bath?' he echoed innocently.

'That woman...Lisa is it?...that you've been scurrying off every Sunday to do recordings with. At least, you *called* them recordings.'

Her tone was only half-joking, so Charles came in quickly, 'And you actually thought I was having a thing with her?'

'You might have been. You're so gorgeous, Charles – at least, I find you so gorgeous – that I imagine every other woman in the world feels the same about you. That's what it's like when you're in love with someone...you're terrified that people are trying to steal them away from you.'

If Charles had needed any proof that he wasn't in love with Cookie Stone, that would have provided it. He was *dying* for someone to steal her away from him. He wanted nothing more than for some nice man, who really *did* think she was beautiful, who adored her for what she was, to come along and sweep her off her feet. If that were to happen, Charles Paris would not create any problems. He would do the decent thing, stand back and concede victory to the newcomer.

But he couldn't see it happening. He couldn't imagine the man had been born who could withstand her constant demands for reassurance. So deeply engrained was the self-doubt about her own attractiveness that all Cookie Stone's prophecies seemed doomed to self-fulfilment.

Still, there was one matter on which he could reassure her, without resorting to lies or half-truths. 'Cookie, I promise you that nothing happened between me and Lisa Wilson yesterday. We like each other fine, but there is never any chance of it becoming a physical relationship in the future.'

Cookie seemed to accept his assertion – which was, to Charles's great regret, the absolute truth – and fortunately she did not enquire about any previous history. But, needless to say, reassurance on one detail did not allay all of Cookie's other anxieties. 'So what is it you're thinking about all the time, Charles, when you look as if you're not here?'

Oh God, he thought, can't I even have my thoughts to myself? Being with Cookie Stone in the real world was claustrophobic enough, without her setting up a monitoring post in his brain as well. But of course that was not what he said. Instead, he tried to fob her off with a half-truth. 'I am rather preoccupied at the moment. There's something I'm trying to find out the truth about. Something rather private.'

Many women in the world would have respected that hint, and discreetly withdrawn from further questioning. Cookie Stone was not amongst their number. 'What is it, Charles?'

'Well, something to do with...You remember that friend of mine who was running the studio in Bath...the one who was terribly drunk the afternoon we recorded the commercial...Mark Lear.'

'Lisa Thing's boyfriend?'

'That's right. Incidentally, he said he'd met you, didn't he?'

'Did he?'

'Yes. That afternoon. Don't you remember?'

She shook her head, making the hair rustle against his naked shoulder. 'Can't recall it. But you say he used to be BBC.'

'Yes. Radio. Continuing Education.'

'I probably got introduced to him in the Ariel Bar at some point. I used to do quite a bit of radio work when I started.'

'Hm.' Charles sighed. 'Well, Mark's death has, kind of, affected me. You know how upset I was in Bath. So I've been trying to find out what really happened there.'

'What, you think it might have been suicide?'

'Yes, or... who can tell?'

'You don't mean you think he might have been murdered, do you?'

'Well...I suppose it's a possibility.'

His words silenced Cookie Stone. Charles couldn't help thinking that if – heaven forbid – his relationship with her continued, he should bear that in mind. Maybe the mention of murder would always silence her. It'd certainly be less exhausting than having to make love to her all the time.

But the silence didn't last for long. 'Who would want to murder him, though?'

'I don't know. Someone who had a secret Mark knew about, and someone who so much didn't want that secret known that they were prepared to silence him for ever. If you remember, he did kind of issue a challenge that afternoon, that he was going to spill the beans about something.'

'Did he? I don't remember. I guess my mind's full of other things too.' Cookie had affected a throaty American voice, and pressed the length of her body against his. Oh God, thought Charles, not again.

But there was an 'again'. After it, out of sheer exhaustion, they both fell asleep.

They were woken by the peremptory buzzing of the entryphone. Charles looked at his watch. Half-past nine. Oh God! Vinnie! Lavinia Bradshaw!

He bustled Cookie into wakefulness. 'For heaven's sake, I've got someone coming to see me!'

'Another woman?' she asked, sleepy but already jealous. 'Yes, she is a woman, but not one that need cause you any anxiety. Please get some clothes on quickly! You've got to get out!'

Charles picked up the entryphone, but Cookie's rampant paranoia had not been appeased. 'She's coming here to your flat at half-past nine in the morning and it needn't cause me any anxiety? You really expect me to believe that, Charles?'

'Yes, I do. Now put some bloody clothes on!' He apologised into the entryphone. 'Sorry, sorry. Look, I'll be right down to let you in if you just wait –'

'But surely,' Lavinia Bradshaw's imperious tones crackled back, 'you can let me in by simply pressing the –?' He cut her off, not without relish.

Shouting at Cookie, which he hadn't done before, had also proved an effective way of silencing her. Another one to bear in mind. She sat on the bed, resentfully pulling on tights, while Charles stumbled into his trousers.

The room looked a mess, fuggy with recent sex. He scrambled the bedspread inadequately over the twisted duvet, and threw open the window to let in cold air as an inadequate means of fumigation.

'Are you ready?' he pleaded once he'd pushed his feet into his shoes.

'Not quite.' Cookie seemed deliberately to have slowed down her dressing.

The entryphone buzzed again, seeming to echo the shrillness of Lavinia Bradshaw's tone.

'Look, I've got to go and let her in. I'll try and delay a bit on the doorstep, but you get down as soon as you can. When you see me, just kind of nod, you know, like you were somebody else living in the block.'

'I see. Still ashamed of me?' asked Cookie.

He countered the resentment in her voice by bellowing, 'Just do as you're bloody told! And I'll see you in Birmingham!'

Once again, the shouting silenced her. Charles crossed to plant a dry kiss on her pouting lips, checked he'd got his keys with him, and went down to open the front door.

'What the hell kept you?' demanded Lavinia Bradshaw. She was expensively dressed, her image sharpened up considerably from the childbound earth mother Charles recalled from their earlier meetings. Whatever her real age, plastic surgery had put her back firmly into her late thirties; and though the reddish-gold of her hair couldn't possibly be natural, it contrived to look natural.

'Sorry, Vinnie. I, er, um... sorry.'

'I didn't *wake* you, did I?' asked Lavinia Bradshaw, to whom the idea was entirely incongruous.

'Good heavens, no. I just, er...' Charles loomed aimlessly, blocking the door.

'Aren't you going to invite me in? It is quite cold out here.'

'Yes, sorry. I, erm...'

Still he hovered, preventing her entrance. Then he heard the welcome sound of footsteps behind him. He turned with relief to see a fully dressed Cookie tiptoeing demurely down the stairs.

She was not an actress for nothing. 'Good morning, Mr Paris,' she said without interest, as she passed him.

On the doorstep, Cookie came face to face with Mark Lear's widow. 'I know you, don't I?' said Lavinia Bradshaw.

'No, I don't think so,' replied Cookie Stone, before hurrying off down Hereford Road towards Westbourne Grove.

Chapter Fifteen

WHEN IT came to sniffs of disapproval, Lavinia Bradshaw left Charles's Bath landlady standing. Sniffs of disapproval were what her face did best. Maybe the fining-down of plastic surgery had sharpened its ability, but Charles seemed to remember the Vinnie of old had a pretty good line in withering scorn.

That was certainly the expression with which she greeted the interior of his flat. The cold blast of early November air which came in through the window did not seem to have dispelled the stuffiness of recent body contact, merely spread it more evenly around the room.

Lavinia Bradshaw focused her disapproval on the window. 'I'm all in favour of fresh air, Charles, but there is a limit.'

'Yes, sorry, I...' He closed the window, sealing in the night's fustiness. 'Could I offer you a cup of coffee or –?'

'No, thank you.' Lavinia Bradshaw's refusal may not have been prompted by the room's insalubrity, but that was certainly the way it came across.

'OK, fine.' He gestured to a chair for Lavinia. She looked at it dubiously. He hurried forward to remove a few weeks' shirts and socks. Very gingerly, Lavinia Bradshaw sat down, allowing her skirt minimum contact with the chair's doubtful surface. Charles perched with unconvincing insouciance on the edge of the bed. 'So what can I do for you?'

'Needless to say, it's about Mark. I've –'

'Oh, I hope you don't mind my interrupting, Vinnie...'

She clearly did. If her face hadn't already given him that information, he would have got it from the coldness with which she said, 'I'm no longer called "Vinnie". Everyone calls me "Lavinia" these days.'

'Oh, sorry. Lavinia. No, well, the thing is, before you start, just a quick question. That girl...that woman...who came down the stairs when I let you in –'

'Or seemed very unwilling to let me in, and kept me waiting on the doorstep.'

'Yes, yes, all right. I'm sorry about that. But that woman...you seemed to know her.'

'Well, I recognised her. We had met before.'

'And did Mark know her?'

'He'd met her too.' But she didn't want to be diverted. 'Charles, I'm not here to discuss passing acquaintances. I'm here to talk about Mark's death.'

'Yes, but –'

'Now let me tell you, I am not getting involved in this business for sentimental reasons. Once I finally left Mark, the only question in my mind was how on earth I'd managed to stay with him for so long. I put up with his drinking, his infidelities. I cooked for him, virtually brought up the children single-handed. Any debt I might have had to Mark I have paid over and over again.

'So I'm not raking through the sordid circumstances of his death for any reason other than the purely practical.' She then went on to confirm Lisa's assessment of the situation. Mark's life had been heavily insured, with a policy designed to benefit their children. But now the insurance company was kicking up a fuss, and had started the police re-investigating what had caused her husband's death. 'Basically, they're suggesting it could have been suicide and, if it was, that invalidates the policy. I didn't pay out all that money in premiums not to get the payoff, so I'm determined to prove that Mark didn't kill himself. Have you any reason to believe that he might have done, Charles?'

The direct question put him in a difficult position. Yes, Charles did have a reason to believe that Mark Lear hadn't killed himself, but only because he knew his friend to have been murdered. Lisa had found the door to the little dead room locked. So far she had been extremely unwilling to pass that information on to the police. For Charles to pass it on now to Lavinia Bradshaw might be regarded as a betrayal of Lisa, because he couldn't envisage Lavinia keeping quiet about it. She would ensure that the police's investigation was very quickly redirected.

'Come on, Charles!' Lavinia Bradshaw made him feel as if he was back at prep school, doing badly in one of Miss Pybus's quick-fire mental arithmetic tests. 'Apparently you were with Mark the afternoon he died. Did he say anything that could have led you to believe he was about to take his own life?'

'Well, he was severely depressed, and he was drinking heavily.'

Lavinia Bradshaw snorted. 'That is no surprise to me at all. I gather he'd pretty soon regretted setting up house in Bath with that slut.'

Charles resisted the temptation to come to Lisa Wilson's defence, as he went on, 'And yes, he did say things that could have been interpreted as expressing suicidal intentions. He said he felt old, he had nothing to look forward to, he couldn't see the point of going on.'

That prompted another derisive snort. In the course of their married life, Lavinia had heard Mark maundering on on similar lines far too often to take it seriously.

Charles endorsed her reaction. 'But though, quoted out of context, those words might have come from someone who was genuinely suicidal, you know and I know that Mark often said things like that.'

'Yes. And I always treated them with the contempt they deserved. Do you know, he even rang me that afternoon?'

'The afternoon he died?'

'Yes.'

'What did he say?'

'Oh, the usual maudlin rubbish. He was extremely drunk. He did all the nonsense about how we should never have split up, and how he still hoped we could get back together again, and how he loved me and the children, and how his life wasn't worth living without us. I'd heard it all many times before.'

'Did you tell the police about this?'

Lavinia Bradshaw was affronted by the suggestion. 'No, of course I didn't! They'd have immediately interpreted that as a sign that he was suicidal. Whereas, as you know, in his cups Mark was always saying things like that. And he didn't mean a word of them.'

'No. Probably not. I mean, of course – to play devil's advocate for a moment – there is always the Last Straw Syndrome to consider. He'd gone on saying that kind of stuff all his life, but eventually perhaps there came a point when the pressures on him were so great that –'

'Poppycock!' Lavinia Bradshaw snapped briskly. 'Mark was a shallow poseur. Like his emotions and his enthusiasms, his depressions were never more than skin-deep.'

It was chilling to hear the depth of resentment in her voice, a resentment that had been simmering away for more than twenty years of marriage.

'Well, I'm not so sure...' said Charles, trying to be loyal to his friend's memory, though rather afraid that she had assessed her ex-husband all too accurately.

'It's true!' Lavinia Bradshaw smoothed down her skirt, as if somehow to separate it from the contamination of Charles Paris's armchair. 'But is there anything else, Charles? Any actual proof you could bring forward to make it clear once and for all that Mark did not deliberately take his own life?'

'But if he didn't...' asked Charles cautiously, 'then how did he die?'

'Of drink and stupidity. He was so drunk when he went into the little studio that he passed out, and didn't wake up, even when he started to suffocate. It was an accident,' Lavinia Bradshaw announced with unarguable finality.

'Yes, quite possibly...'

'Everyone knows it was. It's only the bloody insurance company trying to duck out of its obligations, as usual. Come on, Charles. I told you. I need proof that my ex-husband didn't commit suicide.'

'Well, look...' he hedged, 'I can't actually supply that proof at the moment...'

'Oh, for heaven's sake!' Lavinia Bradshaw had no patience with such shilly-shallying.

'...but I can make a suggestion.'

'Then make it!'

'Yes, all right. Erm...' He had to phrase the next bit carefully. 'The person who found Mark's body was Lisa Wilson...'

'His latest bit of stuff.'

Charles didn't waste time taking issue with the description. 'I should think if anyone knows the detail of what actually happened to Mark, it'd be her.'

That seemed the fairest thing to do. Put the two women in contact and let them sort it out between them. If Lavinia Bradshaw was really determined to find out about her ex-husband's death, then she'd have to overcome her scruples and speak to his 'latest bit of stuff'. Whether or not Lisa Wilson would come across with the goods, admit she'd found the studio doors locked.., well, that was up to her.

Charles thought the probability was that the two women would communicate, and Lisa would share all she knew. If they could overcome their instinctive antipathy, they'd recognise that co-operation was in both their interests. Lavinia Bradshaw was determined to secure her ex-husband's insurance money, and Lisa Wilson wanted to nail Mark's killer. Her attempts to achieve that with the help of Charles Paris having proved less than successful, she would probably be ready to try another approach.

They were two determined women. If they worked together, Charles didn't give much for the murderer's chances of escaping detection for ever.

Lavinia Bradshaw wasn't pleased by Charles's suggestion. She had the feeling that he was holding something back, that he could tell her more. But, in spite of her fierce badgering, he didn't give in.

It was in the middle of the badgering that his phone rang. 'Excuse me,' said Charles and picked up the receiver. Lavinia Bradshaw's mouth went into a little moue of annoyance at the interruption.

'Charles, it's Maurice.'

'Ah, hello. Maurice, if you could make it quick...'

'What's this, Charles? Hurrying me off the phone? I might be ringing about a fabulous offer of a year's very lucrative work.'

'Are you?'

'No. As it happens, I'm not.'

'Well then, if you could make it quickish...I've got someone with me.'

'Oh, Charles. Another of your little lady friends, is it?'

'No. Well, it is a lady, but –'

'Say no more. My lips are sealed. Your secret is safe with me.'

'Maurice...' Charles was tired, and his patience was not inexhaustible. 'What is it you're calling about?'

'You may remember,' said Maurice Skellern with lofty dignity, 'that some time ago you asked me to find out about some gay porn tapes, produced by the late Mark Lear...'

'Yes, of course.'

'Well, I have been continuing my investigations into that matter, and I have found out the names of the actors who were involved.'

Maurice stopped dead. If there was one thing he loved doing, it was to dictate the pace of his revelations.

'Yes, Maurice, yes. Go on, tell me. Who?'

'A very interesting list of names it turns out to be...' the agent went on with infuriating slowness.

'I'm sure it does. Who are they, Maurice?'

Realising that he had squeezed the last drop of potential melodrama out of the situation, Maurice gave Charles the names. And he was right. A very interesting list it did turn out to be.

When Charles had finished scribbling down the names, he said his grateful goodbyes and put the phone down. Lavinia Bradshaw looked extremely peeved at having been kept waiting so long. 'And that's really it, Charles, is it? You have nothing to tell me, except that I should get in touch with this Liza Wilson girl?' She deliberately pronounced the name wrong.

'Yes, 'fraid so.'

She snorted at the inadequacy of his information. 'Well, I'd better go. If you find out anything else, you've got my number.'

'Yes. If I do get anything, I'll certainly let you know. Then we can ensure that justice is done.'

Lavinia Bradshaw tossed her red-gold hair angrily. 'I don't give a damn about justice. I just want the insurance money.'

Charles Paris was seeing her off on the doorstep when another thought came to him. 'That phone call Mark made to you the afternoon he died...'

'Yes. What about it?'

'How did it end? Did you put the phone down on him?'

'No. I was about to, because I had to go out for a hairdresser's appointment. But in fact it was Mark who ended the conversation. He said he had to ring off because someone had just come into the studio.'

'Really? Did he say who that person was?'

'Now let me think...' Lavinia Bradshaw tried to piece the recollection together. 'He did call out, "Hello..." and then I think he said a name, but...'

'Try to remember. It could be very important.'

'Why?'

Suddenly Charles realised that, through all her bluster, Lavinia Bradshaw was in fact not very bright. 'Because,' he explained, 'whoever it was was probably the last person to see Mark alive.'

'Yes, yes,' she said thoughtfully.

'And you haven't mentioned how the phone call ended to the police?'

'No, of course not, Charles. Really, you are dense. Suppose that person, whoever it was, got more of Mark's drunken ramblings of self-pity. Then they might have got the impression that he was suicidal.'

'That's true. Have the police actually talked to you about the phone call? Because presumably they could check who Mark did ring that day.'

'They haven't been in touch yet, no.' A sly look came into her eyes. 'And, if they are, I have a perfectly good cover story ready. Mark rang me to check what one of the girls wanted for her birthday.'

'Which of the girls?'

'Claudia. It was her birthday the next week.'

'Oh, is she the one who's ill? Mark mentioned –'

'Claudia is absolutely fine, thank you,' she said sharply. The slyness came back into her face, and was transformed into self-satisfaction as Lavinia Bradshaw went on, 'People about to commit suicide do not on the whole spend their last hours planning what they're going to give their children as birthday presents, do they?'

'No.'

The glee at her own cleverness gave way to a sudden recollection. 'Ooh, I've just remembered the name Mark said, the name of the person who'd come into the studio. It didn't mean anything to me.'

'No, but then you don't know any of the people who were doing the recording that afternoon.'

'That's true.'

'So tell me what Mark said. The name might mean something to me.'

She told him the name. It did mean something to Charles Paris.

'One other thing, Lavinia...' They had said their goodbyes and she had started off down Hereford Road.

'What now?' she asked crossly.

'That woman who was coming out of the house when you arrived...'

'What about her?'

'Where was it you and Mark met her?'

'It was in the hospital.'

'Hospital?'

'Private clinic, I should say. God, the prices they charge in those places! You pay out all that money in medical insurance, but they still have the nerve to –'

'I hope you don't mind my asking, Lavinia, but what were you in the clinic for?'

'No, I don't mind. Unlike some women, I'm very proud of my new body.'

'So you were in for plastic surgery?'

'That's right. Bags under the eyes, breasts, bum, the whole shooting match.'

'And Cookie – the woman we saw this morning – was in the clinic at the same time? And that's when Mark met her?'

'Yes. God knows why he bothered coming to see me. I'd made it abundantly clear by then that there was nothing left between us, but he insisted on turning up and whingeing away in the lounge for an hour or so.'

'And that woman was in the lounge at the same time?'

'Some of it, yes. I introduced them, you know, casually, the way one does.' She looked at her watch with irritation. 'I'm sorry, Charles, I really must be –'

'Just one more question, Lavinia...Do you happen to remember why Cookie – that woman – was actually in the clinic?'

She let out a harsh little laugh. 'Well, of course I remember. She was having the same as me.'

'Bags under the eyes, breasts, bum, the whole shooting match?'

'Exactly,' said Lavinia Bradshaw, and set off briskly down Hereford Road.

Chapter Sixteen

BEFORE Charles left for Birmingham, he made a couple of phone calls. One was to Lisa Wilson to warn her that she might be contacted by Lavinia Bradshaw. He didn't spell out the details, but made it clear that she would have the option of telling Mark's ex-wife about the locked studio door. Whether she did or not was up to her.

Their conversation was civilised, even friendly. No one listening in would have detected that they'd ever been lovers, or that less than twenty-four hours previously one of them had announced they were no longer lovers.

Charles's second call was to the actors' union, Equity. He had a useful contact in the membership records there, who supplied him with the information he required.

By then, the confusions of the morning had not left Charles time to do as he'd intended and take the tour's dirty clothes to the launderette. Have to wait till Birmingham, he thought resignedly, as he scooped last week's dirty shirts, socks and underwear back into his suitcase (which felt uncomfortably light without its customary ballast of a Bell's bottle). By then he was so close to the train departure time, he had to take a cab to Euston.

He'd hoped to sleep for the hour and forty minutes of the train journey. He was utterly exhausted after the emotional upheavals of the previous few days – not to mention two virtually sleepless nights spent listening to Cookie Stone.

But sleep didn't come. His mind was too full. And, mostly, it was Cookie Stone who filled it.

A lot of details fell into place. The unusual firmness of her breasts, for a start. Charles Paris wondered whether, unwittingly, he'd recently had his first encounter with silicon.

But his other thoughts about Cookie Stone were more serious. She was an extraordinarily neurotic woman, of that there could not be any doubt. And she was deeply anxious about her attractiveness, or lack of it, to the opposite sex. She was also, regrettably, in love with Charles Paris.

He wondered just how deep Cookie's insecurities went, and what kinds of erratic behaviour they might drive her to. Finding out that she'd had plastic surgery fitted the overall picture, filled in a few more pieces in the jigsaw of her personality.

Except in cases of extreme deformity, the decision to have plastic surgery can never be a random one. The patient must be expecting some payback for the pain and inconvenience. In most cases, there must be some level of expectation that the transformation of the body will lead to some kind of transformation in the life. Lack of self-esteem, based on feelings of unattractiveness, the theory runs, will vanish when the external appearance has been adjusted.

And clearly it could work. For Lavinia Bradshaw, the plastic surgery of which she was so proud had been part of the reinvention of herself. Vinnie, wife of Mark Lear, the coping earth mother in droopy cardigans, had been transformed into Lavinia Bradshaw, designer clotheshorse, with a new body to complement her new lover.

But had Cookie Stone's transformation been so effective? From hints she'd dropped, Charles gathered Cookie's sex-life had been pretty inactive in the months before she met him. It was even likely that he was her first post-operation lover. Maybe for her, to have ensnared a lover – and a lover who called her 'beautiful' – was an endorsement of her decision to have the plastic surgery. It had worked!

But how would someone as deeply insecure as Cookie Stone react to the danger that her lover might find out what had happened? Did Charles believe that the body he evidently enjoyed making love to was the real thing? Would his discovery that it was in fact a patched-up, reconditioned body make him 'go off' her?

That was Cookie's greatest fear. That was the phrase that occurred most often in her monologues of self-doubt. 'Are you sure you haven't gone off me, Charles?' 'That hasn't made you go off me, has it, Charles?' 'You would say if you'd gone off me, wouldn't you, Charles?'

Yet again, Charles Paris asked himself the recurrent question:

How on earth did I manage to get myself into this? How can I ever break it to someone who's paranoid that I'm about to go off her, that I was never really 'on' her in the first place?

And with this came the even darker, more uncomfortable question: What lengths would someone like Cookie Stone go to, to prevent her lover from finding out that she'd had plastic surgery?

Mark Lear had definitely recognised her that afternoon in the studio. At the time, he didn't seem to know where he recognised her *from*, but his words might have been enough to set Cookie's ever-present paranoia racing. And the challenges he was flinging out about uncovering people's secrets could have applied as much to her as to anyone else in the studio.

Charles didn't like the thought. So long as there were other possibilities to be considered, he'd rather not think it. But the thought wouldn't leave his mind, and troubled him all the way up to Birmingham.

He walked from New Street Station to the theatre. It was not so much that he needed the exercise – though he undoubtedly did – but that he wanted to compose his mind for the confrontation ahead. Now so many pieces of the puzzle had slotted into place, Charles Paris didn't want to screw up on the final details.

He felt very low. He didn't really notice the splendours of Birmingham city centre, so totally transformed since the last time he'd been there. He was too full of his own thoughts.

He passed a lot of pubs, most of which were open all day. The pull of a large Bell's was almost agonisingly strong, but he resisted it. After the confrontation, maybe...after that night's show... after the end of the Birmingham run...then perhaps he'd have a drink. He knew that was how alcoholics had to think, one step at a time. Give yourself small targets, and try to meet them. Meet one target, and set up another one a little bit further away. And so on.

God, it was a boring prospect. But Charles Paris was determined to keep trying. What Lisa Wilson had said to him the night before had really hurt.

He stopped in a square, now dominated by a modern fountain above a large circular pool. He sat on the low wall of the pool and took out of his pocket the list of names he'd scribbled down that morning at Maurice Skellern's dictation. The names of the actors who'd been involved in the gay porn tapes Mark Lear had produced more than twenty years before.

There were six names. Henry Heaney. Stanley Murphy. Bernard Miles. Geoffrey Thomas. Robert Stephens. And Ransome George.

It was nearly three when he got to the theatre, a dead time on a day when the company weren't called till four-thirty. The set had been erected; the lighting plan – or rather the computer disks that contained it – had been installed. The theatre waited only for the cast to come, to hear a few notes on the slight differences of staging required by the new theatre. They would then do a leisurely walk-through of a couple of moments that might need minimal changes of blocking, probably have a brief break before the six fifty-five 'half', and at seven-thirty *Not On Your Wife!* would have yet another opening, this time hopefully to delight the good burghers of Birmingham. The tour had settled into a kind of rhythm.

Though the theatre was silent, Charles knew it was not unoccupied. Somewhere in unseen offices administrators would be at work. Backstage, final adjustments would be being made by the stage management. In the dressing rooms various actors would be going through their pre-performance rituals. Though it was one in a long sequence of them, this was still a kind of first night, and not even the most blasé of actors would have dared claim that he or she approached it with no nerves at all.

Charles Paris found the person he was looking for in the Green Room, sitting on a sofa, open copy of *Not On Your Wife!* on lap.

'Hi,' said Charles, and received a distracted answering 'Hi.'

'I've been looking for you.'

'Oh?'

'I wanted to have a word.'

'Uh-uh.'

'It's in relation to the death of Mark Lear.'

'Mark Lear?' But the puzzlement in the echo had been a bit contrived. The name was familiar.

'You remember...the drunk who produced that radio commercial in Bath.'

'Oh yes. Yes, with you.'

'The man who died that same day.'

'I heard about that. Terrible tragedy.' The response was automatic, uninterested.

'Some people,' Charles began slowly, 'are of the view that his death wasn't an accident...'

'Suicide, you mean? He certainly seemed in a pretty tense emotional state.'

'No, not suicide. Murder.'

'Really?'

'His girlfriend found the body the next morning. The doors to the studio he was in were locked.'

'Good heavens. Did she tell the police?'

'No. For reasons of her own, she didn't.'

'Oh.' Was Charles being hypersensitive to detect relief in the reaction?

'I'm pretty sure,' Charles went on, 'that Mark Lear was murdered.'

'If you say so.' A shrug, again uninterested.

'...by one of the people who was in the studio recording the commercial that afternoon.'

'What? Why, for God's sake? Most of us were meeting him for the first time that day.'

'No. In fact, Mark had met quite a few of us before, as it happened.'

'Really?'

'Being in the BBC, he'd worked with a lot of actors and actresses.'

'Ah. I didn't know he'd been in the BBC.'

Was that a straight lie? Charles didn't bother to investigate, but went on, 'He didn't do all his work for the BBC. Did a bit of moonlighting as well.'

'Really?'

'Yes. In particular, over twenty years ago, Mark Lear was involved in producing some pornographic audio tapes.'

'Was he?'

'Gay pornographic audio tapes.'

'I'm surprised there's a market for that kind of thing. I can understand people wanting videos, but –'

'There was a market then. Video hadn't really caught on in a big way.'

'Ah.'

'Anyway...' Charles Paris plunged boldly in. 'It's my belief that that afternoon in the studio, Mark Lear recognised somebody who'd worked on those tapes with him all that time ago. And when he said he was going to write a book exposing the things that went on in and around the BBC, that individual took it as a direct threat. He was so worried about his secret being exposed that, later in the afternoon, he returned to the studios, persuaded Mark Lear to go into the small dead room, perhaps even supplied him with a bottle of Scotch to take in there – and then locked the doors on him.'

'Interesting theory,' was all he got by way of response. 'I'm intrigued why you choose to tell me about it.'

'Because I'm convinced that you are the person who killed Mark Lear.'

'What? Oh, really!' The response was amused, rather than shocked. 'And what on earth gave you that idea?'

'Well, I asked myself who had most to lose by a revelation of what some might regard as a sordid past.' Charles took Maurice Skellern's list of names out of his pocket. 'I've a list here of the actors who were involved in recording the porn tapes. There's only one name here that appears on the *Not On Your Wife!* programme, and that person was definitely in the studio to hear Mark Lear make his threat.'

'Who are we talking about?'

'Ransome George.'

'For heaven's sake. Ran wouldn't worry about having done porn stuff. He'd glory in it. It's the kind of thing he'd dine out on.'

'I agree. I also happen to know that Ransome George has an alibi for the time of the murder. And that he has a very comfortable, ongoing blackmail system operating in connection with those audio tapes. So he was never going to upset the apple-cart, was he? No, Ran may be a creep and a blackmailer, but I've got to look for someone else in the role of murderer, haven't I?'

'So it would seem.'

'Going back to my question of who had most to lose...well, the obvious candidate was Bernard Walton.'

The figure on the sofa was silent.

'Because the situation for someone like Bernard Walton is different from old Ran's. It matters rather more what a star did in the past – particularly when that star is currently involved in a high-profile campaign to turn the tide of violence and smut in the media.'

Still not a sound from the sofa.

'Yes, the name "Bernard Walton" would definitely be of interest to the tabloids, wouldn't it? "Mr Squeaky-Clean in Gay Sex Revelation".'

'Working on a gay sex tape doesn't necessarily mean someone's gay,' came an objection from the sofa.

'I agree. God, you don't have to tell me – of all people – to what subterranean depths of work an impoverished actor will sink. But the average tabloid reader doesn't know much about the world of the theatre. Probably tends not to be very imaginative, either. For the average tabloid reader, the news that a well-known public figure once took part in a gay porn recording...well, it's the kind of dirt that sticks. Wouldn't do a popular figure any good at all. Certainly rule out the chances of a knighthood – and could also have a nasty effect on the box office of any show they might be involved in.'

The figure on the sofa had reverted to sullen silence.

'So I think it would have been very definitely worth keeping that particular secret quiet…even if keeping it quiet necessitated the murder of one drunken old has-been. Better surely that Mark Lear should die than that the precious image of Bernard Walton should be sullied.'

'I'm not denying or confirming what you suggest,' the accused said lightly, 'but I'd be very interested to know how you'd set about proving your allegations.'

That was indeed the problem. Charles felt sure he was right, but the evidence remained extremely thin on the ground. Still, no need to let his quarry know that. 'Mark Lear was on the phone to his ex-wife when you came into the studio that afternoon. She heard him greet you by name.'

This revelation produced a moment of discomfiture, but it soon passed.

'You're going to need more than that.'

'Maybe.'

'Assuming...' again the voice was light, almost teasing. 'Assuming there was any truth in what you're saying, can I ask what put you on to me?'

'I wasn't sure till this morning, when I got the list of names of people who'd been involved in the porn recordings. Then I asked myself: Who actually had most to lose if the truth came out? And I looked at the names, and two stuck out like sore thumbs.'

'Which two?'

'Bernard Miles and Robert Stephens. Both very big names in the theatre at the time those recordings were made. Bernard Miles was running the Mermaid, and I think Robert Stephens was still married to Maggie Smith. He was half of the golden couple of British theatre. There is no way, at that stage of Robert Stephens's career – or of Bernard Miles's career – that either of them would have been involved in recording pornographic audio cassettes. So there was only one conclusion possible. If it wasn't the famous Bernard Miles and the famous Robert Stephens, then it must have been another Bernard Miles and another Robert Stephens.

'Now, the making of porn cassettes is a pretty hole-in-the-corner business. No names billed on the outside of the pack…young actors, new to the business, paid off in cash…so Equity rules wouldn't have applied. But in the professional theatre it'd be different. And I'm sure I don't need to remind you of that basic Equity rule, that an actor's name is his stock-in-trade. You can't have two Equity members with the same name. So if your parents christen you Anthony Hopkins, or Ian McKellen, and you want to be an actor…bad luck, sunshine, it's already been bagged – you have to change your name.

'The same would have applied twenty years ago if you had been christened Bernard Miles or Robert Stephens. Ordinary enough names, nothing wrong with them as names, but sadly there were actors who'd already laid claim to them.' No response from the sofa. 'It was Curt Greenfield who told me that

Bernard Walton's family name was Miles. I didn't realise the significance of the information at the time. It was only this morning when I got this list that I realised, in his early days, when he was trying to get a foothold in the business, Bernard Walton would still have been known as "Bernard Miles". So the name had to be changed.'

There was a sullen 'Yes' from the sofa.

'Only a small change, in that case. Just the surname. Whereas you changed "Robert Stephens" into something a little bit more exotic, didn't you?'

'Yes,' said Tony Delaunay. 'I did.'

At that moment further revelations were deferred by the crackle of a voice from the tannoy. 'Could Tony Delaunay come up to the lighting gallery, please? We've got a bit of a problem.'

The company manager rose lithely from the Green Room sofa. 'Well, if they've got a problem, I'd better go and sort it out,' he said, redefining his raison d'être. Wherever there was a problem on the show, it was a point of honour for him to sort it out. His loyalty to Parrott Fashion Productions was total, but there was also the issue of his own self-esteem. Tony Delaunay prided himself on being equal to any challenge that his work might throw up. And, if that challenge was the threat of adverse publicity to the star of *Not On Your Wife!*, and a resultant diminution of box office takings, then Tony Delaunay would have regarded it as a point of honour for him to sort that out too.

He stopped at the door and, looking back sardonically at Charles Paris, said, 'Still be very interested to know how you propose to prove the allegations you've just made.' He grinned infuriatingly and, with a brisk shake of his shoulders, spelled out the reason why he had murdered Mark Lear. 'Can't hang about, though. The show must go on, love.'

Chapter Seventeen

CHARLES Paris's frustration was intense. He knew he was right. Tony Delaunay had virtually admitted he was right. And yet, as the company manager had so enjoyed telling him, Charles had no proof.

The unattractive prospect loomed of two more months touring *Not On Your Wife!*, with Tony Delaunay's impudent smile constantly reminding him of his powerlessness. Throughout the Birmingham week Charles fumed. Apart from anything else, he felt such a sense of anti-climax. He had psyched himself up for the encounter, had had his confrontation with the murderer, and yet at the end of it seemed no further advanced. The whole situation was infuriating.

Charles's fury did not, however, arise from a righteous sense of justice cheated. Mark Lear's death seemed less shocking with the passage of time, even perhaps – given the direction in which his friend had seemed to be heading – a merciful release. It was hard to imagine Mark undergoing the kind of total character change which would have been needed for him to start enjoying life again.

But, whatever his victim's prospects had been, Tony Delaunay was still a murderer. And some atavistic instinct in Charles Paris told him that murderers shouldn't be allowed to get away with their crimes.

All through the Birmingham week, one thought dominated Charles's mind. There must be some way of nailing the bastard.

An idea came to him on the Sunday between Birmingham and Brighton. Back at Hereford Road, he had been greeted by his accumulated post, piled carelessly on a hall shelf by the various Amazonian Swedish girls who occupied the other flats.

There wasn't much of interest. There was very rarely much of interest in Charles Paris's post. He was a lax correspondent, and there's a basic rule that, if you don't send out many letters, you don't get many replies. Nor was his career sufficiently busy to generate a great deal of professional correspondence.

So most of what Charles did get was junk mail. Finance companies, apparently ignorant of his appalling repayment record, kept trying to issue him with new credit cards. Book clubs attempted to lure him into their webs with offers of 50p hardbacks. Insurance companies earnestly asked him, 'What would happen if you were suddenly unable to work?' Since Charles's answer to this was: 'It would be par for the course, my career's always been like that', all such communications tended to get filed in his wastepaper basket.

And then of course there were the bills. Charles Paris had a system with bills. He would pile them up on the mantelpiece of his room until the majority were red, then suddenly indulge in a cathartic orgy of payment, closing his mind to the cheques' combined and simultaneous impact on his beleaguered bank account.

It was a bill, however, which suggested another approach to the problem of Tony Delaunay. It was Charles Paris's telephone bill.

Telephone bills still had a slight air of novelty for him. For many years Charles's sole means of communication with the outside world had been the payphone on the landing at Hereford Road. But that had vanished in the refurbishment which had turned a houseful of 'bedsitters' into a houseful of 'studio flats'. So, along with facing considerably increased rent demands, Charles had also been forced into organising himself a phone line. An answering machine quickly followed, and he was no longer reliant on the erratic message service of the Swedish girls. Charles Paris had at last put a tentative toe into the waters of modern technology, and he was repeatedly astonished at how he'd ever managed to conduct his life without it.

He didn't reckon he used the phone that much, but every time a bill arrived it was still a nasty shock. On this occasion, however, the size of the sum owing wasn't what struck him. It was the fact that his bill was itemised.

There is no defence against that list of figures. The total demanded may seem outrageous, but when one sees every transaction laid out in such detail, argument becomes impossible.

Itemised bills, Charles had decided, must have had a profound influence on the nation's morals. Together with the 'last number redial' facility and the '1471' method of monitoring the most recent incoming call, itemised bills must have severely clipped the wings of the average adulterer.

But it wasn't moral considerations that were uppermost in Charles's mind at that moment. He realised that an itemised phone bill might help him to reconstruct Mark Lear's last hours.

Charles looked at his watch. It was early on the Sunday afternoon. Though he had spent a night at her flat, Lisa Wilson had never volunteered her home phone number to him, but Charles thought it was worth trying the studio. Lisa seemed prepared to work every hour there was to get her business up and running.

Sure enough, she was there, doing some tape editing. She didn't sound particularly surprised to hear from him – or indeed particularly interested.

Charles leapt straight in. 'Lisa, I've been thinking about the phone...'

'What?'

'The phone calls Mark made on the afternoon he died.'

There was a sudden change in her tone. 'How did you know?' she asked sharply.

Charles was bewildered. 'What?'

'How did you work it out?'

'Well,' he floundered, 'it just seemed kind of logical...that we know he used the phone and...'

'And do you think I should tell the police?'

'Erm...'

'I mean, if I didn't tell them that the doors were locked, I can't really tell them about the phone either.'

'What about the phone?' he asked helplessly.

But Lisa Wilson was so caught up in her own thoughts, she imagined Charles knew more than he did. 'The fact that I found the cordless phone in the little dead room with him.'

'And you moved it?'

'I had to.'

'Why?'

'The redial button.'

'Mm?'

'I pressed the redial button on the phone.' A sob came into her voice. 'And I found out that the last number Mark had dialled...probably when he was dying...was the number of the married man who...'

'The one you spent the night with?'

'Yes.' Her voice was taut with pain. 'I'd told him all about this guy...you know, when Mark and I started going out together...so he knew the name. I didn't know he'd got the phone number. He must've copied it out of my address book...and when he was dying, that was the last number...He must've known I was deceiving him...He must've been trying to contact me...'

She was too upset to say any more. Charles asked gently, 'And did he get through? Did he talk to...your friend?'

'No. The guy's a writer. The number's the office where he works. He wasn't there. Mark must've got the answering machine.'

'But, so far as you know, he didn't leave a message?'

'No. I'd have heard.'

'Hm. So you took the phone out of the studio, and put it back on its base, so that the police wouldn't get on to...your friend?'

'Yes. And I dialled another number, so that the redial button wouldn't give it away.'

'But the police would still be able to find out what calls he made. It's all logged somewhere.'

'I know. I wasn't thinking very clearly. I'd just found Mark dead. I was feeling so guilty...'

'And the calls'd be on your itemised phone bill, anyway.'

'Right. Of course they would.'

'Have you had a phone bill recently? I mean, a phone bill that covers the day Mark died?'

'Yes. One came last week. I didn't check it. I didn't think...'
'Have you got it there? Look for calls after three-thirty.'
'Mm.' There was a rustling of papers. 'I never thought of looking at this.' After a moment's silence, she announced, 'He only made three calls after three-thirty that day.'
'And the last one was to your friend?'
'Yes. That was at 17:02. For under a minute. He must've just listened to the ansaphone message and hung up.'
'When were the other calls?'
'One at 15:42.'
'And that was presumably to...' Charles reeled off Lavinia Bradshaw's number.
'Yes. That lasted six minutes, twelve seconds...'
'And was interrupted by the murderer coming into the studio.'
'Was it? Charles, how do you know –?'
'Don't worry, I'll explain in a moment. What was the third call?'
'That was at 16:37. It lasted twelve minutes, nine seconds.'
'And what was the number?'
'It was the same one.'
'What, you mean – your friend?'
'No, Charles. It was another call to his ex-wife.'
'Really?' said Charles Paris.

The Bradshaws' house was in Blackheath, large and imposing. Lavinia's second husband also had money. Pooling their resources had made for a very lavish life-style indeed. The husband was away on business that weekend, but Lavinia was quite happy for Charles Paris to come round. 'Anything that's going to help get this wretched insurance business sorted out,' she said when he rang her. But no, she hadn't yet got round to talking to Lisa Wilson. It was clearly not a task she relished, though her greed would probably not allow it to be deferred for ever.

The sitting room into which she ushered him demonstrated the impersonal luxury that only an interior designer can bring to a house. It seemed to be for demonstration purposes only, too neat ever to be lived in by real human beings. The curtains billowed too lavishly; the cushions were scattered too artlessly; the gas flames licked too politely around the unchanging ceramic lumps of coal.

It was late afternoon. Lavinia Bradshaw offered him tea or coffee, but nothing stronger. Charles declined.

'I want to check about the phone calls Mark made the afternoon he died.'

'Well, I told you. He rang me, and maundered on as usual. All that self-pitying nonsense.'

'And then he was interrupted by the arrival of Tony Delaunay.'

'Tony somebody, certainly. He definitely said "Tony". Perhaps you should talk to this Tony.'

'I have talked to him.'

'And did he say anything that proved it wasn't suicide?'

'Erm...Well...' Charles had to remind himself that Lavinia knew nothing of the suspicions of murder. He would have to edit what he said carefully.

'Before we go on to that, could I just check about the phone calls?'

'Phone calls? There was only one. I had to go out to the hairdresser's. I had an appointment at four.'

'Mark called this number again at four thirty-seven.'

'Well, I wasn't here. He certainly didn't talk to me again.

'He talked to somebody for twelve minutes and nine seconds.'

The line of Lavinia Bradshaw's mouth hardened. 'Oh, did he?' She rose briskly from the sofa, 'I'll go and get her.'

The girl looked ghastly. The loose print dress, worn undoubtedly on her mother's orders to obscure the precise outlines of her body, perversely had the opposite effect. It drew attention to the matchstick thinness of her legs, the disproportionate swellings of her joints. In the same way, the thick Alice band, intended to cover her hair, simply drew attention to its sparseness.

'This is Claudia.'

'Hello. I'm Charles Paris.'

The girl looked at him without interest. She seemed preoccupied. Her eyes were unfocused, but had a glint of deviousness in them.

'Claudia darling, sit down.'

She obeyed, placing herself gingerly on the edge of an armchair, as if her skin was not thick enough to cushion her against the hardness of its upholstery.

'Claudia, did you talk to Daddy on the phone the afternoon he died?'

The girl moved her head round slowly to look at her mother, but said nothing.

'Claudia, I asked you a question.' Still silence. 'Come on, darling, this is important. Important for you. It might affect whether or not you get the money from Daddy's insurance.'

The girl's gaunt face took on a slight sneer at the mention of money. Her mother was predictably stung by the reaction. 'Claudia! I've had enough of this nonsense! I've been very tolerant over the last months, let you do your own thing, indulge all your silly faddishness...but this is something important. You must tell us whether or not you spoke to Daddy on the afternoon he died!'

'It really would help if you could tell us,' said Charles, more softly.

The skull-like face turned from its mother towards Charles Paris, and fixed the same look of challenging contempt on him.

Lavinia Bradshaw rose to her feet in fury. 'Claudia! Will you please do as you're told!'

The girl raised thin arms to wrap around her body, but it was not a gesture of fear. The sleeve on her dress slipped down to reveal the narrow straight line of her forearm and the ugly knob of an elbow.

'Claudia!'

'Do you think perhaps I could speak to her on her own?' asked Charles Paris gently.

'Why didn't you tell her, Claudia?'

'Because she's not interested. She didn't care about Daddy at all.'

From the moment that Lavinia had stomped huffily out of the room, the girl had made no difficulty about answering Charles's questions. Her silence – and probably her anorexia too – was a weapon in a private battle with her mother. She didn't need to deploy it against anyone else.

'Some people might take the view...' Charles started cautiously, 'that her attitude was justified...that your father didn't treat your mother very well.'

'I don't care how he treated her. He was always nice to me. But once she'd walked out, she wouldn't let us see him. The other two didn't mind, but...'

'Did you try to get to see him?'

'It was difficult...being away at university and...He didn't get in touch much. And I was worried...I didn't know whether he wanted to see me.'

'And was that...I mean, when they split up...was that when you started to get ill?'

'I'm not ill,' said Claudia Lear, with total conviction. 'I'm fine.'

'Well, when you started to lose weight...'

'Maybe.' She shrugged. Then she let out a little laugh. 'Mummy's livid about it, you know. To match her new, tarted-up image, what she wants her daughters to be is three perfectly groomed designer accessories.' She opened out her skeletal arms, and said with a note of triumph, 'Well, she can't take me anywhere, can she?'

'No. Going back to what I was saying, Claudia...'

'Hm?'

'Why didn't you tell your mother about your father's call?'

'Because it was nothing to do with her. All she cares about is this bloody insurance. Daddy wasn't a person for her, just a means of getting some more money.'

'So, if you did have proof that he didn't commit suicide, you wouldn't tell your mother about it?'

'Why should I? Let her sweat. I hope she doesn't get the insurance money.'

'It's not her you'd be doing out of it, though. It'd be you and your sisters.'

The bony shoulders shrugged. 'Who cares? We'll get plenty of money one day.' She chuckled. 'I don't mind paying a bit to see Mummy pissed off.'

'And do your sisters share your view?'

'God knows. I doubt it. They're a couple of mercenary bitches, just like Mummy.'

'Hm...And when your father rang you, Claudia, that afternoon, would you say he sounded suicidal?'

'No. If he had, I'd have told everyone. Mummy would've been really furious.'

'So how did he sound?'

Claudia Lear drew her thin lips together as she tried to think of the right word. 'Kind of... resigned, I think.'

'Resigned to the fact that he was going to die?'

'Maybe, but he didn't say that. I mean, he was very drunk and sleepy, so it was difficult to say exactly what he meant.' She looked at Charles with sudden pride. 'He did say he loved me, though.'

'I'm sure he loved you, Claudia.'

'Yes.' She nodded with quiet satisfaction.

'So... what exactly did he say?'

'Well, he rambled, but...He said he'd got himself into something he couldn't get out of...that he was locked in...'

'"Locked in"? He did actually use the expression "locked in"?'

'Yes. I suppose he meant some business thing he'd got involved in...'

'What else did he say? Did he mention anyone by name?'

'Tony. He mentioned someone called Tony. Tony...Delaney?'

'Delaunay.'

'Yes, that's right. He said: "Tony Delaunay's got me locked into this, and there's no way out."' A nostalgic smile came to the girl's thin lips. 'And then he said he loved me.'

Chapter Eighteen

INSPECTOR CRUTTENDEN looks with amazement at Nicky, then back at Bob and Gilly.
INSPECTOR CRUTTENDEN: But let me get this straight. *(He points at Bob.)* If you're not having an affair with this young lady, Nicky, who are you having an affair with? Bob looks round the stage in desperation. He looks hopefully at Willie.
WILLIE: No, no, you can't be having an affair with me. *(He smiles winsomely at Ted.)* I'm having an affair with Ted.
TED: No, you're not. This whole thing's a ghastly misunderstanding.
WILLIE *(taking his hand)*: Don't you worry your pretty little head about it.
TED: Ooh-er.
INSPECTOR CRUTTENDEN *(to Bob)*: So who are you having an affair with?
BOB: Erm...*(brainwave)* I'm having an affair with Ted too.
WILLIE *(slapping Ted's face)*: You two-timing slut!
TED: Ooh-er.
WILLIE *(turning on Bob)*: And you're no better, you...*(slapping Bob's face)* ...you Judas!
During the ensuing dialogue, Ted creeps away to hide out of sight under the table, which he approaches from behind.
LOUISE: Look, for heaven's sake, can we get some sense into all this, please! Ted is my husband...
INSPECTOR CRUTTENDEN *(taking out notebook to make notes)*: Right.
GILLY: And Bob is my husband...
INSPECTOR CRUTTENDEN *(making a note)*: Right.
LOUISE *(turning to look at Nick y)*: And Nicky is...
GILLY: *(also turning to look at Nick y)*: Yes, Nicky is...
INSPECTOR CRUTTENDEN: Come on, the young lady must be somebody's mistress.
LOUISE: Yes, yes, she's... erm...
GILLY: I say, you wouldn't like her to be your mistress, would you, Inspector?
INSPECTOR CRUTTENDEN *(looking lasciviously at Nicky and really attracted by the idea)*: Well, I wouldn't say no. Wouldn't mind a bit of... *(recovering himself and going back into his mournful mode)* No, I am very happily married to Mrs Cruttenden. Worse luck. *(turning beadily on Louise and Gilly)* Now come on – who's this young lady's lover?

Suddenly, as if goosed from behind, Aubrey shoots out from under the tablecloth, where he has been hidden since Act One. He still has his trousers round his ankles.

AUBREY: Ooof!

GILLY AND LOUISE *(triumphantly turning to point at Aubrey)*: He is!

During the ensuing dialogue, Ted emerges from beneath the table. Pulling the tablecloth over him as if it can make him disappear, he tiptoes towards the French windows.

AUBREY: What am I?

GILLY *(pointing to Nick y)*: You're this young lady's lover.

AUBREY: Am I? *(looking at Nicky and very much liking what he sees)* Fwoor! You know I've always fancied the younger woman.

NICKY *(looking at Aubrey and very much liking what she sees)*: And I've always fancied the older man.

They go into a clinch.

GILLY *(beaming at Inspector Cruttenden)*: So everything's turned out all right.

LOUISE *(also beaming at Inspector Cruttenden)*: Yes, and you can go back to the station.

INSPECTOR CRUTTENDEN: Yes. *(He turns to go to the front door, then suddenly stops and has a thought. He turns back.)* Except...

GILLY: Except what?

INSPECTOR CRUTTENDEN: I came here looking for an escaped convict.

LOUISE: Ginger Little.

INSPECTOR CRUTTENDEN: That's right, who is known to be in this vicinity, dressed as an Arab terrorist.

LOUISE: Oh yes.

By this point, Ted has reached the French windows, and is about to open them. With the tablecloth over his head, he does indeed look like an Arab terrorist.

GILLY *(pointing at him)*: Look, there he is!

Ted tries to escape, as the rest of the cast chase him round the stage. He trips, and all the rest of the cast pile up on top of him in a breathless heap. Ted's head is covered with the tablecloth. There is a moment's silence, then Ted lifts up the edge of the tablecloth and looks out at the audience.

TED: Ooh-er.

THE CURTAIN FALLS FOR THE END OF THE PLAY.

That was the fifth ending they'd tried. They'd introduced it for the Brighton week, which followed on from Birmingham. It didn't work any better than the previous four endings. Bill Blunden, however, was not disheartened. He knew his plays took a long time to get right. If *Not On Your Wife!* didn't come together this time round, he was quite reconciled to the thought of its doing another tour the following year.

For Charles Paris, the continuation of the tour was not relaxing. Though he'd spelled out in considerable detail to Cookie Stone that their relationship wasn't working and needed to end, she seemed unable to take this idea on board. He would still continually find her looking at him wistfully with her soulful, surgically debagged eyes, waiting for some sign of his relenting. She clearly believed it was only a matter of time before he saw the error of his ways and came back to the haven of her waiting arms.

Being out of a relationship with Cookie was, in its own way, as exhausting as being in one. Charles Paris couldn't wait for the tour to come to an end.

Cookie Stone wasn't the only reason he felt that during the Brighton and Newcastle weeks. There was also the unresolved problem of Tony Delaunay.

Charles had had to be careful how he handled Claudia Lear. The girl's antipathy to her mother was so strong that he had to try to keep Lavinia out of it. Eventually he decided his only possible approach was complete honesty. He shared his suspicions with Claudia, told her he thought that Mark Lear had been murdered by Tony Delaunay.

It was a risk, but it paid off. Though the girl had had no suspicions of foul play, once the idea was planted in her mind, it generated fury and a strong desire for revenge. She was determined to bring to book the man who had killed her neglectful but beloved 'Daddy'.

So, that very Sunday evening, while Charles was still there, and her mother still out of the room, Claudia Lear had rung the police in Bath.

And then…nothing happened. Or at least, so far as Charles Paris was concerned, nothing seemed to happen. Throughout the Brighton week, he kept catching Tony Delaunay's eye, only to be further goaded by the company manager's complacent smile of immunity.

One early evening, towards the end of the Brighton week, Charles tried to enlist Ransome George's help to nail the murderer. Ran had been involved in the original recordings, surely he'd be prepared to investigate further. Charles bought his fellow-actor a pre-show drink and tentatively raised the topic.

'Forget it,' Ran said with a complacent smile. 'I'm doing very nicely as it is. No way I'm going to upset the apple-cart.'

'What do you mean – "doing very nicely as it is"?'

Ransome George gave the grin that, later in the evening, would bring the house down halfway through Act Two, and confirmed Charles's long-held suspicions. 'Look, I've known about Bernard Walton's involvement in those recordings for years, haven't I? And the more famous he's got, the more it's been in his interests for me to keep quiet about it. That's what I mean by "doing very nicely".'

'So you don't deny that you're blackmailing Bernard?'

'Ugly word – blackmail,' said Ran, in a way that would drag a laugh from the most recalcitrant audience in the country. 'Let's just say we have an agreement.'

'How many other people do you have "agreements" with? I suppose you've been blackmailing Tony Delaunay for years as well?'

'No. It wouldn't matter to Tony. He's gay, anyway. And, apart from that, he's not a star. Nobody's that interested in what a company manager gets up to.' Even when it's murder, thought Charles. 'But with Bernard,' Ran went on, 'it works just fine, has done for years. Mind you...' He looked with sudden suspicion at Charles. 'Now you know all the details, I wouldn't advise you to start trying to do the same thing.'

'What, blackmailing Bernard, you mean?'

'Mm.'

Charles was affronted by the suggestion. 'I can assure you, Ran, there is no danger that I would ever do that.'

'Good.' Ransome George sat back with another sleek, complacent smile. 'Because at the moment the deal I have with Bernard is perfect. I get regular money – never ask too much, you know, doesn't do to be greedy in this sort of business. And then he sees to it I get parts in a lot of his shows too. Same kind of deal as he does for you, eh, Charles?'

Charles Paris was so flabbergasted by the accusation that, before he realised what he was doing, he'd lent Ran a tenner.

It was in Newcastle that the situation changed. For the first few days, Charles's frustration at his own impotence was as great as it had been in Brighton. Then suddenly, on the Wednesday, Tony Delaunay wasn't there. He'd been around for the matinée, but by the time the evening performance started, he had gone. By the beginning of the following week, in Cardiff, a new company manager had been appointed by Parrott Fashion Productions.

Details of what had happened to Tony filtered slowly through the *Not On Your Wife!* company. Plain clothes policemen had apparently arrived at the theatre in Newcastle to interview him, and he had left in their company. Nobody knew why, and, preoccupied – like most actors – with themselves, nobody was that interested in the reasons for his departure.

By the time Tony Delaunay came to trial, charged with the murder of Mark Lear, the tour was over. Individual actors may have been shocked over their breakfast newspapers, but there was no company left to experience communal hysteria.

Not for the first time in his life, Charles Paris wondered how closely the police investigations had been shadowing his own. Even though their official enquiry didn't possess Lisa Wilson's information about the studio doors having been locked, some kind of researches must have been going on, to be presented at the adjourned inquest on Mark Lear. The police too must have been checking out the phone calls he made on the day of his death. And surely they too, in time, would have made contact with Claudia Lear.

Charles didn't talk to the girl again, though he often wondered about her, and how – if at all – her self-destructive relationship with her mother would be resolved. Lavinia Bradshaw had tried to reinvent herself, but Claudia's anorexia was part of the cost of that transformation, a constant reminder that the past can never be completely cut off.

Charles did speak to Lavinia once again. She was delighted by the news that her husband had been murdered. That meant there was no longer any threat to her insurance money.

Charles also heard from Lisa Wilson a few times over the next months. She had been given a fairly rough time by the Bath police for withholding information. At one stage there had been talk of charges against her, but in the event none materialised.

Once that threat had dissipated, her telephone conversations with Charles became less frequent, and finally ceased. Lisa Wilson seemed to be managing to make a new start. Business at the studios, she told him in one of her last calls, was really picking up. At the same time she mentioned casually that she was into a new relationship, which 'seems quite promising – at least he's a teetotaller for a change'.

So was Charles at that point, but he didn't think it worth mentioning the fact to Lisa Wilson. Whatever there might have been between them was now long gone. Besides, although she had been the motive force which made him give up drink, now he was doing it for himself. The abstinence made his evenings very long and slow, but he did feel healthier for it. Also, he needed some kind of self-punishment.

He found a letter at Hereford Road on the Sunday between the Bristol week and the Manchester week. He didn't recognise the name or address on the notepaper.

Dear Mr Paris,
I am writing to inform you of the death of my sister Ruth. As you probably know, she had been in and out of hospital for some months, and so in some ways her passing on must have been a relief to her. I have been through her address book, and am writing to all the people in it to inform them of the sad news, and also to say that a funeral service will be held.

But the date had passed. Charles felt bad. He'd had no idea Ruth was so ill. It compounded his general sense of being an emotional cactus, someone whom no woman could approach without getting hurt.

He kept meaning to ring Frances. But he didn't.

The *Manchester Evening News* gave his performance as Aubrey one of those notices that Charles knew he would never be able to flush out of his mind. 'Charles Paris,' it ran, 'acts as if having a love affair is only marginally preferable to an attack of piles.'

Two months after the *Not On Your Wife!* tour ended, Maurice Skellern rang to say that Charles had been offered another three-month tour. Again of *Not On Your Wife!* Bill Blunden's slow process of perfecting the comic machinery of his play was set to continue for another crawl around the provinces.

Charles Paris's first reaction was to say 'No', and he knew his first reactions were always right. He was sick of the play, for one thing. And he couldn't face another three months of reproach from Cookie Stone.

On the other hand...he had no alternative prospects for the year ahead, the bank balance was dwindling, and three months' work remained three months' work. Then again, as Maurice Skellern said, 'There's always the chance it'll "come in" Charles. When you're on West End money, you won't regret all those endless months of touring, will you?'

So Charles Paris said 'Yes'.

In fact, sure enough, a year later *Not On Your Wife!*, finally rewritten to Bill Blunden's satisfaction, did 'come in' to the West End, for the start of what proved to be a very long and successful run.

There were a few cast changes, though. Pippa Trewin hadn't even done the second tour, because she was playing the lead in a movie. And for the West End run, Cookie Stone was replaced by an actress straight out of drama school. The girl was really not old enough for the part, but she was Pippa Trewin's younger sister. Mind you, she'd changed her name to Samantha Driver. Like Pippa before her, she didn't want anyone to think she was getting preferential treatment just because she was the daughter of Patti Urquhart and Julian Strange.

Oh, and in the West End, the part of Aubrey was played by an actor called George Birkett.

Charles Paris was philosophical about all this. Bloody annoyed, but philosophical. He'd long since given up the expectation that life would be fair.

Possibly to compound its unfairness, in the Queen's next Birthday Honours, Bernard Walton was knighted for 'charitable work and services to the theatre'.

The day Charles Paris agreed to do the second tour of *Not On Your Wife!*, he felt in need of a little celebration. It wasn't that he was celebrating the decision; more that he wanted to shut his mind to the fact that he'd made the decision.

And he had done nearly two months off the booze. That was almost unprecedented. He had proved he wasn't an alcoholic. He could take it or leave it, stop whenever he wanted to. He deserved a little treat.

So that evening Charles Paris went out and got drunk – two-second pause – merry – two-second pause – tiddly – two-second pause – tipsy – two-second pause – blotto – two-second pause – pissed – two-second pause – rat-arsed...

Lightning Source UK Ltd.
Milton Keynes UK
UKOW041122031212

203110UK00001B/121/A